Geoffrey Chaucer

The Canterbury Tales

with an Introduction by Catherine Wells-Cole,
and Bibliography

This edition published 1995 by Wordsworth Editions Ltd,
Cumberland House, Crib Street, Ware, Hertfordshire SG12 9ET.

ISBN 1-85326-436-9

Printed and bound in Great Britain by
Mackays of Chatham PLC, Chatham, Kent.

INTRODUCTION

NOWADAYS the *Canterbury Tales* is Chaucer's most popular and widely read work, and one of the best-known poems in Middle English. This has not always been the case; earlier generations valued Chaucer more for his French-influenced dream poems like *The Book of the Duchess*, or the Italian-inspired tragic love story of *Troilus and Criseyde*. But the energy and variety of the *Tales*, held in the narrative framework of a pilgrimage to Canterbury, has seemed since at least the early 19th century to give the fullest impression of Chaucer's mastery of narrative technique and also of his sophisticated ease with language.

Chaucer is regarded as the first English poet because he more or less turned the English language into an appropriate medium for poetry as his writing career progressed. He was born in London in the early 1340s, the son of a wealthy wine merchant, but he was educated for a career in public service in various royal courts. The first documentary reference to him is from 1357, in the records of Elizabeth, Countess of Ulster, daughter-in-law of Edward II; Chaucer was probably a page in her household. It is, ironically, because of his secretarial and diplomatic duties at court, not because of his fame as a poet, that Chaucer's life is so unusually well documented. During the 1360s and later he appears frequently in the records as an 'esquire', one of a group of administrative officials at court. Until the accession of Richard II in 1377 English was not the main court language; since 1066 the 'prestige vernacular' had been a form of French known as Anglo-Norman. This, or Parisian French, was the language in which the court absorbed its literature: Chaucer produced much early poetry in French and was influenced by French works such as the *Roman de la Rose* by Jean de Meun and Guillaume de Lorris, part of which he translated into English. It was therefore neither automatic nor inevitable that Chaucer would write his major works in

English; his friend and fellow-poet John Gower wrote in Latin and Anglo-Norman as well as English. It has been argued that the readable quality that makes Chaucer's poetry so attractive centuries after it was written comes from experiments and innovations he was compelled to make using a relatively unpolished language; late 14th century English had no 'high style', no rhetorical inflatedness that might have alienated later readers.

Throughout his working life, Chaucer combined his activities as poet with a demanding salaried employment. In 1374 he was appointed controller of export duty on wool and leather leaving the port of London. He continued to work and travel on royal business; it seems likely that on a visit to Lombardy in 1378 he acquired copies of poetry by the most famous Italian writers of the time: Dante, Petrarch and Boccaccio. His own writing shows a profound Italian influence, particularly that of Boccaccio, whose *Filostrato* and *Teseida* gave him the basis for *Troilus and Criseyde* and the *Knight's Tale* respectively.

Troilus, his greatest finished work, was written between 1381 and 1386; in the latter year he also became Member of Parliament for Kent. Although his poetry was celebrated during his lifetime, John Burrow points out that Chaucer was buried in Westminster Abbey because he was a good servant of the king, not because he was a poet. From 1389 to 1391 he held the arduous post of Clerk of the King's Works; he had probably already started work on the *Canterbury Tales*, and was engaged on it until his death in 1400.

The *Canterbury Tales* is a collection of stories held within the framing narrative of a group of pilgrims on the way to the shrine of St Thomas à Becket at Canterbury, one of the most popular destinations for pilgrims in England. The device of a framing narrative was popular in the Middle Ages; Boccaccio uses it in the *Decameron* and Chaucer himself had done so in the *Legend of Good Women*. What is unusual about the *Tales*, however, is its range and variety of narrative voices, its many different kinds of story and its changes of mood and tone. The poem opens with a *General Prologue*, which gives an extended and sharply observed description of all the pilgrims assembled at the Tabard Inn in Southwark. They include no really aristocratic characters, and none who are really poor, but within these limits Chaucer presents a broad sweep of 14th century social types, from the idealised portrayals of the Knight, Parson and Plowman to the more worldly Merchant and Wife of Bath and unattractive figures like the Pardoner and the Reeve. Although the *General Prologue* provides a wealth of individual detail about these characters, from the Wife's red stockings and gap-teeth to the threadbare coat of the Clerk of Oxford, its concern is with types and occupational 'estates' rather than with specific individuals. In this respect, like so much else of Chaucer's poetry, it belongs within medieval literary convention: here, the genre known as 'estates satire'.

The *Prologue* does, however, provide a dynamic and lively cast of characters to undertake the two or three days' journey to Canterbury. Medieval pilgrims travelled in groups for security, but also, as the *Tales* makes clear, for enjoyment and 'felaweship'. Chaucer himself soon becomes one of the jolly party but, although he embarks on two tales in his own right, his voice does not control the narrative. He leaves pilgrims and stories free to speak for themselves, and this in turn frees him, not only from the censure some of the more scurrilous tales might provoke, but also from passing moral or spiritual judgement on the many questions and dilemmas the *Tales* pose. It is left to Harry Bailly, the jovial Host of the Tabard, to accompany the pilgrims and act as master of ceremonies. It is he who urges them not to ride along 'dumb as stones', but instead to tell stories: two each on the way to Canterbury and another two on the way back. The one who tells the best story will be treated to supper by the rest on their return to Southwark.

As there are, besides Chaucer, 30 pilgrims identified in the *General Prologue*, this would result in 120 tales; the poems as it stands has only 24, and this is not only because it was unfinished at Chaucer's death but also because he seems to have revised his original intention in the course of writing.

The tales are in no final order, some of them fragmentary and incomplete, others not properly matched to their teller; and all readings of the poem must take account of these problems. There are more than 80 manuscripts of the *Canterbury Tales*, but none is in Chaucer's own hand or even appears to have been edited by him. Because they were produced at different stages of the composition of the poem, over some twelve or thirteen years, the manuscripts place the tales in many different orders: later editors have had to use their judgement to establish the most coherent groupings of all these fragmentary texts. Thus in Group C, the Physician's and Pardoner's tales are connected to each other by some linking dialogue between the two men and the Host, but there is no dialogue at the beginning or end of the Group to connect either tale with any of the others, or to show where they might belong in the larger framework. At other points in the poem critics have convincingly argued for an overall design, most notably in a sequence of tales known as the Marriage Group – principally the *Wife of Bath's Tale*, the *Clerk's Tale*, the *Merchant's Tale* and the *Franklin's Tale*. Although Chaucer never explicitly claims to be doing so, these tales can be read as a debate about issues of authority and freedom in marriage. The Marriage Group can also be taken as an example of what might be termed the 'dramatic' reading of the *Tales*, which sees them as primarily revelations of character. This reading is endorsed by the vivid and often quarrelsome relationships which develop between pilgrims and which make the framework of the poem as enjoyable as the stories.

The Franklin, for example, is full of praise for the (unfinished) tale of the Squire, perhaps revealing his own social insecurity in the wish that his son were 'a man of suich discrecioun' as the Squire himself. The Pardoner rudely interrupts the Wife of Bath's lengthy *Prologue*, and the Friar comments on it, laughingly, 'This is a long preamble of a tale!' Chaucer's own first attempt at a story, the *Tale of Sir Thopas*, which reads like a parody of all the poetic clichés of the day, is forcibly ended by the Host because it is, in his words, 'rym dogerel' and 'nat worth a tord!' Yet although Chaucer's framework is clearly much more than a peg to hang stories on, it seems reductive to read the *Tales* primarily in terms of character. The moral complexity and emotional range of the *Knight's Tale*, for example, give it a poetic individuality which supersedes the personality of its teller. The same is true of the *Franklin's Tale*, whose subtle and intricate concern with 'gentillesse' is much more than the product of its narrator's social anxiety.

The real triumph and achievement of the *Canterbury Tales* is in its astonishing stylistic variety. It is the last work of a writer who had absorbed everything the English, French and Italian traditions could teach him and who was now demonstrating his mastery of narrative. Not only do the *Tales* offer examples of every kind of story told in the Middle Ages – romances, saints' lives, moral tales, stories of sexual trickery or *fabliaux* – but within each of these categories Chaucer rings changes and tests limits. His three *fabliaux*, the *Miller's Tale*, the *Reeve's Tale* and the *Merchant's Tale*, all show a husband cuckolded by a younger man; yet they are all, as C. David Benson points out, utterly different in mood and implication. For each tale Chaucer creates a distinctive poetic tone, appropriate to the tale itself; the poem encompasses the dignified pathos of Griselda in the *Clerk's Tale*: 'And she ay sad and constant as a wal'; the panic of Dorigen in the *Franklin's*: 'but when she saugh the grisly rokkes blade,/For verray feere so wolde hir herte quake'; and the philosophical acceptance of the *Knight's*: 'This world nys but a thurghfare ful of wo,/And we been pilgrymes, passynge to and fro.' They are all held together, despite the seriousness of individual tales and the sombre final note of Chaucer's *Retraction*, in a poem which seems ultimately comic and humane, and which has delighted readers for hundreds of years.

Catherine Wells-Cole
Roehampton Institute, London

FURTHER READING

P. Boitani, ed: *The Cambridge Chaucer Companion*
D. Burnley: *A Guide to Chaucer's Language*
J. Burrow: *Medieval Writers and Their Work*
S.S. Hussey: *Chaucer: An Introduction*
J. Mann: *Chaucer and Medieval Estates Satire*
D. Pearsall: *The Life of Geoffrey Chaucer*

CONTENTS

THE CANTERBURY TALES

THE CANTERBURY TALES

THE PROLOGUE

Here biginneth the Book of the Tales of Caunterbury

WHAN that Aprille with his shoures sote
The droghte of Marche hath perced to the rote,
And bathed every veyne in swich licour,
Of which vertu engendred is the flour;
Whan Zephirus eek with his swete breeth
Inspired hath in every holt and heeth
The tendre croppes, and the yonge sonne
Hath in the Ram his halfe cours y-ronne,
And smale fowles maken melodye,
That slepen al the night with open yë,
(So priketh hem nature in hir corages):
Than longen folk to goon on pilgrimages
(And palmers for to seken straunge strondes)
To ferne halwes, couthe in sondry londes;
And specially, from every shires ende
Of Engelond, to Caunterbury they wende,
The holy blisful martir for to seke,
That hem hath holpen, whan that they were seke.
  Bifel that, in that seson on a day,
In Southwerk at the Tabard as I lay
Redy to wenden on my pilgrimage
To Caunterbury with ful devout corage,
At night was come in-to that hostelrye
Wel nyne and twenty in a companye,
Of sondry folk, by aventure y-falle
In felawshipe, and pilgrims were they alle,
That toward Caunterbury wolden ryde;
The chambres and the stables weren wyde,
And wel we weren esed atte beste.
And shortly, whan the sonne was to reste,
So hadde I spoken with hem everichon,
That I was of hir felawshipe anon,

And made forward erly for to ryse,
To take our wey, ther as I yow devyse.
But natheles, whyl I have tyme and space,
Er that I ferther in this tale pace,
Me thinketh it acordaunt to resoun,
To telle yow al the condicioun
Of ech of hem, so as it semed me,
And whiche they weren, and of what degree;
And eek in what array that they were inne:
And at a knight than wol I first biginne.
A KNIGHT ther was, and that a worthy man,
That fro the tyme that he first bigan
To ryden out, he loved chivalrye,
Trouthe and honour, fredom and curteisye.
Ful worthy was he in his lordes werre,
And therto hadde he riden (no man ferre)
As wel in Cristendom as hethenesse,
And ever honoured for his worthinesse.
At Alisaundre he was, whan it was wonne;
Ful ofte tyme he hadde the bord bigonne
Aboven alle naciouns in Pruce.
In Lettow hadde he reysed and in Ruce,
No Cristen man so ofte of his degree.
In Gernade at the sege eek hadde he be
Of Algezir, and riden in Belmarye.
At Lyeys was he, and at Satalye,
Whan they were wonne; and in the Grete See
At many a noble aryve hadde he be.
At mortal batailles hadde he been fiftene,
And foughten for our feith at Tramissene
In listes thryes, and ay slayn his fo.
This ilke worthy knight had been also
Somtyme with the lord of Palatye,
Ageyn another hethen in Turkye:
And evermore he hadde a sovereyn prys.
And though that he were worthy, he was wys,
And of his port as meke as is a mayde.
He never yet no vileinye ne sayde
In al his lyf, un-to no maner wight.
He was a verray parfit gentil knight.

But for to tellen yow of his array,
His hors were gode, but he was nat gay.
Of fustian he wered a gipoun
Al bismotered with his habergeoun;
For he was late y-come from his viage,
And wente for to doon his pilgrimage.
With him ther was his sone, a yong SQUYER,
A lovyere, and a lusty bacheler,
With lokkes crulle, as they were leyd in presse.
Of twenty yeer of age he was, I gesse.
Of his stature he was of evene lengthe,
And wonderly deliver, and greet of strengthe.
And he had been somtyme in chivachye,
In Flaundres, in Artoys, and Picardye,
And born him wel, as of so litel space,
In hope to stonden in his lady grace.
Embrouded was he, as it were a mede
Al ful of fresshe floures, whyte and rede.
Singinge he was, or floytinge, al the day;
He was as fresh as is the month of May.
Short was his goune, with sleves longe and wyde.
Wel coude he sitte on hors, and faire ryde.
He coude songes make and wel endyte,
Juste and eek daunce, and wel purtreye and wryte.
So hote he lovede, that by nightertale
He sleep namore than dooth a nightingale.
Curteys he was, lowly, and servisable,
And carf biforn his fader at the table.
A YEMAN hadde he, and servaunts namo
At that tyme, for him liste ryde so;
And he was clad in cote and hood of grene;
A sheef of pecok-arwes brighte and kene
Under his belt he bar ful thriftily;
(Wel coude he dresse his takel yemanly:
His arwes drouped noght with fetheres lowe),
And in his hand he bar a mighty bowe.
A not-heed hadde he, with a broun visage.
Of wode-craft wel coude he al the usage.
Upon his arm he bar a gay bracer,
And by his syde a swerd and a bokeler,

And on that other syde a gay daggere,
Harneised wel, and sharp as point of spere;
A Cristofre on his brest of silver shene.
An horn he bar, the bawdrik was of grene;
A forster was he, soothly, as I gesse.
  Ther was also a Nonne, a PRIORESSE,
That of hir smyling was ful simple and coy:
Hir gretteste ooth was but by sëynt Loy;
And she was cleped madame Eglentyne.
Ful wel she song the service divyne,
Entuned in hir nose ful semely;
And Frensh she spak ful faire and fetisly,
After the scole of Stratford atte Bowe,
For Frensh of Paris was to hir unknowe.
At mete wel y-taught was she with-alle;
She leet no morsel from hir lippes falle,
Ne wette hir fingres in hir sauce depe.
Wel coude she carie a morsel, and wel kepe,
That no drope ne fille up-on hir brest.
In curteisye was set ful muche hir lest.
Hir over lippe wyped she so clene,
That in hir coppe was no ferthing sene
Of grece, whan she dronken hadde hir draughte.
Ful semely after hir mete she raughte,
And sikerly she was of greet disport,
And ful plesaunt, and amiable of port,
And peyned hir to countrefete chere
Of court, and been estatlich of manere,
And to ben holden digne of reverence.
But, for to speken of hir conscience,
She was so charitable and so pitous,
She wolde wepe, if that she sawe a mous
Caught in a trappe, if it were deed or bledde.
Of smale houndes had she, that she fedde
With rosted flesh, or milk and wastel-breed.
But sore weep she if oon of hem were deed,
Or if men smoot it with a yerde smerte:
And al was conscience and tendre herte.
Ful semely hir wimpel pinched was;
Hir nose tretys; hir eyen greye as glas;

Hir mouth ful smal, and ther-to softe and reed;
But sikerly she hadde a fair forheed;
It was almost a spanne brood, I trowe;
For, hardily, she was nat undergrowe.
Ful fetis was hir cloke, as I was war.
Of smal coral aboute hir arm she bar
A peire of bedes, gauded al with grene;
And ther-on heng a broche of gold ful shene,
On which ther was first write a crowned A,
And after, *Amor vincit omnia.*
  Another NONNE with hir hadde she,
That was hir chapeleyne, and PREESTES THREE.
  A MONK ther was, a fair for the maistrye,
An out-rydere, that lovede venerye;
A manly man, to been an abbot able.
Ful many a deyntee hors hadde he in stable:
And, whan he rood, men mighte his brydel here
Ginglen in a whistling wind as clere,
And eek as loude as dooth the chapel-belle
Ther as this lord was keper of the celle.
The reule of seint Maure or of seint Beneit,
By-cause that it was old and som-del streit,
This ilke monk leet olde thinges pace,
And held after the newe world the space.
He yaf nat of that text a pulled hen,
That seith, that hunters been nat holy men;
Ne that a monk, whan he is cloisterlees,
Is lykned til a fish that is waterlees;
This is to seyn, a monk out of his cloistre.
But thilke text held he nat worth an oistre;
And I seyde, his opinioun was good.
What sholde he studie, and make himselven wood,
Upon a book in cloistre alwey to poure,
Or swinken with his handes, and laboure,
As Austin bit? How shal the world be served?
Lat Austin have his swink to him reserved.
Therfore he was a pricasour aright;
Grehoundes he hadde, as swifte as fowel in flight;
Of priking and of hunting for the hare
Was al his lust, for no cost wolde he spare.

I seigh his sleves purfiled at the hond
With grys, and that the fyneste of a lond
And, for to festne his hood under his chin,
He hadde of gold y-wroght a curious pin:
A love-knotte in the gretter ende ther was.
His heed was balled, that shoon as any glas,
And eek his face, as he had been anoint.
He was a lord ful fat and in good point;
His eyen stepe, and rollinge in his heed,
That stemed as a forneys of a leed;
His botes souple, his hors in greet estat.
Now certeinly he was a fair prelat;
He was nat pale as a for-pyned goost.
A fat swan loved he best of any roost.
His palfrey was as broun as is a berye.
A FRERE ther was, a wantown and a merye,
A limitour, a ful solempne man.
In alle the ordres foure is noon that can
So muche of daliaunce and fair langage.
He hadde maad ful many a mariage
Of yonge wommen, at his owne cost.
Un-to his ordre he was a noble post.
Ful wel biloved and famulier was he
With frankeleyns over-al in his contree,
And eek with worthy wommen of the toun:
For he had power of confessioun,
As seyde him-self, more than a curat,
For of his ordre he was licentiat.
Ful swetely herde he confessioun,
And plesaunt was his absolucioun;
He was an esy man to yeve penaunce
Ther as he wiste to han a good pitaunce;
For unto a povre ordre for to yive
Is signe that a man is wel y-shrive.
For if he yaf, he dorste make avaunt,
He wiste that a man was repentaunt.
For many a man so hard is of his herte,
He may nat wepe al-thogh him sore smerte.
Therfore, in stede of weping and preyeres,
Men moot yeve silver to the povre freres.

His tipet was ay farsed ful of knyves
And pinnes, for to yeven faire wyves.
And certeinly he hadde a mery note;
Wel coude he singe and pleyen on a rote.
Of yeddinges he bar utterly the prys.
His nekke whyt was as the flour-de-lys;
Ther-to he strong was as a champioun.
He knew the tavernes wel in every toun,
And everich hostiler and tappestere
Bet than a lazar or a beggestere;
For un-to swich a worthy man as he
Acorded nat, as by his facultee,
To have with seke lazars aqueyntaunce.
It is nat honest, it may nat avaunce
For to delen with no swich poraille,
But al with riche and sellers of vitaille.
And over-al, ther as profit sholde aryse,
Curteys he was, and lowly of servyse.
Ther nas no man no-wher so vertuous.
He was the beste beggere in his hous;
And yaf a certeyn ferme for the graunt;
Noon of his bretheren cam ther in his haunt;
For thogh a widwe hadde noght a sho,
So plesaunt was his '*In principio,*'
Yet wolde he have a ferthing, er he wente.
His purchas was wel bettre than his rente.
And rage he coude, as it were right a whelpe.
In love-dayes ther coude he muchel helpe.
For there he was nat lyk a cloisterer,
With a thredbar cope, as is a povre scoler,
But he was lyk a maister or a pope.
Of double worsted was his semi-cope,
That rounded as a belle out of the presse.
Somwhat he lipsed, for his wantownesse,
To make his English swete up-on his tonge;
And in his harping, whan that he had songe,
His eyen twinkled in his heed aright,
As doon the sterres in the frosty night.
This worthy limitour was cleped Huberd.
  A MARCHANT was ther with a forked berd,

In mottelee, and hye on horse he sat,
Up-on his heed a Flaundrish bever hat;
His botes clasped faire and fetisly.
His resons he spak ful solempnely,
Souninge alway th'encrees of his winning.
He wolde the see were kept for any thing
Bitwixe Middelburgh and Orewelle.
Wel coude he in eschaunge sheeldes selle.
This worthy man ful wel his wit bisette;
Ther wiste no wight that he was in dette,
So estatly was he of his governaunce,
With his bargaynes, and with his chevisaunce.
For sothe he was a worthy man with-alle,
But sooth to seyn, I noot how men him calle.
A CLERK ther was of Oxenford also,
That un-to logik hadde longe y-go.
As lene was his hors as is a rake,
And he nas nat right fat, I undertake;
But loked holwe, and ther-to soberly.
Ful thredbar was his overest courtepy;
For he had geten him yet no benefyce,
Ne was so worldly for to have offyce.
For him was lever have at his beddes heed
Twenty bokes, clad in blak or reed,
Of Aristotle and his philosophye,
Than robes riche, or fithele, or gay sautrye.
But al be that he was a philosophre,
Yet hadde he but litel gold in cofre;
But al that he mighte of his freendes hente,
On bokes and on lerninge he it spente,
And bisily gan for the soules preye
Of hem that yaf him wher-with to scoleye.
Of studie took he most cure and most hede.
Noght o word spak he more than was nede,
And that was seyd in forme and reverence,
And short and quik, and ful of hy sentence.
Souninge in moral vertu was his speche,
And gladly wolde he lerne, and gladly teche.
A SERGEANT OF THE LAWE, war and wys,
That often hadde been at the parvys,

Ther was also, ful riche of excellence.
Discreet he was, and of greet reverence:
He semed swich, his wordes weren so wyse.
Justyce he was ful often in assyse,
By patente, and by pleyn commissioun;
For his science, and for his heigh renoun
Of fees and robes hadde he many oon.
So greet a purchasour was no-wher noon.
Al was fee simple to him in effect,
His purchasing mighte nat been infect.
No-wher so bisy a man as he ther nas,
And yet he semed bisier than he was.
In termes hadde he caas and domes alle,
That from the tyme of king William were falle.
Therto he coude endyte, and make a thing,
Ther coude no wight pinche at his wryting;
And every statut coude he pleyn by rote.
He rood but hoomly in a medlee cote
Girt with a ceint of silk, with barres smale;
Of his array telle I no lenger tale.
A FRANKELEYN was in his companye;
Whyt was his berd, as is the dayesye.
Of his complexioun he was sangwyn.
Wel loved he by the morwe a sop in wyn.
To liven in delyt was ever his wone,
For he was Epicurus owne sone,
That heeld opinioun, that pleyn delyt
Was verraily felicitee parfyt.
An housholdere, and that a greet, was he;
Seint Julian he was in his contree.
His breed, his ale, was alwey after oon;
A bettre envyned man was no-wher noon.
With-oute bake mete was never his hous,
Of fish and flesh, and that so plentevous,
It snewed in his hous of mete and drinke,
Of alle deyntees that men coude thinke.
After the sondry sesons of the yeer,
So chaunged he his mete and his soper.
Ful many a fat partrich hadde he in mewe,
And many a breem and many a luce in stewe.

Wo was his cook, but-if his sauce were
Poynaunt and sharp, and redy al his gere.
His table dormant in his halle alway
Stood redy covered al the longe day.
At sessiouns ther was he lord and sire ;
Ful ofte tyme he was knight of the shire.
An anlas and a gipser al of silk
Heng at his girdel, whyt as morne milk.
A shirreve hadde he been, and a countour ;
Was no-wher such a worthy vavasour.
  An Haberdassher and a Carpenter,
A Webbe, a Dyere, and a Tapicer,
Were with us eek, clothed in o liveree,
Of a solempne and greet fraternitee.
Ful fresh and newe hir gere apyked was ;
Hir knyves were y-chaped noght with bras,
But al with silver, wroght ful clene and weel,
Hir girdles and hir pouches every-deel.
Wel semed ech of hem a fair burgeys,
To sitten in a yeldhalle on a deys.
Everich, for the wisdom that he can,
Was shaply for to been an alderman.
For catel hadde they y-nogh and rente,
And eek hir wyves wolde it wel assente
And elles certein were they to blame.
It is ful fair to been y-clept '*ma dame*,'
And goon to vigilyës al bifore,
And have a mantel royalliche y-bore.
  A Cook they hadde with hem for the nones,
To boille the chiknes with the marybones,
And poudre-marchant tart, and galingale.
Wel coude he knowe a draughte of London ale.
He coude roste, and sethe, and broille, and frye,
Maken mortreux, and wel bake a pye.
But greet harm was it, as it thoughte me,
That on his shine a mormal hadde he ;
For blankmanger, that made he with the beste.
  A Shipman was ther, woning fer by weste :
For aught I woot, he was of Dertemouthe.
He rood up-on a rouncy, as he couthe.

In a gowne of falding to the knee.
A daggere hanging on a laas hadde he
Aboute his nekke under his arm adoun.
The hote somer had maad his hewe al broun;
And, certeinly, he was a good felawe.
Ful many a draughte of wyn had he y-drawe
From Burdeux-ward, whyl that the chapman sleep.
Of nyce conscience took he no keep.
If that he faught, and hadde the hyer hond,
By water he sente hem hoom to every lond.
But of his craft to rekene wel his tydes,
His stremes and his daungers him bisydes,
His herberwe and his mone, his lode-menage,
Ther nas noon swich from Hulle to Cartage.
Hardy he was, and wys to undertake;
With many a tempest hadde his berd been shake.
He knew wel alle the havenes, as they were,
From Gootlond to the cape of Finistere,
And every cryke in Britayne and in Spayne;
His barge y-cleped was the Maudelayne.
  With us ther was a DOCTOUR OF PHISYK,
In al this world ne was ther noon him lyk
To speke of phisik and of surgerye;
For he was grounded in astronomye.
He kepte his pacient a ful greet del
In houres, by his magik naturel.
Wel coude he fortunen the ascendent
Of his images for his pacient.
He knew the cause of everich maladye,
Were it of hoot or cold, or moiste, or drye,
And where engendred, and of what humour;
He was a verrey parfit practisour.
The cause y-knowe, and of his harm the rote,
Anon he yaf the seke man his bote.
Ful redy hadde he his apothecaries,
To sende him drogges and his letuaries,
For ech of hem made other for to winne;
Hir frendschipe nas nat newe to biginne.
Wel knew he th'olde Esculapius,
And Deiscorides, and eek Rufus,

Old Ypocras, Haly, and Galien ;
Serapion, Razis, and Avicen ;
Averrois, Damascien, and Constantyn ;
Bernard, and Gatesden, and Gilbertyn.
Of his diete mesurable was he,
For it was of no superfluitee,
But of greet norissing and digestible.
His studie was but litel on the bible.
In sangwin and in pers he clad was al,
Lyned with taffata and with sendal ;
And yet he was but esy of dispence ;
He kepte that he wan in pestilence.
For gold in phisik is a cordial,
Therfore he lovede gold in special.
  A good WYF was ther of bisyde BATHE,
But she was som-del deef, and that was scathe.
Of clooth-making she hadde swiche an haunt,
She passed hem of Ypres and of Gaunt.
In al the parisshe wyf ne was ther noon
That to th' offring bifore hir sholde goon ;
And if ther dide, certeyn, so wrooth was she,
That she was out of alle charitee.
Hir coverchiefs ful fyne were of ground ;
I dorste swere they weyeden ten pound
That on a Sonday were upon hir heed.
Hir hosen weren of fyn scarlet reed,
Ful streite y-teyd, and shoos ful moiste and newe.
Bold was hir face, and fair, and reed of hewe.
She was a worthy womman al hir lyve,
Housbondes at chirche-dore she hadde fyve,
Withouten other companye in youthe ;
But therof nedeth nat to speke as nouthe.
And thryes hadde she been at Jerusalem ;
She hadde passed many a straunge streem ;
At Rome she hadde been, and at Boloigne,
In Galice at seint Jame, and at Coloigne.
She coude muche of wandring by the weye :
Gat-tothed was she, soothly for to seye.
Up-on an amblere esily she sat,
Y-wimpled wel, and on hir heed an hat

As brood as is a bokeler or a targe ;
A foot-mantel aboute hir hipes large,
And on hir feet a paire of spores sharpe.
In felawschip wel coude she laughe and carpe.
Of remedyes of love she knew perchaunce,
For she coude of that art the olde daunce.
 A good man was ther of religioun,
And was a povre PERSOUN of a toun ;
But riche he was of holy thoght and werk.
He was also a lerned man, a clerk,
That Cristes gospel trewely wolde preche ;
His parisshens devoutly wolde he teche.
Benigne he was, and wonder diligent,
And in adversitee ful pacient ;
And swich he was y-preved ofte sythes.
Ful looth were him to cursen for his tythes,
But rather wolde he yeven, out of doute,
Un-to his povre parisshens aboute
Of his offring, and eek of his substaunce.
He coude in litel thing han suffisaunce.
Wyd was his parisshe, and houses fer a-sonder,
But he ne lafte nat, for reyn ne thonder,
In siknes nor in meschief, to visyte
The ferreste in his parisshe, muche and lyte,
Up-on his feet, and in his hand a staf.
This noble ensample to his sheep he yaf,
That first he wroghte, and afterward he taughte ;
Out of the gospel he tho wordes caughte ;
And this figure he added eek ther-to,
That if gold ruste, what shal iren do ?
For if a preest be foul, on whom we truste,
No wonder is a lewed man to ruste ;
And shame it is, if a preest take keep,
A shiten shepherde and a clene sheep.
Wel oghte a preest ensample for to yive,
By his clennesse, how that his sheep shold live.
He sette nat his benefice to hyre,
And leet his sheep encombred in the myre,
And ran to London, un-to sëynt Poules,
To seken him a chaunterie for soules,

Or with a bretherhed to been withholde ;
But dwelte at hoom, and kepte wel his folde,
So that the wolf ne made it nat miscarie ;
He was a shepherde and no mercenarie.
And though he holy were, and vertuous,
He was to sinful man nat despitous,
Ne of his speche daungerous ne digne,
But in his teching discreet and benigne.
To drawen folk to heven by fairnesse
By good ensample, was his bisinesse :
But it were any persone obstinat,
What-so he were, of heigh or lowe estat,
Him wolde he snibben sharply for the nones.
A bettre preest, I trowe that nowher noon is.
He wayted after no pompe and reverence,
Ne maked him a spyced conscience,
But Cristes lore, and his apostles twelve,
He taughte, and first he folwed it himselve.
With him ther was a PLOWMAN, was his brother,
That hadde y-lad of dong ful many a fother,
A trewe swinker and a good was he,
Livinge in pees and parfit charitee.
God loved he best with al his hole herte
At alle tymes, thogh him gamed or smerte,
And thanne his neighebour right as himselve.
He wolde thresshe, and ther-to dyke and delve,
For Cristes sake, for every povre wight,
Withouten hyre, if it lay in his might.
His tythes payed he ful faire and wel,
Bothe of his propre swink and his catel.
In a tabard he rood upon a mere.
Ther was also a Reve and a Millere,
A Somnour and a Pardoner also,
A Maunciple, and my-self ; ther were namo.
The MILLER was a stout carl, for the nones,
Ful big he was of braun, and eek of bones ;
That proved wel, for over-al ther he cam,
At wrastling he wolde have alwey the ram.
He was short-sholdred, brood, a thikke knarre,
Ther nas no dore that he nolde heve of harre,

Or breke it, at a renning, with his heed.
His berd as any sowe or fox was reed,
And ther-to brood, as though it were a spade.
Up-on the cop right of his nose he hade
A werte, and ther-on stood a tuft of heres,
Reed as the bristles of a sowes eres;
His nose-thirles blake were and wyde.
A swerd and bokeler bar he by his syde;
His mouth as greet was as a greet forneys.
He was a janglere and a goliardeys,
And that was most of sinne and harlotryes.
Wel coude he stelen corn, and tollen thryes;
And yet he hadde a thombe of gold, pardee.
A whyt cote and a blew hood wered he.
A baggepype wel coude he blowe and sowne,
And ther-with-al he broghte us out of towne.
  A gentil MAUNCIPLE was ther of a temple,
Of which achatours mighte take exemple
For to be wyse in bying of vitaille
For whether that he payde, or took by taille,
Algate he wayted so in his achat,
That he was ay biforn and in good stat.
Now is nat that of God a ful fair grace,
That swich a lewed mannes wit shal pace
The wisdom of an heep of lerned men?
Of maistres hadde he mo than thryes ten,
That were of lawe expert and curious;
Of which ther were a doseyn in that hous
Worthy to been stiwardes of rente and lond
Of any lord that is in Engelond,
To make him live by his propre good,
In honour dettelees, but he were wood,
Or live as scarsly as him list desire;
And able for to helpen al a shire
In any cas that mighte falle or happe;
And yit this maunciple sette hir aller cappe.
  The REVE was a sclendre colerik man,
His berd was shave as ny as ever he can.
His heer was by his eres round y-shorn.
His top was dokked lyk a preest biforn

Ful longe were his legges, and ful lene,
Y-lyk a staf, ther was no calf y-sene.
Wel coude he kepe a gerner and a binne ;
Ther was noon auditour coude on him winne.
Wel wiste he, by the droghte, and by the reyn,
The yelding of his seed, and of his greyn.
His lordes sheep, his neet, his dayerye,
His swyn, his hors, his stoor, and his pultrye,
Was hoolly in this reves governing,
And by his covenaunt yaf the rekening,
Sin that his lord was twenty yeer of age ;
Ther coude no man bringe him in arrerage.
Ther nas baillif, ne herde, ne other hyne,
That he ne knew his sleighte and his covyne ;
They were adrad of him, as of the deeth.
His woning was ful fair up-on an heeth,
With grene treës shadwed was his place.
He coude bettre than his lord purchace.
Ful riche he was astored prively,
His lord wel coude he plesen subtilly,
To yeve and lene him of his owne good,
And have a thank, and yet a cote and hood.
In youthe he lerned hadde a good mister ;
He was a wel good wrighte, a carpenter.
This reve sat up-on a ful good stot,
That was al pomely grey, and highte Scot.
A long surcote of pers up-on he hade,
And by his syde he bar a rusty blade.
Of Northfolk was this reve, of which I telle,
Bisyde a toun men clepen Baldeswelle.
Tukked he was, as is a frere, aboute,
And ever he rood the hindreste of our route.
A SOMNOUR was ther with us in that place,
That hadde a fyr-reed cherubinnes face,
For sawcefleem he was, with eyen narwe.
As hoot he was, and lecherous, as a sparwe ;
With scalled browes blake, and piled berd ;
Of his visage children were aferd.
Ther nas quik-silver, litarge, ne brimstoon,
Boras, ceruce, ne oille of tartre noon,

Ne oynement that wolde clense and byte,
That him mighte helpen of his whelkes whyte,
Nor of the knobbes sittinge on his chekes.
Wel loved he garleek, oynons, and eek lekes,
And for to drinken strong wyn, reed as blood.
Than wolde he speke, and crye as he were wood.
And whan that he wel dronken hadde the wyn,
Than wolde he speke no word but Latyn.
A fewe termes hadde he, two or three,
That he had lerned out of som decree;
No wonder is, he herde it al the day;
And eek ye knowen wel, how that a jay
Can clepen 'Watte,' as well as can the pope.
But who-so coude in other thing him grope,
Thanne hadde he spent al his philosophye;
Ay '*Questio quid iuris*' wolde he crye.
He was a gentil harlot and a kinde;
A bettre felawe sholde men noght finde.
He wolde suffre, for a quart of wyn,
A good felawe to have his concubyn
A twelf-month, and excuse him atte fulle:
Ful privoly a finch eek coude he pulle.
And if he fond o-wher a good felawe,
He wolde techen him to have non awe,
In swich cas, of the erchedeknes curs,
But-if a mannes soule were in his purs;
For in his purs he sholde y-punisshed be.
'Purs is the erchedeknes helle,' seyde he.
But wel I woot he lyed right in dede;
Of cursing oghte ech gilty man him drede—
For curs wol slee, right as assoilling saveth—
And also war him of a *significavit*.
In daunger hadde he at his owne gyse
The yonge girles of the diocyse,
And knew hir counseil, and was al hir reed.
A gerland hadde he set up-on his heed,
As greet as it were for an ale-stake;
A bokeler hadde he maad him of a cake.
With him ther rood a gentil PARDONER
Of Rouncival, his freend and his compeer.

That streight was comen fro the court of Rome.
Ful loude he song, 'Com hider, love, to me.'
This somnour bar to him a stif burdoun,
Was never trompe of half so greet a soun.
This pardoner hadde heer as yelow as wex,
But smothe it heng, as dooth a strike of flex ;
By ounces henge his lokkes that he hadde,
And ther-with he his shuldres overspradde ;
But thinne it lay, by colpons oon and oon ;
But hood, for jolitee, ne wered he noon,
For it was trussed up in his walet.
Him thoughte, he rood al of the newe jet ;
Dischevele, save his cappe, he rood al bare.
Swiche glaringe eyen hadde he as an hare.
A vernicle hadde he sowed on his cappe.
His walet lay biforn him in his lappe,
Bret-ful of pardoun come from Rome al hoot.
A voys he hadde as smal as hath a goot.
No berd hadde he, ne never sholde have,
As smothe it was as it were late y-shave ;
I trowe he were a gelding or a mare.
But of his craft, fro Berwik into Ware,
Ne was ther swich another pardoner.
For in his male he hadde a pilwe-beer,
Which that, he seyde, was our lady veyl :
He seyde, he hadde a gobet of the seyl
That sëynt Peter hadde, whan that he wente
Up-on the see, til Jesu Crist him hente.
He hadde a croys of latoun, ful of stones,
And in a glas he hadde pigges bones.
But with thise relikes, whan that he fond
A povre person dwelling up-on lond,
Up-on a day he gat him more moneye
Than that the person gat in monthes tweye.
And thus, with feyned flaterye and japes,
He made the person and the peple his apes.
But trewely to tellen, atte laste,
He was in chirche a noble ecclesiaste.
Wel coude he rede a lessoun or a storie
But alderbest he song an offertorie ;

For wel he wiste, whan that song was songe
He moste preche, and wel affyle his tonge,
To winne silver, as he ful wel coude;
Therefore he song so meriely and loude.
Now have I told you shortly, in a clause,
Th'estat, th'array, the nombre, and eek the cause
Why that assembled was this companye
In Southwerk, at this gentil hostelrye,
That highte the Tabard, faste by the Belle.
But now is tyme to yow for to telle
How that we baren us that ilke night,
Whan we were in that hostelrye alight.
And after wol I telle of our viage,
And al the remenaunt of our pilgrimage.
But first I pray yow, of your curteisye,
That ye n'arette it nat my vileinye,
Thogh that I pleynly speke in this matere,
To telle yow hir wordes and hir chere;
Ne thogh I speke hir wordes properly.
For this ye knowen al-so wel as I,
Who-so shal telle a tale after a man,
He moot reherce, as ny as ever he can,
Everich a word, if it be in his charge,
Al speke he never so rudeliche and large;
Or elles he moot telle his tale untrewe,
Or feyne thing, or finde wordes newe.
He may nat spare, al-thogh he were his brother;
He moot as wel seye o word as another.
Crist spak him-self ful brode in holy writ,
And wel ye woot, no vileinye is it.
Eek Plato seith, who-so that can him rede,
The wordes mote be cosin to the dede.
Also I prey yow to foryeve it me,
Al have I nat set folk in hir degree
Here in this tale, as that they sholde stonde;
My wit is short, ye may wel understonde.
Greet chere made our hoste us everichon,
And to the soper sette us anon;
And served us with vitaille at the beste.
Strong was the wyn, and wel to drinke us leste.

A semely man our hoste was with-alle
For to han been a marshal in an halle;
A large man he was with eyen stepe,
A fairer burgeys is ther noon in Chepe:
Bold of his speche, and wys, and wel y-taught,
And of manhod him lakkede right naught.
Eek therto he was right a mery man,
And after soper pleyen he bigan,
And spak of mirthe amonges othere thinges,
Whan that we hadde maad our rekeninges;
And seyde thus: 'Now, lordinges, trewely,
Ye been to me right welcome hertely:
For by my trouthe, if that I shal nat lye,
I ne saugh this yeer so mery a companye
At ones in this herberwe as is now.
Fayn wolde I doon yow mirthe, wiste I how.
And of a mirthe I am right now bithoght,
To doon yow ese, and it shal coste noght.
  Ye goon to Caunterbury; God yow spede,
The blisful martir quyte yow your mede.
And wel I woot, as ye goon by the weye,
Ye shapen yow to talen and to pleye;
For trewely, confort ne mirthe is noon
To ryde by the weye doumb as a stoon;
And therfore wol I maken yow disport,
As I seyde erst, and doon yow som confort.
And if yow lyketh alle, by oon assent,
Now for to stonden at my jugement,
And for to werken as I shal yow seye,
To-morwe, whan ye ryden by the weye,
Now, by my fader soule, that is deed,
But ye be merye, I wol yeve yow myn heed.
Hold up your hond, withouten more speche.'
  Our counseil was nat longe for to seche;
Us thoughte it was noght worth to make it wys,
And graunted him withouten more avys.
And bad him seye his verdit, as him leste.
  'Lordinges,' quod he, 'now herkneth for the beste;
But tak it not, I prey yow, in desdeyn;
This is the poynt, to speken short and pleyn

That ech of yow, to shorte with your weye,
In this viage, shal telle tales tweye,
To Caunterbury-ward, I mene it so,
And hom-ward he shal tellen othere two,
Of aventures that whylom han bifalle.
And which of yow that bereth him best of alle,
That is to seyn, that telleth in this cas
Tales of best sentence and most solas,
Shal have a soper at our aller cost
Here in this place, sitting by this post,
Whan that we come agayn fro Caunterbury.
And for to make yow the more mery,
I wol my-selven gladly with yow ryde,
Right at myn owne cost, and be your gyde.
And who-so wol my jugement withseye
Shal paye al that we spenden by the weye.
And if ye vouche-sauf that it be so,
Tel me anon, with-outen wordes mo,
And I wol erly shape me therfore.'
This thing was graunted, and our othes swore
With ful glad herte, and preyden him also
That he wold vouche-sauf for to do so,
And that he wolde been our governour,
And of our tales juge and reportour,
And sette a soper at a certeyn prys;
And we wold reuled been at his devys,
In heigh and lowe; and thus, by oon assent,
We been acorded to his jugement.
And ther-up-on the wyn was fet anon;
We dronken, and to reste wente echon,
With-outen any lenger taryinge.
A-morwe, whan that day bigan to springe,
Up roos our host, and was our aller cok,
And gadrede us togidre, alle in a flok,
And forth we riden, a litel more than pas,
Un-to the watering of seint Thomas.
And there our host bigan his hors areste,
And seyde; 'Lordinges, herkneth, if yow leste.
Ye woot your forward, and I it yow recorde.
If even-song and morwe-song acorde,

Lat see now who shal telle the firste tale.
As ever mote I drinke wyn or ale,
Who-so be rebel to my jugement
Shal paye for al that by the weye is spent.
Now draweth cut, er that we ferrer twinne ;
He which that hath the shortest shal biginne.
Sire knight,' quod he, ' my maister and my lord,
Now draweth cut, for that is myn acord.
Cometh neer,' quod he, ' my lady prioresse ;
And ye, sir clerk, lat be your shamfastnesse,
Ne studieth noght ; ley hond to, every man.'
  Anon to drawen every wight bigan,
And shortly for to tellen, as it was,
Were it by aventure, or sort, or cas,
The sothe is this, the cut fil to the knight,
Of which ful blythe and glad was every wight ;
And telle he moste his tale, as was resoun,
By forward and by composicioun,
As ye han herd ; what nedeth wordes mo ?
And whan this gode man saugh it was so,
As he that wys was and obedient
To kepe his forward by his free assent,
He seyde : ' Sin I shal beginne the game,
What, welcome be the cut, a Goddes name !
Now lat us ryde, and herkneth what I seye.'
  And with that word we riden forth our weye ;
And he bigan with right a mery chere
His tale anon, and seyde in this manere.

Here endeth the prolog of this book ; and here biginneth the first tale, which is the Knightes Tale.

THE KNIGHTES TALE

Iamque domos patrias, Scithice post aspera gentis
Prelia, laurigero, &c. [Statius, *Theb.* xii. 519.]

WHYLOM, as olde stories tellen us,
Ther was a duk that highte Theseus;
Of Athenes he was lord and governour,
And in his tyme swich a conquerour,
That gretter was ther noon under the sonne.
Ful many a riche contree hadde he wonne;
What with his wisdom and his chivalrye,
He conquered al the regne of Femenye,
That whylom was y-cleped Scithia;
And weddede the quene Ipolita,
And broghte hir hoom with him in his contree
With muchel glorie and greet solempnitee,
And eek hir yonge suster Emelye.
And thus with victorie and with melodye
Lete I this noble duk to Athenes ryde,
And al his hoost, in armes, him bisyde.
And certes, if it nere to long to here,
I wolde han told yow fully the manere,
How wonnen was the regne of Femenye
By Theseus, and by his chivalrye;
And of the grete bataille for the nones
Bitwixen Athenës and Amazones;
And how asseged was Ipolita,
The faire hardy quene of Scithia;
And of the feste that was at hir weddinge,
And of the tempest at hir hoom-cominge;
But al that thing I moot as now forbere.
I have, God woot, a large feeld to ere,
And wayke been the oxen in my plough.
The remenant of the tale is long y-nough.
I wol nat letten eek noon of this route;
Lat every felawe telle his tale aboute.

And lat see now who shal the soper winne;
And ther I lefte, I wol ageyn biginne.
  This duk, of whom I make mencioun,
When he was come almost unto the toun,
In al his wele and in his moste pryde,
He was war, as he caste his eye asyde,
Wher that ther kneled in the hye weye
A companye of ladies, tweye and tweye,
Ech after other, clad in clothes blake;
But swich a cry and swich a wo they make,
That in this world nis creature livinge,
That herde swich another weymentinge;
And of this cry they nolde never stenten,
Til they the reynes of his brydel henten.
  'What folk ben ye, that at myn hoom-cominge
Perturben so my feste with cryinge?'
Quod Theseus, 'have ye so greet envye
Of myn honour, that thus compleyne and crye?
Or who hath yow misboden, or offended?
And telleth me if it may been amended;
And why that ye ben clothed thus in blak?'
  The eldest lady of hem alle spak,
When she hadde swowned with a deedly chere,
That it was routhe for to seen and here,
And seyde: 'Lord, to whom Fortune hath yiven
Victorie, and as a conquerour to liven,
Noght greveth us your glorie and your honour;
But we biseken mercy and socour.
Have mercy on our wo and our distresse.
Som drope of pitee, thurgh thy gentilesse,
Up-on us wrecched wommen lat thou falle.
For certes, lord, ther nis noon of us alle,
That she nath been a duchesse or a quene;
Now be we caitifs, as it is wel sene:
Thanked be Fortune, and hir false wheel,
That noon estat assureth to be weel.
And certes, lord, t'abyden your presence,
Here in the temple of the goddesse Clemence
We han ben waytinge al this fourtenight;
Now help us, lord, sith it is in thy might.

I wrecche, which that wepe and waille thus,
Was whylom wyf to king Capaneus,
That starf at Thebes, cursed be that day!
And alle we, that been in this array,
And maken al this lamentacioun,
We losten alle our housbondes at that toun,
Whyl that the sege ther-aboute lay.
And yet now th'olde Creon, weylaway!
The lord is now of Thebes the citee,
Fulfild of ire and of iniquitee,
He, for despyt, and for his tirannye,
To do the dede bodyes vileinye,
Of alle our lordes, whiche that ben slawe,
Hath alle the bodyes on an heep y-drawe,
And wol nat suffren hem, by noon assent,
Neither to been y-buried nor y-brent,
But maketh houndes ete hem in despyt.'
And with that word, with-outen more respyt,
They fillen gruf, and cryden pitously,
'Have on us wrecched wommen som mercy,
And lat our sorwe sinken in thyn herte.'
This gentil duk doun from his courser sterte
With herte pitous, whan he herde hem speke.
Him thoughte that his herte wolde breke,
Whan he saugh hem so pitous and so mat,
That whylom weren of so greet estat.
And in his armes he hem alle up hente,
And hem conforteth in ful good entente;
And swoor his ooth, as he was trewe knight,
He wolde doon so ferforthly his might
Up-on the tyraunt Creon hem to wreke,
That al the peple of Grece sholde speke
How Creon was of Theseus y-served,
As he that hadde his deeth ful wel deserved.
And right anoon, with-outen more abood,
His baner he desplayeth, and foorth rood
To Thebes-ward, and al his host bisyde;
No neer Athenës wolde he go ne ryde,
Ne take his ese fully half a day,
But onward on his wey that night he lay;

And sente anoon Ipolita the quene,
And Emelye hir yonge suster shene,
Un-to the toun of Athenës to dwelle;
And forth he rit; ther nis namore to telle.
The rede statue of Mars, with spere and targe,
So shyneth in his whyte baner large,
That alle the feeldes gliteren up and doun;
And by his baner born is his penoun
Of gold ful riche, in which ther was y-bete
The Minotaur, which that he slough in Crete.
Thus rit this duk, thus rit this conquerour,
And in his host of chivalrye the flour,
Til that he cam to Thebes, and alighte
Faire in a feeld, ther as he thoghte fighte.
But shortly for to speken of this thing,
With Creon, which that was of Thebes king,
He faught, and slough him manly as a knight
In pleyn bataille, and putte the folk to flight;
And by assaut he wan the citee after,
And rente adoun bothe wal, and sparre, and rafter;
And to the ladyes he restored agayn
The bones of hir housbondes that were slayn,
To doon obséquies, as was tho the gyse.
But it were al to long for to devyse
The grete clamour and the waymentinge
That the ladyes made at the brenninge
Of the bodyes, and the grete honour
That Theseus, the noble conquerour,
Doth to the ladyes, whan they from him wente;
But shortly for to telle is myn entente.
Whan that this worthy duk, this Theseus,
Hath Creon slayn, and wonne Thebes thus,
Stille in that feeld he took al night his reste,
And dide with al the contree as him leste.
To ransake in the tas of bodyes dede,
Hem for to strepe of harneys and of wede,
The pilours diden bisinesse and cure,
After the bataille and disconfiture.
And so bifel, that in the tas they founde,
Thurgh-girt with many a grevous blody wounde,

Two yonge knightes ligging by and by,
Bothe in oon armes, wroght ful richely,
Of whiche two, Arcita hight that oon,
And that other knight hight Palamon.
Nat fully quike, ne fully dede they were,
But by hir cote-armures, and by hir gere,
The heraudes knewe hem best in special,
As they that weren of the blood royal
Of Thebes, and of sustren two y-born.
Out of the tas the pilours han hem torn,
And han hem caried softe un-to the tente
Of Theseus, and he ful sone hem sente
To Athenës, to dwellen in prisoun
Perpetuelly, he nolde no raunsoun.
And whan this worthy duk hath thus y-don,
He took his host, and hoom he rood anon
With laurer crowned as a conquerour;
And there he liveth, in joye and in honour,
Terme of his lyf; what nedeth wordes mo?
And in a tour, in angwish and in wo,
Dwellen this Palamoun and eek Arcite,
For evermore, ther may no gold hem quyte.
This passeth yeer by yeer, and day by day,
Til it fil ones, in a morwe of May,
That Emelye, that fairer was to sene
Than is the lilie upon his stalke grene,
And fressher than the May with floures newe—
For with the rose colour stroof hir hewe,
I noot which was the fairer of hem two—
Er it were day, as was hir wone to do,
She was arisen, and al redy dight;
For May wol have no slogardye a-night.
The sesoun priketh every gentil herte,
And maketh him out of his sleep to sterte,
And seith, 'Arys, and do thyn observaunce.'
This maked Emelye have remembraunce
To doon honour to May, and for to ryse.
Y-clothed was she fresh, for to devyse;
Hir yelow heer was broyded in a tresse,
Bihinde hir bak, a yerde long, I gesse.

And in the gardin, at the sonne up-riste,
She walketh up and doun, and as hir liste
She gadereth floures, party whyte and rede,
To make a sotil gerland for hir hede,
And as an aungel hevenly she song.
The grete tour, that was so thikke and strong,
Which of the castel was the chief dongeoun,
(Ther-as the knightes weren in prisoun,
Of whiche I tolde yow, and tellen shal)
Was evene joynant to the gardin-wal,
Ther as this Emelye hadde hir pleyinge.
Bright was the sonne, and cleer that morweninge,
And Palamon, this woful prisoner,
As was his wone, by leve of his gayler,
Was risen, and romed in a chambre on heigh,
In which he al the noble citee seigh,
And eek the gardin, ful of braunches grene,
Ther-as this fresshe Emelye the shene
Was in hir walk, and romed up and doun.
This sorweful prisoner, this Palamoun,
Goth in the chambre, roming to and fro,
And to him-self compleyning of his wo ;
That he was born, ful ofte he seyde, 'alas !'
And so bifel, by aventure or cas,
That thurgh a window, thikke of many a barre
Of yren greet, and square as any sparre,
He caste his eye upon Emelya,
And ther-with-al he bleynte, and cryde 'a !'
As though he stongen were un-to the herte.
And with that cry Arcite anon up-sterte,
And seyde, 'Cosin myn, what eyleth thee,
That art so pale and deedly on to see ?
Why crydestow ? who hath thee doon offence ?
For Goddes love, tak al in pacience
Our prisoun, for it may non other be ;
Fortune hath yeven us this adversitee.
Som wikke aspect or disposicioun
Of Saturne, by sum constellacioun,
Hath yeven us this, al-though we hadde it sworn ;
So stood the heven whan that we were born ;

We moste endure it : this is the short and pleyn.'
This Palamon answerde, and seyde ageyn,
'Cosyn, for sothe, of this opinioun
Thou hast a veyn imaginacioun.
This prison caused me nat for to crye.
But I was hurt right now thurgh-out myn yë
In-to myn herte, that wol my bane be.
The fairnesse of that lady that I see
Yond in the gardin romen to and fro,
Is cause of al my crying and my wo.
I noot wher she be womman or goddesse ;
But Venus is it, soothly, as I gesse.'
And ther-with-al on kneës doun he fil,
And seyde : 'Venus, if it be thy wil
Yow in this gardin thus to transfigure
Bifore me, sorweful wrecche creature,
Out of this prisoun help that we may scapen.
And if so be my destinee be shapen
By eterne word to dyen in prisoun,
Of our linage have som compassioun,
That is so lowe y-broght by tirannye.'
And with that word Arcite gan espye
Wher-as this lady romed to and fro.
And with that sighte hir beautee hurte him so,
That, if that Palamon was wounded sore,
Arcite is hurt as muche as he, or more.
And with a sigh he seyde pitously :
'The fresshe beautee sleeth me sodeynly
Of hir that rometh in the yonder place ;
And, but I have hir mercy and hir grace,
That I may seen hir atte leeste weye,
I nam but deed ; ther nis namore to seye.'
This Palamon, whan he tho wordes herde,
Dispitously he loked, and answerde :
'Whether seistow this in ernest or in pley?'
'Nay,' quod Arcite, 'in ernest, by my fey !
God help me so, me list ful yvele pleye.'
This Palamon gan knitte his browes tweye :
'It nere,' quod he, 'to thee no greet honour
For to be fals, ne for to be traytour

To me, that am thy cosin and thy brother
Y-sworn ful depe, and ech of us til other,
That never, for to dyen in the peyne,
Til that the deeth departe shal us tweyne,
Neither of us in love to hindren other,
Ne in non other cas, my leve brother ;
But that thou sholdest trewely forthren me
In every cas, and I shal forthren thee.
This was thyn ooth, and myn also, certeyn ;
I wot right wel, thou darst it nat withseyn.
Thus artow of my counseil, out of doute.
And now thou woldest falsly been aboute
To love my lady, whom I love and serve,
And ever shal, til that myn herte sterve.
Now certes, fals Arcite, thou shalt nat so.
I loved hir first, and tolde thee my wo
As to my counseil, and my brother sworn
To forthre me, as I have told biforn.
For which thou art y-bounden as a knight
To helpen me, if it lay in thy might,
Or elles artow fals, I dar wel seyn.'
  This Arcitë ful proudly spak ageyn,
'Thou shalt,' quod he, 'be rather fals than I ;
But thou art fals, I telle thee utterly ;
For *par amour* I loved hir first er thow.
What wiltow seyn ? thou wistest nat yet now
Whether she be a womman or goddesse !
Thyn is affeccioun of holinesse,
And myn is love, as to a creature ;
For which I tolde thee myn aventure
As to my cosin, and my brother sworn.
I pose, that thou lovedest hir biforn ;
Wostow nat wel the olde clerkes sawe,
That "who shal yeve a lover any lawe ?"
Love is a gretter lawe, by my pan,
Than may be yeve to any erthly man.
And therefore positif lawe and swich decree
Is broke al-day for love, in ech degree.
A man moot nedes love, maugree his heed.
He may nat fleen it, thogh he sholde be deed,

Al be she mayde, or widwe, or elles wyf.
And eek it is nat lykly, al thy lyf,
To stonden in hir grace ; namore shal I ;
For wel thou woost thy-selven, verraily,
That thou and I be dampned to prisoun
Perpetuelly ; us gayneth no raunsoun.
We stryve as dide the houndes for the boon,
They foughte al day, and yet hir part was noon ;
Ther cam a kyte, whyl that they were wrothe,
And bar awey the boon bitwixe hem bothe.
And therfore, at the kinges court, my brother,
Ech man for him-self, ther is non other.
Love if thee list ; for I love and ay shal ;
And soothly, leve brother, this is al.
Here in this prisoun mote we endure,
And everich of us take his aventure.'

Greet was the stryf and long bitwixe hem tweye,
If that I hadde leyser for to seye ;
But to th'effect. It happed on a day,
(To telle it yow as shortly as I may)
A worthy duk that highte Perotheus,
That felawe was un-to duk Theseus
Sin thilke day that they were children lyte,
Was come to Athenes, his felawe to visyte,
And for to pleye, as he was wont to do,
For in this world he loved no man so :
And he loved him as tendrely ageyn.
So wel they loved, as olde bokes seyn,
That whan that oon was deed, sothly to telle,
His felawe wente and soghte him doun in helle ;
But of that story list me nat to wryte.
Duk Perotheus loved wel Arcite,
And hadde him knowe at Thebes yeer by yere ;
And fynally, at requeste and preyere
Of Perotheus, with-oute any raunsoun,
Duk Theseus him leet out of prisoun,
Freely to goon, wher that him liste over-al,
In swich a gyse, as I you tellen shal.

This was the forward, pleynly for t'endyte,
Bitwixen Theseus and him Arcite :

That if so were, that Arcite were y-founde
Ever in his lyf, by day or night or stounde
In any contree of this Theseus,
And he were caught, it was acorded thus,
That with a swerd he sholde lese his heed;
Ther nas non other remedye ne reed,
But taketh his leve, and homward he him spedde;
Let him be war, his nekke lyth to wedde!
 How greet a sorwe suffreth now Arcite!
The deeth he feleth thurgh his herte smyte;
He wepeth, wayleth, cryeth pitously;
To sleen him-self he wayteth prively.
He seyde, 'Allas that day that I was born!
Now is my prison worse than biforn;
Now is me shape eternally to dwelle
Noght in purgatorie, but in helle.
Allas! that ever knew I Perotheus!
For elles hadde I dwelled with Theseus
Y-fetered in his prisoun ever-mo.
Than hadde I been in blisse, and nat in wo.
Only the sighte of hir, whom that I serve,
Though that I never hir grace may deserve,
Wolde han suffised right y-nough for me.
O dere cosin Palamon,' quod he,
'Thyn is the victorie of this aventure,
Ful blisfully in prison maistow dure;
In prison? certes nay, but in paradys!
Wel hath fortune y-turned thee the dys,
That hast the sighte of hir, and I th'absence.
For possible is, sin thou hast hir presence,
And art a knight, a worthy and an able,
That by som cas, sin fortune is chaungeable,
Thou mayst to thy desyr som-tyme atteyne.
But I, that am exyled, and bareyne
Of alle grace, and in so greet despeir,
That ther nis erthe, water, fyr, ne eir,
Ne creature, that of hem maked is,
That may me helpe or doon confort in this:
Wel oughte I sterve in wanhope and distresse;
Farwel my lyf, my lust, and my gladnesse!

Allas, why pleynen folk so in commune
Of purveyaunce of God, or of fortune,
That yeveth hem ful ofte in many a gyse
Wel bettre than they can hem-self devyse ?
Som man desyreth for to han richesse,
That cause is of his mordre or greet siknesse.
And som man wolde out of his prison fayn,
That in his hous is of his meynee slayn.
Infinite harmes been in this matere ;
We witen nat what thing we preyen here.
We faren as he that dronke is as a mous ;
A dronke man wot wel he hath an hous,
But he noot which the righte wey is thider ;
And to a dronke man the wey is slider.
And certes, in this world so faren we ;
We seken faste after felicitee,
But we goon wrong ful often, trewely.
Thus may we seyen alle, and namely I,
That wende and hadde a greet opinioun,
That, if I mighte escapen from prisoun,
Than hadde I been in joye and perfit hele,
Ther now I am exyled fro my wele
Sin that I may nat seen yow, Emelye,
I nam but deed ; ther nis no remedye.'
Up-on that other syde Palamon,
Whan that he wiste Arcite was agon,
Swich sorwe he maketh, that the grete tour
Resouneth of his youling and clamour.
The pure fettres on his shines grete
Weren of his bittre salte teres wete.
'Allas !' quod he, 'Arcita, cosin myn,
Of al our stryf, God woot, the fruyt is thyn.
Thow walkest now in Thebes at thy large,
And of my wo thou yevest litel charge.
Thou mayst, sin thou hast wisdom and manhede,
Assemblen alle the folk of our kinrede,
And make a werre so sharp on this citee,
That by som aventure, or som tretee,
Thou mayst have hir to lady and to wyf,
For whom that I mot nedes lese my lyf.

For, as by wey of possibilitee,
Sith thou art at thy large, of prison free,
And art a lord, greet is thyn avauntage,
More than is myn, that sterve here in a cage.
For I mot wepe and wayle, whyl I live,
With al the wo that prison may me yive,
And eek with peyne that love me yiveth also,
That doubleth al my torment and my wo.'
Ther-with the fyr of jelousye up-sterte
With-inne his brest, and hente him by the herte
So woodly, that he lyk was to biholde
The box-tree, or the asshen dede and colde.
Tho seyde he ; 'O cruel goddes, that governe
This world with binding of your word eterne,
And wryten in the table of athamaunt
Your parlement, and your eterne graunt,
What is mankinde more un-to yow holde
Than is the sheep, that rouketh in the folde ?
For slayn is man right as another beste,
And dwelleth eek in prison and areste,
And hath siknesse, and greet adversitee,
And ofte tymes giltelees, pardee !
What governaunce is in this prescience,
That giltelees tormenteth innocence ?
And yet encreseth this al my penaunce,
That man is bounden to his observaunce,
For Goddes sake, to letten of his wille,
Ther as a beest may al his lust fulfille.
And whan a beest is deed, he hath no peyne ;
But man after his deeth moot wepe and pleyne,
Though in this world he have care and wo :
With-outen doute it may stonden so.
Th' answere of this I lete to divynis,
But wel I woot, that in this world gret pyne is.
Allas ! I see a serpent or a theef,
That many a trewe man hath doon mescheef,
Goon at his large, and wher him list may turne.
But I mot been in prison thurgh Saturne,
And eek thurgh Juno, jalous and eek wood,
That hath destroyed wel ny al the blood

Of Thebes, with his waste walles wyde.
And Venus sleeth me on that other syde
For jelousye, and fere of him Arcite.'
  Now wol I stinte of Palamon a lyte,
And lete him in his prison stille dwelle,
And of Arcita forth I wol yow telle.
  The somer passeth, and the nightes longe
Encresen double wyse the peynes stronge
Bothe of the lovere and the prisoner.
I noot which hath the wofullere mester.
For shortly for to seyn, this Palamoun
Perpetuelly is dampned to prisoun,
In cheynes and in fettres to ben deed;
And Arcite is exyled upon his heed
For ever-mo as out of that contree,
Ne never-mo he shal his lady see.
  Yow loveres axe I now this questioun,
Who hath the worse, Arcite or Palamoun?
That oon may seen his lady day by day,
But in prison he moot dwelle alway.
That other wher him list may ryde or go,
But seen his lady shal he never-mo.
Now demeth as yow liste, ye that can,
For I wol telle forth as I bigan.

Explicit prima Pars.

Sequitur pars secunda.

  Whan that Arcite to Thebes comen was,
Ful ofte a day he swelte and seyde 'allas,'
For seen his lady shal he never-mo.
And shortly to concluden al his wo,
So muche sorwe had never creature
That is, or shal, whyl that the world may dure.
His sleep, his mete, his drink is him biraft,
That lene he wex, and drye as is a shaft.
His eyen holwe, and grisly to biholde;
His hewe falwe, and pale as asshen colde,
And solitarie he was, and ever allone,
And wailling al the night, making his mone.

And if he herde song or instrument,
Then wolde he wepe, he mighte nat be stent;
So feble eek were his spirits, and so lowe,
And chaunged so, that no man coude knowe
His speche nor his vois, though men it herde.
And in his gere, for al the world he ferde
Nat oonly lyk the loveres maladye
Of Hereos, but rather lyk manye
Engendred of humour malencolyk,
Biforen, in his celle fantastyk.
And shortly, turned was al up-so-doun
Bothe habit and eek disposicioun
Of him, this woful lovere daun Arcite.
What sholde I al-day of his wo endyte?
Whan he endured hadde a yeer or two
This cruel torment, and this peyne and wo,
At Thebes, in his contree, as I seyde,
Up-on a night, in sleep as he him leyde,
Him thoughte how that the winged god Mercurie
Biforn him stood, and bad him to be murye.
His slepy yerde in hond he bar uprighte;
An hat he werede up-on his heres brighte.
Arrayed was this god (as he took keep)
As he was whan that Argus took his sleep;
And seyde him thus: 'T'Athénës shaltou wende;
Ther is thee shapen of thy wo an ende.'
And with that word Arcite wook and sterte.
'Now trewely, how sore that me smerte,'
Quod he, 't'Athénës right now wol I fare;
Ne for the drede of deeth shal I nat spare
To see my lady, that I love and serve;
In hir presence I recche nat to sterve.'
And with that word he caughte a greet mirour,
And saugh that chaunged was al his colour,
And saugh his visage al in another kinde.
And right anoon it ran him in his minde,
That, sith his face was so disfigured
Of maladye, the which he hadde endured,
He mighte wel, if that he bar him lowe,
Live in Athénes ever-more unknowe,

And seen his lady wel ny day by day.
And right anon he chaunged his array,
And cladde him as a povre laborer,
And al allone, save oonly a squyer,
That knew his privetee and al his cas,
Which was disgysed povrely, as he was,
T'Athénës is he goon the nexte way.
And to the court he wente up-on a day,
And at the gate he profreth his servyse,
To drugge and drawe, what so men wol devyse.
And shortly of this matere for to seyn,
He fil in office with a chamberleyn,
The which that dwelling was with Emelye;
For he was wys, and coude soon aspye
Of every servaunt, which that serveth here.
Wel coude he hewen wode, and water bere,
For he was yong and mighty for the nones,
And ther-to he was strong and big of bones
To doon that any wight can him devyse.
A yeer or two he was in this servyse,
Page of the chambre of Emelye the brighte;
And 'Philostrate' he seide that he highte.
But half so wel biloved a man as he
Ne was ther never in court, of his degree;
He was so gentil of condicioun,
That thurghout al the court was his renoun.
They seyden, that it were a charitee
That Theseus wolde enhauncen his degree,
And putten him in worshipful servyse,
Ther as he mighte his vertu excercyse.
And thus, with-inne a whyle, his name is spronge
Bothe of his dedes, and his goode tonge,
That Theseus hath taken him so neer
That of his chambre he made him a squyer,
And yaf him gold to mayntene his degree;
And eek men broghte him out of his contree
From yeer to yeer, ful prively, his rente;
But honestly and slyly he it spente,
That no man wondred how that he it hadde.
And three yeer in this wyse his lyf he ladde,

And bar him so in pees and eek in werre,
Ther nas no man that Theseus hath derre.
And in this blisse lete I now Arcite,
And speke I wol of Palamon a lyte.
In derknesse and horrible and strong prisoun
This seven yeer hath seten Palamoun,
Forpyned, what for wo and for distresse;
Who feleth double soor and hevinesse
But Palamon? that love destreyneth so,
That wood out of his wit he gooth for wo;
And eek therto he is a prisoner
Perpetuelly, noght oonly for a yeer.
Who coude ryme in English proprely
His martirdom? for sothe, it am nat I;
Therefore I passe as lightly as I may.
It fel that in the seventhe yeer, in May,
The thridde night, (as olde bokes seyn,
That al this storie tellen more pleyn,)
Were it by aventure or destinee,
(As, whan a thing is shapen, it shal be,)
That, sone after the midnight, Palamoun,
By helping of a freend, brak his prisoun,
And fleeth the citee, faste as he may go;
For he had yive his gayler drinke so
Of a clarree, maad of a certeyn wyn,
With nercotikes and opie of Thebes fyn,
That al that night, thogh that men wolde him shake,
The gayler sleep, he mighte nat awake;
And thus he fleeth as faste as ever he may.
The night was short, and faste by the day,
That nedes-cost he moste him-selven hyde,
And til a grove, faste ther besyde,
With dredful foot than stalketh Palamoun.
For shortly, this was his opinioun,
That in that grove he wolde him hyde al day,
And in the night than wolde he take his way
To Thebes-ward, his freendes for to preye
On Theseus to helpe him to werreye;
And shortly, outher he wolde lese his lyf,
Or winnen Emelye un-to his wyf;

This is th'effect and his entente pleyn.
  Now wol I torne un-to Arcite ageyn,
That litel wiste how ny that was his care,
Til that fortune had broght him in the snare.
  The bisy larke, messager of day,
Saluëth in hir song the morwe gray;
And fyry Phebus ryseth up so brighte,
That al the orient laugheth of the lighte,
And with his stremes dryeth in the greves
The silver dropes, hanging on the leves.
And Arcite, that is in the court royal
With Theseus, his squyer principal,
Is risen, and loketh on the myrie day.
And, for to doon his observaunce to May,
Remembring on the poynt of his desyr,
He on a courser, sterting as the fyr,
Is riden in-to the feeldes, him to pleye,
Out of the court, were it a myle or tweye;
And to the grove, of which that I yow tolde,
By aventure, his wey he gan to holde,
To maken him a gerland of the greves,
Were it of wodebinde or hawethorn-leves,
And loude he song ageyn the sonne shene:
'May, with alle thy floures and thy grene,
Wel-come be thou, faire fresshe May,
I hope that I som grene gete may.'
And from his courser, with a lusty herte,
In-to the grove ful hastily he sterte,
And in a path he rometh up and doun,
Ther-as, by aventure, this Palamoun
Was in a bush, that no man mighte him see,
For sore afered of his deeth was he.
No-thing ne knew he that it was Arcite:
God wot he wolde have trowed it ful lyte.
But sooth is seyd, gon sithen many yeres,
That 'feeld hath eyen, and the wode hath eres.'
It is ful fair a man to bere him evene,
For al-day meteth men at unset stevene.
Ful litel woot Arcite of his felawe,
That was so ny to herknen al his sawe,

For in the bush he sitteth now ful stille.
  Whan that Arcite had romed al his fille,
And songen al the roundel lustily,
In-to a studie he fil sodeynly,
As doon thise loveres in hir queynte geres,
Now in the croppe, now doun in the breres,
Now up, now doun, as boket in a welle.
Right as the Friday, soothly for to telle,
Now it shyneth, now it reyneth faste,
Right so can gery Venus overcaste
The hertes of hir folk ; right as hir day
Is gerful, right so chaungeth she array.
Selde is the Friday al the wyke y-lyke.
  Whan that Arcite had songe, he gan to syke,
And sette him doun with-outen any more :
'Alas ! ' quod he, ' that day that I was bore !
How longe, Juno, thurgh thy crueltee,
Woltow werreyen Thebes the citee ?
Allas ! y-broght is to confusioun
The blood royal of Cadme and Amphioun ;
Of Cadmus, which that was the firste man
That Thebes bulte, or first the toun bigan,
And of the citee first was crouned king,
Of his linage am I, and his of-spring
By verray ligne, as of the stok royal :
And now I am so caitif and so thral,
That he, that is my mortal enemy,
I serve him as his squyer povrely.
And yet doth Juno me wel more shame,
For I dar noght biknowe myn owne name ;
But ther-as I was wont to highte Arcite,
Now highte I Philostrate, noght worth a myte.
Allas ! thou felle Mars, allas ! Juno,
Thus hath your ire our kinrede al fordo,
Save only me, and wrecched Palamoun,
That Theseus martyreth in prisoun.
And over al this, to sleen me utterly,
Love hath his fyry dart so brenningly
Y-stiked thurgh my trewe careful herte,
That shapen was my deeth erst than my sherte.

Ye sleen me with your eyen, Emelye;
Ye been the cause wherfor that I dye.
Of al the remenant of myn other care
Ne sette I nat the mountaunce of a tare,
So that I coude don aught to your plesaunce!'
And with that word he fil doun in a traunce
A longe tyme; and after he up-sterte.
This Palamoun, that thoughte that thurgh his herte
He felte a cold swerd sodeynliche glyde,
For ire he quook, no lenger wolde he byde.
And whan that he had herd Arcites tale,
As he were wood, with face deed and pale,
He sterte him up out of the buskes thikke,
And seyde: 'Arcite, false traitour wikke,
Now artow hent, that lovest my lady so,
For whom that I have al this peyne and wo,
And art my blood, and to my counseil sworn,
As I ful ofte have told thee heer-biforn,
And hast by-japed here duk Theseus,
And falsly chaunged hast thy name thus;
I wol be deed, or elles thou shalt dye.
Thou shalt nat love my lady Emelye,
But I wol love hir only, and namo;
For I am Palamoun, thy mortal fo.
And though that I no wepne have in this place,
But out of prison am astert by grace,
I drede noght that outher thou shalt dye,
Or thou ne shalt nat loven Emelye.
Chees which thou wilt, for thou shalt nat asterte.'
This Arcitë, with ful despitous herte,
Whan he him knew, and hadde his tale herd,
As fiers as leoun, pulled out a swerd,
And seyde thus: 'by God that sit above,
Nere it that thou art sik, and wood for love,
And eek that thou no wepne hast in this place,
Thou sholdest never out of this grove pace,
That thou ne sholdest dyen of myn hond.
For I defye the seurtee and the bond
Which that thou seyst that I have maad to thee.
What, verray fool, think wel that love is free,

And I wol love hir, maugre al thy might!
But, for as muche thou art a worthy knight,
And wilnest to darreyne hir by batayle,
Have heer my trouthe, to-morwe I wol nat fayl
With-outen witing of any other wight,
That here I wol be founden as a knight,
And bringen harneys right y-nough for thee;
And chees the beste, and leve the worste for me.
And mete and drinke this night wol I bringe
Y-nough for thee, and clothes for thy beddinge.
And, if so be that thou my lady winne,
And slee me in this wode ther I am inne,
Thou mayst wel have thy lady, as for me.'
This Palamon answerde: 'I graunte it thee.'
And thus they been departed til a-morwe,
When ech of hem had leyd his feith to borwe.
  O Cupide, out of alle charitee!
O regne, that wolt no felawe have with thee!
Ful sooth is seyd, that love ne lordshipe
Wol noght, his thankes, have no felaweshipe;
Wel finden that Arcite and Palamoun.
Arcite is riden anon un-to the toun,
And on the morwe, er it were dayes light,
Ful prively two harneys hath he dight,
Bothe suffisaunt and mete to darreyne
The bataille in the feeld bitwix hem tweyne.
And on his hors, allone as he was born,
He carieth al this harneys him biforn;
And in the grove, at tyme and place y-set,
This Arcite and this Palamon ben met.
Tho chaungen gan the colour in hir face;
Right as the hunter in the regne of Trace,
That stondeth at the gappe with a spere,
Whan hunted is the leoun or the bere,
And hereth him come russhing in the greves,
And breketh bothe bowes and the leves,
And thinketh, 'heer cometh my mortel enemy,
With-oute faile, he moot be deed, or I;
For outher I mot sleen him at the gappe,
Or he mot sleen me, if that me mishappe:'

So ferden they, in chaunging of hir hewe,
As fer as everich of hem other knewe.
Ther nas no good day, ne no saluing;
But streight, with-outen word or rehersing,
Everich of hem halp for to armen other,
As freendly as he were his owne brother;
And after that, with sharpe speres stronge
They foynen ech at other wonder longe.
Thou mightest wene that this Palamoun
In his fighting were a wood leoun,
And as a cruel tygre was Arcite:
As wilde bores gonne they to smyte,
That frothen whyte as foom for ire wood.
Up to the ancle foghte they in hir blood.
And in this wyse I lete hem fighting dwelle;
And forth I wol of Theseus yow telle.
  The destinee, ministre general,
That executeth in the world over-al
The purveyaunce, that God hath seyn biforn,
So strong it is, that, though the world had sworn
The contrarie of a thing, by ye or nay,
Yet somtyme it shal fallen on a day
That falleth nat eft with-inne a thousand yere.
For certeinly, our appetytes here,
Be it of werre, or pees, or hate, or love,
Al is this reuled by the sighte above.
This mene I now by mighty Theseus,
That for to honten is so desirous,
And namely at the grete hert in May,
That in his bed ther daweth him no day,
That he nis clad, and redy for to ryde
With hunte and horn, and houndes him bisyde.
For in his hunting hath he swich delyt,
That it is al his joye and appetyt
To been him-self the grete hertes bane:
For after Mars he serveth now Diane.
  Cleer was the day, as I have told er this,
And Theseus, with alle joye and blis,
With his Ipolita, the fayre quene,
And Emelye, clothed al in grene,

On hunting be they riden royally.
And to the grove, that stood ful faste by,
In which ther was an hert, as men him tolde,
Duk Theseus the streighte wey hath holde.
And to the launde he rydeth him ful right,
For thider was the hert wont have his flight,
And over a brook, and so forth on his weye.
This duk wol han a cours at him, or tweye,
With houndes, swiche as that him list comaunde.
  And whan this duk was come un-to the launde,
Under the sonne he loketh, and anon
He was war of Arcite and Palamon,
That foughten breme, as it were bores two;
The brighte swerdes wenten to and fro
So hidously, that with the leeste strook
It seemed as it wolde felle an ook;
But what they were, no-thing he ne woot.
This duk his courser with his spores smoot,
And at a stert he was bitwix hem two,
And pulled out a swerd and cryed, 'ho!
Namore, up peyne of lesing of your heed.
By mighty Mars, he shal anon be deed,
That smyteth any strook, that I may seen!
But telleth me what mister men ye been,
That been so hardy for to fighten here
With-outen juge or other officere,
As it were in a listes royally?'
  This Palamon answerde hastily
And seyde: 'sire, what nedeth wordes mo?
We have the deeth deserved bothe two.
Two woful wrecches been we, two caytyves,
That been encombred of our owne lyves;
And as thou art a rightful lord and juge,
Ne yeve us neither mercy ne refuge,
But slee me first, for seynte charitee;
But slee my felawe eek as wel as me.
Or slee him first; for, though thou knowe it lyte,
This is thy mortal fo, this is Arcite,
That fro thy lond is banished on his heed,
For which he hath deserved to be deed.

For this is he that cam un-to thy gate,
And seyde, that he highte Philostrate.
Thus hath he japed thee ful many a yeer,
And thou has maked him thy chief squyer:
And this is he that loveth Emelye.
For sith the day is come that I shal dye,
I make pleynly my confessioun,
That I am thilke woful Palamoun,
That hath thy prison broken wikkedly.
I am thy mortal fo, and it am I
That loveth so hote Emelye the brighte,
That I wol dye present in hir sighte.
Therfore I axe deeth and my juwyse;
But slee my felawe in the same wyse,
For bothe han we deserved to be slayn.'
  This worthy duk answerde anon agayn,
And seyde, 'This is a short conclusioun:
Youre owne mouth, by your confessioun,
Hath dampned you, and I wol it recorde,
It nedeth noght to pyne yow with the corde.
Ye shul be deed, by mighty Mars the rede!'
  The quene anon, for verray wommanhede,
Gan for to wepe, and so dide Emelye,
And alle the ladies in the companye.
Gret pitee was it, as it thoughte hem alle,
That ever swich a chaunce sholde falle;
For gentil men they were, of greet estat,
And no-thing but for love was this debat;
And sawe hir blody woundes wyde and sore;
And alle cryden, bothe lasse and more,
'Have mercy, lord, up-on us wommen alle!'
And on hir bare knees adoun they falle,
And wolde have kist his feet ther-as he stood,
Til at the laste aslaked was his mood;
For pitee renneth sone in gentil herte.
And though he first for ire quook and sterte,
He hath considered shortly, in a clause,
The trespas of hem bothe, and eek the cause:
And al-though that his ire hir gilt accused
Yet in his reson he hem bothe excused;

As thus: he thoghte wel, that every man
Wol helpe him-self in love, if that he can,
And eek delivere him-self out of prisoun;
And eek his herte had compassioun
Of wommen, for they wepen ever in oon;
And in his gentil herte he thoghte anoon,
And softe un-to himself he seyde: 'fy
Up-on a lord that wol have no mercy,
But been a leoun, bothe in word and dede,
To hem that been in repentaunce and drede
As wel as to a proud despitous man
That wol maynteyne that he first bigan!
That lord hath litel of discrecioun,
That in swich cas can no divisioun,
But weyeth pryde and humblesse after oon.'
And shortly, whan his ire is thus agoon,
He gan to loken up with eyen lighte,
And spak thise same wordes al on highte:—
'The god of love, a! *benedicite*,
How mighty and how greet a lord is he!
Ayeins his might ther gayneth none obstacles,
He may be cleped a god for his miracles;
For he can maken at his owne gyse
Of everich herte, as that him list devyse.
Lo heer, this Arcite and this Palamoun,
That quitly weren out of my prisoun,
And mighte han lived in Thebes royally,
And witen I am hir mortal enemy,
And that hir deeth lyth in my might also;
And yet hath love, maugree hir eyen two,
Y-broght hem hider bothe for to dye!
Now loketh, is nat that an heigh folye?
Who may been a fool, but-if he love?
Bihold, for Goddes sake that sit above,
Se how they blede! be they noght wel arrayed?
Thus hath hir lord, the god of love, y-payed
Hir wages and hir fees for hir servyse!
And yet they wenen for to been ful wyse
That serven love, for aught that may bifalle!
But this is yet the beste game of alle,

That she, for whom they han this jolitee,
Can hem ther-for as muche thank as me :
She woot namore of al this hote fare,
By God, than woot a cokkow or an hare !
But al mot been assayed, hoot and cold ;
A man mot been a fool, or yong or old ;
I woot it by my-self ful yore agoon :
For in my tyme a servant was I oon.
And therfore, sin I knowe of loves peyne,
And woot how sore it can a man distreyne,
As he that hath ben caught ofte in his las,
I yow foryeve al hoolly this trespas,
At requeste of the quene that kneleth here,
And eek of Emelye, my suster dere.
And ye shul bothe anon un-to me swere,
That never-mo ye shul my contree dere,
Ne make werre up-on me night ne day,
But been my freendes in al that ye may ;
I yow foryeve this trespas every del.'
And they him swore his axing fayre and wel,
And him of lordshipe and of mercy preyde,
And he hem graunteth grace, and thus he seyde :
  ' To speke of royal linage and richesse,
Though that she were a quene or a princesse,
Ech of yow bothe is worthy, doutelees,
To wedden whan tyme is, but nathelees
I speke as for my suster Emelye,
For whom ye have this stryf and jelousye ;
Ye woot your-self, she may not wedden two
At ones, though ye fighten ever-mo :
That oon of yow, al be him looth or leef,
He moot go pypen in an ivy-leef ;
This is to seyn, she may nat now han bothe,
Al be ye never so jelous, ne so wrothe.
And for-thy I yow putte in this degree,
That ech of yow shal have his destinee
As him is shape ; and herkneth in what wyse ;
Lo, heer your ende of that I shal devyse.
  My wil is this, for plat conclusioun,
With-outen any replicacioun,

If that yow lyketh, tak it for the beste,
That everich of yow shal gon wher him leste
Frely, with-outen raunson or daunger;
And this day fifty wykes, fer ne ner,
Everich of yow shal bringe an hundred knightes,
Armed for listes up at alle rightes,
Al redy to darreyne hir by bataille.
And this bihote I yow, with-outen faille,
Up-on my trouthe, and as I am a knight,
That whether of yow bothe that hath might,
This is to seyn, that whether he or thou
May with his hundred, as I spak of now,
Sleen his contrarie, or out of listes dryve,
Him shal I yeve Emelya o wyve,
To whom that fortune yeveth so fair a grace.
The listes shal I maken in this place,
And God so wisly on my soule rewe,
As I shal even juge been and trewe.
Ye shul non other ende with me maken,
That oon of yow ne shal be deed or taken.
And if yow thinketh this is wel y-sayd,
Seyeth your avys, and holdeth yow apayd.
This is your ende and your conclusioun.'
  Who loketh lightly now but Palamoun?
Who springeth up for joye but Arcite?
Who couthe telle, or who couthe it endyte,
The joye that is maked in the place
Whan Theseus hath doon so fair a grace?
But doun on knees wente every maner wight,
And thanked him with al her herte and might,
And namely the Thebans ofte sythe.
And thus with good hope and with herte blythe
They take hir leve, and hom-ward gonne they ryde
To Thebes, with his olde walles wyde.

Explicit secunda pars.

Sequitur pars tercia.

  I trowe men wolde deme it necligence,
If I foryete to tellen the dispence

Of Theseus, that goth so bisily
To maken up the listes royally;
That swich a noble theatre as it was,
I dar wel seyn that in this world ther nas.
The circuit a myle was aboute,
Walled of stoon, and diched al with-oute.
Round was the shap, in maner of compas,
Ful of degrees, the heighte of sixty pas,
That, whan a man was set on o degree,
He letted nat his felawe for to see.
  Est-ward ther stood a gate of marbel whyt,
West-ward, right swich another in the opposit.
And shortly to concluden, swich a place
Was noon in erthe, as in so litel space;
For in the lond ther nas no crafty man,
That geometrie or ars-metrik can,
Ne purtreyour, ne kerver of images,
That Theseus ne yaf him mete and wages
The theatre for to maken and devyse.
And for to doon his ryte and sacrifyse,
He est-ward hath, up-on the gate above,
In worship of Venus, goddesse of love,
Don make an auter and an oratorie;
And west-ward, in the minde and in memorie
Of Mars, he maked hath right swich another,
That coste largely of gold a fother.
And north-ward, in a touret on the wal,
Of alabastre whyt and reed coral
An oratorie riche for to see,
In worship of Dyane of chastitee,
Hath Theseus don wroght in noble wyse.
  But yet hadde I foryeten to devyse
The noble kerving, and the portreitures,
The shap, the countenaunce, and the figures,
That weren in thise oratories three.
  First in the temple of Venus maystow see
Wroght on the wal, ful pitous to biholde,
The broken slepes, and the sykes colde;
The sacred teres, and the waymenting:
The fyry strokes of the desiring,

That loves servaunts in this lyf enduren ;
The othes, that hir covenants assuren ;
Plesaunce and hope, desyr, fool-hardinesse,
Beautee and youthe, bauderie, richesse,
Charmes and force, lesinges, flaterye,
Dispense, bisynesse, and jelousye,
That wered of yelwe goldes a gerland,
And a cokkow sitting on hir hand ;
Festes, instruments, caroles, daunces,
Lust and array, and alle the circumstaunces
Of love, whiche that I rekne and rekne shal,
By ordre weren peynted on the wal,
And mo than I can make of mencioun.
For soothly, al the mount of Citheroun,
Ther Venus hath hir principal dwelling,
Was shewed on the wal in portreying,
With al the gardin, and the lustinesse.
Nat was foryeten the porter Ydelnesse,
Ne Narcisus the faire of yore agon,
Ne yet the folye of king Salamon,
Ne yet the grete strengthe of Hercules—
Th'enchauntements of Medea and Circes—
Ne of Turnus, with the hardy fiers corage,
The riche Cresus, caytif in servage.
Thus may ye seen that wisdom ne richesse,
Beautee ne sleighte, strengthe, ne hardinesse,
Ne may with Venus holde champartye ;
For as hir list the world than may she gye.
Lo, alle thise folk so caught were in hir las,
Til they for wo ful ofte seyde ' allas ! '
Suffyceth heer ensamples oon or two,
And though I coude rekne a thousand mo.
  The statue of Venus, glorious for to see,
Was naked fleting in the large see,
And fro the navele doun all covered was
With wawes grene, and brighte as any glas.
A citole in hir right hand hadde she,
And on hir heed, ful semely for to see,
A rose gerland, fresh and wel smellinge ;
Above hir heed hir dowves flikeringe.

Biforn hir stood hir sone Cupido,
Up-on his shuldres winges hadde he two;
And blind he was, as it is ofte sene;
A bowe he bar and arwes brighte and kene.
  Why sholde I noght as wel eek telle yow al
The portreiture, that was up-on the wal
With-inne the temple of mighty Mars the rede?
Al peynted was the wal, in lengthe and brede,
Lyk to the estres of the grisly place,
That highte the grete temple of Mars in Trace,
In thilke colde frosty regioun,
Ther-as Mars hath his sovereyn mansioun.
  First on the wal was peynted a foreste,
In which ther dwelleth neither man ne beste,
With knotty knarry bareyn treës olde
Of stubbes sharpe and hidous to biholde;
In which ther ran a rumbel and a swough,
As though a storm sholde bresten every bough:
And downward from an hille, under a bente,
Ther stood the temple of Mars armipotente,
Wroght al of burned steel, of which thentree
Was long and streit, and gastly for to see.
And ther-out cam a rage and such a vese,
That it made al the gates for to rese.
The northren light in at the dores shoon,
For windowe on the wal ne was ther noon,
Thurgh which men mighten any light discerne.
The dores were alle of adamant eterne,
Y-clenched overthwart and endelong
With iren tough; and, for to make it strong,
Every piler, the temple to sustene,
Was tonne-greet, of iren bright and shene.
  Ther saugh I first the derke imagining
Of felonye, and al the compassing;
The cruel ire, reed as any glede;
The pykepurs, and eek the pale drede;
The smyler with the knyf under the cloke;
The shepne brenning with the blake smoke;
The treson of the mordring in the bedde;
The open werre, with woundes al bibledde;

Contek, with blody knyf and sharp manace;
Al ful of chirking was that sory place.
The sleere of him-self yet saugh I ther,
His herte-blood hath bathed al his heer;
The nayl y-driven in the shode a-night;
The colde deeth, with mouth gaping upright.
Amiddes of the temple sat meschaunce,
With disconfort and sory contenaunce.
Yet saugh I woodnesse laughing in his rage;
Armed compleint, out-hees, and fiers outrage.
The careyne in the bush, with throte y-corve:
A thousand slayn, and nat of qualm y-storve;
The tiraunt, with the prey by force y-raft;
The toun destroyed, ther was no-thing laft.
Yet saugh I brent the shippes hoppesteres;
The hunte strangled with the wilde beres:
The sowe freten the child right in the cradel;
The cook y-scalded, for al his longe ladel.
Noght was foryeten by th'infortune of Marte;
The carter over-riden with his carte,
Under the wheel ful lowe he lay adoun.
Ther were also, of Martes divisioun,
The barbour, and the bocher, and the smith
That forgeth sharpe swerdes on his stith.
And al above, depeynted in a tour,
Saw I conquest sittinge in greet honour,
With the sharpe swerde over his heed
Hanginge by a sotil twynes threed.
Depeynted was the slaughtre of Julius,
Of grete Nero, and of Antonius;
Al be that thilke tyme they were unborn,
Yet was hir deeth depeynted ther-biforn,
By manasinge of Mars, right by figure;
So was it shewed in that portreiture
As is depeynted in the sterres above,
Who shal be slayn or elles deed for love.
Suffyceth oon ensample in stories olde,
I may not rekne hem alle, thogh I wolde.
 The statue of Mars up-on a carte stood,
Armed, and loked grim as he were wood;

And over his heed ther shynen two figures
Of sterres, that been cleped in scriptures,
That oon Puella, that other Rubeus.
This god of armes was arrayed thus :—
A wolf ther stood biforn him at his feet
With eyen rede, and of a man he eet ;
With sotil pencel was depeynt this storie,
In redoutinge of Mars and of his glorie.
  Now to the temple of Diane the chaste
As shortly as I can I wol me haste,
To telle yow al the descripcioun.
Depeynted been the walles up and doun
Of hunting and of shamfast chastitee.
Ther saugh I how woful Calistopee,
Whan that Diane agreved was with here,
Was turned from a womman til a bere,
And after was she maad the lode-sterre ;
Thus was it peynt, I can say yow no ferre ;
Hir sone is eek a sterre, as men may see.
Ther saugh I Dane, y-turned til a tree,
I mene nat the goddesse Diane,
But Penneus doughter, which that highte Dane.
Ther saugh I Attheon an hert y-maked,
For vengeaunce that he saugh Diane al naked ;
I saugh how that his houndes have him caught,
And freten him, for that they knewe him naught.
Yet peynted was a litel forther-moor,
How Atthalante hunted the wilde boor,
And Meleagre, and many another mo,
For which Diane wroghte him care and wo.
Ther saugh I many another wonder storie,
The whiche me list nat drawen to memorie.
This goddesse on an hert ful hye seet,
With smale houndes al aboute hir feet ;
And undernethe hir feet she hadde a mone,
Wexing it was, and sholde wanie sone.
In gaude grene hir statue clothed was,
With bowe in honde, and arwes in a cas.
Hir eyen caste she ful lowe adoun,
Ther Pluto hath his derke regioun

A womman travailinge was hir biforn,
But, for hir child so longe was unborn,
Ful pitously Lucyna gan she calle,
And seyde, 'help, for thou mayst best of alle.'
Wel couthe he peynten lyfly that it wroghte,
With many a florin he the hewes boghte.
Now been thise listes maad, and Theseus,
That at his grete cost arrayed thus
The temples and the theatre every del,
Whan it was doon, him lyked wonder wel.
But stinte I wol of Theseus a lyte,
And speke of Palamon and of Arcite.
The day approcheth of hir retourninge,
That everich sholde an hundred knightes bringe,
The bataille to darreyne, as I yow tolde;
And til Athénes, hir covenant for to holde,
Hath everich of hem broght an hundred knightes
Wel armed for the werre at alle rightes.
And sikerly, ther trowed many a man
That never, sithen that the world bigan,
As for to speke of knighthod of hir hond,
As fer as God hath maked see or lond,
Nas, of so fewe, so noble a companye.
For every wight that lovede chivalrye,
And wolde, his thankes, han a passant name,
Hath preyed that he mighte ben of that game;
And wel was him, that ther-to chosen was.
For if ther fille to-morwe swich a cas,
Ye knowen wel, that every lusty knight,
That loveth paramours, and hath his might,
Were it in Engelond, or elles-where,
They wolde, hir thankes, wilnen to be there.
To fighte for a lady, *ben'cite!*
It were a lusty sighte for to see.
And right so ferden they with Palamon.
With him ther wenten knightes many oon;
Som wol ben armed in an habergeoun,
In a brest-plat and in a light gipoun;
And somme woln have a peyre plates large;
And somme woln have a Pruce sheld, or a targe;

Somme woln ben armed on hir legges weel,
And have an ax, and somme a mace of steel.
Ther nis no newe gyse, that it nas old.
Armed were they, as I have you told,
Everich after his opinioun.
  Ther maistow seen coming with Palamoun
Ligurge him-self, the grete king of Trace ;
Blak was his berd, and manly was his face.
The cercles of his eyen in his heed,
They gloweden bitwixe yelow and reed :
And lyk a griffon loked he aboute,
With kempe heres on his browes stoute ;
His limes grete, his braunes harde and stronge,
His shuldres brode, his armes rounde and longe.
And as the gyse was in his contree,
Ful hye up-on a char of gold stood he,
With foure whyte boles in the trays.
In-stede of cote-armure over his harnays,
With nayles yelwe and brighte as any gold,
He hadde a beres skin, col-blak, for-old.
His longe heer was kembd bihinde his bak,
As any ravenes fether it shoon for-blak :
A wrethe of gold arm-greet, of huge wighte,
Upon his heed, set ful of stones brighte,
Of fyne rubies and of dyamaunts.
Aboute his char ther wenten whyte alaunts,
Twenty and mo, as grete as any steer,
To hunten at the leoun or the deer,
And folwed him, with mosel faste y-bounde,
Colers of gold, and torets fyled rounde.
An hundred lordes hadde he in his route
Armed ful wel, with hertes sterne and stoute.
  With Arcita, in stories as men finde,
The grete Emetreus, the king of Inde,
Up-on a stede bay, trapped in steel,
Covered in cloth of gold diapred weel,
Cam ryding lyk the god of armes, Mars.
His cote-armure was of cloth of Tars,
Couched with perles whyte and rounde and grete.
His sadel was of brend gold newe y-bete ;

A mantelet upon his shuldre hanginge
Bret-ful of rubies rede, as fyr sparklinge.
His crispe heer lyk ringes was y-ronne,
And that was yelow, and glitered as the sonne.
His nose was heigh, his eyen bright citryn,
His lippes rounde, his colour was sangwyn,
A fewe fraknes in his face y-spreynd,
Betwixen yelow and somdel blak y-meynd,
And as a leoun he his loking caste.
Of fyve and twenty yeer his age I caste.
His berd was wel bigonne for to springe ;
His voys was as a trompe thunderinge.
Up-on his heed he wered of laurer grene
A gerland fresh and lusty for to sene.
Up-on his hand he bar, for his deduyt,
An egle tame, as eny lilie whyt.
An hundred lordes hadde he with him there,
Al armed, sauf hir heddes, in al hir gere,
Ful richely in alle maner thinges.
For trusteth wel, that dukes, erles, kinges,
Were gadered in this noble companye,
For love and for encrees of chivalrye.
Aboute this king ther ran on every part
Ful many a tame leoun and lepart.
And in this wyse thise lordes, alle and some,
Ben on the Sonday to the citee come
Aboute pryme, and in the toun alight.
  This Theseus, this duk, this worthy knight,
Whan he had broght hem in-to his citee,
And inned hem, everich in his degree,
He festeth hem, and dooth so greet labour
To esen hem, and doon hem al honour,
That yet men weneth that no mannes wit
Of noon estat ne coude amenden it.
The minstralcye, the service at the feste,
The grete yiftes to the moste and leste,
The riche array of Theseus paleys,
Ne who sat first ne last up-on the deys,
What ladies fairest been or best daunsinge,
Or which of hem can dauncen best and singe,

Ne who most felingly speketh of love:
What haukes sitten on the perche above,
What houndes liggen on the floor adoun:
Of al this make I now no mencioun;
But al th'effect, that thinketh me the beste;
Now comth the poynt, and herkneth if yow leste.
The Sonday night, er day bigan to springe,
When Palamon the larke herde singe,
Although it nere nat day by houres two,
Yet song the larke, and Palamon also.
With holy herte, and with an heigh corage
He roos, to wenden on his pilgrimage
Un-to the blisful Citherea benigne,
I mene Venus, honurable and digne.
And in hir houre he walketh forth a pas
Un-to the listes, ther hir temple was,
And doun he kneleth, and with humble chere
And herte soor, he seyde as ye shul here.
'Faireste of faire, o lady myn, Venus,
Doughter to Jove and spouse of Vulcanus,
Thou glader of the mount of Citheroun,
For thilke love thou haddest to Adoun,
Have pitee of my bittre teres smerte,
And tak myn humble preyer at thyn herte.
Allas! I ne have no langage to telle
Th'effectes ne the torments of myn helle;
Myn herte may myne harmes nat biwreye;
I am so confus, that I can noght seye.
But mercy, lady bright, that knowest weel
My thought, and seest what harmes that I feel,
Considere al this, and rewe up-on my sore,
As wisly as I shal for evermore,
Emforth my might, thy trewe servant be,
And holden werre alwey with chastitee;
That make I myn avow, so ye me helpe.
I kepe noght of armes for to yelpe,
Ne I ne axe nat to-morwe to have victorie,
Ne renoun in this cas, ne veyne glorie
Of pris of armes blowen up and doun,
But I wolde have fully possessioun

Of Emelye, and dye in thy servyse ;
Find thou the maner how, and in what wyse.
I recche nat, but it may bettre be,
To have victorie of hem, or they of me,
So that I have my lady in myne armes.
For though so be that Mars is god of armes,
Your vertu is so greet in hevene above,
That, if yow list, I shal wel have my love.
Thy temple wol I worshipe evermo,
And on thyn auter, wher I ryde or go,
I wol don sacrifice, and fyres bete.
And if ye wol nat so, my lady swete,
Than preye I thee, to-morwe with a spere
That Arcita me thurgh the herte bere.
Thanne rekke I noght, whan I have lost my lyf,
Though that Arcita winne hir to his wyf.
This is th'effect and ende of my preyere,
Yif me my love, thou blisful lady dere.'
  Whan th'orisoun was doon of Palamon,
His sacrifice he dide, and that anon
Ful pitously, with alle circumstaunces,
Al telle I noght as now his observaunces.
But atte laste the statue of Venus shook,
And made a signe, wher-by that he took
That his preyere accepted was that day.
For thogh the signe shewed a delay,
Yet wiste he wel that graunted was his bone ;
And with glad herte he wente him hoom ful sone
  The thridde houre inequal that Palamon
Bigan to Venus temple for to goon,
Up roos the sonne, and up roos Emelye,
And to the temple of Diane gan hye.
Hir maydens, that she thider with hir ladde,
Ful redily with hem the fyr they hadde,
Th'encens, the clothes, and the remenant al
That to the sacrifyce longen shal ;
The hornes fulle of meth, as was the gyse ;
Ther lakked noght to doon hir sacrifyse.
Smoking the temple, ful of clothes faire,
This Emelve, with herte debonaire.

Hir body wessh with water of a welle;
But how she dide hir ryte I dar nat telle,
But it be any thing in general;
And yet it were a game to heren al;
To him that meneth wel, it were no charge:
But it is good a man ben at his large.
Hir brighte heer was kempt, untressed al;
A coroune of a grene ook cerial
Up-on hir heed was set ful fair and mete.
Two fyres on the auter gan she bete,
And dide hir thinges, as men may biholde
In Stace of Thebes, and thise bokes olde.
Whan kindled was the fyr, with pitous chere
Un-to Diane she spak, as ye may here.
'O chaste goddesse of the wodes grene,
To whom bothe heven and erthe and see is sene,
Quene of the regne of Pluto derk and lowe,
Goddesse of maydens, that myn herte hast knowe
Ful many a yeer, and woost what I desire,
As keep me fro thy vengeaunce and thyn ire,
That Attheon aboughte cruelly.
Chaste goddesse, wel wostow that I
Desire to been a mayden al my lyf,
Ne never wol I be no love ne wyf.
I am, thou woost, yet of thy companye,
A mayde, and love hunting and venerye,
And for to walken in the wodes wilde,
And noght to been a wyf, and be with childe.
Noght wol I knowe companye of man.
Now help me, lady, sith ye may and can,
For tho thre formes that thou hast in thee.
And Palamon, that hath swich love to me,
And eek Arcite, that loveth me so sore,
This grace I preye thee with-oute more,
As sende love and pees bitwixe hem two;
And fro me turne awey hir hertes so,
That al hir hote love, and hir desyr,
And al hir bisy torment, and hir fyr
Be queynt, or turned in another place;
And if so be thou wolt not do me grace,

Or if my destinee be shapen so,
That I shal nedes have oon of hem two,
As sende me him that most desireth me.
Bihold, goddesse of clene chastitee,
The bittre teres that on my chekes falle.
Sin thou are mayde, and keper of us alle,
My maydenhede thou kepe and wel conserve,
And whyl I live a mayde, I wol thee serve.'
The fyres brenne up-on the auter clere,
Whyl Emelye was thus in hir preyere;
But sodeinly she saugh a sighte queynte,
For right anon oon of the fyres queynte,
And quiked agayn, and after that anon
That other fyr was queynt, and al agon;
And as it queynte, it made a whistelinge,
As doon thise wete brondes in hir brenninge,
And at the brondes ende out-ran anoon
As it were blody dropes many oon;
For which so sore agast was Emelye,
That she was wel ny mad, and gan to crye,
For she ne wiste what it signifyed;
But only for the fere thus hath she cryed,
And weep, that it was pitee for to he e
And ther-with-al Diane gan appere,
With bowe in hond, right as an hunteresse,
And seyde: 'Doghter, stint thyn hevinesse
Among the goddes hye it is affermed,
And by eterne word write and confermed,
Thou shalt ben wedded un-to oon of tho
That han for thee so muchel care and wo;
But un-to which of hem I may nat telle.
Farwel, for I ne may no lenger dwelle.
The fyres which that on myn auter brenne
Shul thee declaren, er that thou go henne,
Thyn aventure of love, as in this cas.'
And with that word, the arwes in the cas
Of the goddesse clateren faste and ringe,
And forth she wente, and made a vanisshinge;
For which this Emelye astoned was,
And seyde, 'What amounteth this, allas!

I putte me in thy proteccioun,
Diane, and in thy disposicioun.'
And hoom she gooth anon the nexte weye.
This is th'effect, ther is namore to seye.
The nexte houre of Mars folwinge this,
Arcite un-to the temple walked is
Of fierse Mars, to doon his sacrifyse,
With alle the rytes of his payen wyse.
With pitous herte and heigh devocioun,
Right thus to Mars he seyde his orisoun:
'O stronge god, that in the regnes colde
Of Trace honoured art, and lord y-holde,
And hast in every regne and every lond
Of armes al the brydel in thyn hond,
And hem fortunest as thee list devyse,
Accept of me my pitous sacrifyse.
If so be that my youthe may deserve,
And that my might be worthy for to serve
Thy godhede, that I may been oon of thyne,
Than preye I thee to rewe up-on my pyne.
For thilke peyne, and thilke hote fyr,
In which thou whylom brendest for desyr,
Whan that thou usedest the grete beautee
Of fayre yonge fresshe Venus free,
And haddest hir in armes at thy wille,
Al-though thee ones on a tyme misfille
Whan Vulcanus had caught thee in his las,
And fond thee ligging by his wyf, allas!
For thilke sorwe that was in thyn herte,
Have routhe as wel up-on my peynes smerte.
I am yong and unkonning, as thou wost,
And, as I trowe, with love offended most,
That ever was any lyves creature;
For she, that dooth me al this wo endure,
Ne reccheth never wher I sinke or flete.
And wel I woot, er she me mercy hete,
I moot with strengthe winne hir in the place;
And wel I woot, withouten help or grace
Of thee, ne may my strengthe noght availle.
Than help me, lord, to-morwe in my bataille,

For thilke fyr that whylom brente thee
As wel as thilke fyr now brenneth me,
And do that I to-morwe have victorie.
Myn be the travaille, and thyn be the glorie!
Thy soverein temple wol I most honouren
Of any place, and alwey most labouren
In thy plesaunce and in thy craftes stronge,
And in thy temple I wol my baner honge,
And alle the armes of my companye;
And evere-mo, un-to that day I dye,
Eterne fyr I wol biforn thee finde.
And eek to this avow I wol me binde:
My berd, myn heer that hongeth long adoun,
That never yet ne felte offensioun
Of rasour nor of shere, I wol thee yive,
And been thy trewe servant whyl I live.
Now lord, have routhe up-on my sorwes sore,
Yif me victorie, I aske thee namore.'
  The preyere stinte of Arcita the stronge,
The ringes on the temple-dore that honge,
And eek the dores, clatereden ful faste,
Of which Arcita som-what him agaste.
The fyres brende up-on the auter brighte,
That it gan al the temple for to lighte;
And swete smel the ground anon up-yaf,
And Arcita anon his hand up-haf,
And more encens in-to the fyr he caste,
With othere rytes mo; and atte laste
The statue of Mars bigan his hauberk ringe.
And with that soun he herde a murmuringe
Ful lowe and dim, that sayde thus, 'Victorie':
For which he yaf to Mars honour and glorie.
And thus with joye, and hope wel to fare,
Arcite anon un-to his inne is fare,
As fayn as fowel is of the brighte sonne.
  And right anon swich stryf ther is bigonne
For thilke graunting, in the hevene above,
Bitwixe Venus, the goddesse of love,
And Mars, the sterne god armipotente,
That Jupiter was bisy it to stente

Til that the pale Saturnus the colde,
That knew so manye of aventures olde,
Fond in his olde experience an art,
That he ful sone hath plesed every part.
As sooth is sayd, elde hath greet avantage;
In elde is bothe wisdom and usage;
Men may the olde at-renne, and noght at-rede.
Saturne anon, to stinten stryf and drede,
Al be it that it is agayn his kynde,
Of al this stryf he gan remedie fynde.
'My dere doghter Venus,' quod Saturne,
'My cours, that hath so wyde for to turne,
Hath more power than wot any man.
Myn is the drenching in the see so wan;
Myn is the prison in the derke cote;
Myn is the strangling and hanging by the throte;
The murmure, and the cherles rebelling,
The groyning, and the pryvee empoysoning:
I do vengeance and pleyn correccioun
Whyl I dwelle in the signe of the Leoun
Myn is the ruine of the hye halles,
The falling of the toures and of the walles
Up-on the mynour or the carpenter.
I slow Sampsoun in shaking the piler;
And myne be the maladyes colde,
The derke tresons, and the castes olde;
My loking is the fader of pestilence.
Now weep namore, I shal doon diligence
That Palamon, that is thyn owne knight,
Shal have his lady, as thou hast him hight.
Though Mars shal helpe his knight, yet natheles
Bitwixe yow ther moot be som tyme pees,
Al be ye noght of o complexioun,
That causeth al day swich divisioun.
I am thin ayel, redy at thy wille;
Weep thou namore, I wol thy lust fulfille.'
Now wol I stinten of the goddes above,
Of Mars, and of Venus, goddesse of love,
And telle yow, as pleynly as I can,
The grete effect, for which that I bigan.

Explicit tercia pars.

Sequitur pars quarta.

Greet was the feste in Athenes that day,
And eek the lusty seson of that May
Made every wight to been in swich plesaunce,
That al that Monday justen they and daunce,
And spenden it in Venus heigh servyse.
But by the cause that they sholde ryse
Erly, for to seen the grete fight,
Unto hir reste wente they at night.
And on the morwe, whan that day gan springe,
Of hors and harneys, noyse and clateringe
Ther was in hostelryes al aboute ;
And to the paleys rood ther many a route
Of lordes, up-on stedes and palfreys.
Ther maystow seen devysing of herneys
So uncouth and so riche, and wroght so weel
Of goldsmithrie, of browding, and of steel :
The sheeldes brighte, testers, and trappures ;
Gold-hewen helmes, hauberks, cote-armures ;
Lordes in paraments on hir courseres,
Knightes of retenue, and eek squyeres
Nailinge the speres, and helmes bokelinge,
Gigginge of sheeldes, with layneres lacinge ;
Ther as need is, they weren no-thing ydel ;
The fomy stedes on the golden brydel
Gnawinge, and faste the armurers also
With fyle and hamer prikinge to and fro ;
Yemen on fote, and communes many oon
With shorte staves, thikke as they may goon ;
Pypes, trompes, nakers, clarioun es,
That in the bataille blowen blody sounes ;
The paleys ful of peples up and doun,
Heer three, ther ten, holding hir questioun,
Divyninge of thise Theban knightes two.
Somme seyden thus, somme seyde it shal be so ;
Somme helden with him with the blake berd,
Somme with the balled, somme with the thikke-herd ;

Somme sayde, he loked grim and he wolde fighte ;
He hath a sparth of twenty pound of wighte.
Thus was the halle ful of divyninge,
Longe after that the sonne gan to springe.
The grete Theseus, that of his sleep awaked
With minstralcye and noyse that was maked,
Held yet the chambre of his paleys riche,
Til that the Thebane knightes, bothe y-liche
Honoured, were into the paleys fet.
Duk Theseus was at a window set,
Arrayed right as he were a god in trone.
The peple preesseth thider-ward ful sone
Him for to seen, and doon heigh reverence,
And eek to herkne his hest and his sentence
An heraud on a scaffold made an ho,
Til al the noyse of peple was y-do ;
And whan he saugh the peple of noyse al stille,
Tho showed he the mighty dukes wille.
'The lord hath of his heigh discrecioun
Considered, that it were destruccioun
To gentil blood, to fighten in the gyse
Of mortal bataille now in this empryse ;
Wherfore, to shapen that they shul not dye,
He wol his firste purpos modifye.
No man therfor, up peyne of los of lyf,
No maner shot, ne pollax, ne short knyf
Into the listes sende, or thider bringe ;
Ne short swerd for to stoke, with poynt bytinge,
No man ne drawe, ne bere it by his syde.
Ne no man shal un-to his felawe ryde
But o cours, with a sharp y-grounde spere ;
Foyne, if him list, on fote, him-self to were.
And he that is at meschief, shal be take,
And noght slayn, but be broght un-to the stake
That shal ben ordeyned on either syde ;
But thider he shal by force, and ther abyde.
And if so falle, the chieftayn be take
On either syde, or elles slee his make,
No lenger shal the turneyinge laste.
God spede yow ; goth forth, and ley on faste.

With long swerd and with maces fight your fille.
Goth now your wey; this is the lordes wille.'
  The voys of peple touchede the hevene,
So loude cryden they with mery stevene:
'God save swich a lord, that is so good,
He wilneth no destruccioun of blood!'
Up goon the trompes and the melodye.
And to the listes rit the companye
By ordinaunce, thurgh-out the citee large,
Hanged with cloth of gold, and nat with sarge.
Ful lyk a lord this noble duk gan ryde,
Thise two Thebanes up-on either syde;
And after rood the quene, and Emelye
And after that another companye
Of oon and other, after hir degree.
And thus they passen thurgh-out the citee,
And to the listes come they by tyme.
It nas not of the day yet fully pryme,
Whan set was Theseus ful riche and hye,
Ipolita the quene and Emelye,
And other ladies in degrees aboute.
Un-to the seetes preesseth al the route.
And west-ward, thurgh the gates under Marte,
Arcite, and eek the hundred of his parte,
With baner reed is entred right anon;
And in that selve moment Palamon
Is under Venus, est-ward in the place,
With baner whyt, and hardy chere and face.
In al the world, to seken up and doun,
So even with-outen variacioun,
Ther nere swiche companyes tweye.
For ther nas noon so wys that coude seye,
That any hadde of other avauntage
Of worthinesse, ne of estaat, ne age,
So even were they chosen, for to gesse.
And in two renges faire they hem dresse.
Whan that hir names rad were everichoon,
That in hir nombre gyle were ther noon,
Tho were the gates shet, and cryed was loude:
'Do now your devoir, yonge knightes proude!'

The heraudes lefte hir priking up and doun ;
Now ringen trompes loude and clarioun ;
Ther is namore to seyn, but west and est
In goon the speres ful sadly in arest ;
In goth the sharpe spore in-to the syde.
Ther seen men who can juste, and who can ryde ;
Ther shiveren shaftes up-on sheeldes thikke ;
He feleth thurgh the herte-spoon the prikke.
Up springen speres twenty foot on highte ;
Out goon the swerdes as the silver brighte.
The helmes they to-hewen and to-shrede ;
Out brest the blood, with sterne stremes rede.
With mighty maces the bones they to-breste.
He thurgh the thikkeste of the throng gan threste.
Ther stomblen stedes stronge, and doun goth al.
He rolleth under foot as dooth a bal.
He foyneth on his feet with his tronchoun,
And he him hurtleth with his hors adoun.
He thurgh the body is hurt, and sithen y-take,
Maugree his heed, and broght un-to the stake,
As forward was, right ther he moste abyde ;
Another lad is on that other syde.
And som tyme dooth hem Theseus to reste,
Hem to refresshe, and drinken if hem leste.
Ful ofte a-day han thise Thebanes two
Togidre y-met, and wroght his felawe wo ;
Unhorsed hath ech other of hem tweye.
Ther nas no tygre in the vale of Galgopheye,
Whan that hir whelp is stole, whan it is lyte,
So cruel on the hunte, as is Arcite
For jelous herte upon this Palamoun :
Ne in Belmarye ther nis so fel leoun,
That hunted is, or for his hunger wood
Ne of his praye desireth so the blood,
As Palamon to sleen his fo Arcite.
The jelous strokes on hir helmes byte ;
Out renneth blood on both hir sydes rede.
Som tyme an ende ther is of every dede ;
For er the sonne un-to the reste wente,
The stronge king Emetreus gan hente

This Palamon, as he faught with Arcite,
And made his swerd depe in his flesh to byte;
And by the force of twenty is he take
Unyolden, and y-drawe unto the stake.
And in the rescous of this Palamoun
The stronge king Ligurge is born adoun;
And king Emetreus, for al his strengthe,
Is born out of his sadel a swerdes lengthe,
So hitte him Palamon er he were take;
But al for noght, he was broght to the stake.
His hardy herte mighte him helpe naught;
He moste abyde, whan that he was caught
By force, and eek by composicioun.
  Who sorweth now but woful Palamoun,
That moot namore goon agayn to fighte?
And whan that Theseus had seyn this sighte,
Un-to the folk that foghten thus echoon
He cryde, 'Ho! namore, for it is doon!
I wol be trewe juge, and no partye.
Arcite of Thebes shal have Emelye,
That by his fortune hath hir faire y-wonne.'
Anon ther is a noyse of peple bigonne
For joye of this, so loude and heigh withalle,
It semed that the listes sholde falle.
  What can now faire Venus doon above?
What seith she now? what dooth this quene of love?
But wepeth so, for wanting of hir wille,
Til that hir teres in the listes fille;
She seyde: 'I am ashamed, doutelees.'
Saturnus seyde: 'Doghter, hold thy pees.
Mars hath his wille, his knight hath al his bone,
And, by myn heed, thou shalt ben esed sone.'
  The trompes, with the loude minstralcye,
The heraudes, that ful loude yolle and crye,
Been in hir wele for joye of daun Arcite.
But herkneth me, and stinteth now a lyte,
Which a miracle ther bifel anon.
  This fierse Arcite hath of his helm y-don,
And on a courser, for to shewe his face,
He priketh endelong the large place,

Loking upward up-on this Emelye;
And she agayn him caste a freendlich yë,
(For wommen, as to speken in comune,
They folwen al the favour of fortune);
And she was al his chere, as in his herte.
Out of the ground a furie infernal sterte,
From Pluto sent, at requeste of Saturne,
For which his hors for fere gan to turne,
And leep asyde, and foundred as he leep;
And, er that Arcite may taken keep,
He pighte him on the pomel of his heed,
That in the place he lay as he were deed,
His brest to-brosten with his sadel-bowe.
As blak he lay as any cole or crowe,
So was the blood y-ronnen in his face.
Anon he was y-born out of the place
With herte soor, to Theseus paleys.
Tho was he corven out of his harneys,
And in a bed y-brought ful faire and blyve,
For he was yet in memorie and alyve,
And alway crying after Emelye.
  Duk Theseus, with al his companye,
Is comen hoom to Athenes his citee,
With alle blisse and greet solempnitee.
Al be it that this aventure was falle,
He nolde noght disconforten hem alle.
Men seyde eek, that Arcite shal nat dye;
He shal ben heled of his maladye.
And of another thing they were as fayn,
That of hem alle was ther noon y-slayn,
Al were they sore y-hurt, and namely oon,
That with a spere was thirled his brest-boon.
To othere woundes, and to broken armes,
Some hadden salves, and some hadden charmes;
Fermacies of herbes, and eek save
They dronken, for they wolde hir limes have.
For which this noble duk, as he wel can,
Conforteth and honoureth every man,
And made revel al the longe night,
Un-to the straunge lordes, as was right.

Ne ther was holden no disconfitinge,
But as a justes or a tourneyinge;
For soothly ther was no disconfiture,
For falling nis nat but an aventure;
Ne to be lad with fors un-to the stake
Unyolden, and with twenty knightes take.
O persone allone, with-outen mo,
And haried forth by arme, foot, and to,
And eek his stede driven forth with staves,
With footmen, bothe yemen and eek knaves,
It nas aretted him no vileinye,
Ther may no man clepen it cowardye.
  For which anon duk Theseus leet crye,
To stinten alle rancour and envye,
The gree as wel of o syde as of other,
And either syde y-lyk, as otheres brother;
And yaf hem yiftes after hir degree,
And fully heeld a feste dayes three;
And conveyed the kinges worthily
Out of his toun a journee largely.
And hoom wente every man the righte way.
Ther was namore, but 'far wel, have good day!'
Of this bataille I wol namore endyte,
But speke of Palamon and of Arcite.
  Swelleth the brest of Arcite, and the sore
Encreesseth at his herte more and more.
The clothered blood, for any lechecraft,
Corrupteth, and is in his bouk y-laft,
That neither veyne-blood, ne ventusinge,
Ne drinke of herbes may ben his helpinge.
The vertu expulsif, or animal,
Fro thilke vertu cleped natural
Ne may the venim voyden, ne expelle.
The pypes of his longes gonne to swelle,
And every lacerte in his brest adoun
Is shent with venim and corrupcioun.
Him gayneth neither, for to gete his lyf,
Vomyt upward, ne dounward laxatif;
Al is to-brosten thilke regioun,
Nature hath now no dominacioun.

And certeinly, ther nature wol nat wirche,
Far-wel, phisyk ! go ber the man to chirche !
This al and som, that Arcita mot dye,
For which he sendeth after Emelye,
And Palamon, that was his cosin dere ;
Than seyde he thus, as ye shul after here.
'Naught may the woful spirit in myn herte
Declare o poynt of alle my sorwes smerte
To yow, my lady, that I love most ;
But I biquethe the service of my gost
To yow aboven every creature,
Sin that my lyf may no lenger dure.
Allas, the wo ! allas, the peynes stronge,
That I for yow have suffred, and so longe !
Allas, the deeth ! allas, myn Emelye !
Allas, departing of our companye !
Allas, myn hertes quene ! allas, my wyf !
Myn hertes lady, endere of my lyf !
What is this world ? what asketh men to have ?
Now with his love, now in his colde grave
Allone, with-outen any companye.
Far-wel, my swete fo ! myn Emelye !
And softe tak me in your armes tweye,
For love of God, and herkneth what I seye.
I have heer with my cosin Palamon
Had stryf and rancour, many a day a-gon,
For love of yow, and for my jelousye.
And Jupiter so wis my soule gye,
To speken of a servant proprely,
With alle circumstaunces trewely,
That is to seyn, trouthe, honour, and knighthede,
Wisdom, humblesse, estaat, and heigh kinrede,
Fredom, and al that longeth to that art,
So Jupiter have of my soule part,
As in this world right now ne knowe I non
So worthy to ben loved as Palamon,
That serveth yow, and wol don al his lyf.
And if that ever ye shul been a wyf,
Foryet nat Palamon, the gentil man.'
And with that word his speche faille gan,

For from his feet up to his brest was come
The cold of deeth, that hadde him overcome
And yet more-over, in his armes two
The vital strengthe is lost, and al ago.
Only the intellect, with-outen more,
That dwelled in his herte syk and sore,
Gan faillen, when the herte felte deeth,
Dusked his eyen two, and failled breeth.
But on his lady yet caste he his yë ;
His laste word was, 'mercy, Emelye!'
His spirit chaunged hous, and wente ther,
As I cam never, I can nat tellen wher.
Therfor I stinte, I nam no divinistre ;
Of soules finde I nat in this registre,
Ne me ne list thilke opiniouns to telle
Of hem, though that they wryten wher they dwelle.
Arcite is cold, ther Mars his soule gye ;
Now wol I speken forth of Emelye.
  Shrighte Emelye, and howleth Palamon,
And Theseus his suster took anon
Swowninge, and bar hir fro the corps away.
What helpeth it to tarien forth the day,
To tellen how she weep, bothe eve and morwe ?
For in swich cas wommen have swich sorwe,
Whan that hir housbonds been from hem ago,
That for the more part they sorwen so,
Or elles fallen in swich maladye,
That at the laste certeinly they dye.
  Infinite been the sorwes and the teres
Of olde folk, and folk of tendre yeres,
In al the toun, for deeth of this Theban ;
For him ther wepeth bothe child and man ;
So greet a weping was ther noon, certayn,
Whan Ector was y-broght, al fresh y-slayn,
To Troye ; allas ! the pitee that was ther,
Cracching of chekes, rending eek of heer.
'Why woldestow be deed,' thise wommen crye,
'And haddest gold y-nough, and Emelye ?'
No man mighte gladen Theseus,
Savinge his olde fader Egeus,

That knew this worldes transmutacioun,
As he had seyn it chaungen up and doun,
Joye after wo, and wo after gladnesse:
And shewed hem ensamples and lyknesse.
 'Right as ther deyed never man,' quod he,
'That he ne livede in erthe in som degree,
Right so ther livede never man,' he seyde,
'In al this world, that som tyme he ne deyde.
This world nis but a thurghfare ful of wo,
And we ben pilgrimes, passinge to and fro;
Deeth is an ende of every worldly sore.'
And over al this yet seyde he muchel more
To this effect, ful wysly to enhorte
The peple, that they sholde hem reconforte.
 Duk Theseus, with al his bisy cure,
Caste now wher that the sepulture
Of good Arcite may best y-maked be,
And eek most honurable in his degree.
And at the laste he took conclusioun,
That ther as first Arcite and Palamoun
Hadden for love the bataille hem bitwene,
That in that selve grove, swote and grene,
Ther as he hadde his amorous desires,
His compleynt, and for love his hote fires,
He wolde make a fyr, in which th'office
Funeral he mighte al accomplice;
And leet comaunde anon to hakke and hewe
The okes olde, and leye hem on a rewe
In colpons wel arrayed for to brenne;
His officers with swifte feet they renne
And ryde anon at his comaundement.
And after this, Theseus hath y-sent
After a bere, and it al over-spradde
With cloth of gold, the richest that he hadde.
And of the same suyte he cladde Arcite;
Upon his hondes hadde he gloves whyte;
Eek on his heed a croune of laurer grene,
And in his hond a swerd ful bright and kene.
He leyde him bare the visage on the bere,
Therwith he weep that pitee was to here.

And for the peple sholde seen him alle,
Whan it was day, he broghte him to the halle,
That roreth of the crying and the soun.
  Tho cam this woful Theban Palamoun,
With flotery berd, and ruggy asshy heres,
In clothes blake, y-dropped al with teres ;
And, passing othere of weping, Emelye,
The rewfulleste of al the companye.
In as muche as the service sholde be
The more noble and riche in his degree,
Duk Theseus leet forth three stedes bringe,
That trapped were in steel al gliteringe,
And covered with the armes of daun Arcite.
Up-on thise stedes, that weren grete and whyte,
Ther seten folk, of which oon bar his sheeld,
Another his spere up in his hondes heeld ;
The thridde bar with him his bowe Turkeys,
Of brend gold was the cas, and eek the harneys ;
And riden forth a pas with sorweful chere
Toward the grove, as ye shul after here.
The nobleste of the Grekes that ther were
Upon hir shuldres carieden the bere,
With slakke pas, and eyen rede and wete,
Thurgh-out the citee, by the maister-strete,
That sprad was al with blak, and wonder hye
Right of the same is al the strete y-wrye.
Up-on the right hond wente old Egeus,
And on that other syde duk Theseus,
With vessels in hir hand of gold ful fyn,
Al ful of hony, milk, and blood, and wyn ;
Eek Palamon, with ful greet companye ;
And after that cam woful Emelye,
With fyr in honde, as was that tyme the gyse,
To do th'office of funeral servyse.
  Heigh labour, and ful greet apparaillinge
Was at the service and the fyr-makinge,
That with his grene top the heven raughte,
And twenty fadme of brede the armes straughte ;
This is to seyn, the bowes were so brode.
Of stree first ther was leyd ful many a lode.

But how the fyr was maked up on highte,
And eek the names how the treës highte,
As ook, firre, birch, asp, alder, holm, popler,
Wilow, elm, plane, ash, box, chasteyn, lind, laurer,
Mapul, thorn, beech, hasel, ew, whippel-tree,
How they weren feld, shal nat be told for me;
Ne how the goddes ronnen up and doun,
Disherited of hir habitacioun,
In which they woneden in reste and pees,
Nymphes, Faunes, and Amadrides;
Ne how the bestes and the briddes alle
Fledden for fere, whan the wode was falle;
Ne how the ground agast was of the light,
That was nat wont to seen the sonne bright;
Ne how the fyr was couched first with stree,
And than with drye stokkes cloven a three,
And than with grene wode and spycerye,
And than with cloth of gold and with perrye,
And gerlandes hanging with ful many a flour,
The mirre, th'encens, with al so greet odour;
Ne how Arcite lay among al this,
Ne what richesse aboute his body is;
Ne how that Emelye, as was the gyse,
Putte in the fyr of funeral servyse;
Ne how she swowned whan men made the fyr,
Ne what she spak, ne what was hir desyr;
Ne what jeweles men in the fyr tho caste,
Whan that the fyr was greet and brente faste;
Ne how som caste hir sheeld, and som hir spere,
And of hir vestiments, whiche that they were,
And cuppes ful of wyn, and milk, and blood,
Into the fyr, that brente as it were wood;
Ne how the Grekes with an huge route
Thryës riden al the fyr aboute
Up-on the left hand, with a loud shoutinge,
And thryës with hir speres clateringe;
And thryës how the ladies gonne crye;
Ne how that lad was hom-ward Emelye;
Ne how Arcite is brent to asshen colde;
Ne how that liche-wake was y-holde

Al thilke night, ne how the Grekes pleye
The wake-pleyes, ne kepe I nat to seye;
Who wrastleth best naked, with oille enoynt,
Ne who that bar him best, in no disjoynt.
I wol nat tellen eek how that they goon
Hoom til Athenes, whan the pley is doon;
But shortly to the poynt than wol I wende,
And maken of my longe tale an ende.
By processe and by lengthe of certeyn yeres
Al stinted is the moorning and the teres.
Of Grekes, by oon general assent,
Than semed me ther was a parlement
At Athenes, up-on certeyn poynts and cas;
Among the whiche poynts y-spoken was
To have with certeyn contrees alliaunce,
And have fully of Thebans obeisaunce.
For which this noble Theseus anon
Leet senden after gentil Palamon,
Unwist of him what was the cause and why;
But in his blake clothes sorwefully
He cam at his comaundemente in hye.
Tho sente Theseus for Emelye.
Whan they were set, and hust was al the place,
And Theseus abiden hadde a space
Er any word cam from his wyse brest,
His eyen sette he ther as was his lest,
And with a sad visage he syked stille,
And after that right thus he seyde his wille.
'The firste moevere of the cause above,
Whan he first made the faire cheyne of love,
Greet was th'effect, and heigh was his entente;
Wel wiste he why, and what ther-of he mente;
For with that faire cheyne of love he bond
The fyr, the eyr, the water, and the lond
In certeyn boundes, that they may nat flee;
That same prince and that moevere,' quod he,
'Hath stablissed, in this wrecched world adoun,
Certeyne dayes and duracioun
To al that is engendred in this place,
Over the whiche day they may nat pace

Al mowe they yet tho dayes wel abregge;
Ther needeth non auctoritee allegge,
For it is preved by experience,
But that me list declaren my sentence.
Than may men by this ordre wel discerne,
That thilke moevere stable is and eterne.
Wel may men knowe, but it be a fool,
That every part deryveth from his hool.
For nature hath nat take his beginning
Of no party ne cantel of a thing,
But of a thing that parfit is and stable,
Descending so, til it be corrumpable.
And therfore, of his wyse purveyaunce,
He hath so wel biset his ordinaunce,
That speces of thinges and progressiouns
Shullen enduren by successiouns,
And nat eterne be, with-oute lyë:
This maistow understonde and seen at yë.
'Lo the ook, that hath so long a norisshinge
From tyme that it first biginneth springe,
And hath so long a lyf, as we may see,
Yet at the laste wasted is the tree.
'Considereth eek, how that the harde stoon
Under our feet, on which we trede and goon,
Yit wasteth it, as it lyth by the weye.
The brode river somtyme wexeth dreye.
The grete tounes see we wane and wende.
Than may ye see that al this thing hath ende.
'Of man and womman seen we wel also,
That nedeth, in oon of thise termes two,
This is to seyn, in youthe or elles age,
He moot ben deed, the king as shal a page;
Som in his bed, som in the depe see,
Som in the large feeld, as men may se;
Ther helpeth noght, al goth that ilke weye.
Thanne may I seyn that al this thing moot deye.
What maketh this but Jupiter the king?
The which is prince and cause of alle thing,
Converting al un-to his propre welle,
From which it is deryved, sooth to telle.

And here-agayns no creature on lyve
Of no degree availleth for to stryve.
‘Thanne is it wisdom, as it thinketh me,
To maken vertu of necessitee,
And take it wel, that we may nat eschue,
And namely that to us alle is due.
And who-so gruccheth ought, he dooth folye,
And rebel is to him that al may gye.
And certeinly a man hath most honour
To dyen in his excellence and flour,
Whan he is siker of his gode name;
Than hath he doon his freend, ne him, no shame.
And gladder oghte his freend ben of his deeth,
Whan with honour up-yolden is his breeth,
Than whan his name apalled is for age;
For al forgeten is his vasselage.
Than is it best, as for a worthy fame,
To dyen whan that he is best of name.
The contrarie of al this is wilfulnesse.
Why grucchen we? why have we hevinesse,
That good Arcite, of chivalrye flour
Departed is, with duetee and honour,
Out of this foule prison of this lyf?
Why grucchen heer his cosin and his wyf
Of his wel-fare that loved hem so weel?
Can he hem thank? nay, God wot, never a deel,
That bothe his soule and eek hem-self offende,
And yet they mowe hir lustes nat amende.
‘What may I conclude of this longe serie,
But, after wo, I rede us to be merie,
And thanken Jupiter of al his grace?
And, er that we departen from this place,
I rede that we make, of sorwes two,
O parfyt joye, lasting ever-mo;
And loketh now, wher most sorwe is herinne,
Ther wol we first amenden and biginne.
‘Suster,’ quod he, ‘this is my fulle assent,
With al th'avys heer of my parlement,
That gentil Palamon, your owne knight,
That serveth yow with wille, herte, and might,

And ever hath doon, sin that ye first him knewe,
That ye shul, of your grace, up-on him rewe,
And taken him for housbonde and for lord :
Leen me your hond, for this is our acord.
Lat see now of your wommanly pitee.
He is a kinges brother sone, pardee ;
And, though he were a povre bacheler,
Sin he hath served yow so many a yeer,
And had for yow so greet adversitee,
It moste been considered, leveth me ;
For gentil mercy oghte to passen right.'
  Than seyde he thus to Palamon ful right ;
'I trowe ther nedeth litel sermoning
To make yow assente to this thing.
Com neer, and tak your lady by the hond.'
Bitwixen hem was maad anon the bond,
That highte matrimoine or mariage,
By al the counseil and the baronage.
And thus with alle blisse and melodye
Hath Palamon y-wedded Emelye.
And God, that al this wyde world hath wroght,
Sende him his love, that hath it dere a-boght.
For now is Palamon in alle wele,
Living in blisse, in richesse, and in hele ;
And Emelye him loveth so tendrely,
And he hir serveth al-so gentilly,
That never was ther no word hem bitwene
Of jelousye, or any other tene.
Thus endeth Palamon and Emelye ;
And God save al this faire companye !—Amen.

Here is ended the Knightes Tale.

THE MILLERES TALE

Here folwen the wordes bitwene the Host and the Millere.

WHAN that the Knight had thus his tale y-told,
In al the route nas ther yong ne old
That he ne seyde it was a noble storie,
And worthy for to drawen to memorie;
And namely the gentils everichoon.
Our Hoste lough and swoor, 'so moot I goon,
This gooth aright; unbokeled is the male;
Lat see now who shal telle another tale:
For trewely, the game is wel bigonne.
Now telleth ye, sir Monk, if that ye conne,
Sumwhat, to quyte with the Knightes tale.'
The Miller, that for-dronken was al pale,
So that unnethe up-on his hors he sat,
He nolde avalen neither hood ne hat,
Ne abyde no man for his curteisye,
But in Pilates vois he gan to crye,
And swoor by armes and by blood and bones,
'I can a noble tale for the nones,
With which I wol now quyte the Knightes tale.'
  Our Hoste saugh that he was dronke of ale,
And seyde: 'abyd, Robin, my leve brother,
Som bettre man shal telle us first another:
Abyd, and lat us werken thriftily.'
  'By goddes soul,' quod he, 'that wol nat I;
For I wol speke, or elles go my wey.'
Our Hoste answerde: 'tel on, a devel wey!
Thou art a fool, thy wit is overcome.'
  'Now herkneth,' quod the Miller, 'alle and some!

But first I make a protestacioun
That I am dronke, I knowe it by my soun;
And therfore, if that I misspeke or seye,
Wyte it the ale of Southwerk, I yow preye;
For I wol telle a legende and a lyf
Bothe of a Carpenter, and of his wyf,
How that a clerk hath set the wrightes cappe.'
The Reve answerde and seyde, 'stint thy clappe,
Lat be thy lewed dronken harlotrye.
It is a sinne and eek a greet folye
To apeiren any man, or him diffame,
And eek to bringen wyves in swich fame.
Thou mayst y-nogh of othere thinges seyn.'
This dronken Miller spak ful sone ageyn,
And seyde, 'leve brother Osewold,
Who hath no wyf, he is no cokewold.
But I sey nat therfore that thou art oon;
Ther been ful gode wyves many oon,
And ever a thousand gode ayeyns oon badde,
That knowestow wel thy-self, but-if thou madde.
Why artow angry with my tale now?
I have a wyf, pardee, as well as thou,
Yet nolde I, for the oxen in my plogh,
Taken up-on me more than y-nogh,
As demen of my-self that I were oon;
I wol beleve wel that I am noon.
An housbond shal nat been inquisitif
Of goddes privetee, nor of his wyf.
So he may finde goddes foyson there,
Of the remenant nedeth nat enquere.'
What sholde I more seyn, but this Millere
He nolde his wordes for no man forbere,
But tolde his cherles tale in his manere;
Me thinketh that I shal reherce it here.
And ther-fore every gentil wight I preye,
For goddes love, demeth nat that I seye
Of evel entente, but that I moot reherce
Hir tales alle, be they bettre or werse
Or elles falsen som of my matere.
And therfore, who-so list it nat y-here,

Turne over the leef, and chese another tale;
For he shal finde y-nowe, grete and smale,
Of storial thing that toucheth gentillesse,
And eek moralitee and holinesse;
Blameth nat me if that ye chese amis.
The Miller is a cherl, ye knowe wel this:
So was the Reve, and othere many mo,
And harlotrye they tolden bothe two.
Avyseth yow and putte me out of blame;
And eek men shal nat make ernest of game.

Here endeth the prologe.

Here biginneth the Millere his tale.

WHYLOM ther was dwellinge at Oxenford
A riche gnof, that gestes heeld to bord,
And of his craft he was a Carpenter.
With him ther was dwellinge a povre scoler,
Had lerned art, but al his fantasye
Was turned for to lerne astrologye,
And coude a certeyn of conclusiouns
To demen by interrogaciouns,
If that men axed him in certein houres,
Whan that men sholde have droghte or elles shoures,
Or if men axed him what sholde bifalle
Of every thing, I may nat rekene hem alle.
  This clerk was cleped hende Nicholas;
Of derne love he coude and of solas;
And ther-to he was sleigh and ful privee,
And lyk a mayden meke for to see.
A chambre hadde he in that hostelrye
Allone, with-outen any companye,
Ful fetisly y-dight with herbes swote;
And he him-self as swete as is the rote
Of licorys, or any cetewale.
His Almageste and bokes grete and smale,
His astrelabie, longinge for his art,
His augrim-stones layen faire a-part
On shelves couched at his beddes heed:
His presse y-covered with a falding reed.

And al above ther lay a gay sautrye,
On which he made a nightes melodye
So swetely, that al the chambre rong;
And *Angelus ad virginem* he song;
And after that he song the kinges note;
Ful often blessed was his mery throte.
And thus this swete clerk his tyme spente
After his freendes finding and his rente.
This Carpenter had wedded newe a wyf
Which that he lovede more than his lyf;
Of eightetene yeer she was of age.
Jalous he was, and heeld hir narwe in cage,
For she was wilde and yong, and he was old,
And demed him-self ben lyk a cokewold.
He knew nat Catoun, for his wit was rude,
That bad man sholde wedde his similitude.
Men sholde wedden after hir estaat,
For youthe and elde is often at debaat.
But sith that he was fallen in the snare,
He moste endure, as other folk, his care.
Fair was this yonge wyf, and ther-with-al
As any wesele hir body gent and smal.
A ceynt she werede barred al of silk,
A barmclooth eek as whyt as morne milk
Up-on hir lendes, ful of many a gore.
Whyt was hir smok and brouded al bifore
And eek bihinde, on hir coler aboute,
Of col-blak silk, with-inne and eek with-oute.
The tapes of hir whyte voluper
Were of the same suyte of hir coler;
Hir filet brood of silk, and set ful hye:
And sikerly she hadde a likerous yë.
Ful smale y-pulled were hir browes two,
And tho were bent, and blake as any sloo.
She was ful more blisful on to see
Than is the newe pere-jonette tree;
And softer than the wolle is of a wether.
And by hir girdel heeng a purs of lether
Tasseld with silk, and perled with latoun.
In al this world, to seken up and doun.

There nis no man so wys, that coude thenche
So gay a popelote, or swich a wenche.
Ful brighter was the shyning of hir hewe
Than in the tour the noble y-forged newe.
But of hir song, it was as loude and yerne
As any swalwe sittinge on a berne.
Ther-to she coude skippe and make game,
As any kide or calf folwinge his dame.
Hir mouth was swete as bragot or the meeth
Or hord of apples leyd in hey or heeth.
Winsinge she was, as is a joly colt,
Long as a mast, and upright as a bolt.
A brooch she baar up-on hir lowe coler,
As brood as is the bos of a bocler.
Hir shoes were laced on hir legges hye;
She was a prymerole, a pigges-nye
For any lord to leggen in his bedde,
Or yet for any good yeman to wedde.
Now sire, and eft sire, so bifel the cas,
That on a day this hende Nicholas
Fil with this yonge wyf to rage and pleye,
Whyl that hir housbond was at Oseneye,
As clerkes ben ful subtile and ful queynte;
And prively he caughte hir by the queynte,
And seyde, 'y-wis, but if ich have my wille,
For derne love of thee, lemman, I spille.'
And heeld hir harde by the haunche-bones,
And seyde, 'lemman, love me al at-ones,
Or I wol dyen, also god me save!'
And she sprong as a colt doth in the trave,
And with hir heed she wryed faste awey,
And seyde, 'I wol nat kisse thee, by my fey,
Why, lat be,' quod she, 'lat be, Nicholas,
Or I wol crye out "harrow" and "allas."
Do wey your handes for your curteisye!'
This Nicholas gan mercy for to crye,
And spak so faire, and profred hir so faste,
That she hir love him graunted atte laste,
And swoor hir ooth, by seint Thomas of Kent,
That she wol been at his comandement,

Whan that she may hir leyser wel espye.
'Myn housbond is so ful of jalousye,
That but ye wayte wel and been privee,
I woot right wel I nam but deed,' quod she.
'Ye moste been ful derne, as in this cas.'
  'Nay ther-of care thee noght,' quod Nicholas,
'A clerk had litherly biset his whyle,
But-if he coude a carpenter bigyle.'
And thus they been acorded and y-sworn
To wayte a tyme, as I have told biforn.
Whan Nicholas had doon thus everydeel,
And thakked hir aboute the lendes weel,
He kist hir swete, and taketh his sautrye,
And pleyeth faste, and maketh melodye.
  Than fil it thus, that to the parish-chirche,
Cristes owne werkes for to wirche,
This gode wyf wente on an haliday;
Hir forheed shoon as bright as any day,
So was it wasshen whan she leet hir werk.
  Now was ther of that chirche a parish-clerk,
The which that was y-cleped Absolon.
Crul was his heer, and as the gold it shoon,
And strouted as a fanne large and brode;
Ful streight and even lay his joly shode.
His rode was reed, his eyen greye as goos;
With Powles window corven on his shoos,
In hoses rede he wente fetisly.
Y-clad he was ful smal and proprely,
Al in a kirtel of a light wachet;
Ful faire and thikke been the poyntes set.
And ther-up-on he hadde a gay surplys
As whyt as is the blosme up-on the rys.
A mery child he was, so god me save,
Wel coude he laten blood and clippe and shave,
And make a chartre of lond or acquitaunce.
In twenty manere coude he trippe and daunce
After the scole of Oxenforde tho,
And with his legges casten to and fro,
And pleyen songes on a small rubible;
Ther-to he song som-tyme a loud quinible;

And as wel coude he pleye on his giterne.
In al the toun nas brewhous ne taverne
That he ne visited with his solas,
Ther any gaylard tappestere was.
But sooth to seyn, he was somdel squaymous
Of farting, and of speche daungerous.
  This Absolon, that jolif was and gay,
Gooth with a sencer on the haliday,
Sensinge the wyves of the parish faste;
And many a lovely look on hem he caste,
And namely on this carpenteres wyf.
To loke on hir him thoughte a mery lyf,
She was so propre and swete and likerous.
I dar wel seyn, if she had been a mous,
And he a cat, he wolde hir hente anon.
  This parish-clerk, this joly Absolon,
Hath in his herte swich a love-longinge,
That of no wyf ne took he noon offringe;
For curteisye, he seyde, he wolde noon.
The mone, whan it was night, ful brighte shoon,
And Absolon his giterne hath y-take,
For paramours, he thoghte for to wake.
And forth he gooth, jolif and amorous,
Til he cam to the carpenteres hous
A litel after cokkes hadde y-crowe;
And dressed him up by a shot-windowe
That was up-on the carpenteres wal.
He singeth in his vois gentil and smal,
'Now, dere lady, if thy wille be,
I preye yow that ye wol rewe on me,'
Ful wel acordaunt to his giterninge.
This carpenter awook, and herde him singe,
And spak un-to his wyf, and seyde anon,
'What! Alison! herestow nat Absolon
That chaunteth thus under our boures wal?'
And she answerde hir housbond ther-with-al,
'Yis, god wot, John, I here it every-del.'
  This passeth forth; what wol ye bet than wel?
Fro day to day this joly Absolon
So woweth hir, that him is wo bigon.

He waketh al the night and al the day;
He kempte hise lokkes brode, and made him gay;
He woweth hir by menes and brocage,
And swoor he wolde been hir owne page;
He singeth, brokkinge as a nightingale;
He sente hir piment, meeth, and spyced ale,
And wafres, pyping hote out of the glede;
And for she was of toune, he profred mede.
For som folk wol ben wonnen for richesse,
And som for strokes, and som for gentillesse.
Somtyme, to shewe his lightnesse and maistrye,
He pleyeth Herodes on a scaffold hye.
But what availleth him as in this cas?
She loveth so this hende Nicholas,
That Absolon may blowe the bukkes horn;
He ne hadde for his labour but a scorn;
And thus she maketh Absolon hir ape,
And al his ernest turneth til a jape.
Ful sooth is this proverbe, it is no lye,
Men seyn right thus, 'alwey the nye slye
Maketh the ferre leve to be looth.'
For though that Absolon be wood or wrooth,
By-cause that he fer was from hir sighte,
This nye Nicholas stood in his lighte.
Now bere thee wel, thou hende Nicholas!
For Absolon may waille and singe 'allas.'
And so bifel it on a Saterday,
This carpenter was goon til Osenay;
And hende Nicholas and Alisoun
Acorded been to this conclusioun,
That Nicholas shal shapen him a wyle
This sely jalous housbond to bigyle;
And if so be the game wente aright,
She sholde slepen in his arm al night,
For this was his desyr and hir also.
And right anon, with-outen wordes mo,
This Nicholas no lenger wolde tarie,
But doth ful softe un-to his chambre carie
Bothe mete and drinke for a day or tweye,
And to hir housbonde bad hir for to seye,

If that he axed after Nicholas,
She sholde seye she niste where he was,
Of al that day she saugh him nat with yë;
She trowed that he was in maladye,
For, for no cry, hir mayde coude him calle;
He nolde answere, for no-thing that mighte falle.
  This passeth forth al thilke Saterday,
That Nicholas stille in his chambre lay,
And eet and sleep, or dide what him leste,
Til Sonday, that the sonne gooth to reste.
  This sely carpenter hath greet merveyle
Of Nicholas, or what thing mighte him eyle,
And seyde, 'I am adrad, by seint Thomas,
It stondeth nat aright with Nicholas.
God shilde that he deyde sodeynly!
This world is now ful tikel, sikerly;
I saugh to-day a cors y-born to chirche
That now, on Monday last, I saugh him wirche
  Go up,' quod he un-to his knave anoon,
'Clepe at his dore, or knokke with a stoon,
Loke how it is, and tel me boldely.'
  This knave gooth him up ful sturdily,
And at the chambre-dore, whyl that he stood,
He cryde and knokked as that he were wood:—
'What! how! what do ye, maister Nicholay?
How may ye slepen al the longe day?'
  But al for noght, he herde nat a word;
An hole he fond, ful lowe up-on a bord,
Ther as the cat was wont in for to crepe;
And at that hole he looked in ful depe,
And at the laste he hadde of him a sighte.
This Nicholas sat gaping ever up-righte,
As he had kyked on the newe mone.
Adoun he gooth, and tolde his maister sone
In what array he saugh this ilke man.
  This carpenter to blessen him bigan,
And seyde, 'help us, seinte Frideswyde!
A man woot litel what him shal bityde.
This man is falle, with his astromye,
In som woodnesse or in som agonye;

I thoghte ay wel how that it sholde be !
Men sholde nat knowe of goddes privetee.
Ye, blessed be alwey a lewed man,
That noght but only his bileve can !
So ferde another clerk with astromye ;
He walked in the feeldes for to prye
Up-on the sterres, what ther sholde bifalle,
Til he was in a marle-pit y-falle ;
He saugh nat that. But yet, by seint Thomas,
Me reweth sore of hende Nicholas.
He shal be rated of his studying,
If that I may, by Jesus, hevene king !
  Get me a staf, that I may underspore,
Whyl that thou, Robin, hevest up the dore.
He shal out of his studying, as I gesse '—
And to the chambre-dore he gan him dresse.
His knave was a strong carl for the nones,
And by the haspe he haf it up atones ;
In-to the floor the dore fil anon.
This Nicholas sat ay as stille as stoon,
And ever gaped upward in-to the eir.
This carpenter wende he were in despeir,
And hente him by the sholdres mightily,
And shook him harde, and cryde spitously,
'What! Nicholay! what, how! what! loke adoun !
Awake, and thenk on Cristes passioun ;
I crouche thee from elves and fro wightes ! '
Ther-with the night-spel seyde he anon-rightes
On foure halves of the hous aboute,
And on the threshfold of the dore with-oute :—
  'Jesu Crist, and sëynt Benedight,
  Blesse this hous from every wikked wight,
  For nightes verye, the white *paternoster* !—
  Where wentestow, seynt Petres soster ? '
And atte laste this hende Nicholas
Gan for to syke sore, and seyde, ' allas !
Shal al the world be lost eftsones now ? '
  This carpenter answerde, ' what seystow ?
What ! thenk on god, as we don, men that swinke.'
  This Nicholas answerde, ' fecche me drinke ;

And after wol I speke in privetee
Of certeyn thing that toucheth me and thee;
I wol telle it non other man, certeyn.'
  This carpenter goth doun, and comth ageyn,
And broghte of mighty ale a large quart;
And whan that ech of hem had dronke his part,
This Nicholas his dore faste shette,
And doun the carpenter by him he sette.
  He seyde, 'John, myn hoste lief and dere,
Thou shalt up-on thy trouthe swere me here,
That to no wight thou shalt this conseil wreye:
For it is Cristes conseil that I seye,
And if thou telle it man, thou are forlore;
For this vengaunce thou shalt han therfore,
That if thou wreye me, thou shalt be wood!'
'Nay, Crist forbede it, for his holy blood!'
Quod tho this sely man, 'I nam no labbe,
Ne, though I seye, I nam nat lief to gabbe.
Sey what thou wolt, I shal it never telle
To child ne wyf, by him that harwed helle!'
  'Now John,' quod Nicholas, 'I wol nat lye;
I have y-founde in myn astrologye,
As I have loked in the mone bright,
That now, a Monday next, at quarter-night,
Shal falle a reyn and that so wilde and wood,
That half so greet was never Noës flood.
This world,' he seyde, 'in lasse than in an hour
Shal al be dreynt, so hidous is the shour;
Thus shal mankynde drenche and lese hir lyf.'
  This carpenter answerde, 'allas, my wyf!
And shal she drenche? allas! myn Alisoun!'
For sorwe of this he fil almost adoun,
And seyde, 'is ther no remedie in this cas?'
  'Why, yis, for gode,' quod hende Nicholas,
'If thou wolt werken after lore and reed:
Thou mayst nat werken after thyn owene heed.
For thus seith Salomon, that was ful trewe,
"Werk al by conseil, and thou shalt nat rewe."
And if thou werken wolt by good conseil,
I undertake, with-outen mast and seyl,

Yet shal I saven hir and thee and me.
Hastow nat herd how saved was Noë,
Whan that our lord had warned him biforn
That al the world with water sholde be lorn ?'
  'Yis,' quod this carpenter, 'ful yore ago.'
  'Hastow nat herd,' quod Nicholas, 'also
The sorwe of Noë with his felawshipe,
Er that he mighte gete his wyf to shipe ?
Him had be lever, I dar wel undertake,
At thilke tyme, than alle hise wetheres blake,
That she hadde had a ship hir-self allone.
And ther-fore, wostou what is best to done ?
This asketh haste, and of an hastif thing
Men may nat preche or maken tarying.
  Anon go gete us faste in-to this in
A kneding-trogh, or elles a kimelin,
For ech of us, but loke that they be large,
In whiche we mowe swimme as in a barge,
And han ther-inne vitaille suffisant
But for a day ; fy on the remenant !
The water shal aslake and goon away
Aboute pryme up-on the nexte day.
  But Robin may nat wite of this, thy knave,
Ne eek thy mayde Gille I may nat save ;
Axe nat why, for though thou aske me,
I wol nat tellen goddes privetee.
Suffiseth thee, but if thy wittes madde,
To han as greet a grace as Noë hadde.
Thy wyf shal I wel saven, out of doute,
Go now thy wey, and speed thee heeraboute.
  But whan thou hast, for hir and thee and me,
Y-geten us thise kneding-tubbes three,
Than shaltow hange hem in the roof ful hye,
That no man of our purveyaunce spye.
And whan thou thus hast doon as I have seyd,
And hast our vitaille faire in hem y-leyd,
And eek an ax, to smyte the corde atwo
When that the water comth, that we may go,
And broke an hole an heigh, up-on the gable,
Unto the gardin-ward, over the stable,

That we may frely passen forth our way
Whan that the grete shour is goon away—
Than shaltow swimme as myrie, I undertake,
As doth the whyte doke aftir hir drake.
Than wol I clepe, "how ! Alison ! how ! John !
Be myrie, for the flood wol passe anon."
And thou wolt seyn, "hayl, maister Nicholay !
Good morwe, I se thee wel, for it is day."
And than shul we be lordes al our lyf
Of al the world, as Noë and his wyf.
  But of o thyng I warne thee ful right,
Be wel avysed, on that ilke night
That we ben entred in-to shippes bord,
That noon of us ne speke nat a word,
Ne clepe, ne crye, but been in his preyere ;
For it is goddes owne heste dere.
  Thy wyf and thou mote hange fer a-twinne,
For that bitwixe yow shal be no sinne
No more in looking than ther shal in dede ;
This ordinance is seyd, go, god thee spede !
Tomorwe at night, whan men ben alle aslepe,
In-to our kneding-tubbes wol we crepe,
And sitten ther, abyding goddes grace.
Go now thy wey, I have no lenger space
To make of this no lenger sermoning.
Men seyn thus, "send the wyse, and sey no-thing;"
Thou art so wys, it nedeth thee nat teche ;
Go, save our lyf, and that I thee biseche.'
  This sely carpenter goth forth his wey.
Ful ofte he seith 'allas' and 'weylawey,'
And to his wyf he tolde his privetee ;
And she was war, and knew it bet than he,
What al this queynte cast was for to seye.
But nathelees she ferde as she wolde deye,
And seyde, 'allas ! go forth thy wey anon,
Help us to scape, or we ben lost echon ;
I am thy trewe verray wedded wyf ;
Go, dere spouse, and help to save our lyf.'
  Lo ! which a greet thyng is affeccioun !
Men may dye of imaginacioun,

So depe may impressioun be take.
This sely carpenter biginneth quake;
Him thinketh verraily that he may see
Noës flood come walwing as the see
To drenchen Alisoun, his hony dere.
He wepeth, weyleth, maketh sory chere,
He syketh with ful many a sory swogh.
He gooth and geteth him a kneding-trogh,
And after that a tubbe and a kimelin,
And prively he sente hem to his in,
And heng hem in the roof in privetee.
His owne hand he made laddres three,
To climben by the ronges and the stalkes
Un-to the tubbes hanginge in the balkes,
And hem vitailled, bothe trogh and tubbe,
With breed and chese, and good ale in a jubbe,
Suffysinge right y-nogh as for a day.
But er that he had maad al this array,
He sente his knave, and eek his wenche also,
Up-on his nede to London for to go.
And on the Monday, whan it drow to night,
He shette his dore with-oute candel-light,
And dressed al thing as it sholde be.
And shortly, up they clomben alle three;
They sitten stille wel a furlong-way.
'Now, *Pater-noster*, clom!' seyde Nicholay,
And 'clom,' quod John, and 'clom,' seyde Alisoun.
This carpenter seyde his devocioun,
And stille he sit, and biddeth his preyere,
Awaytinge on the reyn, if he it here.
The dede sleep, for wery bisinesse,
Fil on this carpenter right, as I gesse,
Aboute corfew-tyme, or litel more;
For travail of his goost he groneth sore,
And eft he routeth, for his heed mislay.
Doun of the laddre stalketh Nicholay,
And Alisoun, ful softe adoun she spedde;
With-outen wordes mo, they goon to bedde
Ther-as the carpenter is wont to lye.
Ther was the revel and the melodye:

And thus lyth Alison and Nicholas,
In bisinesse of mirthe and of solas,
Til that the belle of laudes gan to ringe,
And freres in the chauncel gonne singe.
This parish-clerk, this amorous Absolon,
That is for love alwey so wo bigon,
Up-on the Monday was at Oseneye
With companye, him to disporte and pleye,
And axed up-on cas a cloisterer
Ful prively after John the carpenter;
And he drough him a-part out of the chirche,
And seyde, 'I noot, I saugh him here nat wirche
Sin Saterday; I trow that he be went
For timber, ther our abbot hath him sent;
For he is wont for timber for to go,
And dwellen at the grange a day or two;
Or elles he is at his hous, certeyn;
Wher that he be, I can nat sothly seyn.'
This Absolon ful joly was and light,
And thoghte, 'now is tyme wake al night;
For sikirly I saugh him nat stiringe
Aboute his dore sin day bigan to springe.
So moot I thryve, I shal, at cokkes crowe,
Ful prively knokken at his windowe
That stant ful lowe up-on his boures wal.
To Alison now wol I tellen al
My love-longing, for yet I shal nat misse
That at the leste wey I shal hir kisse.
Som maner confort shal I have, parfay,
My mouth hath icched al this longe day;
That is a signe of kissing atte leste.
Al night me mette eek, I was at a feste.
Therfor I wol gon slepe an houre or tweye,
And al the night than wol I wake and pleye.'
Whan that the firste cok hath crowe, anon
Up rist this joly lover Absolon,
And him arrayeth gay, at point-devys.
But first he cheweth greyn and lycorys,
To smellen swete, er he had kembd his heer.
Under his tonge a trewe love he beer,

For ther-by wende he to ben gracious.
He rometh to the carpenteres hous,
And stille he stant under the shot-windowe;
Un-to his brest it raughte, it was so lowe;
And softe he cogheth with a semi-soun—
'What do ye, hony-comb, swete Alisoun?
My faire brid, my swete cinamome,
Awaketh, lemman myn, and speketh to me!
Wel litel thenken ye up-on my wo,
That for your love I swete ther I go.
No wonder is thogh that I swelte and swete;
I moorne as doth a lamb after the tete.
Y-wis, lemman, I have swich love-longinge,
That lyk a turtel trewe is my moorninge;
I may nat ete na more than a mayde.'
'Go fro the window, Jakke fool,' she sayde,
'As help me god, it wol nat be "com ba me,"
I love another, and elles I were to blame,
Wel bet than thee, by Jesu, Absolon!
Go forth thy wey, or I wol caste a ston,
And lat me slepe, a twenty devel wey!'
'Allas,' quod Absolon, 'and weylawey!
That trewe love was ever so yvel biset!
Than kisse me, sin it may be no bet,
For Jesus love and for the love of me.'
'Wiltow than go thy wey ther-with?' quod she.
'Ye, certes, lemman,' quod this Absolon.
'Thanne make thee redy,' quod she, 'I come anon;'
And un-to Nicholas she seyde stille,
'Now hust, and thou shalt laughen al thy fille.'
This Absolon doun sette him on his knees,
And seyde, 'I am a lord at alle degrees;
For after this I hope ther cometh more!
Lemman, thy grace, and swete brid, thyn ore!'
The window she undoth, and that in haste,
'Have do,' quod she, 'com of, and speed thee faste,
Lest that our neighebores thee espye.'
This Absolon gan wype his mouth ful drye;
Derk was the night as pich, or as the cole,
And at the window out she putte hir hole,

And Absolon, him fil no bet ne wers,
But with his mouth he kiste hir naked ers
Ful savourly, er he was war of this.
Abak he sterte, and thoghte it was amis,
For wel he wiste a womman hath no berd;
He felte a thing al rough and long y-herd,
And seyde, 'fy! allas! what have I do?'
'Tehee!' quod she, and clapte the window to;
And Absolon goth forth a sory pas.
'A berd, a berd!' quod hende Nicholas,
'By goddes *corpus*, this goth faire and weel!'
This sely Absolon herde every deel,
And on his lippe he gan for anger byte;
And to him-self he seyde, 'I shal thee quyte!'
Who rubbeth now, who froteth now his lippes
With dust, with sond, with straw, with clooth, with chippes,
But Absolon, that seith ful ofte, 'allas!
My soule bitake I un-to Sathanas,
But me wer lever than al this toun,' quod he,
'Of this despyt awroken for to be!
Allas!' quod he, 'allas! I ne hadde y-bleynt!'
His hote love was cold and al y-queynt;
For fro that tyme that he had kiste hir ers,
Of paramours he sette nat a kers,
For he was heled of his maladye;
Ful ofte paramours he gan deffye,
And weep as dooth a child that is y-bete.
A softe paas he wente over the strete
Un-til a smith men cleped daun Gerveys,
That in his forge smithed plough-harneys;
He sharpeth shaar and culter bisily
This Absolon knokketh al esily,
And seyde, 'undo, Gerveys, and that anon.'
'What, who artow?' 'It am I, Absolon.'
'What, Absolon! for Cristes swete tree,
Why ryse ye so rathe, ey, *ben'cite!*
What eyleth yow? som gay gerl, god it woot,
Hath broght yow thus up-on the viritoot;

By sëynt Note, ye woot wel what I mene.'
  This Absolon ne roghte nat a bene
Of al his pley, no word agayn he yaf;
He hadde more tow on his distaf
Than Gerveys knew, and seyde, 'freend so dere,
That hote culter in the chimenee here,
As lene it me, I have ther-with to done,
And I wol bringe it thee agayn ful sone.'
  Gerveys answerde, 'certes, were it gold,
Or in a poke nobles alle untold,
Thou sholdest have, as I am trewe smith;
Ey, Cristes foo! what wol ye do therwith?'
  'Therof,' quod Absolon, 'be as be may;
I shal wel telle it thee to-morwe day'—
And caughte the culter by the colde stele.
Ful softe out at the dore he gan to stele,
And wente un-to the carpenteres wal.
He cogheth first, and knokketh ther-with-al
Upon the windowe, right as he dide er.
  This Alison answerde, 'Who is ther
That knokketh so? I warante it a theef.'
  'Why, nay,' quod he, 'god woot, my swete leef,
I am thyn Absolon, my derling!
Of gold,' quod he, 'I have thee broght a ring;
My moder yaf it me, so god me save,
Ful fyn it is, and ther-to wel y-grave;
This wol I yeve thee, if thou me kisse!'
  This Nicholas was risen for to pisse,
And thoghte he wolde amenden al the jape,
He sholde kisse his ers er that he scape.
And up the windowe dide he hastily,
And out his ers he putteth prively
Over the buttok, to the haunche-bon;
And ther-with spak this clerk, this Absolon,
'Spek, swete brid, I noot nat wher thou art.'
  This Nicholas anon leet flee a fart,
As greet as it had been a thonder-dent,
That with the strook he was almost y-blent;
And he was redy with his iren hoot,
And Nicholas amidde the ers he smoot.

Of gooth the skin an hande-brede aboute,
The hote culter brende so his toute,
And for the smert he wende for to dye.
As he were wood, for wo he gan to crye—
'Help ! water ! water ! help, for goddes herte !'
This carpenter out of his slomber sterte,
And herde oon cryen 'water' as he were wood,
And thoghte, 'Allas ! now comth Nowélis flood !'
He sit him up with-outen wordes mo,
And with his ax he smoot the corde a-two,
And doun goth al ; he fond neither to selle,
Ne breed ne ale, til he cam to the selle
Up-on the floor ; and ther aswowne he lay.
Up sterte hir Alison, and Nicholay,
And cryden 'out' and 'harrow' in the strete.
The neighebores, bothe smale and grete,
In ronnen, for to gauren on this man,
That yet aswowne he lay, bothe pale and wan ;
For with the fal he brosten hadde his arm ;
But stonde he moste un-to his owne harm.
For whan he spak, he was anon bore doun
With hende Nicholas and Alisoun.
They tolden every man that he was wood,
He was agast so of 'Nowélis flood'
Thurgh fantasye, that of his vanitee
He hadde y-boght him kneding-tubbes three,
And hadde hem hanged in the roof above ;
And that he preyed hem, for goddes love,
To sitten in the roof, *par companye.*
The folk gan laughen at his fantasye ;
In-to the roof they kyken and they gape,
And turned al his harm un-to a jape.
For what so that this carpenter answerde,
It was for noght, no man his reson herde ;
With othes grete he was so sworn adoun,
That he was holden wood in al the toun ;
For every clerk anon-right heeld with other.
They seyde, 'the man is wood, my leve brother ;
And every wight gan laughen of this stryf.
Thus swyved was the carpenteres wyf,

For al his keping and his jalousye ;
And Absolon hath kist hir nether yë ;
And Nicholas is scalded in the toute.
This tale is doon, and god save al the route !

Here endeth the Millere his tale.

THE REVES TALE

The prologe of the Reves tale.

Whan folk had laughen at this nyce cas
Of Absolon and hende Nicholas,
Diverse folk diversely they seyde ;
But, for the more part, they loughe and pleyde,
Ne at this tale I saugh no man him greve,
But it were only Osewold the Reve,
By-cause he was of carpenteres craft.
A litel ire is in his herte y-laft,
He gan to grucche and blamed it a lyte.
'So thee'k,' quod he, 'ful wel coude I yow quyte
With blering of a proud milleres yë,
If that me liste speke of ribaudye.
But ik am old, me list not pley for age ;
Gras-tyme is doon, my fodder is now forage,
This whyte top wryteth myne olde yeres,
Myn herte is al-so mowled as myne heres,
But-if I fare as dooth an open-ers ;
That ilke fruit is ever leng the wers,
Til it be roten in mullok or in stree.
We olde men, I drede, so fare we ;
Til we be roten, can we nat be rype ;
We hoppen ay, whyl that the world wol pype.
For in oure wil ther stiketh ever a nayl,
To have an hoor heed and a grene tayl,
As hath a leek ; for thogh our might be goon,
Our wil desireth folie ever in oon.
For whan we may nat doon, than wol we speke ;
Yet in our asshen olde is fyr y-reke.

Foure gledes han we, whiche I shal devyse,
Avaunting, lying, anger, coveityse;
Thise foure sparkles longen un-to elde.
Our olde lemes mowe wel been unwelde,
But wil ne shal nat faillen, that is sooth.
And yet ik have alwey a coltes tooth,
As many a yeer as it is passed henne
Sin that my tappe of lyf bigan to renne.
For sikerly, whan I was bore, anon
Deeth drogh the tappe of lyf and leet it gon;
And ever sith hath so the tappe y-ronne,
Til that almost al empty is the tonne.
The streem of lyf now droppeth on the chimbe;
The sely tonge may wel ringe and chimbe
Of wrecchednesse that passed is ful yore;
With olde folk, save dotage, is namore.'
Whan that our host hadde herd this sermoning,
He gan to speke as lordly as a king;
He seide, 'what amounteth al this wit?
What shul we speke alday of holy writ?
The devel made a reve for to preche,
And of a souter a shipman or a leche.
Sey forth thy tale, and tarie nat the tyme,
Lo, Depeford! and it is half-way pryme.
Lo, Grenewich, ther many a shrewe is inne;
It wer al tyme thy tale to biginne.'
'Now, sires,' quod this Osewold the Reve,
'I pray yow alle that ye nat yow greve,
Thogh I answere and somdel sette his howve;
For leveful is with force force of-showve.
This dronke millere hath y-told us heer,
How that bigyled was a carpenteer,
Peraventure in scorn, for I am oon.
And, by your leve, I shal him quyte anoon;
Right in his cherles termes wol I speke.
I pray to god his nekke mote breke;
He can wel in myn yë seen a stalke,
But in his owne he can nat seen a balke.'

Here biginneth the Reves tale.

At Trumpington, nat fer fro Cantebrigge,
Ther goth a brook and over that a brigge,
Up-on the whiche brook ther stant a melle;
And this is verray soth that I yow telle.
A Miller was ther dwelling many a day;
As eny pecok he was proud and gay.
Pypen he coude and fisshe, and nettes bete,
And turne coppes, and wel wrastle and shete;
And by his belt he baar a long panade,
And of a swerd ful trenchant was the blade.
A joly popper baar he in his pouche;
Ther was no man for peril dorste him touche.
A Sheffeld thwitel baar he in his hose;
Round was his face, and camuse was his nose.
As piled as an ape was his skulle.
He was a market-beter atte fulle.
Ther dorste no wight hand up-on him legge,
That he ne swoor he sholde anon abegge.
A theef he was for sothe of corn and mele,
And that a sly, and usaunt for to stele.
His name was hoten dëynous Simkin.
A wyf he hadde, y-comen of noble kin;
The person of the toun hir fader was.
With hir he yaf ful many a panne of bras,
For that Simkin sholde in his blood allye.
She was y-fostred in a nonnerye;
For Simkin wolde no wyf, as he sayde,
But she were wel y-norissed and a mayde,
To saven his estaat of yomanrye.
And she was proud, and pert as is a pye.
A ful fair sighte was it on hem two;
On haly-dayes biforn hir wolde he go
With his tipet bounden about his heed,
And she cam after in a gyte of reed;
And Simkin hadde hosen of the same.
Ther dorste no wight clepen hir but 'dame.'
Was noon so hardy that wente by the weye
That with hir dorste rage or ones pleye,

But-if he wolde be slayn of Simkin
With panade, or with knyf, or boydekin.
For jalous folk ben perilous evermo,
Algate they wolde hir wyves wenden so.
And eek, for she was somdel smoterlich,
She was as digne as water in a dich;
And ful of hoker and of bisemare.
Hir thoughte that a lady sholde hir spare,
What for hir kinrede and hir nortelrye
That she had lerned in the nonnerye.
A doghter hadde they bitwixe hem two
Of twenty yeer, with-outen any mo,
Savinge a child that was of half-yeer age;
In cradel it lay and was a propre page.
This wenche thikke and wel y-growen was,
With camuse nose and yën greye as glas;
With buttokes brode and brestes rounde and hye,
But right fair was hir heer, I wol nat lye.
The person of the toun, for she was feir,
In purpos was to maken hir his heir
Bothe of his catel and his messuage,
And straunge he made it of hir mariage.
His purpos was for to bistowe hir hye
In-to som worthy blood of auncetrye;
For holy chirches good moot been despended
On holy chirches blood, that is descended.
Therfore he wolde his holy blood honoure,
Though that he holy chirche sholde devoure.
Gret soken hath this miller, out of doute,
With whete and malt of al the land aboute;
And nameliche ther was a greet collegge,
Men clepen the Soler-halle at Cantebregge,
Ther was hir whete and eek hir malt y-grounde.
And on a day it happed, in a stounde,
Sik lay the maunciple on a maladye;
Men wenden wisly that he sholde dye.
For which this miller stal bothe mele and corn
An hundred tyme more than biforn;
For ther-biforn he stal but curteisly,
But now he was a theef outrageously,

For which the wardeyn chidde and made fare.
But ther-of sette the miller nat a tare;
He craketh boost, and swoor it was nat so.
  Than were ther yonge povre clerkes two,
That dwelten in this halle, of which I seye.
Testif they were, and lusty for to pleye,
And, only for hir mirthe and revelrye,
Up-on the wardeyn bisily they crye,
To yeve hem leve but a litel stounde
To goon to mille and seen hir corn y-grounde;
And hardily, they dorste leye hir nekke,
The miller shold nat stele hem half a pekke
Of corn by sleighte, ne by force hem reve;
And at the laste the wardeyn yaf hem leve.
John hight that oon, and Aleyn hight that other;
Of o toun were they born, that highte Strother,
Fer in the north, I can nat telle where.
  This Aleyn maketh redy al his gere,
And on an hors the sak he caste anon.
Forth goth Aleyn the clerk, and also John,
With good swerd and with bokeler by hir syde.
John knew the wey, hem nedede no gyde,
And at the mille the sak adoun he layth.
Aleyn spak first, 'al hayl, Symond, y-fayth;
How fares thy faire doghter and thy wyf?'
  'Aleyn! welcome,' quod Simkin, 'by my lyf,
And John also, how now, what do ye heer?'
  'Symond,' quod John, 'by god, nede has na peer;
Him boës serve him-selve that has na swayn,
Or elles he is a fool, as clerkes sayn.
Our manciple, I hope he wil be deed,
Swa werkes ay the wanges in his heed.
And forthy is I come, and eek Alayn,
To grinde our corn and carie it ham agayn;
I pray yow spede us hethen that ye may.'
  'It shal be doon,' quod Simkin, 'by my fay;
What wol ye doon whyl that it is in hande?'
  'By god, right by the hoper wil I stande,'
Quod John, 'and se how that the corn gas in;
Yet saugh I never, by my fader kin,

How that the hoper wagges til and fra.'
  Aleyn answerde, 'John, and wiltow swa,
Than wil I be bynethe, by my croun,
And se how that the mele falles doun
In-to the trough ; that sal be my disport.
For John, in faith, I may been of your sort ;
I is as ille a miller as are ye.'
  This miller smyled of hir nycetee,
And thoghte, 'al this nis doon but for a wyle ;
They wene that no man may hem bigyle ;
But, by my thrift, yet shal I blere hir yë
For al the sleighte in hir philosophye.
The more queynte crekes that they make,
The more wol I stele whan I take.
In stede of flour, yet wol I yeve hem bren.
"The gretteste clerkes been noght the wysest men."
As whylom to the wolf thus spak the mare ;
Of al hir art I counte noght a tare.'
  Out at the dore he gooth ful prively,
Whan that he saugh his tyme, softely ;
He loketh up and doun til he hath founde
The clerkes hors, ther as it stood y-bounde
Bihinde the mille, under a levesel ;
And to the hors he gooth him faire and wel ;
He strepeth of the brydel right anon.
And whan the hors was loos, he ginneth gon
Toward the fen, ther wilde mares renne,
Forth with wehee, thurgh thikke and thurgh thenne.
  This miller gooth agayn, no word he seyde,
But dooth his note, and with the clerkes pleyde,
Til that hir corn was faire and wel y-grounde.
And whan the mele is sakked and y-bounde,
This John goth out and fynt his hors away,
And gan to crye 'harrow' and 'weylaway !
Our hors is lorn ! Alayn, for goddes banes,
Step on thy feet, com out, man, al at anes !
Allas, our wardeyn has his palfrey lorn.'
This Aleyn al forgat, bothe mele and corn,
Al was out of his mynde his housbondrye.
'What ? whilk way is he geen ?' he gan to crye.

The wyf cam leping inward with a ren,
She seyde, 'allas! your hors goth to the fen
With wilde mares, as faste as he may go.
Unthank come on his hand that bond him so,
And he that bettre sholde han knit the reyne.'
'Allas,' quod John, 'Aleyn, for Cristes peyne,
Lay doun thy swerd, and I wil myn alswa;
I is ful wight, god waat, as is a raa;
By goddes herte he sal nat scape us bathe.
Why nadstow pit the capul in the lathe?
Il-hayl, by god, Aleyn, thou is a fonne!'
This sely clerkes han ful faste y-ronne
To-ward the fen, bothe Aleyn and eek John.
And whan the miller saugh that they were gon,
He half a busshel of hir flour hath take,
And bad his wyf go knede it in a cake.
He seyde, 'I trowe the clerkes were aferd;
Yet can a miller make a clerkes berd
For al his art; now lat hem goon hir weye.
Lo wher they goon, ye, lat the children pleye;
They gete him nat so lightly, by my croun!'
Thise sely clerkes rennen up and doun
With 'keep, keep, stand, stand, jossa, warderere,
Ga whistle thou, and I shal kepe him here!'
But shortly, til that it was verray night,
They coude nat, though they do al hir might,
Hir capul cacche, he ran alwey so faste,
Til in a dich they caughte him atte laste.
Wery and weet, as beste is in the reyn,
Comth sely John, and with him comth Aleyn.
'Allas,' quod John, 'the day that I was born!
Now are we drive til hething and til scorn.
Our corn is stole, men wil us foles calle,
Bathe the wardeyn and our felawes alle,
And namely the miller; weylaway!'
Thus pleyneth John as he goth by the way
Toward the mille, and Bayard in his hond.
The miller sitting by the fyr he fond,
For it was night, and forther mighte they noght;
But, for the love of god, they him bisoght

Of herberwe and of ese, as for hir peny.
The miller seyde agayn, 'if ther be eny,
Swich as it is, yet shal ye have your part.
Myn hous is streit, but ye han lerned art;
Ye conne by argumentes make a place
A myle brood of twenty foot of space.
Lat see now if this place may suffyse,
Or make it roum with speche, as is youre gyse.'
'Now, Symond,' seyde John, 'by seint Cutberd,
Ay is thou mery, and this is faire answerd.
I have herd seyd, man sal taa of twa thinges
Slyk as he fyndes, or taa slyk as he bringes.
But specially, I pray thee, hoste dere,
Get us som mete and drinke, and make us chere,
And we wil payen trewely atte fulle.
With empty hand men may na haukes tulle;
Lo here our silver, redy for to spende.'
This miller in-to toun his doghter sende
For ale and breed, and rosted hem a goos,
And bond hir hors, it sholde nat gon loos;
And in his owne chambre hem made a bed
With shetes and with chalons faire y-spred,
Noght from his owne bed ten foot or twelve.
His doghter hadde a bed, al by hir-selve,
Right in the same chambre, by and by;
It mighte be no bet, and cause why,
Ther was no roumer herberwe in the place.
They soupen and they speke, hem to solace,
And drinken ever strong ale atte beste.
Aboute midnight wente they to reste.
Wel hath this miller vernisshed his heed;
Ful pale he was for-dronken, and nat reed.
He yexeth, and he speketh thurgh the nose
As he were on the quakke, or on the pose.
To bedde he gooth, and with him goth his wyf.
As any jay she light was and jolyf,
So was hir joly whistle wel y-wet.
The cradel at hir beddes feet is set,
To rokken, and to yeve the child to souke.
And whan that dronken al was in the crouke,

To bedde went the doghter right anon;
To bedde gooth Aleyn and also John;
Ther nas na more, hem nedede no dwale.
This miller hath so wisly bibbed ale,
That as an hors he snorteth in his sleep,
Ne of his tayl bihinde he took no keep.
His wyf bar him a burdon, a ful strong,
Men mighte hir routing here two furlong;
The wenche routeth eek *par companye.*
  Aleyn the clerk, that herd this melodye,
He poked John, and seyde, 'slepestow?
Herdestow ever slyk a sang er now?
Lo, whilk a compline is y-mel hem alle!
A wilde fyr up-on thair bodyes falle!
Wha herkned ever slyk a ferly thing?
Ye, they sal have the flour of il ending.
This lange night ther tydes me na reste;
But yet, na fors; al sal be for the beste.
For John,' seyde he, 'als ever moot I thryve
If that I may, yon wenche wil I swyve.
Som esement has lawe y-shapen us;
For John, ther is a lawe that says thus,
That gif a man in a point be y-greved,
That in another he sal be releved.
Our corn is stoln, shortly, it is na nay,
And we han had an il fit al this day.
And sin I sal have neen amendement,
Agayn my los I wil have esement.
By goddes saule, it sal neen other be!'
  This John answerde, 'Alayn, avyse thee,
The miller is a perilous man,' he seyde,
'And gif that he out of his sleep abreyde
He mighte doon us bathe a vileinye.'
  Aleyn answerde, 'I count him nat a flye;'
And up he rist, and by the wenche he crepte.
This wenche lay upright, and faste slepte,
Til he so ny was, er she mighte espye,
That it had been to late for to crye,
And shortly for to seyn, they were at on;
Now pley, Aleyn! for I wol speke of John.

This John lyth stille a furlong-wey or two,
And to him-self he maketh routhe and wo:
'Allas!' quod he, 'this is a wikked jape;
Now may I seyn that I is but an ape.
Yet has my felawe som-what for his harm;
He has the milleris doghter in his arm.
He auntred him, and has his nedes sped,
And I lye as a draf-sek in my bed;
And when this jape is tald another day,
I sal been halde a daf, a cokenay!
I wil aryse, and auntre it, by my fayth!
"Unhardy is unsely," thus men sayth.'
And up he roos and softely he wente
Un-to the cradel, and in his hand it hente,
And baar it softe un-to his beddes feet.
Sone after this the wyf hir routing leet,
And gan awake, and wente hir out to pisse,
And cam agayn, and gan hir cradel misse,
And groped heer and ther, but she fond noon.
'Allas!' quod she, 'I hadde almost misgoon;
I hadde almost gon to the clerkes bed.
Ey, *ben'cite!* thanne hadde I foule y-sped:'
And forth she gooth til she the cradel fond.
She gropeth alwey forther with hir hond,
And fond the bed, and thoghte noght but good,
By-cause that the cradel by it stood,
And niste wher she was, for it was derk;
But faire and wel she creep in to the clerk,
And lyth ful stille, and wolde han caught a sleep.
With-inne a whyl this John the clerk up leep,
And on this gode wyf he leyth on sore.
So mery a fit ne hadde she nat ful yore;
He priketh harde and depe as he were mad.
This joly lyf han thise two clerkes lad
Til that the thridde cok bigan to singe.
Aleyn wex wery in the daweninge,
For he had swonken al the longe night;
And seyde, 'far wel, Malin, swete wight!
The day is come, I may no lenger byde;
But evermo, wher so I go or ryde,

I is thyn awen clerk, swa have I seel!'
'Now dere lemman,' quod she, 'go, far weel!
But er thou go, o thing I wol thee telle,
Whan that thou wendest homward by the melle,
Right at the entree of the dore bihinde,
Thou shalt a cake of half a busshel finde
That was y-maked of thyn owne mele,
Which that I heelp my fader for to stele.
And, gode lemman, god thee save and kepe!'
And with that word almost she gan to wepe.
Aleyn up-rist, and thoughte, 'er that it dawe,
I wol go crepen in by my felawe;'
And fond the cradel with his hand anon.
'By god,' thoghte he, 'al wrang I have misgon;
Myn heed is toty of my swink to-night,
That maketh me that I go nat aright.
I woot wel by the cradel, I have misgo,
Heer lyth the miller and his wyf also.'
And forth he goth, a twenty devel way,
Un-to the bed ther-as the miller lay.
He wende have cropen by his felawe John;
And by the miller in he creep anon,
And caughte hym by the nekke, and softe he spak:
He seyde, 'thou, John, thou swynes-heed, awak
For Cristes saule, and heer a noble game.
For by that lord that called is seint Jame,
As I have thryes, in this shorte night,
Swyved the milleres doghter bolt-upright,
Whyl thow hast as a coward been agast.'
'Ye, false harlot,' quod the miller, 'hast?
A! false traitour! false clerk!' quod he,
'Thou shalt be deed, by goddes dignitee!
Who dorste be so bold to disparage
My doghter, that is come of swich linage?'
And by the throte-bolle he caughte Alayn.
And he hente hym despitously agayn,
And on the nose he smoot him with his fest.
Doun ran the blody streem up-on his brest;
And in the floor, with nose and mouth to-broke,
They walwe as doon two pigges in a poke.

And up they goon, and doun agayn anon,
Til that the miller sporned at a stoon,
And doun he fil bakward up-on his wyf,
That wiste no-thing of this nyce stryf;
For she was falle aslepe a lyte wight
With John the clerk, that waked hadde al night.
And with the fal, out of hir sleep she breyde—
'Help, holy croys of Bromeholm,' she seyde,
'*In manus tuas!* lord, to thee I calle!
Awak, Symond! the feend is on us falle,
Myn herte is broken, help, I nam but deed;
There lyth oon up my wombe and up myn heed;
Help, Simkin, for the false clerkes fighte.'
This John sterte up as faste as ever he mighte,
And graspeth by the walles to and fro,
To finde a staf; and she sterte up also,
And knew the estres bet than dide this John,
And by the wal a staf she fond anon,
And saugh a litel shimering of a light,
For at an hole in shoon the mone bright;
And by that light she saugh hem bothe two,
But sikerly she niste who was who,
But as she saugh a whyt thing in hir yë.
And whan she gan the whyte thing espye,
She wende the clerk hadde wered a volupeer.
And with the staf she drough ay neer and neer,
And wende han hit this Aleyn at the fulle,
And smoot the miller on the pyled skulle,
That doun he gooth and cryde, 'harrow! I dye!'
Thise clerkes bete him weel and lete him lye;
And greythen hem, and toke hir hors anon,
And eek hir mele, and on hir wey they gon.
And at the mille yet they toke hir cake
Of half a busshel flour, ful wel y-bake.
Thus is the proude miller wel y-bete,
And hath y-lost the grinding of the whete,
And payed for the soper every-deel
Of Aleyn and of John, that bette him weel.
His wyf is swyved, and his doghter als;
Lo, swich it is a miller to be fals!

And therfore this proverbe is seyd ful sooth,
'Him thar nat wene wel that yvel dooth;
A gylour shal him-self bigyled be.'
And God, that sitteth heighe in magestee,
Save al this companye grete and smale!
Thus have I quit the miller in my tale.

Here is ended the Reves tale.

THE COKES TALE

The prologe of the Cokes tale.

THE Cook of London, whyl the Reve spak,
For joye, him thoughte, he clawed him on the bak,
'Ha ! ha !' quod he, 'for Cristes passioun,
This miller hadde a sharp conclusioun
Upon his argument of herbergage !
Wel seyde Salomon in his langage,
"Ne bringe nat every man in-to thyn hous ;"
For herberwing by nighte is perilous.
Wel oghte a man avysed for to be
Whom that he broghte in-to his privetee.
I pray to god, so yeve me sorwe and care,
If ever, sith I highte Hogge of Ware,
Herde I a miller bettre y-set a-werk.
He hadde a jape of malice in the derk.
But god forbede that we stinten here ;
And therfore, if ye vouche-sauf to here
A tale of me, that am a povre man,
I wol yow telle as wel as ever I can
A litel jape that fil in our citee.'
  Our host answerde, and seide, 'I graunte it thee;
Now telle on, Roger, loke that it be good ;
For many a pastee hastow laten blood,
And many a Jakke of Dover hastow sold
That hath been twyes hoot and twyes cold.
Of many a pilgrim hastow Cristes curs,
For of thy persly yet they fare the wors,
That they han eten with thy stubbel-goos ;
For in thy shoppe is many a flye loos.

Now telle on, gentil Roger, by thy name.
But yet I pray thee, be nat wrooth for game,
A man may seye ful sooth in game and pley.'
'Thou seist ful sooth,' quod Roger, 'by my fey,
But "sooth pley, quaad pley," as the Fleming seith;
And ther-fore, Herry Bailly, by thy feith,
Be thou nat wrooth, er we departen heer,
Though that my tale be of an hostileer.
But nathelees I wol nat telle it yit,
But er we parte, y-wis, thou shalt be quit.'
And ther-with-al he lough and made chere,
And seyde his tale, as ye shul after here.

Thus endeth the Prologe of the Cokes tale.

Heer bigynneth the Cokes tale.

A Prentis whylom dwelled in our citee.
And of a craft of vitaillers was he ;
Gaillard he was as goldfinch in the shawe,
Broun as a berie, a propre short felawe,
With lokkes blake, y-kempt ful fetisly.
Dauncen he coude so wel and jolily,
That he was cleped Perkin Revelour.
He was as ful of love and paramour
As is the hyve ful of hony swete ;
Wel was the wenche with him mighte mete.
At every brydale wolde he singe and hoppe,
He loved bet the tavern than the shoppe.
For whan ther any ryding was in Chepe,
Out of the shoppe thider wolde he lepe.
Til that he hadde al the sighte y-seyn,
And daunced wel, he wolde nat come ageyn.
And gadered him a meinee of his sort
To hoppe and singe, and maken swich disport.
And ther they setten steven for to mete
To pleyen at the dys in swich a strete.
For in the toune nas ther no prentys,
That fairer coude caste a paire of dys
Than Perkin coude, and ther-to he was free
Of his dispense, in place of privetee.

That fond his maister wel in his chaffare;
For often tyme he fond his box ful bare.
For sikerly a prentis revelour,
That haunteth dys, riot, or paramour,
His maister shal it in his shoppe abye,
Al have he no part of the minstralcye;
For thefte and riot, they ben convertible,
Al conne he pleye on giterne or ribible.
Revel and trouthe, as in a low degree
They been ful wrothe al day, as men may see.
This joly prentis with his maister bood,
Til he were ny out of his prentishood,
Al were he snibbed bothe erly and late,
And somtyme lad with revel to Newgate;
But atte laste his maister him bithoghte,
Up-on a day, whan he his paper soghte,
Of a proverbe that seith this same word,
'Wel bet is roten appel out of hord
Than that it rotie al the remenaunt.'
So fareth it by a riotous servaunt;
It is wel lasse harm to lete him pace,
Than he shende alle the servants in the place.
Therfore his maister yaf him acquitance,
And bad him go with sorwe and with meschance;
And thus this joly prentis hadde his leve.
Now lat him riote al the night or leve.
And for ther is no theef with-oute a louke,
That helpeth him to wasten and to souke
Of that he brybe can or borwe may,
Anon he sente his bed and his array
Un-to a compeer of his owne sort,
That lovede dys and revel and disport,
And hadde a wyf that heeld for countenance
A shoppe, and swyved for hir sustenance.
* * * * * * * *

Of this Cokes tale maked Chaucer na more.

THE TALE OF THE MAN OF LAWE

The wordes of the Hoost to the companye.

Our Hoste sey wel that the brighte sonne
Th'ark of his artificial day had ronne
The fourthe part, and half an houre, and more ;
And though he were not depe expert in lore,
He wiste it was the eightetethe day
Of April, that is messager to May ;
And sey wel that the shadwe of every tree
Was as in lengthe the same quantitee
That was the body erect that caused it.
And therfor by the shadwe he took his wit
That Phebus, which that shoon so clere and brighte,
Degrees was fyve and fourty clombe on highte ;
And for that day, as in that latitude,
It was ten of the clokke, he gan conclude,
And sodeynly he plighte his hors aboute.
'Lordinges,' quod he, 'I warne yow, al this route,
The fourthe party of this day is goon ;
Now, for the love of god and of seint John,
Leseth no tyme, as ferforth as ye may ;
Lordinges, the tyme wasteth night and day,
And steleth from us, what prively slepinge,
And what thurgh necligence in our wakinge,
As dooth the streem, that turneth never agayn,
Descending fro the montaigne in-to playn.
Wel can Senek, and many a philosophre
Biwailen tyme, more than gold in cofre.
"For los of catel may recovered be,
But los of tyme shendeth us," quod he.

It wol nat come agayn, with-outen drede,
Na more than wol Malkins maydenhede,
Whan she hath lost it in hir wantownesse ;
Lat us nat moulen thus in ydelnesse.
Sir man of lawe,' quod he, 'so have ye blis,
Tel us a tale anon, as forward is ;
Ye been submitted thurgh your free assent
To stonde in this cas at my jugement.
Acquiteth yow, and holdeth your biheste,
Than have ye doon your devoir atte leste.'
'Hoste,' quod he, '*depardieux* ich assente,
To breke forward is not myn entente.
Biheste is dette, and I wol holde fayn
Al my biheste ; I can no better seyn.
For swich lawe as man yeveth another wight,
He sholde him-selven usen it by right ;
Thus wol our text ; but natheles certeyn
I can right now no thrifty tale seyn,
But Chaucer, though he can but lewedly
On metres and on ryming craftily,
Hath seyd hem in swich English as he can
Of olde tyme, as knoweth many a man.
And if he have not seyd hem, leve brother,
In o bok, he hath seyd hem in another.
For he hath told of loveres up and doun
Mo than Ovyde made of mencioun
In his Epistelles, that been ful olde.
What sholde I tellen hem, sin they ben tolde ?
In youthe he made of Ceys and Alcion,
And sithen hath he spoke of everichon,
Thise noble wyves and thise loveres eke.
Who-so that wol his large volume seke
Cleped the Seintes Legende of Cupyde,
Ther may he seen the large woundes wyde
Of Lucresse, and of Babilan Tisbee ;
The swerd of Dido for the false Enee ;
The tree of Phillis for hir Demophon ;
The pleinte of Dianire and Hermion,
Of Adriane and of Isiphilee ;
The bareyne yle stonding in the see ;

The dreynte Leander for his Erro;
The teres of Eleyne, and eek the wo
Of Brixseyde, and of thee, Ladomëa;
The crueltee of thee, queen Medëa,
Thy litel children hanging by the hals
For thy Jason, that was of love so fals!
O Ypermistra, Penelopee, Alceste,
Your wyfhod he comendeth with the beste!
  But certeinly no word ne wryteth he
Of thilke wikke ensample of Canacee,
That lovede hir owne brother sinfully;
Of swiche cursed stories I sey "fy";
Or elles of Tyro Apollonius,
How that the cursed king Antiochus
Birafte his doghter of hir maydenhede,
That is so horrible a tale for to rede,
Whan he hir threw up-on the pavement.
And therfor he, of ful avysement,
Nolde never wryte in none of his sermouns
Of swiche unkinde abhominaciouns,
Ne I wol noon reherse, if that I may.
  But of my tale how shal I doon this day?
Me were looth be lykned, doutelees,
To Muses that men clepe Pierides—
Metamorphoseos wot what I mene:—
But nathelees, I recche noght a bene
Though I come after him with hawe-bake;
I speke in prose, and lat him rymes make.'
And with that word he, with a sobre chere,
Bigan his tale, as ye shal after here.

The Prologe of the Mannes Tale of Lawe.

O hateful harm! condicion of poverte!
With thurst, with cold, with hunger so confounded!
To asken help thee shameth in thyn herte;
If thou noon aske, with nede artow so wounded,
That verray nede unwrappeth al thy wounde hid!
Maugree thyn heed, thou most for indigence
Or stele, or begge, or borwe thy despence!

Thou blamest Crist, and seyst ful bitterly,
He misdeparteth richesse temporal;
Thy neighebour thou wytest sinfully,
And seyst thou hast to lyte, and he hath al.
'Parfay,' seistow, 'somtyme he rekne shal,
Whan that his tayl shal brennen in the glede,
For he noght helpeth needfulle in hir nede.'

Herkne what is the sentence of the wyse:—
'Bet is to dyën than have indigence;'
'Thy selve neighebour wol thee despyse;'
If thou be povre, farwel thy reverence!
Yet of the wyse man tak this sentence:—
'Alle the dayes of povre men ben wikke;'
Be war therfor, er thou come in that prikke!

'If thou be povre, thy brother hateth thee,
And alle thy freendes fleen fro thee, alas!'
O riche marchaunts, ful of wele ben ye,
O noble, o prudent folk, as in this cas!
Your bagges been nat filled with *ambes as*,
But with *sis cink*, that renneth for your chaunce;
At Cristemasse merie may ye daunce!

Ye seken lond and see for your winninges,
As wyse folk ye knowen al th'estaat
Of regnes; ye ben fadres of tydinges
And tales, bothe of pees and of debat.
I were right now of tales desolat,
Nere that a marchaunt, goon is many a yere,
Me taughte a tale, which that ye shal here.

Here beginneth the Man of Lawe his Tale

In Surrie whylom dwelte a companye
Of chapmen riche, and therto sadde and trewe,
That wyde-wher senten her spycerye,
Clothes of gold, and satins riche of hewe;
Her chaffar was so thrifty and so newe,
That every wight hath deyntee to chaffare
With hem, and eek to sellen hem hir ware.

Now fel it, that the maistres of that sort
Han shapen hem to Rome for to wende ;
Were it for chapmanhode or for disport,
Non other message wolde they thider sende,
But comen hem-self to Rome, this is the ende ;
And in swich place, as thoughte hem avantage
For her entente, they take her herbergage.

Sojourned han thise marchants in that toun
A certein tyme, as fel to hir plesance.
And so bifel, that th'excellent renoun
Of th'emperoures doghter, dame Custance,
Reported was, with every circumstance,
Un-to thise Surrien marchants in swich wyse,
Fro day to day, as I shal yow devyse.

This was the commune vois of every man—
'Our Emperour of Rome, god him see,
A doghter hath that, sin the world bigan,
To rekne as wel hir goodnesse as beautee,
Nas never swich another as is she ;
I prey to god in honour hir sustene,
And wolde she were of al Europe the quene.

In hir is heigh beautee, with-oute pryde,
Yowthe, with-oute grenehede or folye ;
To alle hir werkes vertu is hir gyde,
Humblesse hath slayn in hir al tirannye.
She is mirour of alle curteisye ;
Hir herte is verray chambre of holinesse,
Hir hand, ministre of fredom for almesse.'

And al this vois was soth, as god is trewe,
But now to purpos lat us turne agayn ;
Thise marchants han doon fraught hir shippes newe,
And, whan they han this blisful mayden seyn,
Hoom to Surryë been they went ful fayn,
And doon her nedes as they han don yore,
And liven in wele ; I can sey yow no more.

Now fel it, that thise marchants stode in grace
Of him, that was the sowdan of Surrye ;

For whan they came from any strange place,
He wolde, of his benigne curteisye,
Make hem good chere, and bisily espye
Tydings of sondry regnes, for to lere
The wondres that they mighte seen or here.

Amonges othere thinges, specially
Thise marchants han him told of dame Custance,
So gret noblesse in ernest, ceriously,
That this sowdan hath caught so gret plesance
To han hir figure in his remembrance,
That al his lust and al his bisy cure
Was for to love hir whyl his lyf may dure.

Paraventure in thilke large book
Which that men clepe the heven, y-writen was
With sterres, whan that he his birthe took,
That he for love shulde han his deeth, allas!
For in the sterres, clerer than is glas,
Is writen, god wot, who-so coude it rede,
The deeth of every man, withouten drede.

In sterres, many a winter ther-biforn,
Was writen the deeth of Ector, Achilles,
Of Pompey, Julius, er they were born;
The stryf of Thebes; and of Ercules,
Of Sampson, Turnus, and of Socrates
The deeth; but mennes wittes been so dulle,
That no wight can wel rede it atte fulle.

This sowdan for his privee conseil sente,
And, shortly of this mater for to pace,
He hath to hem declared his entente,
And seyde hem certein, 'but he mighte have grace
To han Custance with-inne a litel space,
He nas but deed;' and charged hem, in hye,
To shapen for his lyf som remedye.

Diverse men diverse thinges seyden;
They argumenten, casten up and doun
Many a subtil resoun forth they leyden,
They speken of magik and abusioun;

But finally, as in conclusioun,
They can not seen in that non avantage,
Ne in non other wey, save mariage.

Than sawe they ther-in swich difficultee
By wey of resoun, for to speke al playn,
By-cause that ther was swich diversitee
Bitwene hir bothe lawes, that they sayn,
They trowe 'that no cristen prince wolde fayn
Wedden his child under oure lawes swete
That us were taught by Mahoun our prophete.'

And he answerde, 'rather than I lese
Custance, I wol be cristned doutelees;
I mot ben hires, I may non other chese.
I prey yow holde your arguments in pees;
Saveth my lyf, and beeth noght recchelees
To geten hir that hath my lyf in cure;
For in this wo I may not longe endure.'

What nedeth gretter dilatacioun?
I seye, by tretis and embassadrye,
And by the popes mediacioun,
And al the chirche, and al the chivalrye,
That, in destruccioun of Maumetrye,
And in encrees of Cristes lawe dere,
They ben acorded, so as ye shal here;

How that the sowdan and his baronage
And alle his liges shulde y-cristned be,
And he shal han Custance in mariage,
And certein gold, I noot what quantitee,
And her-to founden suffisant seurtee;
This same acord was sworn on eyther syde;
Now, faire Custance, almighty god thee gyde!

Now wolde som men waiten, as I gesse,
That I shulde tellen al the purveyance
That th'emperour, of his grete noblesse,
Hath shapen for his doghter dame Custance.
Wel may men knowe that so gret ordinance
May no man tellen in a litel clause
As was arrayed for so heigh a cause.

Bisshopes ben shapen with hir for to wende,
Lordes, ladyes, knightes of renoun,
And other folk y-nowe, this is the ende ;
And notifyed is thurgh-out the toun
That every wight, with gret devocioun,
Shulde preyen Crist that he this mariage
Receyve in gree, and spede this viage.

The day is comen of hir departinge,
I sey, the woful day fatal is come,
That ther may be no lenger taryinge,
But forthward they hem dressen, alle and some ;
Custance, that was with sorwe al overcome,
Ful pale arist, and dresseth hir to wende ;
For wel she seeth ther is non other ende.

Allas ! what wonder is it though she wepte,
That shal be sent to strange nacioun
Fro freendes, that so tendrely hir kepte,
And to be bounden under subieccioun
Of oon, she knoweth not his condicioun.
Housbondes been alle gode, and han ben yore,
That knowen wyves, I dar say yow no more.

'Fader,' she sayde, 'thy wrecched child Custance,
Thy yonge doghter, fostred up so softe,
And ye, my moder, my soverayn plesance
Over alle thing, out-taken Crist on-lofte,
Custance, your child, hir recomandeth ofte
Un-to your grace, for I shal to Surryë,
Ne shal I never seen yow more with yë.

Allas ! un-to the Barbre nacioun
I moste anon, sin that it is your wille ;
But Crist, that starf for our redempcioun,
So yeve me grace, his hestes to fulfille ;
I, wrecche womman, no fors though I spille.
Wommen are born to thraldom and penance,
And to ben under mannes governance.'

I trowe, at Troye, whan Pirrus brak the wal
Or Ylion brende, at Thebes the citee,

N'at Rome, for the harm thurgh Hanibal
That Romayns hath venquisshed tymes three,
Nas herd swich tendre weping for pitee
As in the chambre was for hir departinge ;
Bot forth she moot, wher-so she wepe or singe.

O firste moeving cruel firmament,
With thy diurnal sweigh that crowdest ay
And hurlest al from Est til Occident,
That naturelly wolde holde another way,
Thy crowding set the heven in swich array
At the beginning of this fiers viage,
That cruel Mars hath slayn this mariage.

Infortunat ascendent tortuous,
Of which the lord is helples falle, allas !
Out of his angle in-to the derkest hous.
O Mars, O Atazir, as in this cas !
O feble mone, unhappy been thy pas !
Thou knittest thee ther thou art nat receyved,
Ther thou were weel, fro thennes artow weyved.

Imprudent emperour of Rome, allas !
Was ther no philosophre in al thy toun ?
Is no tyme bet than other in swich cas ?
Of viage is ther noon eleccioun,
Namely to folk of heigh condicioun,
Nat whan a rote is of a birthe y-knowe ?
Allas ! we ben to lewed or to slowe.

To shippe is brought this woful faire mayde
Solempnely, with every circumstance.
'Now Jesu Crist be with yow alle,' she sayde ;
Ther nis namore but 'farewel ! faire Custance !'
She peyneth hir to make good countenance,
And forth I lete hir sayle in this manere,
And turne I wol agayn to my matere.

The moder of the sowdan, welle of vyces,
Espyëd hath hir sones pleyn entente,
How he wol lete his olde sacrifyces,
And right anon she for hir conseil sente ;

And they ben come, to knowe what she mente.
And when assembled was this folke in-fere,
She sette hir doun, and sayde as ye shal here.

'Lordes,' quod she, 'ye knowen everichon,
How that my sone in point is for to lete
The holy lawes of our Alkaron,
Yeven by goddes message Makomete.
But oon avow to grete god I hete,
The lyf shal rather out of my body sterte
Than Makometes lawe out of myn herte!

What shulde us tyden of this newe lawe
But thraldom to our bodies and penance?
And afterward in helle to be drawe
For we reneyed Mahoun our creance?
But, lordes, wol ye maken assurance,
As I shal seyn, assenting to my lore,
And I shall make us sauf for evermore?'

They sworen and assenten, every man,
To live with hir and dye, and by hir stonde;
And everich, in the beste wyse he can,
To strengthen hir shal alle his freendes fonde:
And she hath this empryse y-take on honde,
Which ye shal heren that I shal devyse,
And to hem alle she spak right in this wyse.

'We shul first feyne us cristendom to take,
Cold water shal not greve us but a lyte;
And I shal swich a feste and revel make,
That, as I trowe, I shal the sowdan quyte.
For though his wyf be cristned never so whyte,
She shal have nede to wasshe awey the rede,
Thogh she a font-ful water with hir lede.'

O sowdanesse, rote of iniquitee,
Virago, thou Semyram the secounde,
O serpent under femininitee,
Lyk to the serpent depe in helle y-bounde,
O feyned womman, al that may confounde
Vertu and innocence, thurgh thy malyce,
Is bred in thee, as nest of every vyce!

O Satan, envious sin thilke day
That thou were chased from our heritage,
Wel knowestow to wommen the olde way !
Thou madest Eva bringe us in servage.
Thou wolt fordoon this cristen mariage.
Thyn instrument so, weylawey the whyle !
Makestow of wommen, whan thou wolt begyle.

This sowdanesse, whom I thus blame and warie,
Leet prively hir conseil goon hir way.
What sholde I in this tale lenger tarie ?
She rydeth to the sowdan on a day,
And seyde him, that she wolde reneye hir lay,
And cristendom of preestes handes fonge,
Repenting hir she hethen was so longe,

Biseching him to doon hir that honour,
That she moste han the cristen men to feste ;
'To plesen hem I wol do my labour.'
The sowdan seith, 'I wol don at your heste,'
And kneling thanketh hir of that requeste.
So glad he was, he niste what to seye ;
She kiste hir sone, and hoom she gooth hir weye.

Explicit prima pars.

Sequitur pars secunda.

Arryved ben this Cristen folk to londe,
In Surrie, with a greet solempne route,
And hastily this sowdan sente his sonde,
First to his moder, and al the regne aboute,
And seyde, his wyf was comen, out of doute,
And preyde hir for to ryde agayn the quene,
The honour of his regne to sustene.

Gret was the prees, and riche was th'array
Of Surriens and Romayns met y-fere ;
The moder of the sowdan, riche and gay,
Receyveth hir with al-so glad a chere
As any moder mighte hir doghter dere,
And to the nexte citee ther bisyde
A softe pas solempnely they ryde.

Noght trowe I the triumphe of Julius,
Of which that Lucan maketh swich a bost,
Was royaller, ne more curious
Than was th'assemblee of this blisful host.
But this scorpioun, this wikked gost,
The sowdanesse, for al hir flateringe,
Caste under this ful mortally to stinge.

The sowdan comth him-self sone after this
So royally, that wonder is to telle,
And welcometh hir with alle joye and blis.
And thus in merthe and joye I lete hem dwelle.
The fruyt of this matere is that I telle.
Whan tyme cam, men thoughte it for the beste
That revel stinte, and men goon to hir reste.

The tyme cam, this olde sowdanesse
Ordeyned hath this feste of which I tolde,
And to the feste Cristen folk hem dresse
In general, ye ! bothe yonge and olde.
Here may men feste and royaltee biholde,
And deyntees mo than I can yow devyse,
But al to dere they boughte it er they ryse.

O sodeyn wo ! that ever art successour
To worldly blisse, spreynd with bitternesse ;
Th'ende of the joye of our worldly labour ;
Wo occupieth the fyn of our gladnesse.
Herke this conseil for thy sikernesse,
Up-on thy glade day have in thy minde
The unwar wo or harm that comth bihinde.

For shortly for to tellen at o word,
The sowdan and the Cristen everichone
Ben al to-hewe and stiked at the bord,
But it were only dame Custance allone.
This olde sowdanesse, cursed crone,
Hath with hir frendes doon this cursed dede,
For she hir-self wolde al the contree lede.

Ne ther was Surrien noon that was converted
That of the conseil of the sowdan woot,

That he nas al to-hewe er he asterted.
And Custance han they take anon, foot-hoot,
And in a shippe al sterelees, god woot,
They han hir set, and bidde hir lerne sayle
Out of Surrye agaynward to Itayle.

A certein tresor that she thider ladde,
And, sooth to sayn, vitaille gret plentee
They han hir yeven, and clothes eek she hadde,
And forth she sayleth in the salte see.
O my Custance, ful of benignitee,
O emperoures yonge doghter dere,
He that is lord of fortune be thy stere !

She blesseth hir, and with ful pitous voys
Un-to the croys of Crist thus seyde she,
'O clere, o welful auter, holy croys,
Reed of the lambes blood full of pitee,
That wesh the world fro the olde iniquitee,
Me fro the feend, and fro his clawes kepe,
That day that I shal drenchen in the depe.

Victorious tree, proteccioun of trewe,
That only worthy were for to bere
The king of heven with his woundes newe,
The whyte lamb, that hurt was with the spere,
Flemer of feendes out of him and here
On which thy limes feithfully extenden,
Me keep, and yif me might my lyf t'amenden.'

Yeres and dayes fleet this creature
Thurghout the see of Grece un-to the strayte
Of Marrok, as it was hir aventure ;
On many a sory meel now may she bayte ;
After her deeth ful often may she wayte,
Er that the wilde wawes wol hir dryve
Un-to the placë, ther she shal arryve.

Men mighten asken why she was not slayn ?
Eek at the feste who mighte hir body save ?
And I answere to that demaunde agayn,
Who saved Daniel in the horrible cave,

Ther every wight save he, maister and knave,
Was with the leoun frete er he asterte ?
No wight but god, that he bar in his herte.

God liste to shewe his wonderful miracle
In hir, for we sholde seen his mighty werkes ;
Crist, which that is to every harm triacle,
By certein menes ofte, as knowen clerkes,
Doth thing for certein ende that ful derk is
To mannes wit, that for our ignorance
Ne conne not knowe his prudent purveyance.

Now, sith she was not at the feste y-slawe,
Who kepte hir fro the drenching in the see ?
Who kepte Jonas in the fisshes mawe
Til he was spouted up at Ninivee ?
Wel may men knowe it was no wight but he
That kepte peple Ebraik fro hir drenchinge,
With drye feet thurgh-out the see passinge.

Who bad the foure spirits of tempest,
That power han t'anoyen land and see,
'Bothe north and south, and also west and est,
Anoyeth neither see, ne land, ne tree ?'
Sothly, the comaundour of that was he,
That fro the tempest ay this womman kepte
As wel whan [that] she wook as whan she slepte.

Wher mighte this womman mete and drinke have ?
Three yeer and more how lasteth hir vitaille ?
Who fedde the Egipcien Marie in the cave,
Or in desert ? no wight but Crist, sans faille.
Fyve thousand folk it was as gret mervaille
With loves fyve and fisshes two to fede.
God sente his foison at hir grete nede.

She dryveth forth in-to our occean
Thurgh-out our wilde see, til, atte laste,
Under an hold that nempnen I ne can,
Fer in Northumberlond the wawe hir caste,
And in the sond hir ship stiked so faste,
That thennes wolde it noght of al a tyde,
The wille of Crist was that she shulde abyde.

The constable of the castel doun is fare
To seen this wrak, and al the ship he soghte,
And fond this wery womman ful of care;
He fond also the tresor that she broghte.
In hir langage mercy she bisoghte
The lyf out of hir body for to twinne,
Hir to delivere of wo that she was inne.

A maner Latin corrupt was hir speche,
But algates ther-by was she understonde;
The constable, whan him list no lenger seche,
This woful womman broghte he to the londe;
She kneleth doun, and thanketh goddes sonde.
But what she was, she wolde no man seye,
For foul ne fair, thogh that she shulde deye.

She seyde, she was so mased in the see
That she forgat hir minde, by hir trouthe;
The constable hath of hir so greet pitee,
And eek his wyf, that they wepen for routhe,
She was so diligent, with-outen slouthe,
To serve and plesen everich in that place,
That alle hir loven that loken on hir face.

This constable and dame Hermengild his wyf
Were payens, and that contree everywhere;
But Hermengild lovede hir right as hir lyf,
And Custance hath so longe sojourned there,
In orisons, with many a bitter tere,
Til Jesu hath converted thurgh his grace
Dame Hermengild, constablesse of that place.

In al that lond no Cristen durste route,
Alle Cristen folk ben fled fro that contree
Thurgh payens, that conquereden al aboute
The plages of the North, by land and see;
To Walis fled the Cristianitee
Of olde Britons, dwellinge in this yle;
Ther was hir refut for the mene whyle.

But yet nere Cristen Britons so exyled
That ther nere somme that in hir privetee
Honoured Crist, and hethen folk bigyled;

And ny the castel swiche ther dwelten three.
That oon of hem was blind, and mighte nat see
But it were with thilke yën of his minde,
With whiche men seen, after that they ben blinde.

Bright was the sonne as in that someres day,
For which the constable and his wyf also
And Custance han y-take the righte way
Toward the see, a furlong wey or two,
To pleyen and to romen to and fro;
And in hir walk this blinde man they mette
Croked and old, with yën faste y-shette.

'In name of Crist,' cryde this blinde Britoun,
'Dame Hermengild, yif me my sighte agayn'
This lady wex affrayed of the soun,
Lest that hir housbond, shortly for to sayn,
Wolde hir for Jesu Cristes love han slayn,
Til Custance made hir bold, and bad hir werche
The wil of Crist, as doghter of his chirche.

The constable wex abasshed of that sight,
And seyde, 'what amounteth al this fare?'
Custance answerde, 'sire, it is Cristes might,
That helpeth folk out of the feendes snare.'
And so ferforth she gan our lay declare,
That she the constable, er that it were eve,
Converted, and on Crist made him bileve.

This constable was no-thing lord of this place
Of which I speke, ther he Custance fond,
But kepte it strongly, many wintres space,
Under Alla, king of al Northumberlond,
That was ful wys, and worthy of his hond
Agayn the Scottes, as men may wel here,
But turne I wol agayn to my matere.

Sathan, that ever us waiteth to bigyle,
Saugh of Custance al hir perfeccioun,
And caste anon how he mighte quyte hir whyle,
And made a yong knight, that dwelte in that toun,
Love hir so hote, of foul affeccioun,

That verraily him thoughte he shulde spille
But he of hir mighte ones have his wille.

He woweth hir, but it availleth noght,
She wolde do no sinne, by no weye ;
And, for despyt, he compassed in his thoght
To maken hir on shamful deth to deye.
He wayteth whan the constable was aweye,
And prively, up-on a night, he crepte
In Hermengildes chambre whyl she slepte.

Wery, for-waked in her orisouns,
Slepeth Custance, and Hermengild also.
This knight, thurgh Sathanas temptaciouns,
Al softely is to the bed y-go,
And kitte the throte of Hermengild a-two,
And leyde the blody knyf by dame Custance,
And wente his wey, ther god yeve him meschance !

Sone after comth this constable hoom agayn,
And eek Alla, that king was of that lond,
And saugh his wyf despitously y-slayn,
For which ful ofte he weep and wrong his hond,
And in the bed the blody knyf he fond
By dame Custance ; allas ! what mighte she seye ?
For verray wo hir wit was al aweye.

To king Alla was told al this meschance,
And eek the tyme, and where, and in what wyse
That in a ship was founden dame Custance,
As heer-biforn that ye han herd devyse.
The kinges herte of pitee gan agryse,
Whan he saugh so benigne a creature
Falle in disese and in misaventure.

For as the lomb toward his deeth is broght,
So stant this innocent bifore the king ;
This false knight that hath this tresoun wroght
Berth hir on hond that she hath doon this thing.
But nathelees, ther was [ful] greet moorning
Among the peple, and seyn, 'they can not gesse
That she hath doon so greet a wikkednesse.

For they han seyn hir ever so vertuous,
And loving Hermengild right as her lyf.'
Of this bar witnesse everich in that hous
Save he that Hermengild slow with his knyf.
This gentil king hath caught a gret motyf
Of this witnesse, and thoghte he wolde enquere
Depper in this, a trouthe for to lere.

Allas! Custance! thou hast no champioun,
Ne fighte canstow nought, so weylawey!
But he, that starf for our redempcioun
And bond Sathan (and yit lyth ther he lay)
So be thy stronge champioun this day!
For, but-if Crist open miracle kythe,
Withouten gilt thou shalt be slayn as swythe.

She sette her doun on knees, and thus she sayde,
'Immortal god, that savedest Susanne
Fro false blame, and thou, merciful mayde,
Mary I mene, doghter to Seint Anne,
Bifore whos child aungeles singe Osanne,
If I be giltlees of this felonye,
My socour be, for elles I shal dye!'

Have ye nat seyn som tyme a pale face,
Among a prees, of him that hath be lad
Toward his deeth, wher-as him gat no grace,
And swich a colour in his face hath had,
Men mighte knowe his face, that was bistad,
Amonges alle the faces in that route:
So stant Custance, and loketh hir aboute.

O quenes, livinge in prosperitee,
Duchesses, and ye ladies everichone,
Haveth som routhe on hir adversitee;
An emperoures doghter stant allone;
She hath no wight to whom to make hir mone.
O blood royal, that stondest in this drede,
Fer ben thy freendes at thy grete nede!

This Alla king hath swich compassioun,
As gentil herte is fulfild of pitee,

That from his yën ran the water doun.
'Now hastily do fecche a book,' quod he,
'And if this knight wol sweren how that she
This womman slow, yet wole we us avyse
Whom that we wole that shal ben our justyse.'

A Briton book, writen with Evangyles,
Was fet, and on this book he swoor anoon
She gilty was, and in the mene whyles
A hand him smoot upon the nekke-boon,
That doun he fil atones as a stoon,
And bothe his yën broste out of his face
In sight of every body in that place.

A vois was herd in general audience,
And seyde, 'thou hast desclaundred giltelees
The doghter of holy chirche in hey presence;
Thus hastou doon, and yet holde I my pees.'
Of this mervaille agast was al the prees;
As mased folk they stoden everichone,
For drede of wreche, save Custance allone.

Greet was the drede and eek the repentance
Of hem that hadden wrong suspeccioun
Upon this sely innocent Custance;
And, for this miracle, in conclusioun,
And by Custances mediacioun,
The king, and many another in that place,
Converted was, thanked be Cristes grace!

This false knight was slayn for his untrouthe
By jugement of Alla hastifly;
And yet Custance hadde of his deeth gret routhe.
And after this Jesus, of his mercy,
Made Alla wedden ful solempnely
This holy mayden, that is so bright and shene,
And thus hath Crist y-maad Custance a quene.

But who was woful, if I shal nat lye,
Of this wedding but Donegild, and na mo.
The kinges moder, ful of tirannye?
Hir thoughte hir cursed herte brast a-two;

She wolde noght hir sone had do so;
Hir thoughte a despit, that he sholde take
So strange a creature un-to his make.

Me list nat of the chaf nor of the stree
Maken so long a tale, as of the corn.
What sholde I tellen of the royaltee
At mariage, or which cours gooth biforn,
Who bloweth in a trompe or in an horn?
The fruit of every tale is for to seye;
They ete, and drinke, and daunce, and singe, and pleye.

They goon to bedde, as it was skile and right;
For, thogh that wyves been ful holy thinges,
They moste take in pacience at night
Swich maner necessaries as been plesinges
To folk that han y-wedded hem with ringes,
And leye a lyte hir holinesse asyde
As for the tyme; it may no bet bityde.

On hir he gat a knave-child anoon,
And to a bishop and his constable eke
He took his wyf to kepe, whan he is goon
To Scotland-ward, his fo-men for to seke;
Now faire Custance, that is so humble and meke,
So longe is goon with childe, til that stille
She halt hir chambre, abyding Cristes wille.

The tyme is come, a knave-child she ber;
Mauricius at the font-stoon they him calle;
This constable dooth forth come a messager,
And wroot un-to his king, that cleped was Alle,
How that this blisful tyding is bifalle,
And othere tydings speedful for to seye;
He tak'th the lettre, and forth he gooth his weye.

This messager, to doon his avantage,
Un-to the kinges moder rydeth swythe,
And salueth hir ful faire in his langage,
'Madame,' quod he, 'ye may be glad and blythe,

And thanke god an hundred thousand sythe;
My lady quene hath child, with-outen doute,
To joye and blisse of al this regne aboute.

Lo, heer the lettres seled of this thing,
That I mot bere with al the haste I may;
If ye wol aught un-to your sone the king,
I am your servant, bothe night and day.'
Donegild answerde, 'as now at this tyme, nay;
But heer al night I wol thou take thy reste,
Tomorwe wol I seye thee what me leste.'

This messager drank sadly ale and wyn,
And stolen were his lettres prively
Out of his box, whyl he sleep as a swyn;
And countrefeted was ful subtilly
Another lettre, wroght ful sinfully,
Un-to the king direct of this matere
Fro his constable, as ye shul after here.

The lettre spak, 'the queen delivered was
Of so horrible a feendly creature,
That in the castel noon so hardy was
That any whyle dorste ther endure.
The moder was an elf, by aventure
Y-come, by charmes or by sorcerye,
And every wight hateth hir companye.'

Wo was this king whan he this lettre had seyn,
But to no wighte he tolde his sorwes sore,
But of his owene honde he wroot ageyn,
'Welcome the sonde of Crist for evermore
To me, that am now lerned in his lore;
Lord, welcome be thy lust and thy plesaunce,
My lust I putte al in thyn ordinaunce!

Kepeth this child, al be it foul or fair,
And eek my wyf, un-to myn hoom-cominge;
Crist, whan him list, may sende me an heir
More agreable than this to my lykinge.'
This lettre he seleth, prively wepinge,
Which to the messager was take sone,
And forth he gooth; ther is na more to done.

O messager, fulfild of dronkenesse,
Strong is thy breeth, thy limes faltren ay,
And thou biwreyest alle secreenesse.
Thy mind is lorn, thou janglest as a jay,
Thy face is turned in a newe array!
Ther dronkenesse regneth in any route,
Ther is no conseil hid, with-outen doute.

O Donegild, I ne have noon English digne
Un-to thy malice and thy tirannye!
And therfor to the feend I thee resigne,
Let him endyten of thy traitorye!
Fy, mannish, fy! o nay, by god, I lye,
Fy, *feendly* spirit, for I dar wel telle,
Though thou heer walke, thy spirit is in helle!

This messager comth fro the king agayn,
And at the kinges modres court he lighte,
And she was of this messager ful fayn,
And plesed him in al that ever she mighte.
He drank, and wel his girdel underpighte.
He slepeth, and he snoreth in his gyse
Al night, un-til the sonne gan aryse.

Eft were his lettres stolen everichon
And countrefeted lettres in this wyse;
'The king comandeth his constable anon,
Up peyne of hanging, and on heigh juÿse,
That he ne sholde suffren in no wyse
Custance in-with his regne for t'abyde
Thre dayes and a quarter of a tyde;

But in the same ship as he hir fond,
Hir and hir yonge sone, and al hir gere,
He sholde putte, and croude hir fro the lond,
And charge hir that she never eft come there.'
O my Custance, wel may thy goost have fere
And sleping in thy dreem been in penance,
When Donegild caste al this ordinance!

This messager on morwe, whan he wook
Un-to the castel halt the nexte wey,

And to the constable he the lettre took;
And whan that he this pitous lettre sey,
Ful ofte he seyde 'allas!' and 'weylawey!'
'Lord Crist,' quod he, 'how may this world endure?
So ful of sinne is many a creature!

O mighty god, if that it be thy wille,
Sith thou art rightful juge, how may it be
That thou wolt suffren innocents to spille,
And wikked folk regne in prosperitee?
O good Custance, allas! so wo is me
That I mot be thy tormentour, or deye
On shames deeth; ther is noon other weye!'

Wepen bothe yonge and olde in al that place,
Whan that the king this cursed lettre sente,
And Custance, with a deedly pale face,
The ferthe day toward hir ship she wente.
But natheles she taketh in good entente
The wille of Crist, and, kneling on the stronde,
She seyde, 'lord! ay wel-com be thy sonde!

He that me kepte fro the false blame
Whyl I was on the londe amonges yow,
He can me kepe from harme and eek fro shame
In salte see, al-thogh I see nat how.
As strong as ever he was, he is yet now.
In him triste I, and in his moder dere,
That is to me my seyl and eek my stere.'

Hir litel child lay weping in hir arm,
And kneling, pitously to him she seyde,
'Pees, litel sone, I wol do thee non harm.'
With that hir kerchef of hir heed she breyde,
And over his litel yën she it leyde;
And in hir arm she lulleth it ful faste,
And in-to heven hir yën up she caste.

'Moder,' quod she, 'and mayde bright, Marye,
Sooth is that thurgh wommannes eggement
Mankind was lorn and damned ay to dye,
For which thy child was on a croys y-rent;

Thy blisful yën sawe al his torment;
Than is ther no comparisoun bitwene
Thy wo and any wo man may sustene.

Thou sawe thy child y-slayn bifor thyn yën,
And yet now liveth my litel child, parfay!
Now, lady bright, to whom alle woful cryën,
Thou glorie of wommanhede, thou faire may,
Thou haven of refut, brighte sterre of day,
Rewe on my child, that of thy gentillesse
Rewest on every rewful in distresse!

O litel child, allas! what is thy gilt,
That never wroughtest sinne as yet, pardee,
Why wil thyn harde fader han thee spilt?
O mercy, dere constable!' quod she;
'As lat my litel child dwelle heer with thee;
And if thou darst not saven him, for blame,
So kis him ones in his fadres name!'

Ther-with she loketh bakward to the londe,
And seyde, 'far-wel, housbond routhelees!'
And up she rist, and walketh doun the stronde
Toward the ship; hir folweth al the prees,
And ever she preyeth hir child to holde his pees;
And taketh hir leve, and with an holy entente
She blesseth hir; and in-to ship she wente.

Vitailled was the ship, it is no drede,
Habundantly for hir, ful longe space,
And other necessaries that sholde nede
She hadde y-nogh, heried be goddes grace!
For wind and weder almighty god purchace,
And bringe hir hoom! I can no bettre seye;
But in the see she dryveth forth hir weye.

Explicit secunda pars.

Sequitur pars tercia.

Alla the king comth hoom, sone after this,
Unto his castel of the which I tolde,

And axeth wher his wyf and his child is.
The constable gan aboute his herte colde,
And pleynly al the maner he him tolde
As ye han herd, I can telle it no bettre,
And sheweth the king his seel and [eek] his lettre,

And seyde, 'lord, as ye comaunded me
Up peyne of deeth, so have I doon, certein.'
This messager tormented was til he
Moste biknowe and tellen, plat and plein,
Fro night to night, in what place he had leyn.
And thus, by wit and subtil enqueringe,
Ymagined was by whom this harm gan springe.

The hand was knowe that the lettre wroot,
And al the venim of this cursed dede,
But in what wyse, certeinly I noot.
Th'effect is this, that Alla, out of drede,
His moder slow, that men may pleinly rede,
For that she traitour was to hir ligeaunce.
Thus endeth olde Donegild with meschaunce.

The sorwe that this Alla, night and day,
Maketh for his wyf and for his child also,
Ther is no tonge that it telle may.
But now wol I un-to Custance go,
That fleteth in the see, in peyne and wo,
Fyve yeer and more, as lyked Cristes sonde,
Er that hir ship approched un-to londe.

Under an hethen castel, atte laste,
Of which the name in my text noght I finde,
Custance and eek hir child the see upcaste.
Almighty god, that saveth al mankinde,
Have on Custance and on hir child som minde,
That fallen is in hethen land eft-sone,
In point to spille, as I shal telle yow sone.

Doun from the castel comth ther many a wight
To gauren on this ship and on Custance.
But shortly, from the castel, on a night,
The lordes styward—god yeve him meschaunce!—

A theef, that had reneyed our creaunce,
Com in-to ship allone, and seyde he sholde
Hir lemman be, wher-so she wolde or nolde.

Wo was this wrecched womman tho bigon,
Hir child cryde, and she cryde pitously;
But blisful Marie heelp hir right anon;
For with hir strugling wel and mightily
The theef fil over bord al sodeinly,
And in the see he dreynte for vengeance;
And thus hath Crist unwemmed kept Custance.

O foule lust of luxurie! lo, thyn ende!
Nat only that thou feyntest mannes minde,
But verraily thou wolt his body shende;
Th'ende of thy werk or of thy lustes blinde
Is compleyning, how many-oon may men finde
That noght for werk som-tyme, but for th'entente
To doon this sinne, ben outher sleyn or shente!

How may this wayke womman han this strengthe
Hir to defende agayn this renegat?
O Golias, unmesurable of lengthe,
How mighte David make thee so mat,
So yong and of armure so desolat?
How dorste he loke up on thy dredful face?
Wel may men seen, it nas but goddes grace!

Who yaf Judith corage or hardinesse
To sleen him, Olofernus, in his tente,
And to deliveren out of wrecchednesse
The peple of god? I seye, for this entente,
That, right as god spirit of vigour sente
To hem, and saved hem out of meschance,
So sente he might and vigour to Custance.

Forth goth hir ship thurgh-out the narwe mouth
Of Jubaltar and Septe, dryving ay,
Som-tyme West, som-tyme North and South,
And som-tyme Est, ful many a wery day,
Til Cristes moder (blessed be she ay!)
Hath shapen, thurgh hir endelees goodnesse,
To make an ende of al hir hevinesse.

Now lat us stinte of Custance but a throwe,
And speke we of the Romain Emperour,
That out of Surrie hath by lettres knowe
The slaughtre of Cristen folk, and dishonour
Don to his doghter by a fals traitour,
I mene the cursed wikked sowdanesse,
That at the feste leet sleen both more and lesse.

For which this emperour hath sent anoon
His senatour, with royal ordinance,
And othere lordes, got wot, many oon,
On Surriens to taken heigh vengeance.
They brennen, sleen, and bringe hem to meschance
Ful many a day ; but shortly, this is the ende,
Homward to Rome they shapen hem to wende.

This senatour repaireth with victorie
To Rome-ward, sayling ful royally,
And mette the ship dryving, as seith the storie,
In which Custance sit ful pitously.
No-thing ne knew he what she was, ne why
She was in swich array ; ne she nil seye
Of hir estaat, althogh she sholde deye.

He bringeth hir to Rome, and to his wyf
He yaf hir, and hir yonge sone also ;
And with the senatour she ladde her lyf.
Thus can our lady bringen out of wo
Woful Custance, and many another mo.
And longe tyme dwelled she in that place,
In holy werkes ever, as was hir grace.

The senatoures wyf hir aunte was,
But for al that she knew hir never the more ;
I wol no lenger tarien in this cas,
But to king Alla, which I spak of yore,
That for his wyf wepeth and syketh sore,
I wol retourne, and lete I wol Custance
Under the senatoures governance.

King Alla, which that hadde his moder slayn,
Upon a day fil in swich repentance,

That, if I shortly tellen shal and plain,
To Rome he comth, to receyven his penance;
And putte him in the popes ordinance
In heigh and low, and Jesu Crist bisoghte
Foryeve his wikked werkes that he wroghte.

The fame anon thurgh Rome toun is born,
How Alla king shal come in pilgrimage,
By herbergeours that wenten him biforn;
For which the senatour, as was usage,
Rood him ageyn, and many of his linage,
As wel to shewen his heighe magnificence
As to don any king a reverence.

Greet chere dooth this noble senatour
To king Alla, and he to him also;
Everich of hem doth other greet honour;
And so bifel that, in a day or two,
This senatour is to king Alla go
To feste, and shortly, if I shal nat lye,
Custances sone wente in his companye.

Som men wolde seyn, at requeste of Custance,
This senatour hath lad this child to feste;
I may nat tellen every circumstance,
Be as be may, ther was he at the leste.
But soth is this, that, at his modres heste,
Biforn Alla, during the metes space,
The child stood, loking in the kinges face.

This Alla king hath of this child greet wonder,
And to the senatour he seyde anon,
'Whos is that faire child that stondeth yonder?'
'I noot,' quod he, 'by god, and by seint John!
A moder he hath, but fader hath he non
That I of woot'—but shortly, in a stounde,
He tolde Alla how that this child was founde.

'But god wot,' quod this senatour also,
'So vertuous a livere in my lyf,
Ne saugh I never as she, ne herde of mo
Of worldly wommen, mayden, nor of wyf;

I dar wel seyn hir hadde lever a knyf
Thurgh-out her breste, than been a womman wikke;
Ther is no man coude bringe hir to that prikke.'

Now was this child as lyk un-to Custance
As possible is a creature to be.
This Alla hath the face in remembrance
Of dame Custance, and ther-on mused he
If that the childes moder were aught she
That was his wyf, and prively he sighte,
And spedde him fro the table that he mighte.

'Parfay,' thoghte he, 'fantome is in myn heed!
I oghte deme, of skilful jugement,
That in the salte see my wyf is deed.'
And afterward he made his argument—
'What woot I, if that Crist have hider y-sent
My wyf by see, as wel as he hir sente
To my contree fro thennes that she wente?'

And, after noon, hoom with the senatour
Goth Alla, for to seen this wonder chaunce.
This senatour dooth Alla greet honour,
And hastifly he sente after Custaunce.
But trusteth weel, hir liste nat to daunce
Whan that she wiste wherefor was that sonde.
Unnethe up-on hir feet she mighte stonde.

When Alla saugh his wyf, faire he hir grette,
And weep, that it was routhe for to see.
For at the firste look he on hir sette
He knew wel verraily that it was she.
And she for sorwe as domb stant as a tree;
So was hir herte shet in hir distresse
Whan she remembred his unkindenesse.

Twyës she swowned in his owne sighte;
He weep, and him excuseth pitously:—
'Now god,' quod he, 'and alle his halwes brighte
So wisly on my soule as have mercy,
That of your harm as giltelees am I
As is Maurice my sone so lyk your face;
Elles the feend me fecche out of this place!'

Long was the sobbing and the bitter peyne
Er that hir woful hertes mighte cesse;
Greet was the pitee for to here hem pleyne,
Thurgh whiche pleintes gan hir wo encresse.
I prey yow al my labour to relesse;
I may nat telle hir wo un-til tomorwe,
I am so wery for to speke of sorwe.

But fynally, when that the sooth is wist
That Alla giltelees was of hir wo,
I trowe an hundred tymes been they kist,
And swich a blisse is ther bitwix hem two
That, save the joye that lasteth evermo,
Ther is non lyk, that any creature
Hath seyn or shal, whyl that the world may dure.

Tho preyde she hir housbond mekely,
In relief of hir longe pitous pyne,
That he wold preye hir fader specially
That, of his magestee, he wolde enclyne
To vouche-sauf som day with him to dyne;
She preyde him eek, he sholde by no weye
Un-to hir fader no word of hir seye.

Som men wold seyn, how that the child Maurice
Doth this message un-to this emperour;
But, as I gesse, Alla was nat so nyce
To him, that was of so sovereyn honour
As he that is of Cristen folk the flour,
Sente any child, but it is bet to deme
He wente him-self, and so it may wel seme.

This emperour hath graunted gentilly
To come to diner, as he him bisoghte;
And wel rede I, he loked bisily
Up-on this child, and on his doghter thoghte.
Alla goth to his in, and, as him oghte,
Arrayed for this feste in every wyse
As ferforth as his conning may suffyse.

The morwe cam, and Alla gan him dresse,
And eek his wyf, this emperour to mete;

And forth they ryde in joye and in gladnesse.
And whan she saugh hir fader in the strete,
She lighte doun, and falleth him to fete.
'Fader,' quod she, 'your yonge child Custance
Is now ful clene out of your remembrance.

I am your doghter Cústancë,' quod she,
'That whylom ye han sent un-to Surrye.
It am I, fader, that in the salte see
Was put allone and dampned for to dye.
Now, gode fader, mercy I yow crye,
Send me namore un-to non hethenesse,
But thonketh my lord heer of his kindenesse.'

Who can the pitous joye tellen al
Bitwix hem three, sin they ben thus y-mette?
But of my tale make an ende I shal;
The day goth faste, I wol no lenger lette.
This glade folk to diner they hem sette;
In joye and blisse at mete I lete hem dwelle
A thousand fold wel more than I can telle.

This child Maurice was sithen emperour
Maad by the pope, and lived Cristenly.
To Cristes chirche he dide greet honour;
But I lete al his storie passen by,
Of Custance is my tale specially.
In olde Romayn gestes may men finde
Maurices lyf; I bere it noght in minde.

This king Alla, whan he his tyme sey,
With his Custance, his holy wyf so swete,
To Engelond been they come the righte wey,
Wher-as they live in joye and in quiete.
But litel whyl it lasteth, I yow hete,
Joye of this world, for tyme wol nat abyde;
Fro day to night it changeth as the tyde.

Who lived ever in swich delyt o day
That him ne moeved outher conscience,
Or ire, or talent, or som kin affray,
Envye, or pryde, or passion, or offence?

I ne seye but for this ende this sentence,
That litel whyl in joye or in plesance
Lasteth the blisse of Alla with Custance.

For deeth, that taketh of heigh and low his rente,
When passed was a yeer, even as I gesse,
Out of this world this king Alla he hente,
For whom Custance hath ful gret hevinesse.
Now lat us preyen god his soule blesse!
And dame Custance, fynally to seye,
Towards the toun of Rome gooth hir weye.

To Rome is come this holy creature,
And fyndeth ther hir frendes hole and sounde:
Now is she scaped al hir aventure;
And whan that she hir fader hath y-founde,
Doun on hir kneës falleth she to grounde;
Weping for tendrenesse in herte blythe,
She herieth god an hundred thousand sythe.

In vertu and in holy almes-dede
They liven alle, and never a-sonder wende;
Til deeth departed hem, this lyf they lede.
And fareth now weel, my tale is at an ende.
Now Jesu Crist, that of his might may sende
Joye after wo, governe us in his grace,
And kepe us alle that ben in this place! Amen.

Here endeth the Tale of the Man of Lawe; and next folweth the Shipmannes Prolog.

THE SHIPMANNES TALE

Here biginneth the Shipmannes Prolog.

Our hoste up-on his stiropes stood anon,
And seyde, 'good men, herkneth everich on;
This was a thrifty tale for the nones!
Sir parish prest,' quod he, 'for goddes bones,
Tel us a tale, as was thy forward yore.
I see wel that ye lerned men in lore
Can moche good, by goddes dignitee!'
  The Persone him answerde, '*ben'cite*!
What eyleth the man, so sinfully to swere?'
  Our hoste answerde, 'O Jankin, be ye there?
I smelle a loller in the wind,' quod he.
'How! good men,' quod our hoste, 'herkneth me;
Abydeth, for goddes digne passioun,
For we shal han a predicacioun;
This loller heer wil prechen us som-what.'
  'Nay, by my fader soule! that shal be nat,'
Seyde the Shipman; 'heer he shal nat preche,
He shal no gospel glosen heer ne teche.
We leve alle in the grete god,' quod he,
'He wolde sowen som difficultee,
Or springen cokkel in our clene corn;
And therfor, hoste, I warne thee biforn,
My joly body shal a tale telle,
And I shal clinken yow so mery a belle,
That I shal waken al this companye;
But it shal nat ben of philosophye,
Ne *physices*, ne termes queinte of lawe;
Ther is but litel Latin in my mawe.'

Here endeth the Shipman his Prolog.

Here biginneth the Shipmannes Tale.

A MARCHANT whylom dwelled at Seint Denys,
That riche was, for which men helde him wys;
A wyf he hadde of excellent beautee,
And compaignable and revelous was she,
Which is a thing that causeth more dispence
Than worth is al the chere and reverence
That men hem doon at festes and at daunces;
Swiche salutaciouns and contenaunces
Passen as dooth a shadwe up-on the wal.
But wo is him that payen moot for al;
The sely housbond, algate he mot paye;
He moot us clothe, and he moot us arraye,
Al for his owene worship richely,
In which array we daunce jolily.
And if that he noght may, par-aventure,
Or elles, list no swich dispence endure,
But thinketh it is wasted and y-lost,
Than moot another payen for our cost,
Or lene us gold, and that is perilous.
  This noble Marchant heeld a worthy hous,
For which he hadde alday so greet repair
For his largesse, and for his wyf was fair,
That wonder is; but herkneth to my tale.
Amonges alle his gestes, grete and smale,
Ther was a monk, a fair man and a bold,
I trowe of thritty winter he was old,
That ever in oon was drawing to that place.
This yonge monk, that was so fair of face,
Aqueinted was so with the gode man,
Sith that hir firste knoweliche bigan,
That in his hous as famulier was he
As it possible is any freend to be.
  And for as muchel as this gode man
And eek this monk, of which that I bigan,
Were bothe two y-born in o village,
The monk him claimeth as for cosinage;
And he again, he seith nat ones nay,
But was as glad ther-of as fowel of day;

For to his herte it was a greet plesaunce.
Thus been they knit with eterne alliaunce,
And ech of hem gan other for t'assure
Of bretherhede, whyl that hir lyf may dure.
  Free was daun John, and namely of dispence,
As in that hous ; and ful of diligence
To doon plesaunce, and also greet costage.
He noght forgat to yeve the leeste page
In al that hous ; but, after hir degree,
He yaf the lord, and sitthe al his meynee,
When that he cam, som maner honest thing ;
For which they were as glad of his coming
As fowel is fayn, whan that the sonne up-ryseth.
Na more of this as now, for it suffyseth.
  But so bifel, this marchant on a day
Shoop him to make redy his array
Toward the toun of Brugges for to fare,
To byën ther a porcioun of ware ;
For which he hath to Paris sent anon
A messager, and preyed hath daun John
That he sholde come to Seint Denys to pleye
With him and with his wyf a day or tweye,
Er he to Brugges wente, in alle wyse.
  This noble monk, of which I yow devyse,
Hath of his abbot, as him list, licence,
By-cause he was a man of heigh prudence,
And eek an officer, out for to ryde,
To seen hir graunges and hir bernes wyde ;
And un-to Seint Denys he comth anon.
Who was so welcome as my lord daun John,
Our dere cosin, ful of curteisye ?
With him broghte he a jubbe of Malvesye,
And eek another, ful of fyn Vernage,
And volatyl, as ay was his usage.
And thus I lete hem ete and drinke and pleye,
This marchant and this monk, a day or tweye.
  The thridde day, this marchant up aryseth,
And on his nedes sadly him avyseth,
And up in-to his countour-hous goth he
To rekene with him-self, as wel may be,

Of thilke yeer, how that it with him stood,
And how that he despended hadde his good;
And if that he encressed were or noon.
His bokes and his bagges many oon
He leith biforn him on his counting-bord;
Ful riche was his tresor and his hord,
For which ful faste his countour-dore he shette;
And eek he nolde that no man sholde him lette
Of his accountes, for the mene tyme;
And thus he sit til it was passed pryme.
  Daun John was risen in the morwe also,
And in the gardin walketh to and fro,
And hath his thinges seyd ful curteisly.
  This gode wyf cam walking prively
In-to the gardin, ther he walketh softe,
And him saleweth, as she hath don ofte.
A mayde child cam in hir companye,
Which as hir list she may governe and gye,
For yet under the yerde was the mayde.
'O dere cosin myn, daun John,' she sayde,
'What eyleth yow so rathe for to ryse?'
'Nece,' quod he, 'it oghte y-nough suffyse
Fyve houres for to slepe up-on a night,
But it were for an old appalled wight,
As been thise wedded men, that lye and dare
As in a forme sit a wery hare,
Were al for-straught with houndes grete and smale.
But, dere nece, why be ye so pale?
I trowe certes that our gode man
Hath yow laboured sith the night bigan,
That yow were nede to resten hastily?'
And with that word he lough ful merily,
And of his owene thought he wex al reed.
  This faire wyf gan for to shake hir heed,
And seyde thus, 'ye, god wot al,' quod she;
'Nay, cosin myn, it stant nat so with me.
For, by that god that yaf me soule and lyf,
In al the reme of France is ther no wyf
That lasse lust hath to that sory pley.
For I may singe "allas" and "weylawey,

That I was born," but to no wight,' quod she,
'Dar I nat telle how that it stant with me.
Wherfore I thinke out of this land to wende,
Or elles of my-self to make an ende,
So ful am I of drede and eek of care.'
This monk bigan up-on this wyf to stare,
And seyde, 'allas, my nece, god forbede
That ye, for any sorwe or any drede,
Fordo your-self; but telleth me your grief;
Paraventure I may, in your meschief,
Conseille or helpe, and therfore telleth me
Al your anoy, for it shal been secree;
For on my porthors here I make an ooth,
That never in my lyf, for lief ne looth,
Ne shal I of no conseil yow biwreye.'
'The same agayn to yow,' quod she, 'I seye;
By god and by this porthors, I yow swere,
Though men me wolde al in-to peces tere,
Ne shal I never, for to goon to helle,
Biwreye a word of thing that ye me telle,
Nat for no cosinage ne alliance,
But verraily, for love and affiance.'
Thus been they sworn, and heer-upon they kiste,
And ech of hem tolde other what hem liste.
'Cosin,' quod she, 'if that I hadde a space,
As I have noon, and namely in this place,
Than wolde I telle a legende of my lyf,
What I have suffred sith I was a wyf
With myn housbonde, al be he your cosyn.'
'Nay,' quod this monk, 'by god and seint Martyn,
He is na more cosin un-to me
Than is this leef that hangeth on the tree!
I clepe him so, by Seint Denys of Fraunce,
To have the more cause of aqueintaunce
Of yow, which I have loved specially
Aboven alle wommen sikerly;
This swere I yow on my professioun.
Telleth your grief, lest that he come adoun,
And hasteth yow, and gooth your wey anon.'
'My dere love,' quod she, 'o my daun John,

Ful lief were me this conseil for to hyde,
But out it moot, I may namore abyde.
Myn housbond is to me the worste man
That ever was, sith that the world bigan.
But sith I am a wyf, it sit nat me
To tellen no wight of our privetee,
Neither a-bedde, ne in non other place;
God shilde I sholde it tellen, for his grace!
A wyf ne shal nat seyn of hir housbonde
But al honour, as I can understonde;
Save un-to yow thus muche I tellen shal;
As help me god, he is noght worth at al
In no degree the value of a flye.
But yet me greveth most his nigardye;
And wel ye woot that wommen naturelly
Desyren thinges sixe, as wel as I.
They wolde that hir housbondes sholde be
Hardy, and wyse, and riche, and ther-to free,
And buxom to his wyf, and fresh a-bedde.
But, by that ilke lord that for us bledde,
For his honour, my-self for to arraye,
A Sonday next, I moste nedes paye
An hundred frankes, or elles am I lorn.
Yet were me lever that I were unborn
Than me were doon a sclaundre or vileinye;
And if myn housbond eek it mighte espye,
I nere but lost, and therfore I yow preye
Lene me this somme, or elles moot I deye.
Daun John, I seye, lene me thise hundred frankes;
Pardee, I wol nat faille yow my thankes,
If that yow list to doon that I yow praye.
For at a certein day I wol yow paye,
And doon to yow what plesance and servyce
That I may doon, right as yow list devyse.
And but I do, god take on me vengeance
As foul as ever had Geniloun of France!'
This gentil monk answerde in this manere;
'Now, trewely, myn owene lady dere,
I have,' quod he, 'on yow so greet a routhe,
That I yow swere and plighte yow my trouthe,

That whan your housbond is to Flaundres fare,
I wol delivere yow out of this care;
For I wol bringe yow an hundred frankes.'
And with that word he caughte hir by the flankes,
And hir embraceth harde, and kiste hir ofte.
'Goth now your wey,' quod he, 'al stille and softe,
And lat us dyne as sone as that ye may;
For by my chilindre it is pryme of day.
Goth now, and beeth as trewe as I shal be.'
'Now, elles god forbede, sire,' quod she,
And forth she gooth, as jolif as a pye,
And bad the cokes that they sholde hem hye,
So that men mighte dyne, and that anon.
Up to hir housbonde is this wyf y-gon,
And knokketh at his countour boldely.
'*Qui la?*' quod he. 'Peter! it am I,'
Quod she, 'what, sire, how longe wol ye faste?
How longe tyme wol ye rekene and caste
Your sommes, and your bokes, and your thinges?
The devel have part of alle swiche rekeninges!
Ye have y-nough, pardee, of goddes sonde;
Com doun to-day, and lat your bagges stonde.
Ne be ye nat ashamed that daun John
Shal fasting al this day elenge goon?
What! lat us here a messe, and go we dyne.'
'Wyf,' quod this man, 'litel canstow devyne
The curious bisinesse that we have.
For of us chapmen, al-so god me save,
And by that lord that cleped is Seint Yve,
Scarsly amonges twelve ten shul thryve,
Continuelly, lastinge un-to our age.
We may wel make chere and good visage,
And dryve forth the world as it may be,
And kepen our estaat in privetee,
Til we be deed, or elles that we pleye
A pilgrimage, or goon out of the weye.
And therfor have I greet necessitee
Up-on this queinte world t'avyse me;
For evermore we mote stonde in drede
Of hap and fortune in our chapmanhede.

To Flaundres wol I go to-morwe at day,
And come agayn, as sone as ever I may.
For which, my dere wyf, I thee biseke,
As be to every wight buxom and meke,
And for to kepe our good be curious,
And honestly governe wel our hous.
Thou hast y-nough, in every maner wyse,
That to a thrifty houshold may suffyse.
Thee lakketh noon array ne no vitaille,
Of silver in thy purs shaltow nat faille.'
And with that word his countour-dore he shette,
And doun he gooth, no lenger wolde he lette,
But hastily a messe was ther seyd,
And spedily the tables were y-leyd,
And to the diner faste they hem spedde;
And richely this monk the chapman fedde.
At-after diner daun John sobrely
This chapman took a-part, and prively
He seyde him thus, 'cosyn, it standeth so,
That wel I see to Brugges wol ye go.
God and seint Austin spede yow and gyde!
I prey yow, cosin, wysly that ye ryde;
Governeth yow also of your diete
Atemprely, and namely in this hete.
Bitwix us two nedeth no strange fare;
Fare-wel, cosyn; god shilde yow fro care.
If any thing ther be by day or night,
If it lye in my power and my might,
That ye me wol comande in any wyse,
It shal be doon, right as ye wol devyse.
O thing, er that ye goon, if it may be,
I wolde prey yow; for to lene me
An hundred frankes, for a wyke or tweye,
For certein beestes that I moste beye,
To store with a place that is oures.
God help me so, I wolde it were youres!
I shal nat faille surely of my day,
Nat for a thousand frankes, a myle-way.
But lat this thing be secree, I yow preye,
For yet to-night thise beestes moot I beye;

And fare-now wel, myn owene cosin dere,
Graunt mercy of your cost and of your chere.'
  This noble marchant gentilly anon
Answerde, and seyde, 'o cosin myn, daun John,
Now sikerly this is a smal requeste;
My gold is youres, whan that it yow leste.
And nat only my gold, but my chaffare;
Take what yow list, god shilde that ye spare.
  But o thing is, ye knowe it wel y-nogh,
Of chapmen, that hir moneye is hir plogh.
We may creaunce whyl we have a name,
But goldlees for to be, it is no game.
Paye it agayn whan it lyth in your ese;
After my might ful fayn wolde I yow plese.'
  Thise hundred frankes he fette forth anon,
And prively he took hem to daun John.
No wight in al this world wiste of this lone,
Savinge this marchant and daun John allone.
They drinke, and speke, and rome a whyle and pleye,
Til that daun John rydeth to his abbeye.
  The morwe cam, and forth this marchant rydeth
To Flaundres-ward; his prentis wel him gydeth,
Til he cam in-to Brugges merily.
Now gooth this marchant faste and bisily
Aboute his nede, and byeth and creaunceth.
He neither pleyeth at the dees ne daunceth;
But as a marchant, shortly for to telle,
He let his lyf, and there I lete him dwelle.
  The Sonday next this Marchant was agon,
To Seint Denys y-comen is daun John,
With crowne and berd all fresh and newe y-shave.
In al the hous ther nas so litel a knave,
Ne no wight elles, that he nas ful fayn,
For that my lord daun John was come agayn.
And shortly to the point right for to gon,
This faire wyf accorded with daun John,
That for thise hundred frankes he sholde al night
Have hir in his armes bolt-upright;
And this acord parfourned was in dede.
In mirthe al night a bisy lyf they lede

Til it was day, that daun John wente his way,
And bad the meynee 'fare-wel, have good day!'
For noon of hem, ne no wight in the toun,
Hath of daun John right no suspecioun.
And forth he rydeth hoom to his abbeye,
Or where him list; namore of him I seye.
  This marchant, whan that ended was the faire,
To Seint Denys he gan for to repaire,
And with his wyf he maketh feste and chere,
And telleth hir that chaffare is so dere,
That nedes moste he make a chevisaunce.
For he was bounde in a reconissaunce
To paye twenty thousand sheeld anon.
For which this marchant is to Paris gon,
To borwe of certein frendes that he hadde
A certein frankes; and somme with him he ladde.
And whan that he was come in-to the toun,
For greet chertee and greet affeccioun,
Un-to daun John he gooth him first, to pleye;
Nat for to axe or borwe of him moneye,
But for to wite and seen of his welfare,
And for to tellen him of his chaffare,
As freendes doon whan they ben met y-fere.
Daun John him maketh feste and mery chere;
And he him tolde agayn ful specially,
How he hadde wel y-boght and graciously,
Thanked be god, al hool his marchandyse.
Save that he moste, in alle maner wyse,
Maken a chevisaunce, as for his beste,
And thanne he sholde been in joye and reste.
  Daun John answerde, 'certes, I am fayn
That ye in hele ar comen hoom agayn.
And if that I were riche, as have I blisse,
Of twenty thousand sheeld shold ye nat misse,
For ye so kindely this other day
Lente me gold; and as I can and may,
I thanke yow, by god and by seint Jame!
But nathelees I took un-to our dame,
Your wyf at hoom, the same gold ageyn
Upon your bench; she woot it wel, certeyn,

By certein tokenes that I can hir telle.
Now, by your leve, I may no lenger dwelle,
Our abbot wol out of this toun anon;
And in his companye moot I gon.
Grete wel our dame, myn owene nece swete,
And fare-wel, dere cosin, til we mete!'
  This Marchant, which that was ful war and wys
Creaunced hath, and payd eek in Parys,
To certeyn Lumbardes, redy in hir hond,
The somme of gold, and gat of hem his bond;
And hoom he gooth, mery as a papejay.
For wel he knew he stood in swich array,
That nedes moste he winne in that viage
A thousand frankes above al his costage.
  His wyf ful redy mette him atte gate,
As she was wont of old usage algate,
And al that night in mirthe they bisette;
For he was riche and cleerly out of dette.
Whan it was day, this marchant gan embrace
His wyf al newe, and kiste hir on hir face,
And up he gooth and maketh it ful tough.
  'Namore,' quod she, 'by god, ye have y-nough!'
And wantounly agayn with him she pleyde;
Til, atte laste, that this Marchant seyde,
'By god,' quod he, 'I am a litel wrooth
With yow, my wyf, al-thogh it be me looth.
And woot ye why? by god, as that I gesse,
That ye han maad a maner straungenesse
Bitwixen me and my cosyn daun John.
Ye sholde han warned me, er I had gon,
That he yow hadde an hundred frankes payed
By redy tokene; and heeld him yvel apayed,
For that I to him spak of chevisaunce,
Me semed so, as by his contenaunce.
But nathelees, by god our hevene king,
I thoghte nat to axe of him no-thing.
I prey thee, wyf, ne do namore so;
Tel me alwey, er that I fro thee go,
If any dettour hath in myn absence
Y-payëd thee; lest, thurgh thy necligence,

I mighte him axe a thing that he hath payed.'
  This wyf was nat afered nor affrayed,
But boldely she seyde, and that anon:
'Marie, I defye the false monk, daun John!
I kepe nat of hise tokenes never a deel;
He took me certein gold, that woot I weel!
What! yvel thedom on his monkes snoute!
For, god it woot, I wende, withouten doute,
That he had yeve it me bycause of yow,
To doon ther-with myn honour and my prow,
For cosinage, and eek for bele chere
That he hath had ful ofte tymes here.
But sith I see I stonde in this disjoint,
I wol answere yow shortly, to the point.
Ye han mo slakker dettours than am I!
For I wol paye yow wel and redily
Fro day to day; and, if so be I faille,
I am your wyf; score it up-on my taille,
And I shal paye, as sone as ever I may.
For, by my trouthe, I have on myn array,
And nat on wast, bistowed every deel.
And for I have bistowed it so weel
For your honour, for goddes sake, I seye,
As be nat wrooth, but lat us laughe and pleye.
Ye shal my joly body have to wedde;
By god, I wol nat paye yow but a-bedde.
Forgive it me, myn owene spouse dere;
Turne hiderward and maketh bettre chere.'
  This marchant saugh ther was no remedye,
And, for to chyde, it nere but greet folye,
Sith that the thing may nat amended be.
'Now, wyf,' he seyde, 'and I foryeve it thee;
But, by thy lyf, ne be namore so large;
Keep bet our good, this yeve I thee in charge.'
Thus endeth now my tale, and god us sende
Taling y-nough, un-to our lyves ende. Amen.

Here endeth the Shipmannes Tale

THE PRIORESSES TALE

Bihold the mery wordes of the Host to the Shipman and to the lady Prioresse.

'Wel seyd, by *corpus dominus*,' quod our hoste,
'Now longe moot thou sayle by the coste,
Sir gentil maister, gentil marineer!
God yeve this monk a thousand last quad yeer!
A ha! felawes! beth ware of swiche a jape!
The monk putte in the mannes hood an ape,
And in his wyves eek, by seint Austin!
Draweth no monkes more un-to your in.
  But now passe over, and lat us seke aboute,
Who shal now telle first, of al this route,
Another tale;' and with that word he sayde,
As curteisly as it had been a mayde,
'My lady Prioresse, by your leve,
So that I wiste I sholde yow nat greve,
I wolde demen that ye tellen sholde
A tale next, if so were that ye wolde.
Now wol ye vouche-sauf, my lady dere?'
  'Gladly,' quod she, and seyde as ye shal here.

Explicit.

The Prologe of the Prioresses Tale.

Domine, dominus noster.

O Lord our lord, thy name how merveillous
Is in this large worlde y-sprad—quod she:—
For noght only thy laude precious
Parfourned is by men of dignitee,

But by the mouth of children thy bountee
Parfourned is, for on the brest soukinge
Som tyme shewen they thyn heryinge.

Wherfor in laude, as I best can or may,
Of thee, and of the whyte lily flour
Which that thee bar, and is a mayde alway,
To telle a storie I wol do my labour;
Not that I may encresen hir honour;
For she hir-self is honour, and the rote
Of bountee, next hir sone, and soules bote.—

O moder mayde! o mayde moder free!
O bush unbrent, brenninge in Moyses sighte,
That ravisedest doun fro the deitee,
Thurgh thyn humblesse, the goost that in th'alighte.
Of whos vertu, whan he thyn herte lighte,
Conceived was the fadres sapience,
Help me to telle it in thy reverence!

Lady! thy bountee, thy magnificence,
Thy vertu, and thy grete humilitee
Ther may no tonge expresse in no science;
For som-tyme, lady, er men praye to thee,
Thou goost biforn of thy benignitee,
And getest us the light, thurgh thy preyere,
To gyden us un-to thy sone so dere.

My conning is so wayk, o blisful quene,
For to declare thy grete worthinesse,
That I ne may the weighte nat sustene,
But as a child of twelf monthe old, or lesse,
That can unnethes any word expresse,
Right so fare I, and therfor I yow preye,
Gydeth my song that I shal of yow seye.

Explicit.

Here biginneth the Prioresses Tale.

Ther was in Asie, in a greet citee,
Amonges Cristen folk, a Jewerye,
Sustened by a lord of that contree
For foule usure and lucre of vilanye,

Hateful to Crist and to his companye;
And thurgh the strete men mighte ryde or wende,
For it was free, and open at either ende.

A litel scole of Cristen folk ther stood
Doun at the ferther ende, in which ther were
Children an heep, y-comen of Cristen blood,
That lerned in that scole yeer by yere
Swich maner doctrine as men used there,
This is to seyn, to singen and to rede,
As smale children doon in hir childhede.

Among thise children was a widwes sone,
A litel clergeon, seven yeer of age,
That day by day to scole was his wone,
And eek also, wher-as he saugh th'image
Of Cristes moder, hadde he in usage,
As him was taught, to knele adoun and seye
His *Ave Marie*, as he goth by the weye.

Thus hath this widwe hir litel sone y-taught
Our blisful lady, Cristes moder dere,
To worshipe ay, and he forgat it naught,
For sely child wol alday sone lere;
But ay, whan I remembre on this matere,
Seint Nicholas stant ever in my presence,
For he so yong to Crist did reverence.

This litel child, his litel book lerninge,
As he sat in the scole at his prymer,
He *Alma redemptoris* herde singe,
As children lerned hir antiphoner;
And, as he dorste, he drough him ner and ner,
And herkned ay the wordes and the note,
Til he the firste vers coude al by rote.

Noght wiste he what this Latin was to seye,
For he so yong and tendre was of age;
But on a day his felaw gan he preye
T'expounden him this song in his langage,
Or telle him why this song was in usage;

This preyde he him to construe and declare
Ful ofte tyme upon his knowes bare.

His felaw, which that elder was than he,
Answerde him thus: 'this song, I have herd seye,
Was maked of our blisful lady free,
Hir to salue, and eek hir for to preye
To been our help and socour whan we deye.
I can no more expounde in this matere;
I lerne song, I can but smal grammere.'

'And is this song maked in reverence
Of Cristes moder?' seyde this innocent;
'Now certes, I wol do my diligence
To conne it al, er Cristemasse is went;
Though that I for my prymer shal be shent,
And shal be beten thryës in an houre,
I wol it conne, our lady for to honoure.'

His felaw taughte him homward prively,
Fro day to day, til he coude it by rote,
And than he song it wel and boldely
Fro word to word, acording with the note;
Twyës a day it passed thurgh his throte,
To scoleward and homward whan he wente;
On Cristes moder set was his entente.

As I have seyd, thurgh-out the Jewerye
This litel child, as he cam to and fro,
Ful merily than wolde he singe, and crye
O Alma redemptoris ever-mo.
The swetnes hath his herte perced so
Of Cristes moder, that, to hir to preye,
He can nat stinte of singing by the weye.

Our firste fo, the serpent Sathanas,
That hath in Jewes herte his waspes nest,
Up swal, and seide, 'O Hebraik peple, allas!
Is this to yow a thing that is honest,
That swich a boy shal walken as him lest
In your despyt, and singe of swich sentence,
Which is agayn your lawes reverence?'

Fro thennes forth the Jewes han conspyred
This innocent out of this world to chace;
An homicyde ther-to han they hyred,
That in an aley hadde a privee place;
And as the child gan for-by for to pace,
This cursed Jew him hente and heeld him faste,
And kitte his throte, and in a pit him caste.

I seye that in a wardrobe they him threwe
Wher-as these Jewes purgen hir entraille.
O cursed folk of Herodes al newe,
What may your yvel entente yow availle?
Mordre wol out, certein, it wol nat faille,
And namely ther th'onour of god shal sprede,
The blood out cryeth on your cursed dede.

'O martir, souded to virginitee,
Now maystou singen, folwing ever in oon
The whyte lamb celestial,' quod she,
'Of which the grete evangelist, seint John,
In Pathmos wroot, which seith that they that goon
Biforn this lamb, and singe a song al newe,
That never, fleshly, wommen they ne knewe.'

This povre widwe awaiteth al that night
After hir litel child, but he cam noght;
For which, as sone as it was dayes light,
With face pale of drede and bisy thoght,
She hath at scole and elles-wher him soght,
Til finally she gan so fer espye
That he last seyn was in the Jewerye.

With modres pitee in hir brest enclosed,
She gooth, as she were half out of hir minde,
To every place wher she hath supposed
By lyklihede hir litel child to finde;
And ever on Cristes moder meke and kinde
She cryde, and atte laste thus she wroghte,
Among the cursed Jewes she him soghte.

She frayneth and she preyeth pitously
To every Jew that dwelte in thilke place,

To telle hir, if hir child wente oght for-by.
They seyde, 'nay'; but Jesu, of his grace,
Yaf in hir thought, inwith a litel space,
That in that place after hir sone she cryde,
Wher he was casten in a pit bisyde.

O grete god, that parfournest thy laude
By mouth of innocents, lo heer thy might!
This gemme of chastitee, this emeraude,
And eek of martirdom the ruby bright,
Ther he with throte y-corven lay upright,
He '*Alma redemptoris*' gan to singe
So loude, that al the place gan to ringe.

The Cristen folk, that thurgh the strete wente,
In coomen, for to wondre up-on this thing,
And hastily they for the provost sente;
He cam anon with-outen tarying,
And herieth Crist that is of heven king,
And eek his moder, honour of mankinde,
And after that, the Jewes leet he binde.

This child with pitous lamentacioun
Up-taken was, singing his song alway;
And with honour of greet processioun
They carien him un-to the nexte abbay.
His moder swowning by the bere lay;
Unnethe might the peple that was there
This newe Rachel bringe fro his bere.

With torment and with shamful deth echon
This provost dooth thise Jewes for to sterve
That of this mordre wiste, and that anon;
He nolde no swich cursednesse observe.
Yvel shal have, that yvel wol deserve.
Therfor with wilde hors he dide hem drawe,
And after that he heng hem by the lawe.

Up-on his bere ay lyth this innocent
Biforn the chief auter, whyl masse laste,
And after that, the abbot with his covent
Han sped hem for to burien him ful faste;

And whan they holy water on him caste,
Yet spak this child, whan spreynd was holy water,
And song—'*O Alma redemptoris mater!*'

This abbot, which that was an holy man
As monkes been, or elles oghten be,
This yonge child to conjure he bigan,
And seyde, 'o dere child, I halse thee,
In vertu of the holy Trinitee,
Tel me what is thy cause for to singe,
Sith that thy throte is cut, to my seminge?'

'My throte is cut un-to my nekke-boon,'
Seyde this child, 'and, as by wey of kinde,
I sholde have deyed, ye, longe tyme agoon,
But Jesu Crist, as ye in bokes finde,
Wil that his glorie laste and be in minde;
And, for the worship of his moder dere,
Yet may I singe "*O Alma*" loude and clere.

This welle of mercy, Cristes moder swete,
I lovede alwey, as after my conninge;
And whan that I my lyf sholde forlete,
To me she cam, and bad me for to singe
This antem verraily in my deyinge,
As ye han herd, and, whan that I had songe,
Me thoughte, she leyde a greyn up-on my tonge.

Wherfor I singe, and singe I moot certeyn
In honour of that blisful mayden free,
Til fro my tonge of-taken is the greyn;
And afterward thus seyde she to me,
"My litel child, now wol I fecche thee
Whan that the greyn is fro thy tonge y-take;
Be nat agast, I wol thee nat forsake."'

This holy monk, this abbot, him mene I,
Him tonge out-caughte, and took a-wey the greyn,
And he yaf up the goost ful softely.
And whan this abbot had this wonder seyn,
His salte teres trikled doun as reyn,
And gruf he fil al plat up-on the grounde,
And stille he lay as he had been y-bounde.

The covent eek lay on the pavement
Weping, and herien Cristes moder dere,
And after that they ryse, and forth ben went,
And toke awey this martir fro his bere,
And in a tombe of marbul-stones clere
Enclosen they his litel body swete;
Ther he is now, god leve us for to mete.

O yonge Hugh of Lincoln, slayn also
With cursed Jewes, as it is notable,
For it nis but a litel whyle ago;
Preye eek for us, we sinful folk unstable,
That, of his mercy, god so merciable
On us his grete mercy multiplye,
For reverence of his moder Marye. Amen.

Here is ended the Prioresses Tale.

SIR THOPAS

Bihold the murye wordes of the Host to Chaucer.

WHAN seyd was al this miracle, every man
As sobre was, that wonder was to see,
Til that our hoste japen tho bigan,
And than at erst he loked up-on me,
And seyde thus, 'what man artow ?' quod he ;
'Thou lokest as thou woldest finde an hare,
For ever up-on the ground I see thee stare.

Approche neer, and loke up merily.
Now war yow, sirs, and lat this man have place ;
He in the waast is shape as wel as I ;
This were a popet in an arm t'enbrace
For any womman, smal and fair of face.
He semeth elvish by his contenaunce,
For un-to no wight dooth he daliaunce.

Sey now somwhat, sin other folk han sayd ;
Tel us a tale of mirthe, and that anoon ;'—
'Hoste,' quod I, 'ne beth nat yvel apayd,
For other tale certes can I noon,
But of a ryme I lerned longe agoon.'
'Ye, that is good,' quod he ; 'ncw shul we here
Som deyntee thing, me thinketh by his chere.'

Explicit.

Here biginneth Chaucers Tale of Thopas.

LISTETH, lordes, in good entent,
And I wol telle verrayment
   Of mirthe and of solas ;

Al of a knyght was fair and gent
In bataille and in tourneyment,
  His name was sir Thopas.

Y-born he was in fer contree,
In Flaundres, al biyonde the see,
  At Popering, in the place;
His fader was a man ful free,
And lord he was of that contree,
  As it was goddes grace.

Sir Thopas wex a doghty swayn,
Whyt was his face as payndemayn,
  His lippes rede as rose;
His rode is lyk scarlet in grayn,
And I yow telle in good certayn,
  He hadde a semely nose.

His heer, his berd was lyk saffroun,
That to his girdel raughte adoun;
  His shoon of Cordewane.
Of Brugges were his hosen broun,
His robe was of ciclatoun,
  That coste many a jane.

He coude hunte at wilde deer,
And ryde an hauking for riveer,
  With grey goshauk on honde;
Ther-to he was a good archeer,
Of wrastling was ther noon his peer,
  Ther any ram shal stonde.

Ful many a mayde, bright in bour,
They moorne for him, paramour,
  Whan hem were bet to slepe;
But he was chast and no lechour,
And sweet as is the bremble-flour
  That bereth the rede hepe.

And so bifel up-on a day,
For sothe, as I yow telle may,
  Sir Thopas wolde out ryde;

He worth upon his stede gray,
And in his honde a launcegay,
  A long swerd by his syde.

He priketh thurgh a fair forest,
Ther-inne is many a wilde best,
  Ye, bothe bukke and hare ;
And, as he priketh north and est,
I telle it yow, him hadde almest
  Bitid a sory care.

Ther springen herbes grete and smale,
The lycorys and cetewale,
  And many a clowe-gilofre ;
And notemuge to putte in ale,
Whether it be moyste or stale,
  Or for to leye in cofre.

The briddes singe, it is no nay,
The sparhauk and the papejay,
  That joye it was to here ;
The thrustelcok made eek his lay,
The wodedowve upon the spray
  She sang ful loude and clere.

Sir Thopas fil in love-longinge
Al whan he herde the thrustel singe,
  And priked as he were wood :
His faire stede in his prikinge
So swatte that men mighte him wringe,
  His sydes were al blood.

Sir Thopas eek so wery was
For prikinge on the softe gras,
  So fiers was his corage,
That doun he leyde him in that plas
To make his stede som solas,
  And yaf him good forage.

'O seinte Marie, *ben'cite !*
What eyleth this love at me
  To binde me so sore ?

Me dremed al this night, pardee,
An elf-queen shal my lemman be,
  And slepe under my gore.

An elf-queen wol I love, y-wis,
For in this world no womman is
  Worthy to be my make
                In toune;
Alle othere wommen I forsake,
And to an elf-queen I me take
  By dale and eek by doune!'

In-to his sadel he clamb anoon,
And priketh over style and stoon
  An elf-queen for t'espye,
Til he so longe had riden and goon
That he fond, in a privee woon,
  The contree of Fairye
                So wilde;
For in that contree was ther noon
That to him dorste ryde or goon,
  Neither wyf ne childe.

Til that ther cam a greet geaunt,
His name was sir Olifaunt,
  A perilous man of dede;
He seyde, 'child, by Termagaunt,
But-if thou prike out of myn haunt,
  Anon I slee thy stede
                With mace.
Heer is the queen of Fayërye,
With harpe and pype and simphonye
  Dwelling in this place.'

The child seyde, 'al-so mote I thee,
Tomorwe wol I mete thee
  Whan I have myn armoure;
And yet I hope, *par ma fay*,
That thou shalt with this launcegay
  Abyen it ful soure;
                Thy mawe

Shal I percen, if I may,
Er it be fully pryme of day,
  For heer thou shalt be slawe.'

Sir Thopas drow abak ful faste;
This geaunt at him stones caste
  Out of a fel staf-slinge;
But faire escapeth child Thopas,
And al it was thurgh goddes gras,
  And thurgh his fair beringe.

Yet listeth, lordes, to my tale
Merier than the nightingale,
  For now I wol yow roune
How sir Thopas with sydes smale,
Priking over hil and dale,
  Is come agayn to toune.

His merie men comanded he
To make him bothe game and glee,
  For nedes moste he fighte
With a geaunt with hevedes three,
For paramour and jolitee
  Of oon that shoon ful brighte.

'Do come,' he seyde, 'my minstrales,
And gestours, for to tellen tales
  Anon in myn arminge;
Of romances that been royales,
Of popes and of cardinales,
  And eek of love-lykinge.'

They fette him first the swete wyn,
And mede eek in a maselyn,
  And royal spicerye
Of gingebreed that was ful fyn,
And lycorys, and eek comyn,
  With sugre that is so trye.

He dide next his whyte lere
Of clooth of lake fyn and clere
  A breech and eek a sherte;

And next his sherte an aketoun,
And over that an habergeoun
  For percinge of his herte ;

And over that a fyn hauberk,
Was al y-wroght of Jewes werk,
  Ful strong it was of plate ;
And over that his cote-armour
As whyt as is a lily-flour,
  In which he wol debate.

His sheeld was al of gold so reed,
And ther-in was a bores heed,
  A charbocle bisyde ;
And there he swoor, on ale and breed,
How that 'the geaunt shal be deed,
  Bityde what bityde !'

His jambeux were of quirboilly,
His swerdes shethe of yvory,
  His helm of laton bright ;
His sadel was of rewel-boon,
His brydel as the sonne shoon,
  Or as the mone light.

His spere was of fyn ciprees,
That bodeth werre, and no-thing pees,
  The heed ful sharpe y-grounde ;
His stede was al dappel-gray,
It gooth an ambel in the way
  Ful softely and rounde
                In londe.
Lo, lordes myne, heer is a fit !
If ye wol any more of it,
  To telle it wol I fonde.

[*The Second Fit.*]

Now hold your mouth, *par charitee*,
Bothe knight and lady free,
  And herkneth to my spelle ;

Of bataille and of chivalry,
And of ladyes love-drury
  Anon I wol yow telle.

Men speke of romances of prys,
Of Horn child and of Ypotys,
  Of Bevis and sir Gy,
Of sir Libeux and Pleyn-damour;
But sir Thopas, he bereth the flour
  Of royal chivalry.

His gode stede al he bistrood,
And forth upon his wey he glood
  As sparkle out of the bronde;
Up-on his crest he bar a tour,
And ther-in stiked a lily-flour,
  God shilde his cors fro shonde!

And for he was a knight auntrous,
He nolde slepen in non hous,
  But liggen in his hode;
His brighte helm was his wonger,
And by him baiteth his dextrer
  Of herbes fyne and gode.

Him-self drank water of the wel,
As did the knight sir Percivel,
  So worthy under wede,
Til on a day——

Here the Host stinteth Chaucer of his Tale of Thopas.

THE TALE OF MELIBEUS

'No more of this, for goddes dignitee,'
Quod oure hoste, 'for thou makest me
So wery of thy verray lewednesse
That, also wisly god my soule blesse,
Myn eres aken of thy drasty speche ;
Now swiche a rym the devel I biteche !
This may wel be rym dogerel,' quod he.
'Why so ?' quod I, 'why wiltow lette me
More of my tale than another man,
Sin that it is the beste rym I can ?'
'By god,' quod he, 'for pleynly, at a word,
Thy drasty ryming is nat worth a tord ;
Thou doost nought elles but despendest tyme,
Sir, at o word, thou shalt no lenger ryme.
Lat see wher thou canst tellen aught in geste,
Or telle in prose somwhat at the leste
In which ther be som mirthe or som doctryne.'
'Gladly,' quod I, 'by goddes swete pyne,
I wol yow telle a litel thing in prose,
That oghte lyken yow, as I suppose,
Or elles, certes, ye been to daungerous.
It is a moral tale vertuous,
Al be it told som-tyme in sondry wyse
Of sondry folk, as I shal yow devyse.
As thus ; ye woot that every evangelist,
That telleth us the peyne of Jesu Crist,
Ne saith nat al thing as his felaw dooth,
But natheles, hir sentence is al sooth,

And alle acorden as in hir sentence,
Al be ther in hir telling difference.
For somme of hem seyn more, and somme lesse,
Whan they his pitous passioun expresse;
I mene of Mark [and] Mathew, Luk and John;
But doutelees hir sentence is al oon.
Therfor, lordinges alle, I yow biseche,
If that ye thinke I varie as in my speche,
As thus, thogh that I telle som-what more
Of proverbes, than ye han herd bifore,
Comprehended in this litel tretis here,
To enforce with the th'effect of my matere,
And thogh I nat the same wordes seye
As ye han herd, yet to yow alle I preye,
Blameth me nat; for, as in my sentence,
Ye shul not fynden moche difference
Fro the sentence of this tretis lyte
After the which this mery tale I wryte.
And therfor herkneth what that I shal seye,
And lat me tellen al my tale, I preye.'

Explicit.

Here biȝinneth Chaucers Tale of Melibee.

§ 1. A yong man called Melibeus, mighty and riche, bigat up-on his wyf that called was Prudence, a doghter which that called was Sophie.

§ 2. Upon a day bifel, that he for his desport is went in-to the feeldes him to pleye. His wyf and eek his doghter hath he left inwith his hous, of which the dores weren fast y-shette. Three of his olde foos han it espyed, and setten laddres to the walles of his hous, and by the windowes been entred, and betten his wyf, and wounded his doghter with fyve mortal woundes in fyve sondry places; this is to seyn, in hir feet, in hir handes, in hir eres, in hir nose, and in hir mouth; and leften hir for deed, and wenten awey.

§ 3. Whan Melibeus retourned was in-to his hous, and saugh al this meschief, he, lyk a mad man. rendinge his clothes, gan to wepe and crye.

§ 4. Prudence his wyf, as ferforth as she dorste, bisoghte him of his weping for to stinte; but nat forthy he gan to crye and wepen ever lenger the more.

§ 5. This noble wyf Prudence remembered hir upon the sentence of Ovide, in his book that cleped is The Remedie of Love, wher-as he seith; 'he is a fool that destourbeth the moder to wepen in the deeth of hir child, til she have wept hir fille, as for a certein tyme; and thanne shal man doon his diligence with amiable wordes hir to reconforte, and preyen hir of hir weping for to stinte.' For which resoun this noble wyf Prudence suffred hir housbond for to wepe and crye as for a certein space; and whan she saugh hir tyme, she seyde him in this wyse. 'Allas, my lord,' quod she, 'why make ye your-self for to be lyk a fool? For sothe, it aperteneth nat to a wys man, to maken swiche a sorwe. Your doghter, with the grace of god, shal warisshe and escape. And al were it so that she right now were deed, ye ne oghte nat as for hir deeth yourself to destroye. Senek seith: "the wise man shal nat take to greet disconfort for the deeth of his children, but certes he sholde suffren it in pacience, as wel as he abydeth the deeth of his owene propre persone."'

§ 6. This Melibeus answerde anon and seyde, 'What man,' quod he, 'sholde of his weping stinte, that hath so greet a cause for to wepe? Jesu Crist, our lord, him-self wepte for the deeth of Lazarus his freend.' Prudence answerde, 'Certes, wel I woot, attempree weping is no-thing defended to him that sorweful is, amonges folk in sorwe, but it is rather graunted him to wepe. The Apostle Paul un-to the Romayns wryteth, "man shal rejoyse with hem that maken joye, and wepen with swich folk as wepen." But thogh attempree weping be y-graunted, outrageous weping certes is defended. Mesure of weping sholde be considered, after the lore that techeth us Senek. "Whan that thy freend is deed," quod he, "lat nat thyne eyen to moyste been of teres, ne to muche drye; althogh the teres come to thyne eyen, lat hem nat falle." And whan thou hast for-goon thy freend, do diligence to gete another freend; and this is more wysdom than for to wepe for thy freend which that thou hast lorn; for ther-inne is no bote. And therfore, if ye governe yow by sapience, put awey sorwe out of your herte. Remembre yow that Jesus Syrak seith: "a man that is joyous and glad in herte, it him conserveth florisshing in his age; but soothly sorweful herte maketh his bones drye." He seith eek thus: "that sorwe in herte sleeth ful many a man." Salomon seith: "that, right as motthes in the shepes flees anoyeth to the clothes, and the smale wormes to the tree, right so anoyeth sorwe to the herte." Wherfore us oghte, as wel in the deeth of our children as in the losse of our goodes temporels, have pacience.

§ 7. Remembre yow up-on the pacient Job, whan he hadde lost his children and his temporel substance, and in his body endured and receyved ful many a grevous tribulacioun; yet seyde he thus: "our lord hath yeven it me, our lord hath biraft it me; right as our lord hath wold, right so it is doon; blessed be the name of our lord."' To thise foreseide thinges answerde Melibeus un-to his wyf Prudence: 'Alle thy wordes,' quod he, 'been sothe, and ther-to profitable; but trewely myn herte is troubled with this sorwe so grevously, that I noot what to done.' 'Lat calle,' quod Prudence, 'thy trewe freendes alle, and thy linage whiche that been wyse; telleth your cas, and herkneth what they seye in conseiling, and yow governe after hir sentence. Salomon seith: "werk alle thy thinges by conseil, and thou shalt never repente."'

§ 8. Thanne, by the conseil of his wyf Prudence, this Melibeus leet callen a greet congregacioun of folk; as surgiens, phisiciens, olde folk and yonge, and somme of hise olde enemys reconsiled as by hir semblaunt to his love and in-to his grace; and ther-with-al ther comen somme of hise neighebores that diden him reverence more for drede than for love, as it happeth ofte. Ther comen also ful many subtile flatereres, and wyse advocats lerned in the lawe.

§ 9. And whan this folk togidre assembled weren, this Melibeus in sorweful wyse shewed hem his cas; and by the manere of his speche it semed that in herte he bar a cruel ire, redy to doon vengeaunce up-on hise foos, and sodeynly desired that the werre sholde biginne; but nathelees yet axed he hir conseil upon this matere. A surgien, by licence and assent of swiche as weren wyse, up roos and un-to Melibeus seyde as ye may here.

§ 10. 'Sir,' quod he, 'as to us surgiens aperteneth, that we do to every wight the beste that we can, wher-as we been with-holde, and to our pacients that we do no damage; wherfore it happeth, many tyme and ofte, that whan twey men han everich wounded other, oon same surgien heleth hem bothe; wherefore un-to our art it is nat pertinent to norice werre, ne parties to supporte. But certes, as to the warisshinge of your doghter, al-be-it so that she perilously be wounded, we shullen do so ententif bisinesse fro day to night, that with the grace of god she shal be hool and sound as sone as is possible.' Almost right in the same wyse the phisiciens answerden, save that they seyden a fewe wordes more: 'That, right as maladyes been cured by hir contraries, right so shul men warisshe werre by vengeaunce.' His neighebores, ful of envye, his feyned freendes that semeden reconsiled, and his flatereres, maden semblant of weping, and empeireden and agreggeden muchel of this matere, in preising greetly Melibee of might, of power, of richesse, and of freendes, despysinge the power of his adversaries, and seiden outrely that he anon sholde wreken him on his foos and biginne werre.

§ 11. Up roos thanne an advocat that was wys, by leve and by conseil of othere that were wyse, and seyde: 'Lordinges, the nede for which we been assembled in this place is a ful hevy thing and an heigh matere, by-cause of the wrong and of the wikkednesse that hath be doon, and eek by resoun of the grete damages that in tyme cominge been possible to fallen for this same cause; and eek by resoun of the grete richesse and power of the parties bothe; for the whiche resouns it were a ful greet peril to erren in this matere. Wherfore, Melibeus, this is our sentence: we conseille yow aboven alle thing, that right anon thou do thy diligence in kepinge of thy propre persone, in swich a wyse that thou ne wante noon espye ne wacche, thy body for to save. And after that we conseille, that in thyn hous thou sette suffisant garnisoun, so that they may as wel thy body as thyn hous defende. But certes, for to moeve werre, or sodeynly for to door vengeaunce, we may nat demen in so litel tyme that it were profitable. Wherfore we axen leyser and espace to have deliberacioun in this cas to deme. For the commune proverbe seith thus: "he that sone demeth, sone shal repente." And eek men seyn that thilke juge is wys, that sone understondeth a matere and juggeth by leyser. For al-be-it so that alle tarying be anoyful, algates it is nat to repreve in yevinge of jugement, ne in vengeance-taking, whan it is suffisant and resonable. And that shewed our lord Jesu Crist by ensample; for whan that the womman that was taken in avoutrie was broght in his presence, to knowen what sholde be doon with hir persone, al-be-it so that he wiste wel him-self what that he wolde answere, yet ne wolde he nat answere sodeynly, but he wolde have deliberacioun, and in the ground he wroot twyes. And by thise causes we axen deliberacioun, and we shal thanne, by the grace of god, conseille thee thing that shal be profitable.'

§ 12. Up stirten thanne the yonge folk at-ones, and the moste partie of that companye han scorned the olde wyse men, and bigonnen to make noyse, and seyden: that, right so as whyl that iren is hoot, men sholden smyte, right so, men sholde wreken hir wronges whyle that they been fresshe and newe; and with loud voys they cryden, 'werre! werre!'

Up roos tho oon of thise olde wyse, and with his hand made contenaunce that men sholde holden hem stille and yeven him audience. 'Lordinges,' quod he, 'ther is ful many a man that cryeth "werre! werre!" that woot ful litel what werre amounteth. Werre at his biginning hath so greet an entree and so large, that every wight may entre whan him lyketh, and lightly finde werre. But, certes, what ende that shal ther-of bifalle, it is nat light to knowe. For sothly, whan that werre is ones bigonne, ther is ful many a child unborn of his moder, that shal sterve yong by-cause of that ilke werre, or elles live in sorwe and dye in wrecchednesse. And ther-fore, er that any werre biginne, men moste have greet conseil and greet deliberacioun.' And whan this olde man wende to enforcen his tale by resons, wel ny alle at-ones bigonne they to ryse for to breken his tale, and beden him ful ofte his wordes for to abregge. For soothly, he that precheth to hem that listen nat heren his wordes, his sermon hem anoyeth. For Jesus Syrak seith: that 'musik in wepinge is anoyous thing'; this is to seyn: as muche availleth to speken bifore folk to whiche his speche anoyeth, as dooth to singe biforn him that wepeth. And whan this wyse man saugh that him wanted audience, al shamefast he sette him doun agayn. For Salomon seith: 'ther as thou ne mayst have noon audience, enforce thee nat to speke.' 'I see wel,' quod this wyse man, 'that the commune proverbe is sooth; that "good conseil wanteth whan it is most nede."'

§ 13. Yet hadde this Melibeus in his conseil many folk, that prively in his ere conseilled him certeyn thing, and conseilled him the contrarie in general audience.

Whan Melibeus hadde herd that the gretteste partie of his conseil weren accorded that he sholde maken werre, anoon he consented to hir conseilling, and fully affermed hir sentence. Thanne dame Prudence, whan that she saugh how that hir housbonde shoop him for to wreken him on his foos, and to biginne werre, she in ful humble wyse, when she saugh hir tyme, seide him thise wordes: 'My lord,' quod she, 'I yow biseche as hertely as I dar and can, ne haste yow nat to faste, and for alle guerdons as yeveth me audience. For Piers Alfonce seith: "who-so that dooth to that other good or harm, haste thee nat to quyten it; for in this wyse thy freend wol abyde, and thyn enemy shal the lenger live in drede." The proverbe seith: "he hasteth wel that wysely can abyde"; and in wikked haste is no profit.'

§ 14. This Melibee answerde un-to his wyf Prudence: 'I purpose nat,' quod he, 'to werke by thy conseil, for many causes and resouns. For certes every wight wolde holde me thanne a fool; this is to seyn, if I, for thy conseilling, wolde chaungen thinges that been ordeyned and affermed by so manye wyse. Secoundly I seye, that alle wommen been wikke and noon good of hem alle. For "of a thousand men," seith Salomon, "I fond a good man: but certes, of alle wommen, good womman fond I never." And also certes, if I governed me by thy conseil, it sholde seme that I hadde yeve to thee over me the maistrie; and god forbede that it so were. For Jesus Syrak seith: "that if the wyf have maistrie, she is contrarious to hir housbonde." And Salomon seith: "never in thy lyf, to thy wyf, ne to thy child, ne to thy freend, ne yeve no power over thyself. For bettre it were that thy children aske of thy persone thinges that hem nedeth, than thou see thy-self in the handes of thy children." And also, if I wolde werke by thy conseilling, certes my conseilling moste som tyme be secree, til it were tyme that it moste be knowe; and this ne may noght be. [For it is writen, that "the janglerie of wommen can hyden thinges that they witen noght." Furthermore, the philosophre seith, "in wikked conseil wommen venquisshe men"; and for thise resouns I ne ow nat usen thy conseil.']

§ 15. Whanne dame Prudence, ful debonairly and with greet pacience, hadde herd al that hir housbonde lyked for to seye, thanne axed she of him licence for to speke, and seyde in this wyse. 'My lord,' quod she, 'as to your firste resoun, certes it may lightly been answered. For I seye, that it is no folie to chaunge conseil whan the thing is chaunged; or elles whan the thing semeth otherweyes than it was biforn. And more-over I seye, that though ye han sworn and bihight to perfourne your emprise, and nathelees ye weyve to perfourne thilke same emprise by juste cause, men sholde nat seyn therefore that ye were a lyer ne forsworn. For the book seith, that "the wyse man maketh no lesing whan he turneth his corage to the bettre." And al-be-it so that your emprise be establissed and ordeyned by greet multitude of folk, yet thar ye nat accomplice thilke same ordinaunce but yow lyke. For the trouthe of thinges and the profit been rather founden in fewe folk that been wyse and ful of resoun, than by greet multitude of folk, ther every man cryeth and clatereth what that him lyketh. Soothly swich multitude is nat honeste. As to the seconde resoun, where-as ye seyn that "alle wommen been wikke," save your grace, certes ye despysen alle wommen in this wyse; and "he that alle despyseth alle displeseth," as seith the book. And Senek seith that "who-so wole have sapience, shal no man dispreise; but he shal gladly techen the science that he can, with-outen presumpcioun or pryde. And swiche thinges as he nought ne can, he shal nat been ashamed to lerne hem and enquere of lasse folk than him-self." And sir, that ther hath been many a good womman, may lightly be preved. For certes, sir, our lord Jesu Crist wolde never have descended to be born of a womman, if alle wommen hadden ben wikke. And after that, for the grete bountee that is in wommen, our lord Jesu Crist, whan he was risen fro deeth to lyve, appeered rather to a womman than to his apostles. And though that Salomon seith, that "he ne fond never womman good," it folweth nat therfore that alle wommen ben wikke. For though that he ne fond no good womman, certes, ful many another man hath founden many a womman ful good and trewe. Or elles per-aventure the entente of Salomon was this; that, as in sovereyn bountee, he fond no womman; this is to seyn, that ther is no wight that hath sovereyn bountee save god allone; as he him-self recordeth in his Evaungelie. For ther nis no creature so good that him ne wanteth somwhat of the perfeccioun of god, that is his maker. Your thridde resoun is this: ye seyn that "if ye governe yow by my conseil, it sholde seme that ye hadde yeve me the maistrie and the lordshipe over your persone." Sir, save your grace, it is nat so. For if it were so, that no man sholde be conseilled but only of hem that hadden lordshipe and maistrie of his persone, men wolden nat be conseilled so ofte. For soothly, thilke man that asketh conseil of a purpos, yet hath he free chois, wheither he wole werke by that conseil or noon. And as to your fourthe resoun, ther ye seyn that "the janglerie of wommen hath hid thinges that they woot noght," as who seith, that "a womman can nat hyde that she woot"; sir, thise wordes been understonde of wommen that been jangleresses and wikked; of whiche wommen, men seyn that "three thinges dryven a man out of his hous; that is to seyn, smoke, dropping of reyn, and wikked wyves"; and of swiche wommen seith Salomon, that "it were bettre dwelle in desert, than with a womman that is riotous." And sir, by your leve, that am nat I; for ye han ful ofte assayed my grete silence and my gret pacience; and eek how wel that I can hyde and hele thinges that men oghte secreely to hyde. And soothly, as to your fifthe resoun, wher-as ye seyn, that "in wikked conseil wommen venquisshe men"; god woot, thilke resoun stant here in no stede. For understond now, ye asken conseil to do wikkednesse; and if ye wole werken wikkednesse, and your wyf restreyneth thilke wikked purpos, and overcometh yow by resoun and by good conseil; certes, your wyf oghte rather to be preised than y-blamed. Thus sholde ye understonde the philosophre that seith, "in wikked conseil wommen venquisshen hir housbondes." And ther-as ye blamen alle wommen and hir resouns, I shal shewe yow by manye ensamples that many a womman hath ben ful good, and yet been; and hir conseils ful hoolsome and profitable. Eek som men han seyd, that "the conseillinge of wommen is outher to dere, or elles to litel of prys." But al-be-it so, that ful many a womman is badde, and hir conseil vile and noght worth, yet han men founde ful many a good womman, and ful discrete and wise in conseillinge. Lo, Jacob, by good conseil of his moder Rebekka, wan the benisoun of Ysaak his fader, and the lordshipe over alle his bretheren. Judith, by hir good conseil, delivered the citee of Bethulie, in which she dwelled, out of the handes of Olofernus, that hadde it biseged and wolde have al destroyed it. Abigail delivered Nabal hir housbonde fro David the king, that wolde have slayn him, and apaysed the ire of the king by hir wit and by hir good conseilling. Hester by hir good conseil enhaunced greetly the peple of god in the regne of Assuerus the king. And the same bountee in good conseilling of many a good womman may men telle. And moreover, whan our lord hadde creat Adam our forme-fader, he seyde in this wyse: "it is nat good to been a man allone; make we to him an help semblable to himself." Here may ye se that, if that wommen were nat goode, and hir conseils goode and profitable, our lord god of hevene wolde never han wroght hem, ne called hem help of man, but rather confusioun of man. And ther seyde ones a clerk in two vers: "what is bettre than gold? Jaspre. What is bettre than jaspre? Wisdom. And what is bettre than wisdom? Womman. And what is bettre than a good womman? No-thing." And sir, by manye of othre resons may ye seen, that manye wommen been goode, and hir conseils goode and profitable. And therfore sir, if ye wol triste to my conseil, I shal restore yow your doghter hool and sound. And eek I wol do to yow so muche, that ye shul have honour in this cause.'

§ 16. Whan Melibee hadde herd the wordes of his wyf Prudence, he seyde thus: 'I see wel that the word of Salomon is sooth; he seith, that "wordes that been spoken discreetly by ordinaunce, been honycombes; for they yeven swetnesse to the soule, and hoolsomnesse to the body." And wyf, by-cause of thy swete wordes, and eek for I have assayed and preved thy grete sapience and thy grete trouthe, I wol governe me by thy conseil in alle thing.'

§ 17. 'Now sir,' quod dame Prudence, 'and sin ye vouche-sauf to been governed by my conseil, I wol enforme yow how ye shul governe your-self in chesinge of your conseillours. Ye shul first, in alle your werkes, mekely biseken to the heighe god that he wol be your conseillour; and shapeth yow to swich entente, that he yeve yow conseil and confort, as taughte Thobie his sone: "at alle tymes thou shalt blesse god, and praye him to dresse thy weyes"; and looke that alle thy conseils been in him for evermore. Seint Jame eek seith: "if any of yow have nede of sapience, axe it of god." And afterward thanne shul ye taken conseil in your-self, and examine wel your thoghtes, of swich thing as yow thinketh that is best for your profit. And thanne shul ye dryve fro your herte three thinges that been contrariouse to good conseil, that is to seyn, ire, coveitise, and hastifnesse.

§ 18. First, he that axeth conseil of him-self, certes he moste been with-outen ire, for manye causes. The firste is this: he that hath greet ire and wratthe in him-self, he weneth alwey that he may do thing that he may nat do. And secoundely, he that is irous and wroth, he ne may nat wel deme; and he that may nat wel deme, may nat wel conseille. The thridde is this; that "he that is irous and wrooth," as seith Senek, "ne may nat speke but he blame thinges"; and with his viciouse wordes he stireth other folk to angre and to ire. And eek sir, ye moste dryve coveitise out of your herte. For the apostle seith, that "coveitise is rote of alle harmes." And trust wel that a coveitous man ne can noght deme ne thinke, but only to fulfille the ende of his coveitise; and certes, that ne may never been accompliced; for ever the more habundaunce that he hath of richesse, the more he desyreth. And sir, ye moste also dryve out of your herte hastifnesse; for certes, ye ne may nat deme for the beste a sodeyn thought that falleth in youre herte, but ye moste avyse yow on it ful ofte. For as ye herde biforn, the commune proverbe is this, that "he that sone demeth, sone repenteth."

§ 19. Sir, ye ne be nat alwey in lyke disposicioun; for certes, som thing that somtyme semeth to yow that it is good for to do, another tyme it semeth to yow the contrarie.

§ 20. Whan ye han taken conseil in your-self, and han demed by good deliberacion swich thing as you semeth best, thanne rede I yow, that ye kepe it secree. Biwrey nat your conseil to no persone, but-if so be that ye wenen sikerly that, thurgh your biwreying, your condicioun shal be to yow the more profitable. For Jesus Syrak seith: "neither to thy foo ne to thy freend discovere nat thy secree ne thy folie; for they wol yeve yow audience and loking and supportacioun in thy presence, and scorne thee in thyn absence." Another clerk seith, that "scarsly shaltou finden any persone that may kepe conseil secreely." The book seith: "whyl that thou kepest thy conseil in thyn herte, thou kepest it in thy prisoun: and whan thou biwreyest thy conseil to any wight, he holdeth thee in his snare." And therefore yow is bettre to hyde your conseil in your herte, than praye him, to whom ye han biwreyed your conseil, that he wole kepen it cloos and stille. For Seneca seith: "if so be that thou ne mayst nat thyn owene conseil hyde, how darstou prayen any other wight thy conseil secreely to kepe?" But nathelees, if thou wene sikerly that the biwreying of thy conseil to a persone wol make thy condicioun to stonden in the bettre plyt, thanne shaltou tellen him thy conseil in this wyse. First, thou shalt make no semblant whether thee were lever pees or werre, or this or that, ne shewe him nat thy wille and thyn entente; for trust wel, that comunly thise conseillours been flatereres, namely the conseillours of grete lordes; for they enforcen hem alwey rather to speken plesante wordes, enclyninge to the lordes lust, than wordes that been trewe or profitable. And therfore men seyn, that "the riche man hath seld good conseil but-if he have it of himself." And after that, thou shalt considere thy freendes and thyne enemys. And as touchinge thy freendes, thou shalt considere whiche of hem been most feithful and most wyse, and eldest and most approved in conseilling. And of hem shalt thou aske thy conseil, as the caas requireth.

§ 21. I seye that first ye shul clepe to your conseil your freendes that been trewe. For Salomon seith: that "right as the herte of a man delyteth in savour that is sote, right so the conseil of trewe freendes yeveth swetenesse to the soule." He seith also: "ther may no-thing be lykned to the trewe freend." For certes, gold ne silver beth nat so muche worth as the gode wil of a trewe freend. And eek he seith, that "a trewe freend is a strong deffense; who-so that it findeth, certes he findeth a greet tresour." Thanne shul ye eek considere, if that your trewe freendes been discrete and wyse. For the book seith: "axe alwey thy conseil of hem that been wyse." And by this same resoun shul ye clepen to your conseil, of your freendes that been of age, swiche as han seyn and been expert in manye thinges, and been approved in conseillinges. For the book seith, that "in olde men is the sapience and in longe tyme the prudence." And Tullius seith: that "grete thinges ne been nat ay accompliced by strengthe, ne by delivernesse of body, but by good conseil, by auctoritee of persones, and by science; the whiche three thinges ne been nat feble by age, but certes they enforcen and encreesen day by day." And thanne shul ye kepe this for a general reule. First shul ye clepen to your conseil a fewe of your freendes that been especiale; for Salomon seith: "manye freendes have thou; but among a thousand chese thee oon to be thy conseillour." For al-be-it so that thou first ne telle thy conseil but to a fewe, thou mayst afterward telle it to mo folk, if it be nede. But loke alwey that thy conseillours have thilke three condiciouns that I have seyd bifore; that is to seyn, that they be trewe, wyse, and of old experience. And werke nat alwey in every nede by oon counseillour allone; for somtyme bihoveth it to been conseilled by manye. For Salomon seith: "salvacioun of thinges is wher-as ther been manye conseillours."

§ 22. Now sith that I have told yow of which folk ye sholde been counseilled, now wol I teche yow which conseil ye oghte to eschewe. First ye shul eschewe the conseilling of foles; for Salomon seith: "taak no conseil of a fool, for he ne can noght conseille but after his owene lust and his affeccioun." The book seith: that "the propretee of a fool is this; he troweth lightly harm of every wight, and lightly troweth alle bountee in himself." Thou shalt eek eschewe the conseilling of alle flatereres, swiche as enforcen hem rather to preise your persone by flaterye than for to telle yow the sothfastnesse of thinges.

§ 23. Wherfore Tullius seith: "amonges alle the pestilences that been in freendshipe, the gretteste is flaterye." And therfore is it more nede that thou eschewe and drede flatereres than any other peple. The book seith: "thou shalt rather drede and flee fro the swete wordes of flateringe preiseres, than fro the egre wordes of thy freend that seith thee thy sothes." Salomon seith, that "the wordes of a flaterere is a snare to cacche with innocents." He seith also, that "he that speketh to his freend wordes of swetnesse and of plesaunce, setteth a net biforn his feet to cacche him." And therfore seith Tullius: "enclyne nat thyne eres to flatereres, ne taketh no conseil of wordes of flaterye." And Caton seith: "avyse thee wel, and eschewe the wordes of swetnesse and of plesaunce." And eek thou shalt eschewe the conseilling of thyne olde enemys that been reconsiled. The book seith: that "no wight retourneth saufly in-to the grace of his olde enemy." And Isope seith: "ne trust nat to hem to whiche thou hast had som-tyme werre or enmitee, ne telle hem nat thy conseil." And Seneca telleth the cause why. "It may nat be," seith he, "that, where greet fyr hath longe tyme endured, that ther ne dwelleth som vapour of warmnesse." And therfore seith Salomon: "in thyn olde foo trust never." For sikerly, though thyn enemy be reconsiled and maketh thee chere of humilitee, and louteth to thee with his heed, ne trust him never. For certes, he maketh thilke feyned humilitee more for his profit than for any love of thy persone; by-cause that he demeth to have victorie over thy persone by swich feyned contenance, the which victorie he mighte nat have by stryf or werre. And Peter Alfonce seith: "make no felawshipe with thyne olde enemys; for if thou do hem bountee, they wol perverten it in-to wikkednesse." And eek thou most eschewe the conseilling of hem that been thy servants, and beren thee greet reverence; for peraventure they seyn it more for drede than for love. And therfore seith a philosophre in this wyse: "ther is no wight parfitly trewe to him that he to sore dredeth." And Tullius seith: "ther nis no might so greet of any emperour, that longe may endure, but-if he have more love of the peple than drede." Thou shalt also eschewe the conseiling of folk that been dronkelewe; for they ne can no conseil hyde. For Salomon seith: "ther is no privetee ther-as regneth dronkenesse." Ye shul also han in suspect the conseilling of swich folk as conseille yow a thing prively, and conseille yow the contrarie openly. For Cassidorie seith: that "it is a maner sleighte to hindre, whan he sheweth to doon a thing openly and werketh prively the contrarie." Thou shalt also have in suspect the conseilling of wikked folk. For the book seith: "the conseilling of wikked folk is alwey ful of fraude:" And David seith: "blisful is that man that hath nat folwed the conseilling of shrewes." Thou shalt also eschewe the conseilling of yong folk; for hir conseil is nat rype.

§ 24. Now sir, sith I have shewed yow of which folk ye shul take your conseil, and of which folk ye shul folwe the conseil, now wol I teche yow how ye shal examine your conseil, after the doctrine of Tullius. In the examininge thanne of your conseillour, ye shul considere manye thinges. Alderfirst thou shalt considere, that in thilke thing that thou purposest, and upon what thing thou wolt have conseil, that verray trouthe be seyd and conserved; this is to seyn, telle trewely thy tale. For he that seith fals may nat wel be conseilled, in that cas of which he lyeth. And after this, thou shalt considere the thinges that acorden to that thou purposest for to do by thy conseillours, if resoun accorde therto; and eek, if thy might may atteine ther-to; and if the more part and the bettre part of thy conseillours acorde ther-to, or no. Thanne shaltou considere what thing shal folwe of that conseilling; as hate, pees, werre, grace, profit, or damage; and manye othere thinges. And in alle thise thinges thou shalt chese the beste, and weyve alle othere thinges. Thanne shaltow considere of what rote is engendred the matere of thy conseil, and what fruit it may conceyve and engendre. Thou shalt eek considere alle thise causes, fro whennes they been sprongen. And whan ye han examined your conseil as I have seyd, and which partie is the bettre and more profitable, and hast approved it by manye wyse folk and olde; thanne shaltou considere, if thou mayst parfourne it and maken of it a good ende. For certes, resoun wol nat that any man sholde biginne a thing, but-if he mighte parfourne it as him oghte. Ne no wight sholde take up-on hym so hevy a charge that he mighte nat bere it. For the proverbe seith: "he that to muche embraceth, distreyneth litel." And Catoun seith: "assay to do swich thing as thou hast power to doon, lest that the charge oppresse thee so sore, that thee bihoveth to weyve thing that thou hast bigonne." And if so be that thou be in doute, whether thou mayst parfourne a thing or noon, chese rather to suffre than biginne. And Piers Alphonce seith: "if thou hast might to doon a thing of which thou most repente thee, it is bettre 'nay' than 'ye';" this is to seyn, that thee is bettre holde thy tonge stille, than for to speke. Thanne may ye understonde by strenger resons, that if thou hast power to parfourne a werk of which thou shalt repente, thanne is it bettre that thou suffre than biginne. Wel seyn they, that defenden every wight to assaye any thing of which he is in doute, whether he may parfourne it or no. And after, whan ye han examined your conseil as I have seyd biforn, and knowen wel that ye may parfourne youre emprise, conferme it thanne sadly til it be at an ende.

§ 25. Now is it resoun and tyme that I shewe yow, whanne, and wherfore, that ye may chaunge your conseil with-outen your repreve. Soothly, a man may chaungen his purpos and his conseil if the cause cesseth, or whan a newe caas bitydeth. For the lawe seith: that "upon thinges that newely bityden bihoveth newe conseil." And Senek seith: "if thy conseil is comen to the eres of thyn enemy, chaunge thy conseil." Thou mayst also chaunge thy conseil if so be that thou finde that, by errour or by other cause, harm or damage may bityde. Also, if thy conseil be dishonest, or elles cometh of dishoneste cause, chaunge thy conseil. For the lawes seyn: that "alle bihestes that been dishoneste been of no value." And eek, if it so be that it be inpossible, or may nat goodly be parfourned or kept.

§ 26. And take this for a general reule, that every conseil that is affermed so strongly that it may nat be chaunged, for no condicioun that may bityde, I seye that thilke conseil is wikked.'

§ 27. This Melibeus, whanne he hadde herd the doctrine of his wyf dame Prudence, answerde in this wyse. 'Dame,' quod he, 'as yet in-to this tyme ye han wel and covenably taught me as in general, how I shal governe me in the chesinge and in the withholdinge of my conseillours. But now wolde I fayn that ye wolde condescende in especial, and telle me how lyketh yow, or what semeth yow, by our conseillours that we han chosen in our present nede.'

§ 28. 'My lord,' quod she, 'I biseke yow in al humblesse, that ye wol nat wilfully replye agayn my resouns, ne distempre your herte thogh I speke thing that yow displese. For god wot that, as in myn entente, I speke it for your beste, for your honour and for your profite eke. And soothly, I hope that your benignitee wol taken it in pacience. Trusteth me wel,' quod she, 'that your conseil as in this caas ne sholde nat, as to speke properly, be called a conseilling, but a mocioun or a moevyng of folye; in which conseil ye han erred in many a sondry wyse.

§ 29. First and forward, ye han erred in th'assemblinge of your conseillours. For ye sholde first have cleped a fewe folk to your conseil, and after ye mighte han shewed it to mo folk, if it hadde been nede. But certes, ye han sodeynly cleped to your conseil a greet multitude of peple, ful chargeant and ful anoyous for to here. Also ye han erred, for there-as ye sholden only have cleped to your conseil your trewe freendes olde and wyse, ye han y-cleped straunge folk, and yong folk, false flatereres, and enemys reconsiled, and folk that doon yow reverence withouten love. And eek also ye have erred, for ye han broght with yow to your conseil ire, covetise, and hastifnesse; the whiche three thinges been contrariouse to every conseil honeste and profitable; the whiche three thinges ye han nat anientissed or destroyed hem, neither in your-self ne in your conseillours, as yow oghte. Ye han erred also, for ye han shewed to your conseillours your talent, and your affeccioun to make werre anon and for to do vengeance; they han espyed by your wordes to what thing ye been enclyned. And therfore han they rather conseilled yow to your talent than to your profit. Ye han erred also, for it semeth that yow suffyseth to han been conseilled by thise conseillours only, and with litel avys; wher-as, in so greet and so heigh a nede, it hadde been necessarie mo conseillours, and more deliberacioun to parfourne your emprise. Ye han erred also, for ye han nat examined your conseil in the forseyde manere, ne in due manere as the caas requireth. Ye han erred also, for ye han maked no divisioun bitwixe your conseillours; this is to seyn, bitwixen your trewe freendes and your feyned conseillours; ne ye han nat knowe the wil of your trewe freendes olde and wyse; but ye han cast alle hir wordes in an hochepot, and enclyned your herte to the more part and to the gretter nombre; and ther been ye condescended. And sith ye wot wel that men shal alwey finde a gretter nombre of foles than of wyse men, and therfore the conseils that been at congregaciouns and multitudes of folk, ther-as men take more reward to the nombre than to the sapience of persones, ye see wel that in swiche conseillinges foles han the maistrie.' Melibeus answerde agayn, and seyde: 'I graunte wel that I have erred; but ther as thou hast told me heer-biforn, that he nis nat to blame that chaungeth hise conseillours in certein caas, and for certeine juste causes, I am al redy to chaunge my conseillours, right as thou wolt devyse. The proverbe seith: that "for to do sinne is mannish, but certes for to persevere longe in sinne is werk of the devel."'

§ 30. To this sentence answerde anon dame Prudence, and seyde: 'Examineth,' quod she, 'your conseil, and lat us see the whiche of hem han spoken most resonably, and taught yow best conseil. And for-as-muche as that the examinacioun is necessarie, lat us biginne at the surgiens and at the phisiciens, that first speken in this matere. I sey yow, that the surgiens and phisiciens han seyd yow in your conseil discreetly, as hem oughte; and in hir speche seyden ful wysly, that to the office of hem aperteneth to doon to every wight honour and profit, and no wight for to anoye; and, after hir craft, to doon greet diligence un-to the cure of hem whiche that they han in hir governaunce. And sir, right as they han answered wysly and discreetly, right so rede I that they been heighly and sovereynly guerdoned for hir noble speche; and eek for they sholde do the more ententif bisinesse in the curacioun of your doghter dere. For al-be-it so that they been your freendes, therfore shal ye nat suffren that they serve yow for noght; but ye oghte the rather guerdone hem and shewe hem your largesse. And as touchinge the proposicioun which that the phisiciens entreteden in this caas, this is to seyn, that, in maladyes, that oon contrarie is warisshed by another contrarie, I wolde fayn knowe how ye understonde thilke text, and what is your sentence.' 'Certes,' quod Melibeus, 'I understonde it in this wyse: that, right as they han doon me a contrarie, right so sholde I doon hem another. For right as they han venged hem on me and doon me wrong, right so shal I venge me upon hem and doon hem wrong; and thanne have I cured oon contrarie by another.'

§ 31. 'Lo, lo!' quod dame Prudence, 'how lightly is every man enclyned to his owene desyr and to his owene plesaunce! Certes,' quod she, 'the wordes of the phisiciens ne sholde nat han been understonden in this wyse. For certes, wikkednesse is nat contrarie to wikkednesse, ne vengeaunce to vengeaunce, ne wrong to wrong; but they been semblable. And therfore, o vengeaunce is nat warisshed by another vengeaunce, ne o wrong by another wrong; but everich of hem encreesceth and aggreggeth other. But certes, the wordes of the phisiciens sholde been understonden in this wyse: for good and wikkednesse been two contraries, and pees and werre, vengeaunce and suffraunce, discord and accord, and manye othere thinges. But certes, wikkednesse shal be warisshed by goodnesse, discord by accord, werre by pees, and so forth of othere thinges. And heerto accordeth Seint Paul the apostle in manye places. He seith: "ne yeldeth nat harm for harm, ne wikked speche for wikked speche; but do wel to him that dooth thee harm, and blesse him that seith to thee harm." And in manye othere places he amonesteth pees and accord. But now wol I speke to yow of the conseil which that was yeven to yow by the men of lawe and the wyse folk, that seyden alle by oon accord as ye han herd bifore; that, over alle thynges, ye sholde doon your diligence to kepen your persone and to warnestore your hous. And seyden also, that in this caas ye oghten for to werken ful avysely and with greet deliberacioun. And sir, as to the firste point, that toucheth to the keping of your persone; ye shul understonde that he that hath werre shal evermore mekely and devoutly preyen biforn alle thinges, that Jesus Crist of his grete mercy wol han him in his proteccioun, and been his sovereyn helping at his nede. For certes, in this world ther is no wight that may be conseilled ne kept suffisantly withouten the keping of our lord Jesu Crist. To this sentence accordeth the prophete David, that seith: "if god ne kepe the citee, in ydel waketh he that it kepeth." Now sir, thanne shul ye committe the keping of your persone to your trewe freendes that been approved and y-knowe; and of hem shul ye axen help your persone for to kepe. For Catoun seith: "if thou hast nede of help, axe it of thy freendes; for ther nis noon so good a phisicien as thy trewe freend." And after this, thanne shul ye kepe yow fro alle straunge folk, and fro lyeres, and have alwey in suspect hir companye. For Piers Alfonce seith: "ne tak no companye by the weye of a straunge man, but-if so be that thou have knowe him of a lenger tyme. And if so be that he falle in-to thy companye paraventure withouten thyn assent, enquere thanne, as subtilly as thou mayst, of his conversacioun and of his lyf bifore, and feyne thy wey; seye that thou goost thider as thou wolt nat go; and if he bereth a spere, hold thee on the right syde, and if he bere a swerd, hold thee on the lift syde." And after this, thanne shul ye kepe yow wysely from alle swich manere peple as I have seyd bifore, and hem and hir conseil eschewe. And after this, thanne shul ye kepe yow in swich manere, that for any presumpcioun of your strengthe, that ye ne dispyse nat ne acounte nat the might of your adversarie so litel, that ye lete the keping of your persone for your presumpcioun; for every wys man dredeth his enemy. And Salomon seith: "weleful is he that of alle hath drede; for certes, he that thurgh the hardinesse of his herte and thurgh the hardinesse of him-self hath to greet presumpcioun, him shal yvel bityde." Thanne shul ye evermore countrewayte embusshements and alle espiaille. For Senek seith: that "the wyse man that dredeth harmes escheweth harmes; ne he ne falleth in-to perils, that perils escheweth." And al-be-it so that it seme that thou art in siker place, yet shaltow alwey do thy diligence in kepinge of thy persone; this is to seyn, ne be nat necligent to kepe thy persone, nat only fro thy gretteste enemys but fro thy leeste enemy. Senek seith: "a man that is wel avysed, he dredeth his leste enemy." Ovide seith: that "the litel wesele wol slee the grete bole and the wilde hert." And the book seith: "a litel thorn may prikke a greet king ful sore; and an hound wol holde the wilde boor." But nathelees, I sey nat thou shalt be so coward that thou doute ther wher-as is no drede. The book seith: that "somme folk han greet lust to deceyve, but yet they dreden hem to be deceyved." Yet shaltou drede to been empoisoned, and kepe yow from the companye of scorneres. For the book seith: "with scorneres make no companye, but flee hir wordes as venim."

§ 32. Now as to the seconde point, wher-as your wyse conseillours conseilled yow to warnestore your hous with gret diligence, I wolde fayn knowe, how that ye understonde thilke wordes, and what is your sentence.'

§ 33. Melibeus answerde and seyde, 'Certes I understande it in this wise; that I shal warnestore myn hous with toures, swiche as han castelles and othere manere edifices, and armure and artelleries, by whiche thinges I may my persone and myn hous so kepen and defenden, that myne enemys shul been in drede myn hous for to approche.'

§ 34. To this sentence answerde anon Prudence; 'warnestoring,' quod she, 'of heighe toures and of grete edifices apperteneth som-tyme to pryde; and eek men make heighe toures and grete edifices with grete costages and with greet travaille; and whan that they been accompliced, yet be they nat worth a stree, but-if they be defended by trewe freendes that been olde and wyse. And understond wel, that the gretteste and strongeste garnison that a riche man may have, as wel to kepen his persone as hise goodes, is that he be biloved amonges his subgets and with hise neighebores. For thus seith Tullius: that "ther is a maner garnison that no man may venquisse ne disconfite, and that is, a lord to be biloved of hise citezeins and of his peple."

§ 35. Now sir, as to the thridde point; wher-as your olde and wise conseillours seyden, that yow ne oghte nat sodeynly ne hastily proceden in this nede, but that yow oghte purveyen and apparaillen yow in this caas with greet diligence and greet deliberacioun; trewely, I trowe that they seyden right wysly and right sooth. For Tullius seith, "in every nede, er thou biginne it, apparaille thee with greet diligence." Thanne seye I, that in vengeance-taking, in werre, in bataille, and in warnestoring, er thow biginne, I rede that thou apparaille thee ther-to, and do it with greet deliberacioun. For Tullius seith: that "long apparailling biforn the bataille maketh short victorie." And Cassidorus seith: "the garnison is stronger whan it is longe tyme avysed."

§ 36. But now lat us speken of the conseil that was accorded by your neighebores, swiche as doon yow reverence withouten love, your olde enemys reconsiled, your flatereres that conseilled yow certeyne thinges prively, and openly conseilleden yow the contrarie; the yonge folk also, that conseilleden yow to venge yow and make werre anon. And certes, sir, as I have seyd biforn, ye han greetly erred to han cleped swich maner folk to your conseil; which conseillours been y-nogh repreved by the resouns aforeseyd. But nathelees, lat us now descende to the special. Ye shuln first procede after the doctrine of Tullius. Certes, the trouthe of this matere or of this conseil nedeth nat diligently enquere; for it is wel wist whiche they been that han doon to yow this trespas and vileinye, and how manye trespassours, and in what manere they han to yow doon al this wrong and al this vileinye. And after this, thanne shul ye examine the seconde condicioun, which that the same Tullius addeth in this matere. For Tullius put a thing, which that he clepeth "consentinge," this is to seyn; who been they and how manye, and whiche been they, that consenteden to thy conseil, in thy wilfulnesse to doon hastif vengeance. And lat us considere also who been they, and how manye been they, and whiche been they, that consenteden to your adversaries. And certes, as to the firste poynt, it is wel knowen whiche folk been they that consenteden to your hastif wilfulnesse; for trewely, alle tho that conseilleden yow to maken sodeyn werre ne been nat your freendes. Lat us now considere whiche been they, that ye holde so greetly your freendes as to your persone. For al-be-it so that ye be mighty and riche, certes ye ne been nat but allone. For certes, ye ne han no child but a doghter; ne ye ne han bretheren ne cosins germayns, ne noon other neigh kinrede, wherfore that your enemys, for drede, sholde stinte to plede with yow or to destroye your persone. Ye knowen also, that your richesses moten been dispended in diverse parties; and whan that every wight hath his part, they ne wollen taken but litel reward to venge thy deeth. But thyne enemys been three, and they han manie children, bretheren, cosins, and other ny kinrede; and, though so were that thou haddest slayn of hem two or three, yet dwellen ther y-nowe to wreken hir deeth and to slee thy persone. And though so be that your kinrede be more siker and stedefast than the kin of your adversarie, yet nathelees your kinrede nis but a fer kinrede; they been but litel sib to yow, and the kin of your enemys been ny sib to hem. And certes, as in that, hir condicioun is bet than youres. Thanne lat us considere also if the conseilling of hem that conseilleden yow to taken sodeyn vengeaunce, whether it accorde to resoun? And certes, ye knowe wel "nay." For as by right and resoun, ther may no man taken vengeance on no wight, but the juge that hath the jurisdiccioun of it, whan it is graunted him to take thilke vengeance, hastily or attemprely, as the lawe requireth. And yet more-over, of thilke word that Tullius clepeth "consentinge," thou shalt considere if thy might and thy power may consenten and suffyse to thy wilfulnesse and to thy conseillours. And certes, thou mayst wel seyn that "nay." For sikerly, as for to speke proprely, we may do no-thing but only swich thing as we may doon rightfully. And certes, rightfully ne mowe ye take no vengeance as of your propre auctoritee. Thanne mowe ye seen, that your power ne consenteth nat ne accordeth nat with your wilfulnesse. Lat us now examine the thridde point that Tullius clepeth "consequent." Thou shalt understonde that the vengeance that thou purposest for to take is the consequent. And ther-of folweth another vengeaunce, peril, and werre; and othere damages with-oute nombre, of whiche we be nat war as at this tyme. And as touchinge the fourthe point, that Tullius clepeth "engendringe," thou shalt considere, that this wrong which that is doon to thee is engendred of the hate of thyne enemys; and of the vengeance-takinge upon that wolde engendre another vengeance, and muchel sorwe and wastinge of richesses, as I seyde.

§ 37. Now sir, as to the point that Tullius clepeth "causes," which that is the laste point, thou shalt understonde that the wrong that thou hast receyved hath certeine causes, whiche that clerkes clepen *Oriens* and *Efficiens*, and *Causa longinqua* and *Causa propinqua*; this is to seyn, the fer cause and the ny cause. The fer cause is almighty god, that is cause of alle thinges. The neer cause is thy three enemys. The cause accidental was hate. The cause material been the fyve woundes of thy doghter. The cause formal is the manere of hir werkinge, that broghten laddres and cloumben in at thy windowes. The cause final was for to slee thy doghter; it letted nat in as muche as in hem was. But for to speken of the fer cause, as to what ende they shul come, or what shal finally bityde of hem in this caas, ne can I nat deme but by conjectinge and by supposinge. For we shul suppose that they shul come to a wikked ende, by-cause that the Book of Decrees seith: "selden or with greet peyne been causes y-broght to good ende whanne they been baddely bigonne."

§ 38. Now sir, if men wolde axe me, why that god suffred men to do yow this vileinye, certes, I can nat wel answere as for no sothfastnesse. For th'apostle seith, that "the sciences and the juggementz of our lord god almighty been ful depe; ther may no man comprehende ne serchen hem suffisantly." Nathelees, by certeyne presumpcions and conjectinges, I holde and bileve that god, which that is ful of justice and of rightwisnesse, hath suffred this bityde by juste cause resonable.

§ 39. Thy name is Melibee, this is to seyn, "a man that drinketh hony." Thou hast y-dronke so muchel hony of swete temporel richesses and delices and honours of this world, that thou art dronken; and hast forgeten Jesu Crist thy creatour; thou ne hast nat doon to him swich honour and reverence as thee oughte. Ne thou ne hast nat wel y-taken kepe to the wordes of Ovide, that seith: "under the hony of the godes of the body is hid the venim that sleeth the soule." And Salomon seith, "if thou hast founden hony, ete of it that suffyseth; for if thou ete of it out of mesure, thou shalt spewe," and be nedy and povre. And peraventure Crist hath thee in despit, and hath turned awey fro thee his face and hise eres of misericorde; and also he hath suffred that thou hast been punisshed in the manere that thow hast y-trespassed. Thou hast doon sinne agayn our lord Crist; for certes, the three enemys of mankinde, that is to seyn, the flessh, the feend, and the world, thou hast suffred hem entre in-to thyn herte wilfully by the windowes of thy body, and hast nat defended thyself suffisantly agayns hir assautes and hir temptaciouns, so that they han wounded thy soule in fyve places; this is to seyn, the deedly sinnes that been entred in-to thyn herte by thy fyve wittes. And in the same manere our lord Crist hath wold and suffred, that thy three enemys been entred in-to thyn hous by the windowes, and han y-wounded thy doghter in the fore-seyde manere.'

§ 40. 'Certes,' quod Melibee, 'I see wel that ye enforce yow muchel by wordes to overcome me in swich manere, that I shal nat venge me of myne enemys; shewinge me the perils and the yveles that mighten falle of this vengeance. But who-so wolde considere in alle vengeances the perils and yveles that mighte sewe of vengeance-takinge, a man wolde never take vengeance, and that were harm; for by the vengeance-takinge been the wikked men dissevered fro the gode men. And they that han wil to do wikkednesse restreyne hir wikked purpos, whan they seen the punissinge and chastysinge of the trespassours.' [And to this answerde dame Prudence: 'Certes,' seyde she, 'I graunte wel that of vengeaunce cometh muchel yvel and muchel good; but vengeaunce-taking aperteneth nat unto everichoon, but only unto juges and unto hem that han jurisdiccioun upon the trespassours.] And yet seye I more, that right as a singuler persone sinneth in takinge vengeance of another man, right so sinneth the juge if he do no vengeance of hem that it han deserved. For Senek seith thus: "that maister," he seith, "is good that proveth shrewes." And as Cassidore seith: "A man dredeth to do outrages, whan he woot and knoweth that it displeseth to the juges and sovereyns." And another seith: "the juge that dredeth to do right, maketh men shrewes." And Seint Paule the apostle seith in his epistle, whan he wryteth un-to the Romayns: that "the juges beren nat the spere with-outen cause;" but they beren it to punisse the shrewes and misdoeres, and for to defende the gode men. If ye wol thanne take vengeance of your enemys, ye shul retourne or have your recours to the juge that hath the jurisdiccion up-on hem; and he shal punisse hem as the lawe axeth and requyreth.'

§ 41. 'A!' quod Melibee, 'this vengeance lyketh me no-thing. I bithenke me now and take hede, how fortune hath norissed me fro my childhede, and hath holpen me to passe many a strong pas. Now wol I assayen hir, trowinge, with goddes help, that she shal helpe me my shame for to venge.'

§ 42. 'Certes,' quod Prudence, 'if ye wol werke by my conseil, ye shul nat assaye fortune by no wey; ne ye shul nat lene or bowe unto hir, after the word of Senek: for "thinges that been folily doon, and that been in hope of fortune, shullen never come to good ende." And as the same Senek seith: "the more cleer and the more shyning that fortune is, the more brotil and the sonner broken she is." Trusteth nat in hir, for she nis nat stidefast ne stable; for whan thow trowest to be most seur or siker of hir help, she wol faille thee and deceyve thee. And wheras ye seyn that fortune hath norissed yow fro your childhede, I seye, that in so muchel shul ye the lasse truste in hir and in hir wit. For Senek seith: "what man that is norissed by fortune, she maketh him a greet fool." Now thanne, sin ye desyre and axe vengeance, and the vengeance that is doon after the lawe and bifore the juge ne lyketh yow nat, and the vengeance that is doon in hope of fortune is perilous and uncertein, thanne have ye noon other remedie but for to have your recours unto the sovereyn juge that vengeth alle vileinyes and wronges; and he shal venge yow after that him-self witnesseth, wher-as he seith: "leveth the vengeance to me, and I shal do it."'

§ 43. Melibee answerde, 'if I ne venge me nat of the vileinye that men han doon to me, I sompne or warne hem that han doon to me that vileinye and alle othere, to do me another vileinye. For it is writen: "if thou take no vengeance of an old vileinye, thou sompnest thyne adversaries to do thee a newe vileinye." And also, for my suffrance, men wolden do to me so muchel vileinye, that I mighte neither bere it ne sustene; and so sholde I been put and holden over lowe. For men seyn: "in muchel suffringe shul manye thinges falle un-to thee whiche thou shalt nat mowe suffre."'

§ 44. 'Certes,' quod Prudence, 'I graunte yow that over muchel suffraunce nis nat good; but yet ne folweth it nat ther-of, that every persone to whom men doon vileinye take of it vengeance; for that aperteneth and longeth al only to the juges, for they shul venge the vileinyes and iniuries. And ther-fore tho two auctoritees that ye han seyd above, been only understonden in the juges; for whan they suffren over muchel the wronges and the vileinyes to be doon withouten punisshinge, they sompne nat a man al only for to do newe wronges, but they comanden it. Also a wys man seith: that "the juge that correcteth nat the sinnere comandeth and biddeth him do sinne." And the juges and sovereyns mighten in hir land so muchel suffre of the shrewes and misdoeres, that they sholden by swich suffrance, by proces of tyme, wexen of swich power and might, that they sholden putte out the juges and the sovereyns from hir places, and atte laste maken hem lesen hir lordshipes.

§ 45. But lat us now putte, that ye have leve to venge yow. I seye ye been nat of might and power as now to venge yow. For if ye wole maken comparisoun un-to the might of your adversaries, ye shul finde in manye thinges, that I have shewed yow er this, that hir condicioun is bettre than youres. And therfore seye I, that it is good as now that ye suffre and be pacient.

§ 46. Forther-more, ye knowen wel that, after the comune sawe, "it is a woodnesse a man to stryve with a strenger or a more mighty man than he is him-self; and for to stryve with a man of evene strengthe, that is to seyn, with as strong a man as he, it is peril; and for to stryve with a weyker man, it is folie." And therfore sholde a man flee stryvinge as muchel as he mighte. For Salomon seith: "it is a greet worship to a man to kepen him fro noyse and stryf." And if it so bifalle or happe that a man of gretter might and strengthe than thou art do thee grevaunce, studie and bisie thee rather to stille the same grevaunce, than for to venge thee. For Senek seith: that "he putteth him in greet peril that stryveth with a gretter man than he is him-self." And Catoun seith: "if a man of hyer estaat or degree, or more mighty than thou, do thee anoy or grevaunce, suffre him; for he that ones hath greved thee may another tyme releve thee and helpe." Yet sette I caas, ye have bothe might and licence for to venge yow. I seye, that ther be ful manye thinges that shul restreyne yow of vengeance-takinge, and make yow for to enclyne to suffre, and for to han pacience in the thinges that han been doon to yow. First and foreward, if ye wole considere the defautes that been in your owene persone, for whiche defautes god hath suffred yow have this tribulacioun, as I have seyd yow heer-biforn. For the poete seith, that "we oghte paciently taken the tribulacions that comen to us, whan we thinken and consideren that we han deserved to have hem." And Seint Gregorie seith: that "whan a man considereth wel the nombre of hise defautes and of his sinnes, the peynes and the tribulaciouns that he suffreth semen the lesse un-to hym; and in-as-muche as him thinketh hise sinnes more hevy and grevous, in-so-muche semeth his peyne the lighter and the esier un-to him." Also ye owen to enclyne and bowe your herte to take the pacience of our lord Jesu Crist, as seith seint Peter in hise epistles: "Jesu Crist," he seith, "hath suffred for us, and yeven ensample to every man to folwe and sewe him; for he dide never sinne, ne never cam ther a vileinous word out of his mouth: whan men cursed him, he cursed hem noght; and whan men betten him, he manaced hem noght." Also the grete pacience, which the seintes that been in paradys han had in tribulaciouns that they han y-suffred, with-outen hir desert or gilt, oghte muchel stiren yow to pacience. Forthermore, ye sholde enforce yow to have pacience, consideringe that the tribulaciouns of this world but litel whyle endure, and sone passed been and goon. And the joye that a man seketh to have by pacience in tribulaciouns is perdurable, after that the apostle seith in his epistle: "the joye of god," he seith, "is perdurable," that is to seyn, everlastinge. Also troweth and bileveth stedefastly, that he nis nat wel y-norissed ne wel y-taught, that can nat have pacience or wol nat receyve pacience. For Salomon seith: that "the doctrine and the wit of a man is knowen by pacience." And in another place he seith: that "he that is pacient governeth him by greet prudence." And the same Salomon seith: "the angry and wrathful man maketh noyses, and the pacient man atempreth hem and stilleth." He seith also: "it is more worth to be pacient than for to be right strong; and he that may have the lordshipe of his owene herte is more to preyse, than he that by his force or strengthe taketh grete citees." And therfore seith seint Jame in his epistle: that "pacience is a greet vertu of perfeccioun."'

§ 47. 'Certes,' quod Melibee, 'I graunte yow, dame Prudence, that pacience is a greet vertu of perfeccioun; but every man may nat have the perfeccioun that ye seken; ne I nam nat of the nombre of right parfite men, for myn herte may never been in pees un-to the tyme it be venged. And al-be-it so that it was greet peril to myne enemys, to do me a vileinye in takinge vengeance up-on me, yet token they noon hede of the peril, but fulfilleden hir wikked wil and hir corage. And therfore, me thinketh men oghten nat repreve me, though I putte me in a litel peril for to venge me, and though I do a greet excesse, that is to seyn, that I venge oon outrage by another.'

§ 48. 'A!' quod dame Prudence, 'ye seyn your wil and as yow lyketh; but in no caas of the world a man sholde nat doon outrage ne excesse for to vengen him. For Cassidore seith: that "as yvel doth he that vengeth him by outrage, as he that doth the outrage." And therfore ye shul venge yow after the ordre of right, that is to seyn by the lawe, and noght by excesse ne by outrage. And also, if ye wol venge yow of the outrage of your adversaries in other maner than right comandeth, ye sinnen; and therfore seith Senek: that "a man shal never vengen shrewednesse by shrewednesse." And if ye seye, that right axeth a man to defenden violence by violence, and fighting by fighting, certes ye seye sooth, whan the defense is doon anon with-outen intervalle or with-outen tarying or delay, for to defenden him and nat for to vengen him. And it bihoveth that a man putte swich attemperance in his defence, that men have no cause ne matere to repreven him that defendeth him of excesse and outrage; for elles were it agayn resoun. Pardee, ye knowen wel, that ye maken no defence as now for to defende yow, but for to venge yow; and so seweth it that ye han no wil to do your dede attemprely. And therfore, me thinketh that pacience is good. For

Salomon seith: that "he that is nat pacient shal have greet harm."'

§ 49. 'Certes,' quod Melibee, 'I graunte yow, that whan a man is inpacient and wroth, of that that toucheth him noght and that aperteneth nat un-to him, though it harme him, it is no wonder. For the lawe seith: that "he is coupable that entremetteth or medleth with swich thyng as aperteneth nat un-to him." And Salomon seith: that "he that entremetteth him of the noyse or stryf of another man, is lyk to him that taketh an hound by the eres." For right as he that taketh a straunge hound by the eres is outherwhyle biten with the hound, right in the same wyse is it resoun that he have harm, that by his inpacience medleth him of the noyse of another man, wher-as it aperteneth nat un-to him. But ye knowen wel that this dede, that is to seyn, my grief and my disese, toucheth me right ny. And therfore, though I be wroth and inpacient, it is no merveille. And savinge your grace, I can nat seen that it mighte greetly harme me though I toke vengeaunce; for I am richer and more mighty than myne enemys been. And wel knowen ye, that by moneye and by havinge grete possessions been all the thinges of this world governed. And Salomon seith: that "alle thinges obeyen to moneye."'

§ 50. Whan Prudence hadde herd hir housbonde avanten him of his richesse and of his moneye, dispreisinge the power of hise adversaries, she spak, and seyde in this wyse: 'certes, dere sir, I graunte yow that ye been rich and mighty, and that the richesses been goode to hem that han wel y-geten hem and wel conne usen hem. For right as the body of a man may nat liven withoute the soule, namore may it live withouten temporel goodes. And by richesses may a man gete him grete freendes. And therfore seith Pamphilles: "if a netherdes doghter," seith he, "be riche, she may chesen of a thousand men which she wol take to hir housbonde; for, of a thousand men, oon wol nat forsaken hir ne refusen hir." And this Pamphilles seith also: "if thou be right happy, that is to seyn, if thou be right riche, thou shalt find a greet nombre of felawes and freendes. And if thy fortune change that thou wexe povre, farewel freendshipe and felaweshipe; for thou shalt be allone with-outen any companye, but-if it be the companye of povre folk." And yet seith this Pamphilles moreover: that "they that been thralle and bond of linage shullen been maad worthy and noble by the richesses." And right so as by richesses ther comen manye goodes, right so by poverte come ther manye harmes and yveles. For greet poverte constreyneth a man to do manye yveles. And therfore clepeth Cassidore poverte "the moder of ruine," that is to seyn, the moder of overthrowinge or fallinge doun. And therfore seith Piers Alfonce: "oon of the gretteste adversitees of this world is whan a free man, by kinde or by burthe, is constreyned by poverte to eten the almesse of his enemy." And the same seith Innocent in oon of hise bokes; he seith: that "sorweful and mishappy is the condicioun of a povre begger; for if he axe nat his mete, he dyeth for hunger; and if he axe, he dyeth for shame; and algates necessitee constreyneth him to axe." And therfore seith Salomon: that "bet it is to dye than for to have swich poverte." And as the same Salomon seith: "bettre it is to dye of bitter deeth than for to liven in swich wyse." By thise resons that I have seid un-to yow, and by manye othere resons that I coude seye, I graunte yow that richesses been goode to hem that geten hem wel, and to hem that wel usen tho richesses. And therfore wol I shewe yow how ye shul have yow, and how ye shul bere yow in gaderinge of richesses, and in what manere ye shul usen hem.

§ 51. First, ye shul geten hem withouten greet desyr, by good leyser sokingly, and nat over hastily. For a man that is to desyringe to gete richesses abaundoneth him first to thefte and to alle other yveles. And therfore seith Salomon: "he that hasteth him to bisily to wexe riche shal be noon innocent." He seith also: that "the richesse that hastily cometh to a man, sone and lightly gooth and passeth fro a man; but that richesse that cometh litel and litel wexeth alwey and multiplyeth." And sir, ye shul geten richesses by your wit and by your travaille un-to your profit; and that with-outen wrong or harm-doinge to any other persone. For the lawe seith: that "ther maketh no man himselven riche, if he do harm to another wight"; this is to seyn, that nature defendeth and forbedeth by right, that no man make himself riche un-to the harm of another persone. And Tullius seith: that "no sorwe ne no drede of deeth, ne no-thing that may falle un-to a man is so muchel agayns nature, as a man to encressen his owene profit to the harm of another man. And though the grete men and the mighty men geten richesses more lightly than thou, yet shaltou nat been ydel ne slow to do thy profit; for thou shalt in alle wyse flee ydelnesse." For Salomon seith: that "ydelnesse techeth a man to do manye yveles." And the same Salomon seith: that "he that travailleth and bisieth him to tilien his land, shal eten breed; but he that is ydel and casteth him to no bisinesse ne occupacioun, shal falle in-to poverte, and dye for hunger." And he that is ydel and slow can never finde covenable tyme for to doon his profit. For ther is a versifiour seith: that "the ydel man excuseth hym in winter, by cause of the grete cold; and in somer, by enchesoun of the hete." For thise causes seith Caton: "waketh and enclyneth nat yow over muchel for to slepe; for over muchel reste norisseth and causeth manye vices." And therfore seith seint Jerome: "doth somme gode dedes, that the devel which is our enemy ne finde yow nat unoccupied. For the devel ne taketh nat lightly un-to his werkinge swiche as he findeth occupied in gode werkes."

§ 52. Thanne thus, in getinge richesses, ye mosten flee ydelnesse. And afterward, ye shul use the richesses, whiche ye have geten by your wit and by your travaille, in swich a manere, that men holde nat yow to scars, ne to sparinge, ne to fool-large, that is to seyn, over-large a spender. For right as men blamen an avaricious man by-cause of his scarsetee and chincherye, in the same wyse is he to blame that spendeth over largely. And therfore seith Caton: "use," he seith, "thy richesses that thou hast geten in swich a manere, that men have no matere ne cause to calle thee neither wrecche ne chinche; for it is a greet shame to a man to have a povere herte and a riche purs." He seith also: "the goodes that thou hast y-geten, use hem by mesure," that is to seyn, spende hem mesurably; for they that folily wasten and despenden the goodes that they han, whan they han namore propre of hir owene, they shapen hem to take the goodes of another man. I seye thanne, that ye shul fleen avarice; usinge your richesses in swich manere, that men seye nat that your richesses been y-buried, but that ye have hem in your might and in your weeldinge. For a wys man repreveth the avaricious man, and seith thus, in two vers: "wher-to and why burieth a man hise goodes by his grete avarice, and knoweth wel that nedes moste he dye; for deeth is the ende of every man as in this present lyf." And for what cause or enchesoun joyneth he him or knitteth he him so faste un-to hise goodes, that alle his wittes mowen nat disseveren him or departen him from hise goodes; and knoweth wel, or oghte knowe, that whan he is deed, he shal no-thing bere with him out of this world? And ther-fore seith seint Augustin: that "the avaricious man is likned un-to helle; that the more it swelweth, the more desyr it hath to swelwe and devoure." And as wel as ye wolde eschewe to be called an avaricious man or chinche, as wel sholde ye kepe yow and governe yow in swich a wyse that men calle yow nat fool-large. Therfore seith Tullius: "the goodes," he seith, "of thyn hous ne sholde nat been hid, ne kept so cloos but that they mighte been opened by pitee and debonaire-tee"; that is to seyn, to yeven part to hem that han greet nede; "ne thy goodes shullen nat been so opene, to been every mannes goodes." Afterward, in getinge of your richesses and in usinge hem, ye shul alwey have three thinges in your herte; that is to seyn, our lord god, conscience, and good name. First, ye shul have god in your herte; and for no richesse ye shullen do no-thing, which may in any manere displese god, that is your creatour and maker. For after the word of Salomon: "it is bettre to have a litel good with the love of god, than to have muchel good and tresour, and lese the love of his lord god." And the prophete seith: that "bettre it is to been a good man and have litel good and tresour, than to been holden a shrewe and have grete richesses." And yet seye I ferthermore, that ye sholde alwey doon your bisinesse to gete yow richesses, so that ye gete hem with good conscience. And th'apostle seith: that "ther nis thing in this world, of which we sholden have so greet joye as whan our conscience bereth us good witnesse." And the wyse man seith: "the substance of a man is ful good, whan sinne is nat in mannes conscience." Afterward, in getinge of your richesses, and in usinge of hem, yow moste have greet bisinesse and greet diligence, that your goode name be alwey kept and conserved. For Salomon seith: that "bettre it is and more it availleth a man to have a good name, than for to have grete richesses." And therfore he seith in another place: "do greet diligence," seith Salomon, "in keping of thy freend and of thy gode name; for it shal lenger abide with thee than any tresour, be it never so precious." And certes he sholde nat be called a gentil man, that after god and good conscience, alle thinges left, ne dooth his diligence and bisinesse to kepen his good name. And Cassidore seith: that "it is signe of a gentil herte, whan a man loveth and desyreth to han a good name." And therfore seith seint Augustin: that "ther been two thinges that arn necessarie and nedefulle, and that is good conscience and good loos; that is to seyn, good conscience to thyn owene persone inward, and good loos for thy neighebore outward." And he that trusteth him so muchel in his gode conscience, that he displeseth and setteth at noght his gode name or loos, and rekketh noght though he kepe nat his gode name. nis but a cruel cherl.

§ 53. Sire, now have I shewed yow how ye shul do in getinge richesses, and how ye shullen usen hem; and I see wel, that for the trust that ye han in youre richesses, ye wole moeve werre and bataille. I conseille yow, that ye biginne no werre in trust of your richesses; for they ne suffysen noght werres to mayntene. And therfore seith a philosophre: "that man that desyreth and wole algates han werre, shal never have suffisaunce; for the richer that he is, the gretter despenses moste he make, if he wole have worship and victorie." And Salomon seith: that "the gretter richesses that a man hath, the mo despendours he hath." And dere sire, al-be-it so that for your richesses ye mowe have muchel folk, yet bihoveth it nat, ne it is nat good, to biginne werre, where-as ye mowe in other manere have pees, un-to your worship and profit. For the victories of batailles that been in this world, lyen nat in greet nombre or multitude of the peple ne in the vertu of man; but it lyth in the wil and in the hand of our lord god almighty. And therfore Judas Machabeus, which was goddes knight, whan he sholde fighte agayn his adversarie that hadde a greet nombre, and a gretter multitude of folk and strenger than was this peple of Machabee, yet he reconforted his litel companye, and seyde right in this wyse: "als lightly," quod he, "may our lord god almighty yeve victorie to a fewe folk as to many folk; for the victorie of bataile cometh nat by the grete nombre of peple, but it cometh from our lord god of hevene." And dere sir, for as muchel as there is no man certein, if he be worthy that god yeve him victorie, [namore than he is certein whether he be worthy of the love of god] or naught, after that Salomon seith, therfore every man sholde greetly drede werres to biginne. And by-cause that in batailles fallen manye perils, and happeth outher-while, that as sone is the grete man sleyn as the litel man; and, as it is written in the seconde book of Kinges, "the dedes of batailles been aventurouse and nothing certeyne; for as lightly is oon hurt with a spere as another." And for ther is gret peril in werre, therfore sholde a man flee and eschewe werre, in as muchel as a man may goodly. For Salomon seith: "he that loveth peril shal falle in peril."'

§ 54. After that Dame Prudence hadde spoken in this manere, Melibee answerde and seyde, 'I see wel, dame Prudence, that by your faire wordes and by your resons that ye han shewed me, that the werre lyketh yow no-thing; but I have nat yet herd your conseil, how I shal do in this nede.'

§ 55. 'Certes,' quod she, 'I conseille yow that ye accorde with youre adversaries, and that ye have pees with hem. For seint Jame seith in hise epistles: that "by concord and pees the smale richesses wexen grete, and by debaat and discord the grete richesses fallen doun." And ye knowen wel that oon of the gretteste and most sovereyn thing, that is in this world, is unitee and pees. And therfore seyde oure lord Jesu Crist to hise apostles in this wyse: "wel happy and blessed been they that loven and purchacen pees; for they been called children of god."' 'A!' quod Melibee, 'now see I wel that ye loven nat myn honour ne my worshipe. Ye knowen wel that myne adversaries han bigonnen this debaat and brige by hir outrage; and ye see wel that they ne requeren ne preyen me nat of pees, ne they asken nat to be reconsiled. Wol ye thanne that I go and meke me and obeye me to hem, and crye hem mercy? For sothe, that were nat my worship. For right as men seyn, that "over-greet homlinesse engendreth dispreysinge," so fareth it by to greet humylitee or mekenesse.'

§ 56. Thanne bigan dame Prudence to maken semblant of wratthe, and seyde, 'certes, sir, sauf your grace, I love your honour and your profit as I do myn owene, and ever have doon; ne ye ne noon other syen never the contrarie. And yit, if I hadde seyd that ye sholde han purchaced the pees and the reconsiliacioun, I ne hadde nat muchel mistaken me, ne seyd amis. For the wyse man seith: "the dissensioun biginneth by another man, and the reconsiling biginneth by thyself." And the prophete seith: "flee shrewednesse and do goodnesse; seke pees and folwe it, as muchel as in thee is." Yet seye I nat that ye shul rather pursue to your adversaries for pees than they shuln to yow; for I knowe wel that ye been so hard-herted, that ye wol do no-thing for me. And Salomon seith: "he that hath over-hard an herte, atte laste he shal mishappe and mistyde."'

§ 57. Whanne Melibee hadde herd dame Prudence maken semblant of wratthe, he seyde in this wyse, 'dame, I prey yow that ye be nat displesed of thinges that I seye; for ye knowe wel that I am angry and wrooth, and that is no wonder; and they that been wrothe witen nat wel what they doon, ne what they seyn. Therfore the prophete seith: that "troubled eyen han no cleer sighte." But seyeth and conseileth me as yow lyketh; for I am redy to do right as ye wol desyre; and if ye repreve me of my folye, I am the more holden to love yow and to preyse yow. For Salomon seith: that "he that repreveth him that doth folye, he shal finde gretter grace than he that deceyveth him by swete wordes."'

§ 58. Thanne seide dame Prudence, 'I make no semblant of wratthe ne anger but for your grete profit. For Salomon seith: "he is more worth, that repreveth or chydeth a fool for his folye, shewinge him semblant of wratthe, than he that supporteth him and preyseth him in his misdoinge, and laugheth at his folye." And this same Salomon seith afterward: that "by the sorweful visage of a man," that is to seyn, by the sory and hevy countenaunce of a man, "the fool correcteth and amendeth him-self."'

§ 59. Thanne seyde Melibee, 'I shal nat conne answere to so manye faire resouns as ye putten to me and shewen. Seyeth shortly your wil and your conseil, and I am al ready to fulfille and parfourne it.'

§ 60. Thanne dame Prudence discovered al hir wil to him, and seyde, 'I conseille yow,' quod she, 'aboven alle thinges, that ye make pees bitwene god and yow; and beth reconsiled un-to him and to his grace. For as I have seyd yow heer-biforn, god hath suffred yow to have this tribulacioun and disese for your sinnes. And if ye do as I sey yow, god wol sende your adversaries un-to yow, and maken hem fallen at your feet, redy to do your wil and your comandements. For Salomon seith: "whan the condicioun of man is plesaunt and likinge to god, he chaungeth the hertes of the mannes adversaries, and constreyneth hem to biseken him of pees and of grace." And I prey yow, lat me speke with your adversaries in privee place; for they shul nat knowe that it be of your wil or your assent. And thanne, whan I knowe hir wil and hir entente, I may conseille yow the more seurly.'

§ 61. 'Dame,' quod Melibee, 'dooth your wil and your lykinge, for I putte me hoolly in your disposicioun and ordinaunce.'

§ 62. Thanne Dame Prudence, whan she saugh the gode wil of her housbonde, delibered and took avys in hir-self, thinkinge how she mighte bringe this nede un-to a good conclusioun and to a good ende. And whan she saugh hir tyme, she sente for thise adversaries to come un-to hir in-to a privee place, and shewed wysly un-to hem the grete goodes that comen of pees, and the grete harmes and perils that been in werre; and seyde to hem in a goodly manere, how that hem oughte have greet repentaunce of the injurie and wrong that they hadden doon to Melibee hir lord, and to hir, and to hir doghter.

§ 63. And whan they herden the goodliche wordes of dame Prudence, they weren so surprised and ravisshed, and hadden so greet joye of hir, that wonder was to telle. 'A! lady!' quod they, 'ye han shewed un-to us "the blessinge of swetnesse," after the sawe of David the prophete; for the reconsilinge which we been nat worthy to have in no manere, but we oghte requeren it with greet contricioun and humilitee, ye of your grete goodnesse have presented unto us. Now see we wel that the science and the conninge of Salomon is ful trewe; for he seith: that "swete wordes multiplyen and encresen freendes, and maken shrewes to be debonaire and meke."

§ 64. 'Certes,' quod they, 'we putten our dede and al our matere and cause al hoolly in your goode wil; and been redy to obeye to the speche and comandement of my lord Melibee. And therfore, dere and benigne lady, we preyen yow and biseke yow as mekely as we conne and mowen, that it lyke un-to your grete goodnesse to fulfillen in dede your goodliche wordes; for we consideren and knowlichen that we han offended and greved my lord Melibee out of mesure; so ferforth, that we be nat of power to maken hise amendes. And therfore we oblige and binden us and our freendes to doon al his wil and hise comandements. But peraventure he hath swich hevinesse and swich wratthe to us-ward, by-cause of our offence, that he wole enjoyne us swich a peyne as we mowe nat bere ne sustene. And therfore, noble lady, we biseke to your wommanly pitee, to taken swich avysement in this nede, that we, ne our freendes, be nat desherited ne destroyed thurgh our folye.'

§ 65. 'Certes,' quod Prudence, 'it is an hard thing and right perilous, that a man putte him al outrely in the arbitracioun and juggement, and in the might and power of hise enemys. For Salomon seith: "leveth me, and yeveth credence to that I shal seyn; I seye," quod he, "ye peple, folk, and governours of holy chirche, to thy sone, to thy wyf, to thy freend, ne to thy brother ne yeve thou never might ne maistrie of thy body, whyl thou livest." Now sithen he defendeth, that man shal nat yeven to his brother ne to his freend the might of his body, by a strenger resoun he defendeth and forbedeth a man to yeven him-self to his enemy. And nathelees I conseille you, that ye mistruste nat my lord. For I woot wel and knowe verraily, that he is debonaire and meke, large, curteys, and nothing desyrous ne coveitous of good ne richesse. For ther nis no-thing in this world that he desyreth, save only worship and honour. Forther-more I knowe wel, and am right seur, that he shal no-thing doon in this nede with-outen my conseil. And I shal so werken in this cause, that, by grace of our lord god, ye shul been reconsiled un-to us.'

§ 66. Thanne seyden they with o vois, 'worshipful lady, we putten us and our goodes al fully in your wil and disposicioun; and been redy to comen, what day that it lyke un-to your noblesse to limite us or assigne us, for to maken our obligacioun and bond as strong as it lyketh un-to your goodnesse; that we mowe fulfille the wille of yow and of my lord Melibee.'

§ 67. Whan dame Prudence hadde herd the answeres of thise men, she bad hem goon agayn prively; and she retourned to hir lord Melibee, and tolde him how she fond hise adversaries ful repentant, knowlechinge ful lowely hir sinnes and trespas, and how they were redy to suffren al peyne, requiringe and preyinge him of mercy and pitee.

§ 68. Thanne seyde Melibee, 'he is wel worthy to have pardoun and foryifnesse of his sinne, that excuseth nat his sinne, but knowlecheth it and repenteth him, axinge indulgence. For Senek seith: "ther is the remissioun and foryifnesse, whereas confessioun is"; for confession is neighebore to innocence. And he seith in another place: "he that hath shame for his sinne and knowlecheth it, is worthy remissioun." And therfore I assente and conferme me to have pees; but it is good that we do it nat with-outen the assent and wil of our freendes.'

§ 69. Thanne was Prudence right glad and joyeful, and seyde, 'Certes, sir,' quod she, 'ye han wel and goodly answered. For right as by the conseil, assent, and help of your freendes, ye han been stired to venge yow and maken werre, right so with-outen hir conseil shul ye nat accorden yow, ne have pees with your adversaries. For the lawe seith: "ther nis no-thing so good by wey of kinde, as a thing to been unbounde by him that it was y-bounde."'

§ 70. And thanne dame Prudence, with-outen delay or taryinge, sente anon hir messages for hir kin, and for hir olde freendes whiche that were trewe and wyse, and tolde hem by ordre, in the presence of Melibee, al this matere as it is aboven expressed and declared;

and preyden hem that they wolde yeven hir avys and conseil, what best were to doon in this nede. And whan Melibees freendes hadde taken hir avys and deliberacioun of the forseide matere, and hadden examined it by greet bisinesse and greet diligence, they yave ful conseil for to have pees and reste; and that Melibee sholde receyve with good herte hise adversaries to foryifnesse and mercy.

§ 71. And whan dame Prudence hadde herd the assent of hir lord Melibee, and the conseil of hise freendes, accorde with hir wille and hir entencioun, she was wonderly glad in hir herte, and seyde: 'ther is an old proverbe,' quod she, 'seith: that "the goodnesse that thou mayst do this day, do it; and abyde nat ne delaye it nat til to-morwe." And therfore I conseille that ye sende your messages, swiche as been discrete and wyse, un-to your adversaries; tellinge hem, on your bihalve, that if they wole trete of pees and of accord, that they shape hem, with-outen delay or tarying, to comen un-to us.' Which thing parfourned was in dede. And whanne thise trespassours and repentinge folk of hir folies, that is to seyn, the adversaries of Melibee, hadden herd what thise messagers seyden un-to hem, they weren right glad and joyeful, and answereden ful mekely and benignely, yeldinge graces and thankinges to hir lord Melibee and to al his companye; and shopen hem, with-outen delay, to go with the messagers, and obeye to the comandement of hir lord Melibee.

§ 72. And right anon they token hir wey to the court of Melibee, and token with hem somme of hir trewe freendes, to maken feith for hem and for to been hir borwes. And whan they were comen to the presence of Melibee, he seyde hem thise wordes: 'it standeth thus,' quod Melibee, 'and sooth it is, that ye, causeless, and with-outen skile and resoun, han doon grete injuries and wronges to me and to my wyf Prudence, and to my doghter also. For ye han entred in-to myn hous by violence, and have doon swich outrage, that alle men knowen wel that ye have deserved the deeth;

and therfore wol I knowe and wite of yow, whether ye wol putte the punissement and the chastysinge and the vengeance of this outrage in the wil of me and of my wyf Prudence; or ye wol nat?'

§ 73. Thanne the wyseste of hem three answerde for hem alle, and seyde: 'sire,' quod he, 'we knowen wel, that we been unworthy to comen un-to the court of so greet a lord and so worthy as ye been. For we han so greetly mistaken us, and han offended and agilt in swich a wyse agayn your heigh lordshipe, that trewely we han deserved the deeth. But yet, for the grete goodnesse and debonairetee that all the world witnesseth of your persone, we submitten us to the excellence and benignitee of your gracious lordshipe, and been redy to obeie to alle your comandements; bisekinge yow, that of your merciable pitee ye wol considere our grete repentaunce and lowe submissioun, and graunten us foryevenesse of our outrageous trespas and offence. For wel we knowe, that your liberal grace and mercy strecchen hem ferther in-to goodnesse, than doon our outrageouse giltes and trespas in-to wikkednesse; al-be-it that cursedly and dampnably we han agilt agayn your heigh lordshipe.'

§ 74. Thanne Melibee took hem up fro the ground ful benignely, and receyved hir obligaciouns and hir bondes by hir othes up-on hir plegges and borwes, and assigned hem a certeyn day to retourne un-to his court, for to accepte and receyve the sentence and jugement that Melibee wolde comande to be doon on hem by the causes afore-seyd; whiche thinges ordeyned, every man retourned to his hous.

§ 75. And whan that dame Prudence saugh hir tyme, she freyned and axed hir lord Melibee, what vengeance he thoughte to taken of hise adversaries?

§ 76. To which Melibee answerde and seyde, 'certes,' quod he, 'I thinke and purpose me fully to desherite hem of al that ever they han, and for to putte hem in exil for ever.'

§ 77. 'Certes,' quod dame Prudence, 'this were a cruel sentence, and muchel agayn resoun. For ye been riche y-nough, and han no nede of other mennes good; and ye mighte lightly in this wyse gete yow a coveitous name, which is a vicious thing, and oghte been eschewed of every good man. For after the sawe of the word of the apostle: "coveitise is rote of alle harmes." And therfore, it were bettre for yow to lese so muchel good of your owene, than for to taken of hir good in this manere. For bettre it is to lesen good with worshipe, than it is to winne good with vileinye and shame. And every man oghte to doon his diligence and his bisinesse to geten him a good name. And yet shal he nat only bisie him in kepinge of his good name, but he shal also enforcen him alwey to do som-thing by which he may renovelle his good name; for it is writen, that "the olde good loos or good name of a man is sone goon and passed, whan it is nat newed ne renovelled." And as touchinge that ye seyn, ye wole exile your adversaries, that thinketh me muchel agayn resoun and out of mesure, considered the power that they han yeve yow up-on hem-self. And it is writen, that "he is worthy to lesen his privilege that misuseth the might and the power that is yeven him." And I sette cas ye mighte enjoyne hem that peyne by right and by lawe, which I trowe ye mowe nat do, I seye, ye mighte nat putten it to execucioun peraventure, and thanne were it lykly to retourne to the werre as it was biforn. And therfore, if ye wole that men do yow obeisance, ye moste demen more curteisly; this is to seyn, ye moste yeven more esy sentences and jugements. For it is writen, that "he that most curteisly comandeth, to him men most obeyen." And therfore, I prey yow that in this necessitee and in this nede, ye caste yow to overcome your herte. For Senek seith: that "he that overcometh his herte, overcometh twyes." And Tullius seith: "ther is no-thing so comendable in a greet lord as whan he is debonaire and meke, and appeseth him lightly." And I prey yow that ye wol forbere now to do vengeance, in swich a manere, that your goode name may be kept and conserved; and that men mowe have cause and matere to preyse yow of pitee and of mercy; and that ye have no cause to repente yow of thing that ye doon. For Senek seith: "he overcometh in an yvel manere, that repenteth him of his victorie." Wherfore I pray yow, lat mercy been in your minde and in your herte, to th'effect and entente that god almighty have mercy on yow in his laste jugement. For seint Jame seith in his epistle: "jugement withouten mercy shal be doon to him, that hath no mercy of another wight."'

§ 78. Whanne Melibee hadde herd the grete skiles and resouns of dame Prudence, and hir wise informaciouns and techinges, his herte gan enclyne to the wil of his wyf, consideringe hir trewe entente; and conformed him anon, and assented fully to werken after hir conseil; and thonked god, of whom procedeth al vertu and alle goodnesse, that him sente a wyf of so greet discrecioun. And whan the day cam that hise adversaries sholde apperen in his presence, he spak unto hem ful goodly, and seyde in this wyse: 'al-be-it so that of your pryde and presumpcioun and folie, and of your necligence and unconninge, ye have misborn yow and trespassed un-to me; yet, for as much as I see and biholde your grete humilitee, and that ye been sory and repentant of your giltes, it constreyneth me to doon yow grace and mercy. Therfore I receyve yow to my grace, and foryeve yow outrely alle the offences, injuries, and wronges, that ye have doon agayn me and myne; to this effect and to this ende, that god of his endelees mercy wole at the tyme of our dyinge foryeven us our giltes that we han trespassed to him in this wrecched world. For doutelees, if we be sory and repentant of the sinnes and giltes whiche we han trespassed in the sighte of our lord god, he is so free and so merciable, that he wole foryeven us our giltes, and bringen us to his blisse that never hath ende. Amen.'

Here is ended Chaucers Tale of Melibee and of Dame Prudence.

THE MONKES TALE

The mery wordes of the Host to the Monk.

Whan ended was my tale of Melibee,
And of Prudence and hir benignitee,
Our hoste seyde, 'as I am faithful man,
And by the precious *corpus Madrian,*
I hadde lever than a barel ale
That goode lief my wyf hadde herd this tale!
For she nis no-thing of swich pacience
As was this Melibeus wyf Prudence.
By goddes bones! whan I bete my knaves,
She bringth me forth the grete clobbed staves,
And cryeth, "slee the dogges everichoon,
And brek hem, bothe bak and every boon."
And if that any neighebor of myne
Wol nat in chirche to my wyf enclyne,
Or be so hardy to hir to trespace,
Whan she comth hoom, she rampeth in my face,
And cryeth, "false coward, wreek thy wyf!
By *corpus* bones! I wol have thy knyf,
And thou shalt have my distaf and go spinne!"
Fro day to night right thus she wol biginne;—
"Allas!" she seith, "that ever I was shape
To wedde a milksop or a coward ape,
That wol be overlad with every wight!
Thou darst nat stonden by thy wyves right!"
This is my lyf, but-if that I wol fighte;
And out at dore anon I moot me dighte,
Or elles I am but lost, but-if that I
Be lyk a wilde leoun fool-hardy.

I woot wel she wol do me slee som day
Som neighebor, and thanne go my wey.
For I am perilous with knyf in honde,
Al be it that I dar nat hir withstonde,
For she is big in armes, by my feith,
That shal he finde, that hir misdooth or seith.
But lat us passe awey fro this matere.
 My lord the Monk,' quod he, 'be mery of chere;
For ye shul telle a tale trewely.
Lo! Rouchestre stant heer faste by!
Ryd forth, myn owene lord, brek nat our game,
But, by my trouthe, I knowe nat your name,
Wher shal I calle yow my lord dan John,
Or dan Thomas, or elles dan Albon?
Of what hous be ye, by your fader kin?
I vow to god, thou hast a ful fair skin,
It is a gentil pasture ther thou goost;
Thou art nat lyk a penaunt or a goost.
Upon my feith, thou art som officer,
Some worthy sexteyn, or som celerer,
For by my fader soule, as to my doom,
Thou art a maister whan thou art at hoom;
No povre cloisterer, ne no novys,
But a governour, wyly and wys.
And therwithal of brawnes and of bones
A wel-faring persone for the nones.
I pray to god, yeve him confusioun
That first thee broghte un-to religioun;
Thou woldest han been a trede-foul aright.
Haddestow as greet a leve, as thou hast might
To parfourne al thy lust in engendrure,
Thou haddest bigeten many a creature.
Alas! why werestow so wyd a cope?
God yeve me sorwe! but, and I were a pope,
Not only thou, but every mighty man,
Thogh he were shorn ful hye upon his pan,
Sholde have a wyf; for al the world is lorn!
Religioun hath take up al the corn
Of treding, and we borel men ben shrimpes!
Of feble trees ther comen wrecched impes.

This maketh that our heires been so sclendre
And feble, that they may nat wel engendre.
This maketh that our wyves wol assaye
Religious folk, for ye may bettre paye
Of Venus payements than mowe we ;
God woot, no lussheburghes payen ye !
But be nat wrooth, my lord, for that I pleye ;
Ful ofte in game a sooth I have herd seye.'
  This worthy monk took al in pacience,
And seyde, 'I wol doon al my diligence,
As fer as souneth in-to honestee,
To telle yow a tale, or two, or three.
And if yow list to herkne hiderward,
I wol yow seyn the lyf of seint Edward ;
Or elles first Tragedies wol I telle
Of whiche I have an hundred in my celle.
Tragedie is to seyn a certeyn storie,
As olde bokes maken us memorie,
Of him that stood in greet prosperitee
And is y-fallen out of heigh degree
Into miserie, and endeth wrecchedly.
And they ben versifyed comunly
Of six feet, which men clepe *exametron.*
In prose eek been endyted many oon,
And eek in metre, in many a sondry wyse.
Lo ! this declaring oughte y-nough suffise.
  Now herkneth, if yow lyketh for to here ;
But first I yow biseke in this matere,
Though I by ordre telle nat thise thinges,
Be it of popes, emperours, or kinges,
After hir ages, as men writen finde,
But telle hem som bifore and som bihinde,
As it now comth un-to my remembraunce ;
Have me excused of myn ignoraunce.'

Explicit.

Here biginneth the Monkes Tale, de Casibus Virorum Illustrium.

I WOL biwayle in maner of Tragedie
The harm of hem that stode in heigh degree,
And fillen so that ther nas no remedie
To bringe hem out of hir adversitee;
For certein, whan that fortune list to flee,
Ther may no man the cours of hir withholde;
Lat no man truste on blind prosperitee;
Be war by thise ensamples trewe and olde.

LUCIFER.

At Lucifer, though he an angel were,
And nat a man, at him I wol biginne;
For, thogh fortune may non angel dere,
From heigh degree yet fel he for his sinne
Doun in-to helle, wher he yet is inne.
O Lucifer! brightest of angels alle,
Now artow Sathanas, that maist nat twinne
Out of miserie, in which that thou art falle.

ADAM.

Lo Adam, in the feld of Damassene,
With goddes owene finger wroght was he,
And nat bigoten of mannes sperme unclene,
And welte al Paradys, saving o tree.
Had never worldly man so heigh degree
As Adam, til he for misgovernaunce
Was drive out of his hye prosperitee
To labour, and to helle, and to meschaunce.

SAMPSON.

Lo Sampson, which that was annunciat
By th'angel, longe er his nativitee,
And was to god almighty consecrat,
And stood in noblesse, whyl he mighte see.
Was never swich another as was he,
To speke of strengthe, and therwith hardinesse;
But to his wyves tolde he his secree,
Through which he slow him-self, for wrecchednesse.

Sampson, this noble almighty champioun,
Withouten wepen save his hondes tweye,
He slow and al to-rente the leoun,
Toward his wedding walking by the weye.
His false wyf coude him so plese and preye
Til she his conseil knew, and she untrewe
Un-to his foos his conseil gan biwreye,
And him forsook, and took another newe.

Three hundred foxes took Sampson for ire,
And alle hir tayles he togider bond,
And sette the foxes tayles alle on fire,
For he on every tayl had knit a brond;
And they brende alle the cornes in that lond,
And alle hir oliveres and vynes eek.
A thousand men he slow eek with his hond,
And had no wepen but an asses cheek.

Whan they were slayn, so thursted him that he
Was wel ny lorn, for which he gan to preye
That god wolde on his peyne han som pitee,
And sende him drinke, or elles moste he deye;
And of this asses cheke, that was dreye,
Out of a wang-tooth sprang anon a welle,
Of which he drank y-nogh, shortly to seye,
Thus heelp him god, as *Judicum* can telle.

By verray force, at Gazan, on a night,
Maugree Philistiens of that citee,
The gates of the toun he hath up-plight,
And on his bak y-caried hem hath he
Hye on an hille, that men mighte hem see.
O noble almighty Sampson, leef and dere,
Had thou nat told to wommen thy secree,
In al this worlde ne hadde been thy pere!

This Sampson never sicer drank ne wyn,
Ne on his heed cam rasour noon ne shere,
By precept of the messager divyn,
For alle his strengthes in his heres were;
And fully twenty winter, yeer by yere,

He hadde of Israel the governaunce.
But sone shal he wepen many a tere,
For wommen shal him bringen to meschaunce!

Un-to his lemman Dalida he tolde
That in his heres al his strengthe lay,
And falsly to his fo-men she him solde.
And sleping in hir barme up-on a day
She made to clippe or shere his heer awey,
And made his fo-men al his craft espyen;
And whan that they him fonde in this array,
They bounde him faste, and putten out his yën.

But er his heer were clipped or y-shave,
Ther was no bond with which men might him binde;
But now is he in prisoun in a cave,
Wher-as they made him at the querne grinde.
O noble Sampson, strongest of mankinde,
O whylom juge in glorie and in richesse,
Now maystow wepen with thyn yën blinde,
Sith thou fro wele art falle in wrecchednesse.

Th'ende of this caytif was as I shal seye;
His fo-men made a feste upon a day,
And made him as hir fool bifore hem pleye,
And this was in a temple of greet array.
But atte last he made a foul affray;
For he two pilers shook, and made hem falle,
And doun fil temple and al, and ther it lay,
And slow him-self, and eek his fo-men alle.

This is to seyn, the princes everichoon,
And eek three thousand bodies wer ther slayn
With falling of the grete temple of stoon.
Of Sampson now wol I na-more seyn.
Beth war by this ensample old and playn
That no men telle hir conseil til hir wyves
Of swich thing as they wolde han secree fayn,
If that it touche hir limmes or hir lyves.

Hercules.

Of Hercules the sovereyn conquerour
Singen his workes laude and heigh renoun;

For in his tyme of strengthe he was the flour.
He slow, and rafte the skin of the leoun;
He of Centauros leyde the boost adoun;
He Arpies slow, the cruel briddes felle;
He golden apples rafte of the dragoun;
He drow out Cerberus, the hound of helle:

He slow the cruel tyrant Busirus,
And made his hors to frete him, flesh and boon;
He slow the firy serpent venimous;
Of Achelois two hornes, he brak oon;
And he slow Cacus in a cave of stoon;
He slow the geaunt Antheus the stronge;
He slow the grisly boor, and that anoon,
And bar the heven on his nekke longe.

Was never wight, sith that the world bigan,
That slow so many monstres as dide he.
Thurgh-out this wyde world his name ran,
What for his strengthe, and for his heigh bountee,
And every reaume wente he for to see.
He was so strong that no man mighte him lette;
At bothe the worldes endes, seith Trophee,
In stede of boundes, he a piler sette.

A lemman hadde this noble champioun,
That highte Dianira, fresh as May;
And, as thise clerkes maken mencioun,
She hath him sent a sherte fresh and gay.
Allas! this sherte, allas and weylaway!
Envenimed was so subtilly with-alle,
That, er that he had wered it half a day,
It made his flesh al from his bones falle.

But nathelees somme clerkes hir excusen
By oon that highte Nessus, that it maked;
Be as be may, I wol hir noght accusen;
But on his bak this sherte he wered al naked,
Til that his flesh was for the venim blaked.
And whan he sey noon other remedye,
In hote coles he hath him-selven raked,
For with no venim deyned him to dye.

Thus starf this worthy mighty Hercules;
Lo, who may truste on fortune any throwe?
For him that folweth al this world of prees,
Er he be war, is ofte y-leyd ful lowe.
Ful wys is he that can him-selven knowe.
Beth war, for whan that fortune list to glose,
Than wayteth she hir man to overthrowe
By swich a wey as he wolde leest suppose.

NABUGODONOSOR (NEBUCHADNEZZAR).

The mighty trone, the precious tresor,
The glorious ceptre and royal magestee
That hadde the king Nabugodonosor,
With tonge unnethe may discryved be.
He twyës wan Jerusalem the citee;
The vessel of the temple he with him ladde.
At Babiloyne was his sovereyn see,
In which his glorie and his delyt he hadde.

The fairest children of the blood royal
Of Israel he leet do gelde anoon,
And maked ech of hem to been his thral.
Amonges othere Daniel was oon,
That was the wysest child of everichoon;
For he the dremes of the king expouned,
Wher-as in Chaldey clerk ne was ther noon
That wiste to what fyn his dremes souned.

This proude king leet make a statue of golde,
Sixty cubytes long, and seven in brede,
To which image bothe yonge and olde
Comaunded he to loute, and have in drede;
Or in a fourneys ful of flambes rede
He shal be brent, that wolde noght obeye.
But never wolde assente to that dede
Daniel, ne his yonge felawes tweye.

This king of kinges proud was and elaat,
He wende that god, that sit in magestee,
Ne mighte him nat bireve of his estaat:
But sodeynly he loste his dignitee,

And lyk a beste him semed for to be,
And eet hay as an oxe, and lay ther-oute;
In reyn with wilde bestes walked he,
Til certein tyme was y-come aboute.

And lyk an egles fetheres wexe his heres,
His nayles lyk a briddes clawes were;
Til god relessed him a certein yeres,
And yaf him wit; and than with many a tere
He thanked god, and ever his lyf in fere
Was he to doon amis, or more trespace,
And, til that tyme he leyd was on his bere,
He knew that god was ful of might and grace.

Balthasar (Belshazzar).

His sone, which that highte Balthasar,
That heeld the regne after his fader day,
He by his fader coude nought be war,
For proud he was of herte and of array;
And eek an ydolastre was he ay.
His hye estaat assured him in pryde.
But fortune caste him doun, and ther he lay,
And sodeynly his regne gan divyde.

A feste he made un-to his lordes alle
Up-on a tyme, and bad hem blythe be,
And than his officeres gan he calle—
'Goth, bringeth forth the vessels,' [tho] quod he,
'Which that my fader, in his prosperitee,
Out of the temple of Jerusalem birafte,
And to our hye goddes thanke we
Of honour, that our eldres with us lafte.'

His wyf, his lordes, and his concubynes
Ay dronken, whyl hir appetytes laste,
Out of thise noble vessels sundry wynes;
And on a wal this king his yën caste,
And sey an hond armlees, that wroot ful faste,
For fere of which he quook and syked sore.
This hond, that Balthasar so sore agaste,
Wroot *Mane*, *techel*, *phares*, and na-more.

In al that lond magicien was noon
That coude expoune what this lettre mente;
But Daniel expouned it anoon,
And seyde, 'king, god to thy fader lente
Glorie and honour, regne, tresour, rente:
And he was proud, and no-thing god ne dradde,
And therfor god gret wreche up-on him sente,
And him birafte the regne that he hadde.

He was out cast of mannes companye,
With asses was his habitacioun,
And eet hey as a beste in weet and drye,
Til that he knew, by grace and by resoun,
That god of heven hath dominacioun
Over every regne and every creature;
And thanne had god of him compassioun,
And him restored his regne and his figure.

Eek thou, that art his sone, art proud also,
And knowest alle thise thinges verraily,
And art rebel to god, and art his fo.
Thou drank eek of his vessels boldely;
Thy wyf eek and thy wenches sinfully
Dronke of the same vessels sondry wynes,
And heriest false goddes cursedly;
Therfor to thee y-shapen ful gret pyne is.

This hand was sent from god, that on the walle
Wroot *mane*, *techel*, *phares*, truste me;
Thy regne is doon, thou weyest noght at alle;
Divyded is thy regne, and it shal be
To Medes and to Perses yeven,' quod he.
And thilke same night this king was slawe,
And Darius occupyeth his degree,
Thogh he therto had neither right ne lawe.

Lordinges, ensample heer-by may ye take
How that in lordshipe is no sikernesse;
For whan fortune wol a man forsake,
She bereth awey his regne and his richesse,

And eek his freendes, bothe more and lesse;
For what man that hath freendes thurgh fortune,
Mishap wol make hem enemys, I gesse:
This proverbe is ful sooth and ful commune.

Cenobia (Zenobia).

Cenobia, of Palimerie quene,
As writen Persiens of hir noblesse,
So worthy was in armes and so kene,
That no wight passed hir in hardinesse,
Ne in linage, ne in other gentillesse.
Of kinges blode of Perse is she descended;
I seye nat that she hadde most fairnesse,
But of hir shape she mighte nat been amended.

From hir childhede I finde that she fledde
Office of wommen, and to wode she wente;
And many a wilde hertes blood she shedde
With arwes brode that she to hem sente.
She was so swift that she anon hem hente,
And whan that she was elder, she wolde kille
Leouns, lepardes, and beres al to-rente,
And in hir armes welde hem at hir wille.

She dorste wilde beestes dennes seke,
And rennen in the montaignes al the night,
And slepen under a bush, and she coude eke
Wrastlen by verray force and verray might
With any yong man, were he never so wight;
Ther mighte no-thing in hir armes stonde.
She kepte hir maydenhod from every wight,
To no man deigned hir for to be bonde.

But atte laste hir frendes han hir maried
To Odenake, a prince of that contree,
Al were it so that she hem longe taried;
And ye shul understonde how that he
Hadde swiche fantasyes as hadde she.
But nathelees, whan they were knit infere,
They lived in joye and in felicitee;
For ech of hem hadde other leef and dere.

Save o thing, that she never wolde assente
By no wey, that he sholde by hir lye
But ones, for it was hir pleyn entente
To have a child, the world to multiplye;
And al-so sone as that she mighte espye
That she was nat with childe with that dede,
Than wolde she suffre him doon his fantasye
Eft-sone, and nat but ones, out of drede.

And if she were with childe at thilke cast,
Na-more sholde he pleyen thilke game
Til fully fourty dayes weren past;
Than wolde she ones suffre him do the same.
Al were this Odenake wilde or tame,
He gat na more of hir, for thus she seyde,
'It was to wyves lecherye and shame
In other cas, if that men with hem pleyde.'

Two sones by this Odenake hadde she,
The whiche she kepte in vertu and lettrure;
But now un-to our tale turne we.
I seye, so worshipful a creature,
And wys therwith, and large with mesure,
So penible in the werre, and curteis eke,
Ne more labour mighte in werre endure,
Was noon, thogh al this world men sholde seke.

Hir riche array ne mighte nat be told
As wel in vessel as in hir clothing;
She was al clad in perree and in gold,
And eek she lafte noght, for noon hunting,
To have of sondry tonges ful knowing,
Whan that she leyser hadde, and for to entende
To lernen bokes was al hir lyking,
How she in vertu mighte hir lyf dispende.

And, shortly of this storie for to trete,
So doughty was hir housbonde and eek she,
That they conquered many regnes grete
In th'orient, with many a fair citee,

Apertenaunt un-to the magestee
Of Rome, and with strong hond helde hem ful faste;
Ne never mighte hir fo-men doon hem flee,
Ay whyl that Odenakes dayes laste.

Hir batailes, who-so list hem for to rede,
Agayn Sapor the king and othere mo,
And how that al this proces fil in dede,
Why she conquered and what title had therto,
And after of hir meschief and hir wo,
How that she was biseged and y-take,
Let him un-to my maister Petrark go,
That writ y-nough of this, I undertake.

When Odenake was deed, she mightily
The regnes heeld, and with hir propre honde
Agayn hir foos she faught so cruelly,
That ther nas king ne prince in al that londe
That he nas glad, if that he grace fonde,
That she ne wolde up-on his lond werreye ;
With hir they made alliaunce by bonde
To been in pees, and lete hir ryde and pleye.

The emperour of Rome, Claudius,
Ne him bifore, the Romayn Galien,
Ne dorste never been so corageous,
Ne noon Ermyn, ne noon Egipcien,
Ne Surrien, ne noon Arabien,
Within the feld that dorste with hir fighte
Lest that she wolde hem with hir hondes slen
Or with hir meynee putten hem to flighte.

In kinges habit wente hir sones two,
As heires of hir fadres regnes alle,
And Hermanno, and Thymalaö
Her names were, as Persiens hem calle.
But ay fortune hath in hir hony galle ;
This mighty quene may no whyl endure.
Fortune out of hir regne made hir falle
To wrecchednesse and to misaventure.

Aurelian, whan that the governaunce
Of Rome cam in-to his hondes tweye,
He shoop up-on this queen to do vengeaunce,
And with his legiouns he took his weye
Toward Cenobie, and, shortly for to seye,
He made hir flee, and atte laste hir hente,
And fettred hir, and eek hir children tweye,
And wan the lond, and hoom to Rome he wente.

Amonges othere thinges that he wan,
Hir char, that was with gold wrought and perree,
This grete Romayn, this Aurelian,
Hath with him lad, for that men sholde it see.
Biforen his triumphe walketh she
With gilte cheynes on hir nekke hanging;
Corouned was she, as after hir degree,
And ful of perree charged hir clothing.

Allas, fortune! she that whylom was
Dredful to kinges and to emperoures,
Now gaureth al the peple on hir, allas!
And she that helmed was in starke stoures,
And wan by force tounes stronge and toures,
Shal on hir heed now were a vitremyte;
And she that bar the ceptre ful of floures
Shal bere a distaf, hir cost for to quyte.

De Petro Rege Ispannie.

O noble, o worthy Petro, glorie of Spayne,
Whom fortune heeld so hy in magestee,
Wel oughten men thy pitous deeth complayne!
Out of thy lond thy brother made thee flee;
And after, at a sege, by subtiltee,
Thou were bitrayed, and lad un-to his tente,
Wher-as he with his owene hond slow thee,
Succeding in thy regne and in thy rente.

The feeld of snow, with th'egle of blak ther-inne,
Caught with the lymrod, coloured as the glede,
He brew this cursednes and al this sinne.
The 'wikked nest' was werker of this nede;

Noght Charles Oliver, that ay took hede
Of trouthe and honour, but of Armorike
Genilon Oliver, corrupt for mede,
Broghte this worthy king in swich a brike.

De Petro Rege de Cipro.

O worthy Petro, king of Cypre, also,
That Alisaundre wan by heigh maistrye,
Ful many a hethen wroghtestow ful wo,
Of which thyn owene liges hadde envye,
And, for no thing but for thy chivalrye,
They in thy bedde han slayn thee by the morwe.
Thus can fortune hir wheel governe and gye,
And out of joye bringe men to sorwe.

De Barnabo de Lumbardia.

Of Melan grete Barnabo Viscounte,
God of delyt, and scourge of Lumbardye,
Why sholde I nat thyn infortune acounte,
Sith in estaat thou clombe were so hye?
Thy brother sone, that was thy double allye,
For he thy nevew was, and sone-in-lawe,
With-inne his prisoun made thee to dye;
But why, ne how, noot I that thou were slawe.

De Hugelino, Comite de Pize.

Of the erl Hugelyn of Pyse the langour
Ther may no tonge telle for pitee;
But litel out of Pyse stant a tour,
In whiche tour in prisoun put was he,
And with him been his litel children three.
The eldeste scarsly fyf yeer was of age.
Allas, fortune! it was greet crueltee
Swiche briddes for to putte in swiche a cage!

Dampned was he to deye in that prisoun,
For Roger, which that bisshop was of Pyse,
Hadde on him maad a fals suggestioun,
Thurgh which the peple gan upon him ryse,

And putten him to prisoun in swich wyse
As ye han herd, and mete and drink he hadde
So smal, that wel unnethe it may suffyse,
And therwith-al it was ful povre and badde.

And on a day bifil that, in that hour,
Whan that his mete wont was to be broght,
The gayler shette the dores of the tour.
He herde it wel,—but he spak right noght,
And in his herte anon ther fil a thoght,
That they for hunger wolde doon him dyen.
'Allas!' quod he, 'allas! that I was wroght!'
Therwith the teres fillen from his yën.

His yonge sone, that three yeer was of age,
Un-to him seyde, 'fader, why do ye wepe?
Whan wol the gayler bringen our potage,
Is ther no morsel breed that ye do kepe?
I am so hungry that I may nat slepe.
Now wolde god that I mighte slepen ever!
Than sholde nat hunger in my wombe crepe;
Ther is no thing, save breed, that me were lever.'

Thus day by day this child bigan to crye,
Til in his fadres barme adoun it lay,
And seyde, 'far-wel, fader, I moot dye,'
And kiste his fader, and deyde the same day.
And whan the woful fader deed it sey,
For wo his armes two he gan to byte,
And seyde, 'allas, fortune! and weylaway!
Thy false wheel my wo al may I wyte!'

His children wende that it for hunger was
That he his armes gnow, and nat for wo,
And seyde, 'fader, do nat so, allas!
But rather eet the flesh upon us two;
Our flesh thou yaf us, tak our flesh us fro
And eet y-nough:' right thus they to him seyde,
And after that, with-in a day or two,
They leyde hem in his lappe adoun, and deyde.

Him-self, despeired, eek for hunger starf;
Thus ended is this mighty Erl of Pyse;
From heigh estaat fortune awey him carf.
Of this Tragedie it oghte y-nough suffyse.
Who-so wol here it in a lenger wyse,
Redeth the grete poete of Itaille,
That highte Dant, for he can al devyse
Fro point to point, nat o word wol he faille.

Nero.

Al-though that Nero were as vicious
As any feend that lyth ful lowe adoun,
Yet he, as telleth us Swetonius,
This wyde world hadde in subjeccioun,
Both Est and West, South and Septemtrioun;
Of rubies, saphires, and of perles whyte
Were alle his clothes brouded up and doun;
For he in gemmes greetly gan delyte.

More delicat, more pompous of array,
More proud was never emperour than he;
That ilke cloth, that he had wered o day,
After that tyme he nolde it never see.
Nettes of gold-thred hadde he gret plentee
To fisshe in Tybre, whan him liste pleye.
His lustes were al lawe in his decree,
For fortune as his freend him wolde obeye.

He Rome brende for his delicacye;
The senatours he slow up-on a day,
To here how men wolde wepe and crye;
And slow his brother, and by his sister lay.
His moder made he in pitous array;
For he hir wombe slitte, to biholde
Wher he conceyved was; so weilawey!
That he so litel of his moder tolde!

No tere out of his yën for that sighte
Ne cam, but seyde, 'a fair womman was she.'
Gret wonder is, how that he coude or mighte
Be domesman of hir dede beautee.

The wyn to bringen him comaunded he,
And drank anon ; non other wo he made.
Whan might is joyned un-to crueltee,
Allas ! to depe wol the venim wade !

In youthe a maister hadde this emperour,
To teche him letterure and curteisye,
For of moralitee he was the flour,
As in his tyme, but-if bokes lye ;
And whyl this maister hadde of him maistrye,
He maked him so conning and so souple
That longe tyme it was er tirannye
Or any vyce dorste on him uncouple.

This Seneca, of which that I devyse,
By-cause Nero hadde of him swich drede,
For he fro vyces wolde him ay chastyse
Discreetly as by worde and nat by dede ;—
'Sir,' wolde he seyn, 'an emperour moot nede
Be vertuous, and hate tirannye'—
For which he in a bath made him to blede
On bothe his armes, til he moste dye.

This Nero hadde eek of acustumaunce
In youthe ageyn his maister for to ryse,
Which afterward him thoughte a greet grevaunce ;
Therfor he made him deyen in this wyse.
But natheles this Seneca the wyse
Chees in a bath to deye in this manere
Rather than han another tormentyse ;
And thus hath Nero slayn his maister dere.

Now fil it so that fortune list no lenger
The hye pryde of Nero to cheryce ;
For though that he were strong, yet was she strenger ;
She thoughte thus, 'by god, I am to nyce
To sette a man that is fulfild of vyce
In heigh degree, and emperour him calle.
By god, out of his sete I wol him tryce ;
When he leest weneth, sonest shal he falle.'

The peple roos up-on him on a night
For his defaute, and whan he it espyed,
Out of his dores anon he hath him dight
Alone, and, ther he wende han ben allyed,
He knokked faste, and ay, the more he cryed,
The faster shette they the dores alle ;
Tho wiste he wel he hadde him-self misgyed,
And wente his wey, no lenger dorste he calle.

The peple cryde and rombled up and doun,
That with his eres herde he how they seyde,
'Wher is this false tyraunt, this Neroun ?'
For fere almost out of his wit he breyde,
And to his goddes pitously he preyde
For socour, but it mighte nat bityde.
For drede of this, him thoughte that he deyde,
And ran in-to a gardin, him to hyde.

And in this gardin fond he cherles tweye
That seten by a fyr ful greet and reed,
And to thise cherles two he gan to preye
To sleen him, and to girden of his heed,
That to his body, whan that he were deed,
Were no despyt y-doon, for his defame.
Him-self he slow, he coude no better reed,
Of which fortune lough, and hadde a game.

De Oloferno (Holofernes).

Was never capitayn under a king
That regnes mo putte in subjeccioun,
Ne strenger was in feeld of alle thing,
As in his tyme, ne gretter of renoun,
Ne more pompous in heigh presumpcioun
Than Oloferne, which fortune ay kiste
So likerously, and ladde him up and doun
Til that his heed was of, er that he wiste.

Nat only that this world hadde him in awe
For lesinge of richesse or libertee,
But he made every man reneye his lawe.
'Nabugodonosor was god,' seyde he,

'Noon other god sholde adoured be.'
Ageyns his heste no wight dar trespace
Save in Bethulia, a strong citee,
Wher Eliachim a prest was of that place.

But tak kepe of the deeth of Olofern;
Amidde his host he dronke lay a night,
With-inne his tente, large as is a bern,
And yit, for al his pompe and al his might,
Judith, a womman, as he lay upright,
Sleping, his heed of smoot, and from his tente
Ful prively she stal from every wight,
And with his heed unto hir toun she wente.

De Rege Anthiocho illustri.

What nedeth it of King Anthiochus
To telle his hye royal magestee,
His hye pryde, his werkes venimous?
For swich another was ther noon as he.
Rede which that he was in Machabee,
And rede the proude wordes that he seyde,
And why he fil fro heigh prosperitee,
And in an hil how wrechedly he deyde.

Fortune him hadde enhaunced so in pryde
That verraily he wende he mighte attayne
Unto the sterres, upon every syde,
And in balance weyen ech montayne,
And alle the flodes of the see restrayne.
And goddes peple hadde he most in hate,
Hem wolde he sleen in torment and in payne,
Wening that god ne mighte his pryde abate.

And for that Nichanor and Thimothee
Of Jewes weren venquisshed mightily,
Unto the Jewes swich an hate hadde he
That he bad greithe his char ful hastily,
And swoor, and seyde, ful despitously,
Unto Jerusalem he wolde eft-sone,
To wreken his ire on it ful cruelly;
But of his purpos he was let ful sone.

God for his manace him so sore smoot
With invisible wounde, ay incurable,
That in his guttes carf it so and boot
That his peynes weren importable.
And certeinly, the wreche was resonable,
For many a mannes guttes dide he peyne ;
But from his purpos cursed and dampnable
For al his smert he wolde him nat restreyne ;

But bad anon apparaillen his host,
And sodeynly, er he of it was war,
God daunted al his pryde and al his bost.
For he so sore fil out of his char,
That it his limes and his skin to-tar,
So that he neither mighte go ne ryde,
But in a chayer men aboute him bar,
Al for-brused, bothe bak and syde.

The wreche of god him smoot so cruelly
That thurgh his body wikked wormes crepte ;
And ther-with-al he stank so horribly,
That noon of al his meynee that him kepte,
Whether so he wook or elles slepte,
Ne mighte noght for stink of him endure.
In this meschief he wayled and eek wepte,
And knew god lord of every creature.

To al his host and to him-self also
Ful wlatsom was the stink of his careyne ;
No man ne mighte him bere to ne fro.
And in this stink and this horrible peyne
He starf ful wrecchedly in a monteyne.
Thus hath this robbour and this homicyde,
That many a man made to wepe and pleyne,
Swich guerdon as bilongeth unto pryde.

De Alexandro.

The storie of Alisaundre is so comune,
That every wight that hath discrecioun
Hath herd somwhat or al of his fortune.
This wyde world, as in conclusioun,

He wan by strengthe, or for his hye renoun
They weren glad for pees un-to him sende.
The pryde of man and beste he leyde adoun,
Wher-so he cam, un-to the worldes ende.

Comparisoun might never yit be maked
Bitwixe him and another conquerour;
For al this world for drede of him hath quaked,
He was of knighthode and of fredom flour;
Fortune him made the heir of hir honour;
Save wyn and wommen, no-thing mighte aswage
His hye entente in armes and labour;
So was he ful of leonyn corage.

What preys were it to him, though I yow tolde
Of Darius, and an hundred thousand mo,
Of kinges, princes, erles, dukes bolde,
Whiche he conquered, and broghte hem in-to wo?
I seye, as fer as man may ryde or go,
The world was his, what sholde I more devyse?
For though I write or tolde you evermo
Of his knighthode, it mighte nat suffyse.

Twelf yeer he regned, as seith Machabee;
Philippes sone of Macedoyne he was,
That first was king in Grece the contree.
O worthy gentil Alisaundre, allas!
That ever sholde fallen swich a cas!
Empoisoned of thyn owene folk thou were;
Thy *sys* fortune hath turned into *as*,
And yit for thee ne weep she never a tere!

Who shal me yeven teres to compleyne
The deeth of gentillesse and of fraunchyse,
That al the world welded in his demeyne,
And yit him thoughte it mighte nat suffyse?
So ful was his corage of heigh empryse.
Allas! who shal me helpe to endyte
False fortune, and poison to despyse,
The whiche two of al this wo I wyte?

De Julio Cesare.

By wisdom, manhede, and by greet labour
Fro humble bed to royal magestee,
Up roos he, Julius the conquerour,
That wan al th'occident by lond and see,
By strengthe of hond, or elles by tretee,
And un-to Rome made hem tributarie;
And sitthe of Rome the emperour was he,
Til that fortune wex his adversarie.

O mighty Cesar, that in Thessalye
Ageyn Pompeius, fader thyn in lawe,
That of th'orient hadde al the chivalrye
As fer as that the day biginneth dawe,
Thou thurgh thy knighthode hast hem take and slawe,
Save fewe folk that with Pompeius fledde,
Thurgh which thou puttest al th'orient in awe.
Thanke fortune, that so wel thee spedde!

But now a litel whyl I wol biwaille
This Pompeius, this noble governour
Of Rome, which that fleigh at this bataille;
I seye, oon of his men, a fals traitour,
His heed of smoot, to winnen him favour
Of Julius, and him the heed he broghte.
Allas, Pompey, of th'orient conquerour,
That fortune unto swich a fyn thee broghte!

To Rome ageyn repaireth Julius
With his triumphe, laureat ful hye,
But on a tyme Brutus Cassius,
That ever hadde of his hye estaat envye,
Ful prively hath maad conspiracye
Ageins this Julius, in subtil wyse,
And cast the place, in whiche he sholde dye
With boydekins, as I shal yow devyse.

This Julius to the Capitolie wente
Upon a day, as he was wont to goon,

And in the Capitolie anon him hente
This false Brutus, and his othere foon,
And stikede him with boydekins anoon
With many a wounde, and thus they lete him lye ;
But never gronte he at no strook but oon,
Or elles at two, but-if his storie lye.

So manly was this Julius at herte
And so wel lovede estaatly honestee,
That, though his deedly woundes sore smerte,
His mantel over his hippes casteth he,
For no man sholde seen his privitee.
And, as he lay on deying in a traunce,
And wiste verraily that deed was he,
Of honestee yit hadde he remembraunce.

Lucan, to thee this storie I recomende,
And to Sweton, and to Valerie also,
That of this storie wryten word and ende,
How that to thise grete conqueroures two
Fortune was first freend, and sithen fo.
No man ne truste up-on hir favour longe,
But have hir in awayt for ever-mo.
Witnesse on alle thise conqueroures stronge.

Cresus.

This riche Cresus, whylom king of Lyde,
Of whiche Cresus Cyrus sore him dradde,
Yit was he caught amiddes al his pryde,
And to be brent men to the fyr him ladde.
But swich a reyn doun fro the welkne shadde
That slow the fyr, and made him to escape ;
But to be war no grace yet he hadde,
Til fortune on the galwes made him gape.

Whan he escaped was, he can nat stente
For to biginne a newe werre agayn.
He wende wel, for that fortune him sente
Swich hap, that he escaped thurgh the rayn,

That of his foos he mighte nat be slayn ;
And eek a sweven up-on a night he mette,
Of which he was so proud and eek so fayn,
That in vengeaunce he al his herte sette.

Up-on a tree he was, as that him thoughte,
Ther Juppiter him wesh, bothe bak and syde,
And Phebus eek a fair towaille him broughte
To drye him with, and ther-for wex his pryde ;
And to his doghter, that stood him bisyde,
Which that he knew in heigh science habounde,
He bad hir telle him what it signifyde,
And she his dreem bigan right thus expounde.

'The tree,' quod she, 'the galwes is to mene,
And Juppiter bitokneth snow and reyn,
And Phebus, with his towaille so clene,
Tho ben the sonne stremes for to seyn ;
Thou shalt anhanged be, fader, certeyn ;
Reyn shal thee wasshe, and sonne shal thee drye ;'
Thus warned she him ful plat and ful pleyn,
His doughter, which that called was Phanye.

Anhanged was Cresus, the proude king,
His royal trone mighte him nat availle.—
Tragedie is noon other maner thing,
Ne can in singing crye ne biwaille,
But for that fortune alwey wol assaille
With unwar strook the regnes that ben proude ;
For when men trusteth hir, than wol she faille,
And covere hir brighte face with a cloude.

Explicit Tragedia.

Here stinteth the Knight the Monk of his Tale.

THE NONNE PREESTES TALE

The prologe of the Nonne Preestes Tale.

'Ho!' quod the knight, 'good sir, na-more of this,
That ye han seyd is right y-nough, y-wis,
And mochel more; for litel hevinesse
Is right y-nough to mochel folk, I gesse.
I seye for me, it is a greet disese
Wher-as men han ben in greet welthe and ese,
To heren of hir sodeyn fal, allas!
And the contrarie is joie and greet solas,
As whan a man hath been in povre estaat,
And clymbeth up, and wexeth fortunat,
And ther abydeth in prosperitee,
Swich thing is gladsom, as it thinketh me,
And of swich thing were goodly for to telle.'
'Ye,' quod our hoste, 'by seint Poules belle,
Ye seye right sooth; this monk, he clappeth loude,
He spak how "fortune covered with a cloude"
I noot never what, and als of a "Tragedie"
Right now ye herde, and parde! no remedie
It is for to biwaille, ne compleyne
That that is doon, and als it is a peyne,
As ye han seyd, to here of hevinesse.
Sir monk, na-more of this, so god yow blesse!
Your tale anoyeth al this companye;
Swich talking is nat worth a boterflye;
For ther-in is ther no desport ne game.
Wherfor, sir Monk, or dan Piers by your name,
I preye yow hertely, telle us somwhat elles,
For sikerly, nere clinking of your belles,

That on your brydel hange on every syde,
By heven king, that for us alle dyde,
I sholde er this han fallen doun for slepe,
Although the slough had never been so depe;
Than had your tale al be told in vayn.
For certeinly, as that thise clerkes seyn,
"Wher-as a man may have noon audience,
Noght helpeth it to tellen his sentence."
And wel I woot the substance is in me,
If any thing shal wel reported be.
Sir, sey somwhat of hunting, I yow preye.'
'Nay,' quod this monk, 'I have no lust to pleye:
Now let another telle, as I have told.'
Than spak our host, with rude speche and bold,
And seyde un-to the Nonnes Preest anon,
'Com neer, thou preest, com hider, thou sir John,
Tel us swich thing as may our hertes glade,
Be blythe, though thou ryde up-on a jade.
What though thyn hors be bothe foule and lene,
If he wol serve thee, rekke nat a bene;
Look that thyn herte be mery evermo.'
'Yis, sir,' quod he, 'yis, host, so mote I go,
But I be mery, y-wis, I wol be blamed:'—
And right anon his tale he hath attamed,
And thus he seyde un-to us everichon,
This swete preest, this goodly man, sir John.

Explicit.

Here biginneth the Nonne Preestes Tale of the Cok and Hen, Chauntecleer and Pertelote.

A POVRE widwe, somdel stape in age,
Was whylom dwelling in a narwe cotage,
Bisyde a grove, stonding in a dale.
This widwe, of which I telle yow my tale,
Sin thilke day that she was last a wyf,
In pacience ladde a ful simple lyf,
For litel was hir catel and hir rente;
By housbondrye, of such as God hir sente,

She fond hir-self, and eek hir doghtren two.
Three large sowes hadde she, and namo,
Three kyn, and eek a sheep that highte Malle,
Ful sooty was hir bour, and eek hir halle,
In which she eet ful many a sclendre meel.
Of poynaunt sauce hir neded never a deel.
No deyntee morsel passed thurgh hir throte;
Hir dyete was accordant to hir cote.
Replecciouu ne made hir never syk;
Attempree dyete was al hir phisyk,
And exercyse, and hertes suffisaunce.
The goute lette hir no-thing for to daunce,
N'apoplexye shente nat hir heed;
No wyn ne drank she, neither whyt ne reed;
Hir bord was served most with whyt and blak,
Milk and broun breed, in which she fond no lak,
Seynd bacoun, and somtyme an ey or tweye,
For she was as it were a maner deye.
  A yerd she hadde, enclosed al aboute
With stikkes, and a drye dich with-oute,
In which she hadde a cok, hight Chauntecleer,
In al the land of crowing nas his peer.
His vois was merier than the mery orgon
On messe-dayes that in the chirche gon;
Wel sikerer was his crowing in his logge,
Than is a clokke, or an abbey orlogge.
By nature knew he ech ascencioun
Of equinoxial in thilke toun;
For whan degrees fiftene were ascended,
Thanne crew he, that it mighte nat ben amended.
His comb was redder than the fyn coral,
And batailed, as it were a castel-wal.
His bile was blak, and as the jeet it shoon;
Lyk asur were his legges, and his toon;
His nayles whytter than the lilie flour,
And lyk the burned gold was his colour.
This gentil cok hadde in his governaunce
Sevene hennes, for to doon al his plesaunce,
Whiche were his sustres and his paramours,
And wonder lyk to him, as of colours.

Of whiche the faireste hewed on hir throte
Was cleped faire damoysele Pertelote.
Curteys she was, discreet, and debonaire,
And compaignable, and bar hir-self so faire,
Sin thilke day that she was seven night old,
That trewely she hath the herte in hold
Of Chauntecleer loken in every lith ;
He loved hir so, that wel was him therwith.
But such a joye was it to here hem singe,
Whan that the brighte sonne gan to springe,
In swete accord, 'my lief is faren in londe.'
For thilke tyme, as I have understonde,
Bestes and briddes coude speke and singe.
And so bifel, that in a daweninge,
As Chauntecleer among his wyves alle
Sat on his perche, that was in the halle,
And next him sat this faire Pertelote,
This Chauntecleer gan gronen in his throte,
As man that in his dreem is drecched sore.
And whan that Pertelote thus herde him rore,
She was agast, and seyde, 'O herte dere,
What eyleth yow, to grone in this manere ?
Ye been a verray sleper, fy for shame !'
And he answerde and seyde thus, 'madame,
I pray yow, that ye take it nat a-grief :
By god, me mette I was in swich meschief
Right now, that yet myn herte is sore afright.
Now god,' quod he, 'my swevene recche aright,
And keep my body out of foul prisoun !
Me mette, how that I romed up and doun
Withinne our yerde, wher-as I saugh a beste,
Was lyk an hound, and wolde han maad areste
Upon my body, and wolde han had me deed.
His colour was bitwixe yelwe and reed ;
And tipped was his tail, and bothe his eres,
With blak, unlyk the remenant of his heres ;
His snowte smal, with glowinge eyen tweye.
Yet of his look for fere almost I deye ;
This caused me my groning, doutelees.'
'Avoy !' quod she, 'fy on yow, hertelees !

Allas!' quod she, 'for, by that god above,
Now han ye lost myn herte and al my love;
I can nat love a coward, by my feith.
For certes, what so any womman seith,
We alle desyren, if it mighte be,
To han housbondes hardy, wyse, and free,
And secree, and no nigard, ne no fool,
Ne him that is agast of every tool,
Ne noon avauntour, by that god above!
How dorste ye seyn for shame unto your love,
That any thing mighte make yow aferd?
Have ye no mannes herte, and han a berd?
Allas! and conne ye been agast of swevenis?
No-thing, god wot, but vanitee, in sweven is.
Swevenes engendren of replecciouns,
And ofte of fume, and of complecciouns,
Whan humours been to habundant in a wight.
Certes this dreem, which ye han met to-night,
Cometh of the grete superfluitee
Of youre rede *colera*, pardee,
Which causeth folk to dreden in here dremes
Of arwes, and of fyr with rede lemes,
Of grete bestes, that they wol hem byte,
Of contek, and of whelpes grete and lyte;
Right as the humour of malencolye
Causeth ful many a man, in sleep, to crye,
For fere of blake beres, or boles blake,
Or elles, blake develes wole hem take.
Of othere humours coude I telle also,
That werken many a man in sleep ful wo;
But I wol passe as lightly as I can.
  Lo Catoun, which that was so wys a man,
Seyde he nat thus, ne do no fors of dremes?
Now, sire,' quod she, 'whan we flee fro the bemes,
For Goddes love, as tak som laxatyf;
Up peril of my soule, and of my lyf,
I counseille yow the beste, I wol nat lye,
That bothe of colere and of malencolye
Ye purge yow; and for ye shul nat tarie,
Though in this toun is noon apotecarie,

I shal my-self to herbes techen yow,
That shul ben for your hele, and for your prow;
And in our yerd tho herbes shal I finde,
The whiche han of hir propretee, by kinde,
To purgen yow binethe, and eek above.
Forget not this, for goddes owene love!
Ye been ful colerik of compleccioun.
Ware the sonne in his ascencioun
Ne fynde yow nat repleet of humours hote;
And if it do, I dar wel leye a grote,
That ye shul have a fevere terciane,
Or an agu, that may be youre bane.
A day or two ye shul have digestyves
Of wormes, er ye take your laxatyves,
Of lauriol, centaure, and fumetere,
Or elles of ellebor, that groweth there,
Of catapuce, or of gaytres beryis,
Of erbe yve, growing in our yerd, that mery is;
Pekke hem up right as they growe, and ete hem in.
Be mery, housbond, for your fader kin!
Dredeth no dreem; I can say yow na-more.'
'Madame,' quod he, '*graunt mercy* of your lore.
But nathelees, as touching daun Catoun,
That hath of wisdom such a greet renoun,
Though that he bad no dremes for to drede,
By god, men may in olde bokes rede
Of many a man, more of auctoritee
Than ever Catoun was, so mote I thee,
That al the revers seyn of his sentence,
And han wel founden by experience,
That dremes ben significaciouns,
As wel of joye as tribulaciouns
That folk enduren in this lyf present.
Ther nedeth make of this noon argument;
The verray preve sheweth it in dede.
Oon of the gretteste auctours that men rede
Seith thus, that whylom two felawes wente
On pilgrimage, in a ful good entente;
And happed so, thay come into a toun,
Wher-as ther was swich congregacioun

Of peple, and eek so streit of herbergage
That they ne founde as muche as o cotage
In which they bothe mighte y-logged be.
Wherfor thay mosten, of necessitee,
As for that night, departen compaignye;
And ech of hem goth to his hostelrye,
And took his logging as it wolde falle.
That oon of hem was logged in a stalle,
Fer in a yerd, with oxen of the plough;
That other man was logged wel y-nough,
As was his aventure, or his fortune,
That us governeth alle as in commune.
  And so bifel, that, longe er it were day,
This man mette in his bed, ther-as he lay,
How that his felawe gan up-on him calle,
And seyde, "allas! for in an oxes stalle
This night I shal be mordred ther I lye.
Now help me, dere brother, er I dye;
In alle haste com to me," he sayde.
This man out of his sleep for fere abrayde;
But whan that he was wakned of his sleep,
He turned him, and took of this no keep;
Him thoughte his dreem nas but a vanitee.
Thus twyës in his sleping dremed he.
And atte thridde tyme yet his felawe
Cam, as him thoughte, and seide, "I am now slawe;
Bihold my blody woundes, depe and wyde!
Arys up erly in the morwe-tyde,
And at the west gate of the toun," quod he,
"A carte ful of dong ther shaltow see,
In which my body is hid ful prively;
Do thilke carte aresten boldely.
My gold caused my mordre, sooth to sayn;"
And tolde him every poynt how he was slayn,
With a ful pitous face, pale of hewe.
And truste wel, his dreem he fond ful trewe;
For on the morwe, as sone as it was day,
To his felawes in he took the way;
And whan that he cam to this oxes stalle,
After his felawe he bigan to calle.

The hostiler answered him anon,
And seyde, "sire, your felawe is agon,
As sone as day he wente out of the toun."
This man gan fallen in suspecioun,
Remembring on his dremes that he mette,
And forth he goth, no lenger wolde he lette,
Unto the west gate of the toun, and fond
A dong-carte, as it were to donge lond,
That was arrayed in the same wyse
As ye han herd the dede man devyse;
And with an hardy herte he gan to crye
Vengeaunce and justice of this felonye:—
"My felawe mordred is this same night,
And in this carte he lyth gapinge upright.
I crye out on the ministres," quod he,
"That sholden kepe and reulen this citee;
Harrow! allas! her lyth my felawe slayn!"
What sholde I more un-to this tale sayn?
The peple out-sterte, and caste the cart to grounde,
And in the middel of the dong they founde
The dede man, that mordred was al newe.
O blisful god, that art so just and trewe!
Lo, how that thou biwreyest mordre alway!
Mordre wol out, that see we day by day.
Mordre is so wlatsom and abhominable
To god, that is so just and resonable,
That he ne wol nat suffre it heled be;
Though it abyde a yeer, or two, or three,
Mordre wol out, this my conclusioun.
And right anoon, ministres of that toun
Han hent the carter, and so sore him pyned,
And eek the hostiler so sore engyned,
That thay biknewe hir wikkednesse anoon,
And were an-hanged by the nekke-boon.
Here may men seen that dremes been to drede.
And certes, in the same book I rede,
Right in the nexte chapitre after this,
(I gabbe nat, so have I joye or blis,)
Two men that wolde han passed over see,
For certeyn cause, in-to a fer contree,

If that the wind ne hadde been contrarie,
That made hem in a citee for to tarie,
That stood ful mery upon an haven-syde.
But on a day, agayn the even-tyde,
The wind gan chaunge, and blew right as hem leste.
Jolif and glad they wente un-to hir reste,
And casten hem ful erly for to saille ;
But to that oo man fil a greet mervaille.
That oon of hem, in sleping as he lay,
Him mette a wonder dreem, agayn the day ;
Him thoughte a man stood by his beddes syde,
And him comaunded, that he sholde abyde,
And seyde him thus, " if thou to-morwe wende,
Thou shalt be dreynt ; my tale is at an ende."
He wook, and tolde his felawe what he mette,
And preyde him his viage for to lette ;
As for that day, he preyde him to abyde.
His felawe, that lay by his beddes syde,
Gan for to laughe, and scorned him ful faste.
" No dreem," quod he, " may so myn herte agaste,
That I wol lette for to do my thinges.
I sette not a straw by thy dreminges,
For swevenes been but vanitees and japes.
Men dreme al-day of owles or of apes,
And eke of many a mase therwithal ;
Men dreme of thing that never was ne shal.
But sith I see that thou wolt heer abyde,
And thus for-sleuthen wilfully thy tyde,
God wot it reweth me ; and have good day."
And thus he took his leve, and wente his way.
But er that he hadde halfe his cours y-seyled,
Noot I nat why, ne what mischaunce it eyled,
But casuelly the shippes botme rente,
And ship and man under the water wente
In sighte of othere shippes it byside,
That with hem seyled at the same tyde.
And therfor, faire Pertelote so dere,
By swiche ensamples olde maistow lere,
That no man sholde been to recchelees
Of dremes, for I sey thee, doutelees,

That many a dreem ful sore is for to drede.
Lo, in the lyf of seint Kenelm, I rede,
That was Kenulphus sone, the noble king
Of Mercenrike, how Kenelm mette a thing ;
A lyte er he was mordred, on a day,
His mordre in his avisioun he say.
His norice him expouned every del
His sweven, and bad him for to kepe him wel
For traisoun ; but he nas but seven yeer old,
And therfore litel tale hath he told
Of any dreem, so holy was his herte.
By god, I hadde lever than my sherte
That ye had rad his legende, as have I.
Dame Pertelote, I sey yow trewely,
Macrobeus, that writ th'avisioun
In Affrike of the worthy Cipioun,
Affermeth dremes, and seith that they been
Warning of thinges that men after seen.
And forther-more, I pray yow loketh wel
In th'olde testament, of Daniel,
If he held dremes any vanitee.
Reed eek of Joseph, and ther shul ye see
Wher dremes ben somtyme (I sey nat alle)
Warning of thinges that shul after falle.
Loke of Egipt the king, daun Pharao,
His bakere and his boteler also,
Wher they ne felte noon effect in dremes.
Who-so wol seken actes of sondry remes,
May rede of dremes many a wonder thing.
Lo Cresus, which that was of Lyde king,
Mette he nat that he sat upon a tree,
Which signified he sholde anhanged be ?
Lo heer Andromacha, Ectores wyf,
That day that Ector sholde lese his lyf,
She dremed on the same night biforn,
How that the lyf of Ector sholde be lorn,
If thilke day he wente in-to bataille ;
She warned him, but it mighte nat availle ;
He wente for to fighte nathelees,
But he was slayn anoon of Achilles.

But thilke tale is al to long to telle,
And eek it is ny day, I may nat dwelle.
Shortly I seye, as for conclusioun,
That I shal han of this avisioun
Adversitee ; and I seye forther-more,
That I ne telle of laxatyves no store,
For they ben venimous, I woot it wel ;
I hem defye, I love hem never a del.
  Now let us speke of mirthe, and stinte al this ;
Madame Pertelote, so have I blis,
Of o thing god hath sent me large grace ;
For whan I see the beautee of your face,
Ye ben so scarlet-reed about your yën,
It maketh al my drede for to dyen ;
For, also siker as *In principio,*
Mulier est hominis confusio ;
Madame, the sentence of this Latin is—
Womman is mannes joye and al his blis.
For whan I fele a-night your softe syde,
Al-be-it that I may nat on you ryde,
For that our perche is maad so narwe, alas !
I am so ful of joye and of solas
That I defye bothe sweven and dreem.'
And with that word he fley doun fro the beem,
For it was day, and eek his hennes alle ;
And with a chuk he gan hem for to calle,
For he had founde a corn, lay in the yerd.
Royal he was, he was namore aferd ;
He fethered Pertelote twenty tyme,
And trad as ofte, er that it was pryme.
He loketh as it were a grim leoun ;
And on his toos he rometh up and doun,
Him deyned not to sette his foot to grounde.
He chukketh, whan he hath a corn y-founde,
And to him rennen thanne his wyves alle.
Thus royal, as a prince is in his halle,
Leve I this Chauntecleer in his pasture ;
And after wol I telle his aventure.
  Whan that the month in which the world bigan,
That highte March, whan god first maked man,

Was complet, and [y]-passed were also,
Sin March bigan, thritty dayes and two,
Bifel that Chauntecleer, in al his pryde,
His seven wyves walking by his syde,
Caste up his eyen to the brighte sonne,
That in the signe of Taurus hadde y-ronne
Twenty degrees and oon, and somwhat more;
And knew by kynde, and by noon other lore,
That it was pryme, and crew with blisful stevene.
'The sonne,' he sayde, 'is clomben up on hevene
Fourty degrees and oon, and more, y-wis.
Madame Pertelote, my worldes blis,
Herkneth thise blisful briddes how they singe,
And see the fresshe floures how they springe;
Ful is myn herte of revel and solas.'
But sodeinly him fil a sorweful cas;
For ever the latter ende of joye is wo.
God woot that worldly joye is sone ago;
And if a rethor coude faire endyte,
He in a cronique saufly mighte it wryte
As for a sovereyn notabilitee.
Now every wys man, lat him herkne me;
This storie is al-so trewe, I undertake,
As is the book of Launcelot de Lake,
That wommen holde in ful gret reverence.
Now wol I torne agayn to my sentence.
A col-fox, ful of sly iniquitee,
That in the grove hadde woned yeres three,
By heigh imaginacioun forn-cast,
The same night thurgh-out the hegges brast
Into the yerd, ther Chauntecleer the faire
Was wont, and eek his wyves, to repaire;
And in a bed of wortes stille he lay,
Til it was passed undern of the day,
Wayting his tyme on Chauntecleer to falle,
As gladly doon thise homicydes alle,
That in awayt liggen to mordre men.
O false mordrer, lurking in thy den!
O newe Scariot, newe Genilon!
False dissimilour, O Greek Sinon,

That broghtest Troye al outrely to sorwe!
O Chauntecleer, acursed be that morwe,
That thou into that yerd flough fro the bemes:
Thou were ful wel y-warned by thy dremes,
That thilke day was perilous to thee.
But what that god forwoot mot nedes be,
After the opinioun of certeyn clerkis.
Witnesse on him, that any perfit clerk is,
That in scole is gret altercacioun
In this matere, and greet disputisoun,
And hath ben of an hundred thousand men.
But I ne can not bulte it to the bren,
As can the holy doctour Augustyn,
Or Boëce, or the bishop Bradwardyn,
Whether that goddes worthy forwiting
Streyneth me nedely for to doon a thing,
(Nedely clepe I simple necessitee);
Or elles, if free choys be graunted me
To do that same thing, or do it noght,
Though god forwoot it, er that it was wroght;
Or if his witing streyneth nevere a del
But by necessitee condicionel.
I wol not han to do of swich matere;
My tale is of a cok, as ye may here,
That took his counseil of his wyf, with sorwe,
To walken in the yerd upon that morwe
That he had met the dreem, that I yow tolde.
Wommennes counseils been ful ofte colde;
Wommannes counseil broghte us first to wo,
And made Adam fro paradys to go,
Ther-as he was ful mery, and wel at ese.—
But for I noot, to whom it mighte displese,
If I counseil of wommen wolde blame,
Passe over, for I seyde it in my game.
Rede auctours, wher they trete of swich matere,
And what thay seyn of wommen ye may here.
Thise been the cokkes wordes, and nat myne;
I can noon harm of no womman divyne.—
  Faire in the sond, to bathe hir merily,
Lyth Pertelote, and alle hir sustres by,

Agayn the sonne ; and Chauntecleer so free
Song merier than the mermayde in the see ;
For Phisiologus seith sikerly,
How that they singen wel and merily.
And so bifel that, as he caste his yë,
Among the wortes, on a boterflye,
He was war of this fox that lay ful lowe.
No-thing ne liste him thanne for to crowe,
But cryde anon, 'cok, cok,' and up he sterte,
As man that was affrayed in his herte.
For naturelly a beest desyreth flee
Fro his contrarie, if he may it see,
Though he never erst had seyn it with his yë.
  This Chauntecleer, whan he gan him espye,
He wolde han fled, but that the fox anon
Seyde, 'Gentil sire, allas ! wher wol ye gon ?
Be ye affrayed of me that am your freend ?
Now certes, I were worse than a feend,
If I to yow wolde harm or vileinye.
I am nat come your counseil for t'espye ;
But trewely, the cause of my cominge
Was only for to herkne how that ye singe.
For trewely ye have as mery a stevene
As eny aungel hath, that is in hevene ;
Therwith ye han in musik more felinge
Than hadde Boëce, or any that can singe.
My lord your fader (god his soule blesse !)
And eek your moder, of hir gentilesse,
Han in myn hous y-been, to my gret ese ;
And certes, sire, ful fayn wolde I yow plese.
But for men speke of singing, I wol saye,
So mote I brouke wel myn eyen tweye,
Save yow, I herde never man so singe,
As dide your fader in the morweninge ;
Certes, it was of herte, al that he song.
And for to make his voys the more strong,
He wolde so peyne him, that with bothe his yën
He moste winke, so loude he wolde cryen,
And stonden on his tiptoon ther-with-al,
And strecche forth his nekke long and smal.

And eek he was of swich discrecioun,
That ther nas no man in no regioun
That him in song or wisdom mighte passe.
I have wel rad in daun Burnel the Asse,
Among his vers, how that ther was a cok,
For that a preestes sone yaf him a knok
Upon his leg, whyl he was yong and nyce,
He made him for to lese his benefyce.
But certeyn, ther nis no comparisoun
Bitwix the wisdom and discrecioun
Of youre fader, and of his subtiltee.
Now singeth, sire, for seinte Charitee,
Let see, conne ye your fader countrefete?'
This Chauntecleer his winges gan to bete,
As man that coude his tresoun nat espye,
So was he ravisshed with his flaterye.
  Allas! ye lordes, many a fals flatour
Is in your courtes, and many a losengeour,
That plesen yow wel more, by my feith,
Than he that soothfastnesse unto yow seith.
Redeth Ecclesiaste of flaterye;
Beth war, ye lordes, of hir trecherye.
  This Chauntecleer stood hye up-on his toos,
Strecching his nekke, and heeld his eyen cloos,
And gan to crowe loude for the nones;
And daun Russel the fox sterte up at ones,
And by the gargat hente Chauntecleer,
And on his bak toward the wode him beer,
For yet ne was ther no man that him sewed.
O destinee, that mayst nat been eschewed!
Allas, that Chauntecleer fleigh fro the bemes!
Allas, his wyf ne roghte nat of dremes!
And on a Friday fil al this meschaunce.
O Venus, that art goddesse of plesaunce,
Sin that thy servant was this Chauntecleer,
And in thy service dide al his poweer,
More for delyt, than world to multiplye,
Why woldestow suffre him on thy day to dye?
O Gaufred, dere mayster soverayn,
That, whan thy worthy king Richard was slayn

With shot, compleynedest his deth so sore,
Why ne hadde I now thy sentence and thy lore,
The Friday for to chyde, as diden ye ?
(For on a Friday soothly slayn was he.)
Than wolde I shewe yow how that I coude pleyne
For Chauntecleres drede, and for his peyne.
  Certes, swich cry ne lamentacioun
Was never of ladies maad, whan Ilioun
Was wonne, and Pirrus with his streite swerd,
Whan he hadde hent king Priam by the berd,
And slayn him (as saith us *Eneydos*),
As maden alle the hennes in the clos,
Whan they had seyn of Chauntecleer the sighte.
But sovereynly dame Pertelote shrighte,
Ful louder than dide Hasdrubales wyf,
Whan that hir housbond hadde lost his lyf,
And that the Romayns hadde brend Cartage ;
She was so ful of torment and of rage,
That wilfully into the fyr she sterte,
And brende hir-selven with a stedfast herte.
O woful hennes, right so cryden ye,
As, whan that Nero brende the citee
Of Rome, cryden senatoures wyves,
For that hir housbondes losten alle hir lyves ;
Withouten gilt this Nero hath hem slayn.
Now wol I torne to my tale agayn :—
  This sely widwe, and eek hir doghtres two,
Herden thise hennes crye and maken wo,
And out at dores sterten they anoon,
And syen the fox toward the grove goon,
And bar upon his bak the cok away ;
And cryden, 'Out ! harrow ! and weylaway !
Ha, ha, the fox ! ' and after him they ran,
And eek with staves many another man ;
Ran Colle our dogge, and Talbot, and Gerland.
And Malkin, with a distaf in hir hand ;
Ran cow and calf, and eek the verray hogges
So were they fered for berking of the dogges
And shouting of the men and wimmen eke,
They ronne so, hem thoughte hir herte breke.

They yelleden as feendes doon in helle ;
The dokes cryden as men wolde hem quelle ;
The gees for fere flowen over the trees ;
Out of the hyve cam the swarm of bees ;
So hidous was the noyse, a ! *benedicite !*
Certes, he Jakke Straw, and his meynee,
Ne made never shoutes half so shrille,
Whan that they wolden any Fleming kille,
As thilke day was maad upon the fox.
Of bras thay broghten bemes, and of box,
Of horn, of boon, in whiche they blewe and pouped,
And therwithal thay shryked and they houped ;
It semed as that heven sholde falle.
Now, gode men, I pray yow herkneth alle !
  Lo, how fortune turneth sodeinly
The hope and pryde eek of hir enemy !
This cok, that lay upon the foxes bak,
In al his drede, un-to the fox he spak,
And seyde, 'sire, if that I were as ye,
Yet sholde I seyn (as wis god helpe me),
Turneth agayn, ye proude cherles alle !
A verray pestilence up-on yow falle !
Now am I come un-to this wodes syde,
Maugree your heed, the cok shal heer abyde ;
I wol him ete in feith, and that anon.'—
The fox answerde, 'in feith, it shal be don,'—
And as he spak that word, al sodeinly
This cok brak from his mouth deliverly,
And heighe up-on a tree he fleigh anon.
And whan the fox saugh that he was y-gon,
'Allas !' quod he, 'O Chauntecleer, allas !
I have to yow,' quod he, 'y-doon trespas,
In-as-muche as I maked yow aferd,
Whan I yow hente, and broghte out of the yerd ;
But, sire, I dide it in no wikke entente ;
Com doun, and I shal telle yow what I mente.
I shal seye sooth to yow, god help me so.'
'Nay than,' quod he, 'I shrewe us bothe two,
And first I shrewe my-self, bothe blood and bones,
If thou bigyle me ofter than ones.

Thou shalt na-more, thurgh thy flaterye,
Do me to singe and winke with myn yë.
For he that winketh, whan he sholde see,
Al wilfully, god lat him never thee!'
'Nay,' quod the fox, 'but god yeve him meschaunce,
That is so undiscreet of governaunce,
That jangleth whan he sholde holde his pees.'
Lo, swich it is for to be recchelees,
And necligent, and truste on flaterye.
But ye that holden this tale a folye,
As of a fox, or of a cok and hen,
Taketh the moralitee, good men.
For seint Paul seith, that al that writen is,
To our doctryne it is y-write, y-wis.
Taketh the fruyt, and lat the chaf be stille.
Now, gode god, if that it be thy wille,
As seith my lord, so make us alle good men;
And bringe us to his heighe blisse. Amen.

Here is ended the Nonne Preestes Tale.

Epilogue to the Nonne Preestes Tale.

'Sir Nonnes Preest,' our hoste seyde anoon,
'Y-blessed be thy breche, and every stoon!
This was a mery tale of Chauntecleer.
But, by my trouthe, if thou were seculer,
Thou woldest been a trede-foul a-right.
For, if thou have corage as thou hast might,
Thee were nede of hennes, as I wene,
Ya, mo than seven tymes seventene.
See, whiche braunes hath this gentil Preest,
So greet a nekke, and swich a large breest!
He loketh as a sperhauk with his yën;
Him nedeth nat his colour for to dyen
With brasil, ne with greyn of Portingale.
Now sire, faire falle yow for youre tale!'
And after that he, with ful mery chere,
Seide to another, as ye shullen here.

THE PHISICIENS TALE

Here folweth the Phisiciens Tale.

THER was, as telleth Titus Livius,
A knight that called was Virginius,
Fulfild of honour and of worthinesse,
And strong of freendes and of greet richesse.
  This knight a doghter hadde by his wyf,
No children hadde he mo in al his lyf.
Fair was this mayde in excellent beautee
Aboven every wight that man may see;
For nature hath with sovereyn diligence
Y-formed hir in so greet excellence,
As though she wolde seyn, 'lo! I, Nature,
Thus can I forme and peynte a creature,
Whan that me list; who can me countrefete?
Pigmalion noght, though he ay forge and bete,
Or grave, or peynte; for I dar wel seyn,
Apelles, Zanzis, sholde werche in veyn,
Outher to grave or peynte or forge or bete,
If they presumed me to countrefete.
For he that is the former principal
Hath maked me his vicaire general,
To forme and peynten erthely creaturis
Right as me list, and ech thing in my cure is
Under the mone, that may wane and waxe,
And for my werk right no-thing wol I axe;
My lord and I ben ful of oon accord;
I made hir to the worship of my lord.
So do I alle myne othere creatures,
What colour that they han, or what figures.'

Thus semeth me that Nature wolde seye.
  This mayde of age twelf yeer was and tweye,
In which that Nature hadde swich delyt.
For right as she can peynte a lilie whyt
And reed a rose, right with swich peynture
She peynted hath this noble creature
Er she were born, up-on hir limes free,
Wher-as by right swiche colours sholde be ;
And Phebus dyed hath hir tresses grete
Lyk to the stremes of his burned hete.
And if that excellent was hir beautee,
A thousand-fold more vertuous was she.
In hir ne lakked no condicioun,
That is to preyse, as by discrecioun.
As wel in goost as body chast was she ;
For which she floured in virginitee
With alle humilitee and abstinence,
With alle attemperaunce and pacience,
With mesure eek of bering and array.
Discreet she was in answering alway ;
Though she were wys as Pallas, dar I seyn,
Hir facound eek ful wommanly and pleyn,
No countrefeted termes hadde she
To seme wys ; but after hir degree
She spak, and alle hir wordes more and lesse
Souninge in vertu and in gentillesse.
Shamfast she was in maydens shamfastnesse,
Constant in herte, and ever in bisinesse
To dryve hir out of ydel slogardye.
Bacus hadde of hir mouth right no maistrye ;
For wyn and youthe doon Venus encrece,
As men in fyr wol casten oile or grece.
And of hir owene vertu, unconstreyned,
She hath ful ofte tyme syk hir feyned,
For that she wolde fleen the companye
Wher lykly was to treten of folye,
As is at festes, revels, and at daunces.
That been occasions of daliaunces
Swich thinges maken children for to be
To sone rype and bold, as men may see,

Which is ful perilous, and hath ben yore.
For al to sone may she lerne lore
Of boldnesse, whan she woxen is a wyf.
  And ye maistresses in your olde lyf,
That lordes doghtres han in governaunce,
Ne taketh of my wordes no displesaunce;
Thenketh that ye ben set in governinges
Of lordes doghtres, only for two thinges;
Outher for ye han kept your honestee,
Or elles ye han falle in freletee,
And knowen wel y-nough the olde daunce,
And han forsaken fully swich meschaunce
For evermo; therfore, for Cristes sake,
To teche hem vertu loke that ye ne slake.
A theef of venisoun, that hath forlaft
His likerousnesse, and al his olde craft,
Can kepe a forest best of any man.
Now kepeth hem wel, for if ye wol, ye can;
Loke wel that ye un-to no vice assente,
Lest ye be dampned for your wikke entente;
For who-so doth, a traitour is certeyn.
And taketh kepe of that that I shal seyn;
Of alle tresons sovereyn pestilence
Is whan a wight bitrayseth innocence.
  Ye fadres and ye modres eek also,
Though ye han children, be it oon or two,
Your is the charge of al hir surveyaunce,
Whyl that they been under your governaunce.
Beth war that by ensample of your livinge,
Or by your necligence in chastisinge,
That they ne perisse; for I dar wel seye,
If that they doon, ye shul it dere abeye.
Under a shepherde softe and necligent
The wolf hath many a sheep and lamb to-rent.
Suffyseth oon ensample now as here,
For I mot turne agayn to my matere.
  This mayde, of which I wol this tale expresse,
So kepte hir-self, hir neded no maistresse;
For in hir living maydens mighten rede,
As in a book, every good word or dede,

That longeth to a mayden vertuous ;
She was so prudent and so bountevous.
For which the fame out-sprong on every syde
Bothe of hir beautee and hir bountee wyde ;
That thurgh that land they preysed hir echone,
That loved vertu, save envye allone,
That sory is of other mennes wele,
And glad is of his sorwe and his unhele ;
(The doctour maketh this descripcioun).
This mayde up-on a day wente in the toun
Toward a temple, with hir moder dere,
As is of yonge maydens the manere.
  Now was ther thanne a justice in that toun,
That governour was of that regioun.
And so bifel, this juge his eyen caste
Up-on this mayde, avysinge him ful faste,
As she cam forby ther this juge stood.
Anon his herte chaunged and his mood,
So was he caught with beautee of this mayde ;
And to him-self ful prively he sayde,
'This mayde shal be myn, for any man.'
  Anon the feend in-to his herte ran,
And taughte him sodeynly, that he by slighte
The mayden to his purpos winne mighte.
For certes, by no force, ne by no mede,
Him thoughte, he was nat able for to spede ;
For she was strong of freendes, and eek she
Confermed was in swich soverayn bountee,
That wel he wiste he mighte hir never winne
As for to make hir with hir body sinne.
For which, by greet deliberacioun,
He sente after a cherl, was in the toun,
Which that he knew for subtil and for bold.
This juge un-to this cherl his tale hath told
In secree wyse, and made him to ensure,
He sholde telle it to no creature,
And if he dide, he sholde lese his heed.
Whan that assented was this cursed reed,
Glad was this juge and maked him greet chere,
And yaf him yiftes preciouse and dere.

Whan shapen was al hir conspiracye
Fro point to point, how that his lecherye
Parfourned sholde been ful subtilly,
As ye shul here it after openly,
Hoom gooth the cherl, that highte Claudius.
This false juge that highte Apius,
So was his name, (for this is no fable,
But knowen for historial thing notable,
The sentence of it sooth is, out of doute),
This false juge gooth now faste aboute
To hasten his delyt al that he may.
And so bifel sone after, on a day,
This false juge, as telleth us the storie,
As he was wont, sat in his consistorie,
And yaf his domes up-on sondry cas.
This false cherl cam forth a ful greet pas,
And seyde, 'lord, if that it be your wille,
As dooth me right up-on this pitous bille,
In which I pleyne up-on Virginius.
And if that he wol seyn it is nat thus,
I wol it preve, and finde good witnesse,
That sooth is that my bille wol expresse.'
The juge answerde, 'of this, in his absence,
I may nat yeve diffinitif sentence.
Lat do him calle, and I wol gladly here;
Thou shalt have al right, and no wrong here.'
Virginius cam, to wite the juges wille,
And right anon was rad this cursed bille;
The sentence of it was as ye shul here.
'To yow, my lord, sire Apius so dere,
Sheweth your povre servant Claudius,
How that a knight, called Virginius,
Agayns the lawe, agayn al equitee,
Holdeth, expres agayn the wil of me,
My servant, which that is my thral by right,
Which fro myn hous was stole up-on a night,
Whyl that she was ful yong; this wol I preve
By witnesse, lord, so that it nat yow greve.
She nis his doghter nat, what so he seye;
Wherfore to yow, my lord the juge, I preye,

Yeld me my thral, if that it be your wille.'
Lo ! this was al the sentence of his bille.
  Virginius gan up-on the cherl biholde,
But hastily, er he his tale tolde,
And wolde have preved it, as sholde a knight,
And eek by witnessing of many a wight,
That it was fals that seyde his adversarie,
This cursed juge wolde no-thing tarie,
Ne here a word more of Virginius,
But yaf his jugement, and seyde thus :—
  'I deme anon this cherl his servant have ;
Thou shalt no lenger in thyn hous hir save.
Go bring hir forth, and put hir in our warde,
The cherl shal have his thral, this I awarde.'
  And whan this worthy knight Virginius,
Thurgh sentence of this justice Apius,
Moste by force his dere doghter yiven
Un-to the juge, in lecherye to liven,
He gooth him hoom, and sette him in his halle,
And leet anon his dere doghter calle,
And, with a face deed as asshen colde,
Upon hir humble face he gan biholde,
With fadres pitee stiking thurgh his herte,
Al wolde he from his purpos nat converte.
  'Doghter,' quod he, 'Virginia, by thy name,
Ther been two weyes, outher deeth or shame,
That thou most suffre ; allas ! that I was bore !
For never thou deservedest wherfore
To dyen with a swerd or with a knyf.
O dere doghter, ender of my lyf,
Which I have fostred up with swich plesaunce,
That thou were never out of my remembraunce !
O doghter, which that art my laste wo.
And in my lyf my laste joye also,
O gemme of chastitee, in pacience
Take thou thy deeth, for this is my sentence.
For love and nat for hate, thou most be deed ;
My pitous hand mot smyten of thyn heed.
Allas ! that ever Apius thee say !
Thus hath he falsly juged thee to-day'—

And tolde hir al the cas, as ye bifore
Han herd ; nat nedeth for to telle it more.
'O mercy, dere fader,' quod this mayde,
And with that word she both hir armes layde
About his nekke, as she was wont to do :
The teres broste out of hir eyen two,
And seyde, 'gode fader, shal I dye ?
Is ther no grace ? is ther no remedye ?'
'No, certes, dere doghter myn,' quod he.
'Thanne yif me leyser, fader myn,' quod she,
'My deeth for to compleyne a litel space ;
For pardee, Jepte yaf his doghter grace
For to compleyne, er he hir slow, allas !
And god it woot, no-thing was hir trespas,
But for she ran hir fader first to see,
To welcome him with greet solempnitee.'
And with that word she fil aswowne anon,
And after, whan hir swowning is agon,
She ryseth up, and to hir fader sayde,
'Blessed be god, that I shal dye a mayde.
Yif me my deeth, er that I have a shame ;
Doth with your child your wil, a goddes name !'
And with that word she preyed him ful ofte,
That with his swerd he wolde smyte softe,
And with that word aswowne doun she fil.
Hir fader, with ful sorweful herte and wil,
Hir heed of smoot, and by the top it hente,
And to the juge he gan it to presente,
As he sat yet in doom in consistorie.
And whan the juge it saugh, as seith the storie,
He bad to take him and anhange him faste.
But right anon a thousand peple in thraste,
To save the knight, for routhe and for pitee,
For knowen was the false iniquitee.
The peple anon hath suspect of this thing,
By manere of the cherles chalanging,
That it was by th'assent of Apius ;
They wisten wel that he was lecherous.
For which un-to this Apius they gon,
And caste him in a prison right anon,

Wher-as he slow him-self ; and Claudius,
That servant was un-to this Apius,
Was demed for to hange upon a tree ;
But that Virginius, of his pitee,
So preyde for him that he was exyled ;
And elles, certes, he had been bigyled.
The remenant were anhanged, more and lesse,
That were consentant of this cursednesse.—
Heer men may seen how sinne hath his meryte !
Beth war, for no man woot whom god wol smyte
In no degree, ne in which maner wyse
The worm of conscience may agryse
Of wikked lyf, though it so privee be,
That no man woot ther-of but god and he.
For be he lewed man, or elles lered,
He noot how sone that he shal been afered.
Therfore I rede yow this conseil take,
Forsaketh sinne, er sinne yow forsake.

Here endeth the Phisiciens Tale.

Words of the Host.

The wordes of the Host to the Phisicien and the Pardoner.

Our Hoste gan to swere as he were wood,
'Harrow !' quod he, 'by nayles and by blood !
This was a fals cherl and a fals justyse !
As shamful deeth as herte may devyse
Come to thise juges and hir advocats !
Algate this sely mayde is slayn, allas !
Allas ! to dere boghte she beautee !
Wherfore I seye al day, as men may see,
That yiftes of fortune or of nature
Ben cause of deeth to many a creature.
Hir beautee was hir deeth, I dar wel sayn ;
Allas ! so pitously as she was slayn !
Of bothe yiftes that I speke of now
Men han ful ofte more harm than prow.
But trewely, myn owene mayster dere,
This is a pitous tale for to here.

But natheles, passe over, is no fors ;
I prey to god, so save thy gentil cors,
And eek thyne urinals and thy jordanes,
Thyn Ypocras, and eek thy Galianes,
And every boist ful of thy letuarie ;
God blesse hem, and our lady seinte Marie !
So mot I theen, thou art a propre man,
And lyk a prelat, by seint Ronyan !
Seyde I nat wel ? I can nat speke in terme ;
But wel I woot, thou doost my herte to erme,
That I almost have caught a cardiacle.
By corpus bones ! but I have triacle,
Or elles a draught of moyste and corny ale,
Or but I here anon a mery tale,
Myn herte is lost for pitee of this mayde.
Thou bel amy, thou Pardoner,' he seyde,
'Tel us som mirthe or japes right anon.'
'It shall be doon,' quod he, 'by seint Ronyon !
But first,' quod he, 'heer at this ale-stake
I wol both drinke, and eten of a cake.'
But right anon thise gentils gonne to crye,
'Nay ! lat him telle us of no ribaudye ;
Tel us som moral thing, that we may lere
Som wit, and thanne wol we gladly here.'
'I graunte, y-wis,' quod he, 'but I mot thinke
Up-on som honest thing, whyl that I drinke.'

THE PARDONERS TALE

Here folweth the Prologe of the Pardoners Tale.

Radix malorum est Cupiditas: Ad Thimotheum, sexto.

'Lordings,' quod he, 'in chirches whan I preche,
I peyne me to han an hauteyn speche,
And ringe it out as round as gooth a belle,
For I can al by rote that I telle.
My theme is alwey oon, and ever was—
"*Radix malorum est Cupiditas.*"
First I pronounce whennes that I come,
And than my bulles shewe I, alle and somme.
Our lige lordes seel on my patente,
That shewe I first, my body to warente,
That no man be so bold, ne preest ne clerk,
Me to destourbe of Cristes holy werk;
And after that than telle I forth my tales,
Bulles of popes and of cardinales,
Of patriarkes, and bishoppes I shewe;
And in Latyn I speke a wordes fewe,
To saffron with my predicacioun,
And for to stire men to devocioun.
Than shewe I forth my longe cristal stones,
Y-crammed ful of cloutes and of bones:
Reliks been they, as wenen they echoon.
Than have I in latoun a sholder-boon
Which that was of an holy Jewes shepe.
"Good men," seye I, "tak of my wordes kepe;
If that this boon be wasshe in any welle,
If cow, or calf, or sheep, or oxe swelle

That any worm hath ete, or worm y-stonge,
Tak water of that welle, and wash his tonge,
And it is hool anon ; and forthermore,
Of pokkes and of scabbe, and every sore
Shal every sheep be hool, that of this welle
Drinketh a draughte ; tak kepe eek what I telle.
If that the good-man, that the bestes oweth,
Wol every wike, er that the cok him croweth,
Fastinge, drinken of this welle a draughte,
As thilke holy Jewe our eldres taughte,
His bestes and his stoor shal multiplye.
And, sirs, also it heleth jalousye ;
For, though a man be falle in jalous rage,
Let maken with this water his potage,
And never shal he more his wyf mistriste,
Though he the sooth of hir defaute wiste ;
Al had she taken preestes two or three.
  Heer is a miteyn eek, that ye may see.
He that his hond wol putte in this miteyn,
He shal have multiplying of his greyn,
Whan he hath sowen, be it whete or otes,
So that he offre pens, or elles grotes.
  Good men and wommen, o thing warne I yow,
If any wight be in this chirche now,
That hath doon sinne horrible, that he
Dar nat, for shame, of it y-shriven be,
Or any womman, be she yong or old,
That hath y-maad hir housbond cokewold,
Swich folk shul have no power ne no grace
To offren to my reliks in this place.
And who-so findeth him out of swich blame,
He wol com up and offre in goddes name,
And I assoille him by the auctoritee
Which that by bulle y-graunted was to me."
  By this gaude have I wonne, yeer by yeer,
An hundred mark sith I was Pardoner.
I stonde lyk a clerk in my pulpet,
And whan the lewed peple is doun y-set,
I preche, so as ye han herd bifore,
And telle an hundred false japes more.

Than peyne I me to strecche forth the nekke,
And est and west upon the peple I bekke,
As doth a dowve sitting on a berne.
Myn hondes and my tonge goon so yerne,
That it is joye to see my bisinesse.
Of avaryce and of swich cursednesse
Is al my preching, for to make hem free
To yeve her pens, and namely un-to me.
For my entente is nat but for to winne,
And no-thing for correccioun of sinne.
I rekke never, whan that they ben beried,
Though that her soules goon a-blakeberied!
For certes, many a predicacioun
Comth ofte tyme of yvel entencioun;
Som for plesaunce of folk and flaterye,
To been avaunced by ipocrisye,
And som for veyne glorie, and som for hate.
For, whan I dar non other weyes debate,
Than wol I stinge him with my tonge smerte
In preching, so that he shal nat asterte
To been defamed falsly, if that he
Hath trespased to my brethren or to me.
For, though I telle noght his propre name,
Men shal wel knowe that it is the same
By signes and by othere circumstances.
Thus quyte I folk that doon us displesances;
Thus spitte I out my venim under hewe
Of holynesse, to seme holy and trewe.
But shortly myn entente I wol devyse;
I preche of no-thing but for coveityse.
Therfor my theme is yet, and ever was—
"*Radix malorum est cupiditas.*"
Thus can I preche agayn that same vyce
Which that I use, and that is avaryce.
But, though my-self be gilty in that sinne,
Yet can I maken other folk to twinne
From avaryce, and sore to repente.
But that is nat my principal entente.
I preche no-thing but for coveityse;
Of this matere it oughte y-nogh suffyse.

Than telle I hem ensamples many oon
Of olde stories, longe tyme agoon:
For lewed peple loven tales olde;
Swich thinges can they wel reporte and holde.
What? trowe ye, the whyles I may preche,
And winne gold and silver for I teche,
That I wol live in povert wilfully?
Nay, nay, I thoghte it never trewely!
For I wol preche and begge in sondry londes;
I wol not do no labour with myn hondes,
Ne make baskettes, and live therby,
Because I wol nat beggen ydelly.
I wol non of the apostles counterfete;
I wol have money, wolle, chese, and whete,
Al were it yeven of the povrest page,
Or of the povrest widwe in a village,
Al sholde hir children sterve for famyne.
Nay! I wol drinke licour of the vyne,
And have a joly wenche in every toun.
But herkneth, lordings, in conclusioun;
Your lyking is that I shal telle a tale.
Now, have I dronke a draughte of corny ale,
By god, I hope I shal yow telle a thing
That shal, by resoun, been at your lyking.
For, though myself be a ful vicious man,
A moral tale yet I yow telle can,
Which I am wont to preche, for to winne.
Now holde your pees, my tale I wol beginne.'

Here biginneth the Pardoners Tale.

In Flaundres whylom was a companye
Of yonge folk, that haunteden folye,
As ryot, hasard, stewes, and tavernes,
Wher-as, with harpes, lutes, and gieternes,
They daunce and pleye at dees bothe day and night,
And ete also and drinken over hir might,
Thurgh which they doon the devel sacrifyse
With-in that develes temple, in cursed wyse,

By superfluitee abhominable ;
Hir othes been so grete and so dampnable,
That it is grisly for to here hem swere ;
Our blissed lordes body they to-tere ;
Hem thoughte Jewes rente him noght y-nough ;
And ech of hem at otheres sinne lough.
And right anon than comen tombesteres
Fetys and smale, and yonge fruytesteres,
Singers with harpes, baudes, wafereres,
Whiche been the verray develes officeres
To kindle and blowe the fyr of lecherye,
That is annexed un-to glotonye ;
The holy writ take I to my witnesse,
That luxurie is in wyn and dronkenesse.
  Lo, how that dronken Loth, unkindely,
Lay by his doghtres two, unwitingly ;
So dronke he was, he niste what he wroghte.
  Herodes, (who-so wel the stories soghte,)
Whan he of wyn was replet at his feste,
Right at his owene table he yaf his heste
To sleen the Baptist John ful giltelees.
  Senek seith eek a good word doutelees ;
He seith, he can no difference finde
Bitwix a man that is out of his minde
And a man which that is dronkelewe,
But that woodnesse, y-fallen in a shrewe,
Persevereth lenger than doth dronkenesse.
O glotonye, ful of cursednesse,
O cause first of our confusioun,
O original of our dampnacioun,
Til Crist had boght us with his blood agayn !
Lo, how dere, shortly for to sayn,
Aboght was thilke cursed vileinye ;
Corrupt was al this world for glotonye !
  Adam our fader, and his wyf also,
Fro Paradys to labour and to wo
Were driven for that vyce, it is no drede ;
For whyl that Adam fasted, as I rede,
He was in Paradys ; and whan that he
Eet of the fruyt defended on the tree,

Anon he was out-cast to wo and peyne.
O glotonye, on thee wel oghte us pleyne!
O, wiste a man how many maladyes
Folwen of excesse and of glotonyes,
He wolde been the more mesurable
Of his diete, sittinge at his table.
Allas! the shorte throte, the tendre mouth,
Maketh that, Est and West, and North and South,
In erthe, in eir, in water men to-swinke
To gete a glotoun deyntee mete and drinke!
Of this matere, o Paul, wel canstow trete,
'Mete un-to wombe, and wombe eek un-to mete,
Shal god destroyen bothe,' as Paulus seith.
Allas! a foul thing is it, by my feith,
To seye this word, and fouler is the dede,
Whan man so drinketh of the whyte and rede,
That of his throte he maketh his privee,
Thurgh thilke cursed superfluitee.
The apostel weping seith ful pitously,
'Ther walken many of whiche yow told have I,
I seye it now weping with pitous voys,
[That] they been enemys of Cristes croys,
Of whiche the ende is deeth, wombe is her god.'
O wombe! O bely! O stinking cod,
Fulfild of donge and of corrupcioun!
At either ende of thee foul is the soun.
How greet labour and cost is thee to finde!
Thise cokes, how they stampe, and streyne, and grinde,
And turnen substaunce in-to accident,
To fulfille al thy likerous talent!
Out of the harde bones knokke they
The mary, for they caste noght a-wey
That may go thurgh the golet softe and swote;
Of spicerye, of leef, and bark, and rote
Shal been his sauce y-maked by delyt,
To make him yet a newer appetyt.
But certes, he that haunteth swich delyces
Is deed, whyl that he liveth in tho vyces.

A lecherous thing is wyn, and dronkenesse
Is ful of stryving and of wrecchednesse.
O dronke man, disfigured is thy face,
Sour is thy breeth, foul artow to embrace,
And thurgh thy dronke nose semeth the soun
As though thou seydest ay 'Sampsoun, Sampsoun';
And yet, god wot, Sampsoun drank never no wyn.
Thou fallest, as it were a stiked swyn;
Thy tonge is lost, and al thyn honest cure;
For dronkenesse is verray sepulture
Of mannes wit and his discrecioun.
In whom that drinke hath dominacioun,
He can no conseil kepe, it is no drede.
Now kepe yow fro the whyte and fro the rede,
And namely fro the whyte wyn of Lepe,
That is to selle in Fish-strete or in Chepe.
This wyn of Spayne crepeth subtilly
In othere wynes, growing faste by,
Of which ther ryseth swich fumositee,
That whan a man hath dronken draughtes three,
And weneth that he be at hoom in Chepe,
He is in Spayne, right at the toune of Lepe,
Nat at the Rochel, ne at Burdeux toun;
And thanne wol he seye, 'Sampsoun, Sampsoun.'
But herkneth, lordings, o word, I yow preye,
That alle the sovereyn actes, dar I seye,
Of victories in th'olde testament,
Thurgh verray god, that is omnipotent,
Were doon in abstinence and in preyere;
Loketh the Bible, and ther ye may it lere.
Loke, Attila, the grete conquerour,
Deyde in his sleep, with shame and dishonour,
Bledinge ay at his nose in dronkenesse;
A capitayn shoulde live in sobrenesse.
And over al this, avyseth yow right wel
What was comaunded un-to Lamuel—
Nat Samuel, but Lamuel, seye I—
Redeth the Bible, and finde it expresly
Of wyn-yeving to hem that han justyse.
Na-more of this, for it may wel suffyse.

And now that I have spoke of glotonye,
Now wol I yow defenden hasardrye.
Hasard is verray moder of lesinges,
And of deceite, and cursed forsweringes,
Blaspheme of Crist, manslaughtre, and wast also
Of catel and of tyme ; and forthermo,
It is repreve and contrarie of honour
For to ben holde a commune hasardour.
And ever the hyër he is of estaat,
The more is he holden desolaat.
If that a prince useth hasardrye,
In alle governaunce and policye
He is, as by commune opinioun,
Y-holde the lasse in reputacioun.
Stilbon, that was a wys embassadour,
Was sent to Corinthe, in ful greet honour,
Fro Lacidomie, to make hir alliaunce.
And whan he cam, him happede, par chaunce,
That alle the grettest that were of that lond,
Pleyinge atte hasard he hem fond.
For which, as sone as it mighte be,
He stal him hoom agayn to his contree,
And seyde, 'ther wol I nat lese my name ;
Ne I wol nat take on me so greet defame,
Yow for to allye un-to none hasardours.
Sendeth othere wyse embassadours ;
For, by my trouthe, me were lever dye,
Than I yow sholde to hasardours allye.
For ye that been so glorious in honours
Shul nat allyen yow with hasardours
As by my wil, ne as by my tretee.'
This wyse philosophre thus seyde he.
Loke eek that, to the king Demetrius
The king of Parthes, as the book seith us,
Sente him a paire of dees of gold in scorn,
For he hadde used hasard ther-biforn ;
For which he heeld his glorie or his renoun
At no value or reputacioun.
Lordes may finden other maner pley
Honeste y-nough to dryve the day awey.

Now wol I speke of othes false and grete
A word or two, as olde bokes trete.
Gret swering is a thing abhominable,
And false swering is yet more reprevable.
The heighe god forbad swering at al,
Witnesse on Mathew ; but in special
Of swering seith the holy Jeremye,
'Thou shalt seye sooth thyn othes, and nat lye,
And swere in dome, and eek in rightwisnesse ;'
But ydel swering is a cursednesse.
Bihold and see, that in the firste table
Of heighe goddes hestes honurable,
How that the seconde heste of him is this—
'Tak nat my name in ydel or amis.'
Lo, rather he forbedeth swich swering
Than homicyde or many a cursed thing ;
I seye that, as by ordre, thus it stondeth ;
This knowen, that his hestes understondeth,
How that the second heste of god is that.
And forther over, I wol thee telle al plat,
That vengeance shal nat parten from his hous,
That of his othes is to outrageous.
'By goddes precious herte, and by his nayles,
And by the blode of Crist, that it is in Hayles,
Seven is my chaunce, and thyn is cink and treye ;
By goddes armes, if thou falsly pleye,
This dagger shal thurgh-out thyn herte go'—
This fruyt cometh of the bicched bones two,
Forswering, ire, falsnesse, homicyde.
Now, for the love of Crist that for us dyde,
Leveth your othes, bothe grete and smale ;
But, sirs, now wol I telle forth my tale.

THISE ryotoures three, of whiche I telle,
Longe erst er pryme rong of any belle,
Were set hem in a taverne for to drinke ;
And as they satte, they herde a belle clinke
Biforn a cors, was caried to his grave ;
That oon of hem gan callen to his knave,

'Go bet,' quod he, 'and axe redily,
What cors is this that passeth heer forby;
And look that thou reporte his name wel.'
'Sir,' quod this boy, 'it nedeth never-a-del.
It was me told, er ye cam heer, two houres;
He was, pardee, an old felawe of youres;
And sodeynly he was y-slayn to-night,
For-dronke, as he sat on his bench upright;
Ther cam a privee theef, men clepeth Deeth,
That in this contree al the peple sleeth,
And with his spere he smoot his herte a-two,
And wente his wey with-outen wordes mo.
He hath a thousand slayn this pestilence:
And, maister, er ye come in his presence,
Me thinketh that it were necessarie
For to be war of swich an adversarie:
Beth redy for to mete him evermore.
Thus taughte me my dame, I sey na-more.'
'By seinte Marie,' seyde this taverner,
'The child seith sooth, for he hath slayn this yeer,
Henne over a myle, with-in a greet village,
Both man and womman, child and hyne, and page.
I trowe his habitacioun be there;
To been avysed greet wisdom it were,
Er that he dide a man a dishonour.'
'Ye, goddes armes,' quod this ryotour,
'Is it swich peril with him for to mete?
I shal him seke by wey and eek by strete,
I make avow to goddes digne bones!
Herkneth, felawes, we three been al ones;
Lat ech of us holde up his hond til other,
And ech of us bicomen otheres brother,
And we wol sleen this false traytour Deeth;
He shal be slayn, which that so many sleeth,
By goddes dignitee, er it be night.'
Togidres han thise three her trouthes plight,
To live and dyen ech of hem for other,
As though he were his owene y-boren brother.
And up they sterte al dronken, in this rage,
And forth they goon towardes that village,

Of which the taverner had spoke biforn,
And many a grisly ooth than han they sworn,
And Cristes blessed body they to-rente—
'Deeth shal be deed, if that they may him hente.'
  Whan they han goon nat fully half a myle,
Right as they wolde han troden over a style,
An old man and a povre with hem mette.
This olde man ful mekely hem grette,
And seyde thus, 'now, lordes, god yow see!'
  The proudest of thise ryotoures three
Answerde agayn, 'what? carl, with sory grace,
Why artow al forwrapped save thy face?
Why livestow so longe in so greet age?'
  This olde man gan loke in his visage,
And seyde thus, 'for I ne can nat finde
A man, though that I walked in-to Inde,
Neither in citee nor in no village,
That wolde chaunge his youthe for myn age;
And therfore moot I han myn age stille,
As longe time as it is goddes wille.
  Ne deeth, allas! ne wol nat han my lyf;
Thus walke I, lyk a restelees caityf,
And on the ground, which is my modres gate,
I knokke with my staf, bothe erly and late,
And seye, "leve moder, leet me in!
Lo, how I vanish, flesh, and blood, and skin!
Allas! whan shul my bones been at reste?
Moder, with yow wolde I chaunge my cheste,
That in my chambre longe tyme hath be,
Ye! for an heyre clout to wrappe me!"
But yet to me she wol nat do that grace,
For which ful pale and welked is my face.
  But, sirs, to yow it is no curteisye
To speken to an old man vileinye,
But he trespasse in worde, or elles in dede.
In holy writ ye may your-self wel rede,
"Agayns an old man, hoor upon his heed,
Ye sholde aryse;" wherfor I yeve yow reed,
Ne dooth un-to an old man noon harm now,
Na-more than ye wolde men dide to yow

In age, if that ye so longe abyde ;
And god be with yow, wher ye go or ryde.
I moot go thider as I have to go.'
 'Nay, olde cherl, by god, thou shalt nat so,'
Seyde this other hasardour anon ;
'Thou partest nat so lightly, by seint John !
Thou spak right now of thilke traitour Deeth,
That in this contree alle our frendes sleeth.
Have heer my trouthe, as thou art his aspye,
Tel wher he is, or thou shalt it abye,
By god, and by the holy sacrament !
For soothly thou art oon of his assent,
To sleen us yonge folk, thou false theef ! '
 'Now, sirs,' quod he, 'if that yow be so leef
To finde Deeth, turne up this croked wey,
For in that grove I lafte him, by my fey,
Under a tree, and ther he wol abyde ;
Nat for your boost he wol him no-thing hyde.
See ye that ook ? right ther ye shul him finde.
God save yow, that boghte agayn mankinde,
And yow amende ! '—thus seyde this olde man.
And everich of thise ryotoures ran,
Til he cam to that tree, and ther they founde
Of florins fyne of golde y-coyned rounde
Wel ny an eighte busshels, as hem thoughte.
No lenger thanne after Deeth they soughte,
But ech of hem so glad was of that sighte,
For that the florins been so faire and brighte,
That doun they sette hem by this precious hord.
The worste of hem he spake the firste word.
 'Brethren,' quod he, 'tak kepe what I seye ;
My wit is greet, though that I bourde and pleye.
This tresor hath fortune un-to us yiven,
In mirthe and jolitee our lyf to liven,
And lightly as it comth, so wol we spende.
Ey ! goddes precious dignitee ! who wende
To-day, that we sholde han so fair a grace ?
But mighte this gold be caried fro this place
Hoom to myn hous, or elles un-to youres—
For wel ye woot that al this gold is oures—

Than were we in heigh felicitee.
But trewely, by daye it may nat be;
Men wolde seyn that we were theves stronge,
And for our owene tresor doon us honge.
This tresor moste y-caried be by nighte
As wysly and as slyly as it mighte.
Wherfore I rede that cut among us alle
Be drawe, and lat see wher the cut wol falle;
And he that hath the cut with herte blythe
Shal renne to the toune, and that ful swythe,
And bringe us breed and wyn ful prively.
And two of us shul kepen subtilly
This tresor wel; and, if he wol nat tarie,
Whan it is night, we wol this tresor carie
By oon assent, wher-as us thinketh best.'
That oon of hem the cut broughte in his fest,
And bad hem drawe, and loke wher it wol falle;
And it fil on the yongeste of hem alle;
And forth toward the toun he wente anon.
And al-so sone as that he was gon,
That oon of hem spak thus un-to that other,
'Thou knowest wel thou art my sworne brother,
Thy profit wol I telle thee anon.
Thou woost wel that our felawe is agon;
And heer is gold, and that ful greet plentee,
That shal departed been among us three.
But natheles, if I can shape it so
That it departed were among us two,
Hadde I nat doon a freendes torn to thee?'
  That other answerde, 'I noot how that may be;
He woot how that the gold is with us tweye,
What shal we doon, what shal we to him seye?'
  'Shal it be conseil?' seyde the firste shrewe,
'And I shal tellen thee, in wordes fewe,
What we shal doon, and bringe it wel aboute.'
  'I graunte,' quod that other, 'out of doute,
That, by my trouthe, I wol thee nat biwreye.'
  'Now,' quod the firste, 'thou woost wel we be tweye,

And two of us shul strenger be than oon.
Look whan that he is set, and right anoon
Arys, as though thou woldest with him pleye;
And I shal ryve him thurgh the sydes tweye
Whyl that thou strogelest with him as in game,
And with thy dagger look thou do the same;
And than shal al this gold departed be,
My dere freend, bitwixen me and thee;
Than may we bothe our lustes al fulfille,
And pleye at dees right at our owene wille.'
And thus acorded been thise shrewes tweye
To sleen the thridde, as ye han herd me seye.
  This yongest, which that wente un-to the toun,
Ful ofte in herte he rolleth up and doun
The beautee of thise florins newe and brighte.
'O lord!' quod he, 'if so were that I mighte
Have al this tresor to my-self allone,
Ther is no man that liveth under the trone
Of god, that sholde live so mery as I!'
And atte laste the feend, our enemy,
Putte in his thought that he shold poyson beye,
With which he mighte sleen his felawes tweye;
For-why the feend fond him in swich lyvinge,
That he had leve him to sorwe bringe,
For this was outrely his fulle entente
To sleen hem bothe, and never to repente.
And forth he gooth, no lenger wolde he tarie,
Into the toun, un-to a pothecarie,
And preyed him, that he him wolde selle
Som poyson, that he mighte his rattes quelle;
And eek ther was a polcat in his hawe,
That, as he seyde, his capouns hadde y-slawe,
And fayn he wolde wreke him, if he mighte,
On vermin, that destroyed him by nighte.
  The pothecarie answerde, 'and thou shalt have
A thing that, al-so god my soule save,
In al this world ther nis no creature,
That ete or dronke hath of this confiture
Noght but the mountance of a corn of whete,
That he ne shal his lyf anon forlete;

Ye, sterve he shal, and that in lasse whyle
Than thou wolt goon a paas nat but a myle ;
This poyson is so strong and violent.'
  This cursed man hath in his hond y-hent
This poyson in a box, and sith he ran
In-to the nexte strete, un-to a man,
And borwed [of] him large botels three ;
And in the two his poyson poured he ;
The thridde he kepte clene for his drinke.
For al the night he shoop him for to swinke
In caryinge of the gold out of that place.
And whan this ryotour, with sory grace,
Had filled with wyn his grete botels three,
To his felawes agayn repaireth he.
  What nedeth it to sermone of it more ?
For right as they had cast his deeth bifore,
Right so they han him slayn, and that anon.
And whan that this was doon, thus spak that oon,
'Now lat us sitte and drinke, and make us merie,
And afterward we wol his body berie.'
And with that word it happed him, par cas,
To take the botel ther the poyson was,
And drank, and yaf his felawe drinke also,
For which anon they storven bothe two.
  But, certes, I suppose that Avicen
Wroot never in no canon, ne in no fen,
Mo wonder signes of empoisoning
Than hadde thise wrecches two, er hir ending.
Thus ended been thise homicydes two,
And eek the false empoysoner also.

  O cursed sinne, ful of cursednesse !
O traytours homicyde, o wikkednesse !
O glotonye, luxurie, and hasardrye !
Thou blasphemour of Crist with vileinye
And othes grete, of usage and of pryde !
Allas ! mankinde, how may it bityde,
That to thy creatour which that thee wroghte,
And with his precious herte-blood thee boghte,

Thou art so fals and so unkinde, allas!
  Now, goode men, god forgeve yow your trespas,
And ware yow fro the sinne of avaryce.
Myn holy pardoun may yow alle waryce,
So that ye offre nobles or sterlinges,
Or elles silver broches, spones, ringes.
Boweth your heed under this holy bulle!
Cometh up, ye wyves, offreth of your wolle!
Your name I entre heer in my rolle anon;
In-to the blisse of hevene shul ye gon;
I yow assoile, by myn heigh power,
Yow that wol offre, as clene and eek as cleer
As ye were born; and, lo, sirs, thus I preche.
And Jesu Crist, that is our soules leche,
So graunte yow his pardon to receyve;
For that is best; I wol yow nat deceyve.
  But sirs, o word forgat I in my tale,
I have relikes and pardon in my male,
As faire as any man in Engelond,
Whiche were me yeven by the popes hond.
If any of yow wol, of devocioun,
Offren, and han myn absolucioun,
Cometh forth anon, and kneleth heer adoun,
And mekely receyveth my pardoun:
Or elles, taketh pardon as ye wende,
Al newe and fresh, at every tounes ende,
So that ye offren alwey newe and newe
Nobles and pens, which that be gode and trewe.
It is an honour to everich that is heer,
That ye mowe have a suffisant pardoneer
T'assoille yow, in contree as ye ryde,
For aventures which that may bityde.
Peraventure ther may falle oon or two
Doun of his hors, and breke his nekke atwo.
Look which a seuretee is it to yow alle
That I am in your felaweship y-falle,
That may assoille yow, bothe more and lasse,
Whan that the soule shal fro the body passe.
I rede that our hoste heer shal biginne,
For he is most envoluped in sinne.

Com forth, sir hoste, and offre first anon,
And thou shalt kisse the reliks everichon,
Ye, for a grote ! unbokel anon thy purs.'
  'Nay, nay,' quod he, 'than have I Cristes curs !
Lat be,' quod he, 'it shal nat be, so thee'ch !
Thou woldest make me kisse thyn old breech,
And swere it were a relik of a seint,
Thogh it were with thy fundement depeint !
But by the croys which that seint Eleyne fond,
I wolde I hadde thy coillons in myn hond
In stede of relikes or of seintuarie ;
Lat cutte hem of, I wol thee helpe hem carie ;
They shul be shryned in an hogges tord.'
  This pardoner answerde nat a word ;
So wrooth he was, no word ne wolde he seye.
  'Now,' quod our host, 'I wol no lenger pleye
With thee, ne with noon other angry man.'
But right anon the worthy Knight bigan,
Whan that he saugh that al the peple lough,
'Na-more of this, for it is right y-nough ;
Sir Pardoner, be glad and mery of chere ;
And ye, sir host, that been to me so dere,
I prey yow that ye kisse the Pardoner.
And Pardoner, I prey thee, drawe thee neer,
And, as we diden, lat us laughe and pleye.'
Anon they kiste, and riden forth hir weye.

Here is ended the Pardoners Tale.

THE TALE OF THE WYF OF BATHE

The Prologe of the Wyves Tale of Bathe

'Experience, though noon auctoritee
Were in this world, were right y-nough to me
To speke of wo that is in mariage;
For, lordinges, sith I twelf yeer was of age,
Thonked be god that is eterne on lyve,
Housbondes at chirche-dore I have had fyve
For I so ofte have y-wedded be;
And alle were worthy men in hir degree.
But me was told certeyn, nat longe agon is,
That sith that Crist ne wente never but onis
To wedding in the Cane of Galilee,
That by the same ensample taughte he me
That I ne sholde wedded be but ones.
Herke eek, lo! which a sharp word for the nones
Besyde a welle Jesus, god and man,
Spak in repreve of the Samaritan:
"Thou hast y-had fyve housbondes," quod he,
"And thilke man, the which that hath now thee,
Is noght thyn housbond:" thus seyde he certeyn;
What that he mente ther-by, I can nat seyn;
But that I axe, why that the fifthe man
Was noon housbond to the Samaritan?
How manye mighte she have in mariage?
Yet herde I never tellen in myn age
Upon this nombre diffinicioun;
Men may devyne and glosen up and doun.

But wel I woot expres, with-oute lye,
God bad us for to wexe and multiplye;
That gentil text can I wel understonde.
Eek wel I woot he seyde, myn housbonde
Sholde lete fader and moder, and take me;
But of no nombre mencioun made he,
Of bigamye or of octogamye;
Why sholde men speke of it vileinye?
  Lo, here the wyse king, dan Salomon;
I trowe he hadde wyves mo than oon;
As, wolde god, it leveful were to me
To be refresshed half so ofte as he!
Which yifte of god hadde he for alle his wyvis!
No man hath swich, that in this world alyve is.
God woot, this noble king, as to my wit,
The firste night had many a mery fit
With ech of hem, so wel was him on lyve!
Blessed be god that I have wedded fyve!
Welcome the sixte, whan that ever he shal.
For sothe, I wol nat kepe me chast in al;
Whan myn housbond is fro the world y-gon,
Som Cristen man shal wedde me anon;
For thanne th'apostle seith, that I am free
To wedde, a godd's half, wher it lyketh me.
He seith that to be wedded is no sinne;
Bet is to be wedded than to brinne.
What rekketh me, thogh folk seye vileinye
Of shrewed Lameth and his bigamye?
I woot wel Abraham was an holy man,
And Jacob eek, as ferforth as I can;
And ech of hem hadde wyves mo than two;
And many another holy man also.
Whan saugh ye ever, in any maner age,
That hye god defended mariage
By expres word? I pray you, telleth me;
Or wher comanded he virginitee?
I woot as wel as ye, it is no drede,
Th'apostel, whan he speketh of maydenhede;
He seyde, that precept ther-of hadde he noon.
Men may conseille a womman to been oon,

But conseilling is no comandement;
He putte it in our owene jugement
For hadde god comanded maydenhede,
Thanne hadde he dampned wedding with the dede;
And certes, if ther were no seed y-sowe,
Virginitee, wher-of than sholde it growe?
Poul dorste nat comanden atte leste
A thing of which his maister yaf noon heste.
The dart is set up for virginitee;
Cacche who so may, who renneth best lat see.
But this word is nat take of every wight,
But ther as god list give it of his might.
I woot wel, that th'apostel was a mayde;
But natheless, thogh that he wroot and sayde,
He wolde that every wight were swich as he,
Al nis but conseil to virginitee;
And for to been a wyf, he yaf me leve
Of indulgence; so it is no repreve
To wedde me, if that my make dye,
With-oute excepcioun of bigamye.
Al were it good no womman for to touche,
He mente as in his bed or in his couche;
For peril is bothe fyr and tow t'assemble;
Ye knowe what this ensample may resemble.
This is al and som, he heeld virginitee
More parfit than wedding in freletee.
Freeltee clepe I, but-if that he and she
Wolde leden al hir lyf in chastitee.
I graunte it wel, I have noon envye,
Thogh maydenhede preferre bigamye;
Hem lyketh to be clene, body and goost,
Of myn estaat I nil nat make no boost.
For wel ye knowe, a lord in his houshold,
He hath nat every vessel al of gold;
Somme been of tree, and doon hir lord servyse.
God clepeth folk to him in sondry wyse,
And everich hath of god a propre yifte,
Som this, som that,—as him lyketh shifte.
Virginitee is greet perfeccioun,
And continence eek with devocioun.

But Crist, that of perfeccioun is welle,
Bad nat every wight he sholde go selle
All that he hadde, and give it to the pore,
And in swich wyse folwe him and his fore.
He spak to hem that wolde live parfitly;
And lordinges, by your leve, that am nat I.
I wol bistowe the flour of al myn age
In th' actes and in fruit of mariage.
  Telle me also, to what conclusioun
Were membres maad of generacioun,
And for what profit was a wight y-wroght?
Trusteth right wel, they wer nat maad for noght.
Glose who-so wole, and seye bothe up and doun,
That they were maked for purgacioun
Of urine, and our bothe thinges smale
Were eek to knowe a femele from a male,
And for noon other cause: sey ye no?
The experience woot wel it is noght so;
So that the clerkes be nat with me wrothe,
I sey this, that they maked been for bothe,
This is to seye, for office, and for ese
Of engendrure, ther we nat god displese.
Why sholde men elles in hir bokes sette,
That man shal yelde to his wyf hir dette?
Now wher-with sholde he make his payement,
If he ne used his sely instrument?
Than were they maad up-on a creature,
To purge uryne, and eek for engendrure.
  But I seye noght that every wight is holde,
That hath swich harneys as I to yow tolde,
To goon and usen hem in engendrure;
Than sholde men take of chastitee no cure.
Crist was a mayde, and shapen as a man,
And many a seint, sith that the world bigan,
Yet lived they ever in parfit chastitee.
I nil envye no virginitee;
Lat hem be breed of pured whete-seed,
And lat us wyves hoten barly-breed;
And yet with barly-breed, Mark telle can,
Our lord Jesu refresshed many a man.

In swich estaat as god hath cleped us
I wol persevere, I nam nat precious.
In wyfhode I wol use myn instrument
As frely as my maker hath it sent.
If I be daungerous, god yeve me sorwe!
Myn housbond shal it have bothe eve and morwe,
Whan that him list com forth and paye his dette.
An housbonde I wol have, I nil nat lette,
Which shal be bothe my dettour and my thral,
And have his tribulacioun with-al
Up-on his flessh, whyl that I am his wyf.
I have the power duringe al my lyf
Up-on his propre body, and noght he.
Right thus th'apostel tolde it un-to me;
And bad our housbondes for to love us weel.
Al this sentence me lyketh every-deel'—
Up sterte the Pardoner, and that anon,
'Now dame,' quod he, 'by god and by seint John,
Ye been a noble prechour in this cas!
I was aboute to wedde a wyf; allas!
What sholde I bye it on my flesh so dere?
Yet hadde I lever wedde no wyf to-yere!'
'Abyde!' quod she, 'my tale is nat bigonne;
Nay, thou shalt drinken of another tonne
Er that I go, shal savoure wors than ale.
And whan that I have told thee forth my tale
Of tribulacioun in mariage,
Of which I am expert in al myn age,
This to seyn, my-self have been the whippe;—
Than maystow chese whether thou wolt sippe
Of thilke tonne that I shal abroche.
Be war of it, er thou to ny approche;
For I shal telle ensamples mo than ten.
Who-so that nil be war by othere men,
By him shul othere men corrected be.
The same wordes wryteth Ptholomee;
Rede in his Almageste, and take it there.'
'Dame, I wolde praye yow, if your wil it were,'
Seyde this Pardoner, 'as ye bigan,
Telle forth your tale, spareth for no man,

And teche us yonge men of your praktike.'
  'Gladly,' quod she, 'sith it may yow lyke.
But yet I praye to al this companye,
If that I speke after my fantasye,
As taketh not a-grief of that I seye;
For myn entente nis but for to pleye.
  Now sires, now wol I telle forth my tale.—
As ever mote I drinken wyn or ale,
I shal seye sooth, tho housbondes that I hadde,
As three of hem were gode and two were badde.
The three men were gode, and riche, and olde;
Unnethe mighte they the statut holde
In which that they were bounden un-to me.
Ye woot wel what I mene of this, pardee!
As help me god, I laughe whan I thinke
How pitously a-night I made hem swinke;
And by my fey, I tolde of it no stoor.
They had me yeven hir gold and hir tresoor;
Me neded nat do lenger diligence
To winne hir love, or doon hem reverence.
They loved me so wel, by god above,
That I ne tolde no deyntee of hir love!
A wys womman wol sette hir ever in oon
To gete hir love, ther as she hath noon.
But sith I hadde hem hoolly in myn hond,
And sith they hadde me yeven all hir lond,
What sholde I taken hede hem for to plese,
But it were for my profit and myn ese?
I sette hem so a-werke, by my fey,
That many a night they songen "weilawey!"
The bacoun was nat fet for hem, I trowe,
That som men han in Essex at Dunmowe.
I governed hem so wel, after my lawe,
That ech of hem ful blisful was and fawe
To bringe me gaye thinges fro the fayre.
They were ful glad whan I spak to hem fayre;
For god it woot, I chidde hem spitously.
  Now herkneth, how I bar me proprely,
Ye wyse wyves, that can understonde.
  Thus shul ye speke and bere hem wrong on honde;

For half so boldely can ther no man
Swere and lyen as a womman can.
I sey nat this by wyves that ben wyse,
But-if it be whan they hem misavyse.
A wys wyf, if that she can hir good,
Shal beren him on hond the cow is wood,
And take witnesse of hir owene mayde
Of hir assent; but herkneth how I sayde.
"Sir olde kaynard, is this thyn array?
Why is my neighebores wyf so gay?
She is honoured over-al ther she goth;
I sitte at hoom, I have no thrifty cloth.
What dostow at my neighebores hous?
Is she so fair? artow so amorous?
What rowne ye with our mayde? *ben'cite!*
Sir olde lechour, lat thy japes be!
And if I have a gossib or a freend,
With-outen gilt, thou chydest as a feend,
If that I walke or pleye un-to his hous!
Thou comest hoom as dronken as a mous,
And prechest on thy bench, with yvel preef!
Thou seist to me, it is a greet meschief
To wedde a povre womman, for costage;
And if that she be riche, of heigh parage,
Than seistow that it is a tormentrye
To suffre hir pryde and hir malencolye.
And if that she be fair, thou verray knave,
Thou seyst that every holour wol hir have;
She may no whyle in chastitee abyde,
That is assailled up-on ech a syde.
Thou seyst, som folk desyre us for richesse,
Som for our shap, and som for our fairnesse;
And som, for she can outher singe or daunce,
And som, for gentillesse and daliaunce;
Som, for hir handes and hir armes smale;
Thus goth al to the devel by thy tale.
Thou seyst, men may nat kepe a castel-wal;
It may so longe assailled been over-al.
And if that she be foul, thou seist that she
Coveiteth every man that she may see;

For as a spaynel she wol on him lepe,
Til that she finde som man hir to chepe;
Ne noon so grey goos goth ther in the lake,
As, seistow, that wol been with-oute make.
And seyst, it is an hard thing for to welde
A thing that no man wol, his thankes, helde.
Thus seistow, lorel, whan thow goost to bedde;
And that no wys man nedeth for to wedde,
Ne no man that entendeth un-to hevene.
With wilde thonder-dint and firy levene
Mote thy welked nekke be to-broke!
  Thow seyst that dropping houses, and eek smoke,
And chyding wyves, maken men to flee
Out of hir owene hous; a! *ben'cite!*
What eyleth swich an old man for to chyde?
  Thow seyst, we wyves wol our vyces hyde
Til we be fast, and than we wol hem shewe;
Wel may that be a proverbe of a shrewe!
  Thou seist, that oxen, asses, hors, and houndes,
They been assayed at diverse stoundes;
Bacins, lavours, er that men hem bye,
Spones and stoles, and al swich housbondrye,
And so been po.tes, clothes, and array;
But folk of wyves maken noon assay
Til they be wedded; olde dotard shrewe!
And than, seistow, we wol oure vices shewe.
  Thou seist also, that it displeseth me
But-if that thou wolt preyse my beautee,
And but thou poure alwey up-on my face,
And clepe me 'faire dame' in every place;
And but thou make a feste on thilke day
That I was born, and make me fresh and gay,
And but thou do to my norice honour,
And to my chamberere with-inne my bour,
And to my fadres folk and his allyes;—
Thus seistow, olde barel ful of lyes!
  And yet of our apprentice Janekyn,
For his crisp heer, shyninge as gold so fyn,
And for he squiereth me bothe up and doun,
Yet hastow caught a fals suspecioun;

I wol hym noght, thogh thou were deed to-morwe.
But tel me this, why hydestow, with sorwe,
The keyes of thy cheste awey fro me ?
It is my good as wel as thyn, pardee.
What wenestow make an idiot of our dame ?
Now by that lord, that called is seint Jame,
Thou shalt nat bothe, thogh that thou were wood,
Be maister of my body and of my good ;
That oon thou shalt forgo, maugree thyne yën ;
What nedeth thee of me to enquere or spyën ?
I trowe, thou woldest loke me in thy cheste !
Thou sholdest seye, 'wyf, go wher thee leste,
Tak your disport, I wol nat leve no talis ;
I knowe yow for a trewe wyf, dame Alis.'
We love no man that taketh kepe or charge
Wher that we goon, we wol ben at our large.
Of alle men y-blessed moot he be,
The wyse astrologien Dan Ptholome,
That seith this proverbe in his Almageste,
'Of alle men his wisdom is the hyeste,
That rekketh never who hath the world in honde.'
By this proverbe thou shalt understonde,
Have thou y-nogh, what thar thee recche or care
How merily that othere folkes fare ?
For certeyn, olde dotard, by your leve,
Ye shul have queynte right y-nough at eve.
He is to greet a nigard that wol werne
A man to lighte his candle at his lanterne ;
He shal have never the lasse light, pardee ;
Have thou y-nough, thee thar nat pleyne thee.
Thou seyst also, that if we make us gay
With clothing and with precious array.
That it is peril of our chastitee ;
And yet, with sorwe, thou most enforce thee,
And seye thise wordes in the apostles name,
'In habit, maad with chastitee and shame,
Ye wommen shul apparaille yow,' quod he,
'And noght in tressed heer and gay perree,
As perles, ne with gold, ne clothes riche ;'
After thy text, ne after thy rubriche

I wol nat wirche as muchel as a gnat.
Thou seydest this, that I was lyk a cat;
For who-so wolde senge a cattes skin,
Thanne wolde the cat wel dwellen in his in;
And if the cattes skin be slyk and gay,
She wol nat dwelle in house half a day,
But forth she wole, er any day be dawed,
To shewe hir skin, and goon a-caterwawed;
This is to seye, if I be gay, sir shrewe,
I wol renne out, my borel for to shewe.
  Sire olde fool, what eyleth thee to spyën?
Thogh thou preye Argus, with his hundred yën,
To be my warde-cors, as he can best,
In feith, he shal nat kepe me but me lest;
Yet coude I make his berd, so moot I thee.
  Thou seydest eek, that ther ben thinges three,
The whiche thinges troublen al this erthe,
And that no wight ne may endure the ferthe;
O leve sir shrewe, Jesu shorte thy lyf!
Yet prechestow, and seyst, an hateful wyf
Y-rekened is for oon of thise meschances.
Been ther none othere maner resemblances
That ye may lykne your parables to,
But-if a sely wyf be oon of tho?
  Thou lykenest wommanes love to helle,
To bareyne lond, ther water may not dwelle.
Thou lyknest it also to wilde fyr;
The more it brenneth, the more it hath desyr
To consume every thing that brent wol be.
Thou seyst, that right as wormes shende a tree,
Right so a wyf destroyeth hir housbonde;
This knowe they that been to wyves bonde."
  Lordinges, right thus, as ye have understonde,
Bar I stifly myne olde housbondes on honde,
That thus they seyden in hir dronkenesse;
And al was fals, but that I took witnesse
On Janekin and on my nece also.
O lord, the peyne I dide hem and the wo,
Ful giltelees, by goddes swete pyne!
For as an hors I coude byte and whyne.

I coude pleyne, thogh I were in the gilt,
Or elles often tyme hadde I ben spilt.
Who-so that first to mille comth, first grint;
I pleyned first, so was our werre y-stint.
They were ful glad t'excusen hem ful blyve
Of thing of which they never agilte hir lyve.
  Of wenches wolde I beren him on honde,
Whan that for syk unnethes mighte he stonde.
Yet tikled it his herte, for that he
Wende that I hadde of him so greet chiertee.
I swoor that al my walkinge out by nighte
Was for t'espye wenches that he dighte;
Under that colour hadde I many a mirthe.
For al swich wit is yeven us in our birthe;
Deceite, weping, spinning god hath yive
To wommen kindely, whyl they may live.
And thus of o thing I avaunte me,
Atte ende I hadde the bettre in ech degree,
By sleighte, or force, or by som maner thing,
As by continuel murmur or grucching;
Namely a-bedde hadden they meschaunce,
Ther wolde I chyde and do hem no plesaunce;
I wolde no lenger in the bed abyde,
If that I felte his arm over my syde,
Til he had maad his raunson un-to me;
Than wolde I suffre him do his nycetee.
And ther-fore every man this tale I telle,
Winne who-so may, for al is for to selle.
With empty hand men may none haukes lure;
For winning wolde I al his lust endure,
And make me a feyned appetyt;
And yet in bacon hadde I never delyt;
That made me that ever I wolde hem chyde.
For thogh the pope had seten hem bisyde,
I wolde nat spare hem at hir owene bord.
For by my trouthe, I quitte hem word for word.
As help me verray god omnipotent,
Thogh I right now sholde make my testament,
I ne owe hem nat a word that it nis quit.
I broghte it so aboute by my wit,

That they moste yeve it up, as for the beste;
Or elles hadde we never been in reste.
For thogh he loked as a wood leoun,
Yet sholde he faille of his conclusioun.
  Thanne wolde I seye, "gode lief, tak keep
How mekely loketh Wilkin oure sheep;
Com neer, my spouse, let me ba thy cheke!
Ye sholde been al pacient and meke,
And han a swete spyced conscience,
Sith ye so preche of Jobes pacience.
Suffreth alwey, sin ye so wel can preche;
And but ye do, certein we shal yow teche
That it is fair to have a wyf in pees.
Oon of us two moste bowen, doutelees;
And sith a man is more resonable
Than womman is, ye moste been suffrable.
What eyleth yow to grucche thus and grone?
Is it for ye wolde have my queynte allone?
Why taak it al, lo, have it every-deel;
Peter! I shrewe yow but ye love it weel!
For if I wolde selle my *bele chose*,
I coude walke as fresh as is a rose;
But I wol kepe it for your owene tooth.
Ye be to blame, by god, I sey yow sooth."
  Swiche maner wordes hadde we on honde.
Now wol I speken of my fourthe housbonde.
  My fourthe housbonde was a revelour,
This is to seyn, he hadde a paramour;
And I was yong and ful of ragerye,
Stiborn and strong, and joly as a pye.
Wel coude I daunce to an harpe smale,
And singe, y-wis, as any nightingale,
Whan I had dronke a draughte of swete wyn.
Metellius, the foule cherl, the swyn,
That with a staf birafte his wyf hir lyf,
For she drank wyn, thogh I hadde been his wyf,
He sholde nat han daunted me fro drinke;
And, after wyn, on Venus moste I thinke:
For al so siker as cold engendreth hayl,
A likerous mouth moste han a likerous tayl.

In womman vinolent is no defence,
This knowen lechours by experience.
But, lord Crist! whan that it remembreth me
Up-on my yowthe, and on my jolitee,
It tikleth me aboute myn herte rote.
Unto this day it dooth myn herte bote
That I have had my world as in my tyme.
But age, allas! that al wol envenyme,
Hath me biraft my beautee and my pith;
Lat go, fare-wel, the devel go therwith!
The flour is goon, ther is na-more to telle,
The bren, as I best can, now moste I selle;
But yet to be right mery wol I fonde
Now wol I tellen of my fourthe housbonde.
I seye, I hadde in herte greet despyt
That he of any other had delyt.
But he was quit, by god and by seint Joce!
I made him of the same wode a croce;
Nat of my body in no foul manere,
But certeinly, I made folk swich chere,
That in his owene grece I made him frye
For angre, and for verray jalousye.
By god, in erthe I was his purgatorie,
For which I hope his soule be in glorie.
For god it woot, he sat ful ofte and song
Whan that his shoo ful bitterly him wrong.
Ther was no wight, save god and he, that wiste,
In many wyse, how sore I him twiste.
He deyde whan I cam fro Jerusalem,
And lyth y-grave under the rode-beem,
Al is his tombe noght so curious
As was the sepulcre of him, Darius,
Which that Appelles wroghte subtilly;
It nis but wast to burie him preciously.
Lat him fare-wel, god yeve his soule reste,
He is now in the grave and in his cheste.
Now of my fifthe housbond wol I telle.
God lete his soule never come in helle!
And yet was he to me the moste shrewe;
That fele I on my ribbes al by rewe,

And ever shal, un-to myn ending-day
But in our bed he was so fresh and gay,
And ther-with-al so wel coude he me glose,
Whan that he wolde han my *bele chose*,
That thogh he hadde me bet on every boon,
He coude winne agayn my love anoon.
I trowe I loved him beste, for that he
Was of his love daungerous to me.
We wommen han, if that I shal nat lye,
In this matere a queynte fantasye;
Wayte what thing we may nat lightly have,
Ther-after wol we crye al-day and crave.
Forbede us thing, and that desyren we;
Prees on us faste, and thanne wol we flee.
With daunger oute we al our chaffare;
Greet prees at market maketh dere ware,
And to greet cheep is holde at litel prys;
This knoweth every womman that is wys.
My fifthe housbonde, god his soule blesse!
Which that I took for love and no richesse,
He som-tyme was a clerk of Oxenford,
And had left scole, and wente at hoom to bord
With my gossib, dwellinge in oure toun,
God have hir soule! hir name was Alisoun.
She knew myn herte and eek my privetee
Bet than our parisshe-preest, so moot I thee!
To hir biwreyed I my conseil al.
For had myn housbonde pissed on a wal,
Or doon a thing that sholde han cost his lyf,
To hir, and to another worthy wyf,
And to my nece, which that I loved weel,
I wolde han told his conseil every-deel.
And so I dide ful often, god it woot,
That made his face ful often reed and hoot
For verray shame, and blamed him-self for he
Had told to me so greet a privetee.
And so bifel that ones, in a Lente,
(So often tymes I to my gossib wente,
For ever yet I lovede to be gay,
And for to walke, in March, Averille, and May,

Fro hous to hous, to here sondry talis),
That Jankin clerk, and my gossib dame Alis,
And I my-self, in-to the feldes wente.
Myn housbond was at London al that Lente ;
I hadde the bettre leyser for to pleye,
And for to see, and eek for to be seye
Of lusty folk ; what wiste I wher my grace
Was shapen for to be, or in what place ?
Therefore I made my visitaciouns,
To vigilies and to processiouns,
To preching eek and to thise pilgrimages,
To pleyes of miracles and mariages,
And wered upon my gaye scarlet gytes.
Thise wormes, ne thise motthes, ne thise mytes,
Upon my peril, frete hem never a deel ;
And wostow why ? for they were used weel.
  Now wol I tellen forth what happed me.
I seye, that in the feeldes walked we,
Til trewely we hadde swich daliance,
This clerk and I, that of my purveyance
I spak to him, and seyde him, how that he,
If I were widwe, sholde wedde me.
For certeinly, I sey for no bobance,
Yet was I never with-outen purveyance
Of mariage, n'of othere thinges eek.
I holde a mouses herte nat worth a leek,
That hath but oon hole for to sterte to,
And if that faille, thanne is al y-do.
  I bar him on honde, he hadde enchanted me ;
My dame taughte me that soutiltee.
And eek I seyde, I mette of him al night ;
He wolde han slayn me as I lay up-right,
And al my bed was ful of verray blood,
But yet I hope that he shal do me good ;
For blood bitokeneth gold, as me was taught.
And al was fals, I dremed of it right naught,
But as I folwed ay my dames lore,
As wel of this as of other thinges more.
  But now sir, lat me see, what I shal seyn ?
A ! ha ! by god, I have my tale ageyn.

Whan that my fourthe housbond was on bere,
I weep algate, and made sory chere,
As wyves moten, for it is usage,
And with my coverchief covered my visage;
But for that I was purveyed of a make,
I weep but smal, and that I undertake.
To chirche was myn housbond born a-morwe
With neighebores, that for him maden sorwe;
And Jankin oure clerk was oon of tho.
As help me god, whan that I saugh him go
After the bere, me thoughte he hadde a paire
Of legges and of feet so clene and faire,
That al myn herte I yaf un-to his hold.
He was, I trowe, a twenty winter old,
And I was fourty, if I shal seye sooth;
But yet I hadde alwey a coltes tooth.
Gat-tothed I was, and that bicam me weel;
I hadde the prente of sëynt Venus seel.
As help me god, I was a lusty oon,
And faire and riche, and yong, and wel bigoon;
And trewely, as myne housbondes tolde me,
I had the beste *quoniam* mighte be.
For certes, I am al Venerien
In felinge, and myn herte is Marcien.
Venus me yaf my lust, my likerousnesse,
And Mars yaf me my sturdy hardinesse.
Myn ascendent was Taur, and Mars ther-inne.
Allas! allas! that ever love was sinne!
I folwed ay myn inclinacioun
By vertu of my constellacioun;
That made me I coude noght withdrawe
My chambre of Venus from a good felawe.
Yet have I Martes mark up-on my face,
And also in another privee place.
For, god so wis be my savacioun,
I ne loved never by no discrecioun,
But ever folwede myn appetyt,
Al were he short or long, or blak or whyt;
I took no kepe, so that he lyked me,
How pore he was, ne eek of what degree.

What sholde I seye, but, at the monthes ende,
This joly clerk Jankin, that was so hende,
Hath wedded me with greet solempnitee,
And to him yaf I al the lond and fee
That ever was me yeven ther-bifore;
But afterward repented me ful sore.
He nolde suffre nothing of my list.
By god, he smoot me ones on the list,
For that I rente out of his book a leef,
That of the strook myn ere wex al deef.
Stiborn I was as is a leonesse,
And of my tonge a verray jangleresse,
And walke I wolde, as I had doon biforn,
From hous to hous, al-though he had it sworn.
For which he often tymes wolde preche,
And me of olde Romayn gestes teche,
How he, Simplicius Gallus, lefte his wyf,
And hir forsook for terme of al his lyf,
Noght but for open-heeded he hir say
Lokinge out at his dore upon a day.
Another Romayn tolde he me by name,
That, for his wyf was at a someres game
With-oute his witing, he forsook hir eke.
And than wolde he up-on his Bible seke
That ilke proverbe of Ecclesiaste,
Wher he comandeth and forbedeth faste,
Man shal nat suffre his wyf go roule aboute;
Than wolde he seye right thus, withouten doute,
"Who-so that buildeth his hous al of salwes,
And priketh his blinde hors over the falwes,
And suffreth his wyf to go seken halwes,
Is worthy to been hanged on the galwes!"
But al for noght, I sette noght an hawe
Of his proverbes n'of his olde sawe,
Ne I wolde nat of him corrected be.
I hate him that my vices telleth me,
And so do mo, god woot! of us than I.
This made him with me wood al outrely;
I nolde noght forbere him in no cas.
Now wol I seye yow sooth, by seint Thomas,

Why that I rente out of his book a leef,
For which he smoot me so that I was deef.
He hadde a book that gladly, night and day,
For his desport he wolde rede alway.
He cleped it Valerie and Theofraste,
At whiche book he lough alwey ful faste.
And eek ther was som-tyme a clerk at Rome,
A cardinal, that highte Seint Jerome,
That made a book agayn Jovinian ;
In whiche book eek ther was Tertulan,
Crisippus, Trotula, and Helowys,
That was abbesse nat fer fro Parys ;
And eek the Parables of Salomon,
Ovydes Art, and bokes many on,
And alle thise wer bounden in o volume.
And every night and day was his custume,
Whan he had leyser and vacacioun
From other worldly occupacioun,
To reden on this book of wikked wyves.
He knew of hem mo legendes and lyves
Than been of gode wyves in the Bible.
For trusteth wel, it is an impossible
That any clerk wol speke good of wyves,
But-if it be of holy seintes lyves,
Ne of noon other womman never the mo.
Who peyntede the leoun, tel me who ?
By god, if wommen hadde writen stories,
As clerkes han with-inne hir oratories,
They wolde han writen of men more wikkednesse
Than all the mark of Adam may redresse.
The children of Mercurie and of Venus
Been in hir wirking ful contrarious ;
Mercurie loveth wisdom and science,
And Venus loveth ryot and dispence.
And, for hir diverse disposicioun,
Ech falleth in otheres exaltacioun ;
And thus, god woot ! Mercurie is desolat
In Pisces, wher Venus is exaltat ;
And Venus falleth ther Mercurie is reysed ;
Therfore no womman of no clerk is preysed.

The clerk, whan he is old, and may noght do
Of Venus werkes worth his olde sho,
Than sit he doun, and writ in his dotage
That wommen can nat kepe hir mariage!
  But now to purpos, why I tolde thee
That I was beten for a book, pardee.
Up-on a night Jankin, that was our syre,
Redde on his book, as he sat by the fyre,
Of Eva first, that, for hir wikkednesse,
Was al mankinde broght to wrecchednesse,
For which that Jesu Crist him-self was slayn,
That boghte us with his herte-blood agayn.
Lo, here expres of womman may ye finde,
That womman was the los of al mankinde.
  Tho redde he me how Sampson loste his heres,
Slepinge, his lemman kitte hem with hir sheres;
Thurgh whiche tresoun loste he bothe his yën.
  Tho redde he me, if that I shal nat lyen,
Of Hercules and of his Dianyre,
That caused him to sette himself a-fyre.
  No-thing forgat he the penaunce and wo
That Socrates had with hise wyves two;
How Xantippa caste pisse up-on his heed;
This sely man sat stille, as he were deed;
He wyped his heed, namore dorste he seyn
But "er that thonder stinte, comth a reyn."
  Of Phasipha, that was the quene of Crete,
For shrewednesse, him thoughte the tale swete;
Fy! spek na-more—it is a grisly thing—
Of hir horrible lust and hir lyking.
  Of Clitemistra, for hir lecherye,
That falsly made hir housbond for to dye,
He redde it with ful good devocioun.
  He tolde me eek for what occasioun
Amphiorax at Thebes loste his lyf;
Myn housbond hadde a legende of his wyf,
Eriphilem, that for an ouche of gold
Hath prively un-to the Grekes told
Wher that hir housbonde hidde him in a place,
For which he hadde at Thebes sory grace.

Of Lyma tolde he me, and of Lucye,
They bothe made hir housbondes for to dye;
That oon for love, that other was for hate;
Lyma hir housbond, on an even late,
Empoysoned hath, for that she was his fo.
Lucya, likerous, loved hir housbond so,
That, for he sholde alwey up-on hir thinke,
She yaf him swich a maner love-drinke,
That he was deed, er it were by the morwe;
And thus algates housbondes han sorwe.
Than tolde he me, how oon Latumius
Compleyned to his felawe Arrius,
That in his gardin growed swich a tree,
On which, he seyde, how that his wyves three
Hanged hem-self for herte despitous.
"O leve brother," quod this Arrius,
"Yif me a plante of thilke blissed tree,
And in my gardin planted shal it be!"
Of latter date, of wyves hath he red,
That somme han slayn hir housbondes in hir bed,
And lete hir lechour dighte hir al the night
Whyl that the corps lay in the floor up-right.
And somme han drive nayles in hir brayn
Whyl that they slepte, and thus they han hem slayn.
Somme han hem yeve poysoun in hir drinke.
He spak more harm than herte may bithinke.
And ther-with-al, he knew of mo proverbes
Than in this world ther growen gras or herbes.
"Bet is," quod he, "thyn habitacioun
Be with a leoun or a foul dragoun,
Than with a womman usinge for to chyde.
Bet is," quod he, "hye in the roof abyde
Than with an angry wyf doun in the hous;
They been so wikked and contrarious;
They haten that hir housbondes loveth ay."
He seyde, "a womman cast hir shame away,
Whan she cast of hir smok;" and forthermo,
"A fair womman, but she be chaast also,
Is lyk a gold ring in a sowes nose."
Who wolde wenen, or who wolde suppose

The wo that in myn herte was, and pyne ?
  And whan I saugh he wolde never fyne
To reden on this cursed book al night,
Al sodeynly three leves have I plight
Out of his book, right as he radde, and eke,
I with my fist so took him on the cheke,
That in our fyr he fil bakward adoun.
And he up-stirte as dooth a wood leoun,
And with his fist he smoot me on the heed,
That in the floor I lay as I were deed.
And when he saugh how stille that I lay,
He was agast, and wolde han fled his way,
Til atte laste out of my swogh I breyde :
" O ! hastow slayn me, false theef ? " I seyde,
" And for my land thus hastow mordred me ?
Er I be deed, yet wol I kisse thee."
  And neer he cam, and kneled faire adoun,
And seyde, " dere suster Alisoun,
As help me god, I shal thee never smyte ;
That I have doon, it is thy-self to wyte.
Foryeve it me, and that I thee biseke "—
And yet eft-sones I hitte him on the cheke,
And seyde, " theef, thus muchel am I wreke ;
Now wol I dye, I may no lenger speke."
But atte laste, with muchel care and wo,
We fille acorded, by us selven two.
He yaf me al the brydel in myn hond
To han the governance of hous and lond,
And of his tonge and of his hond also,
And made him brenne his book anon right tho.
And whan that I hadde geten un-to me,
By maistrie, al the soveraynetee,
And that he seyde, " myn owene trewe wyf,
Do as thee lust the terme of al thy lyf,
Keep thyn honour, and keep eek myn estaat "
After that day we hadden never debaat.
God help me so, I was to him as kinde
As any wyf from Denmark un-to Inde,
And also trewe, and so was he to me.
I prey to god that sit in magestee,

So blesse his soule, for his mercy dere!
Now wol I seye my tale, if ye wol here.'

Biholde the wordes bitween the Somonour and the Frere.

The Frere lough, whan he hadde herd al this,
'Now, dame,' quod he, 'so have I joye or blis,
This is a long preamble of a tale!'
And whan the Somnour herde the Frere gale,
'Lo!' quod the Somnour, 'goddes armes two!
A frere wol entremette him ever-mo.
Lo, gode men, a flye and eek a frere
Wol falle in every dish and eek matere.
What spekestow of preambulacioun?
What! amble, or trotte, or pees, or go sit doun;
Thou lettest our disport in this manere.'
'Ye, woltow so, sir Somnour?' quod the Frere,
'Now, by my feith, I shal, er that I go,
Telle of a Somnour swich a tale or two,
That alle the folk shal laughen in this place.'
'Now elles, Frere, I bishrewe thy face,'
Quod this Somnour, 'and I bishrewe me,
But-if I telle tales two or three
Of freres er I come to Sidingborne,
That I shal make thyn herte for to morne;
For wel I woot thy pacience is goon.'
Our hoste cryde 'pees! and that anoon!'
And seyde, 'lat the womman telle hir tale.
Ye fare as folk that dronken been of ale.
Do, dame, tel forth your tale, and that is best.'
'Al redy, sir,' quod she, 'right as yow lest,
If I have licence of this worthy Frere.'
'Yis, dame,' quod he, 'tel forth, and I wol here.'

Here endeth the Wyf of Bathe hir Prologe.

Here biginneth the Tale of the Wyf of Bathe.

In th'olde dayes of the king Arthour,
Of which that Britons speken greet honour,

Al was this land fulfild of fayerye.
The elf-queen, with hir joly companye,
Daunced ful ofte in many a grene mede;
This was the olde opinion, as I rede.
I speke of manye hundred yeres ago;
But now can no man see none elves mo.
For now the grete charitee and prayeres
Of limitours and othere holy freres,
That serchen every lond and every streem,
As thikke as motes in the sonne-beem,
Blessinge halles, chambres, kichenes, boures,
Citees, burghes, castels, hye toures,
Thropes, bernes, shipnes, dayeryes,
This maketh that ther been no fayeryes.
For ther as wont to walken was an elf,
Ther walketh now the limitour himself
In undermeles and in morweninges,
And seyth his matins and his holy thinges
As he goth in his limitacioun.
Wommen may go saufly up and doun,
In every bush, or under every tree;
Ther is noon other incubus but he,
And he ne wol doon hem but dishonour.
  And so bifel it, that this king Arthour
Hadde in his hous a lusty bacheler,
That on a day cam rydinge fro river;
And happed that, allone as she was born,
He saugh a mayde walkinge him biforn,
Of whiche mayde anon, maugree hir heed,
By verray force he rafte hir maydenheed;
For which oppressioun was swich clamour
And swich pursute un-to the king Arthour,
That dampned was this knight for to be deed
By cours of lawe, and sholde han lost his heed
Paraventure, swich was the statut tho;
But that the quene and othere ladies mo
So longe preyeden the king of grace,
Til he his lyf him graunted in the place,
And yaf him to the quene al at hir wille,
To chese, whether she wolde him save or spille.

The quene thanketh the king with al hir might,
And after this thus spak she to the knight,
Whan that she saugh hir tyme, up-on a day:
'Thou standest yet,' quod she, 'in swich array,
That of thy lyf yet hastow no suretee.
I grante thee lyf, if thou canst tellen me
What thing is it that wommen most desyren?
Be war, and keep thy nekke-boon from yren.
And if thou canst nat tellen it anon,
Yet wol I yeve thee leve for to gon
A twelf-month and a day, to seche and lere
An answere suffisant in this matere.
And suretee wol I han, er that thou pace,
Thy body for to yelden in this place.'
Wo was this knight and sorwefully he syketh;
But what! he may nat do al as him lyketh.
And at the laste, he chees him for to wende,
And come agayn, right at the yeres ende,
With swich answere as god wolde him purveye;
And taketh his leve, and wendeth forth his weyè.
He seketh every hous and every place,
Wher-as he hopeth for to finde grace,
To lerne, what thing wommen loven most;
But he ne coude arryven in no cost,
Wher-as he mighte finde in this matere
Two creatures accordinge in-fere.
Somme seyde, wommen loven best richesse,
Somme seyde, honour, somme seyde, jolynesse;
Somme, riche array, somme seyden, lust abedde,
And ofte tyme to be widwe and wedde.
Somme seyde, that our hertes been most esed,
Whan that we been y-flatered and y-plesed.
He gooth ful ny the sothe, I wol nat lye;
A man shal winne us best with flaterye;
And with attendance, and with bisinesse,
Been we y-lymed, bothe more and lesse.
And somme seyn, how that we loven best
For to be free, and do right as us lest,
And that no man repreve us of our vyce,
But seye that we be wyse, and no-thing nyce.

For trewely, ther is noon of us alle,
If any wight wol clawe us on the galle,
That we nil kike, for he seith us sooth;
Assay, and he shal finde it that so dooth.
For be we never so vicious with-inne,
We wol been holden wyse, and clene of sinne.
  And somme seyn, that greet delyt han we
For to ben holden stable and eek secree,
And in o purpos stedefastly to dwelle,
And nat biwreye thing that men us telle.
But that tale is nat worth a rake-stele;
Pardee, we wommen conne no-thing hele;
Witnesse on Myda; wol ye here the tale?
  Ovyde, amonges othere thinges smale,
Seyde, Myda hadde, under his longe heres,
Growinge up-on his heed two asses eres,
The whiche vyce he hidde, as he best mighte,
Ful subtilly from every mannes sighte,
That, save his wyf, ther wiste of it na-mo.
He loved hir most, and trusted hir also;
He preyede hir, that to no creature
She sholde tellen of his disfigure.
  She swoor him 'nay, for al this world to winne,
She nolde do that vileinye or sinne,
To make hir housbond han so foul a name;
She nolde nat telle it for hir owene shame.'
But nathelees, hir thoughte that she dyde,
That she so longe sholde a conseil hyde;
Hir thoughte it swal so sore aboute hir herte,
That nedely som word hir moste asterte;
And sith she dorste telle it to no man,
Doun to a marreys faste by she ran;
Til she came there, hir herte was a-fyre,
And, as a bitore bombleth in the myre,
She leyde hir mouth un-to the water doun:
'Biwreye me nat, thou water, with thy soun,'
Quod she, 'to thee I telle it, and namo;
Myn housbond hath longe asses eres two!
Now is myn herte all hool, now is it oute;
I mighte no lenger kepe it, out of doute.'

Heer may ye se, thogh we a tyme abyde,
Yet out it moot, we can no conseil hyde;
The remenant of the tale if ye wol here,
Redeth Ovyde, and ther ye may it lere.
  This knight, of which my tale is specially,
Whan that he saugh he mighte nat come therby,
This is to seye, what wommen loven moost,
With-inne his brest ful sorweful was the goost;
But hoom he gooth, he mighte nat sojourne.
The day was come, that hoomward moste he tourne,
And in his wey it happed him to ryde,
In al this care, under a forest-syde,
Wher-as he saugh up-on a daunce go
Of ladies foure and twenty, and yet mo;
Toward the whiche daunce he drow ful yerne,
In hope that som wisdom sholde he lerne.
But certeinly, er he came fully there,
Vanisshed was this daunce, he niste where.
No creature saugh he that bar lyf,
Save on the grene he saugh sittinge a wyf;
A fouler wight ther may no man devyse.
Agayn the knight this olde wyf gan ryse,
And seyde, 'sir knight, heer-forth ne lyth no wey.
Tel me, what that ye seken, by your fey?
Paraventure it may the bettre be;
Thise olde folk can muchel thing,' quod she.
  'My leve mooder,' quod this knight certeyn,
'I nam but deed, but-if that I can seyn
What thing it is that wommen most desyre;
Coude ye me wisse, I wolde wel quyte your hyre.'
  'Plight me thy trouthe, heer in myn hand,' quod she,
'The nexte thing that I requere thee,
Thou shalt it do, if it lye in thy might;
And I wol telle it yow er it be night.'
'Have heer my trouthe,' quod the knight, 'I grante.'
  'Thanne,' quod she, 'I dar me wel avante,
Thy lyf is sauf, for I wol stonde therby,
Up-on my lyf, the queen wol seye as I.

Lat see which is the proudeste of hem alle,
That wereth on a coverchief or a calle,
That dar seye nay, of that I shal thee teche ;
Lat us go forth with-outen lenger speche.'
Tho rouned she a pistel in his ere,
And bad him to be glad, and have no fere.
  Whan they be comen to the court, this knight
Seyde, 'he had holde his day, as he hadde hight,
And redy was his answere,' as he sayde.
Ful many a noble wyf, and many a mayde,
And many a widwe, for that they ben wyse,
The quene hir-self sittinge as a justyse,
Assembled been, his answere for to here ;
And afterward this knight was bode appere.
  To every wight comanded was silence,
And that the knight sholde telle in audience,
What thing that worldly wommen loven best.
This knight ne stood nat stille as doth a best,
But to his questioun anon answerde
With manly voys, that al the court it herde :
  'My lige lady, generally,' quod he,
'Wommen desyren to have sovereyntee
As wel over hir housbond as hir love,
And for to been in maistrie him above ;
This is your moste desyr, thogh ye me kille,
Doth as yow list, I am heer at your wille.'
  In al the court ne was ther wyf ne mayde,
Ne widwe, that contraried that he sayde,
But seyden, 'he was worthy han his lyf.'
  And with that word up stirte the olde wyf,
Which that the knight saugh sittinge in the grene :
'Mercy,' quod she, 'my sovereyn lady quene !
Er that your court departe, do me right.
I taughte this answere un-to the knight ;
For which he plighte me his trouthe there,
The firste thing I wolde of him requere,
He wolde it do, if it lay in his might.
Bifore the court than preye I thee, sir knight,'
Quod she, 'that thou me take un-to thy wyf ;
For wel thou wost that I have kept thy lyf.

If I sey fals, sey nay, up-on thy fey!'
  This knight answerde, 'allas! and weylawey!
I woot right wel that swich was my biheste.
For goddes love, as chees a newe requeste;
Tak al my good, and lat my body go.'
  'Nay than,' quod she, 'I shrewe us bothe two!
For thogh that I be foul, and old, and pore,
I nolde for al the metal, ne for ore,
That under erthe is grave, or lyth above,
But-if thy wyf I were, and eek thy love.'
  'My love?' quod he; 'nay, my dampnacioun!
Allas! that any of my nacioun
Sholde ever so foule disparaged be!'
But al for noght, the ende is this, that he
Constreyned was, he nedes moste hir wedde;
And taketh his olde wyf, and gooth to bedde.
  Now wolden som men seye, paraventure,
That, for my necligence, I do no cure
To tellen yow the joye and al th'array
That at the feste was that ilke day.
To whiche thing shortly answere I shal;
I seye, ther nas no joye ne feste at al,
Ther nas but hevinesse and muche sorwe;
For prively he wedded hir on a morwe,
And al day after hidde him as an oule;
So wo was him, his wyf looked so foule.
  Greet was the wo the knight hadde in his thoght,
Whan he was with his wyf a-bedde y-broght;
He walweth, and he turneth to and fro.
His olde wyf lay smylinge evermo,
And seyde, 'o dere housbond, *ben'cite!*
Fareth every knight thus with his wyf as ye?
Is this the lawe of king Arthures hous?
Is every knight of his so dangerous?
I am your owene love and eek your wyf;
I am she, which that saved hath your lyf;
And certes, yet dide I yow never unright;
Why fare ye thus with me this firste night?
Ye faren lyk a man had lost his wit;
What is my gilt? for godd's love, tel me it,

And it shal been amended, if I may.'
  'Amended?' quod this knight, 'allas! nay, nay!
It wol nat been amended never mo!
Thou art so loothly, and so old also,
And ther-to comen of so lowe a kinde,
That litel wonder is, thogh I walwe and winde.
So wolde god myn herte wolde breste!'
  'Is this,' quod she, 'the cause of your unreste?'
  'Ye, certainly,' quod he, 'no wonder is.'
  'Now, sire,' quod she, 'I coude amende al this,
If that me liste, er it were dayes three,
So wel ye mighte bere yow un-to me.
  But for ye speken of swich gentillesse
As is descended out of old richesse,
That therfore sholden ye be gentil men,
Swich arrogance is nat worth an hen.
Loke who that is most vertuous alway,
Privee and apert, and most entendeth ay
To do the gentil dedes that he can,
And tak him for the grettest gentil man.
Crist wol, we clayme of him our gentillesse,
Nat of our eldres for hir old richesse.
For thogh they yeve us al hir heritage,
For which we clayme to been of heigh parage,
Yet may they nat biquethe, for no-thing,
To noon of us hir vertuous living,
That made hem gentil men y-called be;
And bad us folwen hem in swich degree.
  Wel can the wyse poete of Florence,
That highte Dant, speken in this sentence;
Lo in swich maner rym is Dantes tale:
"Ful selde up ryseth by his branches smale
Prowesse of man; for god, of his goodnesse,
Wol that of him we clayme our gentillesse;"
For of our eldres may we no-thing clayme
But temporel thing, that man may hurte and mayme.
  Eek every wight wot this as wel as I,
If gentillesse were planted naturelly

Un-to a certeyn linage, doun the lyne,
Privee ne apert, than wolde they never fyne
To doon of gentillesse the faire offyce ;
They mighte do no vileinye or vyce.
  Tak fyr, and ber it in the derkeste hous
Bitwix this and the mount of Caucasus
And lat men shette the dores and go thenne ;
Yet wol the fyr as faire lye and brenne,
As twenty thousand men mighte it biholde
His office naturel ay wol it holde,
Up peril of my lyf, til that it dye.
  Heer may ye see wel, how that genterye
Is nat annexed to possessioun,
Sith folk ne doon hir operacioun
Alwey, as dooth the fyr, lo ! in his kinde.
For, god it woot, men may wel often finde
A lordes sone do shame and vileinye
And he that wol han prys of his gentrye
For he was boren of a gentil hous,
And hadde hise eldres noble and vertuous,
And nil him-selven do no gentil dedis,
Ne folwe his gentil auncestre that deed is,
He nis nat gentil, be he duk or erl ;
For vileyns sinful dedes make a cherl.
For gentillesse nis but renomee
Of thyne auncestres, for hir heigh bountee
Which is a strange thing to thy persone.
Thy gentillesse cometh fro god allone ;
Than comth our verray gentillesse of grace,
It was no-thing biquethe us with our place.
  Thenketh how noble, as seith Valerius,
Was thilke Tullius Hostilius,
That out of povert roos to heigh noblesse.
Redeth Senek, and redeth eek Boëce,
Ther shul ye seen expres that it no drede is,
That he is gentil that doth gentil dedis
And therfore, leve housbond, I thus conclude,
Al were it that myne auncestres were rude,
Yet may the hye god, and so hope I,
Grante me grace to liven vertuously.

Thanne am I gentil, whan that I biginne
To liven vertuously and weyve sinne.
And ther-as ye of povert me repreve,
The hye god, on whom that we bileve,
In wilful povert chees to live his lyf.
And certes every man, mayden, or wyf,
May understonde that Jesus, hevene king,
Ne wolde nat chese a vicious living.
Glad povert is an honest thing, certeyn;
This wol Senek and othere clerkes seyn.
Who-so that halt him payd of his poverte,
I holde him riche, al hadde he nat a sherte.
He that coveyteth is a povre wight,
For he wolde han that is nat in his might.
But he that noght hath, ne coveyteth have
Is riche, al-though ye holde him but a knave.
Verray povert, it singeth proprely;
Juvenal seith of povert merily:
"The povre man, whan he goth by the weye,
Bifore the theves he may singe and pleye."
Povert is hateful good, and, as I gesse,
A ful greet bringer out of bisinesse;
A greet amender eek of sapience
To him that taketh it in pacience.
Povert is this, al-though it seme elenge:
Possessioun, that no wight wol chalenge.
Povert ful ofte, whan a man is lowe,
Maketh his god and eek him-self to knowe.
Povert a spectacle is, as thinketh me,
Thurgh which he may his verray frendes see.
And therfore, sire, sin that I noght yow greve,
Of my povert na-more ye me repreve.
Now, sire, of elde ye repreve me;
And certes, sire, thogh noon auctoritee
Were in no book, ye gentils of honour
Seyn that men sholde an old wight doon favour,
And clepe him fader, for your gentillesse;
And auctours shal I finden, as I gesse.
Now ther ye seye, that I am foul and old,
Than drede you noght to been a cokewold;

For filthe and elde, al-so mote I thee,
Been grete wardeyns up-on chastitee.
But nathelees, sin I knowe your delyt,
I shal fulfille your worldly appetyt.
  Chees now,' quod she, 'oon of thise thinges tweye,
To han me foul and old til that I deye,
And be to yow a trewe humble wyf,
And never yow displese in al my lyf,
Or elles ye wol han me yong and fair,
And take your aventure of the repair
That shal be to your hous, by-cause of me,
Or in som other place, may wel be.
Now chees your-selven, whether that yow lyketh.'
  This knight avyseth him and sore syketh,
But atte laste he seyde in this manere,
'My lady and my love, and wyf so dere,
I put me in your wyse governance;
Cheseth your-self, which may be most plesance,
And most honour to yow and me also.
I do no fors the whether of the two;
For as yow lyketh, it suffiseth me.'
  'Thanne have I gete of yow maistrye,' quod she,
'Sin I may chese, and governe as me lest?'
  'Ye certes, wyf,' quod he, 'I holde it best.'
  'Kis me,' quod she, 'we be no lenger wrothe;
For, by my trouthe, I wol be to yow bothe,
This is to seyn, ye, bothe fair and good.
I prey to god that I mot sterven wood,
But I to yow be al-so good and trewe
As ever was wyf, sin that the world was newe.
And, but I be to-morn as fair to sene
As any lady, emperyce, or quene,
That is bitwixe the est and eke the west,
Doth with my lyf and deeth right as yow lest.
Cast up the curtin, loke how that it is.'
  And whan the knight saugh verraily al this,
That she so fair was, and so yong ther-to
For joye he hente hir in his armes two,
His herte bathed in a bath of blisse;
A thousand tyme a-rewe he gan hir kisse.

And she obeyed him in every thing
That mighte doon him plesance or lyking.
  And thus they live, un-to hir lyves ende,
In parfit joye ; and Jesu Crist us sende
Housbondes meke, yonge, and fresshe a-bedde,
And grace t'overbyde hem that we wedde.
And eek I preye Jesu shorte hir lyves
That wol nat be governed by hir wyves ;
And olde and angry nigardes of dispence,
God sende hem sone verray pestilence.

Here endeth the Wyves Tale of Bathe.

THE FRERES TALE

The Prologe of the Freres Tale.

THIS worthy limitour, this noble Frere,
He made alwey a maner louring chere
Upon the Somnour, but for honestee
No vileyns word as yet to him spak he.
But atte laste he seyde un-to the Wyf,
'Dame,' quod he, 'god yeve yow right good lyf!
Ye han heer touched, al-so mote I thee,
In scole-matere greet difficultee;
Ye han seyd muchel thing right wel, I seye;
But dame, here as we ryden by the weye,
Us nedeth nat to speken but of game,
And lete auctoritees, on goddes name,
To preching and to scole eek of clergye
But if it lyke to this companye,
I wol yow of a somnour telle a game.
Pardee, ye may wel knowe by the name,
That of a somnour may no good be sayd;
I praye that noon of you be yvel apayd.
A somnour is a renner up and doun
With mandements for fornicacioun,
And is y-bet at every tounes ende.'
  Our host tho spak, 'a! sire, ye sholde be hende
And curteys, as a man of your estaat;
In companye we wol have no debaat.
Telleth your tale, and lat the Somnour be.
  'Nay,' quod the Somnour, 'lat him seye to me
What so him list; whan it comth to my lot,
By god, I shal him quyten every grot.

I shal him tellen which a greet honour
It is to be a flateringe limitour;
And his offyce I shal him telle, y-wis.'
Our host answerde, 'pees, na-more of this.'
And after this he seyde un-to the Frere,
'Tel forth your tale, leve maister deere.'

Here endeth the Prologe of the Frere.

Here biginneth the Freres Tale.

WHILOM ther was dwellinge in my contree
An erchedeken, a man of heigh degree,
That boldely dide execucioun
In punisshinge of fornicacioun,
Of wicchecraft, and eek of bauderye,
Of diffamacioun, and avoutrye,
Of chirche-reves, and of testaments,
Of contractes, and of lakke of sacraments,
And eek of many another maner cryme
Which nedeth nat rehercen at this tyme;
Of usure, and of symonye also.
But certes, lechours dide he grettest wo;
They sholde singen, if that they were hent:
And smale tytheres weren foule y-shent.
If any persone wolde up-on hem pleyne,
Ther mighte asterte him no pecunial peyne.
For smale tythes and for smal offringe
He made the peple pitously to singe.
For er the bisshop caughte hem with his hook,
They weren in the erchedeknes book.
Thanne hadde he, thurgh his jurisdiccioun,
Power to doon on hem correccioun.
He hadde a Somnour redy to his hond,
A slyer boy was noon in Engelond;
For subtilly he hadde his espiaille,
That taughte him, wher that him mighte availle.
He coude spare of lechours oon or two,
To techen him to foure and twenty mo.
For thogh this Somnour wood were as an hare,
To telle his harlotrye I wol nat spare;

For we been out of his correccioun ;
They han of us no jurisdiccioun,
Ne never shullen, terme of alle hir lyves.
'Peter ! so been the wommen of the styves,'
Quod the Somnour, 'y-put out of my cure !'
'Pees, with mischance and with misaventure,'
Thus seyde our host, 'and lat him telle his tale.
Now telleth forth, thogh that the Somnour gale,
Ne spareth nat, myn owene maister dere.'
This false theef, this Somnour, quod the Frere,
Hadde alwey baudes redy to his hond,
As any hauk to lure in Engelond,
That tolde him al the secree that they knewe ;
For hir acqueyntance was nat come of-newe.
They weren hise approwours prively ;
He took him-self a greet profit therby ;
His maister knew nat alwey what he wan.
With-outen mandement, a lewed man
He coude somne, on peyne of Cristes curs,
And they were gladde for to fille his purs,
And make him grete festes atte nale.
And right as Judas hadde purses smale,
And was a theef, right swich a theef was he ;
His maister hadde but half his duëtee.
He was, if I shal yeven him his laude,
A theef, and eek a Somnour, and a baude.
He hadde eek wenches at his retenue,
That, whether that sir Robert or sir Huwe,
Or Jakke, or Rauf, or who-so that it were,
That lay by hem, they tolde it in his ere ;
Thus was the wenche and he of oon assent.
And he wolde fecche a feyned mandement,
And somne hem to the chapitre bothe two,
And pile the man, and lete the wenche go.
Thanne wolde he seye, 'frend, I shal for thy sake
Do stryken hir out of our lettres blake ;
Thee thar na-more as in this cas travaille ;
I am thy freend, ther I thee may availle.'
Certeyn he knew of bryberyes mo
Than possible is to telle in yeres two.

For in this world nis dogge for the bowe,
That can an hurt deer from an hool y-knowe,
Bet than this Somnour knew a sly lechour,
Or an avouter, or a paramour.
And, for that was the fruit of al his rente,
Therfore on it he sette al his entente.
And so bifel, that ones on a day
This Somnour, ever waiting on his pray,
Rood for to somne a widwe, an old ribybe,
Feyninge a cause, for he wolde brybe.
And happed that he saugh bifore him ryde
A gay yeman, under a forest-syde.
A bowe he bar, and arwes brighte and kene;
He hadde up-on a courtepy of grene;
An hat up-on his hood with frenges blake.
'Sir,' quod this Somnour, 'hayl! and wel a-take!'
'Wel-come,' quod he, 'and every good felawe!
Wher rydestow under this grene shawe?'
Seyde this yeman, 'wiltow fer to day?'
This Somnour him answerde, and seyde, 'nay;
Heer faste by,' quod he, 'is myn entente
To ryden, for to reysen up a rente
That longeth to my lordes duëtee.'
'Artow thanne a bailly?' 'Ye!' quod he.
He dorste nat, for verray filthe and shame,
Seye that he was a somnour, for the name.
'*Depardieux*,' quod this yeman, 'dere brother,
Thou art a bailly, and I am another.
I am unknowen as in this contree;
Of thyn aqueyntance I wolde praye thee,
And eek of brotherhede, if that yow leste.
I have gold and silver in my cheste;
If that thee happe to comen in our shyre,
Al shal be thyn, right as thou wolt desyre.'
'Grantmercy,' quod this Somnour, 'by my feith!'
Everich in otheres hand his trouthe leith,
For to be sworne bretheren til they deye.
In daliance they ryden forth hir weye.
This Somnour, which that was as ful of jangles,
As ful of venim been thise wariangles,

And ever enquering up-on every thing,
'Brother,' quod he, 'where is now your dwelling,
Another day if that I sholde yow seche?'
This yeman him answerde in softe speche,
'Brother,' quod he, 'fer in the north contree,
Wher, as I hope, som-tyme I shal thee see.
Er we departe, I shal thee so wel wisse,
That of myn hous ne shaltow never misse.'
'Now, brother,' quod this Somnour, 'I yow preye,
Teche me, whyl that we ryden by the weye,
Sin that ye been a baillif as am I,
Som subtiltee, and tel me feithfully
In myn offyce how I may most winne;
And spareth nat for conscience ne sinne,
But as my brother tel me, how do ye?'
'Now, by my trouthe, brother dere,' seyde he,
'As I shal tellen thee a feithful tale,
My wages been ful streite and ful smale.
My lord is hard to me and daungerous,
And myn offyce is ful laborous;
And therfore by extorcions I live.
For sothe, I take al that men wol me yive;
Algate, by sleyghte or by violence,
Fro yeer to yeer I winne al my dispence.
I can no bettre telle feithfully.'
'Now, certes,' quod this Somnour, 'so fare I;
I spare nat to taken, god it woot,
But-if it be to hevy or to hoot.
What I may gete in conseil prively,
No maner conscience of that have I;
Nere myn extorcioun, I mighte nat liven,
Ne of swiche japes wol I nat be shriven.
Stomak ne conscience ne knowe I noon;
I shrewe thise shrifte-fadres everichoon.
Wel be we met, by god and by seint Jame!
But, leve brother, tel me than thy name,'
Quod this Somnour; and in this mene whyle,
This yeman gan a litel for to smyle.
'Brother,' quod he, 'wiltow that I thee telle?
I am a feend, my dwelling is in helle.

And here I ryde about my purchasing,
To wite wher men wolde yeve me any thing.
My purchas is th'effect of al my rente.
Loke how thou rydest for the same entente,
To winne good, thou rekkest never how;
Right so fare I, for ryde wolde I now
Un-to the worldes ende for a preye.'
  'A,' quod this Somnour, '*ben'cite*, what sey ye?
I wende ye were a yeman trewely.
Ye han a mannes shap as wel as I;
Han ye figure than determinat
In helle, ther ye been in your estat?'
  'Nay, certeinly,' quod he, 'ther have we noon;
But whan us lyketh, we can take us oon,
Or elles make yow seme we ben shape
Som-tyme lyk a man, or lyk an ape;
Or lyk an angel can I ryde or go.
It is no wonder thing thogh it be so;
A lousy jogelour can deceyve thee,
And pardee, yet can I more craft than he.'
  'Why,' quod the Somnour, 'ryde ye thanne or goon
In sondry shap, and nat alwey in oon?'
  'For we,' quod he, 'wol us swich formes make
As most able is our preyes for to take.'
  'What maketh yow to han al this labour?'
  'Ful many a cause, leve sir Somnour,'
Seyde this feend, 'but alle thing hath tyme.
The day is short, and it is passed pryme,
And yet ne wan I no-thing in this day.
I wol entende to winnen, if I may,
And nat entende our wittes to declare.
For, brother myn, thy wit is al to bare
To understonde, al-thogh I tolde hem thee.
But, for thou axest why labouren we;
For, som-tyme, we ben goddes instruments,
And menes to don his comandements,
Whan that him list, up-on his creatures
In divers art and in divers figures.

With-outen him we have no might, certayn,
If that him list to stonden ther-agayn.
And som-tyme, at our prayere, han we leve
Only the body and nat the soule greve ;
Witnesse on Job, whom that we diden wo.
And som-tyme han we might of bothe two,
This is to seyn, of soule and body eke.
And somtyme be we suffred for to seke
Up-on a man, and doon his soule unreste,
And nat his body, and al is for the beste.
Whan he withstandeth our temptacioun,
It is a cause of his savacioun ;
Al-be-it that it was nat our entente
He sholde be sauf, but that we wolde him hente.
And som-tyme be we servant un-to man,
As to the erchebisshop Seint Dunstan
And to the apostles servant eek was I.'
'Yet tel me,' quod the Somnour, 'feithfully,
Make ye yow newe bodies thus alway
Of elements ? ' the feend answerde, 'nay ;
Som-tyme we feyne, and som-tyme we aryse
With dede bodies in ful sondry wyse,
And speke as renably and faire and wel
As to the Phitonissa dide Samuel.
And yet wol som men seye it was nat he ;
I do no fors of your divinitee.
But o thing warne I thee, I wol nat jape,
Thou wolt algates wite how we ben shape ;
Thou shalt her-afterward, my brother dere,
Com ther thee nedeth nat of me to lere.
For thou shalt by thyn owene experience
Conne in a chayer rede of this sentence
Bet than Virgyle, whyl he was on lyve,
Or Dant also ; now lat us ryde blyve.
For I wol holde companye with thee
Til it be so, that thou forsake me.'
'Nay,' quod this Somnour, 'that shal nat bityde ;
I am a yeman, knowen is ful wyde ;
My trouthe wol I holde as in this cas.
For though thou were the devel Sathanas,

My trouthe wol I holde to my brother,
As I am sworn, and ech of us til other
For to be trewe brother in this cas ;
And bothe we goon abouten our purchas.
Tak thou thy part, what that men wol thee yive,
And I shal myn ; thus may we bothe live.
And if that any of us have more than other,
Lat him be trewe, and parte it with his brother.'
'I graunte,' quod the devel, 'by my fey.'
And with that word they ryden forth hir wey.
And right at the entring of the tounes ende,
To which this Somnour shoop him for to wende,
They saugh a cart, that charged was with hey,
Which that a carter droof forth in his wey.
Deep was the wey, for which the carte stood.
The carter smoot, and cryde, as he were wood,
'Hayt, Brok ! hayt, Scot ! what spare ye for the stones ?
The feend,' quod he, 'yow fecche body and bones,
As ferforthly as ever were ye foled !
So muche wo as I have with yow tholed !
The devel have al, bothe hors and cart and hey !'
This Somnour seyde, 'heer shal we have a pley ;'
And neer the feend he drough, as noght ne were,
Ful prively, and rouned in his ere :
'Herkne, my brother, herkne, by thy feith ;
Herestow nat how that the carter seith ?
Hent it anon, for he hath yeve it thee,
Bothe hey and cart, and eek hise caples three.'
'Nay,' quod the devel, 'god wot, never a deel ;
It is nat his entente, trust me weel.
Axe him thy-self, if thou nat trowest me,
Or elles stint a while, and thou shalt see.'
This carter thakketh his hors upon the croupe,
And they bigonne drawen and to-stoupe ;
'Heyt, now !' quod he, 'ther Jesu Crist yow blesse,
And al his handwerk, bothe more and lesse !
That was wel twight, myn owene lyard boy !
I pray god save thee and sëynt Loy !

Now is my cart out of the slow, pardee!'
'Lo! brother,' quod the feend, 'what tolde I thee?
Heer may ye see, myn owene dere brother,
The carl spak oo thing, but he thoghte another.
Lat us go forth abouten our viage;
Heer winne I no-thing up-on cariage.'
Whan that they comen som-what out of toune,
This Somnour to his brother gan to roune,
'Brother,' quod he, 'heer woneth an old rebekke,
That hadde almost as lief to lese hir nekke
As for to yeve a peny of hir good.
I wol han twelf pens, though that she be wood,
Or I wol sompne hir un-to our offyce;
And yet, god woot, of hir knowe I no vyce.
But for thou canst nat, as in this contree,
Winne thy cost, tak heer ensample of me.'
This Somnour clappeth at the widwes gate.
'Com out,' quod he, 'thou olde viritrate!
I trowe thou hast som frere or preest with thee!'
'Who clappeth?' seyde this widwe, '*ben'cite!*
God save you, sire, what is your swete wille?'
'I have,' quod he, 'of somonce here a bille;
Up peyne of cursing, loke that thou be
To-morn bifore the erchedeknes knee
T'answere to the court of certeyn thinges.'
'Now, lord,' quod she, 'Crist Jesu, king of kinges,
So wisly helpe me, as I ne may.
I have been syk, and that ful many a day.
I may nat go so fer,' quod she, 'ne ryde,
But I be deed, so priketh it in my syde.
May I nat axe a libel, sir Somnour,
And answere there, by my procutour,
To swich thing as men wol opposen me?'
'Yis,' quod this Somnour, 'pay anon, lat se,
Twelf pens to me, and I wol thee acquyte.
I shall no profit han ther-by but lyte;
My maister hath the profit, and nat I.
Com of, and lat me ryden hastily;
Yif me twelf pens, I may no lenger tarie.'
'Twelf pens,' quod she, 'now lady Seinte Marie

So wisly help me out of care and sinne,
This wyde world thogh that I sholde winne,
Ne have I nat twelf pens with-inne myn hold.
Ye knowen wel that I am povre and old ;
Kythe your almesse on me povre wrecche.'
 'Nay than,' quod he, 'the foule feend me fecche
If I th'excuse, though thou shul be spilt !'
 'Alas,' quod she, 'god woot, I have no gilt.'
 'Pay me,' quod he, 'or by the swete seinte Anne,
As I wol bere awey thy newe panne
For dette, which that thou owest me of old,
Whan that thou madest thyn housbond cokewold,
I payde at hoom for thy correccioun.'
 'Thou lixt,' quod she, 'by my savacioun !
Ne was I never er now, widwe ne wyf,
Somoned un-to your court in al my lyf ;
Ne never I nas but of my body trewe !
Un-to the devel blak and rough of hewe
Yeve I thy body and my panne also !'
 And whan the devel herde hir cursen so
Up-on hir knees, he seyde in this manere,
'Now Mabely, myn owene moder dere,
Is this your wil in ernest, that ye seye ?'
 'The devel,' quod she, 'so fecche him er he deye,
And panne and al, but he wol him repente !'
 'Nay, olde stot, that is nat myn entente,'
Quod this Somnour, 'for to repente me,
For any thing that I have had of thee ;
I wolde I hadde thy smok and every clooth !'
 'Now, brother,' quod the devel, 'be nat wrooth ;
Thy body and this panne ben myne by right.
Thou shalt with me to helle yet to-night,
Where thou shalt knowen of our privetee
More than a maister of divinitee :'
And with that word this foule feend him hente ;
Body and soule, he with the devel wente
Wher-as that somnours han hir heritage.
And god, that maked after his image
Mankinde, save and gyde us alle and some ;
And leve this Somnour good man to bicome'

Lordinges, I coude han told yow, quod this Frere,
Hadde I had leyser for this Somnour here,
After the text of Crist [and] Poul and John,
And of our othere doctours many oon,
Swiche peynes, that your hertes mighte agryse,
Al-be-it so, no tonge may devyse,
Thogh that I mighte a thousand winter telle,
The peyne of thilke cursed hous of helle.
But, for to kepe us fro that cursed place,
Waketh, and preyeth Jesu for his grace
So kepe us fro the temptour Sathanas.
Herketh this word, beth war as in this cas ;
The leoun sit in his await alway
To slee the innocent, if that he may.
Disposeth ay your hertes to withstonde
The feend, that yow wolde make thral and bonde.
He may nat tempten yow over your might ;
For Crist wol be your champion and knight.
And prayeth that thise Somnours hem repente
Of hir misdedes, er that the feend hem hente.

Here endeth the Freres Tale.

THE SOMNOURS TALE

The prologe of the Somnours Tale.

THIS Somnour in his stiropes hye stood;
Up-on this Frere his herte was so wood,
That lyk an aspen leef he quook for yre.
  'Lordinges,' quod he, 'but o thing I desyre;
I yow biseke that, of your curteisye,
Sin ye han herd this false Frere lye,
As suffereth me I may my tale telle!
This Frere bosteth that he knoweth helle,
And god it woot, that it is litel wonder;
Freres and feendes been but lyte a-sonder.
For pardee, ye han ofte tyme herd telle,
How that a frere ravisshed was to helle
In spirit ones by a visioun;
And as an angel ladde him up and doun,
To shewen him the peynes that ther were,
In al the place saugh he nat a frere;
Of other folk he saugh y-nowe in wo.
Un-to this angel spak the frere tho:
  "Now, sir," quod he, "han freres swich a grace
That noon of hem shal come to this place?"
  "Yis," quod this angel, "many a millioun!"
And un-to Sathanas he ladde him doun.
"And now hath Sathanas," seith he, "a tayl
Brodder than of a carrik is the sayl.
Hold up thy tayl, thou Sathanas!" quod he,
"Shewe forth thyn ers, and lat the frere see
Wher is the nest of freres in this place!"
And, er that half a furlong-wey of space,

Right so as bees out swarmen from an hyve,
Out of the develes ers ther gonne dryve
Twenty thousand freres in a route,
And thurgh-out helle swarmeden aboute
And comen agayn, as faste as they may gon,
And in his ers they crepten everichon.
He clapte his tayl agayn, and lay ful stille.
This frere, whan he loked hadde his fille
Upon the torments of this sory place,
His spirit god restored of his grace
Un-to his body agayn, and he awook;
But natheles, for fere yet he quook,
So was the develes ers ay in his minde,
That is his heritage of verray kinde.
God save yow alle, save this cursed Frere;
My prologe wol I ende in this manere.'

Here endeth the Prologe of the Somnours Tale.

Here biginneth the Somonour his Tale.

LORDINGES, ther is in Yorkshire, as I gesse,
A mersshy contree called Holdernesse,
In which ther wente a limitour aboute,
To preche, and eek to begge, it is no doute.
And so bifel, that on a day this frere
Had preched at a chirche in his manere,
And specially, aboven every thing,
Excited he the peple in his preching
To trentals, and to yeve, for goddes sake,
Wher-with men mighten holy houses make,
Ther as divyne service is honoured,
Nat ther as it is wasted and devoured,
Ne ther it nedeth nat for to be yive,
As to possessioners, that mowen live,
Thanked be god, in wele and habundaunce.
'Trentals,' seyde he, 'deliveren fro penaunce
Hir freendes soules, as wel olde as yonge,
Ye, whan that they been hastily y-songe;
Nat for to holde a preest joly and gay,
He singeth nat but o masse in a day;

Delivereth out,' quod he, ' anon the soules ;
Ful hard it is with fleshhook or with oules
To been y-clawed, or to brenne or bake ;
Now spede yow hastily, for Cristes sake.'
And whan this frere had seyd al his entente,
With *qui cum patre* forth his wey he wente.
  Whan folk in chirche had yeve him what hem leste,
He wente his wey, no lenger wolde he reste,
With scrippe and tipped staf, y-tukked hye ;
In every hous he gan to poure and prye,
And beggeth mele, and chese, or elles corn.
His felawe hadde a staf tipped with horn,
A peyre of tables al of yvory,
And a poyntel polisshed fetisly,
And wroot the names alwey, as he stood,
Of alle folk that yaf him any good,
Ascaunces that he wolde for hem preye.
' Yeve us a busshel whete, malt, or reye,
A goddes kechil, or a trip of chese,
Or elles what yow list, we may nat chese ;
A goddes halfpeny or a masse-peny,
Or yeve us of your brawn, if ye have eny ·
A dagon of your blanket, leve dame,
Our suster dere, lo ! here I write your name ;
Bacon or beef, or swich thing as ye finde.'
  A sturdy harlot wente ay hem bihinde,
That was hir hostes man, and bar a sak,
And what men yaf hem, leyde it on his bak.
And whan that he was out at dore anon,
He planed awey the names everichon
That he biforn had writen in his tables ;
He served hem with nyfles and with fables.
  ' Nay, ther thou lixt, thou Somnour,' quod the Frere.
  ' Pees,' quod our Host, ' for Cristes moder dere ;
Tel forth thy tale and spare it nat at al.'
So thryve I, quod this Somnour, so I shal.—
  So longe he wente hous by hous, til he
Cam til an hous ther he was wont to be

Refresshed more than in an hundred placis.
Sik lay the gode man, whos that the place is;
Bedrede up-on a couche lowe he lay.
'*Deus hic*,' quod he, 'O Thomas, freend, good day,'
Seyde this frere curteisly and softe.
'Thomas,' quod he, 'god yelde yow! ful ofte
Have I up-on this bench faren ful weel.
Here have I eten many a mery meel;'
And fro the bench he droof awey the cat,
And leyde adoun his potente and his hat,
And eek his scrippe, and sette him softe adoun.
His felawe was go walked in-to toun,
Forth with his knave, in-to that hostelrye
Wher-as he shoop him thilke night to lye.
'O dere maister,' quod this syke man.
'How han ye fare sith that March bigan?
I saugh yow noght this fourtenight or more.'
'God woot,' quod he, 'laboured have I ful sore;
And specially, for thy savacioun
Have I seyd many a precious orisoun.
And for our othere frendes, god hem blesse!
I have to-day been at your chirche at messe,
And seyd a sermon after my simple wit,
Nat al after the text of holy writ;
For it is hard to yow, as I suppose,
And therfore wol I teche yow al the glose.
Glosinge is a glorious thing, certeyn,
For lettre sleeth, so as we clerkes seyn.
Ther have I taught hem to be charitable.
And spende hir good ther it is resonable,
And ther I saugh our dame; a! wher is she?'
'Yond in the yerd I trowe that she be,'
Seyde this man, 'and she wol come anon.'
'Ey, maister! wel-come be ye, by seint John!
Seyde this wyf, 'how fare ye hertely?'
The frere aryseth up ful curteisly,
And hir embraceth in his armes narwe,
And kiste hir swete, and chirketh as a sparwe
With his lippes: 'dame,' quod he, 'right weel,
As he that is your servant every deel.

Thanked be god, that yow yaf soule and lyf,
Yet saugh I nat this day so fair a wyf
In al the chirche, god so save me!'
 'Ye, god amende defautes, sir,' quod she,
'Algates wel-come be ye, by my fey!'
'Graunt mercy, dame, this have I founde alwey.
But of your grete goodnesse, by your leve,
I wolde prey yow that ye nat yow greve,
I wol with Thomas speke a litel throwe.
Thise curats been ful necligent and slowe
To grope tendrely a conscience.
In shrift, in preching is my diligence,
And studie in Petres wordes, and n Poules.
I walke, and fisshe Cristen mennes soules,
To yelden Jesu Crist his propre rente;
To sprede his word is set al myn entente.'
 'Now, by your leve, o dere sir,' quod she,
'Chydeth him weel, for seinte Trinitee.
He is as angry as a pissemyre,
Though that he have al that he can desyre.
Though I him wrye a-night and make him warm,
And on hym leye my leg outher myn arm,
He groneth lyk our boor, lyth in our sty.
Other desport right noon of him have I;
I may nat plese him in no maner cas.'
 'O Thomas! *Je vous dy*, Thomas! Thomas!
This maketh the feend, this moste ben amended.
Ire is a thing that hye god defended,
And ther-of wol I speke a word or two.'
 'Now maister,' quod the wyf, 'er that I go,
What wol ye dyne? I wol go ther-aboute.'
 'Now dame,' quod he, '*Je vous dy sanz doute*,
Have I nat of a capon but the livere,
And of your softe breed nat but a shivere,
And after that a rosted pigges heed,
(But that I nolde no beest for me were deed),
Thanne hadde I with yow hoomly suffisaunce.
I am a man of litel sustenaunce.
My spirit hath his fostring in the Bible.
The body is ay so redy and penyble

To wake, that my stomak is destroyed.
I prey yow, dame, ye be nat anoyed,
Though I so freendly yow my conseil shewe;
By god, I wolde nat telle it but a fewe.'
'Now, sir,' quod she, 'but o word er I go;
My child is deed with-inne thise wykes two,
Sone after that ye wente out of this toun.'
'His deeth saugh I by revelacioun,'
Seith this frere, 'at hoom in our dortour.
I dar wel seyn that, er that half an hour
After his deeth, I saugh him born to blisse
In myn avisioun, so god me wisse!
So dide our sexteyn and our fermerer,
That han been trewe freres fifty yeer;
They may now, god be thanked of his lone,
Maken hir jubilee and walke allone.
And up I roos, and al our covent eke,
With many a tere trikling on my cheke,
Withouten noyse or clateringe of belles;
Te deum was our song and no-thing elles,
Save that to Crist I seyde an orisoun,
Thankinge him of his revelacioun.
For sir and dame, trusteth me right weel,
Our orisons been more effectueel,
And more we seen of Cristes secree thinges
Than burel folk, al-though they weren kinges.
We live in povert and in abstinence,
And burel folk in richesse and despence
Of mete and drinke, and n hir foul delyt.
We han this worldes lust al in despyt.
Lazar and Dives liveden diversly,
And diverse guerdon hadden they ther-by.
Who-so wol preye, he moot faste and be clene,
And fatte his soule and make his body lene.
We fare as seith th'apostle; cloth and fode
Suffysen us, though they be nat ful gode.
The clennesse and the fastinge of us freres
Maketh that Crist accepteth our preyeres.
Lo, Moyses fourty dayes and fourty night
Fasted, er that the heighe god of might

Spak with him in the mountain of Sinay.
With empty wombe, fastinge many a day,
Receyved he the lawe that was writen
With goddes finger; and Elie, wel ye witen,
In mount Oreb, er he hadde any speche
With hye god, that is our lyves leche,
He fasted longe and was in contemplaunce.
Aaron, that hadde the temple in governaunce,
And eek the othere preestes everichon,
In-to the temple whan they sholde gon
To preye for the peple, and do servyse,
They nolden drinken, in no maner wyse,
No drinke, which that mighte hem dronke make,
But there in abstinence preye and wake,
Lest that they deyden; tak heed what I seye.
But they be sobre that for the peple preye,
War that I seye; namore! for it suffyseth.
Our lord Jesu, as holy writ devyseth,
Yaf us ensample of fastinge and preyeres.
Therfor we mendinants, we sely freres,
Been wedded to poverte and continence,
To charitee, humblesse, and abstinence,
To persecucion for rightwisnesse,
To wepinge, misericorde, and clennesse.
And therfor may ye see that our preyeres—
I speke of us, we mendinants, we freres—
Ben to the hye god more acceptable
Than youres, with your festes at the table.
Fro Paradys first, if I shal nat lye,
Was man out chaced for his glotonye;
And chaast was man in Paradys, certeyn.
But herkne now, Thomas, what I shal seyn.
I ne have no text of it, as I suppose,
But I shall finde it in a maner glose,
That specially our swete lord Jesus
Spak this by freres, whan he seyde thus:
"Blessed be they that povre in spirit been."
And so forth al the gospel may ye seen,
Wher it be lyker our professioun,
Or hirs that swimmen in possessioun.

Fy on hir pompe and on hir glotonye!
And for hir lewednesse I hem diffye.
  Me thinketh they ben lyk Jovinian,
Fat as a whale, and walkinge as a swan;
Al vinolent as botel in the spence.
Hir preyer is of ful gret reverence;
Whan they for soules seye the psalm of Davit,
Lo, "buf!" they seye, "*cor meum eructavit!*"
Who folweth Cristes gospel and his fore,
But we that humble been and chast and pore,
Werkers of goddes word, not auditours?
Therfore, right as an hauk up, at a sours,
Up springeth in-to their, right so prayeres
Of charitable and chaste bisy freres
Maken hir sours to goddes eres two.
Thomas! Thomas! so mote I ryde or go,
And by that lord that clepid is seint Yve,
Nere thou our brother, sholdestou nat thryve!
In our chapitre praye we day and night
To Crist, that he thee sende hele and might,
Thy body for to welden hastily.'
  'God woot,' quod he, 'no-thing ther-of fele I;
As help me Crist, as I, in fewe yeres,
Han spended, up-on dyvers maner freres,
Ful many a pound; yet fare I never the bet.
Certeyn, my good have I almost biset.
Farwel, my gold! for it is al ago!'
  The frere answerde, 'O Thomas, dostow so?
What nedeth yow diverse freres seche?
What nedeth him that hath a parfit leche
To sechen othere leches in the toun?
Your inconstance is your confusioun.
Holde ye than me, or elles our covent,
To praye for yow ben insufficient?
Thomas, that jape nis nat worth a myte;
Your maladye is for we han to lyte.
"A! yif that covent half a quarter otes!"
"A! yif that covent four and twenty grotes!"
"A! yif that frere a peny, and lat him go!"
Nay, nay, Thomas! it may no-thing be so.

What is a ferthing worth parted in twelve?
Lo, ech thing that is oned in him-selve
Is more strong than whan it is to-scatered.
Thomas, of me thou shalt nat been y-flatered;
Thou woldest han our labour al for noght.
The hye god, that al this world hath wroght,
Seith that the werkman worthy is his hyre.
Thomas! noght of your tresor I desyre
As for my-self, but that al our covent
To preye for yow is ay so diligent,
And for to builden Cristes owene chirche.
Thomas! if ye wol lernen for to wirche,
Of buildinge up of chirches may ye finde
If it be good, in Thomas lyf of Inde.
Ye lye heer, ful of anger and of yre,
With which the devel set your herte a-fyre,
And chyden heer this sely innocent,
Your wyf, that is so meke and pacient.
And therfor, Thomas, trowe me if thee leste,
Ne stryve nat with thy wyf, as for thy beste;
And ber this word awey now, by thy feith,
Touchinge this thing, lo, what the wyse seith:
"With-in thyn hous ne be thou no leoun;
To thy subgits do noon oppressioun;
Ne make thyne aqueyntances nat to flee."
And Thomas, yet eft-sones I charge thee,
Be war from hir that in thy bosom slepeth;
War fro the serpent that so slyly crepeth
Under the gras, and stingeth subtilly.
Be war, my sone, and herkne paciently,
That twenty thousand men han lost hir lyves,
For stryving with hir lemmans and hir wyves.
Now sith ye han so holy and meke a wyf,
What nedeth yow, Thomas, to maken stryf?
Ther nis, y-wis, no serpent so cruel,
Whan man tret on his tayl, ne half so fel,
As womman is, whan she hath caught an ire;
Vengeance is thanne al that they desyre.
Ire is a sinne, oon of the grete of sevene,
Abhominable un-to the god of hevene;

And to him-self it is destruccion.
This every lewed viker or person
Can seye, how Ire engendreth homicyde.
Ire is, in sooth, executour of pryde.
I coude of Ire seye so muche sorwe,
My tale sholde laste til to-morwe.
And therfor preye I god bothe day and night,
An irous man, god sende him litel might!
It is greet harm and, certes, gret pitee,
To sette an irous man in heigh degree.
  Whilom ther was an irous potestat,
As seith Senek, that, duringe his estaat,
Up-on a day out riden knightes two,
And as fortune wolde that it were so,
That oon of hem cam hoom, that other noght.
Anon the knight bifore the juge is broght,
That seyde thus, "thou hast thy felawe slayn,
For which I deme thee to the deeth, certayn."
And to another knight comanded he,
"Go lede him to the deeth, I charge thee."
And happed, as they wente by the weye
Toward the place ther he sholde deye,
The knight cam, which men wenden had be deed.
Thanne thoughte they, it was the beste reed,
To lede hem bothe to the juge agayn.
They seiden, "lord, the knight ne hath nat slayn
His felawe; here he standeth hool alyve."
"Ye shul be deed," quod he, "so moot I thryve!
That is to seyn, bothe oon, and two, and three!"
And to the firste knight right thus spak he,
"I dampned thee, thou most algate be deed.
And thou also most nedes lese thyn heed,
For thou art cause why thy felawe deyth."
And to the thridde knight right thus he seyth,
"Thou hast nat doon that I comanded thee."
And thus he dide don sleen hem alle three.
  Irous Cambyses was eek dronkelewe,
And ay delyted him to been a shrewe.
And so bifel, a lord of his meynee,
That lovede vertuous moralitee,

Seyde on a day bitwix hem two right thus :
" A lord is lost, if he be vicious ;
And dronkenesse is eek a foul record
Of any man, and namely in a lord.
Ther is ful many an eye and many an ere
Awaiting on a lord, and he noot where.
For goddes love, drink more attemprely ;
Wyn maketh man to lesen wrecchedly
His minde, and eek his limes everichon."
" The revers shaltou se," quod he, " anon ;
And preve it, by thyn owene experience,
That wyn ne dooth to folk no swich offence.
Ther is no wyn bireveth me my might
Of hand ne foot, ne of myn eyen sight "—
And, for despyt, he drank ful muchel more
An hondred part than he had doon bifore ;
And right anon, this irous cursed wrecche
Leet this knightes sone bifore him fecche,
Comandinge him he sholde bifore him stonde.
And sodeynly he took his bowe in honde,
And up the streng he pulled to his ere,
And with an arwe he slow the child right there :
" Now whether have I a siker hand or noon ? "
Quod he, " is al my might and minde agoon ?
Hath wyn bireved me myn eyen sight ? "
What sholde I telle th'answere of the knight ?
His sone was slayn, ther is na-more to seye.
Beth war therfor with lordes how ye pleye.
Singeth *Placebo*, and I shal, if I can,
But-if it be un-to a povre man.
To a povre man men sholde hise vyces telle,
But nat to a lord, thogh he sholde go to helle.
Lo irous Cirus, thilke Percien,
How he destroyed the river of Gysen,
For that an hors of his was dreynt ther-inne,
Whan that he wente Babiloigne to winne.
He made that the river was so smal,
That wommen mighte wade it over-al.
Lo, what seyde he, that so wel teche can
" Ne be no felawe to an irous man.

Ne with no wood man walke by the weye,
Lest thee repente ; " ther is na-more to seye.
Now Thomas, leve brother, lef thyn ire ;
Thou shalt me finde as just as is a squire.
Hold nat the develes knyf ay at thyn herte ;
Thyn angre dooth thee al to sore smerte ;
But shewe to me al thy confessioun.'
'Nay,' quod the syke man, 'by Seint Simoun !
I have be shriven this day at my curat ;
I have him told al hoolly myn estat ;
Nedeth na-more to speke of it,' seith he,
'But if me list of myn humilitee.'
'Yif me thanne of thy gold, to make our cloistre,'
Quod he, 'for many a muscle and many an oistre,
Whan other men han ben ful wel at eyse,
Hath been our fode, our cloistre for to reyse.
And yet, god woot, unnethe the fundement
Parfourned is, ne of our pavement
Nis nat a tyle yet with-inne our wones ;
By god, we owen fourty pound for stones !
Now help, Thomas, for him that harwed helle !
For elles moste we our bokes selle.
And if ye lakke our predicacioun,
Than gooth the world al to destrucccioun.
For who-so wolde us fro this world bireve,
So god me save, Thomas, by your leve,
He wolde bireve out of this world the sonne.
For who can teche and werchen as we conne ?
And that is nat of litel tyme,' quod he ;
'But sith that Elie was, or Elisee,
Han freres been, that finde I of record,
In charitee, y-thanked be our lord.
Now Thomas, help, for seinte Charitee !'
And doun anon he sette him on his knee.
This syke man wex wel ny wood for ire ;
He wolde that the frere had been on-fire
With his false dissimulacioun.
'Swich thing as is in my possessioun,'
Quod he, 'that may I yeven, and non other.
Ye sey me thus, how that I am your brother ?'

'Ye, certes,' quod the frere, 'trusteth weel;
I took our dame our lettre with our seel.'
'Now wel,' quod he, 'and som-what shal I yive
Un-to your holy covent whyl I live,
And in thyn hand thou shalt it have anoon;
On this condicioun, and other noon,
That thou departe it so, my dere brother,
That every frere have also muche as other.
This shaltou swere on thy professioun,
With-outen fraude or cavillacioun.'
'I swere it,' quod this frere, 'upon my feith!'
And ther-with-al his hand in his he leith:
'Lo, heer my feith! in me shal be no lak.'
'Now thanne, put thyn hand doun by my bak,'
Seyde this man, 'and grope wel bihinde;
Bynethe my buttok ther shaltow finde
A thing that I have hid in privetee.'
'A!' thoghte this frere, 'this shal go with me!'
And doun his hand he launcheth to the clifte,
In hope for to finde ther a yifte.
And whan this syke man felte this frere
Aboute his tuwel grope there and here,
Amidde his hand he leet the frere a fart.
Ther nis no capul, drawinge in a cart,
That mighte have lete a fart of swich a soun.
The frere up stirte as doth a wood leoun:
'A! false cherl,' quod he, 'for goddes bones,
This hastow for despyt doon, for the nones!
Thou shalt abye this fart, if that I may!'
His meynee, whiche that herden this affray,
Cam lepinge in, and chaced out the frere;
And forth he gooth, with a ful angry chere,
And fette his felawe, ther-as lay his stoor.
He looked as it were a wilde boor;
He grinte with his teeth, so was he wrooth.
A sturdy pas doun to the court he gooth,
Wher-as ther woned a man of greet honour,
To whom that he was alwey confessour;
This worthy man was lord of that village.
This frere cam, as he were in a rage,

Wher-as this lord sat eting at his bord.
Unnethes mighte the frere speke a word,
Til atte laste he seyde : 'god yow see !'
  This lord gan loke, and seide, '*ben'cite !*
What, frere John, what maner world is this?
I see wel that som thing ther is amis.
Ye loken as the wode were ful of thevis,
Sit doun anon, and tel me what your greef is,
And it shal been amended, if I may.'
  'I have,' quod he, 'had a despyt this day,
God yelde yow ! adoun in your village,
That in this world is noon so povre a page,
That he nolde have abhominacioun
Of that I have receyved in your toun.
And yet ne greveth me no-thing so sore,
As that this olde cherl, with lokkes hore,
Blasphemed hath our holy covent eke.'
  'Now, maister,' quod this lord, 'I yow biseke.'
  'No maister, sire,' quod he, 'but servitour,
Thogh I have had in scole swich honour.
God lyketh nat that "Raby" men us calle,
Neither in market ne in your large halle.'
  'No fors,' quod he, 'but tel me al your grief.'
  'Sire,' quod this frere, 'an odious meschief
This day bitid is to myn ordre and me,
And so *per consequens* to ech degree
Of holy chirche, god amende it sone !'
  'Sir,' quod the lord, 'ye woot what is to done.
Distempre yow noght, ye be my confessour ;
Ye been the salt of the erthe and the savour.
For goddes love your pacience ye holde ;
Tel me your grief :' and he anon him tolde,
As ye han herd biforn, ye woot wel what.
  The lady of the hous ay stille sat,
Til she had herd al what the frere sayde :
'Ey, goddes moder,' quod she, 'blisful mayde !
Is ther oght elles ? telle me feithfully.'
  'Madame,' quod he, 'how thinketh yow her-by?'

'How that me thinketh ?' quod she ; 'so god me speede,
I seye, a cherl hath doon a cherles dede.
What shold I seye ? god lat him never thee !
His syke heed is ful of vanitee,
I hold him in a maner frenesye.'
'Madame,' quod he, 'by god I shal nat lye ;
But I on other weyes may be wreke,
I shal diffame him over-al ther I speke,
This false blasphemour, that charged me
To parte that wol nat departed be,
To every man y-liche, with meschaunce !'
The lord sat stille as he were in a traunce,
And in his herte he rolled up and doun,
'How hadde this cherl imaginacioun
To shewe swich a probleme to the frere ?
Never erst er now herde I of swich matere ;
I trowe the devel putte it in his minde.
In ars-metryke shal ther no man finde,
Biforn this day, of swich a questioun.
Who sholde make a demonstracioun,
That every man sholde have y-liche his part
As of the soun or savour of a fart ?
O nyce proude cherl, I shrewe his face !
Lo, sires,' quod the lord, with harde grace,
'Who ever herde of swich a thing er now ?
To every man y-lyke ? tel me how.
It is an inpossible, it may nat be !
Ey, nyce cherl, god lete him never thee !
The rumblinge of a fart, and every soun,
Nis but of eir reverberacioun,
And ever it wasteth lyte and lyte awey.
Ther is no man can demen, by my fey,
If that it were departed equally.
What, lo, my cherl, lo, yet how shrewedly
Un-to my confessour to-day he spak !
I holde him certeyn a demoniak !
Now ete your mete, and lat the cherl go pleye,
Lat him go honge himself, a devel weye !'

Now stood the lordes squyer at the bord,
That carf his mete, and herde, word by word,
Of alle thinges of which I have yow sayd.
'My lord,' quod he, 'be ye nat yvel apayd;
I coude telle, for a goune-clooth,
To yow, sir frere, so ye be nat wrooth,
How that this fart sholde even deled be
Among your covent, if it lyked me.'
'Tel,' quod the lord, 'and thou shalt have anon
A goune-cloth, by god and by Seint John!'
'My lord,' quod he, 'whan that the weder is fair,
With-outen wind or perturbinge of air,
Lat bringe a cartwheel here in-to this halle,
But loke that it have his spokes alle.
Twelf spokes hath a cartwheel comunly.
And bring me than twelf freres, woot ye why?
For thrittene is a covent, as I gesse.
The confessour heer, for his worthinesse,
Shal parfourne up the nombre of his covent.
Than shal they knele doun, by oon assent,
And to every spokes ende, in this manere,
Ful sadly leye his nose shal a frere.
Your noble confessour, ther god him save,
Shal holde his nose upright, under the nave.
Than shal this cherl, with bely stif and toght
As any tabour, hider been y-broght;
And sette him on the wheel right of this cart,
Upon the nave, and make him lete a fart.
And ye shul seen, up peril of my lyf,
By preve which that is demonstratif,
That equally the soun of it wol wende,
And eek the stink, un-to the spokes ende;
Save that this worthy man, your confessour,
By-cause he is a man of greet honour,
Shal have the firste fruit, as reson is;
The noble usage of freres yet is this,
The worthy men of hem shul first be served;
And certeinly, he hath it weel deserved.
He hath to-day taught us so muchel good
With preching in the pulpit ther he stood,

That I may vouche-sauf, I sey for me,
He hadde the firste smel of fartes three,
And so wolde al his covent hardily;
He bereth him so faire and holily.'
  The lord, the lady, and ech man, save the frere,
Seyde that Jankin spak, in this matere,
As wel as Euclide or [as] Ptholomee.
Touchinge this cherl, they seyde, subtiltee
And heigh wit made him speken as he spak;
He nis no fool, ne no demoniak.
And Jankin hath y-wonne a newe goune.—
My tale is doon; we been almost at toune.

Here endeth the Somnours Tale

THE CLERKES TALE

Here folweth the Prologe of the Clerkes Tale of Oxenford.

'SIR clerk of Oxenford,' our hoste sayde,
'Ye ryde as coy and stille as dooth a mayde,
Were newe spoused, sitting at the bord;
This day ne herde I of your tonge a word.
I trowe ye studie aboute som sophyme,
But Salomon seith, "every thing hath tyme."
  For goddes sake, as beth of bettre chere,
It is no tyme for to studien here.
Telle us som mery tale, by your fey;
For what man that is entred in a pley,
He nedes moot unto the pley assente.
But precheth nat, as freres doon in Lente,
To make us for our olde sinnes wepe,
Ne that thy tale make us nat to slepe.
  Telle us som mery thing of aventures;—
Your termes, your colours, and your figures,
Kepe hem in stoor til so be ye endyte
Heigh style, as whan that men to kinges wryte.
Speketh so pleyn at this tyme, I yow preye,
That we may understonde what ye seye.'
  This worthy clerk benignely answerde,
'Hoste,' quod he, 'I am under your yerde;
Ye han of us as now the governaunce,
And therfor wol I do yow obeisaunce,
As fer as reson axeth, hardily.
I wol yow telle a tale which that I
Lerned at Padowe of a worthy clerk,
As preved by his wordes and his werk.

He is now deed and nayled in his cheste,
I prey to god so yeve his soule reste!
  Fraunceys Petrark, the laureat poete,
Highte this clerk, whos rethoryke sweete
Enlumined al Itaille of poetrye,
As Linian dide of philosophye
Or lawe, or other art particuler;
But deeth, that wol nat suffre us dwellen heer
But as it were a twinkling of an yë,
Hem bothe hath slayn, and alle shul we dyë.
  But forth to tellen of this worthy man,
That taughte me this tale, as I bigan,
I seye that first with heigh style he endyteth,
Er he the body of his tale wryteth,
A proheme, in the which discryveth he
Pemond, and of Saluces the contree,
And speketh of Apennyn, the hilles hye,
That been the boundes of West Lumbardye,
And of Mount Vesulus in special,
Where as the Poo, out of a welle smal,
Taketh his firste springing and his sours,
That estward ay encresseth in his cours
To Emelward, to Ferrare, and Venyse:
The which a long thing were to devyse.
And trewely, as to my jugement,
Me thinketh it a thing impertinent,
Save that he wol conveyen his matere:
But this his tale, which that ye may here.'

Here biginneth the Tale of the Clerk of Oxenford.

THER is, at the west syde of Itaille,
Doun at the rote of Vesulus the colde,
A lusty playne, habundant of vitaille,
Wher many a tour and toun thou mayst biholde,
That founded were in tyme of fadres olde,
And many another delitable sighte,
And Saluces this noble contree highte.

A markis whylom lord was of that londe,
As were his worthy eldres him bifore;
And obeisant and redy to his honde
Were alle his liges, bothe lasse and more.
Thus in delyt he liveth, and hath don yore,
Biloved and drad, thurgh favour of fortune,
Bothe of his lordes and of his commune.

Therwith he was, to speke as of linage,
The gentilleste y-born of Lumbardye,
A fair persone, and strong, and yong of age,
And ful of honour and of curteisye;
Discreet y-nogh his contree for to gye,
Save in somme thinges that he was to blame,
And Walter was this yonge lordes name.

I blame him thus, that he considereth noght
In tyme cominge what mighte him bityde,
But on his lust present was al his thoght,
As for to hauke and hunte on every syde;
Wel ny alle othere cures leet he slyde,
And eek he nolde, and that was worst of alle,
Wedde no wyf, for noght that may bifalle.

Only that point his peple bar so sore,
That flokmele on a day they to him wente,
And oon of hem, that wysest was of lore,
Or elles that the lord best wolde assente
That he sholde telle him what his peple mente,
Or elles coude he shewe wel swich matere,
He to the markis seyde as ye shul here.

'O noble markis, your humanitee
Assureth us and yeveth us hardinesse,
As ofte as tyme is of necessitee
That we to yow mowe telle our hevinesse;
Accepteth, lord, now for your gentillesse,
That we with pitous herte un-to yow pleyne,
And lete your eres nat my voys disdeyne.

Al have I noght to done in this matere
More than another man hath in this place,

Yet for as muche as ye, my lord so dere,
Han alwey shewed me favour and grace,
I dar the better aske of yow a space
Of audience, to shewen our requeste,
And ye, my lord, to doon right as yow leste.

For certes, lord, so wel us lyketh yow
And al your werk and ever han doon, that we
Ne coude nat us self devysen how
We mighte liven in more felicitee,
Save o thing, lord, if it your wille be,
That for to been a wedded man yow leste,
Than were your peple in sovereyn hertes reste.

Boweth your nekke under that blisful yok
Of soveraynetee, noght of servyse,
Which that men clepeth spousaille or wedlok ;
And thenketh, lord, among your thoghtes wyse,
How that our dayes passe in sondry wyse ;
For though we slepe or wake, or rome, or ryde,
Ay fleeth the tyme, it nil no man abyde.

And though your grene youthe floure as yit,
In crepeth age alwey, as stille as stoon,
And deeth manaceth every age, and smit
In ech estaat, for ther escapeth noon :
And al so certein as we knowe echoon
That we shul deye, as uncerteyn we alle
Been of that day whan deeth shal on us falle.

Accepteth than of us the trewe entente,
That never yet refuseden your heste,
And we wol, lord, if that ye wol assente,
Chese yow a wyf in short tyme, atte leste,
Born of the gentilleste and of the meste
Of al this lond, so that it oghte seme
Honour to god and yow, as we can deme.

Deliver us out of al this bisy drede,
And tak a wyf, for hye goddes sake ;
For if it so bifelle, as god forbede,
That thurgh your deeth your linage sholde slake,

And that a straunge successour sholde take
Your heritage, o! wo were us alyve!
Wherfor we pray you hastily to wyve.'

Hir meke preyere and hir pitous chere
Made the markis herte han pitee.
'Ye wol,' quod he, 'myn owene peple dere,
To that I never erst thoghte streyne me.
I me rejoysed of my libertee,
That selde tyme is founde in mariage;
Ther I was free, I moot been in servage.

But nathelees I see your trewe entente,
And truste upon your wit, and have don ay;
Wherfor of my free wil I wol assente
To wedde me, as sone as ever I may.
But ther-as ye han profred me to-day
To chese me a wyf, I yow relesse
That choys, and prey yow of that profre cesse.

For god it woot, that children ofte been
Unlyk her worthy eldres hem bifore;
Bountee comth al of god, nat of the streen
Of which they been engendred and y-bore;
I truste in goddes bountee, and therfore
My mariage and myn estaat and reste
I him bitake; he may don as him leste.

Lat me alone in chesinge of my wyf,
That charge up-on my bak I wol endure;
But I yow preye, and charge up-on your lyf,
That what wyf that I take, ye me assure
To worshipe hir, whyl that hir lyf may dure,
In word and werk, bothe here and everywhere,
As she an emperoures doghter were.

And forthermore, this shal ye swere, that ye
Agayn my choys shul neither grucche ne stryve;
For sith I shal forgoon my libertee
At your requeste, as ever moot I thryve,
Ther as myn herte is set, ther wol I wyve;
And but ye wole assente in swich manere,
I prey yow, speketh na-more of this matere.'

With hertly wil they sworen, and assenten
To al this thing, ther seyde no wight nay;
Bisekinge him of grace, er that they wenten,
That he wolde graunten hem a certein day
Of his spousaille, as sone as ever he may;
For yet alwey the peple som-what dredde
Lest that this markis no wyf wolde wedde.

He graunted hem a day, swich as him leste,
On which he wolde be wedded sikerly,
And seyde, he dide al this at hir requeste;
And they, with humble entente, buxomly,
Knelinge up-on her knees ful reverently
Him thanken alle, and thus they han an ende
Of hir entente, and hoom agayn they wende.

And heer-up-on he to his officeres
Comaundeth for the feste to purveye,
And to his privee knightes and squyeres
Swich charge yaf, as him liste on hem leye;
And they to his comandement obeye,
And ech of hem doth al his diligence
To doon un-to the feste reverence.

Explicit prima pars.

Incipit secunda pars.

Noght fer fro thilke paleys honurable
Ther-as this markis shoop his mariage,
Ther stood a throp, of site delitable,
In which that povre folk of that village
Hadden hir bestes and hir herbergage,
And of hir labour took hir sustenance
After that th'erthe yaf hem habundance.

Amonges thise povre folk ther dwelte a man
Which that was holden povrest of hem alle;
But hye god som tyme senden can
His grace in-to a litel oxes stalle:
Janicula men of that throp him calle.
A doghter hadde he, fair y-nogh to sighte,
And Grisildis this yonge mayden highte.

But for to speke of vertuous beautee,
Than was she oon the faireste under sonne;
For povreliche y-fostred up was she,
No likerous lust was thurgh hir herte y-ronne;
Wel ofter of the welle than of the tonne
She drank, and for she wolde vertu plese,
She knew wel labour, but non ydel ese.

But thogh this mayde tendre were of age,
Yet in the brest of hir virginitee
Ther was enclosed rype and sad corage;
And in greet reverence and charitee
Hir olde povre fader fostred she;
A fewe sheep spinning on feeld she kepte,
She wolde noght been ydel til she slepte.

And whan she hoomward cam, she wolde bringe
Wortes or othere herbes tymes ofte,
The whiche she shredde and seeth for hir livinge,
And made hir bed ful harde and no-thing softe;
And ay she kepte hir fadres lyf on-lofte
With everich obeisaunce and diligence
That child may doon to fadres reverence.

Up-on Grisilde, this povre creature,
Ful ofte sythe this markis sette his yë
As he on hunting rood paraventure;
And whan it fil that he mighte hir espye,
He noght with wantoun loking of folye
His yën caste on hir, but in sad wyse
Up-on hir chere he wolde him ofte avyse,

Commending in his herte hir wommanhede,
And eek hir vertu, passing any wight
Of so yong age, as wel in chere as dede.
For thogh the peple have no greet insight
In vertu, he considered ful right
Hir bountee, and disposed that he wolde
Wedde hir only, if ever he wedde sholde.

The day of wedding cam, but no wight can
Telle what womman that it sholde be;

For which merveille wondred many a man,
And seyden, whan they were in privetee,
'Wol nat our lord yet leve his vanitee ?
Wol he nat wedde ? allas, allas the whyle !
Why wol he thus him-self and us bigyle ?'

But natheles this markis hath don make
Of gemmes, set in gold and in asure,
Broches and ringes, for Grisildis sake,
And of hir clothing took he the mesure
By a mayde, lyk to hir stature,
And eek of othere ornamentes alle
That un-to swich a wedding sholde falle.

The tyme of undern of the same day
Approcheth, that this wedding sholde be ;
And al the paleys put was in array,
Bothe halle and chambres, ech in his degree :
Houses of office stuffed with plentee
Ther maystow seen of deyntevous vitaille,
That may be founde, as fer as last Itaille.

This royal markis, richely arrayed,
Lordes and ladyes in his companye,
The whiche unto the feste were y-prayed,
And of his retenue the bachelrye,
With many a soun of sondry melodye,
Un-to the village, of the which I tolde,
In this array the righte wey han holde.

Grisilde of this, god woot, ful innocent,
That for hir shapen was al this array,
To fecchen water at a welle is went,
And cometh hoom as sone as ever she may.
For wel she hadde herd seyd, that thilke day
The markis sholde wedde, and, if she mighte,
She wolde fayn han seyn som of that sighte.

She thoghte, 'I wol with othere maydens stonde,
That been my felawes, in our dore, and see
The markisesse, and therfor wol I fonde
To doon at hoom, as sone as it may be,

The labour which that longeth un-to me ;
And than I may at leyser hir biholde,
If she this wey un-to the castel holde.'

And as she wolde over hir threshfold goon,
The markis cam and gan hir for to calle ;
And she set doun hir water-pot anoon
Bisyde the threshfold, in an oxes stalle,
And doun up-on hir knees she gan to falle,
And with sad contenance kneleth stille
Til she had herd what was the lordes wille.

This thoghtful markis spak un-to this mayde
Ful sobrely, and seyde in this manere,
'Wher is your fader, Grisildis ?' he sayde.
And she with reverence, in humble chere,
Answerde, 'lord, he is al redy here.'
And in she gooth with-outen lenger lette,
And to the markis she hir fader fette.

He by the hond than took this olde man,
And seyde thus, whan he him hadde asyde,
'Janicula, I neither may ne can
Lenger the plesance of myn herte hyde.
If that thou vouche-sauf, what-so bityde,
Thy doghter wol I take, er that I wende,
As for my wyf, un-to hir lyves ende.

Thou lovest me, I woot it wel, certeyn,
And art my feithful lige man y-bore ;
And al that lyketh me, I dar wel seyn
It lyketh thee, and specially therfore
Tel me that poynt that I have seyd bifore,
If that thou wolt un-to that purpos drawe,
To take me as for thy sone-in-lawe ?'

This sodeyn cas this man astoned so,
That reed he wex, abayst, and al quaking
He stood ; unnethes seyde he wordes mo,
But only thus : 'lord,' quod he, 'my willing
Is as ye wole, ne ayeines your lyking
I wol no-thing ; ye be my lord so dere ;
Right as yow lust governeth this matere.'

'Yet wol I,' quod this markis softely,
'That in thy chambre I and thou and she
Have a collacion, and wostow why?
For I wol axe if it hir wille be
To be my wyf, and reule hir after me;
And al this shal be doon in thy presence,
I wol noght speke out of thyn audience.'

And in the chambre whyl they were aboute
Hir tretis, which as ye shal after here,
The peple cam un-to the hous with-oute,
And wondred hem in how honest manere
And tentifly she kepte hir fader dere.
But outerly Grisildis wondre mighte,
For never erst ne saugh she swich a sighte.

No wonder is thogh that she were astoned
To seen so greet a gest come in that place;
She never was to swiche gestes woned,
For which she loked with ful pale face.
But shortly forth this tale for to chace,
Thise arn the wordes that the markis sayde
To this benigne verray feithful mayde.

'Grisilde,' he seyde, 'ye shul wel understonde
It lyketh to your fader and to me
That I yow wedde, and eek it may so stonde,
As I suppose, ye wol that it so be.
But thise demandes axe I first,' quod he,
'That, sith it shal be doon in hastif wyse,
Wol ye assente, or elles yow avyse?

I seye this, be ye redy with good herte
To al my lust, and that I frely may,
As me best thinketh, do yow laughe or smerte,
And never ye to grucche it, night ne day?
And eek whan I sey "ye," ne sey nat "nay,"
Neither by word ne frowning contenance;
Swer this, and here I swere our alliance.'

Wondring upon this word, quaking for drede,
She seyde, 'lord, undigne and unworthy

Am I to thilke honour that ye me bede ;
But as ye wol your-self, right so wol I.
And heer I swere that never willingly
In werk ne thoght I nil yow disobeye,
For to be deed, though me were looth to deye.'

'This is y-nogh, Grisilde myn ! ' quod he.
And forth he gooth with a ful sobre chere
Out at the dore, and after that cam she,
And to the peple he seyde in this manere,
'This is my wyf,' quod he, 'that standeth here.
Honoureth hir, and loveth hir, I preye,
Who-so me loveth ; ther is na-more to seye.'

And for that no-thing of hir olde gere
She sholde bringe in-to his hous, he bad
That wommen sholde dispoilen hir right there ;
Of which thise ladyes were nat right glad
To handle hir clothes wher-in she was clad.
But natheles this mayde bright of hewe
Fro foot to heed they clothed han al newe.

Hir heres han they kembd, that lay untressed
Ful rudely, and with hir fingres smale
A corone on hir heed they han y-dressed,
And sette hir ful of nowches grete and smale ;
Of hir array what sholde I make a tale ?
Unnethe the peple hir knew for hir fairnesse,
Whan she translated was in swich richesse.

This markis hath hir spoused with a ring
Broght for the same cause, and than hir sette
Up-on an hors, snow-whyt and wel ambling,
And to his paleys, er he lenger lette,
With joyful peple that hir ladde and mette,
Conveyed hir, and thus the day they spende
In revel, til the sonne gan descende.

And shortly forth this tale for to chace,
I seye that to this newe markisesse
God hath swich favour sent hir of his grace,
That it ne semed nat by lyklinesse

That she was born and fed in rudenesse,
As in a cote or in an oxe-stalle,
But norished in an emperoures halle.

To every wight she woxen is so dere
And worshipful, that folk ther she was bore
And from hir birthe knewe hir yeer by yere,
Unnethe trowed they, but dorste han swore
That to Janicle, of which I spak bifore,
She doghter nas, for, as by conjecture,
Hem thoughte she was another creature.

For thogh that ever vertuous was she,
She was encressed in swich excellence
Of thewes gode, y-set in heigh bountee,
And so discreet and fair of eloquence,
So benigne and so digne of reverence,
And coude so the peples herte embrace,
That ech hir lovede that loked on hir face.

Noght only of Saluces in the toun
Publiced was the bountee of hir name,
But eek bisyde in many a regioun,
If oon seyde wel, another seyde the same:
So spradde of hir heigh bountee the fame,
That men and wommen, as wel yonge as olde,
Gon to Saluce, upon hir to biholde.

Thus Walter lowly, nay but royally,
Wedded with fortunat honestetee,
In goddes pees liveth ful esily
At hoom, and outward grace y-nogh had he;
And for he saugh that under low degree
Was ofte vertu hid, the peple him helde
A prudent man, and that is seyn ful selde.

Nat only this Grisildis thurgh hir wit
Coude al the feet of wyfly hoomlinesse,
But eek, whan that the cas requyred it,
The commune profit coude she redresse.
Ther nas discord, rancour, ne hevinesse
In al that lond, that she ne coude apese,
And wysly bringe hem alle in reste and ese

Though that hir housbonde absent were anoon,
If gentil men, or othere of hir contree
Were wrothe, she wolde bringen hem atoon;
So wyse and rype wordes hadde she,
And jugements of so greet equitee,
That she from heven sent was, as men wende,
Peple to save and every wrong t'amende.

Nat longe tyme after that this Grisild
Was wedded, she a doughter hath y-bore,
Al had hir lever have born a knave child.
Glad was this markis and the folk therfore;
For though a mayde child come al bifore,
She may unto a knave child atteyne
By lyklihed, sin she nis nat bareyne.

Explicit secunda pars.

Incipit tercia pars.

Ther fil, as it bifalleth tymes mo,
Whan that this child had souked but a throwe,
This markis in his herte longeth so
To tempte his wyf, hir sadnesse for to knowe,
That he ne mighte out of his herte throwe
This merveillous desyr, his wyf t'assaye,
Needless, god woot, he thoughte hir for t'affraye.

He hadde assayed hir y-nogh bifore,
And fond hir ever good; what neded it
Hir for to tempte and alwey more and more?
Though som men preise it for a subtil wit,
But as for me, I seye that yvel it sit
T'assaye a wyf whan that it is no nede,
And putten her in anguish and in drede.

For which this markis wroghte in this manere;
He cam alone a-night, ther as she lay,
With sterne face and with ful trouble chere,
And seyde thus, 'Grisild,' quod he, 'that day
That I yow took out of your povre array,
And putte yow in estaat of heigh noblesse.
Ye have nat that forgeten, as I gesse.

I seye, Grisild, this present dignitee,
In which that I have put yow, as I trowe,
Maketh yow nat foryetful for to be
That I yow took in povre estaat ful lowe
For any wele ye moot your-selven knowe.
Tak hede of every word that I yow seye,
Ther is no wight that hereth it but we tweye.

Ye woot your-self wel, how that ye cam here
In-to this hous, it is nat longe ago,
And though to me that ye be lief and dere,
Un-to my gentils ye be no-thing so;
They seyn, to hem it is greet shame and wo
For to be subgets and ben in servage
To thee, that born art of a smal village.

And namely, sith thy doghter was y-bore,
Thise wordes han they spoken doutelees;
But I desyre, as I have doon bifore,
To live my lyf with hem in reste and pees;
I may nat in this caas be recchelees.
I moot don with thy doghter for the beste,
Nat as I wolde, but as my peple leste.

And yet, god wot, this is ful looth to me;
But nathelees with-oute your witing
I wol nat doon, but this wol I,' quod he,
'That ye to me assente as in this thing.
Shewe now your pacience in your werking
That ye me highte and swore in your village
That day that maked was our mariage.'

Whan she had herd al this, she noght ameved
Neither in word, or chere, or countenaunce;
For, as it semed, she was nat agreved:
She seyde, 'lord, al lyth in your plesaunce,
My child and I with hertly obeisaunce
Ben youres al, and ye mowe save or spille
Your owene thing; werketh after your wille.

Ther may no-thing, god so my soule save,
Lyken to yow that may displese me;

Ne I desyre no-thing for to have,
Ne drede for to lese, save only ye;
This wil is in myn herte and ay shal be.
No lengthe of tyme or deeth may this deface,
Ne chaunge my corage to another place.'

Glad was this markis of hir answering,
But yet he feyned as he were nat so;
Al drery was his chere and his loking
Whan that he sholde out of the chambre go.
Sone after this, a furlong wey or two,
He prively hath told al his entente
Un-to a man, and to his wyf him sente.

A maner sergeant was this privee man,
The which that feithful ofte he founden hadde
In thinges grete, and eek swich folk wel can
Don execucioun on thinges badde.
The lord knew wel that he him loved and dradde;
And whan this sergeant wiste his lordes wille,
In-to the chambre he stalked him ful stille.

'Madame,' he seyde, 'ye mote foryeve it me,
Thogh I do thing to which I am constreyned;
Ye ben so wys that ful wel knowe ye
That lordes hestes mowe nat been y-feyned;
They mowe wel been biwailled or compleyned,
But men mot nede un-to her lust obeye,
And so wol I; ther is na-more to seye.

This child I am comanded for to take'—
And spak na-more, but out the child he hente
Despitously, and gan a chere make
As though he wolde han slayn it er he wente.
Grisildis mot al suffren and consente;
And as a lamb she sitteth meke and stille,
And leet this cruel sergeant doon his wille.

Suspecious was the diffame of this man,
Suspect his face, suspect his word also;
Suspect the tyme in which he this bigan.
Allas! hir doghter that she lovede so

She wende he wolde han slawen it right tho.
But natheles she neither weep ne syked,
Consenting hir to that the markis lyked.

But atte laste speken she bigan,
And mekely she to the sergeant preyde,
So as he was a worthy gentil man,
That she moste kisse hir child er that it deyde ;
And in her barm this litel child she leyde
With ful sad face, and gan the child to kisse
And lulled it, and after gan it blisse.

And thus she seyde in hir benigne voys,
'Far weel, my child ; I shal thee never see ;
But, sith I thee have marked with the croys,
Of thilke fader blessed mote thou be,
That for us deyde up-on a croys of tree.
Thy soule, litel child, I him bitake,
For this night shaltow dyen for my sake.'

I trowe that to a norice in this cas
It had ben hard this rewthe for to se ;
Wel mighte a mooder than han cryed 'allas !'
But nathelees so sad stedfast was she,
That she endured all adversitee,
And to the sergeant mekely she sayde,
'Have heer agayn your litel yonge mayde.

Goth now,' quod she, 'and dooth my lordes heste,
But o thing wol I preye yow of your grace,
That, but my lord forbad yow, atte leste
Burieth this litel body in som place
That bestes ne no briddes it to-race.'
But he no word wol to that purpos seye,
But took the child and wente upon his weye.

This sergeant cam un-to his lord ageyn,
And of Grisildis wordes and hir chere
He tolde him point for point, in short and playn,
And him presenteth with his doghter dere.
Somwhat this lord hath rewthe in his manere ;
But nathelees his purpos heeld he stille,
As lordes doon, whan they wol han hir wille ;

And bad his sergeant that he prively
Sholde this child ful softe winde and wrappe
With alle circumstances tendrely,
And carie it in a cofre or in a lappe;
But, up-on peyne his heed of for to swappe,
That no man sholde knowe of his entente,
Ne whenne he cam, ne whider that he wente;

But at Bologne to his suster dere,
That thilke tyme of Panik was countesse,
He sholde it take, and shewe hir this matere,
Bisekinge hir to don hir bisinesse
This child to fostre in alle gentilesse;
And whos child that it was he bad hir hyde
From every wight, for oght that may bityde.

The sergeant gooth, and hath fulfild this thing;
But to this markis now retourne we;
For now goth he ful faste imagining
If by his wyves chere he mighte see,
Or by hir word aperceyve that she
Were chaunged; but he never hir coude finde
But ever in oon y-lyke sad and kinde.

As glad, as humble, as bisy in servyse,
And eek in love as she was wont to be,
Was she to him in every maner wyse;
Ne of hir doghter noght a word spak she.
Non accident for noon adversitee
Was seyn in hir, ne never hir doghter name
Ne nempned she, in ernest nor in game.

Explicit tercia pars.

Sequitur pars quarta.

In this estaat ther passed been foure yeer
Er she with childe was; but, as god wolde,
A knave child she bar by this Walter,
Ful gracious and fair for to biholde.
And whan that folk it to his fader tolde,
Nat only he, but al his contree, merie
Was for this child, and god they thanke and herie.

Whan it was two yeer old, and fro the brest
Departed of his norice, on a day
This markis caughte yet another lest
To tempte his wyf yet ofter, if he may.
O needles was she tempted in assay!
But wedded men ye knowe no mesure,
Whan that they finde a pacient creature.

'Wyf,' quod this markis, 'ye han herd er this,
My peple sikly berth our mariage,
And namely, sith my sone y-boren is,
Now is it worse than ever in al our age.
The murmur sleeth myn herte and my corage;
For to myne eres comth the voys so smerte,
That it wel ny destroyed hath myn herte.

Now sey they thus, "whan Walter is agoon,
Then shal the blood of Janicle succede
And been our lord, for other have we noon;"
Swiche wordes seith my peple, out of drede.
Wel oughte I of swich murmur taken hede;
For certeinly I drede swich sentence,
Though they nat pleyn speke in myn audience.

I wolde live in pees, if that I mighte;
Wherfor I am disposed outerly,
As I his suster servede by nighte,
Right so thenke I to serve him prively;
This warne I yow, that ye nat sodeynly
Out of your-self for no wo sholde outraye;
Beth pacient, and ther-of I yow preye.'

'I have,' quod she, 'seyd thus, and ever shal,
I wol no thing, ne nil no thing, certayn,
But as yow list; noght greveth me at al,
Thogh that my doghter and my sone be slayn,
At your comandement, this is to sayn.
I have noght had no part of children tweyne
But first siknesse, and after wo and peyne.

Ye been our lord, doth with your owene thing
Right as yow list; axeth no reed at me.

For, as I lefte at hoom al my clothing,
Whan I first cam to yow, right so,' quod she,
'Lefte I my wil and al my libertee,
And took your clothing; wherfor I yow preye,
Doth your plesaunce, I wol your lust obeye.

And certes, if I hadde prescience
Your wil to knowe er ye your lust me tolde,
I wolde it doon with-outen necligence;
But now I woot your lust and what ye wolde,
Al your plesaunce ferme and stable I holde;
For wiste I that my deeth wolde do yow ese,
Right gladly wolde I dyen, yow to plese.

Deth may noght make no comparisoun
Un-to your love:' and, whan this markis sey
The constance of his wyf, he caste adoun
His yën two, and wondreth that she may
In pacience suffre al this array.
And forth he gooth with drery contenaunce,
But to his herte it was ful greet plesaunce.

This ugly sergeant, in the same wyse
That he hir doghter caughte, right so he,
Or worse, if men worse can devyse,
Hath hent hir sone, that ful was of beautee.
And ever in oon so pacient was she,
That she no chere made of hevinesse,
But kiste hir sone, and after gan it blesse;

Save this; she preyed him that, if he mighte,
Hir litel sone he wolde in erthe grave,
His tendre limes, delicat to sighte,
Fro foules and fro bestes for to save.
But she non answer of him mighte have.
He wente his wey, as him no-thing ne roghte;
But to Boloigne he tendrely it broghte.

This markis wondreth ever lenger the more
Up-on hir pacience, and if that he
Ne hadde soothly knowen ther-bifore,
That parfitly hir children lovede she,

He wolde have wend that of som subtiltee,
And of malice or for cruel corage,
That she had suffred this with sad visage.

But wel he knew that next him-self, certayn,
She loved hir children best in every wyse.
But now of wommen wolde I axen fayn,
If thise assayes mighte nat suffyse?
What coude a sturdy housbond more devyse
To preve hir wyfhod and hir stedfastnesse,
And he continuing ever in sturdinesse?

But ther ben folk of swich condicioun,
That, whan they have a certein purpos take,
They can nat stinte of hir entencioun,
But, right as they were bounden to a stake,
They wol nat of that firste purpos slake.
Right so this markis fulliche hath purposed
To tempte his wyf, as he was first disposed.

He waiteth, if by word or contenance
That she to him was changed of corage:
But never coude he finde variance;
She was ay oon in herte and in visage;
And ay the forther that she was in age,
The more trewe, if that it were possible,
She was to him in love, and more penible.

For which it semed thus, that of hem two
Ther nas but o wil; for, as Walter leste,
The same lust was hir plesance also,
And, god be thanked, al fil for the beste.
She shewed wel, for no worldly unreste
A wyf, as of hir-self, no-thing ne sholde
Wille in effect, but as hir housbond wolde.

The sclaundre of Walter ofte and wyde spradde,
That of a cruel herte he wikkedly,
For he a povre womman wedded hadde,
Hath mordred bothe his children prively.
Swich murmur was among hem comunly.
No wonder is, for to the peples ere
Ther cam no word but that they mordred were.

For which, wher-as his peple ther-bifore
Had loved him wel, the sclaundre of his diffame
Made hem that they him hatede therfore;
To been a mordrer is an hateful name.
But natheles, for ernest ne for game
He of his cruel purpos nolde stente;
To tempte his wyf was set al his entente.

Whan that his doghter twelf yeer was of age,
He to the court of Rome, in subtil wyse
Enformed of his wil, sente his message,
Comaunding hem swiche bulles to devyse
As to his cruel purpos may suffyse,
How that the pope, as for his peples reste,
Bad him to wedde another, if him leste.

I seye, he bad they sholde countrefete
The popes bulles, making mencioun
That he hath leve his firste wyf to lete,
As by the popes dispensacioun,
To stinte rancour and dissencioun
Bitwixe his peple and him; thus seyde the bulle,
The which they han publiced atte fulle.

The rude peple, as it no wonder is,
Wenden ful wel that it had been right so;
But whan thise tydinges cam to Grisildis,
I deme that hir herte was ful wo.
But she, y-lyke sad for evermo,
Disposed was, this humble creature,
Th'adversitee of fortune al t'endure.

Abyding ever his lust and his plesaunce,
To whom that she was yeven, herte and al,
As to hir verray worldly suffisaunce;
But shortly if this storie I tellen shal,
This markis writen hath in special
A lettre in which he sheweth his entente,
And secrely he to Boloigne it sente.

To th'erl of Panik, which that hadde tho
Wedded his suster, preyde he specially

To bringen hoom agayn his children two
In honurable estaat al openly.
But o thing he him preyede outerly,
That he to no wight, though men wolde enquere,
Sholde nat telle, whos children that they were,

But seye, the mayden sholde y-wedded be
Un-to the markis of Saluce anon.
And as this erl was preyed, so dide he;
For at day set he on his wey is goon
Toward Saluce, and lordes many oon,
In riche array, this mayden for to gyde;
Hir yonge brother ryding hir bisyde.

Arrayed was toward hir mariage
This fresshe mayde, ful of gemmes clere;
Hir brother, which that seven yeer was of age,
Arrayed eek ful fresh in his manere.
And thus in greet noblesse and with glad chere,
Toward Saluces shaping hir journey,
Fro day to day they ryden in hir wey.

Explicit quarta pars.

Sequitur quinta pars.

Among al this, after his wikke usage,
This markis, yet his wyf to tempte more
To the uttereste preve of hir corage,
Fully to han experience and lore
If that she were as stedfast as bifore,
He on a day in open audience
Ful boistously hath seyd hir this sentence:

'Certes, Grisilde, I hadde y-nough plesaunce
To han yow to my wyf for your goodnesse,
As for your trouthe and for your obeisaunce,
Nought for your linage ne for your richesse;
But now knowe I in verray soothfastnesse
That in gret lordshipe, if I wel avyse,
Ther is gret servitute in sondry wyse.

I may nat don as every plowman may ;
My peple me constreyneth for to take
Another wyf, and cryen day by day ;
And eek the pope, rancour for to slake,
Consenteth it, that dar I undertake ;
And treweliche thus muche I wol yow seye,
My newe wyf is coming by the weye.

Be strong of herte, and voyde anon hir place,
And thilke dower that ye broghten me
Tak it agayn, I graunte it of my grace ;
Retourneth to your fadres hous,' quod he ;
'No man may alwey han prosperitee ;
With evene herte I rede yow t'endure
The strook of fortune or of aventure.'

And she answerde agayn in pacience,
'My lord,' quod she, 'I woot, and wiste alway
How that bitwixen your magnificence
And my poverte no wight can ne may
Maken comparison ; it is no nay.
I ne heeld me never digne in no manere
To be your wyf, no, ne your chamberere.

And in this hous, ther ye me lady made—
The heighe god take I for my witnesse,
And also wisly he my soule glade—
I never heeld me lady ne maistresse,
But humble servant to your worthinesse,
And ever shal, whyl that my lyf may dure,
Aboven every worldly creature.

That ye so longe of your benignitee
Han holden me in honour and nobleye,
Wher-as I was noght worthy for to be,
That thonke I god and yow, to whom I preye
Foryelde it yow ; there is na-more to seye.
Un-to my fader gladly wol I wende,
And with him dwelle un-to my lyves ende.

Ther I was fostred of a child ful smal,
Til I be deed, my lyf ther wol I lede

A widwe clene, in body, herte, and al.
For sith I yaf to yow my maydenhede,
And am your trewe wyf, it is no drede,
God shilde swich a lordes wyf to take
Another man to housbonde or to make.

And of your newe wyf, god of his grace
So graunte yow wele and prosperitee:
For I wol gladly yelden hir my place,
In which that I was blisful wont to be,
For sith it lyketh yow, my lord,' quod she,
'That whylom weren al myn hertes reste,
That I shal goon, I wol gon whan yow leste.

But ther-as ye me profre swich dowaire
As I first broghte, it is wel in my minde
It were my wrecched clothes, no-thing faire,
The which to me were hard now for to finde.
O gode god! how gentil and how kinde
Ye semed by your speche and your visage
The day that maked was our mariage!

But sooth is seyd, algate I finde it trewe—
For in effect it preved is on me—
Love is noght old as whan that it is newe.
But certes, lord, for noon adversitee,
To dyen in the cas, it shal nat be
That ever in word or werk I shal repente
That I yow yaf myn herte in hool entente.

My lord, ye woot that, in my fadres place,
Ye dede me strepe out of my povre wedé,
And richely me cladden, of your grace.
To yow broghte I noght elles, out of drede,
But feyth and nakednesse and maydenhede.
And here agayn my clothing I restore,
And eek my wedding-ring, for evermore.

The remenant of your jewels redy be
In-with your chambre, dar I saufly sayn;
Naked out of my fadres hous,' quod she,
'I cam, and naked moot I turne agayn.

Al your plesaunce wol I folwen fayn ;
But yet I hope it be nat your entente
That I smoklees out of your paleys wente.

Ye coude nat doon so dishoneste a thing,
That thilke wombe in which your children leye
Sholde, biforn the peple, in my walking,
Be seyn al bare ; wherfor I yow preye,
Lat me nat lyk a worm go by the weye.
Remembre yow, myn owene lord so dere,
I was your wyf, thogh I unworthy were.

Wherfor, in guerdon of my maydenhede,
Which that I broghte, and noght agayn I bere,
As voucheth sauf to yeve me, to my mede,
But swich a smok as I was wont to were,
That I therwith may wrye the wombe of here
That was your wyf ; and heer take I my leve
Of yow, myn owene lord, lest I yow greve.'

'The smok,' quod he, 'that thou hast on thy bak,
Lat it be stille, and ber it forth with thee.'
But wel unnethes thilke word he spak,
But wente his wey for rewthe and for pitee.
Biforn the folk hir-selven strepeth she,
And in hir smok, with heed and foot al bare,
Toward hir fader hous forth is she fare.

The folk hir folwe wepinge in hir weye,
And fortune ay they cursen as they goon ;
But she fro weping kepte hir yën dreye,
Ne in this tyme word ne spak she noon.
Hir fader, that this tyding herde anoon,
Curseth the day and tyme that nature
Shoop him to been a lyves creature.

For out of doute this olde povre man
Was ever in suspect of hir mariage ;
For ever he demed, sith that it bigan,
That whan the lord fulfild had his corage,
Him wolde thinke it were a disparage
To his estaat so lowe for t'alighte,
And voyden hir as sone as ever he mighte

Agayns his doghter hastilich goth he,
For he by noyse of folk knew hir cominge.
And with hir olde cote, as it mighte be,
He covered hir, ful sorwefully wepinge;
But on hir body mighte he it nat bringe.
For rude was the cloth, and more of age
By dayes fele than at hir mariage.

Thus with hir fader, for a certeyn space,
Dwelleth this flour of wyfly pacience,
That neither by hir wordes ne hir face
Biforn the folk, ne eek in hir absence,
Ne shewed she that hir was doon offence;
Ne of hir heigh estaat no remembraunce
Ne hadde she, as by hir countenaunce.

No wonder is, for in hir grete estaat
Hir goost was ever in pleyn humylitee;
No tendre mouth, non herte delicaat,
No pompe, no semblant of royaltee,
But ful of pacient benignitee,
Discreet and prydeles, ay honurable,
And to hir housbonde ever meke and stable.

Men speke of Job and most for his humblesse,
As clerkes, whan hem list, can wel endyte,
Namely of men, but as in soothfastnesse,
Thogh clerkes preyse wommen but a lyte,
Ther can no man in humblesse him acquyte
As womman can, ne can ben half so trewe
As wommen been, but it be falle of-newe.

[*Pars Sexta.*]

Fro Boloigne is this erl of Panik come,
Of which the fame up-sprang to more and lesse,
And in the peples eres alle and some
Was couth eek, that a newe markisesse
He with him broghte, in swich pompe and richesse,
That never was ther seyn with mannes yë
So noble array in al West Lumbardye.

The markis, which that shoop and knew al this,
Er that this erl was come, sente his message
For thilke sely povre Grisildis ;
And she with humble herte and glad visage,
Nat with no swollen thoght in hir corage,
Cam at his heste, and on hir knees hir sette,
And reverently and wysly she him grette.

'Grisild,' quod he, 'my wille is outerly,
This mayden, that shal wedded been to me,
Receyved be to-morwe as royally
As it possible is in myn hous to be.
And eek that every wight in his degree
Have his estaat in sitting and servyse
And heigh plesaunce, as I can best devyse.

I have no wommen suffisaunt certayn
The chambres for t'arraye in ordinaunce
After my lust, and therfor wolde I fayn
That thyn were al swich maner governaunce ;
Thou knowest eek of old al my plesaunce ;
Though thyn array be badde and yvel biseye,
Do thou thy devoir at the leeste weye.'

'Nat only, lord, that I am glad,' quod she,
'To doon your lust, but I desyre also
Yow for to serve and plese in my degree
With-outen feynting, and shal evermo.
Ne never, for no wele ne no wo,
Ne shal the gost with-in myn herte stente
To love yow best with al my trewe entente.'

And with that word she gan the hous to dighte,
And tables for to sette and beddes make ;
And peyned hir to doon al that she mighte,
Preying the chambereres, for goddes sake,
To hasten hem, and faste swepe and shake ;
And she, the moste servisable of alle,
Hath every chambre arrayed and his halle.

Abouten undern gan this erl alighte,
That with him broghte thise noble children tweye,

For which the peple ran to seen the sighte
Of hir array, so richely biseye;
And than at erst amonges hem they seye,
That Walter was no fool, thogh that him leste
To chaunge his wyf, for it was for the beste.

For she is fairer, as they demen alle,
Than is Grisild, and more tendre of age,
And fairer fruit bitwene hem sholde falle,
And more plesant, for hir heigh linage;
Hir brother eek so fair was of visage,
That hem to seen the peple hath caught plesaunce,
Commending now the markis governaunce.—

Auctor. 'O stormy peple! unsad and ever untrewe!
Ay undiscreet and chaunging as a vane,
Delyting ever in rumbel that is newe,
For lyk the mone ay wexe ye and wane;
Ay ful of clapping, dere y-nogh a jane;
Your doom is fals, your constance yvel preveth,
A ful greet fool is he that on yow leveth!'

Thus seyden sadde folk in that citee,
Whan that the peple gazed up and doun,
For they were glad, right for the noveltee,
To han a newe lady of hir toun.
Na-more of this make I now mencioun;
But to Grisilde agayn wol I me dresse,
And telle hir constance and hir bisinesse.—

Ful bisy was Grisilde in every thing
That to the feste was apertinent;
Right noght was she abayst of hir clothing,
Though it were rude and somdel eek to-rent.
But with glad chere to the yate is went,
With other folk, to grete the markisesse,
And after that doth forth hir bisinesse.

With so glad chere his gestes she receyveth,
And conningly, everich in his degree,

That no defaute no man aperceyveth ;
But ay they wondren what she mighte be
That in so povre array was for to see,
And coude swich honour and reverence ;
And worthily they preisen hir prudence.

In al this mene whyle she ne stente
This mayde and eek hir brother to commende
With al hir herte, in ful benigne entente,
So wel, that no man coude hir prys amende.
But atte laste, whan that thise lordes wende
To sitten doun to mete, he gan to calle
Grisilde, as she was bisy in his halle.

'Grisilde,' quod he, as it were in his pley,
'How lyketh thee my wyf and hir beautee ?'
'Right wel,' quod she, 'my lord ; for, in good fey,
A fairer say I never noon than she.
I prey to god yeve hir prosperitee ;
And so hope I that he wol to yow sende
Plesance y-nogh un-to your lyves ende.

O thing biseke I yow and warne also,
That ye ne prikke with no tormentinge
This tendre mayden, as ye han don mo ;
For she is fostred in hir norishinge
More tendrely, and, to my supposinge,
She coude nat adversitee endure
As coude a povre fostred creature.'

And whan this Walter say hir pacience,
Hir glade chere and no malice at al,
And he so ofte had doon to hir offence,
And she ay sad and constant as a wal,
Continuing ever hir innocence overal,
This sturdy markis gan his herte dresse
To rewen up-on hir wyfly stedfastnesse.

'This is y-nogh, Grisilde myn,' quod he,
'Be now na-more agast ne yvel apayed ;
I have thy feith and thy benignitee,
As wel as ever womman was, assayed,

In greet estaat, and povreliche arrayed.
Now knowe I, dere wyf, thy stedfastnesse,'—
And hir in armes took and gan hir kesse.

And she for wonder took of it no keep;
She herde nat what thing he to hir seyde;
She ferde as she had stert out of a sleep,
Til she out of hir masednesse abreyde.
'Grisilde,' quod he, 'by god that for us deyde,
Thou art my wyf, ne noon other I have,
Ne never hadde, as god my soule save!

This is thy doghter which thou hast supposed
To be my wyf; that other feithfully
Shal be myn heir, as I have ay purposed;
Thou bare him in thy body trewely.
At Boloigne have I kept hem prively;
Tak hem agayn, for now maystow nat seye
That thou hast lorn non of thy children tweye.

And folk that otherweyes han seyd of me,
I warne hem wel that I have doon this dede
For no malice ne for no crueltee,
But for t'assaye in thee thy wommanhede,
And nat to sleen my children, god forbede!
But for to kepe hem prively and stille,
Til I thy purpos knewe and al thy wille.'

Whan she this herde, aswowne doun she falleth
For pitous joye, and after hir swowninge
She bothe hir yonge children un-to hir calleth,
And in hir armes, pitously wepinge,
Embraceth hem, and tendrely kissinge
Ful lyk a mooder, with hir salte teres
She batheth bothe hir visage and hir heres.

O, which a pitous thing it was to see
Hir swowning, and hir humble voys to here!
'Grauntmercy, lord, that thanke I yow,' quod she,
'That ye han saved me my children dere!
Now rekke I never to ben deed right here;
Sith I stonde in your love and in your grace,
No fors of deeth, ne whan my spirit pace!

O tendre, o dere, o yonge children myne,
Your woful mooder wende stedfastly
That cruel houndes or som foul vermyne
Hadde eten yow ; but god, of his mercy,
And your benigne fader tendrely
Hath doon yow kept ; ' and in that same stounde
Al sodeynly she swapte adoun to grounde.

And in her swough so sadly holdeth she
Hir children two, whan she gan hem t'embrace,
That with greet sleighte and greet difficultee
The children from hir arm they gonne arace.
O many a teer on many a pitous face
Doun ran of hem that stoden hir bisyde ;
Unnethe abouten hir mighte they abyde.

Walter hir gladeth, and hir sorwe slaketh ;
She ryseth up, abaysed, from hir traunce,
And every wight hir joye and feste maketh,
Til she hath caught agayn hir contenaunce.
Walter hir dooth so feithfully plesaunce,
That it was deyntee for to seen the chere
Bitwixe hem two, now they ben met y-fere.

Thise ladyes, whan that they hir tyme say,
Han taken hir, and in-to chambre goon,
And strepen hir out of hir rude array,
And in a cloth of gold that brighte shoon,
With a coroune of many a riche stoon
Up-on hir heed, they in-to halle hir broghte,
And ther she was honoured as hir oghte.

Thus hath this pitous day a blisful ende,
For every man and womman dooth his might
This day in murthe and revel to dispende
Til on the welkne shoon the sterres light.
For more solempne in every mannes sight
This feste was, and gretter of costage,
Than was the revel of hir mariage.

Ful many a yeer in heigh prosperitee
Liven thise two in concord and in reste,

And richely his doghter maried he
Un-to a lord, oon of the worthieste
Of al Itaille; and than in pees and reste
His wyves fader in his court he kepeth,
Til that the soule out of his body crepeth.

His sone succedeth in his heritage
In reste and pees, after his fader day;
And fortunat was eek in mariage,
Al putte he nat his wyf in greet assay.
This world is nat so strong, it is no nay,
As it hath been in olde tymes yore,
And herkneth what this auctour seith therfore.

This storie is seyd, nat for that wyves sholde
Folwen Grisilde as in humilitee,
For it were importable, though they wolde;
But for that every wight, in his degree,
Sholde be constant in adversitee
As was Grisilde; therfor Petrark wryteth
This storie, which with heigh style he endyteth.

For, sith a womman was so pacient
Un-to a mortal man, wel more us oghte
Receyven al in gree that god us sent;
For greet skile is, he preve that he wroghte.
But he ne tempteth no man that he boghte,
As seith seint Jame, if ye his pistel rede;
He preveth folk al day, it is no drede,

And suffreth us, as for our excercyse,
With sharpe scourges of adversitee
Ful ofte to be bete in sondry wyse;
Nat for to knowe our wil, for certes he,
Er we were born, knew al our freletee;
And for our beste is al his governaunce;
Lat us than live in vertuous suffraunce.

But o word, lordinges, herkneth er I go:—
It were ful hard to finde now a dayes
In al a toun Grisildes three or two;
For, if that they were put to swiche assayes,
The gold of hem hath now so badde alayes

With bras, that thogh the coyne be fair at yë,
It wolde rather breste a-two than plye.

For which heer, for the wyves love of Bathe,
Whos lyf and al hir secte god mayntene
In heigh maistrye, and elles were it scathe,
I wol with lusty herte fresshe and grene
Seyn yow a song to glade yow, I wene,
And lat us stinte of ernestful matere :—
Herkneth my song, that seith in this manere.

Lenvoy de Chaucer.

Grisilde is deed, and eek hir pacience,
And bothe atones buried in Itaille ;
For which I crye in open audience,
No wedded man so hardy be t'assaille
His wyves pacience, in hope to finde
Grisildes, for in certein he shall faille !

O noble wyves, ful of heigh prudence,
Lat noon humilitee your tonge naille,
Ne lat no clerk have cause or diligence
To wryte of yow a storie of swich mervaille
As of Grisildis pacient and kinde ;
Lest Chichevache yow swelwe in hir entraille !

Folweth Ekko, that holdeth no silence,
But evere answereth at the countretaille ;
Beth nat bidaffed for your innocence,
But sharply tak on yow the governaille.
Emprinteth wel this lesson in your minde
For commune profit, sith it may availle.

Ye archewyves, stondeth at defence,
Sin ye be stronge as is a greet camaille ;
Ne suffreth nat that men yow doon offence.
And sclendre wyves, feble as in bataille,
Beth egre as is a tygre yond in Inde ;
Ay clappeth as a mille, I yow consaille.

Ne dreed hem nat, do hem no reverence ;
For though thyn housbonde armed be in maille,
The arwes of thy crabbed eloquence
Shal perce his brest, and eek his aventaille ;
In jalousye I rede eek thou him binde,
And thou shalt make him couche as dooth a quaille.

If thou be fair, ther folk ben in presence
Shew thou thy visage and thyn apparaille ;
If thou be foul, be free of thy dispence,
To gete thee freendes ay do thy travaille ;
Be ay of chere as light as leef on linde,
And lat him care, and wepe, and wringe, and waille!

Here endeth the Clerk of Oxenford his Tale.

THE MARCHANTES TALE

The Prologe of the Marchantes Tale.

'WEPING and wayling, care, and other sorwe
I know y-nogh, on even and a-morwe,'
Quod the Marchaunt, 'and so don othere mo
That wedded been, I trowe that it be so.
For, wel I woot, it fareth so with me.
I have a wyf, the worste that may be;
For thogh the feend to hir y-coupled were,
She wolde him overmacche, I dar wel swere.
What sholde I yow reherce in special
Hir hye malice? she is a shrewe at al.
Ther is a long and large difference
Bitwix Grisildis grete pacience
And of my wyf the passing crueltee.
Were I unbounden, al-so moot I thee!
I wolde never eft comen in the snare.
We wedded men live in sorwe and care;
Assaye who-so wol, and he shal finde
I seye sooth, by seint Thomas of Inde,
As for the more part, I sey nat alle.
God shilde that it sholde so bifalle!
  A! good sir hoost! I have y-wedded be
Thise monthes two, and more nat, pardee;
And yet, I trowe, he that all his lyve
Wyflees hath been, though that men wolde him ryve
Un-to the herte, ne coude in no manere
Tellen so muchel sorwe, as I now here
Coude tellen of my wyves cursednesse!'
  'Now,' quod our hoost, 'Marchaunt, so god yow blesse,

Sin ye so muchel knowen of that art,
Ful hertely I pray yow telle us part.'
  'Gladly,' quod he, 'but of myn owene sore,
For sory herte, I telle may na-more.'

Here biginneth the Marchantes Tale.

WHYLOM ther was dwellinge in Lumbardye
A worthy knight, that born was of Pavye,
In which he lived in greet prosperitee;
And sixty yeer a wyflees man was he,
And folwed ay his bodily delyt
On wommen, ther-as was his appetyt,
As doon thise foles that ben seculeer.
And whan that he was passed sixty yeer,
Were it for holinesse or for dotage,
I can nat seye, but swich a greet corage
Hadde this knight to been a wedded man,
That day and night he dooth al that he can
T'espyen where he mighte wedded be;
Preyinge our lord to granten him, that he
Mighte ones knowe of thilke blisful lyf
That is bitwixe an housbond and his wyf;
And for to live under that holy bond
With which that first god man and womman bond.
'Non other lyf,' seyde he, 'is worth a bene;
For wedlok is so esy and so clene,
That in this world it is a paradys.'
Thus seyde this olde knight, that was so wys.
  And certeinly, as sooth as god is king,
To take a wyf, it is a glorious thing,
And namely whan a man is old and hoor;
Thanne is a wyf the fruit of his tresor.
Than sholde he take a yong wyf and a feir,
On which he mighte engendren him an heir,
And lede his lyf in joye and in solas,
Wher-as thise bacheleres singe 'allas,'
Whan that they finden any adversitee
In love, which nis but childish vanitee.

And trewely it sit wel to be so,
That bacheleres have often peyne and wo;
On brotel ground they builde, and brotelnesse
They finde, whan they wene sikernesse.
They live but as a brid or as a beste,
In libertee, and under non areste,
Ther-as a wedded man in his estaat
Liveth a lyf blisful and ordinaat,
Under the yok of mariage y-bounde;
Wel may his herte in joye and blisse habounde.
For who can be so buxom as a wyf?
Who is so trewe, and eek so ententyf
To kepe him, syk and hool, as is his make?
For wele or wo, she wol him nat forsake.
She nis nat wery him to love and serve,
Thogh that he lye bedrede til he sterve.
And yet somme clerkes seyn, it nis nat so,
Of whiche he, Theofraste, is oon of tho.
What force though Theofraste liste lye?
'Ne take no wyf,' quod he, 'for housbondrye,
As for to spare in houshold thy dispence;
A trewe servant dooth more diligence,
Thy good to kepe, than thyn owene wyf.
For she wol clayme half part al hir lyf;
And if that thou be syk, so god me save,
Thy verray frendes or a trewe knave
Wol kepe thee bet than she that waiteth ay
After thy good, and hath don many a day.'
And if thou take a wyf un-to thyn hold,
Ful lightly maystow been a cokewold.
This sentence, and an hundred thinges worse,
Wryteth this man, ther god his bones corse!
But take no kepe of al swich vanitee;
Deffye Theofraste and herke me.
   A wyf is goddes yifte verraily;
Alle other maner yiftes hardily,
As londes, rentes, pasture, or commune,
Or moebles, alle ben yiftes of fortune,
That passen as a shadwe upon a wal.
But dredelees, if pleynly speke I shal,

A wyf wol laste, and in thyn hous endure,
Wel lenger than thee list, paraventure.
Mariage is a ful gret sacrement;
He which that hath no wyf, I holde him shent;
He liveth helplees and al desolat,
I speke of folk in seculer estaat.
And herke why, I sey nat this for noght,
That womman is for mannes help y-wroght.
The hye god, whan he hadde Adam maked,
And saugh him al allone, bely-naked,
God of his grete goodnesse seyde than,
'Lat us now make an help un-to this man
Lyk to him-self;' and thanne he made him Eve.
Heer may ye se, and heer-by may ye preve,
That wyf is mannes help and his confort,
His paradys terrestre and his disport.
So buxom and so vertuous is she,
They moste nedes live in unitee.
O flesh they been, and o flesh, as I gesse,
Hath but on herte, in wele and in distresse.
A wyf! a! Seinte Marie, *ben'cite!*
How mighte a man han any adversitee
That hath a wyf? certes, I can nat seye.
The blisse which that is bitwixe hem tweye
Ther may no tonge telle, or herte thinke.
If he be povre, she helpeth him to swinke;
She kepeth his good, and wasteth never a deel;
Al that hir housbonde lust, hir lyketh weel;
She seith not ones 'nay,' whan he seith 'ye.'
'Do this,' seith he; 'al redy, sir,' seith she.
O blisful ordre of wedlok precious,
Thou art so mery, and eek so vertuous,
And so commended and appreved eek,
That every man that halt him worth a leek,
Up-on his bare knees oghte al his lyf
Thanken his god that him hath sent a wyf;
Or elles preye to god him for to sende
A wyf, to laste un-to his lyves ende.
For thanne his lyf is set in sikernesse;
He may nat be deceyved, as I gesse,

So that he werke after his wyves reed ;
Than may he boldly beren up his heed,
They been so trewe and ther-with-al so wyse ;
For which, if thou wolt werken as the wyse,
Do alwey so as wommen wol thee rede.
  Lo, how that Jacob, as thise clerkes rede,
By good conseil of his moder Rebekke,
Bond the kides skin aboute his nekke ;
Thurgh which his fadres benisoun he wan.
  Lo, Judith, as the storie eek telle can,
By wys conseil she goddes peple kepte,
And slow him, Olofernus, whyl he slepte.
  Lo Abigayl, by good conseil how she
Saved hir housbond Nabal, whan that he
Sholde han be slayn ; and loke, Ester also
By good conseil delivered out of wo
The peple of god, and made him, Mardochee,
Of Assuere enhaunced for to be.
  Ther nis no-thing in gree superlatyf,
As seith Senek, above an humble wyf.
  Suffre thy wyves tonge, as Caton bit ;
She shal comande, and thou shalt suffren it ;
And yet she wol obeye of curteisye.
A wyf is keper of thyn housbondrye ;
Wel may the syke man biwaille and wepe,
Ther-as ther nis no wyf the hous to kepe.
I warne thee, if wysly thou wolt wirche,
Love wel thy wyf, as Crist loveth his chirche.
If thou lovest thy-self, thou lovest thy wyf ;
No man hateth his flesh, but in his lyf
He fostreth it, and therfore bidde I thee,
Cherisse thy wyf, or thou shalt never thee.
Housbond and wyf, what so men jape or pleye,
Of worldly folk holden the siker weye ;
They been so knit, ther may noon harm bityde :
And namely, up-on the wyves syde.
For which this Januarie, of whom I tolde,
Considered hath, inwith his dayes olde,
The lusty lyf, the vertuous quiete,
That is in mariage hony-swete ;

And for his freendes on a day he sente,
To tellen hem th'effect of his entente.
With face sad, his tale he hath hem told;
He seyde, 'freendes, I am hoor and old,
And almost, god wot, on my pittes brinke;
Up-on my soule somwhat moste I thinke.
I have my body folily despended;
Blessed be god, that it shal been amended!
For I wol be, certeyn, a wedded man,
And that anoon in al the haste I can,
Un-to som mayde fair and tendre of age.
I prey yow, shapeth for my mariage
Al sodeynly, for I wol nat abyde;
And I wol fonde t'espyen, on my syde,
To whom I may be wedded hastily.
But for-as-muche as ye ben mo than I,
Ye shullen rather swich a thing espyen
Than I, and wher me best were to allyen.
But o thing warne I yow, my freendes dere,
I wol non old wyf han in no manere.
She shal nat passe twenty yeer, certayn;
Old fish and yong flesh wolde I have ful fayn.
Bet is,' quod he, 'a pyk than a pikerel;
And bet than old boef is the tendre veel.
I wol no womman thritty yeer of age,
It is but bene-straw and greet forage.
And eek thise olde widwes, god it woot,
They conne so muchel craft on Wades boot,
So muchel broken harm, whan that hem leste,
That with hem sholde I never live in reste.
For sondry scoles maken sotil clerkis;
Womman of manye scoles half a clerk is.
But certeynly, a yong thing may men gye,
Right as men may warm wex with handes plye.
Wherfore I sey yow pleynly, in a clause,
I wol non old wyf han right for this cause.
For if so were, I hadde swich mischaunce,
That I in hir ne coude han no plesaunce,
Thanne sholde I lede my lyf in avoutrye,
And go streight to the devel, whan I dye.

Ne children sholde I none up-on hir geten;
Yet were me lever houndes had me eten,
Than that myn heritage sholde falle
In straunge hand, and this I tell yow alle.
I dote nat, I woot the cause why
Men sholde wedde, and forthermore wot I,
Ther speketh many a man of mariage,
That woot na-more of it than woot my page,
For whiche causes man sholde take a wyf.
If he ne may nat liven chast his lyf,
Take him a wyf with greet devocioun,
By-cause of leveful procreacioun
Of children, to th'onour of god above,
And nat only for paramour or love;
And for they sholde lecherye eschue,
And yelde hir dettes whan that they ben due;
Or for that ech of hem sholde helpen other
In meschief, as a suster shal the brother;
And live in chastitee ful holily.
But sires, by your leve, that am nat I.
For god be thanked, I dar make avaunt,
I fele my limes stark and suffisaunt
To do al that a man bilongeth to;
I woot my-selven best what I may do.
Though I be hoor, I fare as dooth a tree
That blosmeth er that fruyt y-woxen be;
A blosmy tree nis neither drye ne deed.
I fele me nowher hoor but on myn heed;
Myn herte and alle my limes been as grene
As laurer thurgh the yeer is for to sene.
And sin that ye han herd al myn entente,
I prey yow to my wil ye wole assente.'
  Diverse men diversely him tolde
Of mariage manye ensamples olde.
Somme blamed it, somme preysed it, certeyn;
But atte laste, shortly for to seyn,
As al day falleth altercacioun
Bitwixen freendes in disputisoun,
Ther fil a stryf bitwixe his bretheren two,
Of whiche that oon was cleped Placebo,

Justinus soothly called was that other.
  Placebo seyde, 'o Januarie, brother,
Ful litel nede had ye, my lord so dere,
Conseil to axe of any that is here;
But that ye been so ful of sapience,
That yow ne lyketh, for your heighe prudence,
To weyven fro the word of Salomon.
This word seyde he un-to us everichon:
"Wirk alle thing by conseil," thus seyde he,
"And thanne shaltow nat repente thee."
But though that Salomon spak swich a word,
Myn owene dere brother and my lord,
So wisly god my soule bringe at reste,
I hold your owene conseil is the beste.
For brother myn, of me tak this motyf,
I have now been a court-man al my lyf.
And god it woot, though I unworthy be,
I have stonden in ful greet degree
Abouten lordes of ful heigh estaat;
Yet hadde I never with noon of hem debaat.
I never hem contraried, trewely;
I woot wel that my lord can more than I.
What that he seith, I holde it ferme and stable;
I seye the same, or elles thing semblable.
A ful gret fool is any conseillour,
That serveth any lord of heigh honour,
That dar presume, or elles thenken it,
That his conseil sholde passe his lordes wit.
Nay, lordes been no foles, by my fay;
Ye han your-selven shewed heer to-day
So heigh sentence, so holily and weel,
That I consente and conferme every-deel
Your wordes alle, and your opinioun.
By god, ther nis no man in al this toun
N'in al Itaille, that coude bet han sayd;
Crist halt him of this conseil wel apayd.
And trewely, it is an heigh corage
Of any man, that stapen is in age,
To take a yong wyf; by my fader kin,
Your herte hangeth on a joly pin.

Doth now in this matere right as yow leste,
For finally I holde it for the beste.'
  Justinus, that ay stille sat and herde,
Right in this wyse to Placebo answerde:
'Now brother myn, be pacient, I preye,
Sin ye han seyd, and herkneth what I seye.
Senek among his othere wordes wyse
Seith, that a man oghte him right wel avyse,
To whom he yeveth his lond or his catel.
And sin I oghte avyse me right wel
To whom I yeve my good awey fro me,
Wel muchel more I oghte avysed be
To whom I yeve my body; for alwey
I warne yow wel, it is no childes pley
To take a wyf with-oute avysement.
Men moste enquere, this is myn assent,
Wher she be wys, or sobre, or dronkelewe,
Or proud, or elles other-weys a shrewe;
A chydester, or wastour of thy good,
Or riche, or poore, or elles mannish wood.
Al-be-it so that no man finden shal
Noon in this world that trotteth hool in al,
Ne man ne beest, swich as men coude devyse;
But nathelees, it oghte y-nough suffise
With any wyf, if so were that she hadde
Mo gode thewes than hir vyces badde;
And al this axeth leyser for t'enquere.
For god it woot, I have wept many a tere
Ful prively, sin I have had a wyf.
Preyse who-so wole a wedded mannes lyf,
Certein, I finde in it but cost and care,
And observances, of alle blisses bare.
And yet, god woot, my neighebores aboute,
And namely of wommen many a route,
Seyn that I have the moste stedefast wyf,
And eek the mekeste oon that bereth lyf.
But I wot best wher wringeth me my sho.
Ye mowe, for me, right as yow lyketh do;
Avyseth yow, ye been a man of age,
How that ve entren in-to mariage,

And namely with a yong wyf and a fair.
By him that made water, erthe, and air,
The yongest man that is in al this route
Is bisy y-nogh to bringen it aboute
To han his wyf allone, trusteth me.
Ye shul nat plese hir fully yeres three,
This is to seyn, to doon hir ful plesaunce.
A wyf axeth ful many an observaunce.
I prey yow that ye be nat yvel apayd.'
'Wel,' quod this Januarie, 'and hastow sayd?
Straw for thy Senek, and for thy proverbes,
I counte nat a panier ful of herbes
Of scole-termes; wyser men than thow,
As thou hast herd, assenteden right now
To my purpos; Placebo, what sey ye?'
'I seye, it is a cursed man,' quod he,
'That letteth matrimoine, sikerly.'
And with that word they rysen sodeynly,
And been assented fully, that he sholde
Be wedded whanne him list and wher he wolde.
Heigh fantasye and curious bisinesse
Fro day to day gan in the soule impresse
Of Januarie aboute his mariage.
Many fair shap, and many a fair visage
Ther passeth thurgh his herte, night by night.
As who-so toke a mirour polished bright,
And sette it in a commune market-place,
Than sholde he see many a figure pace
By his mirour; and, in the same wyse,
Gan Januarie inwith his thoght devyse
Of maydens, whiche that dwelten him bisyde.
He wiste nat wher that he mighte abyde.
For if that oon have beautee in hir face,
Another stant so in the peples grace
For hir sadnesse, and hir benignitee,
That of the peple grettest voys hath she.
And somme were riche, and hadden badde name.
But nathelees, bitwixe ernest and game,
He atte laste apoynted him on oon,
And leet alle othere from his herte goon,

And chees hir of his owene auctoritee ;
For love is blind al day, and may nat see.
And whan that he was in his bed y-broght,
He purtreyed, in his herte and in his thoght,
Hir fresshe beautee and hir age tendre,
Hir myddel smal, hir armes longe and sclendre,
Hir wyse governaunce, hir gentillesse,
Hir wommanly beringe and hir sadnesse.
And whan that he on hir was condescended,
Him thoughte his chois mighte nat ben amended.
For whan that he him-self concluded hadde,
Him thoughte ech other mannes wit so badde,
That inpossible it were to replye
Agayn his chois, this was his fantasye.
His freendes sente he to at his instaunce,
And preyed hem to doon him that plesaunce,
That hastily they wolden to him come ;
He wolde abregge hir labour, alle and some.
Nedeth na-more for him to go ne ryde,
He was apoynted ther he wolde abyde.
  Placebo cam, and eek his freendes sone,
And alderfirst he bad hem alle a bone,
That noon of hem none argumentes make
Agayn the purpos which that he hath take ;
'Which purpos was plesant to god,' seyde he,
'And verray ground of his prosperitee.'
  He seyde, ther was a mayden in the toun,
Which that of beautee hadde greet renoun,
Al were it so she were of smal degree ;
Suffyseth him hir youthe and hir beautee.
Which mayde, he seyde, he wolde han to his wyf,
To lede in ese and holinesse his lyf.
And thanked god, that he mighte han hire al,
That no wight of his blisse parten shal.
And preyde hem to labouren in this nede,
And shapen that he faille nat to spede ;
For thanne, he seyde, his spirit was at ese.
'Thanne is,' quod he, 'no-thing may me displese,
Save o thing priketh in my conscience,
The which I wol reherce in your presence.

I have,' quod he, 'herd seyd, ful yore ago,
Ther may no man han parfite blisses two,
This is to seye, in erthe and eek in hevene.
For though he kepe him fro the sinnes sevene,
And eek from every branche of thilke tree,
Yet is ther so parfit felicitee,
And so greet ese and lust in mariage,
That ever I am agast, now in myn age,
That I shal lede now so mery a lyf,
So delicat, with-outen wo and stryf,
That I shal have myn hevene in erthe here.
For sith that verray hevene is boght so dere,
With tribulacioun and greet penaunce,
How sholde I thanne, that live in swich plesaunce
As alle wedded men don with hir wyvis,
Come to the blisse ther Crist eterne on lyve is?
This is my drede, and ye, my bretheren tweye,
Assoilleth me this questioun, I preye.'
Justinus, which that hated his folye,
Answerde anon, right in his japerye;
And for he wolde his longe tale abregge,
He wolde noon auctoritee allegge,
But seyde, 'sire, so ther be noon obstacle
Other than this, god of his hye miracle
And of his mercy may so for yow wirche,
That, er ye have your right of holy chirche,
Ye may repente of wedded mannes lyf,
In which ye seyn ther is no wo ne stryf.
And elles, god forbede but he sente
A wedded man him grace to repente
Wel ofte rather than a sengle man!
And therfore, sire, the beste reed I can,
Dispeire yow noght, but have in your memorie,
Paraunter she may be your purgatorie!
She may be goddes mene, and goddes whippe;
Than shal your soule up to hevene skippe
Swifter than dooth an arwe out of the bowe!
I hope to god, her-after shul ye knowe,
That their nis no so greet felicitee
In mariage, ne never-mo shal be,

That yow shal lette of your savacioun,
So that ye use, as skile is and resoun,
The lustes of your wyf attemprely,
And that ye plese hir nat to amorously,
And that ye kepe yow eek from other sinne.
My tale is doon :—for my wit is thinne.
Beth nat agast her-of, my brother dere.'—
(But lat us waden out of this matere.
The Wyf of Bathe, if ye han understonde,
Of mariage, which we have on honde,
Declared hath ful wel in litel space).—
'Fareth now wel, god have yow in his grace.'
 And with this word this Justin and his brother
Han take hir leve, and ech of hem of other.
For whan they sawe it moste nedes be,
They wroghten so, by sly and wys tretee,
That she, this mayden, which that Maius highte,
As hastily as ever that she mighte,
Shal wedded be un-to this Januarie.
I trowe it were to longe yow to tarie,
If I yow tolde of every scrit and bond,
By which that she was feffed in his lond ;
Or for to herknen of hir riche array.
But finally y-comen is the day
That to the chirche bothe be they went
For to receyve the holy sacrement.
Forth comth the preest, with stole aboute his nekke,
And bad hir be lyk Sarra and Rebekke,
In wisdom and in trouthe of mariage ;
And seyde his orisons, as is usage,
And crouched hem, and bad god sholde hem blesse,
And made al siker-y-nogh with holinesse.
 Thus been they wedded with solempnitee,
And at the feste sitteth he and she
With other worthy folk up-on the deys.
Al ful of joye and blisse is the paleys,
And ful of instruments and of vitaille,
The moste deyntevous of al Itaille.
Biforn hem stoode swiche instruments of soun,
That Orpheus, ne of Thebes Amphioun,

Ne maden never swich a melodye.
  At every cours than cam loud minstralcye,
That never tromped Joab, for to here,
Nor he, Theodomas, yet half so clere,
At Thebes, whan the citee was in doute.
Bacus the wyn hem skinketh al aboute,
And Venus laugheth up-on every wight.
For Januarie was bicome hir knight,
And wolde bothe assayen his corage
In libertee, and eek in mariage;
And with hir fyrbrond in hir hand aboute
Daunceth biforn the bryde and al the route.
And certeinly, I dar right wel seyn this,
Ymenëus, that god of wedding is,
Saugh never his lyf so mery a wedded man.
Hold thou thy pees, thou poete Marcian,
That wrytest us that ilke wedding murie
Of hir, Philologye, and him, Mercurie,
And of the songes that the Muses songe.
To smal is bothe thy penne, and eek thy tonge,
For to descryven of this mariage.
Whan tendre youthe hath wedded stouping age,
Ther is swich mirthe that it may nat be writen;
Assayeth it your-self, than may ye witen
If that I lye or noon in this matere.
  Maius, that sit with so benigne a chere,
Hir to biholde it semed fayëryë;
Quene Ester loked never with swich an yë
On Assuer, so meke a look hath she.
I may yow nat devyse al hir beautee;
But thus muche of hir beautee telle I may,
That she was lyk the brighte morwe of May,
Fulfild of alle beautee and plesaunce.
  This Januarie is ravisshed in a traunce
At every time he loked on hir face;
But in his herte he gan hir to manace,
That he that night in armes wolde hir streyne
Harder than ever Paris dide Eleyne.
But nathelees, yet hadde he greet pitee,
That thilke night offenden hir moste he;

And thoughte, 'allas! o tendre creature!
Now wolde god ye mighte wel endure
Al my corage, it is so sharp and kene;
I am agast ye shul it nat sustene.
But god forbede that I dide al my might!
Now wolde god that it were woxen night,
And that the night wolde lasten evermo.
I wolde that al this peple were ago.'
And finally, he doth al his labour,
As he best mighte, savinge his honour,
To haste hem fro the mete in subtil wyse.
The tyme cam that reson was to ryse;
And after that, men daunce and drinken faste,
And spyces al aboute the hous they caste;
And ful of joye and blisse is every man;
All but a squyer, highte Damian,
Which carf biforn the knight ful many a day.
He was so ravisshed on his lady May,
That for the verray peyne he was ny wood;
Almost he swelte and swowned ther he stood.
So sore hath Venus hurt him with hir brond,
As that she bar it daunsinge in hir hond.
And to his bed he wente him hastily;
Na-more of him as at this tyme speke I.
But ther I lete him wepe y-nough and pleyne,
Til fresshe May wol rewen on his peyne.
O perilous fyr, that in the bedstraw bredeth!
O famulier foo, that his servyce bedeth!
O servant traitour, false hoomly hewe,
Lyk to the naddre in bosom sly untrewe,
God shilde us alle from your aqueyntaunce!
O Januarie, dronken in plesaunce
Of mariage, see how thy Damian,
Thyn owene squyer and thy borne man,
Entendeth for to do thee vileinye.
God graunte thee thyn hoomly fo t'espye.
For in this world nis worse pestilence
Than hoomly foo al day in thy presence.
Parfourned hath the sonne his ark diurne,
No lenger may the body of him sojurne

On th'orisonte, as in that latitude.
Night with his mantel, that is derk and rude,
Gan oversprede the hemisperie aboute;
For which departed is this lusty route
Fro Januarie, with thank on every syde.
Hom to hir houses lustily they ryde,
Wher-as they doon hir thinges as hem leste,
And whan they sye hir tyme, goon to reste.
Sone after that, this hastif Januarie
Wolde go to bedde, he wolde no lenger tarie.
He drinketh ipocras, clarree, and vernage
Of spyces hote, t'encresen his corage;
And many a letuarie hadde he ful fyn,
Swiche as the cursed monk dan Constantyn
Hath writen in his book *de Coitu*;
To eten hem alle, he nas no-thing eschu.
And to his privee freendes thus seyde he:
'For goddes love, as sone as it may be,
Lat voyden al this hous in curteys wyse.'
And they han doon right as he wol devyse.
Men drinken, and the travers drawe anon;
The bryde was broght a-bedde as stille as stoon;
And whan the bed was with the preest y-blessed,
Out of the chambre hath every wight him dressed.
And Januarie hath faste in armes take
His fresshe May, his paradys, his make.
He lulleth hir, he kisseth hir ful ofte
With thikke bristles of his berd unsofte,
Lyk to the skin of houndfish, sharp as brere,
For he was shave al newe in his manere.
He rubbeth hir aboute hir tendre face,
And seyde thus, 'allas! I moot trespace
To yow, my spouse, and yow gretly offende,
Er tyme come that I wil doun descende.
But nathelees, considereth this,' quod he,
'Ther nis no werkman, what-so-ever he be,
That may bothe werke wel and hastily;
This wol be doon at leyser parfitly.
It is no fors how longe that we pleye;
In trewe wedlok wedded be we tweye;

And blessed be the yok that we been inne,
For in our actes we mowe do no sinne.
A man may do no sinne with his wyf,
Ne hurte him-selven with his owene knyf;
For we han leve to pleye us by the lawe.'
Thus laboureth he til that the day gan dawe;
And than he taketh a sop in fyn clarree,
And upright in his bed than sitteth he,
And after that he sang ful loude and clere,
And kiste his wyf, and made wantoun chere.
He was al coltish, ful of ragerye,
And ful of jargon as a flekked pye.
The slakke skin aboute his nekke shaketh,
Whyl that he sang; so chaunteth he and craketh.
But god wot what that May thoughte in hir herte,
Whan she him saugh up sittinge in his sherte,
In his night-cappe, and with his nekke lene;
She preyseth nat his pleying worth a bene.
Than seide he thus, 'my reste wol I take;
Now day is come, I may no lenger wake.'
And doun he leyde his heed, and sleep til pryme.
And afterward, whan that he saugh his tyme,
Up ryseth Januarie; but fresshe May
Holdeth hir chambre un-to the fourthe day,
As usage is of wyves for the beste.
For every labour som-tyme moot han reste,
Or elles longe may he nat endure;
This is to seyn, no lyves creature,
Be it of fish, or brid, or beest, or man.
  Now wol I speke of woful Damian,
That languissheth for love, as ye shul here;
Therfore I speke to him in this manere:
I seye, 'O sely Damian, allas!
Answere to my demaunde, as in this cas,
How shaltow to thy lady fresshe May
Telle thy wo? She wole alwey seye "nay";
Eek if thou speke, she wol thy wo biwreye;
God be thyn help, I can no bettre seye.'
  This syke Damian in Venus fyr
So brenneth, that he dyeth for desyr;

For which he putte his lyf in aventure,
No lenger mighte he in this wyse endure;
But prively a penner gan he borwe,
And in a lettre wroot he al his sorwe,
In manere of a compleynt or a lay,
Un-to his faire fresshe lady May.
And in a purs of silk, heng on his sherte,
He hath it put, and leyde it at his herte.
The mone that, at noon, was, thilke day
That Januarie hath wedded fresshe May,
In two of Taur, was in-to Cancre gliden;
So longe hath Maius in hir chambre biden,
As custume is un-to thise nobles alle.
A bryde shal nat eten in the halle,
Til dayes foure or three dayes atte leste
Y-passed been; than lat hir go to feste.
The fourthe day compleet fro noon to noon,
Whan that the heighe masse was y-doon,
In halle sit this Januarie, and May
As fresh as is the brighte someres day.
And so bifel, how that this gode man
Remembred him upon this Damian,
And seyde, 'Seinte Marie! how may this be,
That Damian entendeth nat to me?
Is he ay syk, or how may this bityde?'
His squyeres, whiche that stoden ther bisyde,
Excused him by-cause of his siknesse,
Which letted him to doon his bisinesse;
Noon other cause mighte make him tarie.
'That me forthinketh,' quod this Januarie,
'He is a gentil squyer, by my trouthe!
If that he deyde, it were harm and routhe;
He is as wys, discreet, and as secree
As any man I woot of his degree;
And ther-to manly and eek servisable,
And for to been a thrifty man right able.
But after mete, as sone as ever I may,
I wol my-self visyte him and eek May,
To doon him al the confort that I can.'
And for that word him blessed every man,

That, of his bountee and his gentillesse,
He wolde so conforten in siknesse
His squyer, for it was a gentil dede.
'Dame,' quod this Januarie, 'tak good hede,
At-after mete ye, with your wommen alle,
Whan ye han been in chambre out of this halle,
That alle ye go see this Damian;
Doth him disport, he is a gentil man;
And telleth him that I wol him visyte,
Have I no-thing but rested me a lyte;
And spede yow faste, for I wole abyde
Til that ye slepe faste by my syde.'
And with that word he gan to him to calle
A squyer, that was marchal of his halle,
And tolde him certeyn thinges, what he wolde.
  This fresshe May hath streight hir wey y-holde,
With alle hir wommen, un-to Damian.
Doun by his beddes syde sit she than,
Confortinge him as goodly as she may.
This Damian, whan that his tyme he say,
In secree wise his purs, and eek his bille,
In which that he y-writen hadde his wille,
Hath put in-to hir hand, with-outen more,
Save that he syketh wonder depe and sore,
And softely to hir right thus seyde he:
'Mercy! and that ye nat discovere me;
For I am deed, if that this thing be kid.'
This purs hath she inwith hir bosom hid,
And wente hir wey; ye gete namore of me.
But un-to Januarie y-comen is she,
That on his beddes syde sit ful softe.
He taketh hir, and kisseth hir ful ofte,
And leyde him doun to slepe, and that anon.
She feyned hir as that she moste gon
Ther-as ye woot that every wight mot nede.
And whan she of this bille hath taken hede,
She rente it al to cloutes atte laste,
And in the privee softely it caste.
  Who studieth now but faire fresshe May?
Adoun by olde Januarie she lay,

That sleep, til that the coughe hath him awaked;
Anon he preyde hir strepen hir al naked;
He wolde of hir, he seyde, han som plesaunce,
And seyde, hir clothes dide him encombraunce,
And she obeyeth, be hir lief or looth.
But lest that precious folk be with me wrooth,
How that he wroghte, I dar nat to yow telle;
Or whether hir thoughte it paradys or helle;
But here I lete hem werken in hir wyse
Til evensong rong, and that they moste aryse.
Were it by destinee or aventure,
Were it by influence or by nature,
Or constellacion, that in swich estat
The hevene stood, that tyme fortunat
Was for to putte a bille of Venus werkes
(For alle thing hath tyme, as seyn thise clerkes)
To any womman, for to gete hir love,
I can nat seye; but grete god above,
That knoweth that non act is causelees,
He deme of al, for I wol holde my pees.
But sooth is this, how that this fresshe May
Hath take swich impression that day,
For pitee of this syke Damian,
That from hir herte she ne dryve can
The remembraunce for to doon him ese.
'Certeyn,' thoghte she, 'whom that this thing displese,
I rekke noght, for here I him assure,
To love him best of any creature,
Though he na-more hadde than his sherte.'
Lo, pitee renneth sone in gentil herte.
Heer may ye se how excellent franchyse
In wommen is, whan they hem narwe avyse.
Som tyrant is, as ther be many oon,
That hath an herte as hard as any stoon,
Which wolde han lete him sterven in the place
Wel rather than han graunted him hir grace;
And hem rejoysen in hir cruel pryde,
And rekke nat to been an homicyde.

This gentil May, fulfilled of pitee,
Right of hir hande a lettre made she,
In which she graunteth him hir verray grace;
Ther lakketh noght but only day and place,
Wher that she mighte un-to his lust suffyse:
For it shal be right as he wol devyse.
And whan she saugh hir time, up-on a day,
To visite this Damian goth May,
And sotilly this lettre doun she threste
Under his pilwe, rede it if him leste.
She taketh him by the hand, and harde him twiste
So secrely, that no wight of it wiste,
And bad him been al hool, and forth she wente
To Januarie, whan that he for hir sente.
Up ryseth Damian the nexte morwe,
Al passed was his siknesse and his sorwe.
He kembeth him, he proyneth him and pyketh,
He dooth al that his lady lust and lyketh;
And eek to Januarie he gooth as lowe
As ever dide a dogge for the bowe.
He is so plesant un-to every man,
(For craft is al, who-so that do it can)
That every wight is fayn to speke him good;
And fully in his lady grace he stood.
Thus lete I Damian aboute his nede,
And in my tale forth I wol procede.
Somme clerkes holden that felicitee
Stant in delyt, and therefor certeyn he,
This noble Januarie, with al his might,
In honest wyse, as longeth to a knight,
Shoop him to live ful deliciously.
His housinge, his array, as honestly
To his degree was maked as a kinges.
Amonges othere of his honest thinges,
He made a gardin, walled al with stoon;
So fair a gardin woot I nowher noon.
For out of doute, I verraily suppose,
That he that wroot the Romance of the Rose
Ne coude of it the beautee wel devyse;
Ne Priapus ne mighte nat suffyse,

Though he be god of gardins, for to telle
The beautee of the gardin and the welle,
That stood under a laurer alwey grene.
Ful ofte tyme he, Pluto, and his quene,
Proserpina, and al hir fayërye
Disporten hem and maken melodye
Aboute that welle, and daunced, as men tolde.
  This noble knight, this Januarie the olde,
Swich deintee hath in it to walke and pleye,
That he wol no wight suffren bere the keye
Save he him-self; for of the smale wiket
He bar alwey of silver a smal cliket,
With which, whan that him leste, he it unshette.
And whan he wolde paye his wyf hir dette
In somer seson, thider wolde he go,
And May his wyf, and no wight but they two;
And thinges whiche that were nat doon a-bedde,
He in the gardin parfourned hem and spedde.
And in this wyse, many a mery day,
Lived this Januarie and fresshe May.
But worldly joye may nat alwey dure
To Januarie, ne to no creature.
  O sodeyn hap, o thou fortune instable,
Lyk to the scorpioun so deceivable,
That flaterest with thyn heed when thou wolt stinge;
Thy tayl is deeth, thurgh thyn enveniminge.
O brotil joye! o swete venim queynte!
O monstre, that so subtilly canst peynte
Thy yiftes, under hewe of stedfastnesse,
That thou deceyvest bothe more and lesse!
Why hastow Januarie thus deceyved,
That haddest him for thy ful frend receyved?
And now thou hast biraft him bothe hise yën,
For sorwe of which desyreth he to dyen.
  Allas! this noble Januarie free,
Amidde his lust and his prosperitee,
Is woxen blind, and that al sodeynly.
He wepeth and he wayleth pitously;

And ther-with-al the fyr of jalousye,
Lest that his wyf sholde falle in som folye,
So brente his herte, that he wolde fayn
That som man bothe him and hir had slayn.
For neither after his deeth, nor in his lyf,
Ne wolde he that she were love ne wyf,
But ever live as widwe in clothes blake,
Soul as the turtle that lost hath hir make.
But atte laste, after a monthe or tweye,
His sorwe gan aswage, sooth to seye;
For whan he wiste it may noon other be,
He paciently took his adversitee;
Save, out of doute, he may nat forgoon
That he nas jalous evermore in oon;
Which jalousye it was so outrageous,
That neither in halle, n'in noon other hous,
Ne in noon other place, never-the-mo,
He nolde suffre hir for to ryde or go,
But-if that he had hand on hir alway;
For which ful ofte wepeth fresshe May,
That loveth Damian so benignely,
That she mot outher dyen sodeynly,
Or elles she mot han him as hir leste;
She wayteth whan hir herte wolde breste.
Up-on that other syde Damian
Bicomen is the sorwefulleste man
That ever was; for neither night ne day
Ne mighte he speke a word to fresshe May,
As to his purpos, of no swich matere,
But-if that Januarie moste it here,
That hadde an hand up-on hir evermo.
But nathelees, by wryting to and fro
And privee signes, wiste he what she mente;
And she knew eek the fyn of his entente.
O Januarie, what mighte it thee availle,
Thou mightest see as fer as shippes saille?
For also good is blind deceyved be,
As be deceyved whan a man may see.
Lo, Argus, which that hadde an hondred yën,
For al that ever he coude poure or pryen,

Yet was he blent; and, god wot, so ben mo,
That wenen wisly that it be nat so.
Passe over is an ese, I sey na-more.
This fresshe May, that I spak of so yore,
In warme wex hath emprented the cliket,
That Januarie bar of the smale wiket,
By which in-to his gardin ofte he wente.
And Damian, that knew al hir entente,
The cliket countrefeted prively;
Ther nis na-more to seye, but hastily
Som wonder by this cliket shal bityde,
Which ye shul heren, if ye wole abyde.
O noble Ovyde, ful sooth seystou, god woot!
What sleighte is it, thogh it be long and hoot,
That he nil finde it out in som manere?
By Piramus and Tesbee may men lere;
Thogh they were kept ful longe streite overal,
They been accorded, rouninge thurgh a wal,
Ther no wight coude han founde out swich a sleighte.
But now to purpos; er that dayes eighte
Were passed, er the monthe of Juil, bifil
That Januarie hath caught so greet a wil,
Thurgh egging of his wyf, him for to pleye
In his gardin, and no wight but they tweye,
That in a morwe un-to this May seith he:
'Rys up, my wyf, my love, my lady free;
The turtles vois is herd, my douve swete;
The winter is goon, with alle his reynes wete;
Com forth now, with thyn eyën columbyn!
How fairer been thy brestes than is wyn!
The gardin is enclosed al aboute;
Com forth, my whyte spouse; out of doute,
Thou hast me wounded in myn herte, o wyf!
No spot of thee ne knew I al my lyf.
Com forth, and lat us taken our disport;
I chees thee for my wyf and my confort.'
Swiche olde lewed wordes used he;
On Damian a signe made she,

That he sholde go biforen with his cliket:
This Damian thanne hath opened the wiket,
And in he stirte, and that in swich manere,
That no wight mighte it see neither y-here;
And stille he sit under a bush anoon.
  This Januarie, as blind as is a stoon,
With Maius in his hand, and no wight mo,
In-to his fresshe gardin is ago,
And clapte to the wiket sodeynly.
  'Now, wyf,' quod he, 'heer nis but thou and I,
That art the creature that I best love.
For, by that lord that sit in heven above,
Lever ich hadde dyen on a knyf,
Than thee offende, trewe dere wyf!
For goddes sake, thenk how I thee chees,
Noght for no coveityse, doutelees,
But only for the love I had to thee.
And though that I be old, and may nat see,
Beth to me trewe, and I shal telle yow why.
Three thinges, certes, shul ye winne ther-by;
First, love of Crist, and to your-self honour,
And al myn heritage, toun and tour;
I yeve it yow, maketh chartres as yow leste;
This shal be doon to-morwe er sonne reste.
So wisly god my soule bringe in blisse,
I prey yow first, in covenant ye me kisse.
And thogh that I be jalous, wyte me noght.
Ye been so depe enprented in my thoght,
That, whan that I considere your beautee,
And ther-with-al the unlykly elde of me
I may nat, certes, thogh I sholde dye,
Forbere to been out of your companye
For verray love; this is with-outen doute.
Now kis me, wyf, and lat us rome aboute.'
  This fresshe May, whan she thise wordes herde,
Benignely to Januarie answerde,
But first and forward she bigan to wepe,
'I have,' quod she, 'a soule for to kepe
As wel as ye, and also myn honour,
And of my wyfhod thilke tendre flour,

Which that I have assured in your hond,
Whan that the preest to yow my body bond;
Wherfore I wole answere in this manere
By the leve of yow, my lord so dere:
I prey to god, that never dawe the day
That I ne sterve, as foule as womman may,
If ever I do un-to my kin that shame,
Or elles I empeyre so my name,
That I be fals; and if I do that lakke,
Do strepe me and put me in a sakke,
And in the nexte river do me drenche.
I am a gentil womman and no wenche.
Why speke ye thus? but men ben ever untrewe,
And wommen have repreve of yow ay newe.
Ye han non other contenance, I leve,
But speke to us of untrust and repreve.'
  And with that word she saugh wher Damian
Sat in the bush, and coughen she bigan,
And with hir finger signes made she,
That Damian sholde climbe up-on a tree,
That charged was with fruit, and up he wente;
For verraily he knew al hir entente,
And every signe that she coude make
Wel bet than Januarie, hir owene make.
For in a lettre she had told him al
Of this matere, how he werchen shal.
And thus I lete him sitte up-on the pyrie,
And Januarie and May rominge myrie.
  Bright was the day, and blew the firmament,
Phebus of gold his stremes doun hath sent,
To gladen every flour with his warmnesse.
He was that tyme *in Geminis*, as I gesse,
But litel fro his declinacioun
Of Cancer, Jovis exaltacioun.
And so bifel, that brighte morwe-tyde,
That in that gardin, in the ferther syde,
Pluto, that is the king of fayërye,
And many a lady in his companye,
Folwinge his wyf, the quene Proserpyne,
Ech after other, right as any lyne—

Whyl that she gadered floures in the mede,
In Claudian ye may the story rede,
How in his grisly carte he hir fette :—
This king of fairye thanne adoun him sette
Up-on a bench of turves, fresh and grene,
And right anon thus seyde he to his quene.
 'My wyf,' quod he, 'ther may no wight sey nay ;
Th'experience so preveth every day
The treson whiche that wommen doon to man.
Ten hondred thousand [stories] telle I can
Notable of your untrouthe and brotilnesse.
O Salomon, wys, richest of richesse,
Fulfild of sapience and of worldly glorie,
Ful worthy been thy wordes to memorie
To every wight that wit and reson can.
Thus preiseth he yet the bountee of man :
" Amonges a thousand men yet fond I oon,
But of wommen alle fond I noon."
 Thus seith the king that knoweth your wikkednesse ;
And Jesus *filius Syrak*, as I gesse,
Ne speketh of yow but selde reverence.
A wilde fyr and corrupt pestilence
So falle up-on your bodies yet to-night !
Ne see ye nat this honurable knight,
By-cause, allas ! that he is blind and old,
His owene man shal make him cokewold ;
Lo heer he sit, the lechour, in the tree.
Now wol I graunten, of my magestee,
Un-to this olde blinde worthy knight
That he shal have ayeyn his eyen sight,
Whan that his wyf wold doon him vileinye ;
Than shal he knowen al hir harlotrye
Both in repreve of hir and othere mo.'
 'Ye shal,' quod Proserpyne, 'wol ye so ;
Now, by my modres sires soule I swere,
That I shal yeven hir suffisant answere,
And alle wommen after, for hir sake ;
That, though they be in any gilt y-take,

With face bold they shulle hem-self excuse,
And bere hem doun that wolden hem accuse.
For lakke of answer, noon of hem shal dyen.
Al hadde man seyn a thing with bothe his yën,
Yit shul we wommen visage it hardily,
And wepe, and swere, and chyde subtilly,
So that ye men shul been as lewed as gees.
What rekketh me of your auctoritees ?
  I woot wel that this Jew, this Salomon,
Fond of us wommen foles many oon.
But though that he ne fond no good womman,
Yet hath ther founde many another man
Wommen ful trewe, ful gode, and vertuous.
Witnesse on hem that dwelle in Cristes hous,
With martirdom they preved hir constance.
The Romayn gestes maken remembrance
Of many a verray trewe wyf also.
But sire, ne be nat wrooth, al-be-it so,
Though that he seyde he fond no good womman,
I prey yow take the sentence of the man ;
He mente thus, that in sovereyn bontee
Nis noon but god, that sit in Trinitee.
  Ey ! for verray god, that nis but oon,
What make ye so muche of Salomon ?
What though he made a temple, goddes hous ?
What though he were riche and glorious ?
So made he eek a temple of false goddis,
How mighte he do a thing that more forbode is ?
Pardee, as faire as ye his name emplastre,
He was a lechour and an ydolastre ;
And in his elde he verray god forsook.
And if that god ne hadde, as seith the book,
Y-spared him for his fadres sake, he sholde
Have lost his regne rather than he wolde.
I sette noght of al the vileinye,
That ye of wommen wryte, a boterflye.
I am a womman, nedes moot I speke,
Or elles swelle til myn herte breke.
For sithen he seyde that we ben jangleresses,
As ever hool I mote brouke my tresses,

I shal nat spare, for no curteisye,
To speke him harm that wolde us vileinye.'
'Dame,' quod this Pluto, 'be no lenger wrooth ;
I yeve it up ; but sith I swoor myn ooth
That I wolde graunten him his sighte ageyn,
My word shal stonde, I warne yow, certeyn.
I am a king, it sit me noght to lye.'
'And I,' quod she, 'a queene of fayërye.
Hir answere shal she have, I undertake :
Lat us na-more wordes heer-of make.
For sothe, I wol no lenger yow contrarie.'
Now lat us turne agayn to Januarie,
That in the gardin with his faire May
Singeth, ful merier than the papejay,
'Yow love I best, and shal, and other noon.'
So longe aboute the aleyes is he goon,
Til he was come agaynes thilke pyrie,
Wher-as this Damian sitteth ful myrie
An heigh, among the fresshe leves grene.
This fresshe May, that is so bright and shene,
Gan for to syke, and seyde, 'allas, my syde !
Now sir,' quod she, 'for aught that may bityde,
I moste han of the peres that I see,
Or I mot dye, so sore longeth me
To eten of the smale peres grene.
Help, for hir love that is of hevene quene !
I telle yow wel, a womman in my plyt
May han to fruit so greet an appetyt,
That she may dyen, but she of it have.'
'Allas !' quod he, 'that I ne had heer a knave
That coude climbe ; allas ! allas !' quod he,
'That I am blind.' 'Ye, sir, no fors,' quod she :
'But wolde ye vouche-sauf, for goddes sake,
The pyrie inwith your armes for to take,
(For wel I woot that ye mistruste me)
Thanne sholde I climbe wel y-nogh,' quod she,
'So I my foot mighte sette upon your bak.'
'Certes,' quod he, 'ther-on shal be no lak,
Mighte I yow helpen with myn herte blood.'
He stoupeth doun, and on his bak she stood.

And caughte hir by a twiste, and up she gooth.
Ladies, I prey yow that ye be nat wrooth;
I can nat glose, I am a rude man.
And sodeynly anon this Damian
Gan pullen up the smok, and in he throng.
And whan that Pluto saugh this grete wrong,
To Januarie he gaf agayn his sighte,
And made him see, as wel as ever he mighte.
And whan that he hadde caught his sighte agayn,
Ne was ther never man of thing so fayn.
But on his wyf his thoght was evermo;
Up to the tree he caste his eyen two,
And saugh that Damian his wyf had dressed
In swich manere, it may nat ben expressed
But if I wolde speke uncurteisly:
And up he yaf a roring and a cry
As doth the moder whan the child shal dye:
'Out! help! allas! harrow!' he gan to crye,
'O stronge lady store, what dostow?'
And she answerde, 'sir, what eyleth yow?
Have pacience, and reson in your minde,
I have yow holpe on bothe your eyen blinde.
Up peril of my soule, I shal nat lyen,
As me was taught, to hele with your yën,
Was no-thing bet to make yow to see
Than strugle with a man up-on a tree.
God woot, I dide it in ful good entente.'
'Strugle!' quod he, 'ye, algate in it wente!
God yeve yow bothe on shames deeth to dyen!
He swyved thee, I saugh it with myne yën,
And elles be I hanged by the hals!'
'Thanne is,' quod she, 'my medicyne al fals;
For certeinly, if that ye mighte see,
Ye wolde nat seyn thise wordes un-to me:
Ye han som glimsing and no parfit sighte.'
'I see,' quod he, 'as wel as ever I mighte,
Thonked be god! with bothe myne eyen two,
And by my trouthe, me thoughte he dide thee so.'
'Ye maze, maze, gode sire,' quod she,
'This thank have I for I have maad yow see;

Allas!' quod she, 'that ever I was so kinde!'
'Now, dame,' quod he, 'lat al passe out of minde.
Com doun, my lief, and if I have missayd,
God help me so, as I am yvel apayd.
But, by my fader soule, I wende han seyn,
How that this Damian had by thee leyn,
And that thy smok had leyn up-on his brest.'
'Ye, sire,' quod she, 'ye may wene as yow lest;
But, sire, a man that waketh out of his sleep,
He may nat sodeynly wel taken keep
Up-on a thing, ne seen it parfitly,
Til that he be adawed verraily;
Right so a man, that longe hath blind y-be,
Ne may nat sodeynly so wel y-see,
First whan his sighte is newe come ageyn,
As he that hath a day or two y-seyn.
Til that your sighte y-satled be a whyle,
Ther may ful many a sighte yow bigyle.
Beth war, I prey yow; for, by hevene king,
Ful many a man weneth to seen a thing,
And it is al another than it semeth.
He that misconceyveth, he misdemeth.'
And with that word she leep doun fro the tree.
This Januarie, who is glad but he?
He kisseth hir, and clippeth hir ful ofte,
And on hir wombe he stroketh hir ful softe,
And to his palays hoom he hath hir lad.
Now, gode men, I pray yow to be glad.
Thus endeth heer my tale of Januarie;
God blesse us and his moder Seinte Marie!

Here is ended the Marchantes Tale of Januarie.

Epilogue to the Marchantes Tale.

'Ey! goddes mercy!' seyde our Hoste tho,
'Now swich a wyf I pray god kepe me fro!
Lo, whiche sleightes and subtilitees
In wommen been! for ay as bisy as bees

Ben they, us sely men for to deceyve,
And from a sothe ever wol they weyve;
By this Marchauntes Tale it preveth weel.
But doutelees, as trewe as any steel
I have a wyf, though that she povre be;
But of hir tonge a labbing shrewe is she,
And yet she hath an heep of vyces mo;
Ther-of no fors, lat alle swiche thinges go.
But, wite ye what? in conseil be it seyd,
Me reweth sore I am un-to hir teyd.
For, and I sholde rekenen every vyce
Which that she hath, y-wis, I were to nyce,
And cause why; it sholde reported be
And told to hir of somme of this meynee;
Of whom, it nedeth nat for to declare,
Sin wommen connen outen swich chaffare;
And eek my wit suffyseth nat ther-to
To tellen al; wherfor my tale is do.'

THE SQUIERES TALE

The Squire's Prologue.

'Squier, com neer, if it your wille be,
And sey somwhat of love; for, certes, ye
Connen ther-on as muche as any man.'
'Nay, sir,' quod he, 'but I wol seye as I can
With hertly wille; for I wol nat rebelle
Agayn your lust; a tale wol I telle.
Have me excused if I speke amis,
My wil is good; and lo, my tale is this.'

Here biginneth the Squieres Tale.

At Sarray, in the land of Tartarye,
Ther dwelte a king, that werreyed Russye,
Thurgh which ther deyde many a doughty man.
This noble king was cleped Cambinskan,
Which in his tyme was of so greet renoun
That ther nas no-wher in no regioun
So excellent a lord in alle thing;
Him lakked noght that longeth to a king.
As of the secte of which that he was born
He kepte his lay, to which that he was sworn;
And ther-to he was hardy, wys, and riche,
And piëtous and just, alwey y-liche;
Sooth of his word, benigne and honurable,
Of his corage as any centre stable;
Yong, fresh, and strong, in armes desirous
As any bacheler of al his hous.
A fair persone he was and fortunat,
And kepte alwey so wel royal estat,
That ther was nowher swich another man.
This noble king, this Tartre Cambinskan

Hadde two sones on Elpheta his wyf,
Of whiche th'eldeste highte Algarsyf,
That other sone was cleped Cambalo.
A doghter hadde this worthy king also,
That yongest was, and highte Canacee.
But for to telle yow al hir beautee,
It lyth nat in my tonge, n'in my conning;
I dar nat undertake so heigh a thing.
Myn English eek is insufficient;
It moste been a rethor excellent,
That coude his colours longing for that art,
If he sholde hir discryven every part.
I am non swich, I moot speke as I can.
And so bifel that, whan this Cambinskan
Hath twenty winter born his diademe,
As he was wont fro yeer to yeer, I deme,
He leet the feste of his nativitee
Don cryen thurghout Sarray his citee,
The last Idus of March, after the yeer.
Phebus the sonne ful joly was and cleer;
For he was neigh his exaltacioun
In Martes face, and in his mansioun
In Aries, the colerik hote signe.
Ful lusty was the weder and benigne,
For which the foules, agayn the sonne shene,
What for the seson and the yonge grene,
Ful loude songen hir affecciouns;
Hem semed han geten hem protecciouns
Agayn the swerd of winter kene and cold.
This Cambinskan, of which I have yow told,
In royal vestiment sit on his deys,
With diademe, ful heighe in his paleys,
And halt his feste, so solempne and so riche
That in this world ne was ther noon it liche.
Of which if I shal tellen al th'array,
Than wolde it occupye a someres day;
And eek it nedeth nat for to devyse
At every cours the ordre of hir servyse.
I wol nat tellen of hir strange sewes,
Ne of hir swannes, ne of hir heronsewes.

Eek in that lond, as tellen knightes olde,
Ther is som mete that is ful deyntee holde,
That in this lond men recche of it but smal;
Ther nis no man that may reporten al.
I wol nat tarien yow, for it is pryme,
And for it is no fruit but los of tyme;
Un-to my firste I wol have my recours.
  And so bifel that, after the thridde cours,
Whyl that this king sit thus in his nobleye,
Herkninge his minstralles hir thinges pleye
Biforn him at the bord deliciously,
In at the halle-dore al sodeynly
Ther cam a knight up-on a stede of bras,
And in his hand a brood mirour of glas.
Upon his thombe he hadde of gold a ring,
And by his syde a naked swerd hanging;
And up he rydeth to the heighe bord.
In al the halle ne was ther spoke a word
For merveille of this knight; him to biholde
Ful bisily ther wayten yonge and olde.
  This strange knight, that cam thus sodeynly,
Al armed save his heed ful richely,
Saluëth king and queen, and lordes alle,
By ordre, as they seten in the halle,
With so heigh reverence and obeisaunce
As wel in speche as in contenaunce,
That Gawain, with his olde curteisye,
Though he were come ageyn out of Fairye,
Ne coude him nat amende with a word.
And after this, biforn the heighe bord,
He with a manly voys seith his message,
After the forme used in his langage,
With-outen vyce of sillable or of lettre;
And, for his tale sholde seme the bettre,
Accordant to his wordes was his chere,
As techeth art of speche hem that it lere;
Al-be-it that I can nat soune his style,
Ne can nat climben over so heigh a style,
Yet seye I this, as to commune entente,
Thus muche amounteth al that ever he mente,

If it so be that I have it in minde.
He seyde, 'the king of Arabie and of Inde,
My lige lord, on this solempne day
Saluëth yow as he best can and may,
And sendeth yow, in honour of your feste,
By me, that am al redy at your heste,
This stede of bras, that esily and wel
Can, in the space of o day naturel,
This is to seyn, in foure and twenty houres,
Wher-so yow list, in droghte or elles shoures,
Beren your body in-to every place
To which your herte wilneth for to pace
With-outen wem of yow, thurgh foul or fair;
Or, if yow list to fleen as hye in the air
As doth an egle, whan him list to sore,
This same stede shal bere yow ever-more
With-outen harm, til ye be ther yow leste,
Though that ye slepen on his bak or reste;
And turne ayeyn, with wrything of a pin.
He that it wroghte coude ful many a gin;
He wayted many a constellacioun
Er he had doon this operacioun;
And knew ful many a seel and many a bond.
This mirour eek, that I have in myn hond,
Hath swich a might, that men may in it see
Whan ther shal fallen any adversitee
Un-to your regne or to your-self also;
And openly who is your freend or foo.
And over al this, if any lady bright
Hath set hir herte on any maner wight,
If he be fals, she shal his treson see,
His newe love and al his subtiltee
So openly, that ther shal no-thing hyde.
Wherfor, ageyn this lusty someres tyde,
This mirour and this ring, that ye may see,
He hath sent to my lady Canacee,
Your excellente doghter that is here.
The vertu of the ring, if ye wol here,
Is this; that, if hir lust it for to were
Up-on hir thombe, or in hir purs it bere,

Ther is no foul that fleeth under the hevene
That she ne shal wel understonde his stevene,
And knowe his mening openly and pleyn,
And answere him in his langage ageyn.
And every gras that groweth up-on rote
She shal eek knowe, and whom it wol do bote,
Al be his woundes never so depe and wyde.
 This naked swerd, that hangeth by my syde,
Swich vertu hath, that what man so ye smyte,
Thurgh-out his armure it wol kerve and byte,
Were it as thikke as is a branched ook;
And what man that is wounded with the strook
Shal never be hool til that yow list, of grace,
To stroke him with the platte in thilke place
Ther he is hurt: this is as muche to seyn
Ye mote with the platte swerd ageyn
Stroke him in the wounde, and it wol close;
This is a verray sooth, with-outen glose,
It failleth nat whyl it is in your hold.'
 And whan this knight hath thus his tale told,
He rydeth out of halle, and doun he lighte.
His stede, which that shoon as sonne brighte,
Stant in the court, as stille as any stoon.
This knight is to his chambre lad anon,
And is unarmed and to mete y-set.
 The presents been ful royally y-fet,
This is to seyn, the swerd and the mirour,
And born anon in-to the heighe tour
With certeine officers ordeyned therfore;
And un-to Canacee this ring was bore
Solempnely, ther she sit at the table.
But sikerly, with-outen any fable,
The hors of bras, that may nat be remewed,
It stant as it were to the ground y-glewed.
Ther may no man out of the place it dryve
For noon engyn of windas or polyve;
And cause why, for they can nat the craft.
And therefore in the place they han it laft
Til that the knight hath taught hem the manere
To voyden him, as ye shal after here.

Greet was the prees, that swarmeth to and fro,
To gauren on this hors that stondeth so;
For it so heigh was, and so brood and long,
So wel proporcioned for to ben strong,
Right as it were a stede of Lumbardye;
Ther-with so horsly, and so quik of yë
As it a gentil Poileys courser were.
For certes, fro his tayl un-to his ere,
Nature ne art ne coude him nat amende
In no degree, as al the peple wende.
But evermore hir moste wonder was,
How that it coude goon, and was of bras;
It was of Fairye, as the peple semed.
Diverse folk diversely they demed;
As many hedes, as many wittes ther been.
They murmureden as dooth a swarm of been,
And maden skiles after hir fantasyes,
Rehersinge of thise olde poetryes,
And seyden, it was lyk the Pegasee,
The hors that hadde winges for to flee;
Or elles it was the Grekes hors Synon,
That broghte Troye to destruccion,
As men may in thise olde gestes rede.
'Myn herte,' quod oon, 'is evermore in drede;
I trowe som men of armes been ther-inne,
That shapen hem this citee for to winne.
It were right good that al swich thing were knowe.'
Another rowned to his felawe lowe,
And seyde, 'he lyeth, it is rather lyk
An apparence y-maad by som magyk,
As jogelours pleyen at thise festes grete.'
Of sondry doutes thus they jangle and trete,
As lewed peple demeth comunly
Of thinges that ben maad more subtilly
Than they can in her lewednes comprehende;
They demen gladly to the badder ende.
And somme of hem wondred on the mirour,
That born was up in-to the maister-tour,
How men mighte in it swiche thinges see.
Another answerde, and seyde it mighte wel be

Naturelly, by composiciouns
Of angles and of slye reflexiouns,
And seyden, that in Rome was swich oon.
They speken of Alocen and Vitulon,
And Aristotle, that writen in hir lyves
Of queynte mirours and of prospectyves,
As knowen they that han hir bokes herd.
 And othere folk han wondred on the swerd
That wolde percen thurgh-out every-thing;
And fille in speche of Thelophus the king,
And of Achilles with his queynte spere,
For he coude with it bothe hele and dere,
Right in swich wyse as men may with the swerd
Of which right now ye han your-selven herd.
They speken of sondry harding of metal,
And speke of medicynes ther-with-al,
And how, and whanne, it sholde y-harded be;
Which is unknowe algates unto me.
 Tho speke they of Canaceës ring,
And seyden alle, that swich a wonder thing
Of craft of ringes herde they never non,
Save that he, Moyses, and king Salomon
Hadde a name of konning in swich art.
Thus seyn the peple, and drawen hem apart.
But nathelees, somme seyden that it was
Wonder to maken of fern-asshen glas,
And yet nis glas nat lyk asshen of fern;
But for they han y-knowen it so fern,
Therfore cesseth her jangling and her wonder.
As sore wondren somme on cause of thonder,
On ebbe, on flood, on gossomer, and on mist,
And alle thing, til that the cause is wist.
Thus jangle they and demen and devyse,
Til that the king gan fro the bord aryse.
 Phebus hath laft the angle meridional,
And yet ascending was the beest royal,
The gentil Leon, with his Aldiran,
Whan that this Tartre king, this Cambinskan,
Roos fro his bord, ther that he sat ful hye.
Toforn him gooth the loude minstralcye,

Til he cam to his chambre of parements,
Ther as they sownen diverse instruments,
That it is lyk an heven for to here.
Now dauncen lusty Venus children dere,
For in the Fish hir lady sat ful hye,
And loketh on hem with a freendly yë.
This noble king is set up in his trone.
This strange knight is fet to him ful sone,
And on the daunce he gooth with Canacee.
Heer is the revel and the jolitee
That is nat able a dul man to devyse.
He moste han knowen love and his servyse,
And been a festlich man as fresh as May,
That sholde yow devysen swich array.
Who coude telle yow the forme of daunces,
So uncouthe and so fresshe contenaunces,
Swich subtil loking and dissimulinges
For drede of jalouse mennes aperceyvinges ?
No man but Launcelot, and he is deed.
Therefor I passe of al this lustiheed ;
I seye na-more, but in this jolynesse
I lete hem, til men to the soper dresse.
The styward bit the spyces for to hye,
And eek the wyn, in al this melodye.
The usshers and the squyers ben y-goon ;
The spyces and the wyn is come anoon.
They ete and drinke ; and whan this hadde an ende,
Un-to the temple, as reson was, they wende.
The service doon, they soupen al by day.
What nedeth yow rehercen hir array ?
Ech man wot wel, that at a kinges feeste
Hath plentee, to the moste and to the leeste,
And deyntees mo than been in my knowing.
At-after soper gooth this noble king
To seen this hors of bras, with al the route
Of lordes and of ladyes him aboute.
Swich wondring was ther on this hors of bras
That, sin the grete sege of Troye was,
Ther-as men wondreden on an hors also,
Ne was ther swich a wondring as was tho.

But fynally the king axeth this knight
The vertu of this courser and the might,
And preyede him to telle his governaunce.
  This hors anoon bigan to trippe and daunce,
Whan that this knight leyde hand up-on his reyne,
And seyde, 'sir, ther is na-more to seyne,
But, whan yow list to ryden any-where,
Ye moten trille a pin, stant in his ere,
Which I shall telle yow bitwix vs two.
Ye mote nempne him to what place also
Or to what contree that yow list to ryde.
And whan ye come ther as yow list abyde,
Bidde him descende, and trille another pin,
For ther-in lyth the effect of al the gin,
And he wol doun descende and doon your wille;
And in that place he wol abyde stille,
Though al the world the contrarie hadde y-swore;
He shal nat thennes ben y-drawe n'y-bore.
Or, if yow liste bidde him thennes goon,
Trille this pin, and he wol vanishe anoon
Out of the sighte of every maner wight,
And come agayn, be it by day or night,
When that yow list to clepen him ageyn
In swich a gyse as I shal to yow seyn
Bitwixe yow and me, and that ful sone.
Ryde whan yow list, ther is na-more to done.'
  Enformed whan the king was of that knight,
And hath conceyved in his wit aright
The maner and the forme of al this thing,
Thus glad and blythe, this noble doughty king
Repeireth to his revel as biforn.
The brydel is un-to the tour y-born,
And kept among his jewels leve and dere.
The hors vanisshed, I noot in what manere,
Out of hir sighte; ye gete na-more of me.
But thus I lete in lust and Iolitee
This Cambynskan his lordes festeyinge,
Til wel ny the day bigan to springe.

Explicit prima pars.

Sequitur pars secunda.

The norice of digestioun, the slepe,
Gan on hem winke, and bad hem taken kepe,
That muchel drink and labour wolde han reste;
And with a galping mouth hem alle he keste,
And seyde, 'it was tyme to lye adoun,
For blood was in his dominacioun;
Cherissheth blood, natures freend,' quod he.
They thanken him galpinge, by two, by three,
And every wight gan drawe him to his reste,
As slepe hem bad; they toke it for the beste.
Hir dremes shul nat been y-told for me;
Ful were hir hedes of fumositee,
That causeth dreem, of which ther nis no charge.
They slepen til that it was pryme large,
The moste part, but it were Canacee;
She was ful mesurable, as wommen be.
For of hir fader hadde she take leve
To gon to reste, sone after it was eve;
Hir liste nat appalled for to be,
Nor on the morwe unfestlich for to see;
And slepte hir firste sleep, and thanne awook.
For swich a joye she in hir herte took
Both of hir queynte ring and hir mirour,
That twenty tyme she changed hir colour;
And in hir slepe, right for impressioun
Of hir mirour, she hadde a visioun.
Wherfore, er that the sonne gan up glyde,
She cleped on hir maistresse hir bisyde,
And seyde, that hir liste for to ryse.
  Thise olde wommen that been gladly wyse,
As is hir maistresse, answerde hir anoon,
And seyde, 'madame, whider wil ye goon
Thus erly? for the folk ben alle on reste.'
'I wol,' quod she, 'aryse, for me leste
No lenger for to slepe, and walke aboute.'
  Hir maistresse clepeth wommen a gret route,
And up they rysen, wel a ten or twelve;
Up ryseth fresshe Canacee hir-selve,

As rody and bright as dooth the yonge sonne,
That in the Ram is four degrees up-ronne ;
Noon hyer was he, whan she redy was ;
And forth she walketh esily a pas,
Arrayed after the lusty seson sote
Lightly, for to pleye and walke on fote ;
Nat but with fyve or six of hir meynee ;
And in a trench, forth in the park, goth she.
The vapour, which that fro the erthe glood,
Made the sonne to seme rody and brood ;
But nathelees, it was so fair a sighte
That it made alle hir hertes for to lighte,
What for the seson and the morweninge,
And for the foules that she herde singe ;
For right anon she wiste what they mente
Right by hir song, and knew al hir entente.
  The knotte, why that every tale is told,
If it be taried til that lust be cold
Of hem that han it after herkned yore,
The savour passeth ever lenger the more,
For fulsomnesse of his prolixitee.
And by the same reson thinketh me,
I sholde to the knotte condescende,
And maken of hir walking sone an ende.
  Amidde a tree fordrye, as whyt as chalk,
As Canacee was pleying in hir walk,
Ther sat a faucon over hir heed ful hye,
That with a pitous voys so gan to crye
That all the wode resouned of hir cry.
Y-beten hath she hir-self so pitously
With bothe hir winges, til the rede blood
Ran endelong the tree ther-as she stood.
And ever in oon she cryde alwey and shrighte,
And with hir beek hir-selven so she prighte,
That ther nis tygre, ne noon so cruel beste,
That dwelleth either in wode or in foreste
That nolde han wept, if that he wepe coude,
For sorwe of hir, she shrighte alwey so loude.
For ther nas never yet no man on lyve—
If that I coude a faucon wel discryve—

That herde of swich another of fairnesse,
As wel of plumage as of gentillesse
Of shap, and al that mighte y-rekened be.
A faucon peregryn than semed she
Of fremde land ; and evermore, as she stood,
She swowneth now and now for lakke of blood,
Til wel neigh is she fallen fro the tree.
  This faire kinges doghter, Canacee,
That on hir finger bar the queynte ring,
Thurgh which she understood wel every thing
That any foul may in his ledene seyn,
And coude answere him in his ledene ageyn,
Hath understonde what this faucon seyde,
And wel neigh for the rewthe almost she deyde.
And to the tree she gooth ful hastily,
And on this faucon loketh pitously,
And heeld hir lappe abrood, for wel she wiste
The faucon moste fallen fro the twiste,
When that it swowned next, for lakke of blood.
A longe while to wayten hir she stood
Till atte laste she spak in this manere
Un-to the hauk, as ye shul after here.
  'What is the cause, if it be for to telle,
That ye be in this furial pyne of helle ?'
Quod Canacee un-to this hauk above.
'Is this for sorwe of deeth or los of love ?
For, as I trowe, thise ben causes two
That causen moost a gentil herte wo ;
Of other harm it nedeth nat to speke.
For ye your-self upon your-self yow wreke,
Which proveth wel, that either love or drede
Mot been encheson of your cruel dede,
Sin that I see non other wight yow chace.
For love of god, as dooth your-selven grace
Or what may ben your help ; for west nor eest
Ne sey I never er now no brid ne beest
That ferde with him-self so pitously.
Ye slee me with your sorwe, verraily ;
I have of yow so gret compassioun.
For goddes love, com fro the tree adoun ;

And, as I am a kinges doghter trewe,
If that I verraily the cause knewe
Of your disese, if it lay in my might,
I wolde amende it, er that it were night,
As wisly helpe me gret god of kinde !
And herbes shal I right y-nowe y-finde
To hele with your hurtes hastily.'
Tho shrighte this faucon more pitously
Than ever she dide, and fil to grounde anoon,
And lyth aswowne, deed, and lyk a stoon,
Til Canacee hath in hir lappe hir take
Un-to the tyme she gan of swough awake.
And, after that she of hir swough gan breyde,
Right in hir haukes ledene thus she seyde :—
'That pitee renneth sone in gentil herte,
Feling his similitude in peynes smerte,
Is preved al-day, as men may it see,
As wel by werk as by auctoritee ;
For gentil herte kytheth gentillesse.
I see wel, that ye han of my distresse
Compassioun, my faire Canacee,
Of verray wommanly benignitee
That nature in your principles hath set.
But for non hope for to fare the bet,
But for to obeye un-to your herte free,
And for to maken other be war by me,
As by the whelp chasted is the leoun,
Right for that cause and that conclusioun,
Whyl that I have a leyser and a space,
Myn harm I wol confessen, er I pace.'
And ever, whyl that oon hir sorwe tolde,
That other weep, as she to water wolde.
Til that the faucon bad hir to be stille ;
And, with a syk, right thus she seyde hir wille.
'Ther I was bred (allas ! that harde day !)
And fostred in a roche of marbul gray
So tendrely, that nothing eyled me,
I niste nat what was adversitee,
Til I coude flee ful hye under the sky.
Tho dwelte a tercelet me faste by,

That semed welle of alle gentillesse ;
Al were he ful of treson and falsnesse,
It was so wrapped under humble chere,
And under hewe of trouthe in swich manere,
Under plesance, and under bisy peyne,
That no wight coude han wend he coude feyne,
So depe in greyn he dyed his coloures.
Right as a serpent hit him under floures
Til he may seen his tyme for to byte,
Right so this god of love, this ypocryte,
Doth so his cerimonies and obeisaunces,
And kepeth in semblant alle his observances
That sowneth in-to gentillesse of love.
As in a toumbe is al the faire above,
And under is the corps, swich as ye woot,
Swich was this ypocryte, bothe cold and hoot,
And in this wyse he served his entente,
That (save the feend) non wiste what he mente.
Til he so longe had wopen and compleyned,
And many a yeer his service to me feyned,
Til that myn herte, to pitous and to nyce,
Al innocent of his crouned malice,
For-fered of his deeth, as thoughte me,
Upon his othes and his seuretee,
Graunted him love, on this condicioun,
That evermore myn honour and renoun
Were saved, bothe privee and apert ;
This is to seyn, that, after his desert,
I yaf him al myn herte and al my thoght—
God woot and he, that otherwyse noght—
And took his herte in chaunge for myn for ay.
But sooth is seyd, gon sithen many a day,
"A trew wight and a theef thenken nat oon."
And, whan he saugh the thing so fer y-goon
That I had graunted him fully my love,
In swich a gyse as I have seyd above,
And yeven him my trewe herte, as free
As he swoor he his herte yaf to me ;
Anon this tygre, ful of doublenesse,
Fil on his knees with so devout humblesse,

With so heigh reverence, and, as by his chere,
So lyk a gentil lovere of manere,
So ravisshed, as it semed, for the joye,
That never Jason, ne Parys of Troye,
Jason ? certes, ne non other man,
Sin Lameth was, that alderfirst bigan
To loven two, as writen folk biforn,
Ne never, sin the firste man was born,
Ne coude man, by twenty thousand part,
Countrefete the sophimes of his art ;
Ne were worthy unbokele his galoche,
Ther doublenesse or feyning sholde approche.
Ne so coude thanke a wight as he did me !
His maner was an heven for to see
Til any womman, were she never so wys ;
So peynted he and kembde at point-devys
As wel his wordes as his contenaunce.
And I so lovede him for his obeisaunce,
And for the trouthe I demed in his herte,
That, if so were that any thing him smerte,
Al were it never so lyte, and I it wiste,
Me thoughte, I felte deeth myn herte twiste.
And shortly, so ferforth this thing is went,
That my wil was his willes instrument ;
This is to seyn, my wil obeyed his wil
In alle thing, as fer as reson fil,
Keping the boundes of my worship ever.
Ne never hadde I thing so leef, ne lever.
As him, god woot ! ne never shal na-mo.
  This lasteth lenger than a yeer or two.
That I supposed of him noght but good.
But fynally, thus atte laste it stood,
That fortune wolde that he moste twinne
Out of that place which that I was inne.
Wher me was wo, that is no questioun ;
I can nat make of it discripcioun ;
For o thing dar I tellen boldely,
I knowe what is the peyne of deth ther-by ;
Swich harm I felte for he ne mighte bileve.
So on a day of me he took his leve,

So sorwefully eek, that I wende verraily
That he had felt as muche harm as I,
Whan that I herde him speke, and saugh his hewe.
But nathelees, I thoughte he was so trewe,
And eek that he repaire sholde ageyn
With-inne a litel whyle, sooth to seyn;
And reson wolde eek that he moste go
For his honour, as ofte it happeth so,
That I made vertu of necessitee,
And took it wel, sin that it moste be.
As I best mighte, I hidde fro him my sorwe,
And took him by the hond, seint John to borwe,
And seyde him thus: "lo, I am youres al;
Beth swich as I to yow have been, and shal."
What he answerde, it nedeth noght reherce,
Who can sey bet than he, who can do werse?
Whan he hath al wel seyd, thanne hath he doon.
"Therfor bihoveth him a ful long spoon
That shal ete with a feend," thus herde I seye.
So atte laste he moste forth his weye,
And forth he fleeth, til he cam ther him leste.
Whan it cam him to purpos for to reste,
I trowe he hadde thilke text in minde,
That "alle thing, repeiring to his kinde,
Gladeth him-self"; thus seyn men, as I gesse;
Men loven of propre kinde newfangelnesse,
As briddes doon that men in cages fede.
For though thou night and day take of hem hede,
And strawe hir cage faire and softe as silk,
And yeve hem sugre, hony, breed and milk,
Yet right anon, as that his dore is uppe,
He with his feet wol spurne adoun his cuppe,
And to the wode he wol and wormes ete;
So newefangel been they of hir mete,
And loven novelryes of propre kinde;
No gentillesse of blood [ne] may hem binde.
So ferde this tercelet, allas the day!
Though he were gentil born, and fresh and gay,
And goodly for to seen, and humble and free,
He saugh up-on a tyme a kyte flee,

And sodeynly he loved this kyte so,
That al his love is clene fro me ago,
And hath his trouthe falsed in this wyse ;
Thus hath the kyte my love in hir servyse,
And I am lorn with-outen remedye ! '
And with that word this faucon gan to crye,
And swowned eft in Canaceës barme.
  Greet was the sorwe, for the haukes harme,
That Canacee and alle hir wommen made ;
They niste how they mighte the faucon glade
But Canacee hom bereth hir in hir lappe,
And softely in plastres gan hir wrappe,
Ther as she with hir beek had hurt hir-selve.
Now can nat Canacee but herbes delve
Out of the grounde, and make salves newe
Of herbes precious, and fyne of hewe,
To helen with this hauk ; fro day to night
She dooth hir bisinesse and al hir might.
And by hir beddes heed she made a mewe,
And covered it with veluëttes blewe,
In signe of trouthe that is in wommen sene.
And al with-oute, the mewe is peynted grene,
In which were peynted alle thise false foules,
As beth thise tidifs, tercelets, and oules,
Right for despyt were peynted hem bisyde,
And pyes, on hem for to crye and chyde.
  Thus lete I Canacee hir hauk keping ;
I wol na-more as now speke of hir ring,
Til it come eft to purpos for to seyn
How that this faucon gat hir love ageyn
Repentant, as the storie telleth us,
By mediacioun of Cambalus,
The kinges sone, of whiche I yow tolde.
But hennes-forth I wol my proces holde
To speke of aventures and of batailles,
That never yet was herd so grete mervailles.
  First wol I telle yow of Cambinskan,
That in his tyme many a citee wan ;
And after wol I speke of Algarsyf,
How that he wan Theodora to his wyf,

For whom ful ofte in greet peril he was,
Ne hadde he ben holpen by the stede of bras;
And after wol I speke of Cambalo,
That faught in listes with the bretheren two
For Canacee, er that he mighte hir winne.
And ther I lefte I wol ageyn biginne.

Explicit secunda pars.

Incipit pars tercia.

Appollo whirleth up his char so hye,
Til that the god Mercurius hous the slye—

(*Unfinished.*)

Here folwen the wordes of the Frankelin to the Squier, and the wordes of the Host to the Frankelin.

'In feith, Squier, thou hast thee wel y-quit,
And gentilly I preise wel thy wit,'
Quod the Frankeleyn, 'considering thy youthe,
So feelingly thou spekest, sir, I allow the!
As to my doom, there is non that is here
Of eloquence that shal be thy pere,
If that thou live; god yeve thee good chaunce,
And in vertu sende thee continuaunce!
For of thy speche I have greet deyntee.
I have a sone, and, by the Trinitee,
I hadde lever than twenty pound worth lond,
Though it right now were fallen in myn hond,
He were a man of swich discrecioun
As that ye been! fy on possessioun
But-if a man be vertuous with-al.
I have my sone snibbed, and yet shal,
For he to vertu listeth nat entende;
But for to pleye at dees, and to despende,
And lese al that he hath, is his usage.
And he hath lever talken with a page
Than to comune with any gentil wight
Ther he mighte lerne gentillesse aright.'

'Straw for your gentillesse,' quod our host;
'What, frankeleyn? pardee, sir, wel thou wost
That eche of yow mot tellen atte leste
A tale or two, or breken his biheste.'
'That knowe I wel, sir,' quod the frankeleyn;
'I prey yow, haveth me nat in desdeyn
Though to this man I speke a word or two.'
'Telle on thy tale with-outen wordes mo.'
'Gladly, sir host,' quod he, 'I wol obeye
Un-to your wil; now herkneth what I seye.
I wol yow nat contrarien in no wyse
As fer as that my wittes wol suffyse;
I prey to god that it may plesen yow,
Than woot I wel that it is good y-now.'

THE FRANKELEYNS TALE

The Prologe of the Frankeleyns Tale.

THISE olde gentil Britons in hir dayes
Of diverse aventures maden layes,
Rymeyed in hir firste Briton tonge ;
Which layes with hir instruments they songe,
Or elles redden hem for hir plesaunce ;
And oon of hem have I in remembraunce,
Which I shal seyn with good wil as I can.
  But sires, by-cause I am a burel man,
At my biginning first I yow biseche
Have me excused of my rude speche ;
I lerned never rethoryk certeyn ;
Thing that I speke, it moot be bare and pleyn.
I sleep never on the mount of Pernaso,
Ne lerned Marcus Tullius Cithero,
Colours ne knowe I none, with-outen drede,
But swiche colours as growen in the mede,
Or elles swiche as men dye or peynte.
Colours of rethoryk ben me to queynte ;
My spirit feleth noght of swich matere.
But if yow list, my tale shul ye here.

Here biginneth the Frankeleyns Tale.

IN Armorik, that called is Britayne,
Ther was a knight that loved and dide his payne
To serve a lady in his beste wyse ;
And many a labour, many a greet empryse
He for his lady wroghte, er she were wonne.
For she was oon, the faireste under sonne,

And eek therto come of so heigh kinrede,
That wel unnethes dorste this knight, for drede,
Telle hir his wo, his peyne, and his distresse.
But atte laste, she, for his worthinesse,
And namely for his meke obeysaunce,
Hath swich a pitee caught of his penaunce,
That prively she fil of his accord
To take him for hir housbonde and hir lord,
Of swich lordshipe as men han over hir wyves ;
And for to lede the more in blisse hir lyves,
Of his free wil he swoor hir as a knight,
That never in al his lyf he, day ne night,
Ne sholde up-on him take no maistrye
Agayn hir wil, ne kythe hir jalousye,
But hir obeye, and folwe hir wil in al
As any lovere to his lady shal ;
Save that the name of soveraynetee,
That wolde he have for shame of his degree.
  She thanked him, and with ful greet humblesse
She seyde, ‘ sire, sith of your gentillesse
Ye profre me to have so large a reyne,
Ne wolde never god bitwixe us tweyne,
As in my gilt, were outher werre or stryf.
Sir, I wol be your humble trewe wyf,
Have heer my trouthe, til that myn herte breste.’
Thus been they bothe in quiete and in reste.
  For o thing, sires, saufly dar I seye,
That frendes everich other moot obeye,
If they wol longe holden companye.
Love wol nat ben constreyned by maistrye ;
Whan maistrie comth, the god of love anon
Beteth hise winges, and farewel ! he is gon !
Love is a thing as any spirit free ;
Wommen of kinde desiren libertee,
And nat to ben constreyned as a thral ;
And so don men, if I soth seyen shal.
Loke who that is most pacient in love,
He is at his avantage al above.
Pacience is an heigh vertu certeyn ;
For it venquisseth, as thise clerkes seyn,

Thinges that rigour sholde never atteyne.
For every word men may nat chyde or pleyne.
Lerneth to suffre, or elles, so moot I goon,
Ye shul it lerne, wher-so ye wole or noon.
For in this world, certein, ther no wight is,
That he ne dooth or seith som-tyme amis.
Ire, siknesse, or constellacioun,
Wyn, wo, or chaunginge of complexioun
Causeth ful ofte to doon amis or speken.
On every wrong a man may nat be wreken;
After the tyme, moste be temperaunce
To every wight that can on governaunce.
And therfore hath this wyse worthy knight,
To live in ese, suffrance hir bihight,
And she to him ful wisly gan to swere
That never sholde ther be defaute in here.
 Heer may men seen an humble wys accord;
Thus hath she take hir servant and hir lord,
Servant in love, and lord in mariage;
Than was he bothe in lordship and servage;
Servage? nay, but in lordshipe above,
Sith he hath bothe his lady and his love;
His lady, certes, and his wyf also,
The which that lawe of love acordeth to.
And whan he was in this prosperitee,
Hoom with his wyf he gooth to his contree,
Nat fer fro Penmark, ther his dwelling was,
Wher-as he liveth in blisse and in solas.
 Who coude telle, but he had wedded be,
The joye, the ese, and the prosperitee
That is bitwixe an housbonde and his wyf?
A yeer and more lasted this blisful lyf,
Til that the knight of which I speke of thus,
That of Kayrrud was cleped Arveragus,
Shoop him to goon, and dwelle a yeer or tweyne
In Engelond, that cleped was eek Briteyne,
To seke in armes worship and honour;
For al his lust he sette in swich labour;
And dwelled ther two yeer, the book seith thus.
 Now wol I stinte of this Arveragus,

And speken I wole of Dorigene his wyf,
That loveth hir housbonde as hir hertes lyf.
For his absence wepeth she and syketh,
As doon thise noble wyves whan hem lyketh.
She moorneth, waketh, wayleth, fasteth, pleyneth ;
Desyr of his presence hir so distreyneth,
That al this wyde world she sette at noght.
Hir frendes, whiche that knewe hir hevy thoght,
Conforten hir in al that ever they may ;
They prechen hir, they telle hir night and day,
That causelees she sleeth hir-self, allas !
And every confort possible in this cas
They doon to hir with al hir bisinesse,
Al for to make hir leve hir hevinesse.
By proces, as ye knowen everichoon,
Men may so longe graven in a stoon,
Til som figure ther-inne emprented be.
So longe han they conforted hir, til she
Receyved hath, by hope and by resoun,
Th'emprenting of hir consolacioun,
Thurgh which hir grete sorwe gan aswage ;
She may nat alwey duren in swich rage.
And eek Arveragus, in al this care,
Hath sent hir lettres hoom of his welfare,
And that he wol come hastily agayn ;
Or elles hadde this sorwe hir herte slayn.
Hir freendes sawe hir sorwe gan to slake,
And preyede hir on knees, for goddes sake,
To come and romen hir in companye,
Awey to dryve hir derke fantasye.
And finally, she graunted that requeste ;
For wel she saugh that it was for the beste.
Now stood hir castel faste by the see,
And often with hir freendes walketh she
Hir to disporte up-on the bank an heigh,
Wher-as she many a ship and barge seigh
Seilinge hir cours, wher-as hem liste go ;
But than was that a parcel of hir wo.
For to hir-self ful ofte 'allas !' seith she,
'Is ther no ship, of so manye as I see,

Wol bringen hom my lord ? than were myn herte
Al warisshed of his bittre peynes smerte.'
  Another tyme ther wolde she sitte and thinke
And caste hir eyen dounward fro the brinke.
But whan she saugh the grisly rokkes blake,
For verray fere so wolde hir herte quake,
That on hir feet she mighte hir noght sustene.
Than wolde she sitte adoun upon the grene,
And pitously in-to the see biholde,
And seyn right thus, with sorweful sykes colde :
  'Eterne god, that thurgh thy purveyaunce
Ledest the world by certein governaunce,
In ydel, as men seyn, ye no-thing make ;
But, lord, thise grisly feendly rokkes blake,
That semen rather a foul confusioun
Of werk than any fair creacioun
Of swich a parfit wys god and a stable,
Why han ye wroght this werk unresonable ?
For by this werk, south, north, ne west, ne eest,
Ther nis y-fostred man, ne brid, ne beest ;
It dooth no good, to my wit, but anoyeth.
See ye nat, lord, how mankinde it destroyeth ?
An hundred thousand bodies of mankinde
Han rokkes slayn, al be they nat in minde,
Which mankinde is so fair part of thy werk
That thou it madest lyk to thyn owene merk.
Than semed it ye hadde a greet chiertee
Toward mankinde ; but how than may it be
That ye swiche menes make it to destroyen,
Whiche menes do no good, but ever anoyen ?
I woot wel clerkes wol seyn, as hem leste,
By arguments, that al is for the beste,
Though I ne can the causes nat y-knowe.
But thilke god, that made wind to blowe,
As kepe my lord ! this my conclusioun ;
To clerkes lete I al disputisoun.
But wolde god that alle thise rokkes blake
Were sonken in-to helle for his sake !
Thise rokkes sleen myn herte for the fere.'
Thus wolde she seyn, with many a pitous tere.

Hir freendes sawe that it was no disport
To romen by the see, but disconfort;
And shopen for to pleyen somwher elles.
They leden hir by riveres and by welles,
And eek in othere places delitables;
They dauncen, and they pleyen at ches and tables.
So on a day, right in the morwe-tyde,
Un-to a gardin that was ther bisyde,
In which that they had maad hir ordinaunce
Of vitaille and of other purveyaunce,
They goon and pleye hem al the longe day.
And this was on the sixte morwe of May,
Which May had peynted with his softe shoures
This gardin ful of leves and of floures;
And craft of mannes hand so curiously
Arrayed hadde this gardin, trewely,
That never was ther gardin of swich prys,
But-if it were the verray paradys.
Th' odour of floures and the fresshe sighte
Wolde han maad any herte for to lighte
That ever was born, but-if to gret siknesse,
Or to gret sorwe helde it in distresse;
So ful it was of beautee with plesaunce.
At-after diner gonne they to daunce,
And singe also, save Dorigen allone,
Which made alwey hir compleint and hir mone;
For she ne saugh him on the daunce go,
That was hir housbonde and hir love also.
But nathelees she moste a tyme abyde,
And with good hope lete hir sorwe slyde.
Up-on this daunce, amonges othere men,
Daunced a squyer biforen Dorigen,
That fressher was and jolyer of array,
As to my doom, than is the monthe of May.
He singeth, daunceth, passinge any man
That is, or was, sith that the world bigan.
Ther-with he was, if men sholde him discryve,
Oon of the beste faringe man on-lyve;
Yong, strong, right vertuous, and riche and wys,
And wel biloved, and holden in gret prys.

And shortly, if the sothe I tellen shal,
Unwiting of this Dorigen at al,
This lusty squyer, servant to Venus,
Which that y-cleped was Aurelius,
Had loved hir best of any creature
Two yeer and more, as was his aventure,
But never dorste he telle hir his grevaunce ;
With-outen coppe he drank al his penaunce.
He was despeyred, no-thing dorste he seye,
Save in his songes somwhat wolde he wreye
His wo, as in a general compleyning ;
He seyde he lovede, and was biloved no-thing.
Of swich matere made he manye layes,
Songes, compleintes, roundels, virelayes,
How that he dorste nat his sorwe telle,
But languissheth, as a furie dooth in helle ;
And dye he moste, he seyde, as dide Ekko
For Narcisus, that dorste nat telle hir wo.
In other manere than ye here me seye,
Ne dorste he nat to hir his wo biwreye ;
Save that, paraventure, som-tyme at daunces,
Ther yonge folk kepen hir observaunces,
It may wel be he loked on hir face
In swich a wyse, as man that asketh grace ;
But no-thing wiste she of his entente.
Nathelees, it happed, er they thennes wente,
By-cause that he was hir neighebour,
And was a man of worship and honour,
And hadde y-knowen him of tyme yore,
They fille in speche ; and forth more and more
Un-to his purpos drough Aurelius,
And whan he saugh his tyme, he seyde thus :
'Madame,' quod he, 'by god that this world made,
So that I wiste it mighte your herte glade,
I wolde, that day that your Arveragus
Wente over the see, that I, Aurelius,
Had went ther never I sholde have come agayn ;
For wel I woot my service is in vayn.

My guerdon is but bresting of myn herte ;
Madame, reweth upon my peynes smerte ;
For with a word ye may me sleen or save,
Heer at your feet god wolde that I were grave !
I ne have as now no leyser more to seye ;
Have mercy, swete, or ye wol do me deye ! '
  She gan to loke up-on Aurelius :
' Is this your wil,' quod she, ' and sey ye thus ?
Never erst,' quod she, ' ne wiste I what ye mente.
But now, Aurelie, I knowe your entente,
By thilke god that yaf me soule and lyf,
Ne shal I never been untrewe wyf
In word ne werk, as fer as I have wit :
I wol ben his to whom that I am knit ;
Tak this for fynal answer as of me.'
But after that in pley thus seyde she :
  ' Aurelie,' quod she, ' by heighe god above,
Yet wolde I graunte yow to been your love,
Sin I yow see so pitously complayne ;
Loke what day that, endelong Britayne,
Ye remoeve alle the rokkes, stoon by stoon,
That they ne lette ship ne boot to goon—
I seye, whan ye han maad the coost so clene
Of rokkes, that ther nis no stoon y-sene,
Than wol I love yow best of any man ;
Have heer my trouthe in al that ever I can.'
' Is ther non other grace in yow ? ' quod he.
' No, by that lord,' quod she, ' that maked me !
For wel I woot that it shal never bityde.
Lat swiche folies out of your herte slyde.
What deyntee sholde a man han in his lyf
For to go love another mannes wyf,
That hath hir body whan so that him lyketh ? '
  Aurelius ful ofte sore syketh ;
Wo was Aurelie, whan that he this herde,
And with a sorweful herte he thus answerde :
  ' Madame,' quod he, ' this were an inpossible !
Than moot I dye of sodein deth horrible.'
And with that word he turned him anoon.
Tho come hir othere freendes many oon,

And in the aleyes romeden up and doun,
And no-thing wiste of this conclusioun,
But sodeinly bigonne revel newe
Til that the brighte sonne loste his hewe;
For th'orisonte hath reft the sonne his light;
This is as muche to seye as it was night.
And hoom they goon in joye and in solas,
Save only wrecche Aurelius, allas!
He to his hous is goon with sorweful herte;
He seeth he may nat fro his deeth asterte.
Him semed that he felte his herte colde;
Up to the hevene his handes he gan holde,
And on his knowes bare he sette him doun,
And in his raving seyde his orisoun.
For verray wo out of his wit he breyde.
He niste what he spak, but thus he seyde;
With pitous herte his pleynt hath he bigonne
Un-to the goddes, and first un-to the sonne:
He seyde, 'Appollo, god and governour
Of every plaunte, herbe, tree and flour,
That yevest, after thy declinacioun,
To ech of hem his tyme and his sesoun,
As thyn herberwe chaungeth lowe or hye,
Lord Phebus, cast thy merciable yë
On wrecche Aurelie, which that am but lorn.
Lo, lord! my lady hath my deeth y-sworn
With-oute gilt, but thy benignitee
Upon my dedly herte have som pitee!
For wel I woot, lord Phebus, if yow lest,
Ye may me helpen, save my lady, best.
Now voucheth sauf that I may yow devyse
How that I may been holpe and in what wyse.
Your blisful suster, Lucina the shene,
That of the see is chief goddesse and quene,
Though Neptunus have deitee in the see,
Yet emperesse aboven him is she:
Ye knowen wel, lord, that right as hir desyr
Is to be quiked and lightned of your fyr,
For which she folweth yow ful bisily,
Right so the see desyreth naturelly

To folwen hir, as she that is goddesse
Bothe in the see and riveres more and lesse.
Wherfore, lord Phebus, this is my requeste—
Do this miracle, or do myn herte breste—
That now, next at this opposicioun,
Which in the signe shal be of the Leoun,
As preyeth hir so greet a flood to bringe,
That fyve fadme at the leeste it overspringe
The hyeste rokke in Armorik Briteyne ;
And lat this flood endure yeres tweyne ;
Than certes to my lady may I seye :
" Holdeth your heste, the rokkes been aweye."
  Lord Phebus, dooth this miracle for me ;
Preye hir she go no faster cours than ye ;
I seye, preyeth your suster that she go
No faster cours than ye thise yeres two.
Than shal she been evene atte fulle alway,
And spring-flood laste bothe night and day.
And, but she vouche-sauf in swiche manere
To graunte me my sovereyn lady dere,
Prey hir to sinken every rok adoun
In-to hir owene derke regioun
Under the ground, ther Pluto dwelleth inne,
Or never-mo shal I my lady winne.
Thy temple in Delphos wol I barefoot seke ;
Lord Phebus, see the teres on my cheke,
And of my peyne have som compassioun.'
And with that word in swowne he fil adoun,
And longe tyme he lay forth in a traunce.
  His brother, which that knew of his penaunce,
Up caughte him and to bedde he hath him broght.
Dispeyred in this torment and this thoght
Lete I this woful creature lye ;
Chese he, for me, whether he wol live or dye.
  Arveragus, with hele and greet honour,
As he that was of chivalrye the flour,
Is comen hoom, and othere worthy men.
O blisful artow now, thou Dorigen,
That hast thy lusty housbonde in thyne armes,
The fresshe knight, the worthy man of armes,

That loveth thee, as his owene hertes lyf.
No-thing list him to been imaginatyf
If any wight had spoke, whyl he was oute,
To hire of love ; he hadde of it no doute.
He noght entendeth to no swich matere,
But daunceth, justeth, maketh hir good chere ;
And thus in joye and blisse I lete hem dwelle,
And of the syke Aurelius wol I telle.
In langour and in torment furious
Two yeer and more lay wrecche Aurelius,
Er any foot he mighte on erthe goon ;
Ne confort in this tyme hadde he noon,
Save of his brother, which that was a clerk ;
He knew of al this wo and al this werk.
For to non other creature certeyn
Of this matere he dorste no word seyn.
Under his brest he bar it more secree
Than ever dide Pamphilus for Galathee.
His brest was hool, with-oute for to sene,
But in his herte ay was the arwe kene.
And wel ye knowe that of a sursanure
In surgerye is perilous the cure,
But men mighte touche the arwe, or come therby.
His brother weep and wayled prively,
Til atte laste him fil in remembraunce,
That whyl he was at Orliens in Fraunce,
As yonge clerkes, that been likerous
To reden artes that been curious,
Seken in every halke and every herne
Particuler sciences for to lerne,
He him remembred that, upon a day,
At Orliens in studie a book he say
Of magik naturel, which his felawe,
That was that tyme a bacheler of lawe,
Al were he ther to lerne another craft,
Had prively upon his desk y-laft ;
Which book spak muchel of the operaciouns,
Touchinge the eighte and twenty mansiouns
That longen to the mone, and swich folye,
As in our dayes is nat worth a flye ;

For holy chirches feith in our bileve
Ne suffreth noon illusion us to greve.
And whan this book was in his remembraunce,
Anon for joye his herte gan to daunce,
And to him-self he seyde prively :
'My brother shal be warisshed hastily ;
For I am siker that ther be sciences,
By whiche men make diverse apparences
Swiche as thise subtile tregetoures pleye.
For ofte at festes have I wel herd seye,
That tregetours, with-inne an halle large,
Have maad come in a water and a barge,
And in the halle rowen up and doun.
Somtyme hath semed come a grim leoun ;
And somtyme floures springe as in a mede ;
Somtyme a vyne, and grapes whyte and rede ;
Somtyme a castel, al of lym and stoon ;
And whan hem lyked, voyded it anoon.
Thus semed it to every mannes sighte.
  Now than conclude I thus, that if I mighte
At Orliens som old felawe y-finde,
That hadde this mones mansions in minde,
Or other magik naturel above,
He sholde wel make my brother han his love.
For with an apparence a clerk may make
To mannes sighte, that alle the rokkes blake
Of Britaigne weren y-voyded everichon,
And shippes by the brinke comen and gon,
And in swich forme endure a day or two ;
Than were my brother warisshed of his wo.
Than moste she nedes holden hir biheste,
Or elles he shal shame hir atte leste.'
  What sholde I make a lenger tale of this ?
Un-to his brotheres bed he comen is,
And swich confort he yaf him for to gon
To Orliens, that he up stirte anon,
And on his wey forthward thanne is he fare,
In hope for to ben lissed of his care.
  Whan they were come almost to that citee,
But-if it were a two furlong or three,

A yong clerk rominge by him-self they mette,
Which that in Latin thriftily hem grette,
And after that he seyde a wonder thing:
'I knowe,' quod he, 'the cause of your coming':
And er they ferther any fote wente,
He tolde hem al that was in hir entente.
This Briton clerk him asked of felawes
The whiche that he had knowe in olde dawes;
And he answerde him that they dede were,
For which he weep ful ofte many a tere.
Doun of his hors Aurelius lighte anon,
And forth with this magicien is he gon
Hoom to his hous, and made hem wel at ese.
Hem lakked no vitaille that mighte hem plese;
So wel arrayed hous as ther was oon
Aurelius in his lyf saugh never noon.
He shewed him, er he wente to sopeer,
Forestes, parkes ful of wilde deer;
Ther saugh he hertes with hir hornes hye,
The gretteste that ever were seyn with yë.
He saugh of hem an hondred slayn with houndes,
And somme with arwes blede of bittre woundes.
He saugh, whan voided were thise wilde deer,
Thise fauconers upon a fair river,
That with hir haukes han the heron slayn.
Tho saugh he knightes justing in a playn;
And after this, he dide him swich plesaunce,
That he him shewed his lady on a daunce
On which him-self he daunced, as him thoughte.
And whan this maister, that this magik wroughte,
Saugh it was tyme, he clapte his handes two,
And farewel! al our revel was ago.
And yet remoeved they never out of the hous,
Whyl they saugh al this sighte merveillous,
But in his studie, ther-as his bookes be,
They seten stille, and no wight but they three.
To him this maister called his squyer,
And seyde him thus: 'is redy our soper?
Almost an houre it is, I undertake,
Sith I yow bad our soper for to make,

Whan that thise worthy men wenten with me
In-to my studie, ther-as my bookes be.'
'Sire,' quod this squyer, 'whan it lyketh yow,
It is al redy, though ye wol right now.'
'Go we than soupe,' quod he, 'as for the beste;
This amorous folk som-tyme mote han reste.'
At-after soper fille they in tretee,
What somme sholde this maistres guerdon be,
To remoeven alle the rokkes of Britayne,
And eek from Gerounde to the mouth of Sayne.
He made it straunge, and swoor, so god him save,
Lasse than a thousand pound he wolde nat have,
Ne gladly for that somme he wolde nat goon.
Aurelius, with blisful herte anoon,
Answerde thus, 'fy on a thousand pound!
This wyde world, which that men seye is round,
I wolde it yeve, if I were lord of it.
This bargayn is ful drive, for we ben knit.
Ye shal be payed trewely, by my trouthe!
But loketh now, for no necligence or slouthe,
Ye tarie us heer no lenger than to-morwe.'
'Nay,' quod this clerk, 'have heer my feith to borwe.'
To bedde is goon Aurelius whan him leste,
And wel ny al that night he hadde his reste;
What for his labour and his hope of blisse,
His woful herte of penaunce hadde a lisse.
Upon the morwe, whan that it was day,
To Britaigne toke they the righte way,
Aurelius, and this magicien bisyde,
And been descended ther they wolde abyde;
And this was, as the bokes me remembre,
The colde frosty seson of Decembre.
Phebus wex old, and hewed lyk latoun,
That in his hote declinacioun
Shoon as the burned gold with stremes brighte;
But now in Capricorn adoun he lighte,
Wher-as he shoon ful pale, I dar wel seyn.
The bittre frostes, with the sleet and reyn,

Destroyed hath the grene in every yerd.
Janus sit by the fyr, with double berd,
And drinketh of his bugle-horn the wyn.
Biforn him stant braun of the tusked swyn,
And 'Nowel' cryeth every lusty man.
  Aurelius, in al that ever he can,
Doth to his maister chere and reverence,
And preyeth him to doon his diligence
To bringen him out of his peynes smerte,
Or with a swerd that he wolde slitte his herte.
  This subtil clerk swich routhe had of this man,
That night and day he spedde him that he can,
To wayte a tyme of his conclusioun;
This is to seye, to make illusioun,
By swich an apparence or jogelrye,
I ne can no termes of astrologye,
That she and every wight sholde wene and seye,
That of Britaigne the rokkes were aweye,
Or elles they were sonken under grounde.
So atte laste he hath his tyme y-founde
To maken his japes and his wrecchednesse
Of swich a supersticious cursednesse.
His tables Toletanes forth he broght,
Ful wel corrected, ne ther lakked noght,
Neither his collect ne his expans yeres,
Ne his rotes ne his othere geres,
As been his centres and his arguments,
And his proporcionels convenients
For his equacions in every thing.
And, by his eighte spere in his wirking,
He knew ful wel how fer Alnath was shove
Fro the heed of thilke fixe Aries above
That in the ninthe speere considered is;
Ful subtilly he calculed al this.
  Whan he had founde his firste mansioun,
He knew the remenant by proporcioun;
And knew the arysing of his mone weel,
And in whos face, and terme, and every-deel;
And knew ful weel the mones mansioun
Acordaunt to his operacioun,

And knew also his othere observaunces
For swiche illusiouns and swiche meschaunces
As hethen folk used in thilke dayes;
For which no lenger maked he delayes,
But thurgh his magik, for a wyke or tweye,
It semed that alle the rokkes were aweye.
  Aurelius, which that yet despeired is
Wher he shal han his love or fare amis,
Awaiteth night and day on this miracle;
And whan he knew that ther was noon obstacle,
That voided were thise rokkes everichon,
Doun to his maistres feet he fil anon,
And seyde, 'I woful wrecche, Aurelius,
Thanke yow, lord, and lady myn Venus,
That me han holpen fro my cares colde:'
And to the temple his wey forth hath he holde,
Wher-as he knew he sholde his lady see.
And whan he saugh his tyme, anon-right he,
With dredful herte and with ful humble chere,
Salewed hath his sovereyn lady dere:
  'My righte lady,' quod this woful man,
'Whom I most drede and love as I best can,
And lothest were of al this world displese,
Nere it that I for yow have swich disese,
That I moste dyen heer at your foot anon,
Noght wolde I telle how me is wo bigon;
But certes outher moste I dye or pleyne;
Ye slee me giltelees for verray peyne.
But of my deeth, thogh that ye have no routhe,
Avyseth yow, er that ye breke your trouthe.
Repenteth yow, for thilke god above,
Er ye me sleen by-cause that I yow love.
For, madame, wel ye woot what ye han hight;
Nat that I chalange any thing of right
Of yow my sovereyn lady, but your grace;
But in a gardin yond, at swich a place,
Ye woot right wel what ye bihighten me;
And in myn hand your trouthe plighten ye
To love me best, god woot, ye seyde so,
Al be that I unworthy be therto.

Madame, I speke it for the honour of yow,
More than to save myn hertes lyf right now;
I have do so as ye comanded me;
And if ye vouche-sauf, ye may go see.
Doth as yow list, have your biheste in minde,
For quik or deed, right ther ye shul me finde;
In yow lyth al, to do me live or deye;—
But wel I woot the rokkes been aweye!'
He taketh his leve, and she astonied stood,
In al hir face nas a drope of blood;
She wende never han come in swich a trappe:
'Allas!' quod she, 'that ever this sholde happe
For wende I never, by possibilitee,
That swich a monstre or merveille mighte be!
It is agayns the proces of nature:'
And hoom she gooth a sorweful creature.
For verray fere unnethe may she go,
She wepeth, wailleth, al a day or two,
And swowneth, that it routhe was to see;
But why it was, to no wight tolde she;
For out of toune was goon Arveragus.
But to hir-self she spak, and seyde thus,
With face pale and with ful sorweful chere,
In hir compleynt, as ye shul after here:
'Allas,' quod she, 'on thee, Fortune, I pleyne,
That unwar wrapped hast me in thy cheyne;
For which, t'escape, woot I no socour
Save only deeth or elles dishonour;
Oon of thise two bihoveth me to chese.
But nathelees, yet have I lever lese
My lyf than of my body have a shame,
Or knowe my-selven fals, or lese my name,
And with my deth I may be quit, y-wis.
Hath ther nat many a noble wyf, er this,
And many a mayde y-slayn hir-self, allas!
Rather than with hir body doon trespas?
Yis, certes, lo, thise stories beren witnesse;
Whan thretty tyraunts, ful of cursednesse,
Had slayn Phidoun in Athenes, atte feste,
They comanded his doghtres for t'areste,

And bringen hem biforn hem in despyt
Al naked, to fulfille hir foul delyt,
And in hir fadres blood they made hem daunce
Upon the pavement, god yeve hem mischaunce!
For which thise woful maydens, ful of drede,
Rather than they wolde lese hir maydenhede,
They prively ben stirt in-to a welle,
And dreynte hem-selven, as the bokes telle.
They of Messene lete enquere and seke
Of Lacedomie fifty maydens eke,
On whiche they wolden doon hir lecherye;
But was ther noon of al that companye
That she nas slayn, and with a good entente
Chees rather for to dye than assente
To been oppressed of hir maydenhede.
Why sholde I thanne to dye been in drede?
Lo, eek, the tiraunt Aristoclides
That loved a mayden, heet Stimphalides,
Whan that hir fader slayn was on a night,
Un-to Dianes temple goth she right,
And hente the image in hir handes two,
Fro which image wolde she never go.
No wight ne mighte hir handes of it arace,
Til she was slayn right in the selve place.
Now sith that maydens hadden swich despyt
To been defouled with mannes foul delyt,
Wel oghte a wyf rather hir-selven slee
Than be defouled, as it thinketh me.
What shal I seyn of Hasdrubales wyf,
That at Cartage birafte hir-self hir lyf?
For whan she saugh that Romayns wan the toun,
She took hir children alle, and skipte adoun
In-to the fyr, and chees rather to dye
Than any Romayn dide hir vileinye.
Hath nat Lucresse y-slayn hir-self, allas!
At Rome, whanne she oppressed was
Of Tarquin, for hir thoughte it was a shame
To liven whan she hadde lost hir name?
The sevene maydens of Milesie also
Han slayn hem-self, for verray drede and wo,

Rather than folk of Gaule hem sholde oppresse.
Mo than a thousand stories, as I gesse,
Coude I now telle as touchinge this matere.
  Whan Habradate was slayn, his wyf so dere
Hirselven slow, and leet hir blood to glyde
In Habradates woundes depe and wyde,
And seyde, " my body, at the leeste way,
Ther shal no wight defoulen, if I may."
  What sholde I mo ensamples heer-of sayn,
Sith that so manye han hem-selven slayn
Wel rather than they wolde defouled be ?
I wol conclude, that it is bet for me
To sleen my-self, than been defouled thus.
I wol be trewe un-to Arveragus,
Or rather sleen my-self in som manere,
As dide Demociones doghter dere,
By-cause that she wolde nat defouled be.
  O Cedasus ! it is ful greet pitee,
To reden how thy doghtren deyde, allas !
That slowe hem-selven for swich maner cas.
  As greet a pitee was it, or wel more,
The Theban mayden, that for Nichanore
Hir-selven slow, right for swich maner wo.
  Another Theban mayden dide right so ;
For oon of Macedoine hadde hir oppressed,
She with hir deeth hir maydenhede redressed.
  What shal I seye of Nicerates wyf,
That for swich cas birafte hir-self hir lyf ?
  How trewe eek was to Alcebiades
His love, that rather for to dyen chees
Than for to suffre his body unburied be !
Lo which a wyf was Alcestè,' quod she.
  ' What seith Omer of gode Penalopee ?
Al Grece knoweth of hir chastitee.
  Pardee, of Laodomya is writen thus,
That whan at Troye was slayn Protheselaus,
No lenger wolde she live after his day.
  The same of noble Porcia telle I may ;
With-oute Brutus coude she nat live,
To whom she hadde al hool hir herte yive.

The parfit wyfhod of Arthemesye
Honoured is thurgh al the Barbarye.
O Teuta, queen! thy wyfly chastitee
To alle wyvès may a mirour be.
The same thing I seye of Bilia,
Of Rodogone, and eek Valeria.'
Thus pleyned Dorigene a day or tweye,
Purposinge ever that she wolde deye.
But nathelees, upon the thridde night,
Hom cam Arveragus, this worthy knight,
And asked hir, why that she weep so sore?
And she gan wepen ever lenger the more.
'Allas!' quod she, 'that ever was I born!
Thus have I seyd,' quod she, 'thus have I sworn'—
And told him al as ye han herd bifore;
It nedeth nat reherce it yow na-more.
This housbond with glad chere, in freendly wyse,
Answerde and seyde as I shal yow devyse:
'Is ther oght elles, Dorigen, but this?'
'Nay, nay,' quod she, 'god help me so, as wis;
This is to muche, and it were goddes wille.'
'Ye, wyf,' quod he, 'lat slepen that is stille;
It may be wel, paraventure, yet to-day.
Ye shul your trouthe holden, by my fay!
For god so wisly have mercy on me,
I hadde wel lever y-stiked for to be,
For verray love which that I to yow have,
But-if ye sholde your trouthe kepe and save.
Trouthe is the hyeste thing that man may kepe:'—
But with that word he brast anon to wepe,
And seyde, 'I yow forbede, up peyne of deeth,
That never, whyl thee lasteth lyf ne breeth,
To no wight tel thou of this aventure.
As I may best, I wol my wo endure,
Ne make no contenance of hevinesse,
That folk of yow may demen harm or gesse.'
And forth he cleped a squyer and a mayde:
'Goth forth anon with Dorigen,' he sayde,
'And bringeth hir to swich a place anon.'
They take hir leve, and on hir wey they gon;

But they ne wiste why she thider wente.
He nolde no wight tellen his entente.
  Paraventure an heep of yow, y-wis,
Wol holden him a lewed man in this,
That he wol putte his wyf in jupartye;
Herkneth the tale, er ye up-on hir crye.
She may have bettre fortune than yow semeth;
And whan that ye han herd the tale, demeth.
  This squyer, which that highte Aurelius,
On Dorigen that was so amorous,
Of aventure happed hir to mete
Amidde the toun, right in the quikkest strete,
As she was boun to goon the wey forth-right
Toward the gardin ther-as she had hight.
And he was to the gardinward also;
For wel he spyed, whan she wolde go
Out of hir hous to any maner place.
But thus they mette, of aventure or grace;
And he saleweth hir with glad entente,
And asked of hir whiderward she wente?
  And she answerde, half as she were mad,
'Un-to the gardin, as myn housbond bad,
My trouthe for to holde, allas! allas!'
  Aurelius gan wondren on this cas,
And in his herte had greet compassioun
Of hir and of hir lamentacioun,
And of Arveragus, the worthy knight,
That bad hir holden al that she had hight,
So looth him was his wyf sholde breke hir trouthe;
And in his herte he caughte of this greet routhe,
Consideringe the beste on every syde,
That fro his lust yet were him lever abyde
Than doon so heigh a cherlish wrecchednesse
Agayns franchyse and alle gentillesse;
For which in fewe wordes seyde he thus:
  'Madame, seyth to your lord Arveragus,
That sith I see his grete gentillesse
To yow, and eek I see wel your distresse,

That him were lever han shame (and that were routhe)
Than ye to me sholde breke thus your trouthe,
I have wel lever ever to suffre wo
Than I departe the love bitwix yow two.
I yow relesse, madame, in-to your hond
Quit every surement and every bond,
That ye han maad to me as heer-biforn,
Sith thilke tyme which that ye were born.
My trouthe I plighte, I shal yow never repreve
Of no biheste, and here I take my leve,
As of the treweste and the beste wyf
That ever yet I knew in al my lyf.
But every wyf be-war of hir biheste,
On Dorigene remembreth atte leste.
Thus can a squyer doon a gentil dede,
As well as can a knight, with-outen drede.'
  She thonketh him up-on hir knees al bare,
And hoom un-to hir housbond is she fare,
And tolde him al as ye han herd me sayd;
And be ye siker, he was so weel apayd,
That it were inpossible me to wryte;
What sholde I lenger of this cas endyte?
  Arveragus and Dorigene his wyf
In sovereyn blisse leden forth hir lyf.
Never eft ne was ther angre hem bitwene;
He cherisseth hir as though she were a quene;
And she was to him trewe for evermore.
Of thise two folk ye gete of me na-more.
  Aurelius, that his cost hath al forlorn,
Curseth the tyme that ever he was born:
'Allas,' quod he, 'allas! that I bihighte
Of pured gold a thousand pound of wighte
Un-to this philosophre! how shal I do?
I see na-more but that I am fordo.
Myn heritage moot I nedes selle,
And been a begger; heer may I nat dwelle,
And shamen al my kinrede in this place,
But I of him may gete bettre grace.

But nathelees, I wol of him assaye,
At certeyn dayes, yeer by yeer, to paye,
And thanke him of his grete curteisye;
My trouthe wol I kepe, I wol nat lye.'
  With herte soor he gooth un-to his cofre,
And broghte gold un-to this philosophre,
The value of fyve hundred pound, I gesse,
And him bisecheth, of his gentillesse,
To graunte him dayes of the remenaunt,
And seyde, 'maister, I dar wel make avaunt,
I failled never of my trouthe as yit;
For sikerly my dette shal be quit
Towardes yow, how-ever that I fare
To goon a-begged in my kirtle bare.
But wolde ye vouche sauf, up-on seurtee,
Two yeer or three for to respyten me,
Than were I wel; for elles moot I selle
Myn heritage; ther is na-more to telle.'
  This philosophre sobrely answerde,
And seyde thus, whan he thise wordes herde:
'Have I nat holden covenant un-to thee?'
'Yes, certes, wel and trewely,' quod he.
'Hastow nat had thy lady as thee lyketh?'
'No, no,' quod he, and sorwefully he syketh.
'What was the cause? tel me if thou can.'
Aurelius his tale anon bigan,
And tolde him al, as ye han herd bifore;
It nedeth nat to yow reherce it more.
  He seide, 'Arveragus, of gentillesse,
Had lever dye in sorwe and in distresse
Than that his wyf were of hir trouthe fals.'
The sorwe of Dorigen he tolde him als,
How looth hir was to been a wikked wyf,
And that she lever had lost that day hir lyf,
And that hir trouthe she swoor, thurgh innocence:
'She never erst herde speke of apparence;
That made me han of hir so greet pitee.
And right as frely as he sente hir me,
As frely sente I hir to him ageyn.
This al and som, ther is na-more to seyn.'

This philosophre answerde, 'leve brother,
Everich of yow dide gentilly til other.
Thou art a squyer, and he is a knight;
But god forbede, for his blisful might,
But-if a clerk coude doon a gentil dede
As wel as any of yow, it is no drede!
Sire, I relesse thee thy thousand pound,
As thou right now were cropen out of the ground,
Ne never er now ne haddest knowen me.
For sire, I wol nat take a peny of thee
For al my craft, ne noght for my travaille.
Thou hast y-payed wel for my vitaille;
It is y-nogh, and farewel, have good day:'
And took his hors, and forth he gooth his way.
Lordinges, this question wolde I aske now,
Which was the moste free, as thinketh yow?
Now telleth me, er that ye ferther wende.
I can na-more, my tale is at an ende.

Here is ended the Frankeleyns Tale.

THE SECONDE NONNES TALE

The Prologe of the Seconde Nonnes Tale.

THE ministre and the norice un-to vyces,
Which that men clepe in English ydelnesse,
That porter of the gate is of delyces,
T'eschue, and by hir contrarie hir oppresse,
That is to seyn, by leveful bisinesse,
Wel oghten we to doon al our entente,
Lest that the feend thurgh ydelnesse us hente.

For he, that with his thousand cordes slye
Continuelly us waiteth to biclappe,
Whan he may man in ydelnesse espye,
He can so lightly cacche him in his trappe,
Til that a man be hent right by the lappe,
He nis nat war the feend hath him in honde;
Wel oughte us werche, and ydelnes withstonde.

And though men dradden never for to dye,
Yet seen men wel by reson doutelees,
That ydelnesse is roten slogardye,
Of which ther never comth no good encrees;
And seen, that slouthe hir holdeth in a lees
Only to slepe, and for to ete and drinke,
And to devouren al that othere swinke.

And for to putte us fro swich ydelnesse,
That cause is of so greet confusioun,
I have heer doon my feithful bisinesse,
After the legende, in translacioun
Right of thy glorious lyf and passioun,
Thou with thy gerland wroght of rose and lilie;
Thee mene I, mayde and martir, seint Cecilie!

Inuocacio ad Mariam.

AND thou that flour of virgines art alle,
Of whom that Bernard list so wel to wryte,
To thee at my biginning first I calle;
Thou comfort of us wrecches, do me endyte
Thy maydens deeth, that wan thurgh hir meryte
The eternal lyf, and of the feend victorie,
As man may after reden in hir storie.

Thou mayde and mooder, doghter of thy sone,
Thou welle of mercy, sinful soules cure,
In whom that god, for bountee, chees to wone,
Thou humble, and heigh over every creature,
Thou nobledest so ferforth our nature,
That no desdeyn the maker hadde of kinde,
His sone in blode and flesh to clothe and winde.

Withinne the cloistre blisful of thy sydes
Took mannes shap the eternal love and pees,
That of the tryne compas lord and gyde is,
Whom erthe and see and heven, out of relees,
Ay herien; and thou, virgin wemmelees,
Bar of thy body, and dweltest mayden pure,
The creatour of every creature.

Assembled is in thee magnificence
With mercy, goodnesse, and with swich pitee
That thou, that art the sonne of excellence,
Nat only helpest hem that preyen thee,
But ofte tyme, of thy benignitee,
Ful frely, er that men thyn help biseche,
Thou goost biforn, and art hir lyves leche.

Now help, thou meke and blisful fayre mayde,
Me, flemed wrecche, in this desert of galle;
Think on the womman Cananee, that sayde
That whelpes eten somme of the crommes alle
That from hir lordes table been y-falle;
And though that I, unworthy sone of Eve,
Be sinful, yet accepte my bileve.

And, for that feith is deed with-outen werkes,
So for to werken yif me wit and space,
That I be quit fro thennes that most derk is!
O thou, that art so fayr and ful of grace,
Be myn advocat in that heighe place
Ther-as withouten ende is songe 'Osanne,'
Thou Cristes mooder, doghter dere of Anne!

And of thy light my soule in prison lighte,
That troubled is by the contagioun
Of my body, and also by the wighte
Of erthly luste and fals affeccioun;
O haven of refut, o salvacioun
Of hem that been in sorwe and in distresse,
Now help, for to my werk I wol me dresse.

Yet preye I yow that reden that I wryte,
Foryeve me, that I do no diligence
This ilke storie subtilly to endyte;
For both have I the wordes and sentence
Of him that at the seintes reverence
The storie wroot, and folwe hir legende,
And prey yow, that ye wol my werk amende.

Interpretacio nominis Cecilie, quam ponit frater Iacobus Ianuensis in Legenda Aurea.

First wolde I yow the name of seint Cecilie
Expoune, as men may in hir storie see,
It is to seye in English 'hevenes lilie,'
For pure chastnesse of virginitee;
Or, for she whytnesse hadde of honestee,
And grene of conscience, and of good fame
The sote savour, 'lilie' was hir name.

Or Cecile is to seye 'the wey to blinde,'
For she ensample was by good techinge;
Or elles Cecile, as I writen finde,
Is joyned, by a maner conjoininge
Of 'hevene' and 'Lia'; and heer, in figuringe,
The 'heven' is set for thoght of holinesse,
And 'Lia' for hir lasting bisinesse.

Cecile may eek be seyd in this manere,
'Wanting of blindnesse,' for hir grete light
Of sapience, and for hir thewes clere;
Or elles, lo! this maydens name bright
Of 'hevene' and 'leos' comth, for which by right
Men mighte hir wel 'the heven of peple' calle,
Ensample of gode and wyse werkes alle.

For 'leos' 'peple' in English is to seye,
And right as men may in the hevene see
The sonne and mone and sterres every weye,
Right so men gostly, in this mayden free,
Seyen of feith the magnanimitee,
And eek the cleernesse hool of sapience,
And sondry werkes, brighte of excellence.

And right so as thise philosophres wryte
That heven is swift and round and eek brenninge,
Right so was fayre Cecilie the whyte
Ful swift and bisy ever in good werkinge,
And round and hool in good perseveringe,
And brenning ever in charitee ful brighte;
Now have I yow declared what she highte.

Explicit.

Here biginneth the Seconde Nonnes Tale, of the lyf of Seinte Cecile.

THIS mayden bright Cecilie, as hir lyf seith,
Was comen of Romayns, and of noble kinde,
And from hir cradel up fostred in the feith
Of Crist, and bar his gospel in hir minde;
She never cessed, as I writen finde,
Of hir preyere, and god to love and drede,
Biseking him to kepe hir maydenhede.

And when this mayden sholde unto a man
Y-wedded be, that was ful yong of age,
Which that y-cleped was Valerian,
And day was comen of hir mariage,

She, ful devout and humble in hir corage,
Under hir robe of gold, that sat ful fayre,
Had next hir flesh y-clad hir in an heyre.

And whyl the organs maden melodye,
To god alone in herte thus sang she;
'O lord, my soule and eek my body gye
Unwemmed, lest that I confounded be:'
And, for his love that deyde upon a tree,
Every seconde or thridde day she faste,
Ay biddinge in hir orisons ful faste.

The night cam, and to bedde moste she gon
With hir housbonde, as ofte is the manere,
And prively to him she seyde anon,
'O swete and wel biloved spouse dere,
Ther is a conseil, and ye wolde it here,
Which that right fain I wolde unto yow seye,
So that ye swere ye shul me nat biwreye.'

Valerian gan faste unto hir swere,
That for no cas, ne thing that mighte be,
He sholde never-mo biwreyen here;
And thanne at erst to him thus seyde she,
'I have an angel which that loveth me,
That with greet love, wher-so I wake or slepe,
Is redy ay my body for to kepe.

And if that he may felen, out of drede,
That ye me touche or love in vileinye,
He right anon wol slee yow with the dede,
And in your yowthe thus ye shulden dye;
And if that ye in clene love me gye,
He wol yow loven as me, for your clennesse,
And shewen yow his joye and his brightnesse.'

Valerian, corrected as god wolde,
Answerde agayn, 'if I shal trusten thee,
Lat me that angel see, and him biholde;
And if that it a verray angel be,
Than wol I doon as thou hast preyed me;
And if thou love another man, for sothe
Right with this swerd than wol I slee yow bothe.'

Cecile answerde anon right in this wyse,
'If that yow list, the angel shul ye see,
So that ye trowe on Crist and yow baptyse.
Goth forth to Via Apia,' quod she,
'That fro this toun ne stant but myles three,
And, to the povre folkes that ther dwelle,
Sey hem right thus, as that I shal yow telle.

Telle hem that I, Cecile, yow to hem sente,
To shewen yow the gode Urban the olde,
For secree nedes and for good entente.
And whan that ye seint Urban han biholde,
Telle him the wordes whiche I to yow tolde;
And whan that he hath purged yow fro sinne,
Thanne shul ye see that angel, er ye twinne.'

Valerian is to the place y-gon,
And right as him was taught by his lerninge,
He fond this holy olde Urban anon
Among the seintes buriels lotinge.
And he anon, with-outen taryinge,
Dide his message; and whan that he it tolde,
Urban for joye his hondes gan up holde.

The teres from his yën leet he falle—
'Almighty lord, O Jesu Crist,' quod he,
'Sower of chast conseil, herde of us alle,
The fruit of thilke seed of chastitee
That thou hast sowe in Cecile, tak to thee!
Lo, lyk a bisy bee, with-outen gyle,
Thee serveth ay thyn owene thral Cecile!

For thilke spouse, that she took but now
Ful lyk a fiers leoun, she sendeth here,
As meke as ever was any lamb, to yow!'
And with that worde, anon ther gan appere
An old man, clad in whyte clothes clere,
That hadde a book with lettre of golde in honde,
And gan biforn Valerian to stonde.

Valerian as deed fil doun for drede
Whan he him saugh, and he up hente him tho,

And on his book right thus he gan to rede—
'Oo Lord, oo feith, oo god with-outen mo,
Oo Cristendom, and fader of alle also,
Aboven alle and over al everywhere'—
Thise wordes al with gold y-writen were.

Whan this was rad, than seyde this olde man,
'Levestow this thing or no? sey ye or nay.'
'I leve al this thing,' quod Valerian,
'For sother thing than this, I dar wel say,
Under the hevene no wight thinke may.'
Tho vanisshed th'olde man, he niste where,
And pope Urban him cristened right there.

Valerian goth hoom, and fint Cecilie
With-inne his chambre with an angel stonde;
This angel hadde of roses and of lilie
Corones two, the which he bar in honde;
And first to Cecile, as I understonde,
He yaf that oon, and after gan he take
That other to Valerian, hir make.

'With body clene and with unwemmed thoght
Kepeth ay wel thise corones,' quod he;
'Fro Paradys to yow have I hem broght.
Ne never-mo ne shal they roten be,
Ne lese her sote savour, trusteth me;
Ne never wight shal seen hem with his yë,
But he be chaast and hate vileinyë.

And thou, Valerian, for thou so sone
Assentedest to good conseil also,
Sey what thee list, and thou shalt han thy bone.'
'I have a brother,' quod Valerian tho,
'That in this world I love no man so.
I pray yow that my brother may han grace
To knowe the trouthe, as I do in this place.'

The angel seyde, 'god lyketh thy requeste,
And bothe, with the palm of martirdom,
Ye shullen come unto his blisful feste.'
And with that word Tiburce his brother com.

And whan that he the savour undernom
Which that the roses and the lilies caste,
With-inne his herte he gan to wondre faste,

And seyde, 'I wondre, this tyme of the yeer,
Whennes that sote savour cometh so
Of rose and lilies that I smelle heer.
For though I hadde hem in myn hondes two,
The savour mighte in me no depper go.
The sote smel that in myn herte I finde
Hath chaunged me al in another kinde.'

Valerian seyde, 'two corones han we,
Snow-whyte and rose-reed, that shynen clere,
Whiche that thyn yën han no might to see;
And as thou smellest hem thurgh my preyere,
So shaltow seen hem, leve brother dere,
If it so be thou wolt, withouten slouthe,
Bileve aright and knowen verray trouthe.'

Tiburce answerde, 'seistow this to me
In soothnesse, or in dreem I herkne this?'
'In dremes,' quod Valerian, 'han we be
Unto this tyme, brother myn, y-wis.
But now at erst in trouthe our dwelling is.'
'How woostow this,' quod Tiburce, 'in what wyse?'
Quod Valerian, 'that shal I thee devyse.

The angel of god hath me the trouthe y-taught
Which thou shalt seen, if that thou wolt reneye
The ydoles and be clene, and elles naught.'—
And of the miracle of thise corones tweye
Seint Ambrose in his preface list to seye;
Solempnely this noble doctour dere
Commendeth it, and seith in this manere:

The palm of martirdom for to receyve,
Seinte Cecile, fulfild of goddes yifte,
The world and eek hir chambre gan she weyve;
Witnes Tyburces and Valerians shrifte,

To whiche god of his bountee wolde shifte
Corones two of floures wel smellinge,
And made his angel hem the corones bringe :

The mayde hath broght thise men to blisse above ;
The world hath wist what it is worth, certeyn,
Devocioun of chastitee to love.—
Tho shewede him Cecile al open and pleyn
That alle ydoles nis but a thing in veyn ;
For they been dombe, and therto they been deve,
And charged him his ydoles for to leve.

'Who so that troweth nat this, a beste he is,'
Quod tho Tiburce, 'if that I shal nat lye.'
And she gan kisse his brest, that herde this,
And was ful glad he coude trouthe espye.
'This day I take thee for myn allye,'
Seyde this blisful fayre mayde dere ;
And after that she seyde as ye may here :

'Lo, right so as the love of Crist,' quod she,
'Made me thy brotheres wyf, right in that wyse
Anon for myn allye heer take I thee,
Sin that thou wolt thyn ydoles despyse.
Go with thy brother now, and thee baptyse,
And make thee clene ; so that thou mowe biholde
The angels face of which thy brother tolde.'

Tiburce answerde and seyde, 'brother dere,
First tel me whider I shal, and to what man ?'
'To whom ?' quod he, 'com forth with right good
chere,
I wol thee lede unto the pope Urban.'
'Til Urban ? brother myn Valerian,'
Quod tho Tiburce, 'woltow me thider lede ?
Me thinketh that it were a wonder dede.

Ne menestow nat Urban,' quod he tho,
'That is so ofte dampned to be deed,
And woneth in halkes alwey to and fro,
And dar nat ones putte forth his heed ?
Men sholde him brennen in a fyr so reed

If he were founde, or that men mighte him spye;
And we also, to bere him companye—

And whyl we seken thilke divinitee
That is y-hid in hevene prively,
Algate y-brend in this world shul we be!'
To whom Cecile answerde boldely,
'Men mighten dreden wel and skilfully
This lyf to lese, myn owene dere brother,
If this were livinge only and non other.

But ther is better lyf in other place,
That never shal be lost, ne drede thee noght,
Which goddes sone us tolde thurgh his grace;
That fadres sone hath alle thinges wroght;
And al that wroght is with a skilful thoght,
The goost, that fro the fader gan procede,
Hath sowled hem, withouten any drede.

By word and by miracle goddes sone,
Whan he was in this world, declared here
That ther was other lyf ther men may wone.'
To whom answerde Tiburce, 'O suster dere,
Ne seydestow right now in this manere,
Ther nis but o god, lord in soothfastnesse;
And now of three how maystow bere witnesse?'

'That shal I telle,' quod she, 'er I go.
Right as a man hath sapiences three,
Memorie, engyn, and intellect also,
So, in o being of divinitee,
Three persones may ther right wel be.'
Tho gan she him ful bisily to preche
Of Cristes come and of his peynes teche,

And many pointes of his passioun;
How goddes sone in this world was withholde,
To doon mankinde pleyn remissioun,
That was y-bounde in sinne and cares colde:
Al this thing she unto Tiburce tolde.
And after this Tiburce, in good entente,
With Valerian to pope Urban he wente,

That thanked god; and with glad herte and light
He cristned him, and made him in that place
Parfit in his lerninge, goddes knight.
And after this Tiburce gat swich grace,
That every day he saugh, in tyme and space,
The angel of god; and every maner bone
That he god axed, it was sped ful sone.

It were ful hard by ordre for to seyn
How many wondres Jesus for hem wroghte;
But atte laste, to tellen short and pleyn,
The sergeants of the toun of Rome hem soghte,
And hem biforn Almache the prefect broghte,
Which hem apposed, and knew al hir entente,
And to the image of Jupiter hem sente,

And seyde, 'who so wol nat sacrifyse,
Swap of his heed, this is my sentence here.'
Anon thise martirs that I yow devyse,
Oon Maximus, that was an officere
Of the prefectes and his corniculere,
Hem hente; and whan he forth the seintes ladde,
Him-self he weep, for pitee that he hadde.

Whan Maximus had herd the seintes lore,
He gat him of the tormentoures leve,
And ladde hem to his hous withoute more;
And with hir preching, er that it were eve,
They gonnen fro the tormentours to reve,
And fro Maxime, and fro his folk echone
The false feith, to trowe in god allone.

Cecilie cam, whan it was woxen night,
With preestes that hem cristned alle y-fere;
And afterward, whan day was woxen light,
Cecile hem seyde with a ful sobre chere,
'Now, Cristes owene knightes leve and dere,
Caste alle awey the werkes of derknesse,
And armeth yow in armure of brightnesse.

Ye han for sothe y-doon a greet bataille,
Your cours is doon, your feith han ye conserved,

Goth to the corone of lyf that may nat faille;
The rightful juge, which that ye han served,
Shall yeve it yow, as ye han it deserved.'
And whan this thing was seyd as I devyse,
Men ladde hem forth to doon the sacrifyse.

But whan they weren to the place broght,
To tellen shortly the conclusioun,
They nolde encense ne sacrifice right noght,
But on hir knees they setten hem adoun
With humble herte and sad devocioun,
And losten bothe hir hedes in the place.
Hir soules wenten to the king of grace.

This Maximus, that saugh this thing bityde,
With pitous teres tolde it anon-right,
That he hir soules saugh to heven glyde
With angels ful of cleernesse and of light,
And with his word converted many a wight;
For which Almachius dide him so to-bete
With whippe of leed, til he his lyf gan lete.

Cecile him took and buried him anoon
By Tiburce and Valerian softely,
Withinne hir burying-place, under the stoon.
And after this Almachius hastily
Bad his ministres fecchen openly
Cecile, so that she mighte in his presence
Doon sacrifyce, and Jupiter encense.

But they, converted at hir wyse lore,
Wepten ful sore, and yaven ful credence
Unto hir word, and cryden more and more,
'Crist, goddes sone withouten difference,
Is verray god, this is al our sentence,
That hath so good a servant him to serve;
This with o voys we trowen, thogh we sterve!'

Almachius, that herde of this doinge,
Bad fecchen Cecile, that he might hir see,
And alderfirst, lo! this was his axinge,
'What maner womman artow?' tho quod he.
'I am a gentil womman born,' quod she.

'I axe thee,' quod he, 'thogh it thee greve,
Of thy religioun and of thy bileve.'

'Ye han bigonne your question folily,'
Quod she, 'that wolden two answeres conclude
In oo demande ; ye axed lewedly.'
Almache answerde unto that similitude,
'Of whennes comth thyn answering so rude ?'
'Of whennes ?' quod she, whan that she was
freyned,
'Of conscience and of good feith unfeyned.'

Almachius seyde, 'ne takestow non hede
Of my power ?' and she answerde him this—
'Your might,' quod she, 'ful litel is to drede ;
For every mortal mannes power nis
But lyk a bladdre, ful of wind, y-wis.
For with a nedles poynt, whan it is blowe,
May al the boost of it be leyd ful lowe.'

'Ful wrongfully bigonne thou,' quod he,
'And yet in wrong is thy perseveraunce ;
Wostow nat how our mighty princes free
Han thus comanded and maad ordinaunce,
That every Cristen wight shal han penaunce
But-if that he his Cristendom withseye,
And goon al quit, if he wol it reneye ?'

'Your princes erren, as your nobley dooth,'
Quod tho Cecile, 'and with a wood sentence
Ye make us gilty, and it is nat sooth ;
For ye, that knowen wel our innocence,
For as muche as we doon a reverence
To Crist, and for we bere a Cristen name,
Ye putte on us a cryme, and eek a blame.

But we that knowen thilke name so
For vertuous, we may it nat withseye.'
Almache answerde, 'chees oon of thise two,
Do sacrifyce, or Cristendom reneye,
That thou mowe now escapen by that weye.'
At which the holy blisful fayre mayde
Gan for to laughe, and to the juge seyde,

'O juge, confus in thy nycetee,
Woltow that I reneye innocence,
To make me a wikked wight?' quod she;
'Lo! he dissimuleth here in audience,
He stareth and woodeth in his advertence!'
To whom Almachius, 'unsely wrecche,
Ne woostow nat how far my might may strecche?

Han noght our mighty princes to me yeven,
Ye, bothe power and auctoritee
To maken folk to dyen or to liven?
Why spekestow so proudly than to me?'
'I speke noght but stedfastly,' quod she,
'Nat proudly, for I seye, as for my syde,
We haten deedly thilke vyce of pryde.

And if thou drede nat a sooth to here,
Than wol I shewe al openly, by right,
That thou hast maad a ful gret lesing here.
Thou seyst, thy princes han thee yeven might
Bothe for to sleen and for to quiken a wight;
Thou, that ne mayst but only lyf bireve,
Thou hast non other power ne no leve!

But thou mayst seyn, thy princes han thee maked
Ministre of deeth; for if thou speke of mo,
Thou lyest, for thy power is ful naked.'
'Do wey thy boldnes,' seyde Almachius tho,
'And sacrifyce to our goddes, er thou go;
I recche nat what wrong that thou me profre,
For I can suffre it as a philosophre;

But thilke wronges may I nat endure
That thou spekest of our goddes here,' quod he.
Cecile answerede, 'O nyce creature,
Thou seydest no word sin thou spak to me
That I ne knew therwith thy nycetee;
And that thou were, in every maner wyse,
A lewed officer and a veyn justyse.

Ther lakketh no-thing to thyn utter yën
That thou nart blind, for thing that we seen alle

That it is stoon, that men may wel espyen,
That ilke stoon a god thou wolt it calle.
I rede thee, lat thyn hand upon it falle,
And taste it wel, and stoon thou shalt it finde,
Sin that thou seest nat with thyn yën blinde.

It is a shame that the peple shal
So scorne thee, and laughe at thy folye;
For comunly men woot it wel overal,
That mighty god is in his hevenes hye,
And thise images, wel thou mayst espye,
To thee ne to hem-self mowe nought profyte,
For in effect they been nat worth a myte.'

Thise wordes and swiche othere seyde she,
And he weex wroth, and bad men sholde hir lede
Hom til hir hous, 'and in hir hous,' quod he,
'Brenne hir right in a bath of flambes rede.'
And as he bad, right so was doon in dede;
For in a bath they gonne hir faste shetten,
And night and day greet fyr they under betten.

The longe night and eek a day also,
For al the fyr and eek the bathes hete,
She sat al cold, and felede no wo,
It made hir nat a drope for to swete.
But in that bath hir lyf she moste lete;
For he, Almachius, with ful wikke entente
To sleen hir in the bath his sonde sente.

Three strokes in the nekke he smoot hir tho,
The tormentour, but for no maner chaunce
He mighte noght smyte al hir nekke a-two;
And for ther was that tyme an ordinaunce,
That no man sholde doon man swich penaunce
The ferthe strook to smyten, softe or sore,
This tormentour ne dorste do na-more.

But half-deed, with hir nekke y-corven there,
He lefte hir lye, and on his wey is went.
The Cristen folk, which that aboute hir were,
With shetes han the blood ful faire y-hent.

Three dayes lived she in this torment,
And never cessed hem the feith to teche;
That she hadde fostred, hem she gan to preche;

And hem she yaf hir moebles and hir thing,
And to the pope Urban bitook hem tho,
And seyde, 'I axed this at hevene king,
To han respyt three dayes and na-mo,
To recomende to yow, er that I go,
Thise soules, lo! and that I mighte do werche
Here of myn hous perpetuelly a cherche.'

Seint Urban, with his deknes, prively
The body fette, and buried it by nighte
Among his othere seintes honestly.
Hir hous the chirche of seint Cecilie highte;
Seint Urban halwed it, as he wel mighte;
In which, into this day, in noble wyse,
Men doon to Crist and to his seint servyse.

Here is ended the Seconde Nonnes Tale.

THE CHANOUNS YEMANNES TALE

The prologe of the Chanons Yemannes Tale.

WHAN ended was the lyf of seint Cecyle,
Er we had riden fully fyve myle,
At Boghton under Blee us gan atake
A man, that clothed was in clothes blake,
And undernethe he hadde a whyt surplys.
His hakeney, that was al pomely grys,
So swatte, that it wonder was to see;
It semed he had priked myles three.
The hors eek that his yeman rood upon
So swatte, that unnethe mighte it gon.
Aboute the peytrel stood the foom ful hye,
He was of fome al flekked as a pye.
A male tweyfold on his croper lay,
It semed that he caried lyte array.
Al light for somer rood this worthy man,
And in myn herte wondren I bigan
What that he was, til that I understood
How that his cloke was sowed to his hood;
For which, when I had longe avysed me,
I demed him som chanon for to be.
His hat heng at his bak doun by a laas,
For he had riden more than trot or paas;
He had ay priked lyk as he were wood.
A clote-leef he hadde under his hood
For swoot, and for to kepe his heed from hete.
But it was joye for to seen him swete!
His forheed dropped as a stillatorie,
Were ful of plantain and of paritorie.

And whan that he was come, he gan to crye,
'God save,' quod he, 'this joly companye!
Faste have I priked,' quod he, 'for your sake,
By-cause that I wolde yow atake,
To ryden in this mery companye.'
His yeman eek was ful of curteisye,
And seyde, 'sires, now in the morwe-tyde
Out of your hostelrye I saugh you ryde,
And warned heer my lord and my soverayn,
Which that to ryden with yow is ful fayn,
For his desport; he loveth daliaunce.'
'Freend, for thy warning god yeve thee good chaunce,'
Than seyde our host, 'for certes, it wolde seme
Thy lord were wys, and so I may wel deme;
He is ful jocund also, dar I leye.
Can he oght telle a mery tale or tweye,
With which he glade may this companye?'
'Who, sire? my lord? ye, ye, withouten lye,
He can of murthe, and eek of jolitee
Nat but ynough; also sir, trusteth me,
And ye him knewe as wel as do I,
Ye wolde wondre how wel and craftily
He coude werke, and that in sondry wyse.
He hath take on him many a greet empryse,
Which were ful hard for any that is here
To bringe aboute, but they of him it lere.
As homely as he rit amonges yow,
If ye him knewe, it wolde be for your prow;
Ye wolde nat forgoon his aqueyntaunce
For mochel good, I dar leye in balaunce
Al that I have in my possessioun.
He is a man of heigh discrecioun,
I warne you wel, he is a passing man.'
'Wel,' quod our host, 'I pray thee, tel me than,
Is he a clerk, or noon? tel what he is.'
'Nay, he is gretter than a clerk, y-wis,'
Seyde this yeman, 'and in wordes fewe,
Host, of his craft som-what I wol yow shewe.

I seye, my lord can swich subtilitee—
(But al his craft ye may nat wite at me ;
And som-what helpe I yet to his werking)—
That al this ground on which we been ryding,
Til that we come to Caunterbury toun,
He coude al clene turne it up-so-doun,
And pave it al of silver and of gold.'
And whan this yeman hadde thus y-told
Unto our host, he seyde, '*ben'cite !*
This thing is wonder merveillous to me,
Sin that thy lord is of so heigh prudence,
By-cause of which men sholde him reverence,
That of his worship rekketh he so lyte ;
His oversloppe nis nat worth a myte,
As in effect, to him, so mote I go !
It is al baudy and to-tore also.
Why is thy lord so sluttish, I thee preye,
And is of power better cloth to beye,
If that his dede accorde with thy speche ?
Telle me that, and that I thee biseche.'
'Why ?' quod this yeman, 'wherto axe ye me ?
God help me so, for he shal never thee !
(But I wol nat avowe that I seye,
And therfor kepe it secree, I yow preye).
He is to wys, in feith, as I bileve ;
That that is overdoon, it wol nat preve
Aright, as clerkes seyn, it is a vyce.
Wherfor in that I holde him lewed and nyce.
For whan a man hath over-greet a wit,
Ful oft him happeth to misusen it ;
So dooth my lord, and that me greveth sore.
God it amende, I can sey yow na-more.'
'Ther-of no fors, good yeman,' quod our host ;
'Sin of the conning of thy lord thou wost,
Tel how he dooth, I pray thee hertely,
Sin that he is so crafty and so sly.
Wher dwellen ye, if it to telle be ?'
'In the suburbes of a toun,' quod he,
'Lurkinge in hernes and in lanes blinde,
Wher-as thise robbours and thise theves by kinde

Holden hir privee fereful residence,
As they that dar nat shewen hir presence;
So faren we, if I shal seye the sothe.'
 'Now,' quod our host, 'yit lat me talke to the;
Why artow so discoloured of thy face?'
 'Peter!' quod he, 'god yeve it harde grace,
I am so used in the fyr to blowe,
That it hath chaunged my colour, I trowe.
I am nat wont in no mirour to prye,
But swinke sore and lerne multiplye.
We blondren ever and pouren in the fyr,
And for al that we fayle of our desyr,
For ever we lakken our conclusioun.
To mochel folk we doon illusioun,
And borwe gold, be it a pound or two,
Or ten, or twelve, or many sommes mo,
And make hem wenen, at the leeste weye,
That of a pound we coude make tweye!
Yet is it fals, but ay we han good hope
It for to doon, and after it we grope.
But that science is so fer us biforn,
We mowen nat, al-though we hadde it sworn,
It overtake, it slit awey so faste;
It wol us maken beggers atte laste.'
 Whyl this yeman was thus in his talking,
This chanoun drough him neer, and herde al thing
Which this yeman spak, for suspecioun
Of mennes speche ever hadde this chanoun.
For Catoun seith, that he that gilty is
Demeth al thing be spoke of him, y-wis.
That was the cause he gan so ny him drawe
To his yeman, to herknen al his sawe.
And thus he seyde un-to his yeman tho,
'Hold thou thy pees, and spek no wordes mo,
For if thou do, thou shalt it dere abye;
Thou sclaundrest me heer in this companye,
And eek discoverest that thou sholdest hyde.'
 'Ye,' quod our host, 'telle on, what so bityde;
Of al his threting rekke nat a myte!'
'In feith,' quod he, 'namore I do but lyte.'

And whan this chanon saugh it wolde nat be,
But his yeman wolde telle his privetee,
He fledde awey for verray sorwe and shame.
'A!' quod the yeman, 'heer shal aryse game,
Al that I can anon now wol I telle.
Sin he is goon, the foule feend him quelle!
For never her-after wol I with him mete
For peny ne for pound, I yow bihete!
He that me broghte first unto that game,
Er that he dye, sorwe have he and shame!
For it is ernest to me, by my feith;
That fele I wel, what so any man seith.
And yet, for al my smerte and al my grief,
For al my sorwe, labour, and meschief,
I coude never leve it in no wyse.
Now wolde god my wit mighte suffyse
To tellen al that longeth to that art!
But natheles yow wol I tellen part;
Sin that my lord is gon, I wol nat spare;
Swich thing as that I knowe, I wol declare.'—

Here endeth the Prologe of the Chanouns Yemannes Tale.

Here biginneth the Chanouns Yeman his Tale.

[*Prima Pars.*]

WITH this chanoun I dwelt have seven yeer,
And of his science am I never the neer.
Al that I hadde, I have y-lost ther-by:
And god wot, so hath many mo than I.
Ther I was wont to be right fresh and gay
Of clothing and of other good array,
Now may I were an hose upon myn heed;
And wher my colour was bothe fresh and reed,
Now is it wan and of a leden hewe;
Who-so it useth, sore shal he rewe.
And of my swink yet blered is myn yë,
Lo! which avantage is to multiplye!

That slyding science hath me maad so bare,
That I have no good, wher that ever I fare;
And yet I am endetted so ther-by
Of gold that I have borwed, trewely,
That whyl I live, I shal it quyte never.
Lat every man be war by me for ever!
What maner man that casteth him ther-to,
If he continue, I holde his thrift y-do.
So helpe me god, ther-by shal he nat winne,
But empte his purs, and make his wittes thinne.
And whan he, thurgh his madnes and folye,
Hath lost his owene good thurgh jupartye,
Thanne he excyteth other folk ther-to,
To lese hir good as he him-self hath do.
For unto shrewes joye it is and ese
To have hir felawes in peyne and disese;
Thus was I ones lerned of a clerk.
Of that no charge, I wol speke of our werk.
  Whan we been ther as we shul exercyse
Our elvish craft, we semen wonder wyse,
Our termes been so clergial and so queynte.
I blowe the fyr til that myn herte feynte.

  What sholde I tellen ech proporcioun
Of thinges whiche that we werche upon,
As on fyve or sixe ounces, may wel be,
Of silver or som other quantitee,
And bisie me to telle yow the names
Of orpiment, brent bones, yren squames,
That into poudre grounden been ful smal?
And in an erthen potte how put is al,
And salt y-put in, and also papeer,
Biforn thise poudres that I speke of heer,
And wel y-covered with a lampe of glas,
And mochel other thing which that ther was?
And of the pot and glasses enluting,
That of the eyre mighte passe out no-thing?
And of the esy fyr and smart also,
Which that was maad, and of the care and wo

That we hadde in our matires sublyming,
And in amalgaming and calcening
Of quik-silver, y-clept Mercurie crude ?
For alle our sleightes we can nat conclude.
Our orpiment and sublymed Mercurie,
Our grounden litarge eek on the porphurie,
Of ech of thise of ounces a certeyn
Nought helpeth us, our labour is in veyn.
Ne eek our spirites ascencioun,
Ne our materes that lyen al fixe adoun,
Mowe in our werking no-thing us avayle.
For lost is al our labour and travayle,
And al the cost, a twenty devel weye,
Is lost also, which we upon it leye.
Ther is also ful many another thing
That is unto our craft apertening ;
Though I by ordre hem nat reherce can,
By-cause that I am a lewed man,
Yet wol I telle hem as they come to minde,
Though I ne can nat sette hem in hir kinde ;
As bole armoniak, verdegrees, boras,
And sondry vessels maad of erthe and glas,
Our urinales and our descensories,
Violes, croslets, and sublymatories,
Cucurbites, and alembykes eek,
And othere swiche, dere y-nough a leek.
Nat nedeth it for to reherce hem alle,
Watres rubifying and boles galle,
Arsenik, sal armoniak, and brimstoon ;
And herbes coude I telle eek many oon,
As egremoine, valerian, and lunarie,
And othere swiche, if that me liste tarie.
Our lampes brenning bothe night and day,
To bringe aboute our craft, if that we may.
Our fourneys eek of calcinacioun,
And of watres albificacioun,
Unslekked lym, chalk, and gleyre of an ey,
Poudres diverse, asshes, dong, pisse, and cley,
Cered pokets, sal peter, vitriole ;
And divers fyres maad of wode and cole ;

Sal tartre, alkaly, and sal preparat,
And combust materes and coagulat,
Cley maad with hors or mannes heer, and oile
Of tartre, alum, glas, berm, wort, and argoile,
Resalgar, and our materes enbibing;
And eek of our materes encorporing,
And of our silver citrinacioun,
Our cementing and fermentacioun,
Our ingottes, testes, and many mo.
I wol yow telle, as was me taught also,
The foure spirites and the bodies sevene,
By ordre, as ofte I herde my lord hem nevene.
The firste spirit quik-silver called is,
The second orpiment, the thridde, y-wis,
Sal armoniak, and the ferthe brimstoon.
The bodies sevene eek, lo! hem heer anoon:
Sol gold is, and Luna silver we threpe,
Mars yren, Mercurie quik-silver we clepe,
Saturnus leed, and Jupiter is tin,
And Venus coper, by my fader kin!
This cursed craft who-so wol exercyse,
He shal no good han that him may suffyse;
For al the good he spendeth ther-aboute,
He lese shal, ther-of have I no doute.
Who-so that listeth outen his folye,
Lat him come forth, and lerne multiplye;
And every man that oght hath in his cofre
Lat him appere, and wexe a philosofre.
Ascaunce that craft is so light to lere?
Nay, nay, god woot, al be he monk or frere,
Preest or chanoun, or any other wight,
Though he sitte at his book bothe day and night,
In lernyng of this elvish nyce lore,
Al is in veyn, and parde, mochel more!
To lerne a lewed man this subtiltee,
Fy! spek nat ther-of, for it wol nat be;
Al conne he letterure, or conne he noon,
As in effect, he shal finde it al oon.
For bothe two, by my savacioun,
Concluden, in multiplicacioun,

Y-lyke wel, whan they han al y-do;
This is to seyn, they faylen bothe two.
Yet forgat I to maken rehersaille
Of watres corosif and of limaille,
And of bodyes mollificacioun,
And also of hir induracioun,
Oiles, ablucions, and metal fusible,
To tellen al wolde passen any bible
That o-wher is; wherfor, as for the beste,
Of alle thise names now wol I me reste.
For, as I trowe, I have yow told y-nowe
To reyse a feend, al loke he never so rowe.
A! nay! lat be; the philosophres stoon,
Elixir clept, we sechen faste echoon;
For hadde we him, than were we siker y-now.
But, unto god of heven I make avow,
For al our craft, whan we han al y-do,
And al our sleighte, he wol nat come us to.
He hath y-maad us spenden mochel good,
For sorwe of which almost we wexen wood,
But that good hope crepeth in our herte,
Supposinge ever, though we sore smerte,
To be releved by him afterward;
Swich supposing and hope is sharp and hard;
I warne yow wel, it is to seken ever;
That futur temps hath maad men to dissever,
In trust ther-of, from al that ever they hadde.
Yet of that art they can nat wexen sadde,
For unto hem it is a bitter swete;
So semeth it; for nadde they but a shete
Which that they mighte wrappe hem inne a-night,
And a bak to walken inne by day-light,
They wolde hem selle and spenden on this craft;
They can nat stinte til no-thing be laft.
And evermore, wher that ever they goon,
Men may hem knowe by smel of brimstoon;
For al the world, they stinken as a goot;
Her savour is so rammish and so hoot,
That, though a man from hem a myle be,
The savour wol infecte him, trusteth me;

Lo, thus by smelling and threedbare array,
If that men liste, this folk they knowe may.
And if a man wol aske hem prively,
Why they been clothed so unthriftily,
They right anon wol rownen in his ere,
And seyn, that if that they espyed were,
Men wolde hem slee, by-cause of hir science;
Lo, thus this folk bitrayen innocence!
  Passe over this; I go my tale un-to.
Er than the pot be on the fyr y-do,
Of metals with a certein quantitee,
My lord hem tempreth, and no man but he—
Now he is goon, I dar seyn boldely—
For, as men seyn, he can don craftily;
Algate I woot wel he hath swich a name,
And yet ful ofte he renneth in a blame;
And wite ye how? ful ofte it happeth so,
The pot to-breketh, and farewel! al is go!
Thise metals been of so greet violence,
Our walles mowe nat make hem resistence,
But if they weren wroght of lym and stoon;
They percen so, and thurgh the wal they goon,
And somme of hem sinken in-to the ground—
Thus han we lost by tymes many a pound—
And somme are scatered al the floor aboute,
Somme lepe in-to the roof; with-outen doute,
Though that the feend noght in our sighte him shewe,
I trowe he with us be, that ilke shrewe!
In helle wher that he is lord and sire,
Nis ther more wo, ne more rancour ne ire.
Whan that our pot is broke, as I have sayd,
Every man chit, and halt him yvel apayd.
  Som seyde, it was long on the fyr-making,
Som seyde, nay! it was on the blowing;
(Than was I fered, for that was myn office);
'Straw!' quod the thridde, 'ye been lewed and nyce,
It was nat tempred as it oghte be.'
'Nay!' quod the ferthe, 'stint, and herkne me;

By-cause our fyr ne was nat maad of beech,
That is the cause, and other noon, so theech !'
I can nat telle wher-on it was long,
But wel I wot greet stryf is us among.
'What !' quod my lord, 'ther is na-more to done,
Of thise perils I wol be war eft-sone ;
I am right siker that the pot was crased.
Be as be may, be ye no-thing amased ;
As usage is, lat swepe the floor as swythe,
Plukke up your hertes, and beth gladde and blythe.'
The mullok on an hepe y-sweped was,
And on the floor y-cast a canevas,
And al this mullok in a sive y-throwe,
And sifted, and y-piked many a throwe.
'Pardee,' quod oon, 'somwhat of our metal
Yet is ther heer, though that we han nat al.
Al-though this thing mishapped have as now,
Another tyme it may be wel y-now,
Us moste putte our good in aventure ;
A marchant, parde ! may nat ay endure
Trusteth me wel, in his prosperitee ;
Somtyme his good is drenched in the see,
And somtym comth it sauf un-to the londe.'
'Pees !' quod my lord, 'the next tyme I wol fonde
To bringe our craft al in another plyte ;
And but I do, sirs, lat me han the wyte ;
Ther was defaute in som-what, wel I woot.'
Another seyde, the fyr was over hoot :—
But, be it hoot or cold, I dar seye this,
That we concluden evermore amis.
We fayle of that which that we wolden have,
And in our madnesse evermore we rave.
And whan we been togidres everichoon,
Every man semeth a Salomon.
But al thing which that shyneth as the gold
Nis nat gold, as that I have herd it told ;
Ne every appel that is fair at yë
Ne is nat good, what-so men clappe or crye.

Right so, lo ! fareth it amonges us ;
He that semeth the wysest, by Jesus !
Is most fool, whan it cometh to the preef ;
And he that semeth trewest is a theef ;
That shul ye knowe, er that I fro yow wende,
By that I of my tale have maad an ende.

Explicit prima pars.

Et sequitur pars secunda.

Ther is a chanoun of religioun
Amonges us, wolde infecte al a toun,
Though it as greet were as was Ninivee,
Rome, Alisaundre, Troye, and othere three.
His sleightes and his infinit falsnesse
Ther coude no man wryten, as I gesse,
Thogh that he mighte liven a thousand yeer.
In al this world of falshede nis his peer ;
For in his termes so he wolde him winde,
And speke his wordes in so sly a kinde,
Whan he commune shal with any wight,
That he wol make him doten anon right,
But it a feend be, as him-selven is.
Ful many a man hath he bigyled er this,
And wol, if that he live may a whyle ;
And yet men ryde and goon ful many a myle
Him for to seke and have his aqueyntaunce,
Noght knowinge of his false governaunce.
And if yow list to yeve me audience,
I wol it tellen heer in your presence.
But worshipful chanouns religious,
Ne demeth nat that I sclaundre your hous,
Al-though my tale of a chanoun be.
Of every ordre som shrewe is, parde,
And god forbede that al a companye
Sholde rewe a singuler mannes folye.
To sclaundre yow is no-thing myn entente,
But to correcten that is mis I mente.
This tale was nat only told for yow,
But eek for othere mo ; ye woot wel how

That, among Cristes apostelles twelve,
Ther nas no traytour but Judas him-selve.
Than why sholde al the remenant have blame
That giltlees were? by yow I seye the same.
Save only this, if ye wol herkne me,
If any Judas in your covent be,
Remeveth him bitymes, I yow rede,
If shame or los may causen any drede.
And beth no-thing displesed, I yow preye,
But in this cas herkneth what I shal seye.

In London was a preest, an annueleer,
That therin dwelled hadde many a yeer,
Which was so plesaunt and so servisable
Unto the wyf, wher-as he was at table,
That she wolde suffre him no-thing for to paye
For bord ne clothing, wente he never so gaye;
And spending-silver hadde he right y-now.
Therof no fors; I wol procede as now,
And telle forth my tale of the chanoun,
That broghte this preest to confusioun.
This false chanoun cam up-on a day
Unto this preestes chambre, wher he lay,
Biseching him to lene him a certeyn
Of gold, and he wolde quyte it him ageyn.
'Lene me a mark,' quod he, 'but dayes three,
And at my day I wol it quyten thee.
And if so be that thou me finde fals,
Another day do hange me by the hals!'
This preest him took a mark, and that as swythe,
And this chanoun him thanked ofte sythe,
And took his leve, and wente forth his weye,
And at the thridde day broghte his moneye,
And to the preest he took his gold agayn,
Wherof this preest was wonder glad and fayn.
'Certes,' quod he, 'no-thing anoyeth me
To lene a man a noble, or two or three,
Or what thing were in my possessioun,
Whan he so trewe is of condicioun,

That in no wyse he breke wol his day;
To swich a man I can never seye nay.'
'What!' quod this chanoun, 'sholde I be untrewe?
Nay, that were thing y-fallen al of-newe.
Trouthe is a thing that I wol ever kepe
Un-to that day in which that I shal crepe
In-to my grave, and elles god forbede;
Bileveth this as siker as is your crede.
God thanke I, and in good tyme be it sayd,
That ther was never man yet yvel apayd
For gold ne silver that he to me lente,
Ne never falshede in myn herte I mente.
And sir,' quod he, 'now of my privetee,
Sin ye so goodlich han been un-to me,
And kythed to me so greet gentillesse,
Somwhat to quyte with your kindenesse,
I wol yow shewe, and, if yow list to lere,
I wol yow teche pleynly the manere,
How I can werken in philosophye.
Taketh good heed, ye shul wel seen at yë,
That I wol doon a maistrie er I go.'
'Ye,' quod the preest, 'ye, sir, and wol ye so?
Marie! ther-of I pray yow hertely!'
'At your comandement, sir, trewely,'
Quod the chanoun, 'and elles god forbede!'
Lo, how this theef coude his servyse bede!
Ful sooth it is, that swich profred servyse
Stinketh, as witnessen thise olde wyse;
And that ful sone I wol it verifye
In this chanoun, rote of al trecherye,
That ever-more delyt hath and gladnesse—
Swich feendly thoughtes in his herte impresse—
How Cristes peple he may to meschief bringe;
God kepe us from his fals dissimulinge!
Noght wiste this preest with whom that he delte,
Ne of his harm cominge he no-thing felte.
O sely preest! O sely innocent!
With coveityse anon thou shalt be blent!

O gracelees, ful blind is thy conceit,
No-thing ne artow war of the deceit
Which that this fox y-shapen hath to thee!
His wyly wrenches thou ne mayst nat flee.
Wherfor, to go to the conclusioun
That refereth to thy confusioun,
Unhappy man! anon I wol me hye
To tellen thyn unwit and thy folye,
And eek the falsnesse of that other wrecche,
As ferforth as that my conning may strecche.
  This chanoun was my lord, ye wolden wene?
Sir host, in feith, and by the hevenes quene,
It was another chanoun, and nat he,
That can an hundred fold more subtiltee!
He hath bitrayed folkes many tyme;
Of his falshede it dulleth me to ryme.
Ever whan that I speke of his falshede,
For shame of him my chekes wexen rede;
Algates, they biginnen for to glowe,
For reednesse have I noon, right wel I knowe,
In my visage; for fumes dyverse
Of metals, which ye han herd me reherce,
Consumed and wasted han my reednesse.
Now tak heed of this chanouns cursednesse!
  'Sir,' quod he to the preest, 'lat your man gon
For quik-silver, that we it hadde anon;
And lat him bringen ounces two or three;
And whan he comth, as faste shul ye see
A wonder thing, which ye saugh never er this.'
  'Sir,' quod the preest, 'it shal be doon, y-wis.'
He bad his servant fecchen him this thing,
And he al redy was at his bidding,
And wente him forth, and cam anon agayn
With this quik-silver, soothly for to sayn,
And took thise ounces three to the chanoun;
And he hem leyde fayre and wel adoun,
And bad the servant coles for to bringe,
That he anon mighte go to his werkinge.
  The coles right anon weren y-fet,
And this chanoun took out a crosselet

Of his bosom, and shewed it the preest.
'This instrument,' quod he, 'which that thou seest,
Tak in thyn hand, and put thy-self ther-inne
Of this quik-silver an ounce, and heer biginne,
In the name of Crist, to wexe a philosofre.
Ther been ful fewe, whiche that I wolde profre
To shewen hem thus muche of my science.
For ye shul seen heer, by experience,
That this quik-silver wol I mortifye
Right in your sighte anon, withouten lye,
And make it as good silver and as fyn
As ther is any in your purs or myn,
Or elleswher, and make it malliable;
And elles, holdeth me fals and unable
Amonges folk for ever to appere!
I have a poudre heer, that coste me dere,
Shal make al good, for it is cause of al
My conning, which that I yow shewen shal.
Voydeth your man, and lat him be ther-oute,
And shet the dore, whyls we been aboute
Our privetee, that no man us espye
Whyls that we werke in this philosophye.'
Al as he bad, fulfilled was in dede,
This ilke servant anon-right out yede,
And his maister shette the dore anon,
And to hir labour speedily they gon.
  This preest, at this cursed chanouns bidding,
Up-on the fyr anon sette this thing,
And blew the fyr, and bisied him ful faste;
And this chanoun in-to the croslet caste
A poudre, noot I wher-of that it was
Y-maad, other of chalk, other of glas,
Or som-what elles, was nat worth a flye
To blynde with the preest; and bad him hye
The coles for to couchen al above
The croslet; 'for, in tokening I thee love,'
Quod this chanoun, 'thyn owene hondes two
Shul werche al thing which that shal heer be do.'
  'Graunt mercy,' quod the preest, and was ful glad,
And couched coles as the chanoun bad.

And whyle he bisy was, this feendly wrecche,
This fals chanoun, the foule feend him fecche!
Out of his bosom took a bechen cole,
In which ful subtilly was maad an hole,
And ther-in put was of silver lymaille
An ounce, and stopped was, with-outen fayle,
The hole with wex, to kepe the lymail in.
And understondeth, that this false gin
Was nat maad ther, but it was maad bifore;
And othere thinges I shal telle more
Herafterward, which that he with him broghte;
Er he cam ther, him to bigyle he thoghte,
And so he dide, er that they wente a-twinne;
Til he had terved him, coude he not blinne.
It dulleth me whan that I of him speke,
On his falshede fayn wolde I me wreke,
If I wiste how; but he is heer and ther:
He is so variaunt, he abit no-wher.
  But taketh heed now, sirs, for goddes love!
He took his cole of which I spak above,
And in his hond he baar it prively.
And whyls the preest couchede busily
The coles, as I tolde yow er this,
This chanoun seyde, 'freend, ye doon amis;
This is nat couched as it oghte be;
But sone I shal amenden it,' quod he.
'Now lat me medle therwith but a whyle,
For of yow have I pitee, by seint Gyle!
Ye been right hoot, I see wel how ye swete,
Have heer a cloth, and wype awey the wete.'
And whyles that the preest wyped his face,
This chanoun took his cole with harde grace,
And leyde it above, up-on the middeward
Of the croslet, and blew wel afterward,
Til that the coles gonne faste brenne.
  'Now yeve us drinke,' quod the chanoun thenne,
'As swythe al shal be wel, I undertake;
Sitte we doun, and lat us mery make.'
And whan that this chanounes bechen cole
Was brent, al the lymaille, out of the hole,

Into the croslet fil anon adoun;
And so it moste nedes, by resoun,
Sin it so even aboven couched was;
But ther-of wiste the preest no-thing, alas!
He demed alle the coles y-liche good,
For of the sleighte he no-thing understood.
And whan this alkamistre saugh his tyme,
'Rys up,' quod he, 'sir preest, and stondeth by me;
And for I woot wel ingot have ye noon,
Goth, walketh forth, and bring us a chalk-stoon;
For I wol make oon of the same shap
That is an ingot, if I may han hap.
And bringeth eek with yow a bolle or a panne,
Ful of water, and ye shul see wel thanne
How that our bisinesse shal thryve and preve.
And yet, for ye shul han no misbileve
Ne wrong conceit of me in your absence,
I ne wol nat been out of your presence,
But go with yow, and come with yow ageyn.'
The chambre-dore, shortly for to seyn,
They opened and shette, and wente hir weye.
And forth with hem they carieden the keye,
And come agayn with-outen any delay.
What sholde I tarien al the longe day?
He took the chalk, and shoop it in the wyse
Of an ingot, as I shal yow devyse.
  I seye, he took out of his owene sleve
A teyne of silver (yvele mote he cheve!)
Which that ne was nat but an ounce of weighte;
And taketh heed now of his cursed sleighte!
  He shoop his ingot, in lengthe and eek in brede,
Of this teyne, with-outen any drede,
So slyly, that the preest it nat espyde;
And in his sleve agayn he gan it hyde;
And fro the fyr he took up his matere,
And in th'ingot putte it with mery chere,
And in the water-vessel he it caste
Whan that him luste, and bad the preest as faste,
'Look what ther is, put in thyn hand and grope,
Thow finde shalt ther silver, as I hope;

What, devel of helle! sholde it elles be?
Shaving of silver silver is, pardee!'
He putte his hond in, and took up a teyne
Of silver fyn, and glad in every veyne
Was this preest, whan he saugh that it was so.
'Goddes blessing, and his modres also,
And alle halwes have ye, sir chanoun,'
Seyde this preest, 'and I hir malisoun,
But, and ye vouche-sauf to techen me
This noble craft and this subtilitee,
I wol be youre, in al that ever I may!'
Quod the chanoun, 'yet wol I make assay
The second tyme, that ye may taken hede
And been expert of this, and in your nede
Another day assaye in myn absence
This disciplyne and this crafty science.
Lat take another ounce,' quod he tho,
'Of quik-silver, with-outen wordes mo,
And do ther-with as ye han doon er this
With that other, which that now silver is.'
This preest him bisieth in al that he can
To doon as this chanoun, this cursed man,
Comanded him, and faste he blew the fyr,
For to come to th'effect of his desyr.
And this chanoun, right in the mene whyle,
Al redy was, the preest eft to bigyle,
And, for a countenance, in his hande he bar
An holwe stikke (tak keep and be war!)
In the ende of which an ounce, and na-more,
Of silver lymail put was, as bifore
Was in his cole, and stopped with wex weel
For to kepe in his lymail every deel.
And whyl this preest was in his bisinesse,
This chanoun with his stikke gan him dresse
To him anon, and his pouder caste in
As he did er; (the devel out of his skin
Him terve, I pray to god, for his falshede;
For he was ever fals in thoght and dede);
And with this stikke, above the croslet,
That was ordeyned with that false get,

He stired the coles, til relente gan
The wex agayn the fyr, as every man,
But it a fool be, woot wel it mot nede,
And al that in the stikke was out yede,
And in the croslet hastily it fel.
Now gode sirs, what wol ye bet than wel ?
Whan that this preest thus was bigyled ageyn,
Supposing noght but trouthe, soth to seyn,
He was so glad, that I can nat expresse
In no manere his mirthe and his gladnesse ;
And to the chanoun he profred eftsone
Body and good ; 'ye,' quod the chanoun sone,
'Though povre I be, crafty thou shalt me finde ;
I warne thee, yet is ther more bihinde.
Is ther any coper her-inne ?' seyde he.
'Ye,' quod the preest, 'sir, I trowe wel ther be.'
'Elles go bye us som, and that as swythe,
Now, gode sir, go forth thy wey and hy the.'
  He wente his wey, and with the coper cam,
And this chanoun it in his handes nam,
And of that coper weyed out but an ounce.
Al to simple is my tonge to pronounce,
As ministre of my wit, the doublenesse
Of this chanoun, rote of al cursednesse.
He semed freendly to hem that knewe him noght,
But he was feendly bothe in herte and thoght.
It werieth me to telle of his falsnesse,
And nathelees yet wol I it expresse,
To th'entente that men may be war therby,
And for noon other cause, trewely.
  He putte his ounce of coper in the croslet,
And on the fyr as swythe he hath it set,
And caste in poudre, and made the preest to blowe,
And in his werking for to stoupe lowe,
As he dide er, and al nas but a jape ;
Right as him liste, the preest he made his ape ;
And afterward in th'ingot he it caste,
And in the panne putte it at the laste
Of water, and in he putte his owene hond.
And in his sleve (as ye biforn-hond

Herde me telle) he hadde a silver teyne.
He slyly took it out, this cursed heyne—
Unwiting this preest of his false craft—
And in the pannes botme he hath it laft;
And in the water rombled to and fro,
And wonder prively took up also
The coper teyne, noght knowing this preest,
And hidde it, and him hente by the breest,
And to him spak, and thus seyde in his game,
'Stoupeth adoun, by god, ye be to blame,
Helpeth me now, as I dide yow whyl-er,
Putte in your hand, and loketh what is ther.'
This preest took up this silver teyne anon,
And thanne seyde the chanoun, 'lat us gon
With thise three teynes, which that we han wroght,
To som goldsmith, and wite if they been oght.
For, by my feith, I nolde, for myn hood,
But-if that they were silver, fyn and good,
And that as swythe preved shal it be.'
  Un-to the goldsmith with thise teynes three
They wente, and putte thise teynes in assay
To fyr and hamer; mighte no man sey nay,
But that they weren as hem oghte be.
  This sotted preest, who was gladder than he?
Was never brid gladder agayn the day,
Ne nightingale, in the sesoun of May,
Nas never noon that luste bet to singe;
Ne lady lustier in carolinge
Or for to speke of love and wommanhede,
Ne knight in armes to doon an hardy dede
To stonde in grace of his lady dere,
Than had this preest this sory craft to lere;
And to the chanoun thus he spak and seyde,
'For love of god, that for us alle deyde,
And as I may deserve it un-to yow,
What shal this receit coste? telleth now!'
  'By our lady,' quod this chanoun, 'it is dere,
I warne yow wel; for, save I and a frere,
In Engelond ther can no man it make.'
  'No fors,' quod he, 'now, sir, for goddes sake,

What shal I paye ? telleth me, I preye.'
  'Y-wis,' quod he, 'it is ful dere, I seye ;
Sir, at o word, if that thee list it have,
Ye shul paye fourty pound, so god me save !
And, nere the freendship that ye dide er this
To me, ye sholde paye more, y-wis.'
  This preest the somme of fourty pound anon
Of nobles fette, and took hem everichon
To this chanoun, for this ilke receit ;
Al his werking nas but fraude and deceit.
  'Sir preest,' he seyde, 'I kepe han no loos
Of my craft, for I wolde it kept were cloos ;
And as ye love me, kepeth it secree ;
For, and men knewe al my subtilitee,
By god, they wolden han so greet envye
To me, by-cause of my philosophye,
I sholde be deed, ther were non other weye.'
  'God it forbede !' quod the preest, 'what sey ye ?'
Yet hadde I lever spenden al the good
Which that I have (and elles wexe I wood !)
Than that ye sholden falle in swich mescheef.'
  'For your good wil, sir, have ye right good preef,'
Quod the chanoun, 'and far-wel, grant mercy !'
He wente his wey and never the preest him sy
After that day ; and whan that this preest sholde
Maken assay, at swich tyme as he wolde,
Of this receit, far-wel ! it wolde nat be !
Lo, thus byjaped and bigyled was he !
Thus maketh he his introduccioun
To bringe folk to hir destruccioun.—
  Considereth, sirs, how that, in ech estaat,
Bitwixe men and gold ther is debaat
So ferforth, that unnethes is ther noon.
This multiplying blent so many oon,
That in good feith I trowe that it be
The cause grettest of swich scarsetee.
Philosophres speken so mistily
In this craft, that men can nat come therby,

For any wit that men han now a-dayes.
They mowe wel chiteren, as doon thise jayes,
And in her termes sette hir lust and peyne,
But to hir purpos shul they never atteyne.
A man may lightly lerne, if he have aught,
To multiplye, and bringe his good to naught!
Lo! swich a lucre is in this lusty game,
A mannes mirthe it wol torne un-to grame,
And empten also grete and hevy purses,
And maken folk for to purchasen curses
Of hem, that han hir good therto y-lent.
O! fy! for shame! they that han been brent,
Allas! can they nat flee the fyres hete?
Ye that it use, I rede ye it lete,
Lest ye lese al; for bet than never is late.
Never to thryve were to long a date.
Though ye prolle ay, ye shul it never finde;
Ye been as bolde as is Bayard the blinde,
That blundreth forth, and peril casteth noon;
He is as bold to renne agayn a stoon
As for to goon besydes in the weye.
So faren ye that multiplye, I seye.
If that your yën can nat seen aright,
Loke that your minde lakke nought his sight.
For, though ye loke never so brode, and stare,
Ye shul nat winne a myte on that chaffare,
But wasten al that ye may rape and renne.
Withdrawe the fyr, lest it to faste brenne;
Medleth na-more with that art, I mene,
For, if ye doon, your thrift is goon ful clene.
And right as swythe I wol yow tellen here,
What philosophres seyn in this matere.
Lo, thus seith Arnold of the Newe Toun,
As his Rosarie maketh mencioun;
He seith right thus, with-outen any lye.
'Ther may no man Mercurie mortifye,
But it be with his brother knowleching.
How that he, which that first seyde this thing,
Of philosophres fader was, Hermes;
He seith, how that the dragoun, douteles,

Ne deyeth nat, but-if that he be slayn
With his brother; and that is for to sayn,
By the dragoun, Mercurie and noon other
He understood; and brimstoon by his brother,
That out of *sol* and *luna* were y-drawe.
And therfor,' seyde he, 'tak heed to my sawe,
Let no man bisy him this art for to seche,
But-if that he th'entencioun and speche
Of philosophres understonde can;
And if he do, he is a lewed man.
For this science and this conning,' quod he,
'Is of the secree of secrees, parde.'
  Also ther was a disciple of Plato,
That on a tyme seyde his maister to,
As his book Senior wol bere witnesse,
And this was his demande in soothfastnesse:
'Tel me the name of the privy stoon?'
  And Plato answerde unto him anoon,
'Tak the stoon that Titanos men name.'
  'Which is that?' quod he. 'Magnesia is the same,'
Seyde Plato. 'Ye, sir, and is it thus?
This is *ignotum per ignotius*.
What is Magnesia, good sir, I yow preye?'
  'It is a water that is maad, I seye,
Of elementes foure,' quod Plato.
  'Tel me the rote, good sir,' quod he tho,
'Of that water, if that it be your wille?'
  'Nay, nay,' quod Plato, 'certein, that I nille.
The philosophres sworn were everichoon,
That they sholden discovere it un-to noon,
Ne in no book it wryte in no manere;
For un-to Crist it is so leef and dere
That he wol nat that it discovered be,
But wher it lyketh to his deitee
Man for t'enspyre, and eek for to defende
Whom that him lyketh; lo, this is the ende.'
  Thanne conclude I thus; sith god of hevene
Ne wol nat that the philosophres nevene

How that a man shal come un-to this stoon,
I rede, as for the beste, lete it goon.
For who-so maketh god his adversarie,
As for to werken any thing in contrarie
Of his wil, certes, never shal he thryve,
Thogh that he multiplye terme of his lyve.
And ther a poynt; for ended is my tale;
God sende every trewe man bote of his bale!—
Amen.

Here is ended the Chanouns Yemannes Tale.

THE MAUNCIPLES TALE

Here folweth the Prologe of the Maunciples Tale.

WITE ye nat wher ther stant a litel toun
Which that y-cleped is Bob-up-and-doun,
Under the Blee, in Caunterbury weye ?
Ther gan our hoste for to jape and pleye,
And seyde, 'sirs, what ! Dun is in the myre !
Is ther no man, for preyere ne for hyre,
That wol awake our felawe heer bihinde ?
A theef mighte him ful lightly robbe and binde.
See how he nappeth ! see, for cokkes bones,
As he wol falle from his hors at ones.
Is that a cook of Londoun, with meschaunce ?
Do him come forth, he knoweth his penaunce,
For he shal telle a tale, by my fey !
Al-though it be nat worth a botel hey.
Awake, thou cook,' quod he, 'god yeve thee sorwe,
What eyleth thee to slepe by the morwe ?
Hastow had fleen al night, or artow dronke,
Or hastow with som quene al night y-swonke,
So that thou mayst nat holden up thyn heed ?'
  This cook, that was ful pale and no-thing reed,
Seyde to our host, 'so god my soule blesse,
As ther is falle on me swich hevinesse,
Noot I nat why, that me were lever slepe
Than the beste galoun wyn in Chepe.'
  'Wel,' quod the maunciple, 'if it may doon ese
To thee, sir cook, and to no wight displese
Which that heer rydeth in this companye,
And that our host wol, of his curteisye,

I wol as now excuse thee of thy tale ;
For, in good feith, thy visage is ful pale,
Thyn yën daswen eek, as that me thinketh,
And wel I woot, thy breeth ful soure stinketh,
That sheweth wel thou art not wel disposed ;
Of me, certein, thou shalt nat been y-glosed.
Se how he ganeth, lo, this dronken wight,
As though he wolde us swolwe anon-right.
Hold cloos thy mouth, man, by thy fader kin !
The devel of helle sette his foot ther-in !
Thy cursed breeth infecte wol us alle ;
Fy, stinking swyn, fy ! foule moot thee falle !
A ! taketh heed, sirs, of this lusty man.
Now, swete sir, wol ye justen atte fan ?
Ther-to me thinketh ye been wel y-shape !
I trowe that ye dronken han wyn ape,
And that is whan men pleyen with a straw.'
And with this speche the cook wex wrooth and wraw,
And on the maunciple he gan nodde faste
For lakke of speche, and doun the hors him caste,
Wher as he lay, til that men up him took ;
This was a fayr chivachee of a cook !
Allas ! he nadde holde him by his ladel !
And, er that he agayn were in his sadel,
Ther was greet showving bothe to and fro,
To lifte him up, and muchel care and wo,
So unweldy was this sory palled gost.
And to the maunciple thanne spak our host,
'By-cause drink hath dominacioun
Upon this man, by my savacioun
I trowe he lewedly wolde telle his tale.
For, were it wyn, or old or moysty ale,
That he hath dronke, he speketh in his nose,
And fneseth faste, and eek he hath the pose.
He hath also to do more than y-nough
To kepe him and his capel out of slough ;
And, if he falle from his capel eft-sone,
Than shul we alle have y-nough to done,
In lifting up his hevy dronken cors.
Telle on thy tale, of him make I no fors.

But yet, maunciple, in feith thou art to nyce,
Thus openly repreve him of his vyce.
Another day he wol, peraventure,
Reclayme thee, and bringe thee to lure;
I mene, he speke wol of smale thinges,
As for to pinchen at thy rekeninges,
That wer not honeste, if it cam to preef.'
'No,' quod the maunciple, 'that were a greet mescheef!
So mighte he lightly bringe me in the snare.
Yet hadde I lever payen for the mare
Which he rit on, than he sholde with me stryve;
I wol nat wratthe him, al-so mote I thryve!
That that I spak, I seyde it in my bourde;
And wite ye what? I have heer, in a gourde,
A draught of wyn, ye, of a rype grape,
And right anon ye shul seen a good jape.
This cook shal drinke ther-of, if I may;
Up peyne of deeth, he wol nat seye me nay!'
And certeinly, to tellen as it was,
Of this vessel the cook drank faste, allas!
What neded him? he drank y-nough biforn.
And whan he hadde pouped in this horn,
To the maunciple he took the gourde agayn;
And of that drinke the cook was wonder fayn,
And thanked him in swich wyse as he coude.
Than gan our host to laughen wonder loude,
And seyde, 'I see wel, it is necessarie,
Wher that we goon, good drink we with us carie;
For that wol turne rancour and disese
T'acord and love, and many a wrong apese.
O thou Bachus, y-blessed be thy name,
That so canst turnen ernest in-to game!
Worship and thank be to thy deitee!
Of that matere ye gete na-more of me.
Tel on thy tale, maunciple, I thee preye.'
'Wel, sir,' quod he, 'now herkneth what I seye.'

Thus endeth the Prologe of the Manciple.

Here biginneth the Maunciples Tale of the Crowe.

WHAN Phebus dwelled here in this erthe adoun,
As olde bokes maken mencioun
He was the moste lusty bachiler
In al this world, and eek the beste archer;
He slow Phitoun, the serpent, as he lay
Slepinge agayn the sonne upon a day;
And many another noble worthy dede
He with his bowe wroghte, as men may rede.
  Pleyen he coude on every minstralcye,
And singen, that it was a melodye,
To heren of his clere vois the soun.
Certes the king of Thebes, Amphioun,
That with his singing walled that citee,
Coude never singen half so wel as he.
Therto he was the semelieste man
That is or was, sith that the world bigan.
What nedeth it his fetures to discryve?
For in this world was noon so fair on lyve.
He was ther-with fulfild of gentillesse,
Of honour, and of parfit worthinesse.
  This Phebus, that was flour of bachelrye,
As wel in fredom as in chivalrye,
For his desport, in signe eek of victorie
Of Phitoun, so as telleth us the storie,
Was wont to beren in his hand a bowe.
  Now had this Phebus in his hous a crowe,
Which in a cage he fostred many a day,
And taughte it speken, as men teche a jay.
Whyt was this crowe, as is a snow-whyt swan,
And countrefete the speche of every man
He coude, whan he sholde telle a tale.
Ther-with in al this world no nightingale
Ne coude, by an hondred thousand deel,
Singen so wonder merily and weel.
  Now had this Phebus in his hous a wyf,
Which that he lovede more than his lyf,
And night and day dide ever his diligence
Hir for to plese, and doon hir reverence,

Save only, if the sothe that I shal sayn,
Jalous he was, and wolde have kept hir fayn ;
For him were looth by-japed for to be.
And so is every wight in swich degree ;
But al in ydel, for it availleth noght.
A good wyf, that is clene of werk and thoght,
Sholde nat been kept in noon await, certayn ;
And trewely, the labour is in vayn
To kepe a shrewe, for it wol nat be.
This holde I for a verray nycetee,
To spille labour, for to kepe wyves ;
Thus writen olde clerkes in hir lyves.
But now to purpos, as I first bigan :
This worthy Phebus dooth all that he can
To plesen hir, weninge by swich plesaunce,
And for his manhede and his governaunce,
That no man sholde han put him from hir grace.
But god it woot, ther may no man embrace
As to destreyne a thing, which that nature
Hath naturelly set in a creature.
Tak any brid, and put it in a cage,
And do al thyn entente and thy corage
To fostre it tendrely with mete and drinke,
Of alle deyntees that thou canst bithinke,
And keep it al-so clenly as thou may ;
Al-though his cage of gold be never so gay,
Yet hath this brid, by twenty thousand fold,
Lever in a forest, that is rude and cold,
Gon ete wormes and swich wrecchednesse.
For ever this brid wol doon his bisinesse
To escape out of his cage, if he may ;
His libertee this brid desireth ay.
Lat take a cat, and fostre him wel with milk,
And tendre flesh, and make his couche of silk,
And lat him seen a mous go by the wal ;
Anon he weyveth milk, and flesh, and al,
And every deyntee that is in that hous,
Swich appetyt hath he to ete a mous.
Lo, here hath lust his dominacioun,
And appetyt flemeth discrecioun.

A she-wolf hath also a vileins kinde ;
The lewedeste wolf that she may finde,
Or leest of reputacion wol she take,
In tyme whan hir lust to han a make.
Alle thise ensamples speke I by thise men
That been untrewe, and no-thing by wommen.
For men han ever a likerous appetyt
On lower thing to parfourne hir delyt
Than on hir wyves, be they never so faire,
Ne never so trewe, ne so debonaire.
Flesh is so newefangel, with meschaunce,
That we ne conne in no-thing han plesaunce
That souneth in-to vertu any whyle.
This Phebus, which that thoghte upon no gyle,
Deceyved was, for al his jolitee ;
For under him another hadde she,
A man of litel reputacioun,
Noght worth to Phebus in comparisoun.
The more harm is ; it happeth ofte so,
Of which ther cometh muchel harm and wo.
And so bifel, whan Phebus was absent,
His wyf anon hath for hir lemman sent ;
Hir lemman ? certes, this is a knavish speche !
Foryeveth it me, and that I yow biseche.
The wyse Plato seith, as ye may rede,
The word mot nede accorde with the dede.
If men shal telle proprely a thing,
The word mot cosin be to the werking.
I am a boistous man, right thus seye I,
Ther nis no difference, trewely,
Bitwixe a wyf that is of heigh degree,
If of hir body dishonest she be,
And a povre wenche, other than this—
If it so be, they werke bothe amis—
But that the gentile, in estaat above,
She shal be cleped his lady, as in love ;
And for that other is a povre womman,
She shal be cleped his wenche, or his lemman.
And, god it woot, myn owene dere brother,
Men leyn that oon as lowe as lyth that other.

Right so, bitwixe a titlelees tiraunt
And an outlawe, or a theef erraunt,
The same I seye, ther is no difference.
To Alisaundre told was this sentence;
That, for the tyrant is of gretter might,
By force of meynee for to sleen doun-right,
And brennen hous and hoom, and make al plain,
Lo! therfor is he cleped a capitain;
And, for the outlawe hath but smal meynee,
And may nat doon so greet an harm as he,
Ne bringe a contree to so greet mescheef,
Men clepen him an outlawe or a theef.
But, for I am a man noght textuel,
I wol noght telle of textes never a del;
I wol go to my tale, as I bigan.
Whan Phebus wyf had sent for hir lemman,
Anon they wroghten al hir lust volage.
The whyte crowe, that heng ay in the cage,
Biheld hir werk, and seyde never a word.
And whan that hoom was come Phebus, the lord,
This crowe sang 'cokkow! cokkow! cokkow!'
'What, brid?' quod Phebus, 'what song singestow?
Ne were thow wont so merily to singe
That to myn herte it was a rejoisinge
To here thy vois? allas! what song is this?'
'By god,' quod he, 'I singe nat amis;
Phebus,' quod he, 'for al thy worthinesse,
For al thy beautee and thy gentilesse,
For al thy song and al thy minstralcye,
For al thy waiting, blered is thyn yë
With oon of litel reputacioun,
Noght worth to thee, as in comparisoun,
The mountance of a gnat; so mote I thryve!
For on thy bed thy wyf I saugh him swyve.'
What wol ye more? the crowe anon him tolde,
By sadde tokenes and by wordes bolde,
How that his wyf had doon hir lecherye,
Him to gret shame and to gret vileinye;

And tolde him ofte, he saugh it with his yën.
This Phebus gan aweyward for to wryen,
Him thoughte his sorweful herte brast a-two ;
His bowe he bente, and sette ther-inne a flo,
And in his ire his wyf thanne hath he slayn.
This is th'effect, ther is na-more to sayn ;
For sorwe of which he brak his minstralcye,
Bothe harpe, and lute, and giterne, and sautrye ;
And eek he brak his arwes and his bowe.
And after that, thus spak he to the crowe :
'Traitour,' quod he, 'with tonge of scorpioun,
Thou hast me broght to my confusioun !
Allas ! that I was wroght ! why nere I deed ?
O dere wyf, O gemme of lustiheed,
That were to me so sad and eek so trewe,
Now lystow deed, with face pale of hewe,
Ful giltelees, that dorste I swere, y-wis !
O rakel hand, to doon so foule amis !
O trouble wit, O ire recchelees,
That unavysed smytest giltelees !
O wantrust, ful of fals suspecioun,
Where was thy wit and thy discrecioun ?
O every man, be-war of rakelnesse,
Ne trowe no-thing with-outen strong witnesse ;
Smyt nat to sone, er that ye witen why,
And beeth avysed wel and sobrely
Er ye doon any execucioun,
Up-on your ire, for suspecioun.
Allas ! a thousand folk hath rakel ire
Fully fordoon, and broght hem in the mire.
Allas ! for sorwe I wol my-selven slee !'
And to the crowe, 'O false theef !' seyde he,
'I wol thee quyte anon thy false tale !
Thou songe whylom lyk a nightingale ;
Now shaltow, false theef, thy song forgon,
And eek thy whyte fetheres everichon,
Ne never in al thy lyf ne shaltou speke.
Thus shal men on a traitour been awreke ;
Thou and thyn of-spring ever shul be blake,
Ne never swete noise shul ye make,

But ever crye agayn tempest and rayn,
In tokeninge that thurgh thee my wyf is slayn.'
And to the crowe he stirte, and that anon,
And pulled his whyte fetheres everichon,
And made him blak, and refte him al his song,
And eek his speche, and out at dore him slong
Un-to the devel, which I him bitake;
And for this caas ben alle crowes blake.—
Lordings, by this ensample I yow preye,
Beth war, and taketh kepe what I seye:
Ne telleth never no man in your lyf
How that another man hath dight his wyf;
He wol yow haten mortally, certeyn.
Daun Salomon, as wyse clerkes seyn,
Techeth a man to kepe his tonge wel;
But as I seyde, I am noght textuel.
But nathelees, thus taughte me my dame:
'My sone, thenk on the crowe, a goddes name:
My sone, keep wel thy tonge and keep thy freend.
A wikked tonge is worse than a feend.
My sone, from a feend men may hem blesse;
My sone, god of his endelees goodnesse
Walled a tonge with teeth and lippes eke,
For man sholde him avyse what he speke.
My sone, ful ofte, for to muche speche,
Hath many a man ben spilt, as clerkes teche;
But for a litel speche avysely
Is no men shent, to speke generally.
My sone, thy tonge sholdestow restreyne
At alle tyme, but whan thou doost thy peyne
To speke of god, in honour and preyere.
The firste vertu, sone, if thou wolt lere,
Is to restreyne and kepe wel thy tonge.—
Thus lerne children whan that they ben yonge.—
My sone, of muchel speking yvel-avysed,
Ther lasse speking hadde y-nough suffysed,
Comth muchel harm, thus was me told and taught.
In muchel speche sinne wanteth naught.
Wostow wher-of a rakel tonge serveth?
Right as a swerd forcutteth and forkerveth

An arm a-two, my dere sone, right so
A tonge cutteth frendship al a-two.
A jangler is to god abhominable;
Reed Salomon, so wys and honurable;
Reed David in his psalmes, reed Senekke.
My sone, spek nat, but with thyn heed thou bekke.
Dissimule as thou were deef, if that thou here
A jangler speke of perilous matere.
The Fleming seith, and lerne it, if thee leste,
That litel jangling causeth muchel reste.
My sone, if thou no wikked word hast seyd,
Thee thar nat drede for to be biwreyd;
But he that hath misseyd, I dar wel sayn,
He may by no wey clepe his word agayn.
Thing that is seyd, is seyd; and forth it gooth,
Though him repente, or be him leef or looth.
He is his thral to whom that he hath sayd
A tale, of which he is now yvel apayd.
My sone, be war, and be non auctour newe
Of tydinges, whether they ben false or trewe.
Wher-so thou come, amonges hye or lowe,
Kepe wel thy tonge, and thenk up-on the crowe.'

Here is ended the Maunciples Tale of the Crowe.

THE PERSONES TALE

Here folweth the Prologe of the Persones Tale.

BY that the maunciple hadde his tale al ended,
The sonne fro the south lyne was descended
So lowe, that he nas nat, to my sighte,
Degreës nyne and twenty as in highte.
Foure of the clokke it was tho, as I gesse:
For eleven foot, or litel more or lesse,
My shadwe was at thilke tyme, as there,
Of swich feet as my lengthe parted were
In six feet equal of proporcioun.
Ther-with the mones exaltacioun,
I mene Libra, alwey gan ascende,
As we were entringe at a thropes ende;
For which our host, as he was wont to gye,
As in this caas, our joly companye,
Seyde in this wyse, 'lordings everichoon,
Now lakketh us no tales mo than oon.
Fulfild is my sentence and my decree;
I trowe that we han herd of ech degree.
Almost fulfild is al myn ordinaunce;
I prey to god, so yeve him right good chaunce,
That telleth this tale to us lustily.
Sir preest,' quod he, 'artow a vicary?
Or art a person? sey sooth, by thy fey!
Be what thou be, ne breke thou nat our pley;
For every man, save thou, hath told his tale,
Unbokel, and shewe us what is in thy male;
For trewely, me thinketh, by thy chere,
Thou sholdest knitte up wel a greet matere.

Tel us a tale anon, for cokkes bones!'
  This Persone him answerde, al at ones,
'Thou getest fable noon y-told for me;
For Paul, that wryteth unto Timothee,
Repreveth hem that weyven soothfastnesse,
And tellen fables and swich wrecchednesse.
Why sholde I sowen draf out of my fest,
Whan I may sowen whete, if that me lest?
For which I seye, if that yow list to here
Moralitee and vertuous matere,
And thanne that ye wol yeve me audience,
I wol ful fayn, at Cristes reverence,
Do yow plesaunce leefful, as I can.
But trusteth wel, I am a Southren man,
I can nat geste—rum, ram, ruf—by lettre,
Ne, god wot, rym holde I but litel bettre;
And therfor, if yow list, I wol nat glose.
I wol yow telle a mery tale in prose
To knitte up al this feeste, and make an ende.
And Jesu, for his grace, wit me sende
To shewe yow the wey, in this viage,
Of thilke parfit glorious pilgrimage
That highte Jerusalem celestial.
And, if ye vouche-sauf, anon I shal
Biginne upon my tale, for whiche I preye
Telle your avys, I can no bettre seye.
But nathelees, this meditacioun
I putte it ay under correccioun
Of clerkes, for I am nat textuel;
I take but the sentens, trusteth wel.
Therfor I make protestacioun
That I wol stonde to correccioun.'
  Up-on this word we han assented sone,
For, as us semed, it was for to done,
To enden in som vertuous sentence,
And for to yeve him space and audience;
And bede our host he sholde to him seye,
That alle we to telle his tale him preye.
  Our host hadde the wordes for us alle:—
'Sir preest,' quod he, 'now fayre yow bifalle!

Sey what yow list, and we wol gladly here '—
And with that word he seyde in this manere—
' Telleth,' quod he, ' your meditacioun.
But hasteth yow, the sonne wol adoun ;
Beth fructuous, and that in litel space,
And to do wel god sende yow his grace ! '

Explicit prohemium.

Here biginneth the Persones Tale.

Jer. 6°. *State super vias et videte et interrogate de viis antiquis, que sit via bona ; et ambulate in ea, et inuenietis refrigerium animabus vestris, &c.*

§ 1. Our swete lord god of hevene, that no man wol perisse, but wole that we comen alle to the knoweleche of him, and to the blisful lyf that is perdurable, amonesteth us by the prophete Jeremie, that seith in this wyse : ' stondeth upon the weyes, and seeth and axeth of olde pathes (that is to seyn, of olde sentences) which is the goode wey ; and walketh in that wey, and ye shul finde refresshinge for your soules,' &c. Manye been the weyes espirituels that leden folk to oure Lord Jesu Crist, and to the regne of glorie. Of whiche weyes, ther is a ful noble wey and a ful covenable, which may nat faile to man ne to womman, that thurgh sinne hath misgoon fro the righte wey of Jerusalem celestial ; and this wey is cleped Penitence, of which man sholde gladly herknen and enquere with al his herte ; to witen what is Penitence, and whennes it is cleped Penitence, and in how manye maneres been the accions or werkinges of Penitence, and how manye spyces ther been of Penitence, and whiche thinges apertenen and bihoven to Penitence, and whiche thinges destourben Penitence.

§ 2. Seint Ambrose seith, that ' Penitence is the pleyninge of man for the gilt that he hath doon, and na-more to do any thing for which him oghte to pleyne.' And som doctour seith : ' Penitence is the waymentinge of man, that sorweth for his sinne and pyneth himself for he hath misdoon.' Penitence, with certeyne circumstances, is verray repentance of a man that halt him-self in sorwe and other peyne for hise giltes. And for he shal be verray penitent, he shal first biwailen the sinnes that he hath doon, and stidefastly purposen in his herte to have shrift of mouthe, and to doon satisfaccioun, and never to doon thing for which him oghte more to biwayle or to compleyne, and to continue in goode werkes: or elles his repentance may nat availle. For as seith seint Isidre: 'he is a japer and a gabber, and no verray repentant, that eftsoone dooth thing, for which him oghte repente.' Wepinge, and nat for to stinte to doon sinne, may nat avaylle. But nathelees, men shal hope that every tyme that man falleth, be it never so ofte, that he may arise thurgh Penitence, if he have grace: but certeinly it is greet doute. For as seith Seint Gregorie: 'unnethe aryseth he out of sinne, that is charged with the charge of yvel usage.' And therfore repentant folk, that stinte for to sinne, and forlete sinne er that sinne forlete hem, holy chirche holdeth hem siker of hir savacioun. And he that sinneth, and verraily repenteth him in his laste ende, holy chirche yet hopeth his savacioun, by the grete mercy of oure lord Jesu Crist, for his repentaunce; but tak the siker wey.

§ 3. And now, sith I have declared yow what thing is Penitence, now shul ye understonde that ther been three accions of Penitence. The firste accion of Penitence is, that a man be baptized after that he hath sinned. Seint Augustin seith: 'but he be penitent for his olde sinful lyf, he may nat biginne the newe clene lif.' For certes, if he be baptized withouten penitence of his olde gilt, he receiveth the mark of baptisme, but nat the grace ne the remission of his sinnes, til he have repentance verray. Another defaute is this, that men doon deedly sinne after that they han received baptisme. The thridde defaute is, that men fallen in venial sinnes after hir baptisme, fro day to day. Ther-of seith Seint Augustin, that 'penitence of goode and humble folk is the penitence of every day.'

§ 4. The speces of Penitence been three. That oon

of hem is solempne, another is commune, and the thridde is privee. Thilke penance that is solempne, is in two maneres; as to be put out of holy chirche in lente, for slaughtre of children, and swich maner thing. Another is, whan a man hath sinned openly, of which sinne the fame is openly spoken in the contree; and thanne holy chirche by jugement destreineth him for to do open penaunce. Commune penaunce is that preestes enjoinen men comunly in certeyn caas; as for to goon, peraventure, naked in pilgrimages, or barefoot. Privee penaunce is thilke that men doon alday for privee sinnes, of whiche we shryve us prively and receyve privee penaunce.

§ 5. Now shaltow understande what is bihovely and necessarie to verray parfit Penitence. And this stant on three thinges; Contricioun of herte, Confessioun of Mouth, and Satisfaccioun. For which seith Seint John Crisostom: 'Penitence destreyneth a man to accepte benignely every peyne that him is enjoyned, with contricion of herte, and shrift of mouth, with satisfaccion; and in werkinge of alle maner humilitee.' And this is fruitful Penitence agayn three thinges in whiche we wratthe oure lord Jesu Crist: this is to seyn, by delyt in thinkinge, by recchelesnesse in spekinge, and by wikked sinful werkinge. And agayns thise wikkede giltes is Penitence, that may be lykned un-to a tree.

§ 6. The rote of this tree is Contricion, that hydeth him in the herte of him that is verray repentant, right as the rote of a tree hydeth him in the erthe. Of the rote of Contricion springeth a stalke, that bereth braunches and leves of Confession, and fruit of Satisfaccion. For which Crist seith in his gospel: 'dooth digne fruit of Penitence'; for by this fruit may men knowe this tree, and nat by the rote that is hid in the herte of man, ne by the braunches ne by the leves of Confession. And therefore oure Lord Jesu Crist seith thus: 'by the fruit of hem ye shul knowen hem.' Of this rote eek springeth a seed of grace, the which seed is moder of sikernesse, and this seed is egre and hoot. The grace of this seed springeth of god, thurgh remembrance of the day of dome and on the peynes of helle. Of this matere seith Salomon, that 'in the drede of god man forleteth his sinne.' The hete of this seed is the love of god, and the desiring of the joye perdurable. This hete draweth the herte of a man to god, and dooth him haten his sinne. For soothly, ther is no-thing that savoureth so wel to a child as the milk of his norice, ne no-thing is to him more abhominable than thilke milk whan it is medled with other mete. Right so the sinful man that loveth his sinne, him semeth that it is to him most swete of any-thing; but fro that tyme that he loveth sadly our lord Jesu Crist, and desireth the lif perdurable, ther nis to him no-thing more abhominable. For soothly, the lawe of god is the love of god; for which David the prophete seith: 'I have loved thy lawe and hated wikkednesse and hate'; he that loveth god kepeth his lawe and his word. This tree saugh the prophete Daniel in spirit, up-on the avision of the king Nabugodonosor, whan he conseiled him to do penitence. Penaunce is the tree of lyf to hem that it receiven, and he that holdeth him in verray penitence is blessed; after the sentence of Salomon.

§ 7. In this Penitence or Contricion man shal understonde foure thinges, that is to seyn, what is Contricion: and whiche been the causes that moeven a man to Contricion: and how he sholde be contrit: and what Contricion availleth to the soule. Thanne is it thus: that Contricion is the verray sorwe that a man receiveth in his herte for his sinnes, with sad purpos to shryve him, and to do penaunce, and nevermore to do sinne. And this sorwe shal been in this manere, as seith seint Bernard: 'it shal been hevy and grevous, and ful sharpe and poinant in herte.' First, for man hath agilt his lord and his creatour; and more sharpe and poinant, for he hath agilt his fader celestial; and yet more sharpe and poinant, for he hath wrathed and agilt him that boghte him; which with his precious blood hath delivered us fro the bondes of sinne, and fro the crueltee of the devel and fro the peynes of helle.

§ 8. The causes that oghte moeve a man to Contricion been six. First, a man shal remembre him of hise sinnes; but loke he that thilke remembrance ne be to him no delyt by no wey, but greet shame and sorwe for his gilt. For Job seith: 'sinful men doon werkes worthy of Confession.' And therfore seith Ezechie: 'I wol remembre me alle the yeres of my lyf, in bitternesse of myn herte.' And god seith in the Apocalips: 'remembreth yow fro whennes that ye been falle'; for biforn that tyme that ye sinned, ye were the children of god, and limes of the regne of god; but for your sinne ye been woxen thral and foul, and membres of the feend, hate of aungels, sclaundre of holy chirche, and fode of the false serpent; perpetuel matere of the fyr of helle. And yet more foul and abhominable, for ye trespassen so ofte tyme, as doth the hound that retourneth to eten his spewing. And yet be ye fouler for your longe continuing in sinne and your sinful usage, for which ye be roten in your sinne, as a beest in his dong. Swiche manere of thoghtes maken a man to have shame of his sinne, and no delyt, as god seith by the prophete Ezechiel: 'ye shal remembre yow of youre weyes, and they shuln displese yow.' Sothly, sinnes been the weyes that leden folk to helle.

§ 9. The seconde cause that oghte make a man to have desdeyn of sinne is this: that, as seith seint Peter, 'who-so that doth sinne is thral of sinne'; and sinne put a man in greet thraldom. And therfore seith the prophete Ezechiel: 'I wente sorweful in desdayn of my-self.' And certes, wel oghte a man have desdayn of sinne, and withdrawe him from that thraldom and vileinye. And lo, what seith Seneca in this matere. He seith thus: 'though I wiste that neither god ne man ne sholde nevere knowe it, yet wolde I have desdayn for to do sinne.' And the same Seneca also seith: 'I am born to gretter thinges than to be thral to my body, or than for to maken of my body a thral.' Ne a fouler thral may no man ne womman maken of his body, than for to yeven his body to sinne. Al were it the fouleste cherl, or the fouleste womman that liveth, and leest of value, yet is he thanne more foule and more in servitute. Evere fro the hyer degree that man falleth, the more is he thral, and more to god and to the world vile and abhominable. O gode god, wel oghte man have desdayn of sinne; sith that, thurgh sinne, ther he was free, now is he maked bonde. And therfore seyth Seint Augustin: 'if thou hast desdayn of thy servant, if he agilte or sinne, have thou thanne desdayn that thou thy-self sholdest do sinne.' Take reward of thy value, that thou ne be to foul to thy-self. Allas! wel oghten they thanne have desdayn to been servauntz and thralles to sinne, and sore been ashamed of hemself, that god of his endelees goodnesse hath set hem in heigh estaat, or yeven hem wit, strengthe of body, hele, beautee, prosperitee, and boghte hem fro the deeth with his herte blood, that they so unkindely, agayns his gentilesse, quyten him so vileinsly, to slaughtre of hir owene soules. O gode god, ye wommen that been of so greet beautee, remembreth yow of the proverbe of Salomon, that seith: 'he lykneth a fair womman, that is a fool of hir body, lyk to a ring of gold that were in the groyn of a sowe.' For right as a sowe wroteth in everich ordure, so wroteth she hir beautee in the stinkinge ordure of sinne.

§ 10. The thridde cause that oghte moeve a man to Contricion, is drede of the day of dome, and of the horrible peynes of helle. For as seint Jerome seith: 'at every tyme that me remembreth of the day of dome, I quake; for whan I ete or drinke, or what-so that I do, evere semeth me that the trompe sowneth in myn ere: riseth up, ye that been dede, and cometh to the jugement.' O gode god, muchel oghte a man to drede swich a jugement, 'ther-as we shullen been alle,' as seint Poul seith, 'biforn the sete of oure lord Jesu Crist'; wher-as he shal make a general congregacion, wher-as no man may been absent. For certes, there availleth noon essoyne ne excusacion. And nat only that oure defautes shullen be juged, but eek that alle oure werkes shullen openly be knowe. And as seith Seint Bernard: 'ther ne shal no pledinge availle, ne no sleighte; we shullen yeven rekeninge of everich ydel word.' Ther shul we han a juge that may nat been deceived ne corrupt. And why? For, certes, alle our thoghtes been discovered as to him; ne for preyere ne for mede he shal nat been corrupt. And therfore seith Salomon: 'the wratthe of god ne wol nat spare no wight, for preyere ne for yifte'; and therfore, at the day of doom, ther nis noon hope to escape. Wherfore, as seith Seint Anselm: 'ful greet angwissh shul the sinful folk have at that tyme; ther shal the sterne and wrothe juge sitte above, and under him the horrible put of helle open to destroyen him that moot biknowen hise sinnes, whiche sinnes openly been shewed biforn god and biforn every creature. And on the left syde, mo develes than herte may bithinke, for to harie and drawe the sinful soules to the pyne of helle. And with-inne the hertes of folk shal be the bytinge conscience, and with-oute-forth shal be the world al brenninge. Whider shal thanne the wrecched sinful man flee to hyden him? Certes, he may nat hyden him; he moste come forth and shewen him.' For certes, as seith seint Jerome: 'the erthe shal casten him out of him, and the see also; and the eyr also, that shal be ful of thonder-clappes and lightninges.' Now sothly, who-so wel remembreth him of thise thinges, I gesse that his sinne shal nat turne him in-to delyt, but to greet sorwe, for drede of the peyne of helle. And therfore seith Job to god: 'suffre, lord, that I may a whyle biwaille and wepe, er I go with-oute returning to the derke lond, covered with the derknesse of deeth; to the lond of misese and of derknesse, where-as is the shadwe of deeth; where-as ther is noon ordre or ordinance, but grisly drede that evere shal laste.' Lo, here may ye seen that Job preyde respyt a whyle, to biwepe and waille his trespas; for soothly oon day of respyt is bettre than al the tresor of the world. And for-as-muche as a man may acquiten him-self biforn god by penitence in this world, and nat by tresor, therfore sholde he preye to god to yeve him respyt a whyle, to biwepe and biwaillen his trespas. For certes, al the sorwe that a man mighte make fro the beginning of the world, nis but a litel thing at regard of the sorwe of helle. The cause why that Job clepeth helle 'the lond of derknesse'; understondeth that he clepeth it 'londe' or erthe, for it is stable, and nevere shal faille; 'derk,' for he that is in helle hath defaute of light material. For certes, the derke light, that shal come out of the fyr that evere shal brenne, shal turne him al to peyne that is in helle; for it sheweth him to the horrible develes that him tormenten. 'Covered with the derknesse of deeth': that is to seyn, that he that is in helle shal have defaute of the sighte of god; for certes, the sighte of god is the lyf perdurable. 'The derknesse of deeth' been the sinnes that the wrecched man hath doon, whiche that destourben him to see the face of god; right as doth a derk cloude bitwixe us and the sonne. 'Lond of misese': by-cause that ther been three maneres of defautes, agayn three thinges that folk of this world han in this present lyf, that is to seyn, honours, delyces, and richesses. Agayns honour, have they in helle shame and confusion. For wel ye woot that men clepen 'honour' the reverence that man doth to man; but in helle is noon honour ne reverence. For certes, na-more reverence shal be doon there to a king than to a knave. For which god seith by the prophete Jeremye: 'thilke folk that me despysen shul been in despyt.' 'Honour' is eek cleped greet lordshipe; ther shal no man serven other but of harm and torment. 'Honour' is eek cleped greet dignitee and heighnesse; but in helle shul they been al fortroden of develes. And god seith: 'the horrible develes shulle goon and comen up-on the hevedes of the dampned folk.' And this is for-as-muche as, the hyer that they were in this present lyf, the more shulle they been abated and defouled in helle. Agayns the richesses of this world, shul they han misese of poverte; and this poverte shal been in foure thinges: in defaute of tresor, of which that David seith; 'the riche folk, that embraceden and oneden al hir herte to tresor of this world, shul slepe in the slepinge of deeth; and no-thing ne shul they finden in hir handes of al hir tresor.' And more-over, the miseise of helle shal been in defaute of mete and drinke. For god seith thus by Moyses; 'they shul been wasted with hunger, and the briddes of helle shul devouren hem with bitter deeth, and the galle of the dragon shal been hir drinke, and the venim of the dragon hir morsels.' And fortherover, hir miseise shal been in defaute of clothing: for they shulle be naked in body as of clothing, save the fyr in which they brenne and othere filthes; and naked shul they been of soule, of alle manere vertues, which that is the clothing of the soule. Where been thanne the gaye robes and the softe shetes and the smale shertes? Lo, what seith god of hem by the prophete Isaye: 'that under hem shul been strawed motthes, and hir covertures shulle been of wormes of helle.' And forther-over, hir miseise shal been in defaute of freendes; for he nis nat povre that hath goode freendes, but there is no freend; for neither god ne no creature shal been freend to hem, and everich of hem shal haten other with deedly hate. 'The sones and the doghtren shullen rebellen agayns fader and mooder, and kinrede agayns kinrede, and chyden and despysen everich of hem other,' bothe day and night, as god seith by the prophete Michias. And the lovinge children, that whylom loveden so fleshly everich other, wolden everich of hem eten other if they mighte. For how sholden they love hem togidre in the peyne of helle, whan they hated ech of hem other in the prosperitee of this lyf? For truste wel, hir fleshly love was deedly hate; as seith the prophete David: 'who-so that loveth wikkednesse he hateth his soule.' And who-so hateth his owene soule, certes, he may love noon other wight in no manere. And therefore, in helle is no solas ne no frendshipe, but evere the more fleshly kinredes that been in helle, the more cursinges, the more chydinges, and the more deedly hate ther is among hem. And forther-over, they shul have defaute of alle manere delyces; for certes, delyces been after the appetytes of the fyve wittes, as sighte, heringe, smellinge, savoringe, and touchinge. But in helle hir sighte shal be ful of derknesse and of smoke, and therfore ful of teres; and hir heringe, ful of waymentinge and of grintinge of teeth, as seith Jesu Crist; hir nosethirles shullen be ful of stinkinge stink. And as seith Isaye the prophete: 'hir savoring shal be ful of bitter galle.' And touchinge of al hir body, y-covered with 'fyr that nevere shal quenche, and with wormes that nevere shul dyen,' as god seith by the mouth of Isaye. And for-as-muche as they shul nat wene that they may dyen for peyne, and by hir deeth flee fro peyne, that may they understonden by the word of Job, that seith: 'ther-as is the shadwe of deeth.' Certes, a shadwe hath the lyknesse of the thing of which it is shadwe, but shadwe is nat the same thing of which it is shadwe. Right so fareth the peyne of helle; it is lyk deeth for the horrible anguissh, and why? For it peyneth hem evere, as though they sholde dye anon; but certes they shal nat dye. For as seith Seint Gregorie: 'to wrecche caytives shal be deeth with-oute deeth, and ende withouten ende, and defaute with-oute failinge. For hir deeth shal alwey liven, and hir ende shal everemo biginne, and hir defaute shal nat faille.' And therfore seith Seint John the Evangelist: 'they shullen folwe deeth, and they shul nat finde him; and they shul desyren to dye, and deeth shal flee fro hem.' And eek Job seith: that 'in helle is noon ordre of rule.' And al-be-it so that god hath creat alle thinges in right ordre, and no-thing with-outen ordre, but alle thinges been ordeyned and nombred; yet nathelees they that been dampned been no-thing in ordre, ne holden noon ordre. For the erthe ne shal bere hem no fruit. For, as the prophete David seith: 'god shal destroye the fruit of the erthe as fro hem'; ne water ne shal yeve hem no moisture; ne the eyr no refresshing, ne fyr no light. For as seith seint Basilie: 'the brenninge of the fyr of this world shal god yeven in helle to hem that been dampned; but the light and the cleernesse shal be yeven in hevene to hise children'; right as the gode man yeveth flesh to hise children, and bones to his houndes. And for they shullen have noon hope to escape, seith seint Job atte laste: that 'ther shal horrour and grisly drede dwellen with-outen ende.' Horrour is alwey drede of harm that is to come, and this drede shal evere dwelle in the hertes of hem that been dampned. And therefore han they lorn al hir hope, for sevene causes. First, for god that is hir juge shal be with-outen mercy to hem; ne they may nat plese him, ne noon of hise halwes; ne they ne may yeve no-thing for hir raunson; ne they have no vois to speke to him; ne they may nat flee fro peyne; ne they have no goodnesse in hem, that they mowe shewe to delivere hem fro peyne. And therfore seith Salomon: 'the wikked man dyeth; and whan he is deed, he shal have noon hope to escape fro peyne.' Who-so thanne wolde wel understande these peynes, and bithinke him weel that he hath deserved thilke peynes for his sinnes, certes, he sholde have more talent to syken and to wepe than for to singen and to pleye. For as that seith Salomon: 'who-so that hadde the science to knowe the peynes that been establissed and ordeyned for sinne, he wolde make sorwe.' 'Thilke science,' as seith seint Augustin, 'maketh a man to waymenten in his herte.'

§ 11. The fourthe point, that oghte maken a man to have contricion, is the sorweful remembrance of the good that he hath left to doon here in erthe; and eek the good that he hath lorn. Soothly, the gode werkes that he hath left, outher they been the gode werkes that he wroghte er he fel in-to deedly sinne, or elles the gode werkes that he wroghte while he lay in sinne. Soothly, the gode werkes, that he dide biforn that he fil in sinne, been al mortified and astoned and dulled by the ofte sinning. The othere gode werkes, that he wroghte whyl he lay in deedly sinne, they been outrely dede as to the lyf perdurable in hevene. Thanne thilke gode werkes that been mortified by ofte sinning, whiche gode werkes he dide whyl he was in charitee, ne mowe nevere quiken agayn with-outen verray penitence. And ther-of seith god, by the mouth of Ezechiel: that, 'if the rightful man returne agayn from his rightwisnesse and werke wikkednesse, shal he live?' Nay; for alle the gode werkes that he hath wroght ne shul nevere been in remembrance; for he shal dyen in his sinne. And up-on thilke chapitre seith seint Gregorie thus: 'that we shulle understonde this principally; that whan we doon deedly sinne, it is for noght thanne to rehercen or drawen in-to memorie the gode werkes that we han wroght biforn.' For certes, in the werkinge of the deedly sinne, ther is no trust to no good werk that we han doon biforn; that is to seyn, as for to have therby the lyf perdurable in hevene. But nathelees, the gode werkes quiken agayn, and comen agayn, and helpen, and availlen to have the lyf perdurable in hevene, whan we han contricion. But soothly, the gode werkes that men doon whyl they been in deedly sinne, for-as-muche as they were doon in deedly sinne, they may nevere quiken agayn. For certes, thing that nevere hadde lyf may nevere quikene; and nathelees, al-be-it that they ne availle noght to han the lyf perdurable, yet availlen they to abregge of the peyne of helle, or elles to geten temporal richesse, or elles that god wole the rather enlumine and lightne the herte of the sinful man to have repentance; and eek they availlen for to usen a man to doon gode werkes, that the feend have the lasse power of his soule. And thus the curteis lord Jesu Crist wole that no good werk be lost; for in somwhat it shal availle. But for-as-muche as the gode werkes that men doon whyl they been in good lyf, been al mortified by sinne folwinge; and eek, sith that alle the gode werkes that men doon whyl they been in deedly synne, been outrely dede as for to have the lyf perdurable; wel may that man, that no good werke ne dooth, singe thilke newe Frenshe song: '*Jay tout perdu mon temps et mon labour.*' For certes, sinne bireveth a man bothe goodnesse of nature and eek the goodnesse of grace. For soothly, the grace of the holy goost fareth lyk fyr, that may nat been ydel; for fyr faileth anoon as it forleteth his wirkinge, and right so grace fayleth anoon as it forleteth his werkinge. Than leseth the sinful man the goodnesse of glorie, that only is bihight to gode men that labouren and werken. Wel may he be sory thanne, that oweth al his lif to god as longe as he hath lived, and eek as longe as he shal live, that no goodnesse ne hath to paye with his dette to god, to whom he oweth al his lyf. For trust wel, 'he shal yeven acountes,' as seith seint Bernard, 'of alle the godes that han be yeven him in this present lyf, and how he hath hem despended; in so muche that ther shal nat perisse an heer of his heed, ne a moment of an houre ne shal nat perisse of his tyme, that he ne shal yeve of it a rekening.'

§ 12. The fifthe thing that oghte moeve a man to contricion, is remembrance of the passion that oure lord Jesu Crist suffred for oure sinnes. For, as seith seint Bernard: 'whyl that I live, I shal have remembrance of the travailles that oure lord Crist suffred in preching; his werinesse in travailling, hise temptacions whan he fasted, hise longe wakinges whan he preyde, hise teres whan that he weep for pitee of good peple; the wo and the shame and the filthe that men seyden to him; of the foule spitting that men spitte in his face, of the buffettes that men yaven him, of the foule mowes, and of the repreves that men to him seyden; of the nayles with whiche he was nailed to the croys, and of al the remenant of his passion that he suffred for my sinnes, and no-thing for his gilt.' And ye shul understonde, that in mannes sinne is every manere of ordre or ordinance turned up-so-doun. For it is sooth, that god, and reson, and sensualitee, and the body of man been so ordeyned, that everich of thise foure thinges sholde have lordshipe over that other; as thus: god sholde have lordshipe over reson, and reson over sensualitee, and sensualitee over the body of man. But sothly, whan man sinneth, al this ordre or ordinance is turned up-so-doun. And therfore thanne, for-as-muche as the reson of man ne wol nat be subget ne obeisant to god, that is his lord by right, therfore leseth it the lordshipe that it sholde have over sensualitee, and eek over the body of man. And why? For sensualitee rebelleth thanne agayns reson; and by that wey leseth reson the lordshipe over sensualitee and over the body. For right as reson is rebel to god, right so is bothe sensualitee rebel to reson and the body also. And certes, this disordinance and this rebellion oure lord Jesu Crist aboghte up-on his precious body ful dere, and herkneth in which wyse. For-as-muche thanne as reson is rebel to god, therfore is man worthy to have sorwe and to be deed. This suffred oure lord Jesu Crist for man, after that he hadde be bitraysed of his disciple, and distreyned and bounde, 'so that his blood brast out at every nail of hise handes,' as seith seint Augustin. And forther-over, for-as-muchel as reson of man ne wol nat daunte sensualitee whan it may, therfore is man worthy to have shame; and this suffred oure lord Jesu Crist for man, whan they spetten in his visage. And forther-over, for-as-muchel thanne as the caitif body of man is rebel bothe to reson and to sensualitee, therfore is it worthy the deeth. And this suffred oure lord Jesu Crist for man up-on the croys, where-as ther was no part of his body free, with-outen greet peyne and bitter passion. And al this suffred Jesu Crist, that nevere forfeted. And therfore resonably may be seyd of Jesu in this manere: 'to muchel am I peyned for the thinges that I nevere deserved, and to muche defouled for shendshipe that man is worthy to have.' And therfore may the sinful man wel seye, as seith seint Bernard: 'acursed be the bitternesse of my sinne, for which ther moste be suffred so muchel bitternesse.' For certes, after the diverse discordances of oure wikkednesses, was the passion of Jesu Crist ordeyned in diverse thinges, as thus. Certes, sinful mannes soule is bitraysed of the devel by coveitise of temporel prosperitee, and scorned by deceite whan he cheseth fleshly delyces; and yet is it tormented by inpacience of adversitee, and bispet by servage and subjeccion of sinne; and atte laste it is slayn fynally. For this disordinaunce of sinful man was Jesu Crist first bitraysed, and after that was he bounde, that cam for to unbynden us of sinne and peyne. Thanne was he biscorned, that only sholde han been honoured in alle thinges and of alle thinges. Thanne was his visage, that oghte be desired to be seyn of al man-kinde, in which visage aungels desyren to looke, vileynsly bispet. Thanne was he scourged that no-thing hadde agilt; and fynally, thanne was he crucified and slayn. Thanne was acompliced the word of Isaye: 'he was wounded for oure misdedes, and defouled for oure felonies.' Now sith that Jesu Crist took up-on him-self the peyne of alle oure wikkednesses, muchel oghte sinful man wepen and biwayle, that for hise sinnes goddes sone of hevene sholde al this peyne endure.

§ 13. The sixte thing that oghte moeve a man to contricion, is the hope of three thynges; that is to seyn, foryifnesse of sinne, and the yifte of grace wel for to do, and the glorie of hevene, with which god shal guerdone a man for hise gode dedes. And for-as-muche as Jesu Crist yeveth us thise yiftes of his largesse and of his sovereyn bountee, therfore is he cleped *Jesus Nazarenus rex Judeorum.* Jesus is to seyn 'saveour' or 'salvacion,' on whom men shul hope to have foryifnesse of sinnes, which that is proprely salvacion of sinnes. And therfore seyde the aungel to Joseph: 'thou shalt clepen his name Jesus, that shal saven his peple of hir sinnes.' And heer-of seith seint Peter: 'ther is noon other name under hevene that is yeve to any man, by which a man may be saved, but only Jesus.' *Nazarenus* is as muche for to seye as 'florisshinge,' in which a man shal hope, that he that yeveth him remission of sinnes shal yeve him eek grace wel for to do. For in the flour is hope of fruit in tyme cominge; and in foryifnesse of sinnes hope of grace wel for to do. 'I was atte dore of thyn herte,' seith Jesus, 'and cleped for to entre; he that openeth to me shal have foryifnesse of sinne. I wol entre in-to him by my grace, and soupe with him,' by the goode werkes that he shal doon; whiche werkes been the foode of god; 'and he shal soupe with me,' by the grete joye that I shal yeven him. Thus shal man hope, for hise werkes of penaunce, that god shall yeven him his regne; as he bihoteth him in the gospel

§ 14. Now shal a man understonde, in which manere shal been his contricion. I seye, that it shal been universal and total; this is to seyn, a man shal be verray repentant for alle hise sinnes that he hath doon in delyt of his thoght; for delyt is ful perilous. For ther been two manere of consentinges; that oon of hem is cleped consentinge of affeccion, whan a man is moeved to do sinne, and delyteth him longe for to thinke on that sinne; and his reson aperceyveth it wel, that it is sinne agayns the lawe of god, and yet his reson refreyneth nat his foul delyt or talent, though he see wel apertly that it is agayns the reverence of god; al-though his reson ne consente noght to doon that sinne in dede, yet seyn somme doctours that swich delyt that dwelleth longe, it is ful perilous, al be it nevere so lite. And also a man sholde sorwe, namely, for al that evere he hath desired agayn the lawe of god with perfit consentinge of his reson; for ther-of is no doute, that it is deedly sinne in consentinge. For certes, ther is no deedly sinne, that it nas first in mannes thought, and after that in his delyt; and so forth in-to consentinge and in-to dede. Wherfore I seye, that many men ne repenten hem nevere of swiche thoghtes and delytes, ne nevere shryven hem of it, but only of the dede of grete sinnes outward. Wherfore I seye, that swiche wikked delytes and wikked thoghtes been subtile bigyleres of hem that shullen be dampned. More-over, man oghte to sorwe for hise wikkede wordes as wel as for hise wikkede dedes; for certes, the repentance of a singuler sinne, and nat repente of alle hise othere sinnes, or elles repenten him of alle hise othere sinnes, and nat of a singuler sinne, may nat availle. For certes, god almighty is al good; and ther-fore he foryeveth al, or elles right noght. And heer-of seith seint Augustin:

'I woot certeinly that god is enemy to everich sinnere'; and how thanne? He that observeth o sinne, shal he have foryifnesse of the remenaunt of hise othere sinnes? Nay. And forther-over, contricion sholde be wonder sorweful and anguissous, and therfore yeveth him god pleynly his mercy; and therfore, whan my soule was anguissous with-inne me, I hadde remembrance of god that my preyere mighte come to him. Forther-over, contricion moste be continuel, and that man have stedefast purpos to shryven him, and for to amenden him of his lyf. For soothly, whyl contricion lasteth, man may evere have hope of foryifnesse; and of this comth hate of sinne, that destroyeth sinne bothe in himself, and eek in other folk, at his power. For which seith David: 'ye that loven god hateth wikkednesse.' For trusteth wel, to love god is for to love that he loveth, and hate that he hateth.

§ 15. The laste thing that man shal understonde in contricion is this; wher-of avayleth contricion. I seye, that som tyme contricion delivereth a man fro sinne; of which that David seith: 'I seye,' quod David, that is to seyn, 'I purposed fermely to shryve me; and thow, Lord, relesedest my sinne.' And right so as contricion availleth noght, with-outen sad purpos of shrifte, if man have oportunitee, right so litel worth is shrifte or satisfaccion with-outen contricion. And more-over, contricion destroyeth the prison of helle, and maketh wayk and feble alle the strengthes of the develes, and restoreth the yiftes of the holy goost and of alle gode vertues; and it clenseth the soule of sinne, and delivereth the soule fro the peyne of helle, and fro the companye of the devel, and fro the servage of sinne, and restoreth it to alle godes espirituels, and to the companye and communion of holy chirche. And forther-over, it maketh him that whylom was sone of ire to be sone of grace; and alle thise thinges been preved by holy writ. And therfore, he that wolde sette his entente to thise thinges, he were ful wys; for soothly, he ne sholde nat thanne in al his lyf have corage to sinne, but yeven his body and al his herte to the service of Jesu Crist, and ther-of doon him hommage. For soothly, oure swete lord Jesu Crist hath spared us so debonairly in our folies, that if he ne hadde pitee of mannes soule, a sory song we mighten alle singe.

Explicit prima pars Penitentie; et sequitur secunda pars eiusdem.

§ 16. The seconde partie of Penitence is Confession, that is signe of contricion. Now shul ye understonde what is Confession, and whether it oghte nedes be doon or noon, and whiche thinges been covenable to verray Confession.

§ 17. First shaltow understonde that Confession is verray shewinge of sinnes to the preest; this is to seyn 'verray,' for he moste confessen him of alle the condiciouns that bilongen to his sinne, as ferforth as he can. Al moot be seyd, and no thing excused ne hid ne forwrapped, and noght avaunte him of his gode werkes. And forther over, it is necessarie to understonde whennes that sinnes springen, and how they encresen, and whiche they been.

§ 18. Of the springinge of sinnes seith seint Paul in this wise: that 'right as by a man sinne entred first in-to this world, and thurgh that sinne deeth, right so thilke deeth entred in-to alle men that sinneden.' And this man was Adam, by whom sinne entred in-to this world whan he brak the comaundement of god. And therfore, he that first was so mighty that he sholde not have dyed, bicam swich oon that he moste nedes dye, whether he wolde or noon; and all his progenie in this world that in thilke man sinneden. Loke that in th'estaat of innocence, when Adam and Eve naked weren in paradys, and no-thing ne hadden shame of hir nakednesse, how that the serpent, that was most wyly of alle othere bestes that god hadde maked, seyde to the womman: 'why comaunded god to yow, ye sholde nat eten of every tree in paradys?' The womman answerde: 'of the fruit,' quod she, 'of the trees in paradys we feden us; but soothly, of the fruit of the tree that is in the middel of paradys, god forbad us for to ete, ne nat touchen it, lest per-aventure we should dyen.' The serpent seyde to the womman : 'nay, nay, ye shul nat dyen of deeth ; for sothe, god woot, that what day that ye eten ther-of, youre eyen shul opene, and ye shul been as goddes, knowinge good and harm.' The womman thanne saugh that the tree was good to feding, and fair to the eyen, and delytable to the sighte ; she tok of the fruit of the tree, and eet it, and yaf to hir housbonde, and he eet ; and anoon the eyen of hem bothe openeden. And whan that they knewe that they were naked, they sowed of fige-leves a manere of breches to hiden hir membres. There may ye seen that deedly sinne hath first suggestion of the feend, as sheweth here by the naddre ; and afterward, the delyt of the flesh, as sheweth here by Eve ; and after that, the consentinge of resoun, as sheweth here by Adam. For trust wel, thogh so were that the feend tempted Eve, that is to seyn the flesh, and the flesh hadde delyt in the beautee of the fruit defended, yet certes, til that resoun, that is to seyn, Adam, consented to the etinge of the fruit, yet stood he in th'-estaat of innocence. Of thilke Adam toke we thilke sinne original ; for of him fleshly descended be we alle, and engendred of vile and corrupt matere. And whan the soule is put in our body, right anon is contract original sinne ; and that, that was erst but only peyne of concupiscence, is afterward bothe peyne and sinne. And therfore be we alle born sones of wratthe and of dampnacion perdurable, if it nere baptesme that we receyven, which binimeth us the culpe ; but for sothe, the peyne dwelleth with us, as to temptacion, which peyne highte concupiscence. Whan it is wrongfully disposed or ordeyned in man, it maketh him coveite, by coveitise of flesh, fleshly sinne, by sighte of hise eyen as to erthely thinges, and coveitise of hynesse by pryde of herte.

§ 19. Now as for to speken of the firste coveitise, that is, concupiscence after the lawe of oure membres, that weren lawefulliche y-maked and by rightful jugement of god; I seye, for-as-muche as man is nat obeisaunt to god, that is his lord, therfore is the flesh to him disobeisaunt thurgh concupiscence, which yet is cleped norissinge of sinne and occasion of sinne. Therfore, al the whyle that a man hath in him the peyne of concupiscence, it is impossible but he be tempted somtyme, and moeved in his flesh to sinne. And this thing may nat faille as longe as he liveth; it may wel wexe feble and faille, by vertu of baptesme and by the grace of god thurgh penitence; but fully ne shal it nevere quenche, that he ne shal som tyme be moeved in himself, but-if he were al refreyded by siknesse, or by malefice of sorcerie or colde drinkes. For lo, what seith seint Paul: 'the flesh coveiteth agayn the spirit, and the spirit agayn the flesh; they been so contrarie and so stryven, that a man may nat alwey doon as he wolde.' The same seint Paul, after his grete penaunce in water and in lond (in water by night and by day, in greet peril and in greet peyne, in lond, in famine, in thurst, in cold and clothlees, and ones stoned almost to the deeth) yet seyde he: 'allas! I, caytif man, who shal delivere me fro the prisoun of my caytif body?' And seint Jerome, whan he longe tyme hadde woned in desert, where-as he hadde no companye but of wilde bestes, where-as he ne hadde no mete but herbes and water to his drinke, ne no bed but the naked erthe, for which his flesh was blak as an Ethiopen for hete and ny destroyed for cold, yet seyde he: that 'the brenninge of lecherie boiled in al his body.' Wherfore I woot wel sikerly, that they been deceyved that seyn, that they ne be nat tempted in hir body. Witnesse on Seint Jame the Apostel, that seith: that 'every wight is tempted in his owen concupiscence;' that is to seyn, that everich of us hath matere and occasion to be tempted of the norissinge of sinne that is in his body. And therfore seith Seint John the Evaungelist: 'if that we seyn that we beth with-oute sinne, we deceyve us-selve, and trouthe is nat in us.'

§ 20. Now shal ye understonde in what manere that sinne wexeth or encreseth in man. The firste thing is thilke norissinge of sinne, of which I spak biforn, thilke fleshly concupiscence. And after that comth the subjeccion of the devel, this is to seyn, the develes bely, with which he bloweth in man the fyr of fleshly concupiscence. And after that, a man bithinketh him whether he wol doon, or no, thilke thing to which he is tempted. And thanne, if that a man withstonde and weyve the firste entysinge of his flesh and of the feend, thanne is it no sinne; and if it so be that he do nat so, thanne feleth he anon a flambe of delyt. And thanne is it good to be war, and kepen him wel, or elles he wol falle anon in-to consentinge of sinne; and thanne wol he do it, if he may have tyme and place. And of this matere seith Moyses by the devel in this manere: 'the feend seith, I wole chace and pursue the man by wikked suggestion, and I wole hente him by moevynge or stiringe of sinne. I wol departe my pryse or my praye by deliberacion, and my lust shal been accompliced in delyt; I wol drawe my swerd in consentinge:' for certes, right as a swerd departeth a thing in two peces, right so consentinge departeth god fro man: 'and thanne wol I sleen him with myn hand in dede of sinne'; thus seith the feend. For certes, thanne is a man al deed in soule. And thus is sinne accompliced by temptacion, by delyt, and by consentinge; and thanne is the sin cleped actuel.

§ 21. For sothe, sinne is in two maneres; outher it is venial, or deedly sinne. Soothly, whan man loveth any creature more than Jesu Crist oure creatour, thanne is it deedly sinne. And venial synne is it, if man love Jesu Crist lasse than him oghte. For sothe, the dede of this venial sinne is ful perilous; for it amenuseth the love that men sholde han to god more and more. And therfore, if a man charge him-self with manye swiche venial sinnes, certes, but-if so be that he som tyme descharge him of hem by shrifte, they mowe ful lightly amenuse in him al the love that he hath to Jesu Crist; and in this wise skippeth venial in-to deedly sinne. For certes, the more that a man chargeth his soule with venial sinnes, the more is he enclyned to fallen in-to deedly sinne. And therfore, lat us nat be necligent to deschargen us of venial sinnes. For the proverbe seith: that manye smale maken a greet. And herkne this ensample. A greet wawe of the see comth som-tyme with so greet a violence that it drencheth the ship. And the same harm doth somtyme the smale dropes of water, that entren thurgh a litel crevace in-to the thurrok, and in-to the botme of the ship, if men be so necligent that they ne descharge hem nat by tyme. And therfore, althogh ther be a difference bitwixe thise two causes of drenchinge, algates the ship is dreynt. Right so fareth it somtyme of deedly sinne, and of anoyouse veniale sinnes, whan they multiplye in a man so greetly, that thilke worldly thinges that he loveth, thurgh whiche he sinneth venially, is as greet in his herte as the love of god, or more. And therfore, the love of every thing, that is nat biset in god ne doon principally for goddes sake, al-though that a man love it lasse than god, yet is it venial sinne; and deedly sinne, whan the love of any thing weyeth in the herte of man as muchel as the love of god, or more. 'Deedly sinne,' as seith seint Augustin, 'is, whan a man turneth his herte fro god, which that is verray sovereyn bountee, that may nat chaunge, and yeveth his herte to thing that may chaunge and flitte'; and certes, that is every thing, save god of hevene. For sooth is, that if a man yeve his love, the which that he oweth al to god with al his herte, un-to a creature, certes, as muche of his love as he yeveth to thilke creature, so muche he bireveth fro god; and therfore doth he sinne. For he, that is dettour to god, ne yeldeth nat to god al his dette, that is to seyn, al the love of his herte.

§ 22. Now sith man understondeth generally, which is venial sinne, thanne is it covenable to tellen specially of sinnes whiche that many a man per-aventure ne demeth hem nat sinnes, and ne shryveth him nat of the same thinges; and yet nathelees they been sinnes. Soothly, as thise clerkes wryten, this is to seyn, that at every tyme that a man eteth or drinketh more than suffyseth to the sustenaunce of his body, in certein he dooth sinne. And eek whan he speketh more than nedeth, it is sinne. Eke whan he herkneth nat benignely the compleint of the povre. Eke whan he is in hele of body and wol nat faste, whan othere folk faste, with-outen cause resonable. Eke whan he slepeth more than nedeth, or whan he comth by thilke enchesoun to late to chirche, or to othere werkes of charite. Eke whan he useth his wyf, with-outen sovereyn desyr of engendrure, to the honour of god, or for the entente to yelde to his wyf the dette of his body. Eke whan he wol nat visite the sike and the prisoner, if he may. Eke if he love wyf or child, or other worldly thing, more than resoun requyreth. Eke if he flatere or blandishe more than him oghte for any necessitee. Eke if he amenuse or withdrawe the almesse of the povre. Eke if he apparailleth his mete more deliciously than nede is, or ete it to hastily by likerousnesse. Eke if he tale vanitees at chirche or at goddes service, or that he be a talker of ydel wordes of folye or of vileinye; for he shal yelden acountes of it at the day of dome. Eke whan he biheteth or assureth to do thinges that he may nat perfourne. Eke whan that he, by lightnesse or folie, misseyeth or scorneth his neighebore. Eke whan he hath any wikked suspecion of thing, ther he ne woot of it no soothfastnesse. Thise thinges and mo with-oute nombre been sinnes, as seith seint Augustin.

Now shal men understonde, that al-be-it so that noon erthely man may eschue alle venial sinnes, yet may he refreyne him by the brenninge love that he hath to oure lord Jesu Crist, and by preyeres and confession and othere gode werkes, so that it shal but litel greve. For, as seith seint Augustin: 'if a man love god in swiche manere, that al that evere he doth is in the love of god, and for the love of god verraily, for he brenneth in the love of god: loke, how muche that a drope of water that falleth in a fourneys ful of fyr anoyeth or greveth, so muche anoyeth a venial sinne un-to a man that is parfit in the love of Jesu Crist.' Men may also refreyne venial sinne by receyvinge worthily of the precious body of Jesu Crist; by receyving eek of holy water; by almesdede; by general confession of *Confiteor* at masse and at complin; and by blessinge of bisshopes and of preestes, and by othere gode werkes.

Explicit secunda pars Penitentie.

Sequitur de Septem Peccatis Mortalibus et eorum dependenciis circumstanciis et speciebus.

§ 23. Now is it bihovely thing to telle whiche been the deedly sinnes, this is to seyn, chieftaines of sinnes; alle they renne in o lees, but in diverse maneres. Now been they cleped chieftaines for-as-muche as they been chief, and springers of alle othere sinnes. Of the roote of thise sevene sinnes thanne is Pryde, the general rote of alle harmes; for of this rote springen certein braunches, as Ire, Envye, Accidie or Slewthe, Avarice or Coveitise (to commune understondinge), Glotonye, and Lecherye. And everich of thise chief sinnes hath hise braunches and hise twigges, as shal be declared in hir chapitres folwinge.

De Superbia.

§ 24. And thogh so be that no man can outrely telle the nombre of the twigges and of the harmes that cometh of Pryde, yet wol I shewe a partie of hem, as ye shul understonde. Ther is Inobedience, Avauntinge, Ipocrisie, Despyt, Arrogance, Impudence, Swellinge of herte, Insolence, Elacion, Impacience, Strif, Contumacie, Presumpcion, Irreverence, Pertinacie, Veyne Glorie; and many another twig that I can nat declare. Inobedient, is he that disobeyeth for despyt to the comandements of god and to hise sovereyns, and to his goostly fader. Avauntour, is he that bosteth of the harm or of the bountee that he hath doon. Ipocrite, is he that hydeth to shewe him swiche as he is, and sheweth him swiche as he noght is. Despitous, is he that hath desdeyn of his neighebore, that is to seyn, of his evene-cristene, or hath despyt to doon that him oghte to do. Arrogant, is he that thinketh that he hath thilke bountees in him that he hath noght, or weneth that he sholde have hem by hise desertes; or elles he demeth that he be that he nis nat. Impudent, is he that for his pride hath no shame of hise sinnes. Swellinge of herte, is whan a man rejoyseth him of harm that he hath doon. Insolent, is he that despyseth in his jugement alle othere folk as to regard of his value, and of his conning, and of his speking, and of his bering. Elacion, is whan he ne may neither suffre to have maister ne felawe. Impacient, is he that wol nat been y-taught ne undernome of his vyce, and by stryf werreyeth trouthe witingly, and deffendeth his folye. *Contumax*, is he that thurgh his indignacion is agayns everich auctoritee or power of hem that been hise sovereyns. Presumpcion, is whan a man undertaketh an empryse that him oghte nat do, or elles that he may nat do; and that is called Surquidrie. Irreverence, is whan men do nat honour thereas hem oghte to doon, and waiten to be reverenced. Pertinacie, is whan man deffendeth his folye, and trusteth to muchel in his owene wit. Veyne glorie, is for to have pompe and delyt in his temporel hynesse, and glorifie him in this worldly estaat. Janglinge, is whan men speken to muche biforn folk, and clappen as a mille, and taken no kepe what they seye.

§ 25. And yet is ther a privee spece of Pryde, that waiteth first to be salewed er he wole salewe, al be he lasse worth than that other is, per-aventure; and eek he waiteth or desyreth to sitte, or elles to goon above him in the wey, or kisse pax, or been encensed, or goon to offring biforn his neighebore, and swiche semblable thinges; agayns his duetee, per-aventure, but that he hath his herte and his entente in swich a proud desyr to be magnifyed and honoured biforn the peple.

§ 26. Now been ther two maneres of Pryde; that oon of hem is with-inne the herte of man, and that other is withoute. Of whiche soothly thise forseyde thinges, and mo than I have seyd, apertenen to pryde that is in the herte of man; and that othere speces of pryde been with-oute. But natheles that oon of thise speces of pryde is signe of that other, right as the gaye leefsel atte taverne is signe of the wyn that is in the celer. And this is in manye thinges: as in speche and contenaunce, and in outrageous array of clothing; for certes, if ther ne hadde be no sinne in clothing, Crist wolde nat have noted and spoken of the clothing of thilke riche man in the gospel. And, as seith Seint Gregorie, that precious clothing is coupable for the derthe of it, and for his softenesse, and for his strangenesse and degysinesse, and for the superfluitee, or for the inordinat scantnesse of it. Allas! may men nat seen, as in oure dayes, the sinful costlewe array of clothinge, and namely in to muche superfluitee, or elles in to desordinat scantnesse?

§ 27. As to the firste sinne, that is in superfluitee of clothinge, which that maketh it so dere, to harm of the peple; nat only the cost of embroudinge, the degyse endentinge or barringe, oundinge, palinge, windinge, or bendinge, and semblable wast of clooth in vanitee; but ther is also costlewe furringe in hir gounes, so muche pounsoninge of chisels to maken holes, so muche dagginge of sheres; forth-with the superfluitee in lengthe of the forseide gounes, trailinge in the dong and in the myre, on horse and eek on fote, as wel of man as of womman, that al thilke trailing is verraily as in effect wasted, consumed, thredbare, and roten with donge, rather than it is yeven to the povre; to greet damage of the forseyde povre folk. And that in sondry wyse: this is to seyn, that the more that clooth is wasted, the more it costeth to the peple for the scantnesse; and forther-over, if so be that they wolde yeven swich pounsoned and dagged clothing to the povre folk, it is nat convenient to were for hir estaat, ne suffisant to bete hir necessitee, to kepe hem fro the distemperance of the firmament. Upon that other syde, to speken of the horrible disordinat scantnesse of clothing, as been thise cutted sloppes or hainselins, that thurgh hir shortnesse ne covere nat the shameful membres of man, to wikked entente. Allas! somme of hem shewen the boce of hir shap, and the horrible swollen membres, that semeth lyk the maladie of hirnia, in the wrappinge of hir hoses ; and eek the buttokes of hem faren as it were the hindre part of a she-ape in the fulle of the mone. And more-over, the wrecched swollen membres that they shewe thurgh the degysinge, in departinge of hir hoses in whyt and reed, semeth that half hir shameful privee membres weren flayn. And if so be that they departen hire hoses in othere colours, as is whyt and blak, or whyt and blew, or blak and reed, and so forth ; thanne semeth it, as by variance of colour, that half the partie of hir privee membres were corrupt by the fyr of seint Antony, or by cancre, or by other swich meschaunce. Of the hindre part of hir buttokes, it is ful horrible for to see. For certes, in that partie of hir body ther-as they purgen hir stinkinge ordure, that foule partie shewe they to the peple proudly in despyt of honestetee, the which honestetee that Jesu Crist and hise freendes observede to shewen in hir lyve. Now as of the outrageous array of wommen, god woot, that though the visages of somme of hem seme ful chaast and debonaire, yet notifie they in hir array of atyr likerousnesse and pryde. I sey nat that honestetee in clothinge of man or womman is uncovenable, but certes the superfluitee or disordinat scantitee of clothinge is reprevable. Also the sinne of aornement or of apparaille is in thinges that apertenen to rydinge, as in to manye delicat horses that been holden for delyt, that been so faire, fatte, and costlewe ; and also to many a vicious knave that is sustened by cause of hem ; in to curious harneys, as in sadeles, in crouperes, peytrels, and brydles covered with precious clothing and riche, barres and plates of gold and of silver. For which god seith by Zakarie the prophete, 'I wol confounde the ryderes of swiche horses.' This folk taken litel reward of the rydinge of goddes sone of hevene, and of his harneys whan he rood up-on the asse, and ne hadde noon other harneys but the povre clothes of hise disciples ; ne we ne rede nat that evere he rood on other beest. I speke this for the sinne of superfluitee, and nat for reasonable honestetee, wnan reson it requyreth. And forther, certes pryde is greetly notified in holdinge of greet meinee, whan they be of litel profit or of right no profit. And namely, whan that meinee is felonous and damageous to the peple, by hardinesse of heigh lordshipe or by wey of offices. For certes, swiche lordes sellen thanne hir lordshipe to the devel of helle, whanne they sustenen the wikkednesse of hir meinee. Or elles whan this folk of lowe degree, as thilke that holden hostelries, sustenen the thefte of hir hostilers, and that is in many manere of deceites. Thilke manere of folk been the flyes that folwen the hony, or elles the houndes that folwen the careyne. Swiche forseyde folk stranglen spiritually hir lordshipes; for which thus seith David the prophete, 'wikked deeth mote come up-on thilke lordshipes, and god yeve that they mote descenden in-to helle al doun; for in hir houses been iniquitees and shrewednesses,' and nat god of hevene. And certes, but-if they doon amendement, right as god yaf his benison to Laban by the service of Jacob, and to Pharao by the service of Joseph, right so god wol yeve his malison to swiche lordshipes as sustenen the wikkednesse of hir servaunts, but-if they come to amendement. Pryde of the table appereth eek ful ofte; for certes, riche men been cleped to festes, and povre folk been put awey and rebuked. Also in excesse of diverse metes and drinkes; and namely, swiche manere bake metes and dish-metes, brenninge of wilde fyr, and peynted and castelled with papir, and semblable wast; so that it is abusion for to thinke. And eek in to greet preciousnesse of vessel and curiositee of minstralcie, by whiche a man is stired the more to delyces of luxurie, if so be that he sette his herte the lasse up-on oure lord Jesu Crist, certein it is a sinne; and certeinly the delyces mighte been so grete in this caas, that man mighte lightly falle by hem in-to deedly sinne. The especes that sourden of Pryde, soothly whan they sourden of malice ymagined, avysed, and forncast, or elles of usage, been deedly synnes, it is no doute. And whan they sourden by freletee unavysed sodeinly, and sodeinly withdrawen ayein, al been they grevouse sinnes, I gesse that they ne been nat deedly. Now mighte men axe wher-of that Pryde sourdeth and springeth, and I seye: somtyme it springeth of the goodes of nature, and som-tyme of the goodes of fortune, and som-tyme of the goodes of grace. Certes, the goodes of nature stonden outher in goodes of body or in goodes of soule. Certes, goodes of body been hele of body, as strengthe, delivernesse, beautee, gentrye, franchise. Goodes of nature of the soule been good wit, sharp understondynge, subtil engin, vertu naturel, good memorie. Goodes of fortune been richesses, highe degrees of lordshipes, preisinges of the peple. Goodes of grace been science, power to suffre spirituel travaille, benignitee, vertuous contemplacion, withstondinge of temptacion, and semblable thinges. Of whiche for-seyde goodes, certes it is a ful greet folye a man to pryden him in any of hem alle. Now as for to speken of goodes of nature god woot that som-tyme we han hem in nature as muche to oure damage as to oure profit. As, for to speken of hele of body; certes it passeth ful lightly, and eek it is ful ofte encheson of the siknesse of oure soule; for god woot, the flesh is a ful greet enemy to the soule: and therfore, the more that the body is hool, the more be we in peril to falle. Eke for to pryde him in his strengthe of body, it is an heigh folye; for certes, the flesh coveiteth agayn the spirit, and ay the more strong that the flesh is, the sorier may the soule be: and, over al this, strengthe of body and worldly hardinesse causeth ful ofte many a man to peril and meschaunce. Eek for to pryde him of his gentrye is ful greet folye; for ofte tyme the gentrye of the body binimeth the gentrye of the soule; and eek we ben alle of o fader and of o moder; and alle we been of o nature roten and corrupt, both riche and povre. For sothe, oo manere gentrye is for to preise, that apparailleth mannes corage with vertues and moralitees, and maketh him Cristes child. For truste wel, that over what man sinne hath maistrie, he is a verray cherl to sinne.

§ 28. Now been ther generale signes of gentilesse; as eschewinge of vyce and ribaudye and servage of sinne, in word, in werk, and contenance; and usinge vertu, curteisye, and clennesse, and to be liberal, that is to seyn, large by mesure; for thilke that passeth mesure is folye and sinne. Another is, to remembre him of bountee that he of other folk hath receyved. Another is, to be benigne to hise goode subgetis; wherfore, as seith Senek, 'ther is no-thing more covenable to a man of heigh estaat than debonairetee and pitee. And therfore thise flyes that men clepeth bees, whan they maken hir king, they chesen oon that hath no prikke wherwith he may stinge.' Another is, a man to have a noble herte and a diligent, to attayne to heighe vertuouse thinges. Now certes, a man to pryde him in the goodes of grace is eek an outrageous folye; for thilke yiftes of grace that sholde have turned him to goodnesse and to medicine, turneth him to venim and to confusion, as seith seint Gregorie. Certes also, who-so prydeth him in the goodes of fortune, he is a ful greet fool; for som-tyme is a man a greet lord by the morwe, that is a caitif and a wrecche er it be night: and somtyme the richesse of a man is cause of his deeth; somtyme the delyces of a man is cause of the grevous maladye thurgh which he dyeth. Certes, the commendacion of the peple is somtyme ful fals and ful brotel for to triste; this day they preyse, tomorwe they blame. God woot, desyr to have commendacion of the peple hath caused deeth to many a bisy man.

Remedium contra peccatum Superbie.

§ 29. Now sith that so is, that ye han understonde what is pryde, and whiche been the speces of it, and whennes pride sourdeth and springeth; now shul ye understonde which is the remedie agayns the sinne of pryde, and that is, humilitee or mekenesse. That is a vertu, thurgh which a man hath verray knoweleche of him-self, and holdeth of him-self no prys ne deyntee as in regard of hise desertes, consideringe evere his freletee. Now been ther three maneres of humilitee;

as humilitee in herte, and another humilitee in his mouth; the thridde in hise werkes. The humilitee in herte is in foure maneres: that oon is, whan a man holdeth him-self as noght worth biforn god of hevene. Another is, whan he ne despyseth noon other man. The thridde is, whan he rekketh nat thogh men holde him noght worth. The ferthe is, whan he nis nat sory of his humiliacion. Also, the humilitee of mouth is in foure thinges: in attempree speche, and in humblesse of speche, and whan he biknoweth with his owene mouth that he is swich as him thinketh that he is in his herte. Another is, whan he preiseth the bountee of another man, and nothing ther-of amenuseth. Humilitee eek in werkes is in foure maneres: the firste is, whan he putteth othere men biforn him. The seconde is, to chese the loweste place over-al. The thridde is, gladly to assente to good conseil. The ferthe is, to stonde gladly to the award of hise sovereyns, or of him that is in hyer degree; certein, this is a greet werk of humilitee.

Sequitur de Inuidia.

§ 30. After Pryde wol I speken of the foule sinne of Envye, which is, as by the word of the philosophre, sorwe of other mannes prosperitee; and after the word of seint Augustin, it is sorwe of other mannes wele, and joye of othere mennes harm. This foule sinne is platly agayns the holy goost. Al-be-it so that every sinne is agayns the holy goost, yet nathelees, for as muche as bountee aperteneth proprely to the holy goost, and Envye comth proprely of malice, therfore it is proprely agayn the bountee of the holy goost. Now hath malice two speces, that is to seyn, hardnesse of herte in wikkednesse, or elles the flesh of man is so blind, that he considereth nat that he is in sinne, or rekketh nat that he is in sinne; which is the hardnesse of the devel. That other spece of malice is, whan a man werreyeth trouthe, whan he woot that it is trouthe. And eek, whan he werreyeth the grace that god hath yeve to his neighebore; and al this is by Envye. Certes, thanne is

Envye the worste sinne that is. For soothly, alle othere sinnes been som-tyme only agayns o special vertu; but certes, Envye is agayns alle vertues and agayns alle goodnesses; for it is sory of alle the bountees of his neighebore; and in this manere it is divers from alle othere sinnes. For wel unnethe is ther any sinne that it ne hath som delyt in itself, save only Envye, that evere hath in itself anguish and sorwe. The speces of Envye been thise: ther is first, sorwe of other mannes goodnesse and of his prosperitee; and prosperitee is kindely matere of joye; thanne is Envye a sinne agayns kinde. The seconde spece of Envye is joye of other mannes harm; and that is proprely lyk to the devel, that evere rejoyseth him of mannes harm. Of thise two speces comth bakbyting; and this sinne of bakbyting or detraccion hath certeine speces, as thus. Som man preiseth his neighebore by a wikke entente; for he maketh alwey a wikked knotte atte laste ende. Alwey he maketh a 'but' atte laste ende, that is digne of more blame, than worth is al the preisinge. The seconde spece is, that if a man be good and dooth or seith a thing to good entente, the bakbyter wol turne all thilke goodnesse up-so-doun to his shrewed entente. The thridde is, to amenuse the bountee of his neighebore. The fourthe spece of bakbyting is this; that if men speke goodnesse of a man, thanne wol the bakbyter seyn, 'parfey, swich a man is yet bet than he'; in dispreisinge of him that men preise. The fifte spece is this; for to consente gladly and herkne gladly to the harm that men speke of other folk. This sinne is ful greet, and ay encreseth after the wikked entente of the bakbyter. After bakbyting cometh grucching or murmuracion; and somtyme it springeth of inpacience agayns god, and somtyme agayns man. Agayns god it is, whan a man gruccheth agayn the peynes of helle, or agayns poverte, or los of catel, or agayn reyn or tempest; or elles gruccheth that shrewes han prosperitee, or elles for that goode men han adversitee. And alle thise thinges sholde men suffre paciently, for they comen by the rightful jugement and ordinance of god. Somtyme comth grucching of avarice; as Judas grucched agayns the Magdaleyne, whan she enoynte the heved of oure lord Jesu Crist with hir precious oynement. This maner murmure is swich as whan man gruccheth of goodnesse that him-self dooth, or that other folk doon of hir owene catel. Somtyme comth murmure of Pryde; as whan Simon the Pharisee grucched agayn the Magdaleyne, whan she approched to Jesu Crist, and weep at his feet for hir sinnes. And somtyme grucching sourdeth of Envye; whan men discovereth a mannes harm that was privee, or bereth him on hond thing that is fals. Murmure eek is ofte amonges servaunts, that grucchen whan hir sovereyns bidden hem doon leveful thinges; and, for-as-muche as they dar nat openly withseye the comaundements of hir sovereyns, yet wol they seyn harm, and grucche, and murmure prively for verray despyt; whiche wordes men clepen the develes *Pater-noster*, though so be that the devel ne hadde nevere *Pater-noster*, but that lewed folk yeven it swich a name. Som tyme grucching comth of ire or prive hate, that norisseth rancour in herte, as afterward I shal declare. Thanne cometh eek bitternesse of herte; thurgh which bitternesse every good dede of his neighebor semeth to him bitter and unsavory. Thanne cometh discord, that unbindeth alle manere of frendshipe. Thanne comth scorninge, as whan a man seketh occasioun to anoyen his neighebor, al do he never so weel. Thanne comth accusinge, as whan man seketh occasion to anoyen his neighebor, which that is lyk to the craft of the devel, that waiteth bothe night and day to accusen us alle. Thanne comth malignitee, thurgh which a man anoyeth his neighebor prively if he may; and if he noght may, algate his wikked wil ne shal nat wante, as for to brennen his hous prively, or empoysone or sleen hise bestes, and semblable thinges.

Remedium contra peccatum Inuidie.

§ 31. Now wol I speke of the remedie agayns this

foule sinne of Envye. First, is the love of god principal, and loving of his neighebor as him-self; for soothly, that oon ne may nat been withoute that other. And truste wel, that in the name of thy neighebore thou shalt understonde the name of thy brother: for certes alle we have o fader fleshly, and o moder, that is to seyn, Adam and Eve; and eek o fader espirituel, and that is god of hevene. Thy neighebore artow holden for to love, and wilne him alle goodnesse; and therfore seith god, 'love thy neighebore as thyselve,' that is to seyn, to salvacion bothe of lyf and of soule. And more-over, thou shalt love him in word, and in benigne amonestinge, and chastysinge; and conforten him in hise anoyes, and preye for him with al thyn herte. And in dede thou shalt love him in swich wyse, that thou shalt doon to him in charitee as thou woldest that it were doon to thyn owene persone. And therfore, thou ne shalt doon him no damage in wikked word, ne harm in his body, ne in his catel, ne in his soule, by entysing of wikked ensample. Thou shalt nat desyren his wyf, ne none of hise thinges. Understond eek, that in the name of neighebor is comprehended his enemy. Certes man shal loven his enemy by the comandement of god; and soothly thy frend shaltow love in God. I seye, thyn enemy shaltow love for goddes sake, by his comandement. For if it were reson that a man sholde haten his enemy, for sothe god nolde nat receiven us to his love that been hise enemys. Agayns three manere of wronges that his enemy dooth to hym, he shal doon three thinges, as thus. Agayns hate and rancour of herte, he shal love him in herte. Agayns chyding and wikkede wordes, he shal preye for his enemy. And agayn the wikked dede of his enemy, he shal doon him bountee. For Crist seith, 'loveth youre enemys, and preyeth for hem that speke yow harm; and eek for hem that yow chacen and pursewen, and doth bountee to hem that yow haten.' Lo, thus comaundeth us oure lord Jesu Crist, to do to oure enemys. For soothly, nature dryveth us to loven oure freendes, and parfey, oure enemys han more nede to love than our freendes; and they that more nede have, certes, to hem shal men doon goodnesse; and certes, in thilke dede have we remembrance of the love of Jesu Crist, that deyde for hise enemys. And in-as-muche as thilke love is the more grevous to perfourne, in-so-muche is the more gretter the merite; and therfore the lovinge of oure enemy hath confounded the venim of the devel. For right as the devel is disconfited by humilitee, right so is he wounded to the deeth by love of oure enemy. Certes, thanne is love the medicine that casteth out the venim of Envye fro mannes herte. The speces of this pas shullen be more largely in hir chapitres folwinge declared.

Sequitur de Ira.

§ 32. After Envye wol I discryven the sinne of Ire. For soothly, who-so hath envye upon his neighebor, anon he wole comunly finde him a matere of wratthe, in word or in dede, agayns him to whom he hath envye. And as wel comth Ire of Pryde, as of Envye; for soothly, he that is proude or envious is lightly wrooth.

§ 33. This sinne of Ire, after the discryving of seint Augustin, is wikked wil to been avenged by word or by dede. Ire, after the philosophre, is the fervent blood of man y-quiked in his herte, thurgh which he wole harm to him that he hateth. For certes the herte of man, by eschaufinge and moevinge of his blood, wexeth so trouble, that he is out of alle jugement of resoun. But ye shal understonde that Ire is in two maneres; that oon of hem is good, and that other is wikked. The gode Ire is by jalousye of goodnesse, thurgh which a man is wrooth with wikkednesse and agayns wikkednesse; and therfore seith a wys man, that 'Ire is bet than pley.' This Ire is with debonairetee, and it is wrooth withouten bitternesse; nat wrooth agayns the man, but wrooth with the misdede of the man; as seith the prophete David, *Irascimini et nolite peccare.* Now understondeth, that wikked Ire is in two maneres, that is to seyn, sodeyn Ire or hastif Ire, withouten avisement and consentinge of resoun. The mening and the sens of this is, that the resoun of man ne consente nat to thilke sodeyn Ire; and thanne it is venial. Another Ire is ful wikked, that comth of felonye of herte avysed and cast biforn; with wikked wil to do vengeance, and ther.o his resoun consenteth; and soothly this is deedly sinne. This Ire is so displesant to god, that it troubleth his hous and chaceth the holy goost out of mannes soule, and wasteth and destroyeth the lyknesse of god, that is to seyn, the vertu that is in mannes soule; and put in him the lyknesse of the devel, and binimeth the man fro god that is his rightful lord. This Ire is a ful greet plesaunce to the devel; for it is the develes fourneys, that is eschaufed with the fyr of helle. For certes, right so as fyr is more mighty to destroyen erthely thinges than any other element, right so Ire is mighty to destroyen alle spirituel thinges. Loke how that fyr of smale gledes, that been almost dede under asshen, wollen quike agayn whan they been touched with brimstoon; right so Ire wol everemo quiken agayn, whan it is touched by the pryde that is covered in mannes herte. For certes fyr ne may nat comen out of no-thing, but-if it were first in the same thing naturelly; as fyr is drawen out of flintes with steel. And right so as pryde is ofte tyme matere of Ire, right so is rancour norice and keper of Ire. Ther is a maner tree, as seith seint Isidre, that whan men maken fyr of thilke tree, and covere the coles of it with asshen, soothly the fyr of it wol lasten al a yeer or more. And right so fareth it of rancour; whan it is ones conceyved in the hertes of som men, certein, it wol lasten peraventure from oon Estre-day unto another Estre-day, and more. But certes, thilke man is ful fer fro the mercy of god al thilke while.

§ 34. In this forseyde develes fourneys ther forgen three shrewes: Pryde, that ay bloweth and encreseth the fyr by chydinge and wikked wordes. Thanne stant Envye, and holdeth the hote iren upon the herte of man with a peire of longe tonges of long rancour. And thanne stant the sinne of contumelie or stryf and cheeste, and batereth and forgeth by vileyns reprevinges.

Certes, this cursed sinne anoyeth bothe to the man him-self and eek to his neighebor. For soothly, almost al the harm that any man dooth to his neighebore comth of wratthe. For certes, outrageous wratthe doth al that evere the devel him comaundeth ; for he ne spareth neither Crist, ne his swete mooder. And in his outrageous anger and Ire, allas ! allas ! ful many oon at that tyme feleth in his herte ful wikkedly, bothe of Crist and of alle hise halwes. Is nat this a cursed vice ? Yis, certes. Allas ! it binimeth from man his wit and his resoun, and al his debonaire lyf espirituel that sholde kepen his soule. Certes, it binimeth eek goddes due lordshipe, and that is mannes soule, and the love of hise neighebores. It stryveth eek alday agayn trouthe. It reveth him the quiete of his herte, and subverteth his soule.

§ 35. Of Ire comen thise stinkinge engendrures : first hate, that is old wratthe ; discord, thurgh which a man forsaketh his olde freend that he hath loved ful longe. And thanne cometh werre, and every manere of wrong that man dooth to his neighebore, in body or in catel. Of this cursed sinne of Ire cometh eek manslaughtre. And understonde wel, that homicyde, that is manslaughtre, is in dyverse wyse. Som manere of homicyde is spirituel, and som is bodily. Spirituel manslaughtre is in six thinges. First, by hate ; as seint John seith, 'he that hateth his brother is homicyde.' Homicyde is eek by bakbytinge ; of whiche bakbyteres seith Salomon, that 'they han two swerdes with whiche they sleen hir neighebores.' For soothly, as wikke is to binime his good name as his lyf. Homicyde is eek, in yevinge of wikked conseil by fraude ; as for to yeven conseil to areysen wrongful custumes and taillages. Of whiche seith Salomon, 'Leon rorynge and bere hongry been lyke to the cruel lordshipes,' in withholdinge or abregginge of the shepe (or the hyre), or of the wages of servaunts, or elles in usure or in withdrawinge of the almesse of povre folk. For which the wyse man seith, 'fedeth him that almost dyeth for honger' ; for soothly, but-if thou fede him, thou sleest him ; and alle thise been deedly sinnes. Bodily manslaughtre is, whan thow sleest him with thy tonge in other manere; as whan thou comandest to sleen a man, or elles yevest him conseil to sleen a man. Manslaughtre in dede is in foure maneres. That oon is by lawe; right as a justice dampneth him that is coupable to the deeth. But lat the justice be war that he do it rightfully, and that he do it nat for delyt to spille blood, but for kepinge of rightwisenesse. Another homicyde is, that is doon for necessitee, as whan o man sleeth another in his defendaunt, and that he ne may noon otherwise escape from his owene deeth. But certeinly, if he may escape withouten manslaughtre of his adversarie, and sleeth him, he doth sinne, and he shal bere penance as for deedly sinne. Eek if a man, by caas or aventure, shete an arwe or caste a stoon with which he sleeth a man, he is homicyde. Eek if a womman by necligence overlyeth hir child in hir sleping, it is homicyde and deedly sinne. Eek whan man destourbeth concepcion of a child, and maketh a womman outher bareyne by drinkinge venemouse herbes, thurgh which she may nat conceyve, or sleeth a child by drinkes wilfully, or elles putteth certeine material thinges in hir secree places to slee the child; or elles doth unkindely sinne, by which man or womman shedeth hir nature in manere or in place ther-as a child may nat be conceived; or elles, if a womman have conceyved and hurt hir-self, and sleeth the child, yet is it homicyde. What seye we eek of wommen that mordren hir children for drede of worldly shame? Certes, an horrible homicyde. Homicyde is eek if a man approcheth to a womman by desir of lecherye, thurgh which the child is perissed, or elles smyteth a womman witingly, thurgh which she leseth hir child. Alle thise been homicydes and horrible deedly sinnes. Yet comen ther of Ire manye mo sinnes, as wel in word as in thoght and in dede; as he that arretteth upon god, or blameth god, of thing of which he is him-self gilty; or despyseth god and alle hise halwes, as doon thise cursede hasardours in diverse contrees. This cursed sinne doon they, whan they felen in hir hertes ful wikkedly of god and of hise halwes. Also, whan they treten unreverently the sacrement of the auter, thilke sinne is so greet, that unnethe may it been relesed, but that the mercy of god passeth alle hise werkes; it is so greet and he so benigne. Thanne comth of Ire attry angre; whan a man is sharply amonested in his shrifte to forleten his sinne, than wole he be angry and answeren hokerly and angrily, and deffenden or excusen his sinne by unstedefastnesse of his flesh; or elles he dide it for to holde companye with hise felawes, or elles, he seith, the fend entyced him; or elles he dide it for his youthe, or elles his complexioun is so corageous, that he may nat forbere; or elles it is his destinee, as he seith, unto a certein age; or elles, he seith, it cometh him of gentillesse of hise auncestres; and semblable thinges. Alle this manere of folk so wrappen hem in hir sinnes, that they ne wol nat delivere hem-self. For soothly, no wight that excuseth him wilfully of his sinne may nat been delivered of his sinne, til that he mekely biknoweth his sinne. After this, thanne cometh swering, that is expres agayn the comandement of god; and this bifalleth ofte of anger and of Ire. God seith: 'thou shalt nat take the name of thy lord god in veyn or in ydel.' Also oure lord Jesu Crist seith by the word of seint Mathew: '*Nolite iurare omnino*: ne wol ye nat swere in alle manere; neither by hevene, for it is goddes trone; ne by erthe, for it is the bench of his feet; ne by Jerusalem, for it is the citee of a greet king; ne by thyn heed, for thou mayst nat make an heer whyt ne blak. But seyeth by youre word, "ye, ye," and "nay, nay"; and what that is more, it is of yvel,' seith Crist. For Cristes sake, ne swereth nat so sinfully, in dismembringe of Crist by soule, herte, bones, and body. For certes, it semeth that ye thinke that the cursede Jewes ne dismembred nat y-nough the preciouse persone of Crist, but ye dismembre him more. And if so be that the lawe compelle yow to swere, thanne rule yow after the lawe of god in youre swering, as seith Jeremye *quarto capitulo*, '*Iurabis in veritate, in iudicio et in iusticia*: thou shalt kepe three condicions; thou shalt swere in trouthe, in doom, and in rightwisnesse.' This is to seyn, thou shalt swere sooth; for every lesinge is agayns Crist. For Crist is verray trouthe. And think wel this, that every greet swerere, nat compelled lawefully to swere, the wounde shal nat departe from his hous whyl he useth swich unleveful swering. Thou shalt sweren eek in doom, whan thou art constreyned by thy domesman to witnessen the trouthe. Eek thou shalt nat swere for envye ne for favour, ne for mede, but for rightwisnesse; for declaracioun of it to the worship of god and helping of thyne evene-cristene. And therfore, every man that taketh goddes name in ydel, or falsly swereth with his mouth, or elles taketh on him the name of Crist, to be called a Cristene man, and liveth agayns Cristes livinge and his techinge, alle they taken goddes name in ydel. Loke eek what seint Peter seith, *Actuum quarto capitulo*, '*Non est aliud nomen sub celo*,' &c. 'Ther nis noon other name,' seith seint Peter, 'under hevene, yeven to men, in which they mowe be saved;' that is to seyn, but the name of Jesu Crist. Take kepe eek how that the precious name of Crist, as seith seint Paul *ad Philipenses secundo*, '*In nomine Jesu*, &c.: that in the name of Jesu every knee of hevenely creatures, or erthely, or of helle sholden bowe'; for it is so heigh and so worshipful, that the cursede feend in helle sholde tremblen to heren it y-nempned. Thanne semeth it, that men that sweren so horribly by his blessed name, that they despyse him more boldely than dide the cursede Jewes, or elles the devel, that trembleth whan he hereth his name.

§ 36. Now certes, sith that swering, but-if it be lawefully doon, is so heighly deffended, muche worse is forswering falsly, and yet nedelees.

§ 37. What seye we eek of hem that delyten hem in swering, and holden it a gentrie or a manly dede to swere grete othes? And what of hem that, of verray usage, ne cesse nat to swere grete othes, al be the cause nat worth a straw? Certes, this is horrible sinne. Sweringe sodeynly with-oute avysement is eek a sinne. But lat us go now to thilke horrible swering of adjuracioun and conjuracioun, as doon thise false enchauntours or nigromanciens in bacins ful of water, or in a bright swerd, in a cercle, or in a fyr, or in a shulderboon of a sheep. I can nat seye but that they doon cursedly and damnably, agayns Crist and al the feith of holy chirche.

§ 38. What seye we of hem that bileven in divynailes, as by flight or by noyse of briddes, or of bestes, or by sort, by geomancie, by dremes, by chirkinge of dores, or crakkinge of houses, by gnawynge of rattes, and swich manere wrecchednesse? Certes, al this thing is deffended by god and by al holy chirche. For which they been acursed, til they come to amendement, that on swich filthe setten hir bileve. Charmes for woundes or maladye of men, or of bestes, if they taken any effect, it may be peraventure that god suffreth it, for folk sholden yeve the more feith and reverence to his name.

§ 39. Now wol I speken of lesinges, which generally is fals significacioun of word, in entente to deceyven his evene-cristene. Som lesinge is of which ther comth noon avantage to no wight: and som lesinge turneth to the ese or profit of o man, and to disese and damage of another man. Another lesinge is for to saven his lyf or his catel. Another lesinge comth of delyt for to lye, in which delyt they wol forge a long tale, and peynten it with alle circumstaunces, where al the ground of the tale is fals. Som lesinge comth, for he wole sustene his word; and som lesinge comth of recchelesnesse, with-outen avysement; and semblable thinges.

§ 40. Lat us now touche the vyce of flateringe, which ne comth nat gladly but for drede or for coveitise. Flaterye is generally wrongful preisinge. Flatereres been the develes norices, that norissen hise children with milk of losengerie. For sothe, Salomon seith, that 'flaterie is wors than detraccioun.' For somtyme detraccion maketh an hautein man be the more humble, for he dredeth detraccion ; but certes flaterye, that maketh a man to enhauncen his herte and his contenaunce. Flatereres been the develes enchauntours ; for they make a man to wene of him-self be lyk that he nis nat lyk. They been lyk to Judas that bitraysed [god ; and thise flatereres bitraysen] a man to sellen him to his enemy, that is, to the devel. Flatereres been the develes chapelleyns, that singen evere *Placebo.* I rekene flaterye in the vyces of Ire ; for ofte tyme, if o man be wrooth with another, thanne wol he flatere som wight to sustene him in his querele.

§ 41. Speke we now of swich cursinge as comth of irous herte. Malisoun generally may be seyd every maner power of harm. Swich cursinge bireveth man fro the regne of god, as seith seint Paul. And ofte tyme swich cursinge wrongfully retorneth agayn to him that curseth, as a brid that retorneth agayn to his owene nest. And over alle thing men oghten eschewe to cursen hir children, and yeven to the devel hir engendrure, as ferforth as in hem is ; certes, it is greet peril and greet sinne.

§ 42. Lat us thanne speken of chydinge and reproche, whiche been ful grete woundes in mannes herte ; for they unsowen the semes of frendshipe in mannes herte. For certes, unnethes may a man pleynly been accorded with him that hath him openly revyled and repreved in disclaundre. This is a ful grisly sinne, as Crist seith in the gospel. And tak kepe now, that he that repreveth his neighebor, outher he repreveth him by som harm of peyne that he hath on his body, as 'mesel,' 'croked harlot,' or by som sinne that he dooth. Now if he repreve him by harm of peyne, thanne turneth the repreve to Jesu Crist ; for peyne is sent by the rightwys sonde of god, and by his suffrance, be it meselrie, or maheym, or maladye. And if he repreve him uncharitably of sinne, as, 'thou holour,' 'thou dronkelewe harlot,' and so forth ; thanne aperteneth that to the rejoysinge of the devel, that evere hath joye that men doon sinne. And certes, chydinge may nat come but out of a vileyns herte. For after the habundance of the herte speketh the mouth ful ofte. And ye shul understonde that loke, by any wey, whan any man shal chastyse another, that he be war from chydinge or reprevinge. For trewely, but he be war, he may ful lightly quiken the fyr of angre and of wratthe, which that he sholde quenche, and per-aventure sleeth him which that he mighte chastyse with benignitee. For as seith Salomon, 'the amiable tonge is the tree of lyf,' that is to seyn, of lyf espirituel: and sothly, a deslavee tonge sleeth the spirites of him that repreveth, and eek of him that is repreved. Lo, what seith seint Augustin: 'ther is no-thing so lyk the develes child as he that ofte chydeth.' Seint Paul seith eek: 'I, servant of god, bihove nat to chyde.' And how that chydinge be a vileyns thing bitwixe alle manere folk, yet it is certes most uncovenable bitwixe a man and his wyf; for there is nevere reste. And therfore seith Salomon, 'an hous that is uncovered and droppinge, and a chydinge wyf, been lyke.' A man that is in a droppinge hous in many places, though he eschewe the droppinge in o place, it droppeth on him in another place; so fareth it by a chydinge wyf. But she chyde him in o place, she wol chyde him in another. And therfore, 'bettre is a morsel of breed with joye than an hous ful of delyces, with chydinge,' seith Salomon. Seint Paul seith: 'O ye wommen, be ye subgetes to youre housbondes as bihoveth in god; and ye men, loveth youre wyves.' *Ad Colossenses, tertio.*

§ 43. Afterward speke we of scorninge, which is a wikked sinne; and namely, whan he scorneth a man for hise gode werkes. For certes, swiche scorneres faren lyk the foule tode, that may nat endure to smelle the sote savour of the vyne whanne it florissheth. Thise scorneres been parting felawes with the devel; for they han joye whan the devel winneth, and sorwe whan he leseth. They been adversaries of Jesu Crist; for they haten that he loveth, that is to seyn, salvacion of soule.

§ 44. Speke we now of wikked conseil; for he that wikked conseil yeveth is a traytour. For he deceyveth him that trusteth in him, *ut Achitofel ad Absolonem.* But natheless, yet is his wikked conseil first agayn him-self. For, as seith the wyse man, every fals livinge hath this propertee in him-self, that he that wole anoye another man, he anoyeth first him-self. And men shul understonde, that man shal nat taken his conseil of fals folk, ne of angry folk, or grevous folk, ne of folk that loven specially to muchel hir owene profit, ne to muche worldly folk, namely, in conseilinge of soules.

§ 45. Now comth the sinne of hem that sowen and maken discord amonges folk, which is a sinne that Crist hateth outrely ; and no wonder is. For he deyde for to make concord. And more shame do they to Crist, than dide they that him crucifyede ; for god loveth bettre, that frendshipe be amonges folk, than he dide his owene body, the which that he yaf for unitee. Therfore been they lykned to the devel, that evere been aboute to maken discord.

§ 46. Now comth the sinne of double tonge ; swiche as speken faire biforn folk, and wikkedly bihinde ; or elles they maken semblant as though they speke of good entencioun, or elles in game and pley, and yet they speke of wikked entente.

§ 47. Now comth biwreying of conseil, thurgh which a man is defamed ; certes, unnethe may he restore the damage.

Now comth manace, that is an open folye ; for he that ofte manaceth, he threteth more than he may perfourne ful ofte tyme.

Now cometh ydel wordes, that is with-outen profit of him that speketh tho wordes, and eek of him that herkneth tho wordes. Or elles ydel wordes been tho that been nedelees, or with-outen entente of naturel profit. And al-be-it that ydel wordes been som tyme venial sinne, yet sholde men douten hem ; for we shul yeve rekeninge of hem bifore god.

Now comth janglinge, that may nat been withoute sinne. And, as seith Salomon, 'it is a sinne of apert folye.' And therfore a philosophre seyde, whan men axed him how that men sholde plese the peple; and he answerde, 'do many gode werkes, and spek fewe jangles.'

After this comth the sinne of japeres, that been the develes apes; for they maken folk to laughe at hir japerie, as folk doon at the gaudes of an ape. Swiche japeres deffendeth seint Paul. Loke how that vertuouse wordes and holy conforten hem that travaillen in the service of Crist; right so conforten the vileyns wordes and knakkes of japeris hem that travaillen in the service of the devel. Thise been the sinnes that comen of the tonge, that comen of Ire and of othere sinnes mo.

Sequitur remedium contra peccatum Ire.

§ 48. The remedye agayns Ire is a vertu that men clepen Mansuetude, that is Debonairetee; and eek another vertu, that men callen Pacience or Suffrance.

§ 49. Debonairetee withdraweth and refreyneth the stiringes and the moevynges of mannes corage in his herte, in swich manere that they ne skippe nat out by angre ne by Ire. Suffrance suffreth swetely alle the anoyaunces and the wronges that men doon to man outward. Seint Jerome seith thus of debonairetee, that 'it doth noon harm to no wight, ne seith; ne for noon harm that men doon or seyn, he ne eschaufeth nat agayns his resoun.' This vertu som-tyme comth of nature; for, as seith the philosophre, 'a man is a quik thing, by nature debonaire and tretable to goodnesse; but whan debonairetee is enformed of grace, thanne is it the more worth.'

§ 50. Pacience, that is another remedye agayns Ire, is a vertu that suffreth swetely every mannes goodnesse, and is nat wrooth for noon harm that is doon to him. The philosophre seith, that 'pacience is thilke vertu that suffreth debonairely alle the outrages of adversitee and every wikked word.' This vertu maketh a man lyk to god, and maketh him goddes owene dere child, as seith Crist. This vertu disconfiteth thyn enemy. And therfore seith the wyse man, 'if thou wolt venquisse thyn enemy, lerne to suffre.' And thou shalt understonde, that man suffreth foure manere of grevances in outward thinges, agayns the whiche foure he moot have foure manere of paciences.

§ 51. The firste grevance is of wikkede wordes; thilke suffrede Jesu Crist with-outen grucching, ful paciently, whan the Jewes despysed and repreved him ful ofte. Suffre thou therfore paciently; for the wyse man seith: 'if thou stryve with a fool, though the fool be wrooth or though he laughe, algate thou shalt have no reste.' That other grevance outward is to have damage of thy catel. Ther-agayns suffred Crist ful paciently, whan he was despoyled of al that he hadde in this lyf, and that nas but hise clothes. The thridde grevance is a man to have harm in his body. That suffred Crist ful paciently in al his passioun. The fourthe grevance is in outrageous labour in werkes. Wherfore I seye, that folk that maken hir servants to travaillen to grevously, or out of tyme, as on halydayes, soothly they do greet sinne. Heer-agayns suffred Crist full paciently, and taughte us pacience, whan he bar up-on his blissed shulder the croys, up-on which he sholde suffren despitous deeth. Heer may men lerne to be pacient; for certes, noght only Cristen men been pacient for love of Jesu Crist, and for guerdoun of the blisful lyf that is perdurable; but certes, the olde payens, that nevere were Cristene, commendeden and useden the vertu of pacience.

§ 52. A philosophre up-on a tyme, that wolde have beten his disciple for his grete trespas, for which he was greetly amoeved, and broghte a yerde to scourge the child; and whan this child saugh the yerde, he seyde to his maister, 'what thenke ye to do?' 'I wol bete thee,' quod the maister, 'for thy correccion.' 'For sothe,' quod the child, 'ye oghten first correcte youre-self, that han lost al youre pacience for the gilt of a child.' 'For sothe,' quod the maister al wepinge, 'thou seyst sooth; have thou the yerde, my dere sone, and correcte me for myn inpacience.' Of Pacience comth Obedience, thurgh which a man is obedient to

Crist and to alle hem to whiche he oghte to been obedient in Crist. And understond wel that obedience is perfit, whan that a man doth gladly and hastily, with good herte entierly, al that he sholde do. Obedience generally, is to perfourne the doctrine of god and of his sovereyns, to whiche him oghte to ben obeisaunt in alle rightwysnesse.

Sequitur de Accidia.

§ 53. After the sinnes of Envie and of Ire, now wol I speken of the sinne of Accidie. For Envye blindeth the herte of a man, and Ire troubleth a man ; and Accidie maketh him hevy, thoghtful, and wrawe. Envye and Ire maken bitternesse in herte ; which bitternesse is moder of Accidie, and binimeth him the love of all goodnesse. Thanne is Accidie the anguissh of a trouble herte ; and seint Augustin seith : 'it is anoy of goodnesse and joye of harm.' Certes, this is a dampnable sinne ; for it doth wrong to Jesu Crist, in-as-muche as it binimeth the service that men oghte doon to Crist with alle diligence, as seith Salomon. But Accidie dooth no swich diligence ; he dooth alle thing with anoy, and with wrawnesse, slaknesse, and excusacioun, and with ydelnesse and unlust ; for which the book seith : 'acursed be he that doth the service of god necligently.' Thanne is Accidie enemy to everich estaat of man ; for certes, the estaat of man is in three maneres. Outher it is th'estaat of innocence, as was th'estaat of Adam biforn that he fil into sinne ; in which estaat he was holden to wirche, as in heryinge and adouringe of god. Another estaat is the estaat of sinful men, in which estaat men been holden to laboure in preyinge to god for amendement of hir sinnes, and that he wole graunte hem to arysen out of hir sinnes. Another estaat is th'estaat of grace, in which estaat he is holden to werkes of penitence ; and certes, to alle thise thinges is Accidie enemy and contrarie. For he loveth no bisinesse at al. Now certes, this foule sinne Accidie is eek a ful greet enemy to the lyflode of the body ; for it ne hath no purveaunce agayn temporel necessitee ; for it forsleweth and forsluggeth, and destroyeth alle goodes temporeles by reccheleesnesse.

§ 54. The fourthe thinge is, that Accidie is lyk to hem that been in the peyne of helle, by-cause of hir slouthe and of hir hevinesse; for they that been dampned been so bounde, that they ne may neither wel do ne wel thinke. Of Accidie comth first, that a man is anoyed and encombred for to doon any goodnesse, and maketh that god hath abhominacion of swich Accidie, as seith seint Johan.

§ 55. Now comth Slouthe, that wol nat suffre noon hardnesse ne no penaunce. For soothly, Slouthe is so tendre, and so delicat, as seith Salomon, that he wol nat suffre noon hardnesse ne penaunce, and therfore he shendeth al that he dooth. Agayns this rotenherted sinne of Accidie and Slouthe sholde men exercise hem-self to doon gode werkes, and manly and vertuously cacchen corage wel to doon; thinkinge that oure lord Jesu Crist quyteth every good dede, be it never so lyte. Usage of labour is a greet thing; for it maketh, as seith seint Bernard, the laborer to have stronge armes and harde sinwes; and Slouthe maketh hem feble and tendre. Thanne comth drede to biginne to werke any gode werkes; for certes, he that is enclyned to sinne, him thinketh it is so greet an empryse for to undertake to doon werkes of goodnesse, and casteth in his herte that the circumstaunces of goodnesse been so grevouse and so chargeaunt for to suffre, that he dar nat undertake to do werkes of goodnesse, as seith seint Gregorie.

§ 56. Now comth wanhope, that is despeir of the mercy of god, that comth somtyme of to muche outrageous sorwe, and somtyme of to muche drede: imagininge that he hath doon so muche sinne, that it wol nat availlen him, though he wolde repenten him and forsake sinne: thurgh which despeir or drede he abaundoneth al his herte to every maner sinne, as seith seint Augustin. Which dampnable sinne, if that it continue un-to his ende, it is cleped sinning in the holy gost. This horrible sinne is so perilous, that he that is despeired, ther nis no felonye ne no sinne that he douteth for to do; as shewed wel by Judas. Certes, aboven alle sinnes thanne is this sinne most displesant to Crist, and most adversarie. Soothly, he that despeireth him is lyk the coward championn recreant, that seith creant withoute nede. Allas! allas! nedeles is he recreant and nedeles despeired. Certes, the mercy of god is evere redy to every penitent, and is aboven alle hise werkes. Allas! can nat a man bithinke him on the gospel of seint Luk, 15., where-as Crist seith that 'as wel shal ther be joye in hevene upon a sinful man that doth penitence, as up-on nynety and nyne rightful men that neden no penitence?' Loke forther, in the same gospel, the joye and the feste of the gode man that hadde lost his sone, whan his sone with repentaunce was retourned to his fader. Can they nat remembren hem eek, that, as seith seint Luk *xxiii*° *capitulo*, how that the theef that was hanged bisyde Jesu Crist, seyde: 'Lord, remembre of me, whan thou comest in-to thy regne?' 'For sothe,' seyde Crist, 'I seye to thee, to-day shaltow been with me in Paradys.' Certes, ther is noon so horrible sinne of man, that it ne may, in his lyf, be destroyed by penitence, thurgh vertu of the passion and of the deeth of Crist. Allas! what nedeth man thanne to been despeired, sith that his mercy so redy is and large? Axe and have. Thanne cometh Sompnolence, that is, sluggy slombringe, which maketh a man be hevy and dul, in body and in soule; and this sinne comth of Slouthe. And certes, the tyme that, by wey of resoun, men sholde nat slepe, that is by the morwe; but-if ther were cause resonable. For soothly, the morwe-tyde is most covenable, a man to seye his preyeres, and for to thinken on god, and for to honoure god, and to yeven almesse to the povre, that first cometh in the name of Crist. Lo! what seith Salomon: 'who-so wolde by the morwe awaken and seke me, he shal finde.' Thanne cometh Necligence, or recchelesnesse, that rekketh of no-thing. And how that ignoraunce be moder of all harm, certes, Necligence is the norice. Necligence ne doth no fors, whan he shal doon a thing, whether he do it weel or baddely

§ 57. Of the remedie of thise two sinnes, as seith the wyse man, that 'he that dredeth god, he spareth nat to doon that him oghte doon.' And he that loveth god, he wol doon diligence to plese god by his werkes, and abaundone him-self, with al his might, wel for to doon. Thanne comth ydelnesse, that is the yate of alle harmes. An ydel man is lyk to a place that hath no walles; the develes may entre on every syde and sheten at him at discovert, by temptacion on every syde. This ydelnesse is the thurrok of alle wikked and vileyns thoghtes, and of alle jangles, trufles, and of alle ordure. Certes, the hevene is yeven to hem that wol labouren, and nat to ydel folk. Eek David seith: that 'they ne been nat in the labour of men, ne they shul nat been whipped with men,' that is to seyn, in purgatorie. Certes, thanne semeth it, they shul be tormented with the devel in helle, but-if they doon penitence.

§ 58. Thanne comth the sinne that men clepen *Tarditas*, as whan a man is to latrede or taryinge, er he wole turne to god; and certes, that is a greet folye. He is lyk to him that falleth in the dich, and wol nat aryse. And this vyce comth of a fals hope, that he thinketh that he shal live longe; but that hope faileth ful ofte.

§ 59. Thanne comth Lachesse: that is he, that whan he biginneth any good werk, anon he shal forleten it and stinten; as doon they that han any wight to governe, and ne taken of him na-more kepe, anon as they finden any contrarie or any anoy. Thise been the newe shepherdes, that leten hir sheep witingly go renne to the wolf that is in the breres, or do no fors of hir owene governaunce. Of this comth poverte and destruccioun, bothe of spirituel and temporel thinges. Thanne comth a manere coldnesse, that freseth al the herte of man. Thanne comth undevocioun, thurgh which a man is so blent, as seith seint Bernard, and hath swiche langour in soule, that he may neither rede ne singe in holy chirche, ne here ne thinke of no devocioun, ne travaille with hise handes in no good werk, that it nis him unsavory and al apalled. Thanne wexeth he slow and slombry, and sone wol be wrooth, and sone is enclyned to hate and to envye. Thanne comth the sinne of worldly sorwe, swich as is cleped *tristicia*, that sleeth man, as seint Paul seith. For certes, swich sorwe werketh to the deeth of the soule and of the body also; for ther-of comth, that a man is anoyed of his owene lyf. Wherfore swich sorwe shorteth ful ofte the lyf of a man, er that his tyme be come by wey of kinde.

Remedium contra peccatum Accidie.

§ 60. Agayns this horrible sinne of Accidie, and the branches of the same, ther is a vertu that is called *Fortitudo* or Strengthe; that is, an affeccioun thurgh which a man despyseth anoyous thinges. This vertu is so mighty and so vigorous, that it dar withstonde mightily and wysely kepen him-self fro perils that been wikked, and wrastle agayn the assautes of the devel. For it enhaunceth and enforceth the soule, right as Accidie abateth it and maketh it feble. For this *Fortitudo* may endure by long suffraunce the travailles that been convenable.

§ 61. This vertu hath manye speces; and the firste is cleped Magnanimitee, that is to seyn, greet corage. For certes, ther bihoveth greet corage agains Accidie, lest that it ne swolwe the soule by the sinne of sorwe, or destroye it by wanhope. This vertu maketh folk to undertake harde thinges and grevouse thinges, by hir owene wil, wysely and resonably. And for as muchel as the devel fighteth agayns a man more by queyntise and by sleighte than by strengthe, therfore men shal withstonden him by wit and by resoun and by discrecioun. Thanne arn ther the vertues of feith, and hope in god and in hise seintes, to acheve and acomplice the gode werkes in the whiche he purposeth fermely to continue. Thanne comth seuretee or sikernesse; and that is, whan a man ne douteth no travaille in tyme cominge of the gode werkes that a man hath bigonne. Thanne comth Magnificence, that is to seyn, whan a man dooth and perfourneth grete werkes of goodnesse that he hath bigonne; and that is the ende why that men sholde do gode werkes; for in the acomplissinge of grete goode werkes lyth the grete guerdoun. Thanne is ther Constaunce, that is, stablenesse of corage; and this sholde been in herte by stedefast feith, and in mouth, and in beringe, and in chere and in dede. Eke ther been mo speciale remedies agains Accidie, in diverse werkes, and in consideracioun of the peynes of helle, and of the joyes of hevene, and in trust of the grace of the holy goost, that wole yeve him might to perfourne his gode entente.

Sequitur de Auaricia.

§ 62. After Accidie wol I speke of Avarice and of Coveitise, of which sinne seith seint Paule, that 'the rote of alle harmes is Coveitise': *Ad Timotheum, sexto capitulo.* For soothly, whan the herte of a man is confounded in it-self and troubled, and that the soule hath lost the confort of god, thanne seketh he an ydel solas of worldly thinges.

§ 63. Avarice, after the descripcion of seint Augustin, is likerousnesse in herte to have erthely thinges. Som other folk seyn, that Avarice is, for to purchacen manye erthely thinges, and no-thing yeve to hem that han nede. And understond, that Avarice ne stant nat only in lond ne catel, but somtyme in science and in glorie, and in every manere of outrageous thing is Avarice and Coveitise. And the difference bitwixe Avarice and Coveitise is this. Coveitise is for to coveite swiche thinges as thou hast nat; and Avarice is for to withholde and kepe swiche thinges as thou hast, with-oute rightful nede. Soothly, this Avarice is a sinne that is ful dampnable; for al holy writ curseth it, and speketh agayns that vyce; for it dooth wrong to Jesu Crist. For it bireveth him the love that men to him owen, and turneth it bakward agayns alle resoun; and maketh that the avaricious man hath more hope in his catel than in Jesu Crist, and dooth more observance in kepinge of his tresor than he dooth to service of Jesu Crist. And therfore seith seint Paul *ad Ephesios, quinto,* that 'an avaricious man is in the thraldom of ydolatrie.'

§ 64. What difference is bitwixe an ydolastre and an

avaricious man, but that an ydolastre, per aventure, ne hath but o mawmet or two, and the avaricious man hath manye ? For certes, every florin in his cofre is his mawmet. And certes, the sinne of Mawmetrye is the firste thing that God deffended in the ten comaundments, as bereth witnesse *Exodi, capitulo xx°*: 'Thou shalt have no false goddes bifore me, ne thou shalt make to thee no grave thing.' Thus is an avaricious man, that loveth his tresor biforn god, an ydolastre, thurgh this cursed sinne of Avarice. Of Coveitise comen thise harde lordshipes, thurgh whiche men been distreyned by tailages, costumes, and cariages, more than hir duetee or resoun is. And eek they taken of hir bonde-men amerciments, whiche mighten more reasonably ben cleped extorcions than amerciments. Of whiche amerciments and raunsoninge of bondemen, somme lordes stywardes seyn, that it is rightful ; for-as-muche as a cherl hath no temporel thing that it ne is his lordes, as they seyn. But certes, thise lordshipes doon wrong, that bireven hir bonde-folk thinges that they nevere yave hem : *Augustinus de Civitate, libro nono.* Sooth is, that the condicioun of thraldom and the firste cause of thraldom is for sinne ; *Genesis, quinto.*

§ 65. Thus may ye seen that the gilt disserveth thraldom, but nat nature. Wherfore thise lordes ne sholde nat muche glorifyen hem in hir lordshipes, sith that by naturel condicion they been nat lordes of thralles ; but for that thraldom comth first by the desert of sinne. And forther-over, ther-as the lawe seith, that temporel godes of bonde-folk been the godes of hir lordshipes, ye, that is for to understonde, the godes of the emperour, to deffenden hem in hir right, but nat for to robben hem ne reven hem. And therfore seith Seneca : 'thy prudence sholde live benignely with thy thralles.' Thilke that thou clepest thy thralles been goddes peple ; for humble folk been Cristes freendes ; they been contubernial with the lord.

§ 66. Think eek, that of swich seed as cherles springeth, of swich seed springen lordes. As wel may the cherl be saved as the lord. The same deeth that taketh the cherl, swich deeth taketh the lord. Wherfore I rede, do right so with thy cherl, as thou woldest that thy lord dide with thee, if thou were in his plyt. Every sinful man is a cherl to sinne. I rede thee, certes, that thou, lord, werke in swiche wyse with thy cherles, that they rather love thee than drede. I woot wel ther is degree above degree, as reson is; and skile it is, that men do hir devoir ther-as it is due; but certes, extorcions and despit of youre underlinges is dampnable.

§ 67. And forther-over understond wel, that thise conquerours or tiraunts maken ful ofte thralles of hem, that been born of as royal blood as been they that hem conqueren. This name of thraldom was nevere erst couth, til that Noe seyde, that his sone Canaan sholde be thral to hise bretheren for his sinne. What seye we thanne of hem that pilen and doon extorcions to holy chirche? Certes, the swerd, that men yeven first to a knight whan he is newe dubbed, signifyeth that he sholde deffenden holy chirche, and nat robben it ne pilen it; and who so dooth, is traitour to Crist. And, as seith seint Augustin, 'they been the develes wolves, that stranglen the sheep of Jesu Crist'; and doon worse than wolves. For soothly, whan the wolf hath ful his wombe, he stinteth to strangle sheep. But soothly, the pilours and destroyours of goddes holy chirche ne do nat so; for they ne stinte nevere to pile. Now, as I have seyd, sith so is that sinne was first cause of thraldom, thanne is it thus; that thilke tyme that al this world was in sinne, thanne was al this world in thraldom and subjeccioun. But certes, sith the tyme of grace cam, god ordeyned that som folk sholde be more heigh in estaat and in degree, and som folk more lowe, and that everich sholde be served in his estaat and in his degree. And therfore, in somme contrees ther they byen thralles, whan they han turned hem to the feith, they maken hir thralles free out of thraldom. And therfore, certes, the lord oweth to his man that the man oweth to his lord. The Pope calleth him-self servant of the servaunts of god; but for-as-muche as the estaat of holy chirche ne mighte nat han be, ne the commune profit mighte nat han be kept, ne pees and reste in erthe, but-if god hadde ordeyned that som men hadde hyer degree and som men lower: therfore was sovereyntee ordeyned to kepe and mayntene and deffenden hir underlinges or hir subgets in resoun, as ferforth as it lyth in hir power; and nat to destroyen hem ne confounde. Wherfore I seye, that thilke lordes that been lyk wolves, that devouren the possessiouns or the catel of povre folk wrongfully, with-outen mercy or mesure, they shul receyven by the same mesure that they han mesured to povre folk the mercy of Jesu Crist, but-if it be amended. Now comth deceite bitwixe marchant and marchant. And thow shalt understonde, that marchandyse is in two maneres; that oon is bodily, and that other is goostly. That oon is honeste and leveful, and that other is deshoneste and unleveful. Of thilke bodily marchandyse, that is leveful and honeste, is this; that, there-as god hath ordeyned that a regne or a contree is suffisaunt to him-self, thanne is it honeste and leveful, that of habundaunce of this contree, that men helpe another contree that is more nedy. And therfore, ther mote been marchants to bringen fro that o contree to that other hire marchandyses. That other marchandise, that men haunten with fraude and trecherie and deceite, with lesinges and false othes, is cursed and dampnable. Espirituel marchandyse is proprely Symonye, that is, ententif desyr to byen thing espirituel, that is, thing that aperteneth to the seintuarie of god and to cure of the soule. This desyr, if so be that a man do his diligence to parfournen it, al-be-it that his desyr ne take noon effect, yet is it to him a deedly sinne; and if he be ordred, he is irreguler. Certes, Symonye is cleped of Symon Magus, that wolde han boght, for temporel catel, the yifte that god hadde yeven, by the holy goost, to seint Peter and to the apostles. And therfore understond, that bothe he that selleth and he that byeth thinges espirituels, been cleped Symonials; be it by catel, be it by procuringe, or by fleshly preyere of hise freendes, fleshly freendes, or espirituel freendes. Fleshly, in two maneres; as by kinrede or othere freendes. Soothly, if they praye for him that is nat worthy and able, it is Symonye if he take the benefice; and if he be worthy and able, ther nis noon. That other manere is, whan a man or womman preyen for folk to avauncen hem, only for wikked fleshly affeccioun that they have un-to the persone; and that is foul Symonye. But certes, in service, for which men yeven thinges espirituels un-to hir servants, it moot been understonde that the service moot been honeste, and elles nat; and eek that it be with-outen bargayninge, and that the persone be able. For, as seith seint Damasie, 'alle the sinnes of the world, at regard of this sinne, arn as thing of noght'; for it is the gretteste sinne that may be, after the sinne of Lucifer and Antecrist. For, by this sinne, god forleseth the chirche, and the soule that he boghte with his precious blood, by hem that yeven chirches to hem that been nat digne. For they putten in theves, that stelen the soules of Jesu Christ and destroyen his patrimoine. By swiche undigne preestes and curates han lewed men the lasse reverence of the sacraments of holy chirche; and swiche yeveres of chirches putten out the children of Crist, and putten in-to the chirche the develes owene sone. They sellen the soules that lambes sholde kepen to the wolf that strangleth hem. And therfore shul they nevere han part of the pasture of lambes, that is, the blisse of hevene. Now comth hasardrye with hise apurtenaunces, as tables and rafles; of which comth deceite, false othes, chydinges, and alle ravines, blaspheminge and reneyinge of god, and hate of hise neighebores, wast of godes, misspendinge of tyme, and som-tyme manslaughtre. Certes, hasardours ne mowe nat been with-outen greet sinne whyles they haunte that craft. Of avarice comen eek lesinges, thefte, fals witnesse, and false othes. And ye shul understonde that thise been grete sinnes, and expres agayn the comaundements of god, as I have seyd. Fals witnesse is in word and eek in dede. In word, as for to bireve thy neighebores goode name by thy fals witnessing, or bireven him his catel or his heritage by thy fals witnessing; whan thou, for ire or for mede, or for envye, berest fals witnesse, or accusest him or excusest him by thy fals witnesse, or elles excusest thy-self falsly. Ware yow, questemongeres and notaries! Certes, for fals witnessing was Susanna in ful gret sorwe and peyne, and many another mo. The sinne of thefte is eek expres agayns goddes heste, and that in two maneres, corporel and espirituel. Corporel, as for to take thy neighebores catel agayn his wil, be it by force or by sleighte, be it by met or by mesure. By steling eek of false enditements upon him, and in borwinge of thy neighebores catel, in entente nevere to payen it agayn, and semblable thinges. Espirituel thefte is Sacrilege, that is to seyn, hurtinge of holy thinges, or of thinges sacred to Crist, in two maneres; by reson of the holy place, as chirches or chirche-hawes, for which every vileyns sinne that men doon in swiche places may be cleped sacrilege, or every violence in the semblable places. Also, they that withdrawen falsly the rightes that longen to holy chirche. And pleynly and generally, sacrilege is to reven holy thing fro holy place, or unholy thing out of holy place, or holy thing out of unholy place.

Relevacio contra peccatum Avaricie.

§ 68. Now shul ye understonde, that the relevinge of Avarice is misericorde, and pitee largely taken. And men mighten axe, why that misericorde and pitee is relevinge of Avarice? Certes, the avaricious man sheweth no pitee ne misericorde to the nedeful man; for he delyteth him in the kepinge of his tresor, and nat in the rescowinge ne relevinge of his evene-cristene. And therfore speke I first of misericorde. Thanne is misericorde, as seith the philosophre, a vertu, by which the corage of man is stired by the misese of him that is misesed. Up-on which misericorde folweth pitee, in parfourninge of charitable werkes of misericorde. And certes, thise thinges moeven a man to misericorde of Jesu Crist, that he yaf him-self for oure gilt, and suffred deeth for misericorde, and forgaf us oure originale sinnes; and therby relessed us fro the peynes of helle, and amenused the peynes of purgatorie by penitence, and yeveth grace wel to do, and atte laste the blisse of hevene. The speces of misericorde been, as for to lene and for to yeve and to foryeven and relesse, and for to han pitee in herte, and compassioun of the meschief of his evene-cristene, and eek to chastyse there as nede is. Another manere of remedie agayns Avarice is resonable largesse; but soothly, here bihoveth the consideracioun of the grace of Jesu Crist, and of hise temporel goodes, and eek of the godes perdurables that Crist yaf to us; and to han remembrance of the deeth that he shal receyve, he noot whanne, where, ne how; and eek that he shal forgon al that he hath, save only that he hath despended in gode werkes.

§ 69. But for-as-muche as som folk been unmesurable, men oghten eschue fool largesse, that men clepen wast. Certes, he that is fool-large ne yeveth nat his catel, but he leseth his catel. Soothly, what thing that he yeveth for veyne glorie, as to minstrals and to folk, for to beren his renoun in the world, he hath sinne ther-of and noon almesse. Certes, he leseth foule his good, that ne seketh with the yifte of his good no-thing but sinne. He is lyk to an hors that seketh rather to drinken drovy or trouble water than for to drinken water of the clere welle. And for-as-muchel as they yeven ther as they sholde nat yeven, to hem aperteneth thilke malisoun that Crist shal yeven at the day of dome to hem that shullen been dampned.

Sequitur de Gula.

§ 70. After Avarice comth Glotonye, which is expres eek agayn the comandement of god. Glotonye is unmesurable appetyt to ete or to drinke, or elles to doon y-nogh to the unmesurable appetyt and desordeynee coveityse to eten or to drinke. This sinne corrumped al this world, as is wel shewed in the sinne of Adam and of Eve. Loke eek, what seith seint Paul of Glotonye. 'Manye,' seith seint Paul, 'goon, of whiche I have ofte seyd to yow, and now I seye it wepinge, that they been the enemys of the croys of Crist; of whiche the ende is deeth, and of whiche hir wombe is hir god, and hir glorie in confusioun of hem that so saveren erthely thinges.' He that is usaunt to this sinne of Glotonye, he ne may no sinne withstonde. He moot been in servage of alle vyces, for it is the develes hord ther he hydeth him and resteth. This sinne hath manye speces. The firste is dronkenesse, that is the horrible sepulture of mannes resoun; and therfore, whan a man is dronken, he hath lost his resoun; and this is deedly sinne. But soothly, whan that a man is nat wont to strong drinke, and peraventure ne knoweth nat the strengthe of the drinke, or hath feblesse in his heed, or hath travailed, thurgh which he drinketh the more, al be he sodeynly caught with drinke, it is no deedly sinne, but venial. The seconde spece of Glotonye is, that the spirit of a man wexeth al trouble; for dronkenesse bireveth him the discrecioun of his wit. The thridde spece of Glotonye is, whan a man devoureth his mete, and hath no rightful manere of etinge. The fourthe is whan, thurgh the grete habundaunce of his mete, the humours in his body been destempred. The fifthe is, foryetelnesse by to muchel drinkinge; for which somtyme a man foryeteth er the morwe what he dide at even or on the night biforn.

§ 71. In other manere been distinct the speces of Glotonye, after seint Gregorie. The firste is, for to ete biforn tyme to ete. The seconde is, whan a man get him to delicat mete or drinke. The thridde is, whan men taken to muche over mesure. The fourthe is curiositee, with greet entente to maken and apparaillen his mete. The fifthe is, for to eten to gredily. Thise been the fyve fingres of the develes hand, by whiche he draweth folk to sinne.

Remedium contra peccatum Gule.

§ 72. Agayns Glotonye is the remedie Abstinence, as seith Galien; but that holde I nat meritorie, if he do it only for the hele of his body. Seint Augustin wole, that Abstinence be doon for vertu and with pacience. Abstinence, he seith, is litel worth, but-if a man have good wil ther-to, and but it be enforced by pacience and by charitee, and that men doon it for godes sake, and in hope to have the blisse of hevene.

§ 73. The felawes of Abstinence been Attemperaunce, that holdeth the mene in alle thinges: eek Shame, that eschueth alle deshonestee: Suffisance, that seketh no riche metes ne drinkes, ne dooth no fors of to outrageous apparailinge of mete. Mesure also, that restreyneth by resoun the deslavee appetyt of etinge: Sobrenesse also, that restreyneth the outrage of drinke: Sparinge also, that restreyneth the delicat ese to sitte longe at his mete and softely; wherfore som folk stonden of hir owene wil, to eten at the lasse leyser.

Sequitur de Luxuria.

§ 74. After Glotonye, thanne comth Lecherie; for thise two sinnes been so ny cosins, that ofte tyme they wol nat departe. God woot, this sinne is ful displesaunt thing to god; for he seyde himself, 'do no lecherie.' And therfore he putte grete peynes agayns this sinne in the olde lawe. If womman thral were taken in this sinne, she sholde be beten with staves to the deeth. And if she were a gentil womman, she sholde be slayn with stones. And if she were a bisshoppes doghter, she sholde been brent, by goddes comandement. Forther over, by the sinne of Lecherie, god dreynte al the world at the diluge. And after that, he brente fyve citees with thonder-leyt, and sank hem in-to helle.

§ 75. Now lat us speke thanne of thilke stinkinge sinne of Lecherie that men clepe Avoutrie of wedded folk, that is to seyn, if that oon of hem be wedded, or elles bothe. Seint John seith, that avoutiers shullen been in helle in a stank brenninge of fyr and of brimston; in fyr, for the lecherie; in brimston, for the stink of hir ordure. Certes, the brekinge of this sacrement is an horrible thing; it was maked of god himself in paradys, and confermed by Jesu Crist, as witnesseth seint Mathew in the gospel: 'A man shal lete fader and moder, and taken him to his wyf, and they shullen be two in o flesh.' This sacrement bitokneth the knittinge togidre of Crist and of holy chirche. And nat only that god forbad avoutrie in dede, but eek he comanded that thou sholdest nat coveite thy neighebores wyf. In this heeste, seith seint Augustin, is forboden alle manere coveitise to doon lecherie. Lo what seith seint Mathew in the gospel: that 'who-so seeth a womman to coveitise of his lust, he hath doon lecherie with hir in his herte.' Here may ye seen that nat only the dede of this sinne is forboden, but eek the desyr to doon that sinne. This cursed sinne anoyeth grevousliche hem that it haunten. And first, to hir soule; for he oblygeth it to sinne and to peyne of deeth that is perdurable. Un-to the body anoyeth it grevously also, for it dreyeth him, and wasteth, and shent him, and of his blood he maketh sacrifyce to the feend of helle; it wasteth his catel and his substaunce. And certes, if it be a foul thing, a man to waste his catel on wommen, yet is it a fouler thing whan that, for swich ordure, wommen dispenden up-on men hir catel and substaunce. This sinne, as seith the prophete, bireveth man and womman hir gode fame, and al hir honour; and it is ful pleasaunt to the devel; for ther-by winneth he the moste partie of this world. And right as a marchant delyteth him most in chaffare that he hath most avantage of, right so delyteth the feend in this ordure.

§ 76. This is that other hand of the devel, with fyve fingres, to cacche the peple to his vileinye. The firste finger is the fool lookinge of the fool womman and of the fool man, that sleeth, right as the basilicok sleeth folk by the venim of his sighte; for the coveitise of eyen folweth the coveitise of the herte. The seconde finger is the vileyns touchinge in wikkede manere; and ther-fore seith Salomon, that who-so toucheth and handleth a womman, he fareth lyk him that handleth the scorpioun that stingeth and sodeynly sleeth thurgh his enveniminge; as who-so toucheth warm pich, it shent his fingres. The thridde, is foule wordes, that fareth lyk fyr, that right anon brenneth the herte. The fourthe finger is the kissinge; and trewely he were a greet fool that wolde kisse the mouth of a brenninge ovene or of a fourneys. And more fooles been they that kissen in vileinye; for that mouth is the mouth of helle: and namely, thise olde dotardes holours, yet wol they kisse, though they may nat do, and smatre hem. Certes, they been lyk to houndes; for an hound, whan he comth by the roser or by othere busshes, though he may nat pisse, yet wole he heve up his leg and make a contenaunce to pisse. And for that many man weneth that he may nat sinne, for no likerousnesse that he doth with his wyf; certes, that opinion is fals. God woot, a man may sleen him-self with his owene knyf, and make him-selven dronken of his owene tonne. Certes, be it wyf, be it child, or any worldly thing that he loveth biforn god, it is his maumet, and he is an ydolastre. Man sholde loven his wyf by discrecioun, paciently and atemprely; and thanne is she as though it were his suster. The fifthe finger of the develes hand is the stinkinge dede of Lecherie. Certes, the fyve fingres of Glotonie the feend put in the wombe of a man, and with hise fyve fyngres of Lecherie he gripeth him by the reynes, for to throwen him in-to the fourneys of helle; ther-as they shul han the fyr and the wormes that evere shul lasten, and wepinge and wailinge, sharp hunger and thurst, and grimnesse of develes that shullen al to-trede hem, with-outen respit and with-outen ende. Of Lecherie, as I seyde, sourden diverse speces; as fornicacioun, that is bitwixe man and womman that been nat maried; and this is deedly sinne and agayns nature. Al that is enemy and des-truccioun to nature is agayns nature. Parfay, the resoun of a man telleth eek him wel that it is deedly sinne, for-as-muche as god forbad Lecherie. And seint Paul yeveth hem the regne, that nis dewe to no wight but to hem that doon deedly sinne. Another sinne of Lecherie is to bireve a mayden of hir maydenhede; for he that so dooth, certes, he casteth a mayden out of the hyeste degree that is in this present lyf, and bireveth hir thilke precious fruit that the book clepeth 'the hundred fruit.' I ne can seye it noon other weyes in English, but in Latin it highte *Centesimus fructus*.

Certes, he that so dooth is cause of manye damages and vileinyes, mo than any man can rekene; right as he somtyme is cause of alle damages that bestes don in the feeld, that breketh the hegge or the closure; thurgh which he destroyeth that may nat been restored. For certes, na-more may maydenhede be restored than an arm that is smiten fro the body may retourne agayn to wexe. She may have mercy, this woot I wel, if she do penitence; but nevere shal it be that she nas corrupt. And al-be-it so that I have spoken somwhat of Avoutrie, it is good to shewen mo perils that longen to Avoutrie, for to eschue that foule sinne. Avoutrie in Latin is for to seyn, approchinge of other mannes bed, thurgh which tho that whylom weren o flessh abaundone hir bodyes to othere persones. Of this sinne, as seith the wyse man, folwen manye harmes. First, brekinge of feith; and certes, in feith is the keye of Cristendom. And whan that feith is broken and lorn, soothly Cristendom stant veyn and with-outen fruit. This sinne is eek a thefte; for thefte generally is for to reve a wight his thing agayns his wille. Certes, this is the fouleste thefte that may be, whan a womman steleth hir body from hir housbonde and yeveth it to hire holour to defoulen hir; and steleth hir soule fro Crist, and yeveth it to the devel. This is a fouler thefte, than for to breke a chirche and stele the chalice; for thise avoutiers breken the temple of god spiritually, and stelen the vessel of grace, that is, the body and the soule, for which Crist shal destroyen hem, as seith seint Paul. Soothly of this thefte douted gretly Joseph, whan that his lordes wyf preyed him of vileinye, whan he seyde, 'lo, my lady, how my lord hath take to me under my warde al that he hath in this world; ne nothing of hise thinges is out of my power, but only ye that been his wyf. And how sholde I thanne do this wikkednesse, and sinne so horribly agayns god, and agayns my lord? God it forbede.' Allas! al to litel is swich trouthe now y-founde! The thridde harm is the filthe thurgh which they breken the comandement of god, and defoulen the auctour of matrimoine, that is Crist. For certes, in-so-muche as the sacrement of mariage is so noble and so digne, so muche is it gretter sinne for to breken it; for god made mariage in paradys, in the estaat of innocence, to multiplye man-kinde to the service of god. And therfore is the brekinge ther-of more grevous. Of which brekinge comen false heires ofte tyme, that wrongfully occupyen folkes heritages. And therfore wol Crist putte hem out of the regne of hevene, that is heritage to gode folk. Of this brekinge comth eek ofte tyme, that folk unwar wedden or sinnen with hir owene kinrede; and namely thilke harlottes that haunten bordels of thise fool wommen, that mowe be lykned to a commune gonge, where-as men purgen hir ordure. What seye we eek of putours that liven by the horrible sinne of puterie, and constreyne wommen to yelden to hem a certeyn rente of hir bodily puterie, ye, somtyme of his owene wyf or his child; as doon this baudes? Certes, thise been cursede sinnes. Understond eek, that avoutrie is set gladly in the ten comandements bitwixe thefte and manslaughtre; for it is the gretteste thefte that may be; for it is thefte of body and of soule. And it is lyk to homicyde; for it kerveth a-two and breketh a-two hem that first were maked o flesh, and therfore, by the olde lawe of god, they sholde be slayn. But nathelees, by the lawe of Jesu Crist, that is lawe of pitee, whan he seyde to the womman that was founden in avoutrie, and sholde han been slayn with stones, after the wil of the Jewes, as was hir lawe: 'Go,' quod Jesu Crist, 'and have na-more wil to sinne'; or, 'wille na-more to do sinne.' Soothly, the vengeaunce of avoutrie is awarded to the peynes of helle, but-if so be that it be destourbed by penitence. Yet been ther mo speces of this cursed sinne; as whan that oon of hem is religious, or elles bothe; or of folk that been entred in-to ordre, as subdekne or dekne, or preest, or hospitaliers. And evere the hyer that he is in ordre, the gretter is the sinne. The thinges that gretly agreggen hir sinne is the brekinge of hir avow of chastitee, whan they receyved the ordre. And forther-over, sooth is, that holy ordre is chief of al the tresorie of god, and his especial signe and mark of chastitee; to shewe that they been joyned to chastitee, which that is most precious lyf that is. And thise ordred folk been specially tytled to god, and of the special meynee of god; for which, whan they doon deedly sinne, they been the special traytours of god and of his peple; for they liven of the peple, to preye for the peple, and whyle they been suche traitours, hir preyers availen nat to the peple. Preestes been aungeles, as by the dignitee of hir misterye; but for sothe, seint Paul seith, that 'Sathanas transformeth him in an aungel of light.' Soothly, the preest that haunteth deedly sinne, he may be lykned to the aungel of derknesse transformed in the aungel of light; he semeth aungel of light, but for sothe he is aungel of derknesse. Swiche preestes been the sones of Helie, as sheweth in the book of Kinges, that they weren the sones of Belial, that is, the devel Belial is to seyn 'with-outen juge'; and so faren they; hem thinketh they been free, and han no juge, na-more than hath a free bole that taketh which cow that him lyketh in the toun. So faren they by wommen. For right as a free bole is y-nough for al a toun, right so is a wikked preest corrupcioun y-nough for al a parisshe, or for al a contree. Thise preestes, as seith the book, ne conne nat the misterie of preesthode to the peple, ne god ne knowe they nat; they ne helde hem nat apayd, as seith the book, of soden flesh that was to hem offred, but they toke by force the flesh that is rawe. Certes, so thise shrewes ne holden hem nat apayed of rosted flesh and sode flesh, with which the peple fedden hem in greet reverence, but they wole have raw flesh of folkes wyves and hir doghtres. And certes, thise wommen that consenten to hir harlotrie doon greet wrong to Crist and to holy chirche and alle halwes, and to alle soules; for they bireven alle thise him that sholde worshipe Crist and holy chirche, and preye for Cristene soules. And therfore han swiche preestes, and hir lemmanes eek that consenten to hir lecherie, the malisoun of al the court Cristen, til they come to amendement. The thridde spece of avoutrie is som-tyme bitwixe a man and his wyf; and that is whan they take no reward in hir assemblinge, but only to hire fleshly delyt, as seith seint Jerome; and ne rekken of no-thing but that they been assembled; by-cause that they been maried, al is good y-nough, as thinketh to hem. But in swich folk hath the devel power, as seyde the aungel Raphael to Thobie; for in hir assembiinge they putten Jesu Crist out of hir herte, and yeven hem-self to alle ordure. The fourthe spece is, the assemblee of hem that been of hire kinrede, or of hem that been of oon affinitee, or elles with hem with whiche hir fadres or hir kinrede han deled in the sinne of lecherie; this sinne maketh hem lyk to houndes, that taken no kepe to kinrede. And certes, parentele is in two maneres, outher goostly or fleshly; goostly, as for to delen with hise godsibbes. For right so as he that engendreth a child is his fleshly fader, right so is his godfader his fader espirituel. For which a womman may in no lasse sinne assemblen with hir godsib than with hir owene fleshly brother. The fifthe spece is thilke abhominable sinne, of which that no man unnethe oghte speke ne wryte, nathelees it is openly reherced in holy writ. This cursednesse doon men and wommen in diverse entente and in diverse manere; but though that holy writ speke of horrible sinne, certes, holy writ may nat been defouled, na-more than the sonne that shyneth on the mixen. Another sinne aperteneth to lecherie, that comth in slepinge; and this sinne cometh ofte to hem that been maydenes, and eek to hem that been corrupt; and this sinne men clepen pollucioun, that comth in foure maneres. Somtyme, of languissinge of body; for the humours been to ranke and habundaunt in the body of man. Somtyme of infermetee; for the feblesse of the vertu retentif, as phisik maketh mencioun. Somtyme, for surfeet of mete and drinke. And somtyme of vileyns thoghtes, that been enclosed in mannes minde whan he goth to slepe; which may nat been with-oute sinne. For which men moste kepen hem wysely, or elles may men sinnen ful grevously.

Remedium contra peccatum Luxurie.

§ 77. Now comth the remedie agayns Lecherie, and that is, generally, Chastitee and Continence, that restreyneth alle the desordeynee moevinges that comen of fleshly talentes. And evere the gretter merite shal he han, that most restreyneth the wikkede eschaufinges of the ordure of this sinne. And this is in two maneres, that is to seyn, chastitee in mariage, and chastitee in widwehode. Now shaltow understonde, that matrimoine is leefful assemblinge of man and of womman, that receyven by vertu of the sacrement the bond, thurgh which they may nat be departed in al hir lyf, that is to seyn, whyl that they liven bothe. This, as seith the book, is a ful greet sacrement. God maked it, as I have seyd, in paradys, and wolde him-self be born in mariage. And for to halwen mariage, he was at a weddinge, where-as he turned water in-to wyn; which was the firste miracle that he wroghte in erthe biforn hise disciples. Trewe effect of mariage clenseth fornicacioun and replenisseth holy chirche of good linage; for that is the ende of mariage; and it chaungeth deedly sinne in-to venial sinne bitwixe hem that been y-wedded, and maketh the hertes al oon of hem that been y-wedded, as wel as the bodies. This is verray mariage, that was establissed by god er that sinne bigan, whan naturel lawe was in his right point in paradys; and it was ordeyned that o man sholde have but o womman, and o womman but o man, as seith seint Augustin, by manye resouns.

§ 78. First, for mariage is figured bitwixe Crist and holy chirche. And that other is, for a man is heved of a womman; algate, by ordinaunce it sholde be so. For if a womman had mo men than oon, thanne sholde she have mo hevedes than oon, and that were an horrible thing biforn god; and eek a womman ne mighte nat plese to many folk at ones. And also ther ne sholde nevere be pees ne reste amonges hem; for everich wolde axen his owene thing. And forther-over, no man ne sholde knowe his owene engendrure, ne who sholde have his heritage; and the womman sholde been the lasse biloved, fro the time that she were conjoynt to many men.

§ 79. Now comth, how that a man sholde bere him with his wyf; and namely, in two thinges, that is to seyn in suffraunce and reverence, as shewed Crist whan he made first womman. For he ne made hir nat of the heved of Adam, for she sholde nat clayme to greet lordshipe. For ther-as the womman hath the maistrie, she maketh to muche desray; ther neden none ensamples of this. The experience of day by day oghte suffyse. Also certes. god ne made nat womman of the foot of Adam, for she ne sholde nat been holden to lowe; for she can nat paciently suffre: but god made womman of the rib of Adam, for womman sholde be felawe un-to man. Man sholde bere him to his wyf in feith, in trouthe, and in love, as seith seint Paul: that 'a man sholde loven his wyf as Crist loved holy chirche, that loved it so wel that he deyde for it.' So sholde a man for his wyf, if it were nede.

§ 80. Now how that a womman sholde be subget to hir housbonde, that telleth seint Peter. First, in obedience. And eek, as seith the decree, a womman that is a wyf, as longe as she is a wyf, she hath noon auctoritee to swere ne bere witnesse with-oute leve of hir housbonde, that is hir lord; algate, he sholde be so by resoun. She sholde eek serven him in alle honestee, and been attempree of hir array. I wot wel that they sholde setten hir entente to plesen hir housbondes, but nat by hir queyntise of array. Seint Jerome seith, that wyves that been apparailled in silk and in precious purpre ne mowe nat clothen hem in Jesu Crist. What seith seint John eek in this matere? Seint Gregorie eek seith, that no wight seketh precious array but only for veyne glorie, to been honoured the more biforn the peple. It is a greet folye, a womman to have a fair array outward and in hir-self be foul inward. A wyf sholde eek be mesurable in lokinge and in beringe and in laughinge, and discreet in alle hir wordes and hir dedes. And aboven alle worldly thing she sholde loven hir housbonde with al hir herte, and to him be trewe of hir body; so sholdc an housbonde eek be to his wyf. For sith that al the body is the housbondes, so sholde hir herte been, or elles ther is bitwixe hem two, as in that, no parfit mariage. Thanne shal men understonde that for three thinges a man and his wyf fleshly mowen assemble. The firste is in entente of engendrure of children to the service of god, for certes that is the cause fynal of matrimoine. Another cause is, to yelden everich of hem to other the dette of hir bodies, for neither of hem hath power over his owene body. The thridde is, for to eschewe lecherye and vileinye. The ferthe is for sothe deedly sinne. As to the firste, it is meritorie; the seconde also; for, as seith the decree, that she hath merite of chastitee that yeldeth to hir housbonde the dette of hir body, ye, though it be agayn hir lykinge and the lust of hir herte. The thridde manere is venial sinne, and trewely scarsly may ther any of thise be withoute venial sinne, for the corrupcion and for the delyt. The fourthe manere is for to understonde, if they assemble only for amorous love and for noon of the forseyde causes, but for to accomplice thilke brenninge delyt, they rekke nevere how ofte, sothly it is deedly sinne; and yet, with sorwe, somme folk wol peynen hem more to doon than to hir appetyt suffyseth.

§ 81. The seconde manere of chastitee is for to been a clene widewe, and eschue the embracinges of man, and desyren the embracinge of Jesu Crist. Thise been tho that han been wyves and han forgoon hir housbondes, and eek wommen that han doon lecherie and been releeved by Penitence. And certes, if that a wyf coude kepen hir al chaast by licence of hir housbonde, so that she yeve nevere noon occasion that he agilte, it were to hire a greet merite. Thise manere wommen that observen chastitee moste be clene in herte as well as in body and in thoght, and mesurable in clothinge and in contenaunce; and been abstinent in etinge and drinkinge, in spekinge, and in dede. They been the vessel or the boyste of the blissed Magdalene, that fulfilleth holy chirche of good odour. The thridde manere of chastitee is virginitee, and it bihoveth that she be holy in herte and clene of body; thanne is she spouse to Jesu Crist, and she is the lyf of angeles. She is the preisinge of this world, and she is as thise martirs in egalitee; she hath in hir that tonge may nat telle ne herte thinke. Virginitee baar oure lord Jesu Crist, and virgine was him-selve.

§ 82. Another remedie agayns Lecherie is, specially to withdrawen swiche thinges as yeve occasion to thilke vileinye; as ese, etinge and drinkinge; for certes, whan the pot boyleth strongly, the beste remedie is to withdrawe the fyr. Slepinge longe in greet quiete is eek a greet norice to Lecherie.

§ 83. Another remedie agayns Lecherie is, that a man or a womman eschue the companye of hem by whiche he douteth to be tempted; for al-be-it so that the dede is withstonden, yet is ther greet temptacioun. Soothly a whyt wal, although it ne brenne noght fully by stikinge of a candele, yet is the wal blak of the leyt. Ful ofte tyme I rede, that no man truste in his owene perfeccioun, but he be stronger than Sampson, and holier than David, and wyser than Salomon.

§ 84. Now after that I have declared yow, as I can, the sevene deedly sinnes, and somme of hir braunches and hir remedies, soothly, if I coude, I wolde telle yow the ten comandements. But so heigh a doctrine I lete to divines. Natheles, I hope to god they been touched in this tretice, everich of hem alle.

De Confessione.

§ 85. Now for-as-muche as the second partie of Penitence stant in Confessioun of mouth, as I bigan in the firste chapitre, I seye, seint Augustin seith: sinne is every word and every dede, and al that men coveiten agayn the lawe of Jesu Crist; and this is for to sinne in herte, in mouth, and in dede, by thy fyve wittes, that been sighte, heringe, smellinge, tastinge or savouringe, and felinge. Now is it good to understonde that that agreggeth muchel every sinne. Thou shalt considere what thou art that doost the sinne, whether thou be male or femele, yong or old, gentil or thral, free or servant, hool or syk, wedded or sengle, ordred or unordred, wys or fool, clerk or seculer; if she be of thy kinrede, bodily or goostly, or noon; if any of thy kinrede have sinned with hir or noon, and manye mo thinges.

§ 86. Another circumstaunce is this; whether it be doon in fornicacioun, or in avoutrie, or noon; incest, or noon; mayden, or noon; in manere of homicyde, or noon; horrible grete sinnes, or smale; and how longe thou hast continued in sinne. The thridde circumstaunce is the place ther thou hast do sinne; whether in other mennes hous or in thyn owene; in feeld or in chirche, or in chirche-hawe; in chirche dedicat, or noon. For if the chirche be halwed, and man or womman spille his kinde in-with that place by wey of sinne, or by wikked temptacion, the chirche is entredited til it be reconciled by the bishop; and the preest that dide swich a vileinye, to terme of al his lyf, he sholde na-more singe masse; and if he dide, he sholde doon deedly sinne at every tyme that he so songe masse. The fourthe circumstaunce is, by whiche mediatours or by whiche messagers, as for entycement, or for consentement to bere companye with felaweshipe; for many a wrecche, for to bere companye, wil go to the devel of helle. Wher-fore they that eggen or consenten to the sinne been parteners of the sinne, and of the dampnacioun of the sinner. The fifthe circumstaunce is, how manye tymes that he hath sinned, if it be in his minde, and how ofte that he hath falle. For he that ofte falleth in sinne, he despiseth the mercy of god, and encreesseth his sinne, and is unkinde to Crist; and he wexeth the more feble to withstonde sinne, and sinneth the more lightly, and the latter aryseth, and is the more eschew for to shryven him, namely, to him that is his confessour. For which that folk, whan they falle agayn in hir olde folies, outher they forleten hir olde confessours al outrely, or elles they departen hir shrift in diverse places; but soothly, swich departed shrift deserveth no mercy of god of hise sinnes. The sixte circumstaunce is, why that a man sinneth, as by whiche temptacioun; and if himself procure thilke temptacioun, or by the excytinge of other folk; or if he sinne with a womman by force, or by hir owene assent; or if the womman, maugree hir heed, hath been afforced, or noon; this shal she telle; for coveitise, or for poverte, and if it was hir procuringe, or noon; and swiche manere harneys. The seventhe circumstaunce is, in what manere he hath doon his sinne, or how that she hath suffred that folk han doon to hir. And the same shal the man telle pleynly, with alle circumstaunces; and whether he hath sinned with comune bordel-wommen, or noon; or doon his sinne in holy tymes, or noon; in fasting-tymes, or noon; or biforn his shrifte, or after his latter shrifte, and hath, per-aventure, broken ther-fore his penance enjoyned; by whos help and whos conseil; by sorcerie or craft; al moste be told. Alle thise thinges, after that they been grete or smale, engreggen the conscience of man. And eek the preest that is thy juge, may the bettre been avysed of his jugement in yevinge of thy penaunce, and that is after thy contricioun. For understond wel, that after tyme that a man hath defouled his baptesme by sinne, if he wole come to salvacioun, ther is noon other wey but by penitence and shrifte and satisfaccioun; and namely by the two, if ther be a confessour to which he may shryven him; and the thridde, if he have lyf to parfournen it.

§ 87. Thanne shal man looke and considere, that if he wole maken a trewe and a profitable confessioun, ther moste be foure condiciouns. First, it moot been in sorweful bitternesse of herte, as seyde the king Ezekias to god: 'I wol remembre me alle the yeres of my lyf in bitternesse of myn herte.' This condicioun of bitternesse hath fyve signes. The firste is, that confessioun moste be shamefast, nat for to covere ne hyden his sinne, for he hath agilt his god and defouled his soule. And her-of seith seint Augustin: 'the herte travailleth for shame of his sinne'; and for he hath greet shamefastnesse, he is digne to have greet mercy of god. Swich was the confession of the publican, that wolde nat heven up hise eyen to hevene, for he hadde offended god of hevene; for which shamefastnesse he hadde anon the mercy of god. And ther-of seith seint Augustin, that swich shamefast folk been next foryevenesse and remissioun. Another signe is humilitee in confessioun; of which seith seint Peter, 'Humbleth yow under the might of god.' The hond of god is mighty in confession, for ther-by god foryeveth thee thy sinnes; for he allone hath the power. And this humilitee shal been in herte, and in signe outward; for right as he hath humilitee to god in his herte, right so sholde he humble his body outward to the preest that sit in goddes place. For which in no manere, sith that Crist is sovereyn and the preest mene and mediatour bitwixe Crist and the sinnere, and the sinnere is the laste by wey of resoun, thanne sholde nat the sinnere sitte as heighe as his confessour, but knele biforn him or at his feet, but-if maladie destourbe it. For he shal nat taken kepe who sit there, but in whos place that he sitteth. A man that hath trespased to a lord, and comth for to axe mercy and maken his accord, and set him doun anon by the lord, men wolde holden him outrageous, and nat worthy so sone for to have remissioun ne mercy. The thridde signe is, how that thy shrift sholde be ful of teres, if man may; and if man may nat wepe with hise bodily eyen, lat him wepe in herte. Swich was the confession of seint Peter; for after that he hadde forsake Jesu Crist, he wente out and weep ful bitterly. The fourthe signe is, that he ne lette nat for shame to shewen his confessioun. Swich was the confessioun of the Magdelene, that she spared, for no shame of hem that weren atte feste, for to go to oure lord Jesu Crist and biknowe to him hir sinnes. The fifthe signe is, that a man or a womman be obeisant to receyven the penaunce that him is enjoyned for hise sinnes; for certes Jesu Crist, for the giltes of a man, was obedient to the deeth.

§ 88. The seconde condicion of verray confession is, that it be hastily doon; for certes, if a man hadde a deedly wounde, evere the lenger that he taried to warisshe him-self, the more wolde it corrupte and haste him to his deeth; and eek the wounde wolde be the wors for to hele. And right so fareth sinne, that longe tyme is in a man unshewed. Certes, a man oghte hastily shewen hise sinnes for manye causes; as for drede of deeth, that cometh ofte sodenly, and is in no certeyn what tyme it shal be, ne in what place; and eek the drecchinge of o synne draweth in another; and eek the lenger that he tarieth, the ferther he is fro Crist. And if he abyde to his laste day, scarsly may he shryven him or remembre him of hise sinnes, or repenten him, for the grevous maladie of his deeth. And for-as-muche as he ne hath nat in his lyf herkned Jesu Crist, whanne he hath spoken, he shal crye to Jesu Crist at his laste day, and scarsly wol he herkne him. And understond that this condicioun moste han foure thinges. Thy shrift moste be purveyed bifore and avysed; for wikked haste doth no profit; and that a man conne shryve him of hise sinnes, be it of pryde, or of envye, and so forth of the speces and circumstances; and that he have comprehended in his minde the nombre and the greetnesse of hise sinnes, and how longe that he hath leyn in sinne; and eek that he be contrit of hise sinnes, and in stedefast purpos, by the grace of god, nevere eft to falle in sinne; and eek that he drede and countrewaite him-self, that he flee the occasiouns of sinne to whiche he is enclyned. Also thou shalt shryve thee of alle thy sinnes to o man, and nat a parcel to o man and a parcel to another; that is to understonde, in entente to departe thy confessioun as for shame or drede; for it nis but stranglinge of thy soule. For certes, Jesu Crist is entierly al good; in him nis noon inperfeccioun; and therfore outher he foryeveth al parfitly or never a deel. I seye nat that if thou be assigned to the penitauncer for certein sinne, that thou art bounde to shewen him al the remenaunt of thy sinnes, of whiche thou hast be shriven to thy curat, but-if it lyke to thee of thyn humilitee; this is no departinge of shrifte. Ne I seye nat, ther-as I speke of divisioun of confessioun, that if thou have lycence for to shryve thee to a discreet and an honeste preest, where thee lyketh, and by lycence of thy curat, that thou ne mayst wel shryve thee to him of alle thy sinnes. But lat no blotte be bihinde; lat no sinne been untold, as fer as thou hast remembraunce. And whan thou shalt be shriven to thy curat, telle him eek alle the sinnes that thou hast doon sin thou were last y-shriven; this is no wikked entente of divisioun of shrifte.

§ 89. Also the verray shrifte axeth certeine condiciouns. First, that thou shryve thee by thy free wil, noght constreyned, ne for shame of folk, ne for maladie, ne swiche thinges; for it is resoun that he that trespasseth by his free wil, that by his free wil he confesse his trespas; and that noon other man telle his sinne but he him-self, ne he shal nat nayte ne denye his sinne, ne wratthe him agayn the preest for his amonestinge to leve sinne. The seconde condicioun is, that thy shrift be laweful; that is to seyn, that thou that shryvest thee, and eek the preest that hereth thy confessioun, been verraily in the feith of holy chirche; and that a man ne be nat despeired of the mercy of Jesu Crist, as Caym or Judas. And eek a man moot accusen him-self of his owene trespas, and nat another; but he shal blame and wyten him-self and his owene malice of his sinne, and noon other; but nathelees, if that another man be occasioun or entycer of his sinne, or the estaat of a persone be swich thurgh which his sinne is agregged, or elles that he may nat pleynly shryven him but he telle the persone with which he hath sinned; thanne may he telle; so that his entente ne be nat to bakbyte the persone, but only to declaren his confessioun.

§ 90. Thou ne shalt nat eek make no lesinges in thy confessioun; for humilitee, per-aventure, to seyn that thou hast doon sinnes of whiche that thou were nevere gilty. For seint Augustin seith: if thou, by cause of thyn humilitee, makest lesinges on thy-self, though thou ne were nat in sinne biforn, yet artow thanne in sinne thurgh thy lesinges. Thou most eek shewe thy sinne by thyn owene propre mouth, but thou be wexe doumb, and nat by no lettre; for thou that hast doon the sinne, thou shalt have the shame therfore. Thou shalt nat eek peynte thy confessioun by faire subtile wordes, to covere the more thy sinne; for thanne bigylestow thy-self and nat the preest; thou most tellen it pleynly, be it nevere so foul ne so horrible. Thou shalt eek shryve thee to a preest that is discreet to conseille thee, and eek thou shalt nat shryve thee for veyne glorie, ne for ypocrisye, ne for no cause, but only for the doute of Jesu Crist and the hele of thy soule. Thou shalt nat eek renne to the preest sodeynly, to tellen him lightly thy sinne, as who-so telleth a jape or a tale, but avysely and with greet devocioun. And generally, shryve thee ofte. If thou ofte falle, ofte thou aryse by confessioun. And thogh thou shryve thee ofter than ones of sinne, of which thou hast be shriven, it is the more merite. And, as seith seint Augustin, thou shalt have the more lightly relesing and grace of god, bothe of sinne and of peyne. And certes, ones a yere atte leeste wey it is laweful for to been housled; for certes ones a yere alle thinges renovellen.

Explicit secunda pars Penitencie; et sequitur tercia pars eiusdem, de Satisfaccione.

§ 91. Now have I told you of verray Confessioun that is the seconde partie of Penitence.

The thridde partie of Penitence is Satisfaccioun; and that stant most generally in almesse and in bodily peyne. Now been ther three manere of almesses; contricion of herte, where a man offreth himself to god; another is, to han pitee of defaute of hise neighebores; and the thridde is, in yevinge of good conseil goostly and bodily, where men han nede, and namely in sustenaunce of mannes fode. And tak keep, that a man hath need of thise thinges generally; he hath need of fode, he hath nede of clothing, and herberwe, he hath nede of charitable conseil, and visitinge in prisone and in maladie, and sepulture of his dede body. And if thou mayst nat visite the nedeful with thy persone, visite him by thy message and by thy yiftes. Thise been generally almesses or werkes of charitee of hem that han temporel richesses or discrecioun in conseilinge. Of thise werkes shaltow heren at the day of dome.

§ 92. Thise almesses shaltow doon of thyne owene propre thinges, and hastily, and prively if thou mayst; but nathelees, if thou mayst nat doon it prively, thou shalt nat forbere to doon almesse though men seen it; so that it be nat doon for thank of the world, but only for thank of Jesu Crist. For as witnesseth seint Mathew, *capitulo quinto*, 'A citee may nat been hid that is set on a montayne; ne men lighte nat a lanterne and put it under a busshel; but men sette it on a candle-stikke, to yeve light to the men in the hous. Right so shal youre light lighten bifore men, that they may seen youre gode werkes, and glorifie youre fader that is in hevene.'

§ 93. Now as to speken of bodily peyne, it stant in preyeres, in wakinges, in fastinges, in vertuouse techinges of orisouns. And ye shul understonde, that orisouns or preyeres is for to seyn a pitous wil of herte, that redresseth it in god and expresseth it by word outward, to remoeven harmes and to han thinges espirituel and durable, and somtyme temporel thinges; of whiche orisouns, certes, in the orisoun of the *Paternoster*, hath Jesu Crist enclosed most thinges. Certes, it is privileged of three thinges in his dignitee, for which it is more digne than any othere preyere; for that Jesu Crist him-self maked it; and it is short, for it sholde be coud the more lightly, and for to withholden it the more esily in herte, and helpen him-self the ofter with the orisoun; and for a man sholde be the lasse wery to seyen it, and for a man may nat excusen him to lerne it, it is so short and so esy; and for it comprehendeth in it-self alle gode preyeres. The exposicioun of this holy preyere, that is so excellent and digne, I bitake to thise maistres of theologie; save thus muchel wol I seyn: that, whan thou prayest that god sholde foryeve thee thy giltes as thou foryevest hem that agilten to thee, be ful wel war that thou be nat out of charitee. This holy orisoun amenuseth eek venial sinne; and therfore it aperteneth specially to penitence.

§ 94. This preyere moste be trewely seyd and in verray feith, and that men preye to god ordinatly and discreetly and devoutly; and alwey a man shal putten his wil to be subget to the wille of god. This orisoun moste eek been seyd with greet humblesse and ful pure; honestly, and nat to the anoyaunce of any man or womman. It moste eek been continued with the werkes of charitee. It avayleth eek agayn the vyces of the soule; for, as seith seint Jerome, 'By fastinge been saved the vyces of the flesh, and by preyere the vyces of the soule.'

§ 95. After this, thou shalt understonde, that bodily peyne stant in wakinge; for Jesu Crist seith, 'waketh, and preyeth that ye ne entre in wikked temptacioun.' Ye shul understanden also, that fastinge stant in three thinges; in forberinge of bodily mete and drinke, and in forberinge of worldly jolitee, and in forberinge of deedly sinne; this is to seyn, that a man shal kepen him fro deedly sinne with al his might.

§ 96. And thou shalt understanden eek, that god ordeyned fastinge; and to fastinge appertenen foure thinges. Largenesse to povre folk, gladnesse of herte espirituel, nat to been angry ne anoyed, ne grucche for he fasteth; and also resonable houre for to ete by mesure; that is for to seyn, a man shal nat ete in untyme, ne sitte the lenger at his table to ete for he fasteth.

§ 97. Thanne shaltow understonde, that bodily peyne stant in disciplyne or techinge, by word or by wrytinge, or in ensample. Also in weringe of heyres or of stamin. or of haubergeons on hir naked flesh, for Cristes sake, and swiche manere penances. But war thee wel that swiche manere penances on thy flesh ne make nat thyn herte bitter or angry or anoyed of thy-self; for bettre is to caste awey thyn heyre, than for to caste away the sikernesse of Jesu Crist. And therfore seith seint Paul: 'Clothe yow, as they that been chosen of god, in herte of misericorde, debonairetee, suffraunce, and swich manere of clothinge'; of whiche Jesu Crist is more apayed than of heyres, or haubergeons, or hauberkes.

§ 98. Thanne is disciplyne eek in knokkinge of thy brest, in scourginge with yerdes, in knelinges, in tribulacions; in suffringe paciently wronges that been doon to thee, and eek in pacient suffraunce of maladies, or lesinge of worldly catel, or of wyf, or of child, or othere freendes.

§ 99. Thanne shaltow understonde, whiche thinges destourben penaunce; and this is in four maneres, that is, drede, shame, hope, and wanhope, that is, desperacion. And for to speke first of drede; for which he weneth that he may suffre no penaunce; ther-agayns is remedie for to thinke, that bodily penaunce is but short and litel at regard of the peyne of helle, that is so cruel and so long, that it lasteth with-outen ende.

§ 100. Now again the shame that a man hath to shryven him, and namely, thise ypocrites that wolden been holden so parfite that they han no nede to shryven hem; agayns that shame, sholde a man thinke that, by wey of resoun, that he that hath nat been ashamed to doon foule thinges, certes him oghte nat been ashamed to do faire thinges, and that is confessiouns. A man sholde eek thinke, that god seeth and woot alle hise thoghtes and alle hise werkes; to him may no thing been hid ne covered. Men sholden eek remembren hem of the shame that is to come at the day of dome, to hem that been nat penitent and shriven in this present lyf. For alle the creatures in erthe and in helle shullen seen apertly al that they hyden in this world.

§ 101. Now for to speken of the hope of hem that been necligent and slowe to shryven hem, that stant in two maneres. That oon is, that he hopeth for to live longe and for to purchacen muche richesse for his delyt, and thanne he wol shryven him; and, as he seith, him semeth thanne tymely y-nough to come to shrifte. Another is, surquidrie that he hath in Cristes mercy.

Agayns the firste vyce, he shal thinke, that oure lyf is in no sikernesse; and eek that alle the richesses in this world ben in aventure, and passen as a shadwe on the wal. And, as seith seint Gregorie, that it aperteneth to the grete rightwisnesse of god, that nevere shal the peyne stinte of hem that nevere wolde withdrawen hem fro sinne, hir thankes, but ay continue in sinne; for thilke perpetual wil to do sinne shul they han perpetuel peyne.

§ 102. Wanhope is in two maneres: the firste wanhope is in the mercy of Crist; that other is that they thinken, that they ne mighte nat longe persevere in goodnesse. The firste wanhope comth of that he demeth that he hath sinned so greetly and so ofte, and so longe leyn in sinne, that he shal nat be saved. Certes, agayns that cursed wanhope sholde he thinke, that the passion of Jesu Crist is more strong for to unbinde than sinne is strong for to binde. Agayns the seconde wanhope, he shal thinke, that as ofte as he falleth he may aryse agayn by penitence. And thogh he never so longe have leyn in sinne, the mercy of Crist is alwey redy to receiven him to mercy. Agayns the wanhope, that he demeth that he sholde nat longe persevere in goodnesse, he shal thinke, that the feblesse of the devel may no-thing doon but-if men wol suffren him; and eek he shal han strengthe of the help of god, and of al holy chirche, and of the proteccioun of aungels, if him list.

§ 103. Thanne shal men understonde what is the fruit of penaunce; and, after the word of Jesu Crist, it is the endelees blisse of hevene, ther joye hath no contrarioustee of wo ne grevaunce, ther alle harmes been passed of this present lyf; ther-as is the sikernesse fro the peyne of helle; ther-as is the blisful companye, that rejoysen hem everemo, everich of otheres joye; ther-as the body of man, that whylom was foul and derk, is more cleer than the sonne; ther-as the body, that whylom was syk, freele, and feble, and mortal, is inmortal, and so strong and so hool that ther may nothing apeyren it; ther-as ne is neither hunger, thurst, ne cold, but every soule replenissed with the sighte of the parfit knowinge of god. This blisful regne may men purchace by poverte espirituel, and the glorie by lowenesse; the plentee of joye by hunger and thurst, and the reste by travaille; and the lyf by deeth and mortificacion of sinne.

Here taketh the makere of this book his leve.

§ 104. Now preye I to hem alle that herkne this litel tretis or rede, that if ther be any thing in it that lyketh hem, that ther-of they thanken oure lord Jesu Crist, of whom procedeth al wit and al goodnesse. And if ther be any thing that displese hem, I preye hem also that they arrette it to the defaute of myn unconninge, and nat to my wil, that wolde ful fayn have seyd bettre if I hadde had conninge. For oure boke seith, 'al that is writen is writen for oure doctrine'; and that is myn entente. Wherfore I beseke yow mekely for the mercy of god, that ye preye for me, that Crist have mercy on me and foryeve me my giltes:—and namely, of my translacions and endytinges of worldly vanitees, the whiche I revoke in my retracciouns: as is the book of Troilus; The book also of Fame; The book of the nynetene Ladies; The book of the Duchesse; The book of seint Valentynes day of the Parlement of Briddes; The tales of Caunterbury, thilke that sounen in-to sinne; The book of the Leoun; and many another book, if they were in my remembrance; and many a song and many a lecherous lay; that Crist for his grete mercy foryeve me the sinne. But of the translacion of Boece de Consolacione, and othere bokes of Legendes of seintes, and omelies, and moralitee, and devocioun, that thanke I oure lord Jesu Crist and his blisful moder, and alle the seintes of hevene; bisekinge hem that they from hennes-forth, un-to my lyves ende, sende me grace to biwayle my giltes, and to studie to the salvacioun of my soule:—and graunte me grace of verray penitence, confessioun and satisfaccioun to doon in this present lyf; thurgh the benigne grace of him that is king of kinges and preest over alle preestes, that boghte us with the precious blood of his herte; so that I may been oon of hem at the day of dome that shulle be saved: *Qui cum patre, &c.*

Here is ended the book of the Tales of Caunterbury, compiled by Geffrey Chaucer, of whos soule Jesu Crist have mercy. Amen.

NOTE ON THE
LANGUAGE AND METRE

A READER who takes up Chaucer for the first time in an edition like this, which aims at reproducing the text as he wrote it, will probably wonder why the three centuries that have passed since Shakespeare died have changed the language so little, and why two centuries more should make Chaucer's English seem difficult and remote. Difference of dialect will not account for it, for Chaucer was a Londoner, and except where the North-country clerks appear in the *Reeve's Tale*, he writes in the dialect of London, which is Shakespeare's too. Nor are changes in the quality of sounds (important as they are) a main cause of difficulty; for few readers of Shakespeare stop to consider what his pronunciation was, and probably not many of those who read Chaucer for pleasure would gain much by knowing that he pronounced *ou* in *hous, thou*, &c., like our *oo* in 'loose'; or the long *i* sound in *wyde* 'wide', *whyt* 'white', &c. (spelt *y* in this edition to distinguish it from short *i* in *wit*) as in our 'machine'.

Part of the explanation lies in the number of Chaucer's words that have become obsolete (e.g. on p. 1 *ferne* 'distant', *halwes* 'saints', *couthe* 'famous'), and in the much greater number that have changed their meanings (e.g. on the same page *vertu* 'quickening power', *croppes* 'shoots', *fowles* 'birds', *coráges* 'hearts'). Such loss and change go on incessantly; but the attractions of Elizabethan poetry, the conserving power of the language of the Bible, and the place of Shakespeare in modern studies, all tend to keep alive the vocabulary that was in use about 1600: even words and meanings that are no longer used are recognized in print. Besides, from Shakespeare's time to the present there is an unbroken line of authors and works that are commonly read, so that change is concealed by slow gradations. With Chaucer it is otherwise. In the gap of nearly two centuries between the *Canterbury Tales* (about 1386) and the great Elizabethans there is no work that is much read in its original form, and the considerable changes that took place in this interval seem greater than they are because we come upon them abruptly.

Yet the changes in vocabulary are not the most important. It so happens that all the obsolete words on p. 1 occur in one line; and if *ferne* does not survive, its base *far* does; if we have not *halwes* or *couthe* there are memorials of them in 'All Hallows' and 'uncouth'. The changes in grammar and spelling are revolutionary by comparison.

From the earliest times English has been shedding its inflexions. By Chaucer's day they were not more numerous in Northern English than they are in modern English. But in the London area, and so in Chaucer's speech, many inflexions that disappeared in the fifteenth century were still pronounced as separate syllables and had a grammatical value. For our present purposes the regular inflexions are more important than isolated survivals, and the first two pages of the text will usually supply examples.

Nouns. The genitive sing. ends in *-es*, which makes a syllable, e.g. *lord-es werre.* The plural of nouns usually ends in *-es*, e.g. *shour-es sote* 'sweet showers'; *tendre cropp-es* 'tender shoots'. But words of two or more syllables borrowed from French often make the plural in *-s*, e.g. *palmers, pilgrims.*

Adjectives in the plural usually end in *-e*, which is a separate syllable, e.g. *smal-e fowles.* The singular also usually ends in *-e* if it is preceded by a demonstrative word like *the, this, his,* e.g. *the yong-e sonne, his half-e cours.*

Pronoun. The personal pronoun in the 3rd singular is practically modern, but (*h*)*it* has the possessive *his*, never *its*, so that the three examples of *his* on p. 1 are probably not due to personification. For the plural 'they', 'their', 'them', Chaucer uses *they, hir, hem*, and it is easy to confuse the possessive plural *hir* 'their' with the singular *hir* 'her', e.g. at p. 358 (middle) where *hir livinge* means 'their living'. In the 2nd person *thou, thee* are in regular use, though the polite plural *ye* is used in addressing a superior. *You* is always objective and is never confused with *ye* nominative. The relative is commonly *that*; but *which*, and the composite forms *the which, the which that*, are fairly frequent. *Whos* and *whom* are also used as relatives, but the nominative *who* is only an interrogative or indefinite pronoun.

Verb. THE INFINITIVE ends in syllabic *-en* or *-e*: *sek-en* or *sek-e* 'seek'. Shorter forms are *go(on)*, *do(on)*, *be(en)*, *han* 'have'.

THE PRES. INDIC. is normally *y lov-e*, *thou lov-est*, *he lov-eth*, *we* (*ye*, *they*) *lov-en* or *lov-e*, compared with modern 'I love', 'he loves', 'we love', &c. But stems ending in *d*, *t*, *s*, have a short 3rd sing., e. g. *bit* = biddeth, *sit* = sitteth, *rist* = riseth. Note that the 3rd person sing. is the form of a number of impersonal verbs, which take the objective case of the pronoun, e. g. *me thinketh*, *you liketh*, *hir list*.

THE IMPERATIVE PLURAL sometimes ends in *-eth*, sometimes in *-e*, sometimes has no ending: note at p. 20 (foot) *herkneth . . . tak*, and the series at p. 352, which includes a curious Chaucerian usage: *as beth* 'be'.

THE PAST TENSE of weak verbs singular ends in *-e*, e. g. *hadd-e*. All verbs have in the past plural the ending *-en* or *-e*, e. g. *wer-en* beside *wer-e*.

THE PAST PARTICIPLE often has the prefix *y-*, e. g. *y-ronne*, *y-falle*. The ending in strong verbs is *-en* or *-e*, e. g. *holp-en*, *com-e*. In weak verbs the ending *-ed* is a syllable, e. g. *bath-ed*, *inspir-ed*.

This by no means exhausts the list of old endings, but it shows that many forms were a syllable longer in Chaucer's day than they are now, even though the spelling remains unchanged, as in *bathed*, *inspired*, *shires*.

Spelling. The spelling of Chaucerian manuscripts is more phonetic than ours. He pronounced consonant groups like *kn-*, *wr-*, *-gh-*, and *coude*, *vitaille*, *soverayn*, *goost* are truer forms than 'could', 'victuals', 'sovereign', 'ghost'. But modern spelling has sometimes the advantage, e. g. in 'sun', 'sundry', where Chaucer has *sonne*, *sondry* although the sound was *ŭ*, not *o*. Identification of the words will be easier if the following differences from present usage are noted:—*ou* and *ow* were alternatives, e. g. *shoures*. *yow*; so were *ei* : *ey* on the one hand and *ai* : *ay* on the other, and the modern spellings of *feith*, *wey*, *veyne*, *leyde*, *mayde* bear witness to a thorough jumbling since. *aun-* followed by a consonant often represents modern *an-*, e. g. in *straunge*, *Caunterbury*; and *er-* followed by a consonant is often modern *ar-*, e. g. *ferther*. *werre*. The occurrence of double and single letters is different: compare for the consonants *ful*, *al*, *sonne*, *werre*; and for the vowels *maad* 'made', *rote* 'root', *smoot* 'smote', *swete* 'sweet', *leet* 'let'. Observe that modern *ea*, *oa* are represented by *e*, *ee* and *o*, *oo*, e. g. in *seson*, *breeth*, *cloke*, *ooth*.

It might seem that modernized spelling, which is usual in editions of Shakespeare, would be a short cut through these difficulties. Yet the circumstances are not parallel. For as a rule, the number of syllables in a word in Shakespeare's time was the same as it is now; but to modernize Chaucer's spelling is to dock many words of a syllable (*wer-re*, for instance, would become *war*), and to make his smooth-paced verse into the rude jog-trot that Spenser and Dryden and Pope supposed it to be.

Metre. It was Tyrwhitt who recovered the secret of his rhythm about 1775, and the following rough rules apply to all the measures: (1) *-ed*, *-es* are distinct syllables; (2) final *-e* is a distinct syllable, except before a word beginning with a vowel or *h-*, when it is usually elided; (3) in the endings *-ioun*, *-ient*, &c., *-i-* is a syllable, e. g. *con-dic-i-oun*, *nac-i-oun*, *pac-i-ent*, *con-sci-enc-e*; (4) many French words keep their French accentuation, e. g. *licóur*, *melodýe*, *natúre*, *corágés*, *aventúre*. We may now scan two simple lines :—

> And báth|ed éver|y véynẹ | in swích | licóur.
> And smál|e fówl|es mák|en mél|odý|e

Note that *-e* at the line end (e. g. in *melody-e*) makes a syllable; as is shown by rimes like *Rome* : *to me* p. 18 (top); *ba me* : *blame* p. 95 (mid.); *youthe* : *allow the* p. 435 (mid.); *tyme* : *by me* p. 494; *swythe* : *hy the* p. 496 (mid.).

Two more lines (p. 3) will illustrate the elision of *-e* within the verse :—

> Wel coudẹ | he síttẹ | on hórs | and fáir|ë rýd|e.
> He cóud|ë sóng|es mákẹ | and wél | endýt|e.

The rhythm would be monotonous if it were always regular, and in fact Chaucer allows himself many of the liberties which are familiar in later English verse. He may begin the line with a single strong syllable, e. g. p. 8 :—

> Twén|ty bók|es clád | in blák | or réed,

or trippingly, with three syllables, e. g. p. 252 (mid.) :—

> Pékkẹ hem up | right as | they grówẹ | and étẹ | hem ín.

And the regular fall of the natural stress is often varied by inversion: we should not, for instance, read *right ás* in the line last quoted.

GLOSSARY

THE glossary includes hard words and phrases, obsolete meanings and some proper names which might not be recognized. As a rule it is enough to give the usual form of classical names, which can be followed up in a dictionary like Lempriere's. To the names of saints the anniversary is added, as a key to collections such as Alban Butler's *Lives of the Saints*. Any one who bears in mind the remarks on spelling at p. 599 above, will be saved a good deal of searching.

a, *indef. art.* a, one; *al a*, the whole of a.
a, *prep.* on; *a-nighte*, by night; *a three*, in three.
abayst, amazed, abashed.
abegge, abeye, pay for.
a-begged, a begging.
abit = abideth.
a-blakeberied, astray.
abo(u)ghte, paid for; see **abye**.
abood, *pl.* abodes, delay.
abood, *pa. t. sg.* of **abyde**.
aboute, about; in turn.
abrayde, started (up).
abregginge, diminishing.
abroche, to broach.
abusioun, deceit.
abyden, await, abide; refrain.
abye, pay for, suffer for, atone for; *pp. and pa. t.* abo(u)ght(e).
a-caterwawed, a-caterwauling.
accident, outward appearance; change of appearance.
accidie, sloth.
achat, purchase.
achatours, buyers.
acordaunt (to), in accord (with).
acorde, to agree; suit.
acustomaunce; *had of a.*, was accustomed.
adawed, *pp.* awake.
Adoun, Adonis.
adrad, afraid.
Adriane = Ariadne.
aferd, afraid.
affeccioun, desire.
affiance, trust.
afforced, forced.
affrayed, afraid, frightened.
affyle, to make smooth.
after, according to (as); in expectation of (for); *wayte after*, to seek; *after me*, according to my command.
agains, against; in answer to; instead of; before, in the presence of; to meet; near to.
agaynward, back again.
agilte, offended.
ago(n), ago, gone; dead.
agregge, to aggravate.
agrief; *take a.*, take (it) amiss.
agrysen, to be horrified (at).
aketoun, sleeveless tunic.
al, *adj.* all, every; *adv.* quite; *conj.* whether, although; *al on highte*, quite aloud; *al and som(e)*, the whole, one and all; *al so*, so.
alambykes, alembics.
alaunts, boar hounds.
alayes, alloys.
albificacioun, whitening.
alderfirst, first of all; cp. **aller**, *gen. pl.* of **all**.
Aldiran, star in the forepaws of Leo.

alestake, a pole projecting from an ale-house to support a sign or bush.
algate(s), always ; anyway.
Algezir, Algeçiras, taken from the Moors in 1344.
Alisaundre, Alexandria, captured 1365.
alkamistre, alchemist.
Alkaron, the Koran.
Alla, English king (d. 588).
aller, *gen. pl.* of all ; *our aller*, of us all ; *hir aller*, of them all. Cp. **alder-**.
allow, to applaud.
allyed, provided with aid.
Almageste, Ptolemy's 'greatest' work on Astronomy.
almesse, alms.
Alocen, Alhazen, Arabic optician (eleventh century).
aloon, alone ; *her aloon*, by herself.
als(o), **alswa**, also, so, as.
Amadrides, Hamadryads.
amalgaming, making an amalgam (of mercury and another metal).
ambes as, double aces (dice).
amenuse, to diminish.
amerciments, fines.
ameved, **amoeved**, moved, changed ; perturbed.
amonesteth, admonishes ; recommends.
amy, friend.
an, on ; *an heigh*, on high.
anes, once.
anhange, to hang.
anientissed, brought to naught.
anlas, a dagger.
annueleer, chaplain who sings anniversary masses.
annunciat, foretold.
anon(-rightes), immediately.
anoy, trouble, sadness.
anoy-ful, **-ous**, tedious, troublesome, disagreeable.
Antheus, Antaeus.
Antony, *fyr of seint*, erysipelas.
aornement, adornment.
apayse ; see **apese**.
ap(p)alled, made pale ; weakened.
ap(p)arail(len), prepare.
ape, (ape), dupe.
apeiren, injure, impair.
aperceive, perceive.
apert, open, frank.
aperteneth, belongs (to).
apese, **apeise**, appease.
ap(p)osed, questioned.
appreved, approved.
approwours, informers.
apyked, trimmed, adorned.
arace, to tear away.
araise ; see **areysen**.
arches ; see **ark**.
archewyves, masterful wives.
arest, rest (for a spear).
areste, arrest, detention ; restraint.
aret(t)en, account, impute.
areysen, to levy.
a-rewe, in a row.
argoile, crude tartar.
arist = **ariseth**.
ark, sun's daily course.
arm-greet, thick as one's arm.
armipotente, powerful in arms.
armoniak, ammoniac.
Armorik, Brittany.
Arnold of the Newe Toun, Arnoldus de Villa Nova, taught in France (d. 1312).
Arpies, Harpies.
arrerage, arrears.
ars-metryke, arithmetic.

Art, Ovid's *Ars Amatoria*.
artow, art thou.
arwes, arrows.
aryve, arrival, landing.
as, so, like ; *as after*, according to; *as now* (*nouthe*), at present ; *as that*, as soon as ; with imperative, e. g. *as lat*, pray let ; *as lene*, pray lend.
as, an ace (at dice).
ascaunce(s), as if, perhaps.
aslake, diminish, assuage.
asp, aspen tree.
aspect, an (astrological) aspect ; i. e. the position of heavenly bodies relative to one another or to an observer.
assege, to besiege.
assoilen, absolve.
Assuere, Ahasuerus.
assyse, assize, session.
asterte, to escape.
astonyed, amazed.
astored, stored.
astromye (*for* astronomye).
aswowne, in a swoon.
at, at ; as to ; by ; *at his large*, free ; *at on*, at one ; *at yë*, at a glance.
at-after, after.
atake, overtake.
atazir, evil influence.
atempraunce, moderation.
atempre, *adj.* modest ; *v. refl.* control oneself.
athamaunt, adamant.
at-ones, at once.
atoon, at one ; *bringen atoon*, to reconcile.
at-rede, surpass in counsel.
at-renne, to outrun.
attamed, broached.
atte, at the ; *atte beste*, in the best way; *atte hasard*, at dice.
Atthalante, Atalanta.
Attheon, Actaeon.
attry, venomous.
a-twinne, apart.
auctor, author ; original.
auctoritee, authority.
augrim-stones, counters for calculating.
auntre, to risk.
auntrous, adventurous.
Austin, St. Augustine of Hippo, d. 430 (Aug. 28).
avale, to take off.
avaunce, to profit, advance.
avaunt, boast.
aventayle, front of helmet.
aventure, adventure, chance.
Averrois, Moorish physician of Cordova (1126–98).
Avicen, Avicenna (978–1036), Arab physician, wrote the *Canon*, a famous medical text-book.
avoutier, adulterer.
avowtrie, adultery.
avys, advice, deliberation.
avyse, *v.* consider ; *adj.* wary.
avysely, advisedly.
avysement, deliberation.
await, watch ; *have in awayt*, to watch.
awaite, to watch.
awen, own.
aweyward, backwards.
awroken, avenged.
axe, ask ; **axing**, question.
ayeins, against.
ayel, grandfather.

ba, to kiss.
Babilan Tisbee, Thisbe of Babylon.
bachelrye, young men.
Bacus, Bacchus (wine).

bak, rough cloak.
balaunce; *in b.*, in jeopardy.
balke, balk, beam.
balled, bald.
banes, bones.
barbre, barbarous.
barm-clooth, apron.
barme, bosom, lap.
Barnabo Viscounte, Bernabo Visconti of Milan (d. 1385).
basilicok, basilisk.
batailled, battlemented.
bathe, both.
bauderye, coarse mirth.
baudy, dirty.
bawdrik, baldric.
Bayard, proverbial name for a horse.
bechen, made of beech.
bede, to proffer; tell.
bedes, *peire of b.*, rosary.
bedrede, bedridden.
been, *pl.* bees.
beere, bier.
beet, kindle; see bete.
beggestere, (female) beggar.
behette; see bihete.
bekke, to nod.
bel amy, good friend.
bele chere, good cheer.
Belmarye, a N. African state.
bely, pair of bellows.
bely-naked, stark-naked.
beme, trumpet.
bendinge, slant-banding.
benigne, gentle, modest.
bent, grassy slope.
berafte, bereft.
berd, beard; *in the berd*, face to face; *make (his) berd*, deceive (him).
bere, bear; *beren on honde*, accuse; make to believe; *bere thurgh*, pierce.
berm, yeast.
bern, barn.
Bernard, Gordonius, teacher of medicine at Montpellier; wrote *Lilium Medicinae* in 1305.
bet, better.
bete, improve, help; kindle.
Bevis; see the Romance of Sir Beves of Hampton, ed. Kölbing, E.E.T.S.
beye, to buy.
bibbed, imbibed.
bi-bledde, covered with blood.
bicched bones, *i.e.* dice.
bi-clappe, to catch, trap.
bidaffed, befooled.
bidde, to ask; command; pray.
biheste, *n.* promise.
bihete, **bihote**, to promise.
bihovely, needful.
biknowe, confess; *pa. t.* **biknew**.
bileve, to remain behind.
bille, letter; petition.
biscorned, scorned.
biseken, beseech.
bisemare, *n.* scorn.
bisette, used, employed.
biseye, beseen; *wel (yvel) b.*, fair (ill) looking; *richely b.*, splendid.
bismotered, spotted.
bispet, spit upon.
bistad, *hard b.*, in great peril.
bit = biddeth.
bitake, commend, commit.
biteche, to entrust (to).
bitore, bittern.
bitraise, **bitraisshe**, betray.
bitydinge, happening.
biwreye, reveal, betray.
blankmanger, a 'white' dish made of chicken, &c.

Blee, Blean Forest in Kent.
blent, deceived.
blesse, make the sign of the cross (over).
bleynte, blenched.
blinne, to cease.
blosme, blossom.
blyve, quickly.
bobance, presumption, boast.
boce, boss, hump.
boceler, buckler.
bode, *pp.* bidden.
Boece, Boethius, d. 524.
boes, behoves.
boist, box.
boistous, roughly; **-ly**, loudly.
bokeler, buckler.
boket, bucket.
bole armoniak, Armenian clay, a styptic.
bolle, bowl.
Boloigne, (1) Boulogne (*Prologue*); (2) Bologna in Italy.
bombleth, booms.
bonde, bondman.
bone, a boon.
Book of the nynetene Ladies, Chaucer's *Legend of Good Women.*
boost, boast, talk, noise.
boot, *pa. t. sg.* bit.
boras, borax.
bord, table; meal; board.
bordels, brothels.
borel, coarse, common.
borwe, *n.* pledge; *v.* borrow.
bos, boss.
bote, benefit; healing.
boterflye, butterfly.
bouk, trunk (of the body).
boun, prepared.
bountee, goodness.
bourde, *n.* jest; *v.* to jest.
boydekin, dagger.
bracer, **bracer**, a guard for the arm in archery.
Bradwardyn, Abp. Thomas (d. 1349), wrote *de Causa Dei.*
bragot, honeyed ale.
brasil, a reddish dye.
breme, furiously.
bren, bran.
brenne, to burn; see **brinne**.
brenningly, fervently.
brere, briar.
breste, **brast**, **brosten**, burst.
bretful, **brat-**, brimful.
bretherhed, brotherhood.
breyde, to awake; snatch.
brige, contention.
brike, snare, dilemma.
brinne, to burn.
Brixseyde, Briseis.
brocage, mediation.
Brok, Badger (name for a horse).
brokkinge, warbling.
Bromeholm, in Norfolk, where a fragment of the True Cross was kept.
brond, firebrand.
brood, **brode**, broad.
brotel, brittle; insecure.
brouded, embroidered.
brouke, enjoy, use.
browding, embroidery.
broyded, braided.
Brutus Cassius, a confusion of the two persons Brutus and Cassius.
brybe, steal, filch.
bryberyes, ways of robbing.
bukkes horn, *blowe the*, have one's pains for nothing.
bulde, build: *pp.* **bulte**.
bulte, to boult, sift.
burdoun, bass.

burel, unlettered; see **borel**.
buriels, tombs.
burned, burnished.
Burnel the Asse, the *Speculum Stultorum* of Nigel Wireker, printed by T. Wright, *Anglo-Latin Satirists of the Twelfth Century*, vol. 1.
busk, bush.
but if, unless.
buxom, obedient.
by and by, in order.

caas, circumstance, cases.
calcening, calcination.
Calistopee, nymph Callisto.
calle, head-dress.
camaille, camel.
Cambinskan, Gengis Khan, Milton's Cambuscan.
camuse, flat, snub.
can, (I) know.
Cantebrigge, Cambridge.
cantel, portion.
Capaneus, one of the seven kings who besieged Thebes.
capel, **capul**, horse.
cappe, cap; *set the wrightes cappe*, made a fool of him.
cardiacle, heart-disease.
careful, sorrowful.
careyne, carcase.
cariage, tolls, dues.
carl, man, rustic.
carpe, to talk.
carrik, barge.
cas, accident, occasion; *to dyen in the cas*, though death be the result; see **caas**.
Cassidori, Cassiodorus, d. 575.
cast, *n.* plan; occasion.
caste, to reckon (on); contrive.
casuelly, by accident.
catapuce, garden spurge.
catel, goods, chattels.
Catoun, Dionysius Cato, supposed author of a collection of Moral Distichs.
cavillacioun, cavilling.
Cedasus, Scedasus (in Plutarch).
cered, waxed, sealed.
cerial ook, holm oak.
certein, sure(ly); *c. gold*, a stated sum; *a c.*, a fixed quantity.
ceruce, white lead.
cetewale, valerian.
ceynt, girdle.
Ceys, Ceyx (in Ovid, *Metamorphoses* xi).
chaffare, wares; trade; matters.
chalons, blankets.
chamberere, maidservant.
champartye, equality.
chanon, canon.
chapman, trader.
chapman-hede, trade.
charbocle, carbuncle (stone).
charge, care; burden; *of that no c.*, it matters not.
chargeant, burdensome.
chasted, *pp.* taught.
chasteyn, chestnut.
chaunterie, endowment for singing masses.
cheep, bargain.
che(e)se, to choose.
cheeste, wrangling.
chepe, to bargain.
Chepe, Cheapside (London).
chere, countenance; manner.
cheve, thrive, succeed.
chevisaunce, dealing; borrowing.
chiertee, affection.
chilindre, small sun-dial.

chichivache, cow-like monster, who grew thin on a diet of patient wives.
chimbe, rim of a barrel.
chimbe, to chime.
chinche(rye), niggard(ry).
chirche-hawe, church-yard.
chirche-reves, church-wardens.
chirketh, chirps.
chisels, scissors.
chit = chideth.
chiteren, to chatter.
chivachee, -ye, feat of horsemanship; expedition.
chydester, a scold.
ciclatoun, a rich cloth.
cink, five (at dice).
Cipioun, Cicero's *Somnium Scipionis*, annotated by Macrobius.
Cithero, Cicero.
citole, a harp.
citrinacioun, turning lemon colour (in alchemy).
clappe, *n.* and *v.* chatter.
clarree, spiced wine.
clawe, to rub.
clepen, to call, summon.
clergeon, chorister.
clergial, learned.
clergye, learning.
cliket, latch-key.
clippe, to embrace.
Clitemistra, Clytemnestra.
clobbed, clubbed.
clom! be silent!
cloos, closed.
clos, closure, enclosure.
clote-leef, burdock leaf.
clothered, clotted.
clowe-gilofre, clove.
cod, bag; stomach.
cokenay, cockney, milksop.
Cokkes = *Goddes*, God's.
cokkow, cuckoo.
colde, to grow cold.
col-fox, fox with black markings.
collacioun, conference.
collects, tables of motions of planets.
Coloigne, Cologne, where pilgrims visited the shrine of the Three Kings.
colours, ornaments of style.
colpons, shreds, bundles.
columbyn, dove-like.
come, *n.* coming.
comestow, comest thou.
commune, *adj.* general; *n.* the commons.
compaignable, companionable.
complexioun, temperament.
composicioun, agreement.
comune, a right of using another's land.
comyn, cummin.
confiture, mixture.
confus, confounded.
conne, can; know how to.
conning, experience, learning.
conseil, council; counsel(lor).
consistorie, court of justice.
constablesse, governor's wife.
Constantyn (the African), became a monk of Monte Cassino, and translated medical works from Arabic (11th cent.).
constellacioun, influence of the stars.
contek, strife.
contenance, gesture, demeanour.
continued, accompanied.

contubernial, familiar.
convertible, equivalent.
cop, top, hill-top.
coppe, cup.
corage, heart, desire.
cordewane, Cordovan leather.
corniculere, assistant.
corrumpable, corruptible.
cors, body
corse, *v.* curse.
cosinage, kinship.
costlewe, costly.
cote, cot ; dungeon.
couched, embroidered.
coude, could, knew (how).
countenance, show, pretext.
countour, auditor ; office.
countretaille, counter-tally ; *at the c.* = back again.
countrewaite, keep watch (over *or* against).
courtepy, short rough coat.
couthe, knew ; *pp.* known.
coveityse, covetousness, lust.
covenable, suitable.
covent, convent of monks.
coverchief, kerchief.
covyne, deceitfulness.
cow, chough ; cp. *Manciple's T.*
cracching, scratching.
craketh, croaks ; roars.
crased, cracked.
creant, *seith c.*, acknowledges defeat.
creaunce, *n.* belief ; *v.* borrow.
crekes, wiles.
cryke. creek.
Crisippus, Chrysippus, Greek writer quoted by Jerome.
Cristofre, image of St. C.
croce, cross, staff.
crop, top ; shoot ; summit.
cropen, *pp.* crept.
croper, **croupe(r)**, crupper.
croslet, crucible.
crouche, mark with the cross.
croude, to thrust.
crouke. pitcher.
crul(le), curly.
crydestow, didst thou cry out.
cucurbites, flasks.
culpe, guilt.
cure, care.
curiositee, fastidiousness.
curious, skilful, careful.
custume, custom ; dues.
cut, lot.
Cutberd, St. Cuthbert (Mar. 20).

daf, fool.
dagged, tagged.
dagon, small piece.
Dalida, Delilah.
Damascien, Johannes Damascenus, reputed author of medical *Aphorisms* translated from Arabic.
dampne, to condemn.
Dan, **Daun**, master, sir.
dare, to doze, be dazed.
Dane, Daphne.
Dant, Dante (d 1321).
darreyne, to contest.
daswen, to be dim.
daunger, control ; liability.
daungerous, forbidding ; sparing ; hard to please.
dawes, days.
daweth, dawns.
debate, do battle.
deduyt, pleasure.
de(e)dly, mortal.
deer, wild animals.
defence, denial.
defendaunt, defence.
defende, forbid ; defend.
degyse, *adj.* elaborate.

Deiscorides, Dioscorides, Greek physician (2nd cent.).
delicacye, amusement.
delit(able), delight(ful).
deliver, active, clever.
delyces, delights.
demeyne, dominion.
depardieux, 'in God's name.'
departe, to divide.
Depeford, Deptford.
depper, *comp.* more deeply.
dere, to harm.
dere (*ynough a*), not worth a.
derne, secret.
derre, *comp.* more dearly.
descensories, vessels for extracting oil.
desclaundred, slandered.
deshonestee, unseemliness.
deslavee, foul; unbridled.
desordeynee, inordinate.
despence, expenditure.
despitous, angry, scornful.
desray, confusion.
destreyne, dis-, constrain, vex.
devoir, duty.
devys, direction; wish.
devyse, narrate, explain.
dextrer, war-horse.
deye, dairywoman.
deynous, arrogant.
deyntee, *n.* worth; pleasure.
deys, platform, daïs.
dighte, prepare, array.
digne, worthy.
dilatacioun, diffuseness.
dischevele, dishevelled.
discryven, to describe.
disese, distress, unrest.
disjoynt, difficulty.
disparage, *n.* and *v.* dishonour.
distemperaunce, inclemency.
distempre, to vex.
divinistre, diviner.
divisioun, distinction.
divynailes, divinations.
domesman, judge.
doom, judgement, sentence.
do(on), do; cause; *with infin.*, e.g. *don strepen*, cause to be stripped; *do wey*, cease.
dortour, dormitory.
dradde, feared.
draf, *n.* refuse, chaff.
draf-sek, sack of chaff.
drasty, filthy, worthless.
drecched, vexed, troubled.
dreechinge, *n.* prolonging.
dredful, cautious, afraid.
drenchen, to drown; *pa. t.* dreynte.
dresse, to prepare.
drogges, drugs.
dronkelewe, drunken.
drough, drew.
drovy, dirty, turbid.
drugge, to drudge.
Dun is in the myre, game in which Dun, a log representing a horse, must be pulled out of the mire.
dure, endure; live.
dwale, sleeping draught.
dy, *je vous dy*, I tell you.

echoon, each one, every one.
eek, also.
eft, again.
eftsone(s), soon after; again.
egalitee, equality.
eggement, incitement.
Egipcien Marie, St. Mary of Egypt (April 2).
egre, bitter, keen.
egremoine, agrimony (plant).
elenge, miserable.
Eleyne, Helen of Troy.
Elie, Elijah.

Elisee, Elisha.
ellebor, hellebore.
elvish, abstracted, 'daft'.
embrouded, embroidered.
embusshements, ambuscades.
Emelward, *to E.*, towards Emilia (N. Italy).
emforth, to the extent of.
empeireden, made worse.
emplastre, to whitewash.
emprenting, impression.
empte, to empty.
enbibing, absorption.
encense, to offer incense.
enchesoun, occasion.
encrees, increase.
encressen, to increase, enrich.
endelong, all along.
endyte, to write; compose.
Enee, Aeneas.
engreggen, to burden.
engyn, wit; cunning.
engyned, tortured.
enhauncen, to raise.
enhorte, to exhort.
enluting, daubing with clay.
enoynt, anointed.
entende, to attend (to).
entredited, interdicted.
entremette, to interfere.
entreteden, discussed.
envoluped, enveloped.
envyned, supplied with wine.
erbe-yve, buck's horn (herb).
ere, to plough.
erme, to grieve.
Ermyn, an Armenian.
erraunt, wandering.
Erro, Hero.
erst, at first; *e. than*, before.
eschaufen, to heat; be angry.
eschew, *adj.* averse.
Esculapius, Greek god of medicine.
ese, to entertain.
esement, benefit.
especes, varieties.
espiaille, set of spies.
essoyne, excuse.
estatlich, stately.
estres, recesses, interior.
even(e), average; *adv.* closely.
evene-cristene, fellow Christian.
everich, each, every.
everichoon, every one.
ew, yew-tree.
exametron, hexameter.
expans, separate(ly).
ey, egg.
eyle, to ail.
Ezekias, Hezekiah.

facounde, eloquence.
fader, *gen.* father's.
fadme, fathoms.
fair(nesse), good(ness).
falding, coarse cloth.
falle, to happen.
falwe, yellow; brown.
falwes, fallow ground.
fan, quintain, mark to tilt at.
fantome, delusion.
fare, conduct; fuss.
faren, to go; behave; *pa. t.* **ferde**.
farsed, stuffed.
fawe, fain.
fay, **fey**, faith.
feendly, fiendish.
feet, feat; acts.
feffed (in), endowed (with).
fele, many.
Femenye, women, the Amazons.
fen, Arabic name for the subsections of Avicenna's *Canon*.
fer, **ferre**, **ferreste**, far, &c.

ferd(e), went; behaved.
fere, companion.
fered, afraid.
ferforth(ly), thoroughly.
ferly, strange.
fermacies, remedies.
ferme, rent.
fermerere, infirmary keeper.
fern(e), distant; long ago.
fern-asshen, fern-ashes.
ferthe, fourth.
ferthing, morsel.
fest, fist.
festeyinge, feasting.
festlich, festive.
fet, fetched.
fether, wing.
fetis(ly), elegant(ly).
feyntest, enfeeblest.
finch, *pulle a f.*, pluck a dupe.
finding, provision.
fint = findeth.
fit, turn; canto; stave.
fithele, fiddle.
fixe, solidified.
fla(u)mbe, flame.
fleen, *pl.* fleas.
fleete, flete, to float.
flemen, to banish.
flemer, banisher.
flex, flax.
fley, flew.
flo, arrow.
flokmele, in crowds.
flotery, dishevelled.
flough, flew.
floytinge, playing on the flute.
fneseth, (he) snorts.
folily, foolishly.
fonde, try to persuade.
fonge, to take, receive.
fonne, fool.
fontstoon, font.
fool-large, overlavish.
foot-hot, instantly.
for, for; because of, to prevent.
for-, *intensive prefix* (a) *with adjs.* 'very', as: **for-blak**, very black; **for-dry, for-old.** (b) *with verbs*, as: **for-brused**, badly bruised; **-cutten**, to cut to pieces; **-do**, to destroy; **-dronken, -fered**, very drunk, afraid; **-gon**, lost; **-kerveth**, hews in pieces; **-laft**, abandoned; **-leseth**, loses utterly; **-leten**, to abandon; **-pyned**, wasted away; **-sleuthen**, to waste in sloth; **-sluggeth**, spoils; **-straught**, distracted; **-troden**, trodden under foot; **-waked**, worn out with watching; **-wrapped**, wrapped up.
fore, path, track.
forfeted, did wrong.
forme-fader, first parent, Adam.
forn-cast, premeditated.
forneys, furnace.
fors; *no fors*, no matter.
forster, forester.
forthren, help.
forth-right, directly.
forthy, therefore; *nat f.*, nevertheless.
fortunen, to favour; presage.
forward, covenant.
forwiting, foreknowledge.
forwoot, foreknew.
foryelde, to requite.
foryetelnesse, forgetfulness.
foryeten, to forget.
foryeve, to forgive.
fother, cart-load.
foundred, stumbled.

foyne, to thrust.
foyson, plenty.
fraknes, freckles.
franchyse, liberality.
frayne, freyne, to ask.
freele, frail.
fremde, foreign.
frenesye, madness.
frenges, fringes.
freten, to consume.
frote, to rub.
fruytesteres, fruit-vendors.
fumetere, fumitory (herb).
fumositee, headiness.
furial, raging.

gabbe, to talk idly.
gadeling, vagabond.
gaillard, joyous.
gale, to sing, exclaim.
Galgopheye, Gargaphie (Ovid, *Metamorphoses* iii, 156).
galianes, medicines.
Galien, Gallienus (d. 268), Roman emperor (p. 234).
Galien, Galen, Greek physician (2nd cent. A. D.) and the great authority in the Middle Ages.
galle, sore place.
galoun, gallon (of).
galping, gaping.
galwes, gallows.
gamed, it pleased.
gan, *with infin. forms past tense*, e.g. *gan calle*, called.
ganeth, yawns.
gargat, throat.
garnisoun, garrison.
gas, goes (Northern dialect).
Gatesden (John), Oxford physician (d. 1361); wrote *Rosa Anglica.*
gat-toothed, with teeth wide apart; wanton (?).
gaude, trick, pranks.
gauded (*with green*), with large green beads separating the decades (of a rosary).
gaude-green, yellowish green.
Gaufred, Geoffrey de Vinsauf (about 1200), lamented Richard I in his *Poetria Novella.*
Gaunt, Ghent.
gaure, to stare.
gayler, jailer.
gayneth, avails.
gaytres, dogwood.
geen, gone (Northern form).
Geniloun. Ganelon, who betrayed Charlemagne's army at Roncesvalles.
gent, *adj.* noble; slim.
geomancie, divination by figures made on the earth.
gere, capricious mood; gear.
gerful, gery, changeable.
Gernade, Granada.
gerner, garner.
Geroundo, river Gironde.
geste, (alliterative) romance.
gestour, a story-teller.
get, contrivance.
gif, if.
gigginge, strapping.
Gilbertyn, Gilbertus Anglicus, English physician (12th–13th cent.).
gin, snare; contrivance.
ginne, to begin.
gipoun, short vest.
gipser, purse.
girden, to strike.
girles, youths.
giterne, guitar.
glader, one who cheers.

glede, gleed, glowing coal.
gleyre, white of egg.
glimsing, glimmering.
glood, *pa. t.* glided.
glose, to flatter; explain.
gnof, churl.
gnow, gnawed.
gobet, morsel.
godsib, sponsor.
goldes, marigolds.
golet, gullet, throat.
goliardeys, buffoon.
gonge, privy.
gonne(n), began; did.
goot, goat.
Gootland, Gottland.
gore, gusset, garment; *under my g.*, beside me.
gost(ly), spirit(ually).
governaille, mastery.
grame, anger.
gras-tyme, spring-time of life.
graunges, granaries.
gra(u)nt mercy! many thanks!
grayn, a scarlet dye.
gree, pleasure; superiority.
greithe, to prepare.
grenehede, immaturity.
Grete See, E. Mediterranean.
greve, grove.
greyn, cardamom, a spice.
grinte, gnashed.
gronte, groaned.
grope, to examine.
grot, particle, bit.
grote, a Dutch coin, groat.
groyn, snout.
groyning, murmuring.
grucche, to grumble.
gruf, *adj.* grovelling.
grys, grey (fur).
guerdons, *for alle g.*, at all costs.
Gy (Sir): see the Romance of Guy of Warwick (ed. Zupitza, E.E.T.S.).
gye, to guide.
gylour, beguiler.
gyse, way, custom; discretion.
Gysen, river in the East called by Herodotus 'Gyndes'.
gyte, skirt; mantle.

Habradates, Abradates (in Xenophon, *Cyropaedia*).
haf, heaved.
hainselins, short jackets.
hakeney, horse.
haliday, holy day, festival.
halke, nook, corner.
hals, neck; throat.
halse, to beseech.
halt = holdeth, keeps.
halwen, to hallow.
halwes, saints; shrines.
Haly, Arab commentator on Galen (10th–11th cent.). Another, Haly Abbas (d. 994), wrote a medical encyclopaedia called *Maliki* or *De Dispositione Regali.*
ham, home (Northern).
han, to have.
handebrede, hand's breadth.
hardily, assuredly.
harie, to drag.
harlot, rascal.
harneys, armour.
harre, hinge.
harrow! *interj.* help!
harwed, harried.
hasard(rye), dice-play.
Hasdrubal, King of Carthage, 146 B.C.
hastow, hast thou.
haubergeoun, coat of mail.
haunt, practice, skill.

haunten, to practise.
hauteyn, loud; haughty.
hawe, hedge, yard.
hawe, haw; *hawe bake*, baked haws; coarse fare.
Hayles, abbey in Gloucestershire where was a relic of the Holy Blood.
hayt! *interj.* come up!
heer, *pl.* **heres**, hair.
heeste, commandment.
heet, *pp.* was called.
helde, to hold.
hele, health.
hele, to conceal.
Helowys, Heloïse, married Abelard (d. 1164).
hende, courteous.
heng, *pa. t* hung.
henne, hence.
hente, to catch, get.
hepe, hip (berry).
heraude, to proclaim.
herbergage, lodging.
herbergeours, harbingers.
herberwe, inn.
herie, to praise, worship.
Hermes, Hermes 'the thrice great', to whom philosophical and alchemical writings were attributed.
herne, corner.
heronsewes, young herons.
hert, hart.
herte-spoon, breast-bone.
herying, praising.
hete, to promise.
hethen, hence.
hething, contempt.
heved, head.
hevinesse, sadness.
hewe (1), hue, mien.
hewe (2), servant.
heyne, wretch.
heyre, hair; hair-shirt.
hight, promised, was called.
highte; *on h.* aloud.
hindreste, hindmost.
hir, *gen. pl.* of them; *poss.* their.
hit = hideth.
hochepot, mixture.
Hogge = Roger.
hoker, scorn.
hold, possession; castle.
holour, adulterer.
holt, wood.
hond, hand; *beren him on h.* accuse.
honest, honourable, seemly.
honestee, goodness, virtue.
honge, to hang.
hool, whole, sound.
hoot, hot.
hoppesteres, dancers.
hostesman, servant to guests at a convent (?), p. 337.
hote, to command; **hoten**, be called.
houndfish, dogfish.
housled, having received the Eucharist.
howve, cap; *sette his h.*, befool.
hunte, hunter.
hust, hushed.
hyne, servant.
Hugelyne of Pyse, Hugelino of Pisa (d. 1289); see *Inferno*, Canto xxxiii.
Hugh (of Lincoln), supposed to have been murdered by Jews 27th Aug., 1255.

I-, prefix of past participle; see **Y-**.
idus, ides.
Iepte, Jeptha.
ie vous dy, I tell you.

ignotum per ignotius (to explain) 'an unknown thing by one more unknown'.
ik, I (Northern).
il-hayl, bad luck (to you).
ilke, same.
impertinent, irrelevant.
impes, grafts, scions.
importable, insufferable.
infect, made of no effect.
in-fere, together, in company.
ingot, a mould for metal.
inned, housed, lodged.
inordinate, unusual.
in principio, 'in the beginning (was the Word)'.
intendestow, dost thou intend?
in-with, within.
Ioce, St. Judoc (13th Dec.).
ipocras, a cordial drink.
irous, angry.
irregular, a sinner against the rule of his order.
is, am, art (Northern).
Isidre, Isidore of Seville, d. 636.
Isiphilee, Hypsipyle.
Isope, Aesop.
ivy-leef, *pipen in an i.*, 'go whistle'.

Jakke of Dover, kind of pie(?).
Jakke Straw, led the London mob against the Flemings in 1381.
jade, miserable hack.
jambeux, leggings.
jane, small coin of Genoa.
janglere, jester, raconteur.
jangleresse, female gossip.
jape, jest, trick.
jeet, jet.
jet, fashion, mode.
Jesus Syrak, i.e. Ecclesiasticus.
Jewerye, a Jews' quarter.
jogelour, juggler.
jolyer, *comp.* handsomer.
jordanes, chamber-pots.
joynant, adjoining.
Jubaltar, Gibraltar.
jubbe, large jug.
Judicum, Book of Judges.
juge (for jug), a yoke.
juste, to joust, tilt.
juyse, judgement, sentence.

Kaynard, dotard.
kechil, small cake.
keep, *take keep*, take heed.
kembe, to comb.
kempe, shaggy, rough.
kers, cress; trifle.
kerver, sculptor.
kid, *pp.* known.
kimelin, a large tub.
kinde, lineage; nature.
kindely, by nature.
kinges note, name of a tune.
kitte, *pa. t.* cut.
knakkes, knacks, tricks.
knarre, thick-set fellow.
knarry, gnarled.
knave, boy, servant.
knowes, *pl.* knees.
knowlecheth, acknowledges.
kyken, peep.
kythe, show, make known.

La(a)s, lace; net.
labbe, tell-tale, blabber.
Lacedomie, Lacedaemonia.
lacerte, muscle.
lachesse, idleness.
ladde, took, carried.
Ladomea, Laodamia.
lady, *gen.* lady's.

lafte, ceased.
lake, fine white linen.
lampe, a thin plate.
Lamuel, Lemuel, Prov. xxxi.
lappe, fold, edge.
large, liberal.
last, 'million' (a vague number).
lathe, barn.
latoun, latten, kind of brass.
latrede, tardy.
Latumius, *for* Pacuvius.
launcegay, kind of lance.
launde, grassy glade.
laureat, laurel-crowned.
laurer, laurel.
lauriol, spurge-laurel.
lavours, basins.
lawe, religion.
lay (law), creed, faith.
layneres, straps, thongs.
lazar, leper.
leche, physician.
ledene, language.
leed, lead (metal); cauldron.
leef, dear; lief.
leefful, lawful.
leefsel, bush; bower.
lees, leash.
leeste, *atte l. wey*, at any rate.
leet, let; caused; left.
legge, to lay.
lemes (1), flames.
lemes (2), limbs.
lendes, loins.
lene, to lend.
leng(er), longer.
Lepe, place near Cadiz.
lere, flesh, skin.
lere, to teach; learn.
lese, to lose.
lesing, falsehood.
lest, pleasure; see list.
lest, it pleases.
let = leadeth.
lette, to hinder; forgo.
Lettow, Lithuania.
lettrure, learning.
letuarie, remedy.
leve, to believe.
leve, dear.
leveful, allowable.
levene, lightning.
lever, *him was l.*, he preferred.
levesel, bower.
lewed, ignorant.
ley, *pa. t.* lied; see lye (2).
leyser, leisure.
leyt, flame.
libel, written accusation.
Libeux, see the Romance of Libeaus Desconus ('the Fair Unknown'), ed. Kaluza, Leipzig 1890.
licentiat, licensed confessor.
liche-wake, watch over a corpse.
lige, liege.
liggen, to lie (down).
Ligurge, Lycurgus.
likerous, wanton; greedy.
limaille, metal filings.
limitour, friar licensed to beg.
lind, lime tree.
Linian, Giovanni di Lignano, Italian jurist (d. 1383).
lipsed, lisped.
lisse, *n.* and *v.* comfort.
list, ear.
list, *n.* pleasure; *v.* it pleases.
litarge, white lead.
lith, limb.
lith = lieth.
litherly, ill, badly.
lixt, liest; see lye (2).
lodemenage, pilotage.
lode sterre, polar star.
logge, resting-place.

loller, lollard.
longes, lungs.
loos, praise, renown.
looth(ly), hideous ; hateful.
lorel, worthless fellow.
lorn, lost.
losengeour, flatterer.
losengerie, flattery.
lotinge, lurking.
lough, laughed.
louke, accomplice.
loute, bow down.
lovedayes, days for settling disputes.
love-drury, love, passion.
luce, fish (pike).
Lumbardes, Lombard financiers.
luna, the moon ; silver.
lunarie, moon-wort.
Lussheburghes, bad coins from Luxemburg.
lustihede, high spirits.
luxurie, wantonness.
lyard, grey.
lye (1), to lie (down).
lye (2), to tell lies.
lye (3), to blaze.
Lyeys, Ayas in Armenia.
lyflode, livelihood.
lyknesse, parable.
Lyma, *for* Livia who poisoned her husband Drusus, A.D. 23.
lymrod, lime-twig.
lyte, *adj.* and *adv.* little.
lyves, living.

madde, to go mad.
Madrian, St. Mathurin (1st Nov.).
maheym, maiming.
Mahoun, Mahomet.
maister-tour, chief tower.
maistresse, governess.
maistrye, *for the m.*, exceedingly.
make, mate ; wife ; husband.
Makomete, Mahomet.
male, bag, wallet.
malefice, evil contrivance.
malgré, in spite of.
malison, curse.
Malvesye, (Napoli di) Malvasia, whence Malmsey wine.
manace, threat(en).
manasinge, threatening.
mandement, summons.
manhede, manliness.
mannish, hard-hearted.
mantelet, short mantle.
manye, mania.
Marcian, Martianus Capella (5th cent.).
Mardochee, Mordecai.
mareys, marsh.
mark (*of Adam*), race of men.
market-beter, swaggerer.
Marrok, Morocco.
mary(bones), marrow(bones).
mased, bewildered.
maselyn, maple-wood bowl.
mat, dejected ; defeated.
maugre(e), in spite of.
maumet(rye), idol(atry).
maunciple, caterer.
may, maiden.
maystow, mayst thou.
mechel, much.
mede, **me(e)th**, mead (drink).
medlee, of mixed colours.
melle, mill.
men, *impers. pron.* one.
mendinants, mendicant friars.
Mercenrike, Mercia.
meritorie, meritorious.
merk, image ; see **mark**.
merveille, marvel.

meschief, *at m.*, beaten.
mesel (-erie), leper (leprosy).
message(r), messenger.
messe, mass.
Messene, Messenia.
meste, most ; greatest.
mester, service.
mesurable, moderate.
met, measure (of capacity).
met(te), dreamt.
meve, to move.
mewe, a coop, cage.
meynee, household.
Middelburgh, in Holland, centre of wool trade 1384–8.
misbileve, suspicion.
misboden, insulted.
misborn, misbehaved.
misdeme, to misjudge.
misdeparte, divide unfairly.
misdoo, to ill-treat.
misericorde, pity.
misese, trouble.
misfille, *pa. t.* went ill with.
misgovernaunce, misconduct.
misgyed, misconducted.
misseye, to slander.
mister, trade ; *what m. men*, what sort of men.
misterye, profession.
mistyde, come to grief.
mixen, dunghill.
mo, more ; others.
moche(l), **muche(l)**, much.
moeve, to stir up.
moevyng, *first m.*, the *primum mobile*—the outermost of the spheres.
mood, anger ; thought.
moot, **mote**, must, may.
moralitee, moral (tale).
mordre, murder.
more, more, greater ; *withouten m.*, without more ado.
mormal, a sore.
mortifye, transmute.
mortreux, thick soup ; stew.
morwe(ninge), morning.
mosel, muzzle.
mottelee, motley array.
motyf, suspicion.
moulen, grow mouldy.
mountance, amount ; value.
mowen, may, can.
mowled, *pp.* decayed.
mullock, rubbish, refuse.
multiplye, make gold & silver.
murye, merry.
muscle, mussel.
Myda, Midas.
mynour, miner, sapper.

n' = *ne*, negative prefix.
na, no ; *namo*, no more.
Nabugodonosor, Nebuchadnezzar.
naddre, adder.
nadstow, hadst thou not ?
nake, naked ; destitute.
nakers, kettle-drums.
nale, *atte n.*, at the ale-house.
nam = *ne am*, am not.
nam, *pa. t.* took.
namely, especially.
narwe, narrow, close.
nas = *ne was*, was not.
nat, not ; *nat but*, only.
nath = *ne hath*, hath not.
natheless, nevertheless.
nay, *it is no n.*, undoubtedly.
nayte, withhold, deny.
ne, not, nor.
nedes-cost, of necessity.
neen, no (Northern).
neet, cattle.
nempnen, name.
ner, nearer.
nercotikes, narcotics.

nere = *ne were*, were not; were it not for.
net-herdes, *gen.* neat-herd's.
nevene, to name.
neveradel, not a bit.
nighter-tale, night.
night-spel, spell against evil by night.
nigromanciens, magicians.
nil = *ne wil*, will not.
niste = *ne wiste*, knew not.
noble, a gold coin.
nobley, nobility; state.
nolde = *ne wolde*, would not.
nones, *for the n.* = for the occasion.
noot = *ne woot*, know not.
norice, *n.* and *v.* nurse; to nourish.
nortelrye, education.
nose-thirles, nostrils.
note, employment, task.
notemuge, nutmeg.
not-heed, cropped head.
nouthe, at present.
nowches, jewelled clasps.
Nowelis = Noe's, Noah's.
nyce, foolish; scrupulous.
nyfles, trifles; fictions.

O, oo, one; see oon.
obeisaunce, obedience.
observe, to countenance.
offensioun, injury.
of-newe, anew, lately.
of-showve, repel.
olifaunt = elephant.
oliveres, olive groves.
Olofernus, Holofernes.
oned(en), united, complete.
ones, oones, once.
on-lofte, aloft
oon, one, alone; *in oon*, alike.
open-ers, medlar-fruit.
open-heeded, with head bared.
opie, opium.
ordinaat, orderly.
ore, grace.
orisonte, the horizon.
orloge, clock.
otes, oats.
other, outher, either, or.
other, second.
ouche, jewelled clasp.
oule (1), owl.
oule (2), flesh-hook.
ounces, little bits.
ounding, waving.
outen, to utter; to exhibit.
out-hees, outcry.
outherwhyle, sometimes.
outraye, lose temper.
outrely, utterly.
out-rydere, monk who rode out to inspect estates.
out-sterte, started out.
out-taken, excepted.
over-al, everywhere.
overbyde, to survive.
overest, uppermost.
overlad, put upon.
oversloppe, upper garment.
overthwart, across.
owen, owe; possess; ought.
o-wher, anywhere.
oynement, ointment.

Padowe, Padua.
Palatye, in Anatolia (?).
Palimerie, Palmyra.
palinge, upright striping.
Pamphilles, Pamphilius Maurilianus, who wrote a *Liber de Amore* (12th century).
pan, skull.
panade, knife.
Panik (not identified).

papeer, pepper.
papejay, popinjay, parrot.
paper, documents.
parage, birth ; rank.
paraments, robes ; tapestry.
paramour(s), lover(s); for love.
pardoner, seller of pardons.
parentele, kinship.
parfay, by my faith.
parfit, perfect.
parfourne, perform.
paritorie, pellitory (herb).
parting-felawes, sharers.
partye, partisan.
Parvys, church porch (of Saint Paul's), where lawyers consulted.
pas, step, foot-pace; grade.
passant- (**-ing**), surpassing.
Pavye, Pavia, N. Italy.
paye, please, satisfy.
payen, pagan.
payndemayn, white bread.
payne, *did his p.*, took pains.
pecok-arwes, arrows feathered with peacock feathers.
pecunial, pecuniary.
Pegasee, Pegasus.
Pemond, Piedmont.
penaunt, penitent.
penible, painstaking.
penitauncer, confessor.
Penmark, Penmarch.
penner, pen-case.
Percivel (**Sir**) ; see the Romance Sir Percyvelle of Galles, ed. Campion & Holthausen, Heidelberg 1913.
pere-jonette, an early pear.
Pernaso, Parnassus.
perree, gems.
pers, a sky-blue stuff.
persly, parsley.
persone, parson.
Petro (**of Cipre**), Pierre de Lusignan (d. 1369).
Petro (**of Spayne**), Peter the Cruel, 1334-69.
peytrel, breast-plate.
Phasipha, Pasiphaë.
philosophre, alchemist.
Phisiologus, a book of 'wonders of the animal world' originally composed in Greek: source of Bestiaries.
Phitonyssa, the witch of Endor.
Phitoun, the python, slain by Apollo.
physices, Aristotle's *Physics*.
Pierides, daughters of Pierus, who for emulating the Muses were turned into magpies.
Piers Alfonce, Petrus Alfonsi (12th cent.), who wrote *Disciplina Clericalis*.
pigges-nye (pig's eye), darling.
pighte (*him*), (he) fell.
pikerel, young pike.
pile, to plunder, rob.
piled, bald, bare.
pilwe (**-beer**), pillow (-case).
piment, spiced wine.
pin, *hang on joly pin*, be gay.
pinche, to cavil ; pleat.
pissemyre, ant.
pistel, epistle, message.
pit, put (Northern).
pitous, compassionate ; sad.
Placebo, an anthem in the Office of the Dead.
plages, coasts, regions.
plat, flat ; certain(ly).
plegges, pledges.
pleyn, full(y) ; frank(ly).
Pleyn-damour, name of a

Knight in Malory, *Morte d'Arthur*, Book ix.
plight(e), plucked, pulled.
plye, to bend.
Poileys, Apulian.
point, *in good p.*, in good case; *at p. devyse*, carefully.
poke, bag.
pokkes, pox.
pollax, pole-axe.
polyve, pulley.
pomel, top, crown.
pomely, dappled.
popelote, pet, darling.
Poperinge, Poperinghe, near Calais.
popet, doll, puppet.
popper, small dagger.
poraille, the poor.
porphurie, porphyry slab.
porthors, breviary.
Portingale, Portugal.
pose, cold in the head.
pose, to assume.
possessioners, endowed clergy.
potente, crutch.
potestat, potentate.
poudre-marchaunt, a tart (i.e. sharp tasting) spice.
pounsoned, pierced.
pouped, blew (a horn).
povre, poor(ly).
Powles window, open work, like the rose window at old St. Paul's.
poynaunt, piquant.
poyntel, stylus, pencil.
predicacioun, sermon.
preef, preve, proof, test.
prees, press, throng.
prefer, be better than
preparat, prepared (salt).
preys, praise.
pricasour, hard rider.
prighte, pricked; see next.
priken, prick, incite, spur.
prikke, a stroke, point.
procutour, proctor.
proheme, prologue.
prolle, to prowl.
propre, own; comely.
propretee, peculiarity.
prospectyves, lenses.
prow, profit.
proyneth, trims, preens.
Pruce, Prussia.
pryme, prime (9 a.m.); *half-way p.*, 7.30 a.m.
prymerole, primrose.
prys, price, prize, esteem.
pulle, pluck; *p. a finch*, befool.
purchace, acquire, provide.
purchas, (illicit) gain.
purchasour, one who feathers his own nest.
pure, very.
purfiled, trimmed.
purpre, purple raiment.
purtreye, portray, draw.
purveyance, providence.
put, pit.
puterie, prostitution.
putours, pimps, procurers.
pye, magpie.
pyke, to make tidy.
pyne, torment; torture.
pyrie, pear-tree.

qua(a)d, evil, bad.
quakke, hoarseness, asthma.
qualm, pestilence.
quarter-night, about 9 p.m.
quelle, to kill.
questio quid iuris, 'the question is, what is the law?'
queynt(e), *pp.* quenched.
querele, quarrel.

quern, hand-mill.
questemongeres, jurymen.
queyntise, finery ; art.
quicken, give life to ; revive.
qui la? who 's there?
quinible, shrill treble.
quirboilly, boiled leather.
quitly, wholly.
quod, said.
quook, quaked.
quyte, requite, ransom.

raa, roe (Northern).
Raby, Rabbi.
rad, *pp.* read.
rage, to disport.
rageryе, wantonness.
rakel(nesse), rash(ness).
rake-stele, rake-handle.
rape (*and renne*), rob and plunder.
rathe(r), soon(er).
raughte, reached.
ravines, thefts.
ravisedest, didst draw down.
Razis, Rhazes, Arab physician (9th–10th cent.); his chief medical treatises are *Continens* and *Almansor.*
rebekke, old woman.
recche (1), *pp.* roghte, reck.
recche (2), to interpret.
recchelees, careless.
reconciled, re-consecrated.
rede, to read ; to counsel.
rede, reed, red.
redoutinge, reverence.
reed, counsel, plan, help.
refreyed, cooled.
refreyne, to curb.
refut, refuge.
regne, realm, dominion.
rek(e)ne, reckon, recount.
relees, *out of r.*, continually.
relente, to melt.
relese, to forgive.
reme, realm.
remewed, removed.
ren, a run ; **renne**, to run.
renably, fluently.
reneye, deny, abjure.
renges, ranks.
renomee, renown.
renovelle, to renew.
rente, income.
repair, company of visitors.
reportour, reporter.
reprevable, reprehensible.
repreve, reproof, shame.
requeren, to entreat, ask.
resalgar, disulphide of arsenic.
rescous, rescue.
rese, to shake.
resons, opinions.
rethor, orator.
reve, steward.
reve, to rob, bereave.
revelous, fond of revelry.
reward, regard.
rewe, row, line, order.
rewel-boon, ivory.
rewthe, pity.
reye, rye.
reynes, loins.
reysed, *pp.* raided, invaded.
ribaudye, jesting.
ribible, kind of fiddle.
ribybe, an old hag.
right (*way*), direct.
rightwisnesse, righteousness.
riote, gambling.
rist = riseth.
rit = rideth.
riveer, river(-bank); *for r.*, by the river-side.
roche, rock.
rode, complexion, redness.

rode-beem, rood-beam.
rody, ruddy.
Romayn Gestes, the collection of Tales called *Gesta Romanorum*.
rombled, groped ; murmured.
ronges, rungs (of ladder).
Ronyan, St. Ronan (7th Feb.).
roof, *pa. t.* pierced.
Rosarie, *Rosarium Philosophorum*, an alchemical treatise by Arnoldus de Villa Nova, q.v.
roser, rose-tree.
rote (1), root.
rote (2), point taken as a basis of calculation in astrology.
rote (3), a small harp.
rotie, to make rotten.
roughte, recked ; cared.
rouketh, cowers.
roule, to gad (about).
roum, roomy ; **roumer**, larger.
Rouncival, a hospital near Charing Cross, London.
rouncy, nag.
rounde, briskly.
roune, to whisper.
route, to snore.
route, to assemble ; move about.
routhe, pity.
rowe, roughly.
rubible, fiddle ; see **ribible**.
rubriche, rubric.
Ruce, Russia.
Rufus, Greek physician of Ephesus (1st – 2nd cent. A.D.).
ruggy, rough.
ryding, jousting.
ryme, **rymeye**, tell in verse.
ryot, riotous living.
ryot(our), roystering, (-er).
rys, spray, twig.

sad, unmoved ; serious.
St. Beneit, St. Benedict (4th Dec.).
St. Denys, near Paris.
St. Jame, famous shrine at Compostella, in Galicia.
St. Julian, (9th Jan.), the pattern of hospitality.
St. Loy, St. Eligius (1st Dec.).
St. Note, St. Neot (28th Oct.).
St. Thomas a Waterings, brook two miles from London on the way to Canterbury.
St. Yve, St. Ivo (25th Apr.).
sakked, put in a sack.
sal, shall (Northern).
sal(peter), salt(petre).
salewe, **salue**, salute.
Saluce(s), Saluzzo, N. Italy.
salwes, willows.
sangwin, blood-red.
sans faille, without fail.
sarge, serge.
Sarray, Tzarev, near Sarepta on the Volga.
Satalye, Adalia (Asia Minor).
sauf (1) safe ; (2) except.
saugh, *pa. t.* saw.
saule, soul (Northern).
sautrye, psaltery, harp.
save, sage (plant).
saveren, to relish, care for.
savourly, enjoyably.
sawcefleem, pimpled.
say, *pa. t.* saw.
Sayne, the Seine.
scalled, scabbed.
Scariot, Judas Iscariot.
scars, parsimonious.
scathe, harm, pity.
sclaundre, ill-fame, scandal.

sclendre, thin, poor.
scole-matere, philosophy.
scoleye, to study.
scrippe, bag.
scrit, deed, document.
seche, to seek.
secree, secret(ly); trusty.
seculer, layman.
see, seat, throne.
see, *God him s.*, God watch over him.
seek, **seke**, sick.
seel, bliss.
seet, *pa. t.* sat.
seeth, *pa. t.* boiled; see **sethe**.
seigh, *pa. t.* saw.
sein, to say.
seinte, holy.
seintuarie, sanctuary.
seistow = sayest thou.
selde, seldom.
selle, foundation-beam.
sely, happy, good, simple.
semblaunt, appearance.
semes, seams.
semicope, short cloak.
semisoun, low noise.
sencer, censer.
sendal, thin silk.
sene, (*to*), (to) look on.
senge, singe; **seynd**, broiled.
Senior, an old book on chemistry is attributed to Senior Zadith.
sentence, meaning, purpose.
Septe, Ceuta (N. Africa).
septemtrioun, north.
Serapion (John), physician (9th cent.).
serchen, to search, go about.
serie, argument.
sermone, to preach, talk.
sermouns, writings.
servage, thraldom.
servant, lover.
servisable, ready to serve.
sethe, to boil.
seur(ly), sure(ly).
sewe, to follow, ensue.
sewes, seasoned dishes.
seyn, *pp.* seen.
seynd, *pp.* broiled; see **senge**.
shaar, ploughshare.
shadwed, shaded.
shamfast(nesse), shy(ness).
shapen, to plan, prepare.
shaply, fit.
shawe, a wood.
sheld, French crown.
shende (shent), to harm, ruin, spoil, scold, blame.
shendshipe, shame.
shene, bright, fair.
shere, pair of shears.
sheten, to shoot.
shette, to shut; *pp.* **shet**.
sheweth, pretends.
shifte, assign, provide.
shilde, defend; forbid.
shine, shin.
shipman, skipper; sailor.
shirreve, sheriff.
shiten, dirty.
shivere, thin slice.
shode, parting of the hair.
shonde, shame, harm.
shoop (him), determined.
shot windowe, casement.
shepne, **shipne**, cow-house.
shrewe, to curse; *pp.* **shrewed**.
shrewe, shrew; rascal.
shrifte-fadres, confessors.
shrighte, **shryked**, shrieked.
shrimpes, weaklings.
shuldre-boon, shoulder-blade.
sib, related, akin.
sicer, strong drink.

Sidingborne, Sittingbourne.
sighte, sighed.
Significavit, writ following excommunication.
siker(ly), sure(ly).
simphonye, a kind of tabour.
sin, since.
sinwes, sinews.
sis-cink, six-five (at dice).
sit = sitteth; befits.
sith(en), since; afterwards.
sive, sieve.
skile, reason, cause.
skilfully, reasonably.
skinketh, pours out.
slee(n), slay; *pa. t.* **slow**; *pp.* **slawe(n)**.
sleep, slept.
sleere, slayer.
sleigh, sly, clever.
sleighte, trick, skill, plan.
slewthe, sloth.
slider, slippery.
slit = slideth.
sloppes, loose garments.
slough, slow, slew.
slyk, (1) sleek; (2) such.
slyly, wisely, cleverly.
smal, slender.
smatre, to smirch.
smerte, pain; *adv.* sharply.
smit = smiteth.
smoterlich, disreputable.
snewed, snowed.
snibben, to chide.
soden, boiled; see **sethe**.
soken, toll, due.
sokingly, gradually.
solas, amusement, comfort.
solempne, festive, grand.
Soler Halle, King's Hall, merged in Trinity Coll., Camb.
somdel, somewhat.
somnour, one who summoned delinquents before an ecclesiastical court.
somonce, summons.
sompne, to summon.
sond, sand.
sonde, message, messenger.
soor, a wound; *adj.* sore.
soper, supper.
sophyme, sophism; problem.
sort, lot, chance.
sorwestow, do you grieve?
soster, sister.
sote, sweet.
sothfastnesse, truth.
sotil, subtle, thin.
souded, devoted.
souke, suck; extract money.
soul, sole, single.
soun, sound.
soun(e), to sound, tend towards.
sourdeth, arises.
sours, source; upward spring.
souter, cobbler.
soutiltee, device.
sowdan, sultan.
sowled, endowed with souls.
space, opportunity; course.
sparhauk, sparrow-hawk.
sparth, battle-axe.
sparwe, sparrow.
spaynel, spaniel.
spede, to succeed, prosper.
speedful, advantageous.
speere, sphere.
spelle, story.
spence, buttery.
spille, to destroy; die.
spitously, maliciously.
spore, spur.
sporne, to stumble.
spousaille, wedding.
springen, sprinkle; *pp.* **spreynd**.

spyced, (too) delicate.
spyces, species.
squames, scales.
squaymous, squeamish.
squiereth, attends.
squire, carpenter's square.
squyer, squire.
stablissed, established.
Stace of Thebes, the *Thebaid* of Statius.
staf-slinge, a powerful sling attached to a stick.
stalkes, uprights of a ladder.
stamin, coarse cloth.
stampe, bray in a mortar.
stank, lake, pool.
stant = standeth.
stape(n), advanced.
starf, *pa. t.* died ; see **storven**.
stele, handle.
stemed, shone, glowed.
stenten, to leave off ; stay.
stepe, glittering.
stere, rudder ; pilot.
sterlinge, silver penny.
sterre, star.
stert, *at a s.*, in a moment.
sterte, to leap (up *or* down).
sterve, die (of famine).
stevene, voice ; *sette s.*, made appointment.
stewe, fish-pond.
stiborn, stubborn.
Stilbon, *for* Chilon.
stillatorie, distilling vessel.
stinte, to cease.
stirte, started.
stith, anvil.
stok, race ; *pl.* logs.
stoke, to stab.
stonde, stand ; be, consist.
stongen, stung, pierced.
stoon, stone ; gem.
stoor, stock ; store.
stopen, advanced.
store, audacious.
storial, historical.
storven, *pp.* died ; see **sterve**.
stot (1) horse ; (2) woman (*abusive*).
stounde, while, time.
stour, conflict, battle.
stra(u)nge, *make it s.*, make difficulties.
strangenesse, estrangement.
straught(e), stretched.
strawen, *pp.* strewn.
stree, a straw.
streen, strain, race.
streite, *pp.* drawn (sword).
streng, string.
strepen, to strip.
streyne, constrain ; clasp.
strike, hank (of flax).
stronde, shore.
strong, difficult ; severe.
stroof, *pa. t.* strove.
Strother, Castle Strother, near Wooller, Northumb.
strouted, spread out.
stubbel-goos, fatted goose.
sturdinesse, sternness.
styves, brothels ; stews.
styward, steward.
subgit, servant.
subjeccion, suggestion.
sublymatories, vessels for sublimation.
suffisaunce, sufficiency, content.
suffrable, patient.
suggestioun, accusation.
surcote, outer garment.
surement, pledge.
surquidrie, arrogance.
Surrie, Syria.
sursanure, wound healed outwardly.

surveyaunce, surveillance.
sustren, sisters.
suyte, *of the same s. of*, matching.
swa, so (Northern).
swal, *pa. t.* swelled.
swap(pe), to strike.
swatte, *pa. t.* sweated.
sweigh, motion.
swelte, fainted, died.
swelwe, to swallow.
swete, to sweat ; *pa. t.* **swatte**.
swevene, a dream.
Sweton(ius), Suetonius.
swich, such.
swink(e), *n.* and *v.* toil, labour.
swo(u)gh, a groan ; swoon ; blast.
swonken, *pp.* toiled.
swoot, sweat.
swote, sweet.
swowne, a swoon.
swythe, quickly.
swyve, to lie with.
sy(e), *pa. t.* saw.
syk(e), *n.* and *v.* sigh.
symonials, simoniacs.
sys, six (at dice).
sythe, time.

T' for *to*, before verb beginning with a vowel, as **t'abyde**, **t'amende**, &c.
taa, to take (Northern).
tabard, short coat ; inn-sign.
table ; *t. dormant*, table fixed for constant use.
tables, backgammon.
taillages, taxes.
taille, tally, score ; credit.
take, to take ; give.
takel, gear, arrows.
talde, told (Northern).
talen, to tell stories.
talent, wish ; appetite.
taling, story-telling.
tapicer, tapestry-maker.
tappestere, woman innkeeper.
tas, heap.
taste, to test, feel.
temple, inn of court.
temps, time.
tene, vexation.
tentifly, attentively.
tercelet, male (falcon).
tercian, fever recurring every third day.
terme(s), *in t.*, precisely.
terrestre, earthly.
Tertulan, Tertullian, 2nd–3rd cent.
terve, to flay, strip.
testers, head-pieces.
testes, testing vessels.
testif, headstrong.
textuel, learned in texts.
teyne, thin metal plate.
th' for *the*, in **thabsence**, **&c.**
thakketh, *v.* strokes, pats.
th'alighte, alighted (in) thee.
thank, *can th.*, give thanks ; (*his*) *th.*, of (his) free will.
thar, need ; it behoves.
thedom, *evil th.*, misfortune.
thee, to thrive ; **theech**, **theek** = *thee ich*, so may I thrive.
th'eir = *the eir*, the air.
Thelophus, Telephus of Mysia.
thenche, to imagine.
thenne, thin.
thenne(s), thence.
Theodomas, Thiodamas (Statius *Thebaid* viii. 279).
Theophrastus, *de Nuptiis*, quoted by Jerome.

ther as, where.
ther-bifore, beforehand.
ther-oute, out in the open.
thewes, habits ; virtues.
thikke-herd, thick-haired.
thilke = *the ilke*, the same.
thing, fact; document; prayer.
thinketh, it seems.
thirled, *pp.* pierced.
this = this is.
tho, (1) those ; (2) then.
tholed, *pp.* suffered.
thonder-dint, thunder-clap.
thonder-leyt, lightning.
threpe, to call.
threshfold, threshold.
threste, to thrust.
thretty, thirty.
thriftily, profitably, well.
thringe, *pa. t.* **throng**, thrust.
throp, village.
throte-bolle, 'Adam's apple '.
throwe, a (little) while.
thrustle-cok, thrush (male).
thryes, thrice.
thurgh-girt, pierced through.
thurrok, hold (of a ship), sink.
thwitel, knife.
tidifs, small birds.
tikel, unstable, frail.
til, to (Northern).
tipet, a strip of cloth, pendant from hood or sleeve.
Tisbee, Thisbe.
to(o), toe ; *pl.* **toon**.
to-, intensive prefix ; e. g. *to-bete*, beat severely, &c.
to-breste, break in pieces.
tode, toad.
to-forn, before.
toght, taut.
to-hewen, hewn in pieces.
Toletanes, of Toledo.
tollen, take toll.
tombesteres, dancing girls, tumblers.
tonne (*-greet*), (large as) a tun.
to-race, to tear in pieces.
tord, piece of dung.
toret, swivel-ring.
torn, a turn.
to-shrede, cut into shreds.
to-stoupe, to bend forward.
to-swinke, to labour greatly.
to-tar, *pa. t.* tore in pieces.
to-trede, to trample.
toty, dizzy.
toute, backside.
to-yere, this year.
Trace, Thrace.
trad, *pa. t.* trod.
Tramissene, in Algeria.
trappures, harness.
trave, frame for unruly horses when being shod.
travers, a curtain, screen.
trays, traces.
trede-foul, treader of hens.
tregetour, a juggler.
trench, alley.
trentals, thirty masses for the dead.
tret = treadeth.
tretable, tractable.
tretis, treaty.
tretys, well-made, shapely.
trewe-love, aromatic herb.
treye, three (at dice).
triacle, remedy.
trille, to twirl, turn.
trip, small piece.
trompes, trumpeters.
tronchoun, spear shaft.
trone, throne.
Trophee, (unexplained).
Trotula, supposed woman writer of medical books.
trufles, trifles.

trussed, packed.
tryce, pull, drag away.
trye, excellent.
tryne compas, three fold world—earth, sky, and sea.
tulle, to entice.
tuwel, hole.
tweyfold, double.
twight, *pp.* pulled.
twinne, to sever, depart.
twiste, a twig, branch.
twyes, twice.
tyden, to befall.
tytled, *pp.* dedicated.

unbrent, unburnt.
unconninge, ignorance.
unconvenable, unfitting.
uncouth, curious, strange.
undermel, early morning.
undern, morning.
undernom(e), perceived; reproved.
underpyghte, stuffed.
underspore, to thrust (under).
undigne, unworthy.
unfestlich, not festive, jaded.
unhardy, cowardly.
unhele, ill-luck; illness.
unkinde, unnatural.
unkonning, unskilful.
unleveful, not permissible.
unlust, disinclination.
unlykly, unpleasing.
unnethe(s), scarcely.
unordred, not belonging to a religious order.
unsad, inconstant.
unsely, unhappy, unlucky.
unset; *at u. steven*, unexpected.
unshette, unlocked.
unshewed, unconfessed.
unslekked, unslacked.
unthank! a curse.
unthriftily, poorly.
untyme, *in u.*, out of season.
unwar, unexpected.
unwelde, impotent.
unwemmed, pure, spotless.
unyolden, without yielding.
up, upon.
up-haf, *pa. t.* uplifted.
uppe, up, *i. e.* open.
up-plight, *pp.* pulled up.
upright, on (one's) back.
up-rist, rises up.
up-riste, uprising.
up-ronne, *pp.* ascended.
up-so-doun, upside-down.
up-yaf, *pa. t.* gave up.
up-yolden, *pp.* yielded up.
Urban, Pope Urban I (d. 230).
usaunt, accustomed.
utter, outward.

Valerie (p. 245), Valerius Maximus.
Valerie, the *Epistola Valerii ad Rufinum* 'Against Marriage', p. 308.
vavasour, sub-vassal.
veluettes, velvets.
Venerian, devoted to Venus.
venerye, hunting.
ventusinge, cupping (in surgery).
Vernage, a white wine.
Vernicle, a copy of St. Veronica's handkerchief with the impression of Christ's face.
vernisshed, varnished.
verrayment, truly.
vertu, (quickening) power.
verye (meaning unknown).
vese, rush of wind.
vessel, plate, silver.
Vesulus, Monte Viso.

viage, voyage, journey.
virelay, kind of ballad.
viritoot (meaning unknown).
viritrate, a hag.
vitaille, victuals.
vitremyte, woman's head-dress.
Vitulon, Vitello, Polish writer on optics (13th cent.).
volage, wanton.
volatyl, fowls.
volupe(e)r, night-cap.
voyden, to get rid of.

waast, waist.
waat, knows (Northern).
wacche, sentinel.
wachet, blue cloth.
Wade, a Teutonic hero; the story is lost.
waden, to wade, pass, go.
wafereres, confectioners.
waiten, to watch; *w. after*, look for.
wake-pleyes, funeral games.
waking, vigils.
walked, *go w.*, go walking.
walwe, to wallow, tumble.
wanges, molar teeth.
wanhope, despair.
wantrust, distrust(ful).
war, aware, wary.
wardecors, body-guard.
warderere! look out behind!
wardrobe, privy.
warente, to protect.
wariangles, shrikes, butcher-birds.
warien, to curse.
warisshe, to cure; be cured.
warnestore, to fortify; garrison.
waryce, to heal, cure.
wastel-breed, finest bread.
wawe, a wave.
wayke, weak.
waymenten, to lament.
webbe, a weaver.
wedde, *to w.*, as a pledge.
weeldinge, power, control.
weep, *pa. t.* wept.
weex, *pa. t.* grew.
welden, control; *pa. t.* **welte.**
weleful, happy, prosperous.
welked, withered.
wem, spot; hurt.
wemmelees, stainless.
wenden, to go.
wenen, to suppose; *pa. t.* **wende.**
were, to defend.
werkes, *v.* ache (Northern *pl.*).
werre, war.
werreye, to make war.
wers, worse.
werte, wart.
wesele, weasel.
wexen, to grow; see **woxen.**
weyen, to weigh.
weymentinge, lamenting.
weyven, turn aside; forsake.
what, why.
whelkes, pimples.
whenne(s), whence.
wher (1) where; (2) whether.
wher-so, whethersoever.
wher-as, whereas: where.
whiche, of what kind.
whilk, which (Northern).
whippeltree, cornel-tree.
whyle, time; *quyte her w.*, take vengeance on her.
whyl-er, formerly.
wight, *a lyte w.*, a little while.
wight, active, swift.
wike, week.
wilde fyr, erysipelas.
wilnen, to desire.

wiltow, wilt thou.
wimple, wimple, head-dress.
windas, windlass.
winsinge, skittish.
wis(ly), certainly, surely.
wisse, to guide, direct.
wit, judgement, discretion.
witen, to know.
withholden, to retain, shut up.
withoute-forth, outwardly.
withseye, renounce, gainsay.
witing, knowledge.
wlatsom, disgusting.
wo, *adj.* unhappy.
wode-binde, honeysuckle.
wode-dowve, wood-pigeon.
wol(n), to will, desire; *woldestow*, would'st thou; *pp.* wold, desired.
wone, to dwell, live.
wone, custom.
wones, houses.
wonger, pillow.
woning, habitation, house.
wood(ly), mad(ly).
woodnesse, madness.
woodeth, *pr. s.* rages.
woot, know; knew.
word, *for* ord, beginning.
wort, unfermented beer.
wortes, herbs, vegetables.
worthen, to be, get (on).
wost, knowest.
wounde, plague, p. 553.
woxen, *pp.* grown, become.
wrang, wrong, amiss (Northern).
wraw(e), angry, fretful.
wrecche, wretch; wretched.
wreche, vengeance.
wrenches, frauds, stratagems.
wreye, reveal, bewray.
wroteth, roots (as a pig).
wrye, to cover.
wrye(n), to turn; twist.
wyde-where, far and wide.
wyn ape, the joyful stage of drunkenness.
wys, wise; *make it w.*, to deliberate, hesitate.
wyte, *n.* and *v.* blame, reproach.

Y-, a prefix to the *pp.* and some infinitives e.g. **y-finde**, **y-here**, &c.
yaf, *pa. t.* gave.
y-bet(en), beaten, stamped. **y-blent**, blinded. **y-bleynt**, blenched. **y-brent**, burnt. **y-chaped**, bound. **y-clenched**, clamped. **y-cleped**, **-clept**, called. **y-corve(n)**, cut. **y-coupled**, wedded. **y-crowe**, crowed.
ydel, *in y.*, in vain.
y-dight, decked.
ydolastre, idolater.
y-do(on), done.
y-dropped, sprinkled.
ye, eye; *pl.* yen.
yeddinges, songs.
yede, went.
yelden, to yield, requite.
yeldhalle, guild-hall.
yelding, *n.* produce.
yelpe, to boast.
yeman, yeoman.
yerde, stick, rod.
yerne, eager(ly), brisk(ly).
yeve, give; **yeveres**, givers.
yexeth, *v.* hiccoughs.
y-fere, together.
y-fet, fetched. **y-geten**, gotten, procured. **y-glosed**, flattered. **y-greved**, harmed. **y-hent**, seized. **y-herd**, covered with hair. **y-holde**, esteemed.

yifte, a gift.
y-kempt, combed. **y-korven**, cut. **y-lad**, led; carted.
y-liche, alike.
y-logged, lodged.
y-lymed, caught, ensnared.
y-mel, among (Northern).
y-meynd, mingled.
y-nempned, named.
y-nogh, enough.
yolde(n), yielded.
yolle, to yell.
youling, loud lamentation.
Ypermistra, Hypermnestra.
y-piked, picked over.
Ypocras, Hippocrates, great Greek physician (5th cent. B.C.)
ypocras, a cordial drink.
Ypotis, a religious legend, ed. Horstmann, *Altenglische Legenden* (1881), p. 341.
y-preved, proved (to be). **y-pulled**, trimmed. **y-queynt**, quenched. **y-quiked**, kindled. **y-raft**, bereft. **y-reke**, raked together.
yren, iron.
y-ronne, *pp.* run; clustered. **y-satled**, settled. **y-schette**, shut. **y-shent**, shamed, blamed. **y-spreynd**, sprinkled. **y-stiked**, stabbed. **y-stint**, stopped. **y-stonge**, stung. **y-storve**, dead. **y-take**, caught.
yve; see **erbe-yve**.
yvele, evil; ill.
y-voyded, removed. **y-wimpled**, wearing a wimple.
y-wis, certainly.
y-woxen, grown.
y-wryen, covered; hidden.

Zanzis, Zeuxis, Greek painter.
Zephirus, west wind.